P9-DYZ-046

CYADOR'S HEIRS

Tor Books by L. E. Modesitt, Jr.

The Saga of Recluce

The Magic of Recluce
The Towers of the Sunset
The Magic Engineer
The Order War
The Death of Chaos
Fall of Angels
The Chaos Balance
The White Order
Colors of Chaos
Magi'i of Cyador
Scion of Cyador
Wellspring of Chaos
Ordermaster
Natural Ordermage
Mage-Guard of Hamor
Arms-Commander
Cyador's Heirs
Heritage of Cyador (forthcoming)

The Corean Chronicles

Legacies
Darknesses
Scepters
Alector's Choice
Cadmian's Choice
Soarer's Choice
The Lord-Protector's Daughter
Lady-Protector

The Imager Portfolio

Imager
Imager's Challenge
Imager's Intrigue
Scholar
Princeps
Imager's Battalion
Antiagon Fire
Rex Regis

The Spellsong Cycle

The Soprano Sorceress
The Spellsong War
Darksong Rising
The Shadow Sorceress
Shadowsinger

The Ecolitan Matter

Empire & Ecolitan (comprising *The Ecolitan Operation* and *The Ecologic Secession*)
Ecolitan Prime (comprising *The Ecologic Envoy* and *The Ecolitan Enigma*)
The Forever Hero (comprising *Dawn for a Distant Earth, The Silent Warrior,* and *In Endless Twilight*)

Timegod's World (comprising *Timediver's Dawn* and *The Timegod*)

The Ghost Books

Of Tangible Ghosts
The Ghost of the Revelator
Ghost of the White Nights
Ghost of Columbia (comprising *Of Tangible Ghosts* and *The Ghost of the Revelator*)

The Hammer of Darkness
The Green Progression
The Parafaith War
Adiamante
Gravity Dreams
The Octagonal Raven
Archform: Beauty
The Ethos Effect
Flash
The Eternity Artifact
The Elysium Commission
Viewpoints Critical
Haze
Empress of Eternity
The One-Eyed Man

L. E. Modesitt, Jr.

CYADOR'S HEIRS

A Tom Doherty Associates Book / New York

This is a work of fiction. All of the characters, organizations, and events portrayed in this novel are either products of the author's imagination or are used fictitiously.

CYADOR'S HEIRS

Maps by Ellisa Mitchell

A Tor Book
Published by Tom Doherty Associates, LLC
175 Fifth Avenue
New York, NY 10010

www.tor-forge.com

Tor® is a registered trademark of Tom Doherty Associates, LLC.

Library of Congress Cataloging-in-Publication Data

Modesitt, L. E., Jr., 1943–
Cyador's heirs / L.E. Modesitt.—First edition.
p. cm.
ISBN 978-0-7653-7477-6 (hardcover)
ISBN 978-1-4668-4310-3 (e-book)
I. Title.
PS3563.O264C93 2014
813'.54—dc23
2013029671

Tor books may be purchased for educational, business, or promotional use. For information on bulk purchases, please contact Macmillan Corporate and Premium Sales Department at 1-800-221-7945, extension 5442, or write specialmarkets@macmillan.com.

First Edition: May 2014

Printed in the United States of America

0 9 8 7 6 5 4 3 2 1

For Kellen Scott Dukes,
heir in his own right

Characters

Lephi	Emperor of Cyador (deceased)
Mairena	Empress of Cyador (deceased)
Kiedron	Duke of Cigoerne, son of Lephi and Mairena
Xeranya	Healer and consort of Kiedron
Emerya	Healer, daughter of Lephi and Mairena
Phortyn	Majer, commander of Mirror Lancers
Jhalet	Submajer, second in command, Mirror Lancers
Altyrn	Majer (stipended), former commander of Mirror Lancers
Maeroja	Consort of Altyrn
Lephi	Eldest son of Kiedron and Xeryana
Lerial	Second son of Kiedron and Xeranya
Ryalah	Daughter of Kiedron and Xeranya
Amaira	Daughter of Emerya
Atroyan	Duke of Afrit
Rhamuel	Arms-Commander of Afrit, brother of Atroyan
Khesyn	Duke of Heldya
Casseon	Duke of Merowey
Tyrsalyn	Third Magus of Cyador, First Magus of Cigoerne
Saltaryn	Magus, tutor of Lerial

NORTHERN
CANDAR
Gulf of Murr
Gulf of Candar
RECLUCE
EASTERN OCEAN
The WORLD
E.Mitchell 1995

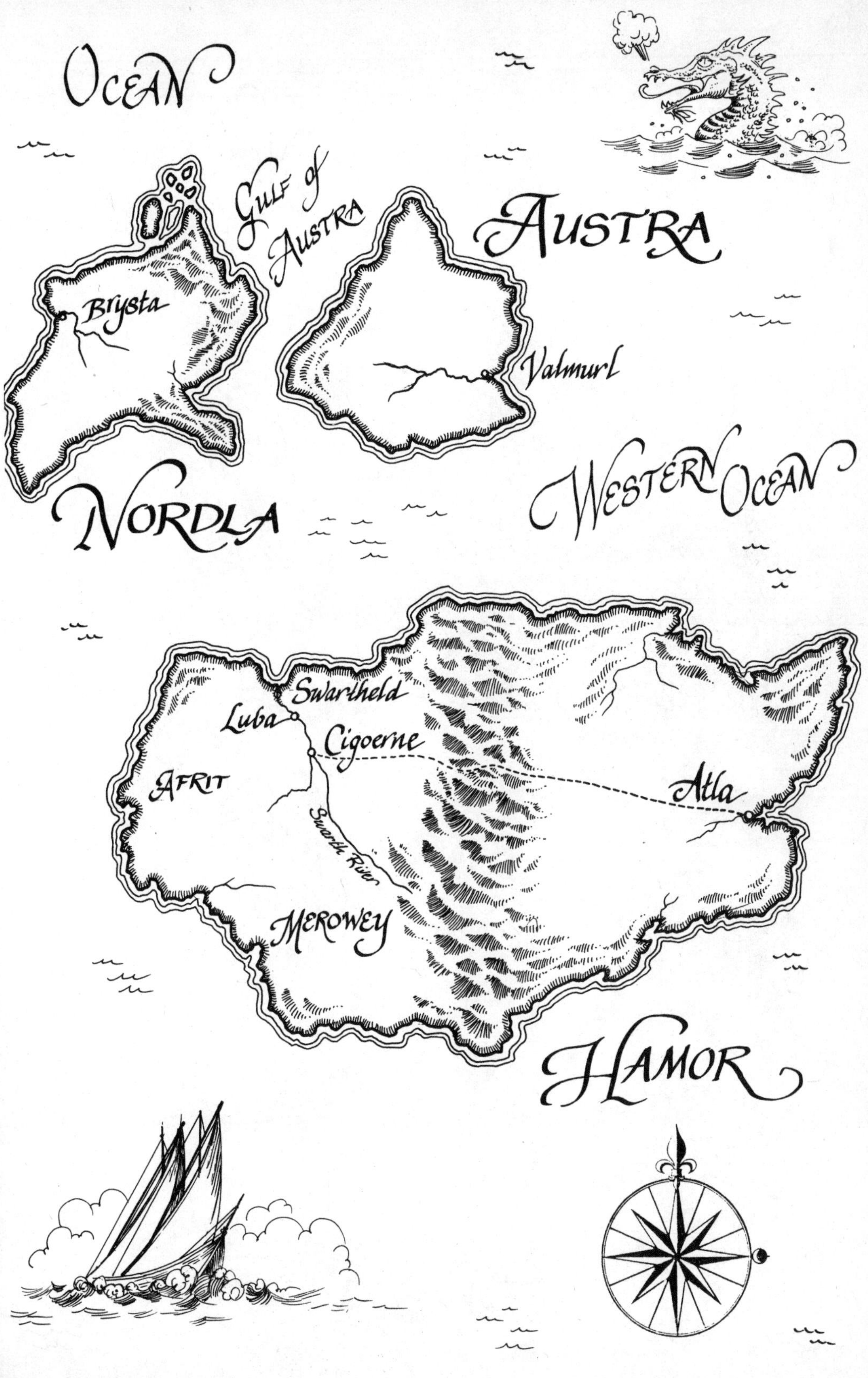

Ocean

Gulf of Austra

Austra

Brysta

Valmurl

Nordla

Western Ocean

Swartheld

Luba

Cigoerne

Afrit

Atla

Swarth River

Merowey

Hamor

Hamor

Dolari
Northpoint
Swartheld
Luba
Guasyra
Cigoerne
Heldya
Highpoint
Quarries
Swarth River
Westyr
Clyan River
Jabuti
Clyanaka
Alsenyi
Kysha
Merowey
Dawhut
Awhut River
Elmari
Nubyat
Sastak
Southern Ocean

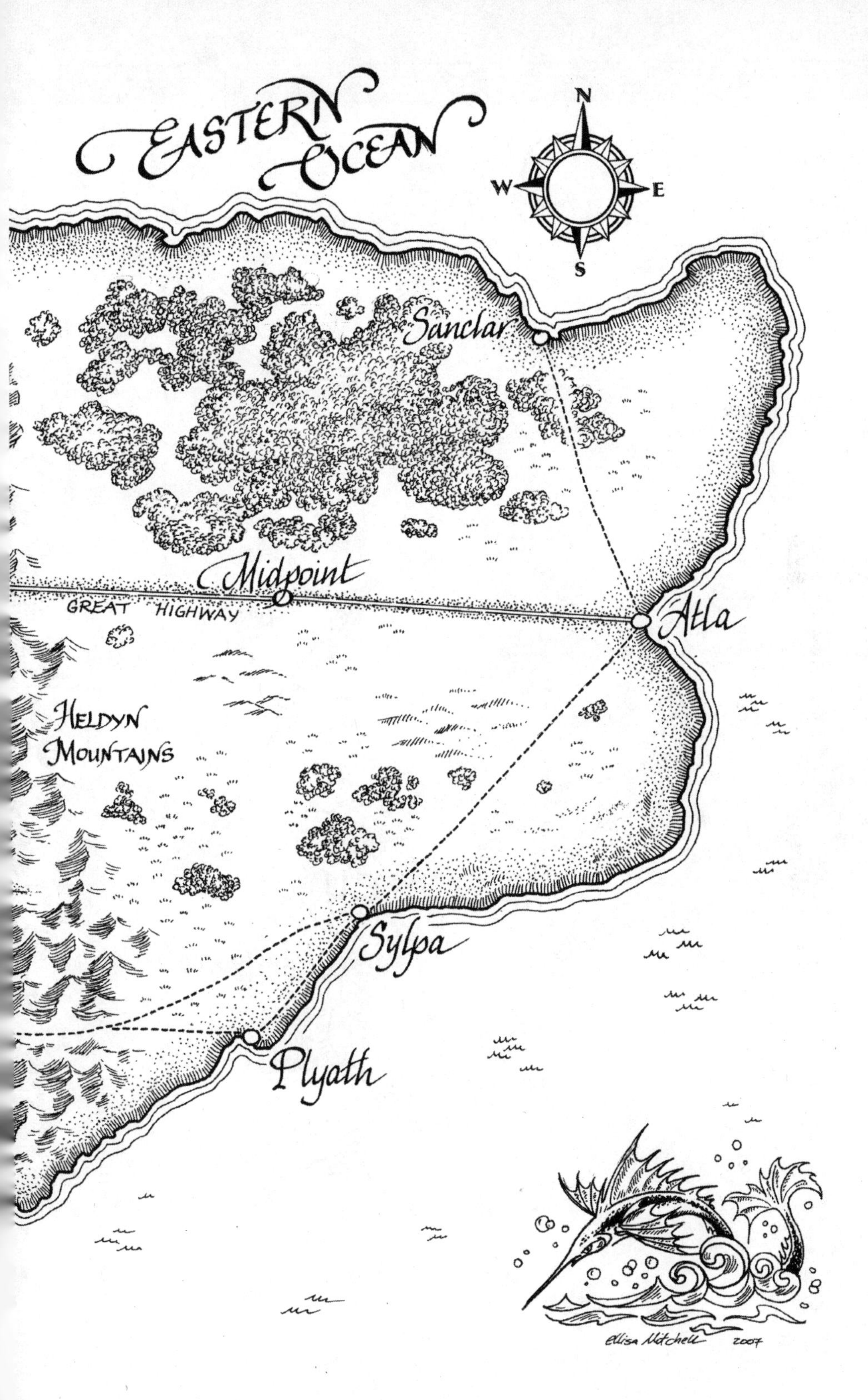

EASTERN OCEAN
N
W
E
S
Sanclar
Midpoint
GREAT HIGHWAY
Atla
HELDYN MOUNTAINS
Sylpa
Plyath
Ellisa Mitchell 2007

PROLOGUE

The boy and the girl sit on a carved wooden bench in the shade beside the small courtyard fountain. He has pale white skin, unruly red hair and a strong straight nose just short of being considered excessive. Her hair is black, as are her eyes, and her skin is smooth, if the light tan of aged parchment. Her name is Kyedra. His is Lerial.

Four guards watch them. Two wear white long-sleeved tunics with faded green trim, and bear scarce cupridium blades in worn scabbards. The other two sport silvered iron breastplates over dull crimson short-sleeved tunics. Their shortswords are of dark iron, carried in oiled leather scabbards that are more like large knife sheaths. The Lancers in green watch the guards in crimson, while the guards in crimson watch the boy. No one watches the girl, who fingers a heavy brocade head scarf that she has let slip to reveal some of her hair and her lower face, an act that would be severely condemned were she of lesser rank, older, or in public.

"Why are your guards called Lancers?" She finally breaks the silence.

"They're supposed to be called Mirror Lancers, but no one except the family or other Lancers calls them that. I forget why." Lerial has not forgotten. He would prefer not to explain, especially when speaking the Hamorian of Afrit, but since the girl just introduced to him as Kyedra less than a quarter glass before speaks no Cyadoran, he has no choice but to speak in her tongue.

Once more, the two do not speak for a time, until the girl asks, "Does your name mean something special in your tongue?"

Lerial considers what he should say for a moment before replying. "My grandfather was the Emperor Lephi. One of my ancestors was the Emperor Kerial. My grandmother felt I should be named after both."

"There are no Emperors in Hamor. There never have been." Her voice is firmly serious.

"They were Emperors of Cyador," declares Lerial.

"The land that the sea destroyed?"

"The sea only destroyed Cyad. That was the capital . . . and maybe Fyrad. The Accursed Forest destroyed most of the other cities and covered the land with endless forest. That was why we came to Hamor."

"My father says you never should have come. He says that Afrit will never be the same."

Lerial knows not to say anything about that. "Why did your father bring you here?"

"He said I should see Cigoerne. He said it was different."

Lerial can feel that there is more she has not said. "Is it?"

Kyedra nods solemnly.

"How is it different?"

"I thought it would be smaller, and that all the people would be taller."

"Why? Because we have held the river for years against the Heldyans?"

"Father doesn't like them. He likes them less than you."

"What about the raiders from the south?"

"He doesn't like them either. They smell bad, he says."

Lerial nods and waits.

"How did you come to Hamor?" Kyedra asks after another long silence.

"You don't know the story?" *Surely, the daughter of the Duke of Afrit should know that,* thinks Lerial.

"I know the sea destroyed Cyador . . . Cyad, anyway. You came across the Great Western Ocean on a white metal ship. You threatened to sink all the ships in the harbor at Swartheld. My grandfather allowed your father—"

"My grandmother. The Empress. Go on."

"My grandfather allowed your grandmother to purchase these lands. That's what I know. Tell me something I don't know."

"My grandmother was the Empress. She gathered the Mirror Lancers and the Magi'i onto the *Kerial.* That was the last fireship. They got out of the harbor at Cyad just before the big waves smashed and swallowed everything. Then they took the ship to Fyrad, but the entire city was gone. There was just a big bay there. All the towns along the coast were gone, too. So she ordered the captain to cross the ocean to Hamor. Some people died. When they got to Swartheld . . . well, you know that part. Then the fireship carried them up the river here, and the Magi'i and the Lancers began to build. My grandmother told them what to do. The fireship stopped the Heldyans and the raiders from Merowey from coming downriver and bothering people. That was what Grandmother promised." Lerial stops and looks at Kyedra, then says, "It wasn't that simple. That's what . . ." He does not finish the sentence, realizing that he doesn't want to admit that it was his mother who had told him that building Cigoerne and expanding the lands controlled by the Magi'i had been anything but simple.

"What about your grandmother?" asks Kyedra.

"I told you about her."

"You said what she did. You didn't say what she was like. Was she ugly, the way . . ." The girl stops.

Lerial does not press, knowing that someone, perhaps her father, had said that about his grandmother. "She was kind to me, but she didn't put up with any misbehavior. She even swatted my brother." *Lephi deserved it. He was hurting the cat that lived in the stable.* "She was grand and tall, and no one argued with her. Not any of the Magi'i or the Mirror Lancers. Not even my father, and certainly not my aunt."

"Your aunt?"

"Emerya."

"She was the healer who saved Uncle Rham, wasn't she?"

"She is." Lerial knows he should not mention that Rham had attempted an ambush that would have killed his aunt, not when his brother the duke—and Kyedra's father—is meeting with his own father. He still thinks Rham was sneaky and evil. He does not even consider saying so.

"Is she your favorite aunt?"

"I suppose so. She's my only aunt. Do you have a favorite aunt?"

"Father only has brothers. They can't have consorts unless he doesn't have children. I have two brothers. They're still little. Do you have other brothers or a sister?"

"Besides my brother Lephi, I have one sister. That's Ryalah. She's just two."

"I wish I had a sister."

Thinking about Ryalah, Lerial can't imagine why anyone would want a sister. He also doesn't want to talk anymore to the strange girl he is supposed to be nice to, but he dutifully asks, "Why?"

"My brothers are always fighting. They play rough."

"Sisters can play rough."

"Not in the palace of the Duke of Afrit. Not in Swartheld." She pauses. "This isn't much of a palace. It's nice, but it's small."

Lerial glances around the north fountain courtyard, some twenty yards on a side. It doesn't seem that small to him, although his mother has told him that it is tiny compared to the vanished Palace of Light.

Cigoerne

I

The sun beats down on the palace, and Lerial tries not to trudge as he makes his way out into the private south courtyard that has always served as the arms practice area for the family—since the palace was completed some ten years earlier. The north and south courtyards are the same size, half that of the main central courtyard, with its multiple fountains and its walled gardens. The north courtyard has two fountains, making it cooler than the south courtyard, with its small single fountain, its paved open area for weapons practice, while the central courtyard boasts four fountains, spaced so that their mist cools the entire open space.

The wooden wand Lerial carries feels heavier than the cupridium blade he will use once his father has decided he is accomplished enough to ride with the Lancers on patrol missions, against either Heldyan border forces or the nomadic raiders that occasionally make their way northward through the grasslands of Merowey.

Lerial knows the heavy feel of the wand comes from what awaits him in sparring with Lephi, who is only three years older, and not that much taller, but far more at ease with a weapon in his hand than is Lerial, whether the weapon is a sabre or a bow or lance, not that Lerial has had any practice with a lance, and little enough with a bow.

"Are you ready?" asks Lephi from the sunlit center of the courtyard, where he stands waiting, raising the heavy wooden wand that approximates a Lancer's sabre.

"I'm coming." Lerial walks from the shadows cast by the three upper levels of the palace and into the sunlight, a brightness whose intensity always seems to surprise him. He can feel the fine grit under the soles of his boots, grit that is everywhere no matter how often the rough courtyard tiles are swept.

Lephi, of course, stands with his back to the sun. Lerial takes a position with the brilliant white sun to his left and motions with his wand for Lephi to move to a point directly across the circle marked in red and black tiles.

"You can't do that in battle," observes Lephi.

"No . . . but I can choose to fight or not and take a position."

"Not always."

Lerial just waits for Lephi to move or attack.

After several moments, Lephi moves, taking a position directly across from his younger brother. Lerial sets his feet, lifts his blade, and concentrates on Lephi and his brother's wand.

Lephi half turns, starts to do what looks to be a thrust, but Lerial knows the movement is a feint, because his brother's feet do not move, nor does he shift his weight. Instead of trying to block a thrust that will not come, Lerial merely holds his guard. Then Lephi suddenly drops and brings his wand up, and Lerial barely can beat down the thrust and has to move to the side.

Wands move quickly, and then even more quickly. Lerial is already sweating heavily with the effort of countering Lephi's constant attacks, thrusts, and counterthrusts . . . and just trying to react.

Abruptly, Lephi turns a thrust into a twisting move that rips Lerial's wand out of his sweaty hand. The older youth grins. "You didn't see that one."

Lerial doesn't reply but moves to the side of the circle to recover his wand. When he picks it up, the grip of the hilt feels rougher in places where grit has clung to the dampness from his hand. Maybe that will help.

In the shadows, he can see Amaira, and her mother, his aunt Emerya, and Ryalah, all three sitting at a small table. Amaira and Ryalah are playing pegboard, but Emerya has been watching the sparring. Why? The other courtyards are cooler. He is still wondering when Lephi speaks.

"That was quick. Do you want to try again?" Lephi lifts his wand.

Lerial considers the invitation, ignoring Lephi's tone, a tone that implies that Lerial is smaller and weaker, and always will be. He smiles, painful as it is. "I won't get any better if I don't keep trying."

"That's the spirit."

Again, Lerial can sense the undertone by which Lephi suggests all the trying in the world won't help Lerial. He finds his teeth clenching. He takes a deep breath and tries to relax before he slowly walks back and takes a position on the edge of the circle.

Lerial and Lephi spar for almost a glass.

By the time they are both exhausted, Lerial's shirt is dripping wet, and he has bruises in too many places. Those bruises would be far worse if Lephi had not pulled his strikes, Lerial knows, and that leaves him feeling even more despondent when he leaves the circle.

Ryalah and Amaira have left, perhaps following Lephi, but Emerya remains at the table near the small fountain.

"You worked hard, Lerial," she says kindly.

"Hard, yes, but not good enough to hold my own." Lerial takes a deep breath. "There ought to be a way for me to do better against Lephi." He tries to keep his words from sounding despondent, even though that is how he feels. He glances at his aunt, whose once shimmering red hair is now mostly white, although he can sense that she still is a strong healer with a core of black order.

"There is . . . if you're willing to work at it," Emerya says quietly.

"There is? Really? Can you show me?"

"If you're willing to pay the price."

The utter seriousness of her tone and the feeling of truthfulness behind her words cools his enthusiasm almost as quickly as a bucket of winter water from the Swarth might have.

"Come see me after dinner. If anyone asks, tell them that I think it's time for you to learn something about battlefield healing."

"Won't that be lying? If it is, Mother will know." If she concentrates.

"I'm supposed to begin teaching you about some healing, and I will. That will help you with bladework."

Lerial can't help but frown.

"Trust me. It will. It will also be harder than practicing with Lephi . . . until you learn how." Emerya smiles. "That's true of every skill worth having, you'll discover."

"You sound like Grandmere."

"Where do you think I learned such matters?" For a moment, Emerya seems to be somewhere else. Abruptly, she smiles. "After dinner, then? My apartments?"

"Thank you. I'll be there." What other choice does he have? No matter how hard Lerial tries, no matter how much instruction he gets from his father, or from Undercaptain Woelyt, Lephi seems to be getting better faster than he is.

He takes his time walking back to his room up on the third level, where the breezes are stronger, but it is a good glass before he has cooled down enough to wash up and change into trousers and a plain pale green shirt for dinner. He walks to the window and stands there, letting the light spring breeze flow past him as he looks to the north, out over the small city that Cigoerne has become just in the years he can remember. Once there was the single pier where the *Kerial* had been moored until operating the fireship had become too dangerous, and Lerial's father had ordered it dismantled and the fittings and metal turned to other uses, with the limited amount of cupridium remaining being chaos-forged into Lancer sabres, lighter and stronger than the heavy iron blades of Afrit or Heldya. Now there are two shorter piers, used mostly for trading vessels . . . and the handful of craft used by the Lancers to patrol the river.

Finally, Lerial makes his way down to the small dining terrace off the main courtyard. There, every evening when the weather is good and when his father is in Cigoerne, the family shares refreshments before dining. At least, Lerial reflects, they have for as long as the palace has been complete, and that has been for not quite eleven years, not that he can remember those first years very clearly.

His mother is already there, sitting at the largest table and talking with his aunt. Unlike Emerya, Xeranya is blond, with shoulder-length curly hair, and freckles that Lerial has inherited across her nose and below her eyes, eyes that are a watery but penetrating green. She has a strong nose, like Lerial, and an equally strong chin, unlike Lerial, whose chin is more modest. She wears a green blouse and loose green pantaloons, what most healers wear, especially in public, where all women also wear loose silky scarves that cover their hair and lower face—or are supposed to do so.

Emerya, dressed in similar fashion, although the green of her garb is slightly darker, nods to Lerial and then looks back to Xeranya. Amaira and Ryalah are at another small table, moving the pegs on the circular board.

"I won!" declares Ryalah. "This time I won!"

"Good, dear," says Xeranya, in the calm voice that Lerial associates with healers, since both his mother and Emerya speak that way, and so did his grandmother, and all were healers. "But please don't shout it to the world. Boasting is very unbecoming."

The brown-eyed and dark-haired Amaira offers an amused smile, and Lerial understands that Ryalah's victory might not have been entirely due to her skill.

That's fine when you're six, but if Lephi tried that now, you'd be furious. As it is, Lerial bridles at his older brother's condescending attitude when they spar.

"Good evening, Mother, Aunt Emerya!" Lephi's cheerful voice comes from behind Lerial. He strides past Lerial toward the refreshment table. There he picks up a glass carafe—the crystal carafes are reserved for meals with officials from Swartheld or with important merchanters—and starts to fill a squarish tumbler with a pale red vintage.

"If you're going to drink wine, Lephi," Xeranya says, "water it."

"Yes, Mother." Lephi smiles.

Lerial can order-sense his brother's anger, and that means both his aunt, and possibly his mother, can as well, but no one says a word.

Lephi pours a small amount of water into the wine and swirls it, then walks over to the large round table that will seat eight, but is occupied only by the two women. He takes a seat on the far side of the table, facing the nearest fountain in the courtyard, a fountain with a set of nozzles that encircle a statue of Lerial and Lephi's grandsire, the Emperor Lephi, and spray a mist that both shrouds the statue and helps cool the courtyard. In turn, Lerial steps to the refreshment table and half fills a pewter mug with the light lager. He joins the others at the "adult" table, taking a place beside Emerya.

"It's been a cool spring, don't you think?" asks Xeranya, clearly changing the subject from whatever she and Emerya had been discussing.

"Cooler than last year, but warmer than two years ago," replies Emerya. "I still think we'll have a hot summer. The river's lower, too, a good yard."

"You think that will affect the maize?"

"Not here, but it will farther downstream, especially south of Luba." Emerya glances toward the archway that leads to the main corridor of the palace.

"Will that mean raiders from Afrit?" asks Lephi.

Lerial can sense the eagerness in his brother's voice. *Because Father has said he can ride on some Lancer patrols?*

"The arms-commander of Afrit has sent a dispatch to your father saying that, if there are raiders, he will be pleased to execute publicly any who are captured, either by our Lancers or his armsmen." Xeranya smiles. "I suspect that dispatch was posted in every Afritan town on our northern border."

"That might not stop them," Lephi declares.

"It will," says Emerya. "The Duke's arms-commander is a man of his word, for better or worse."

Lephi starts to say something—until Xeranya looks at him.

"We don't have problems with Afrit, and we don't need them," Xeranya says, as though Lephi had not even opened his mouth. "If there's a hot summer again this year, we'll have to deal with more marauders from Merowey . . . and who knows what the Duke of Heldya will do?"

Emerya nods.

At that moment, Xeranya glances in the direction of the archway, then smiles in pleasure as a tall and broad-shouldered figure steps onto the terrace. "Kiedron, dear, I was getting worried."

"There's nothing to worry about." The Duke of Cigoerne offers a smile in return as he nears the table. His dark brown hair still shows not a sign of silver, nor do his thick dark eyebrows, nor would any beard he grew, although he has never grown one, not that Lerial recalls. "The tariff inspectors found finished cloth inside cotton bales in a Meroweyan flatboat headed to Swartheld. The trader who owns the flatboat insisted that he'd taken the cargo on good faith . . ."

"I still don't like the idea of the Duke of Cigoerne acting as a tariff justicer for Afrit," declares Xeranya.

"We can use the golds, and they only call for me when it's a question of law."

"But Afrit gets half the golds," says Xeranya.

"We'd both suffer if they paid tariffs to us and then to Afrit," replies Kiedron. "We'd have to patrol the Swarth day and night. Whether they port here or in Swartheld or any of the Afrit river towns, we get a share of the tariffs."

"Not a huge share," rejoins Xeranya. "And we have to rely on the Duke's count."

That, Lerial knows, is always less than it should be, but it is another matter never mentioned except among family—and never by any children.

"It's better than fighting over it, don't you think? Besides, the arrangement means that more traders from the south stop here for provisions and other goods that they can sell downriver without paying tariffs. That's helped build Cigoerne. We can't afford to dream about what cannot yet be. We just need to build, brick by brick. Those tariffs are what funded the ministry building and what pay for not only the river port inspectors but also for some of the tariff collectors and others."

"What did you decide on the cloth smuggler?" asks Emerya smoothly before Xeranya can say more.

"We took a tenth part of the cloth and fined him two golds. He should consider himself fortunate."

Even Lerial knows that the cloth or the proceeds from its sale will not be reported to Duke Atroyan's inspectors. The golds will, because they are recorded on the passage documents.

"He should indeed," declares Xeranya.

"And for dinner?" asks Kiedron, before turning to the refreshment table and pouring a full tumbler of the deep red wine.

"Goat biastras," replies Xeranya. "Young goat."

Lerial wonders from where the cooks had obtained the marinated sweet peppers that surround the strips of braised goat before each tube is batter-dipped and fried. It seems early for peppers.

"The peppers came from the sheltered garden on the south side of the palace, Lerial," explains Emerya.

Her reply to his unspoken question reminds him, again, of how really good healers can sense how people feel even when they say nothing or their faces reveal little, although he suspects his expression might well have been less than impassive.

"Better biastras than burhka," says Kiedron with a smile.

"I think I'd actually prefer the burhka." Xeranya smiles. "We're having that for dinner tomorrow, but I'll tell the cooks to be sparing with the chilies."

Before long, everyone is seated at the long dining table, with Lerial's father at the head, and his mother to his right, and Lephi to his left. Emerya sits beside Lephi and Lerial beside his mother and across from his aunt. Amaira is seated on Lerial's other side, with Ryalah beside Emerya.

Because he serves Amaira before himself, Lerial is one of the last to try a biastra. He hopes that the "young" goat is less gamey than what he has tasted before. Not only is it barely gamey, but the white cream sauce he has drizzled over the biastra is excellent, with the piquancy of a good cheese and a hint of mint. He finishes the first and begins on the second, noting that Amaira has also finished her first. He serves her a second one.

"I see this version of biastra meets with your approval," murmurs his mother with a smile.

"It's excellent," he returns in an equally low voice.

"Have the river patrols seen any signs of raiders or Heldyan patrols?" Lephi asks Kiedron.

"Not so far, but it's not likely to be long. The planting season is over, and usually that's when the raids begin." Kiedron turns to Xeranya. "This is a great improvement, dear. If the cooks can do the same in the future, we should have biastras more often."

"I think that can be managed," replies Xeranya warmly.

"Excellent." Kiedron looks to Emerya. "Have you found any more healers for your school?"

"There are two village girls from Ensenla. They show great promise."

"Ensenla? That's in Afrit," declares Lephi.

"They slipped away because they would not be allowed as healers in

Afrit," explains Emerya. "They are from a peasant background. I'm not about to turn away girls who could be good healers."

Kiedron nods. "See what you can do to suggest that while any of their family are welcome here, they would be wise not to return to Ensenla, even for a visit."

"Their return to Afrit is unlikely. One was beaten so badly for asking to be considered as a healer that some of her bruises have still not healed."

That is something Lerial does not understand. Even in Cyador, children from anywhere had been allowed to try to meet the standards of either the Magi'i or the Lancers. Most didn't make it, but many did, and his grandsire, the Emperor Lephi, had even allowed women to become ironmages.

After that, the conversation veers toward the weather, the river, and how well the family gardens and fields seem to be doing. There are no sweets following the main course. Sweets and desserts are reserved for special occasions . . . or for formal dinners with outsiders.

The first to leave the dining terrace after dinner are Emerya, Amaira, and Ryalah. Ryalah will be put to bed by her mother, not her nurse, because Emerya has refused to turn her daughter over to a nurse except during the day when she is at the Hall of Healing. That has been true from the time of Amaira's birth . . . another family matter that is never discussed. Lerial still recalls the tongue-lashing his mother delivered when he'd insisted on asking why a second time . . . and the fact that she'd said that if it ever came up again, his father would handle the matter.

At age eight, Lerial hadn't been willing to risk that. He still isn't. He just listens.

". . . bows like the Rational Archers used . . ."

". . . ironmages . . . even with cupridium . . . can't get the flexibility . . ."

"Local yew works better . . ."

"We're losing too much of what we had, ser," insists Lephi.

"Your grandmother," interjects Xeranya quietly, "said that trying to reclaim too much at once was foolish."

". . . still seems wrong . . ."

After a time, Lerial looks to his sire.

"You want to leave, Lerial?"

"Yes, ser."

"Where are you going?" asks Kiedron. "Sneaking off somewhere?"

"No, ser. Aunt Emerya said it was time to see if I could learn anything about wound healing . . . after a fight, I mean."

"Well . . . pay attention. That can't hurt. She's a good healer."

"Who needs to be a healer?" asks Lephi. "If you're good enough, you don't need healing."

"Your men might," replies Xeranya. "I've healed more of your father's Lancers than I can recall." Her voice is pleasant and even.

Lephi stiffens at the look she bestows on him and immediately responds. "I can see that. Some of them aren't as good as Father."

And neither are you. But Lerial does not speak those words. Instead, he leaves the dining terrace and makes his way toward the west end of the south corridor on the second level, one of the warmer quarters in the palace, not particularly comfortable in summer. The corridor guard nods politely as Lerial passes and walks to the last doorway on the left. He raps firmly, then eases the door ajar. "Aunt Emerya? I'm here."

"Just take a seat somewhere. I'm still putting Amaira to bed. I'll be there in a moment."

"Please don't hurry for me." Lerial steps into the chamber that serves as sitting room and study for his aunt and closes the door behind himself.

"I won't."

Lerial can hear the hint of a smile in her voice, even from the adjoining sleeping chamber she shares, by choice and not necessity, with her daughter. He takes the straight chair by the window looking out to the south. The inner shutters, closed during the day to keep out the heat that will get worse as spring turns to summer, are open, although with the evening breeze coming out of the north, the sitting room is still uncomfortably warm. To the south are the palace grounds, mostly gardens in tended raised beds with oranges, lemons, limes, and figs. There are no pearapples, for most of Hamor is too hot, except in the far south, in places like Sastok and Plyath, or so he has heard. Pearapples do not travel well, and he has only heard his father, mother, and aunt occasionally lament their absence. Beyond the walls that enclose the gardens and protect the family, not that they need much of that now, are the dwellings and shops that stretch to the south. To the east, of course, and down a gradual slope, is the river. Farther to the west are hills, and the springs that feed the aqueduct that serves the palace. Lerial continues to gaze out the window as he hears his aunt singing.

"There was a pretty little city on a sea of blue,
and a pretty little girl who looked a lot like you,
and the girl and her mother loved the green and white

that flooded from the great grand Palace of Light
when the sun had set and she saw the night
and the stars of glory shined out so bright . . ."

Hearing the song, Lerial couldn't help but think of Amaira. She is eight. She has dark brown curly hair and brown eyes, unlike anyone else in the family. She laughs a lot, also unlike most of the Magi'i and their children. She and Ryalah play together, almost as if they were sisters, rather than cousins. Lerial can't help but like Amaira, but no one has ever talked about her father . . . or who he might have been.

His aunt had never consorted. That he knows. He also knows that she has never been particularly interested in any of the younger Magi'i. Of course, no one pressed her, not when there are so few men among those her age because most of them had died when the Accursed Forest had destroyed the cities of Cyador . . . and Lerial's grandsire and most of the chaos-wielding Magi'i and all but the two companies of Mirror Lancers that his grandmother had used to take the *Kerial* and transport the survivors to Hamor . . . and Cigoerne.

As he half listens and waits, Lerial cannot help but wonder how his grandmere had managed it. The older he got, the more improbable it seemed. Yet it had happened. At the silence from the bedchamber and the sound of the door closing, Lerial stands and turns.

"Are you ready?" asks Emerya.

"I am." He almost says, "ser," but refrains because his aunt doesn't like that form of respect applied to women, even though Grandmother Mairena had insisted on it for herself. But then, there are few women, except healers, in positions of authority in Cigoerne, and none, so far as Lerial knows, in Afrit.

"By the way," asks his aunt, "do you recall from where the name Cigoerne comes?"

"An ancient bird from the Rational Stars," he replies, "like the one on the old, old box that you have."

"That box came from the worlds of the Rational Stars. Your grandmother Mairena said that such boxes were often given to healers, much in the way that healers were given the gold and malachite bracelets in Cyador. But there's an irony in that." Emerya smiles ruefully. "Do you know what it is?"

Lerial frowns. He's never heard about this.

"What skill must good healers have?"

"Control of order."

"What are the colors of order and chaos?"

"Chaos is white, usually mixed with red or orange."

"Gold, not orange."

"Order is black." For a moment, Lerial pauses, then says, involuntarily, "Oh . . . but if they were given white . . ."

"Exactly." Emerya shrugs. "But then, all the old books, the ones lost in Cyad, said that the way everything worked was somehow different in the worlds of the Rational Stars."

"How could that be? How could things be different?"

"They can be. Even here, things are often different from what people say or think. Healing is sometimes like that."

"Is that why it will help me in sparring against Lephi?"

"In time, Lerial. In time. What you need to learn will take time and effort, and you will have to practice what I show you, but only around me or when you are alone. Later, you'll be able to show your mother, but not now."

"What about Father?"

Emerya shakes her head. "Kiedron is like many of the Magi'i. He can sense and use chaos, but he is blind to order. Order-blindness is not infrequent among the Magi'i, but the great Emperors of the past, such as Alyiakal and Lorn, could sense and use both."

"Not Kerial?"

"We don't know about him. There were no records about him, either of his appearance or his magely talents . . . or if he had any." At Lerial's disbelieving look, she adds, "Either he destroyed such records or his nephew did. He had no children, remember?"

Lerial recalls that . . . but only after her reminder.

"Anyway . . . that's why you can't show your father . . . or Lephi. He takes after Kiedron in that respect."

That was something Lerial does not know, and already he has a glimmering of an idea as to why Emerya may be able to help him.

"I'm going to show you something, but you'll have to watch, with your thoughts, the way you do when you sense chaos. Look at the back of my hand."

Lerial does so. For a moment, he can see or sense nothing. Then . . . there is a black fuzziness.

"That's what gathering order looks like. Try to feel what I'm doing."

Sensing what Emerya is doing is far harder than merely observing the result of what she has done, and in moments Lerial can feel the sweat beading on his forehead. "You see why I said this would take time and work?"

"I do."

"You can stop now." Emerya waits a moment, as if to allow Lerial to gather his thoughts and recover, then says, "A good healer only uses order when necessary. For small and shallow wounds that can be cleaned well and quickly, it's better to do that. Clear strong spirits are generally best, but garlic juice will also do, but that can be painful and may require holding the injured man when you apply either spirits or garlic. Then bind the wound and watch. If there is a dull red that strengthens you can apply free order . . . but there is great danger in that, because trying to draw too much free order will take it from you . . . and can kill you. That is why healers are trained slowly and carefully, so that they have experience in knowing how much order is needed and how much they can spare. You are *not* to attempt any healing except with me or another trained healer watching. Do you understand?"

Lerial nods.

"For the next eightday, I want you to watch people the way you just watched me. You're to sense what you can about the order and the chaos in them or around them. You're to do that without actually looking at them. Most times you won't sense more than a white fuzziness or a vague black fuzziness. If you sense more than that, don't say anything to them, but tell me each evening. You're to come and meet with me for a bit every night that you can for the next eightday. Is that clear?"

"Yes, ser." The honorific slips out before Lerial can catch it.

Emerya does not correct him, but only says, "That's all for tonight. Go and get some sleep. That will help all those bruises. Also, I wouldn't spar with Lephi tomorrow."

"I won't." Lerial pauses, then adds, "Thank you."

"You're welcome." Emerya smiles.

As Lerial leaves and walks back toward his own small sleeping chamber, he realizes that he had sensed—or had the feeling—that Emerya has more than one reason for not wanting him to spar with Lephi on threeday.

II

The next morning at breakfast, Lerial concentrates on trying to see either order or chaos patterns in others, beginning with his mother, who has just enough chaos in her system that he senses her as a dark, dark gray—as opposed to his father and Lephi, who, while not a brilliant white, seem to be an off-white. Ryalah and Amaira are close to pure black, as is Emerya, although Ryalah is slightly darker than either her cousin or her aunt. In making his observations, Lerial is especially careful not to look in his aunt's direction. For the next five days, Lerial follows his aunt's instructions as well as he can, reporting to her every evening, when he learns a bit more at each meeting about healing.

On oneday morning, he makes his way into the study off the southern courtyard to meet with Saltaryn, the magus in charge of his instruction in not only reading, writing, mathematics, and rhetoric, but in the understanding and use of chaos and order. Saltaryn stands beside the circular table. He is sandy haired and perhaps twenty-six or twenty-seven. Like all Magi'i he wears white with the crossed lightnings on the breast of his summer tunic.

"Good morning, ser," offers Lerial, as he always does.

"Good morning, Lerial." Saltaryn does not smile, but asks, "What have you been doing over the past eightday?"

"Ser? I'm sorry, but I don't understand. I've done the same things every day as I always do . . . except I haven't sparred with Lephi this eightday. I was too bruised to do that for several days, and he's been riding on a patrol the past few."

"Hmmm . . . Oh, well. These things happen."

"What things, might I ask, ser?"

"You're manifesting more order than chaos, and that's . . . not . . . usual for one of the Magi'i . . . unless you're an order magus or an iron magus. Noerant hasn't been instructing you, has he?"

"Magus Noerant, ser? No, ser. I scarcely even ever see him."

"Well . . . let's get on with your lessons." Saltaryn gestures toward the table, then seats himself.

Lerial sits across from the magus and waits.

Saltaryn takes the candle in the brass holder and sets it between them. "Watch the candle, and tell me what you see." He concentrates, and the wick flares into flame.

Lerial can sense the flash of red-white chaos, as well as the thinnest edging of chaos.

"Well?" asks the white wizard.

"You lit the wick with chaos."

"Just with chaos?"

"Almost entirely. I think . . . I think there was a tiny bit of order directing the chaos."

"Of course. Without direction, chaos is formless. But the less order you can use, the stronger the chaos."

"Doesn't it take more order to control greater amounts of chaos?" asks Lerial.

"It does, but the way a magus handles that order makes a difference. Some require much more order." Saltaryn concentrates, and the candle flame flares and vanishes.

Lerial manages not to frown, surprised that the white wizard has used more chaos to extinguish the flame than it took to light it.

"I want you to try to light the candle," Saltaryn says.

"How?"

"Try to imitate what I did. Focus a tiny bit of chaos at the tip of the candlewick."

Lerial has his doubts, but if Saltaryn can do that, it can be done . . . and Lephi must have done it as well, since his brother can manage some small bolts of chaos.

By the time he leaves the study, Lerial is exhausted. His entire body is covered with sweat, and his undertunic is soaked. But he has managed to light the candle, time after time.

Lighting a candle isn't the same as throwing firebolts. But it is a start.

Since Lephi is not around, Lerial has to practice with someone else, and that ends up being Undercaptain Woelyt—and Woelyt is better than Lephi . . . and not at all sympathetic. By the time Lerial reaches Emerya's quarters after dinner, his entire body aches once more.

"You've been sparring today?" asks Emerya when she leaves the bedchamber and closes the door.

"Not with Lephi. Undercaptain Woelyt."

His aunt shakes her head. "And working with chaos?"

"Yes. How did you know?"

"Because there are chaos fragments swirling around and through you." She shakes her head once more. "You can do it that way, but if you keep it up you'll be dead long before you're even my age."

"Father isn't dead. Neither are you."

"Healers don't handle chaos, and I don't deal with order that way either, since it shortens one's life, if not as much as with chaos. Your father doesn't have the strength you and Lephi have. That comes from your mother."

"Father can throw firebolts, more than Lephi can."

"Not that many, and not for that long, and he can do it better than Lephi right now because he has better control. Lephi will be stronger when he's older."

"How do you know that?"

"What have you been doing for the past days? Haven't you seen?"

Lerial frowns.

"Have you observed your father and Lephi together? Which one glows whiter?"

"Lephi. I thought that was because he's younger."

"That's partly true, but not as much as people think. The ability to handle chaos and order requires a certain skill. Some people have more than others, and it tends to be passed from parents to children. Your grandsire wouldn't have been considered as a magus if he hadn't been Emperor. He had that little ability as a magus. Your grandmother would have been a strong healer if she'd been born to the poorest tradesman or crafter in Cyad."

"That doesn't solve anything. Lephi—"

"I am trying to help you. Complaining and whining won't help."

"What am I supposed to do? I'm of the Magi'i," replies Lerial, a touch of bitterness in his words. "I'm supposed to be a white wizard who can handle a blade with the best."

"You could be a stronger gray magus and still handle a blade. You just can't do it the same way Lephi and your father do. Can you observe the Lancers sparring without being seen?"

"I can't do concealments yet, and I didn't know there were gray Magi'i."

"They have never been many. Most ended up as Mirror Lancer officers. Lorn was likely one. These days, no one is likely to say anything, especially since you're not the eldest. I didn't mean you should try a concealment. I just want you to watch some of them spar. Try to sense how order and chaos move around them. You should see a pattern."

"What sort of pattern?"

Emerya shakes her head, then picks up a small cloth bag tied tightly at the top with twine. She tosses it to Lerial. He catches it without thinking. It is filled with sand.

"Toss it back."

Lerial does so.

"Close your eyes. Go ahead. Close them. Now try to catch the bag."

The bag bounces off his hands. He opens his eyes, then bends and scoops the bag off the woven grass carpet, dyed in green and white, before straightening up.

"Concentrate on me, not the bag. Keep your eyes closed and toss the bag back to me," orders Emerya.

Lerial closes his eyes and lofts the bag back toward where she had been.

"Lerial! I moved. Keep trying to sense where I am."

At the end of close to half a glass Lerial is again soaked in sweat . . . but by then he has a good feel for where the bag will be—and where Emerya is—by the way order flows around her.

"How will this help?"

"Do you need light to see what I'm doing?"

"Oh . . ."

"If you can sense where someone is when the light is bad . . ."

Lerial nods.

"That's not the only reason, but you aren't good enough yet for the second one to be obvious. You'll have to trust me on that."

Lerial smiles. "I can do that." *For you.*

"Now . . . there's something else you need to think about. Chaos comes in different shades of red," explains Emerya. "Tomorrow . . ." She shakes her head. "No . . . tomorrow won't work. Nor threeday. On fourday, you'll come to the Hall of Healing after your lessons. I'll arrange that with Saltaryn and your mother. While you're there, you can see some of the differing shades of chaos. Order isn't quite the same."

"It's all black, but . . ." Lerial frowns. "Aren't there different shades? In some people, it's like the black is deeper, even though it feels like there's no difference in the color."

"How do you know that?" asked his aunt. "I've never mentioned that."

"Ryalah is a brighter black than Amaira. I thought that was because she was younger."

This time, Emerya is the one to frown. "You definitely need more training in order and chaos, especially in order. That might be a problem." After a moment, she adds, "I'd appreciate it if you didn't mention that to anyone quite yet."

"I won't. Will you tell me when I can talk about it?"

"I will." Emerya smiles. "Go and get a good night's sleep. You need it."

After he leaves his aunt's rooms, Lerial realizes that Emerya has never responded directly to his observation about Amaira not showing as deep a sense of order blackness as did Ryalah. *Because her father wasn't of the Magi'i? Or for some other reason? And why was she disturbed about your being able to feel different degrees of order blackness?*

He shakes his head, thinking about how complicated things are getting just because he'd told his aunt about his troubles in sparring with Lephi. *Or would they have gotten complicated anyway?*

III

On fourday, after breakfast, but well before midmorning, Lerial stands outside the stables off the north courtyard of the palace, holding the reins of the brown gelding that has been his mount for the past five years, despite Lephi's scarcely veiled suggestions that a stallion might be more appropriate. He wears the pale green summer trousers and tunic that are worn by either Lancer or healer trainees, not that there are many men who are healers. He has picked a spot where he and the gelding can stand in the narrow shadows that are shrinking moment by moment as he waits for Emerya.

For an instant, he does not recognize the rider who approaches, followed by two Lancer guards, because Emerya is wearing a filmy but largely opaque head scarf that hides her red-streaked, silver-white hair. He immediately mounts and urges the gelding to move up beside his aunt, who is riding a mare, if one nearly as large as Lerial's gelding.

"I'm glad you're ready," Emerya says. "Your father had a few questions I had to answer before I left."

"About me coming with you?"

"He didn't know about that until I told him. When I said it was necessary for you to get better control of your abilities and that I'd talked to Magus Saltaryn, he just nodded. No . . . there were other matters we discussed. If you want to know what they are, you'll have to ask him."

Lerial manages not to frown, since Emerya has to know that he isn't about to ask his father about anything unless Kiedron brings up the subject first. *But then, that's why she said it that way, rather than just saying she wouldn't tell you.*

The courtyard gates are open, and guarded but by a pair of Lancers, both to the eye not that much older than Lerial. Neither gives Emerya, Lerial, or the two Lancer guards more than a passing glance.

Once on the main square in front of the palace, Emerya turns her mare to the left toward the boulevard leading northeast. On the right is the Ministry—the building that holds the high minister, and the tariff inspectors and the well-guarded treasury on the lower level. As he rides past the two-story structure, Lerial looks ahead. While he knows that the Hall of Healing is on a low rise overlooking the river piers, and has even ridden past it more than a few times, he has never been inside the sandstone walls, let alone into the Hall itself.

"What are you going to do today?" he asks.

"What I always do every day. I try to heal people. What you will do is to observe closely and say nothing until I ask you a question or give you permission to speak. Do you understand?"

"Yes, ser."

"Good. I don't want to have to remind you when others are around."

Lerial can understand that, and he wouldn't want to be corrected in front of others, especially healers. He is always happy to be out of the palace, and he begins to study both sides of the boulevard.

Although his parents and Emerya have all assured him that, as cities go, Cigoerne is small, it does not seem that small to Lerial. The palace is located on a flattened ridge almost two kays west of the Swarth River, with the Square of the Magi'i directly before it on the east side. East of the square, beyond the walls around the Ministry, stretching somewhat to the north and south, are larger dwellings, all of two stories, and all with center courtyards and fountains. These house the families of the Magi'i and those of the more senior Lancer officers, those whose rank is overcaptain and higher. As a practical matter, only the majer and the submajers, past and present, have dwellings anywhere close to the square, not that there are even a handful of them.

Even farther east and extending north and south as well are the dwellings of the merchanters. Even closer to the river, and lower, if not low enough to worry about the infrequent floods of the Swarth River, are the houses and shops of the crafters. Just behind the river piers are the structures housing the warehouses and factorages of the merchanters, as well as the shops of various tradesmen.

Lerial remains silent for a time as they ride down the boulevard, which leads directly to the Hall of Healing, just as the boulevard that angles southeast from the square leads to the headquarters of the Lancers, also located on a low rise above the river, with piers for the Lancer river patrol craft below the rise. Finally, he asks, "You never really answered my question about why the Hall of Healing is so far from the palace."

Emerya laughs softly. "You asked that years ago. You couldn't have been more than ten. Do you recall every question you asked when you were told you needed to be older to understand?"

Lerial smiles at the good-humored tone in her voice. "Probably not . . . but I remember the ones I thought were important."

"Sometimes those are the best to remember, but not always. Sometimes, the questions we forget to ask are the ones that are the most important."

Lerial has to think about that for a moment, then realizes that Emerya has still not answered his question. "Why is the Hall of Healing—"

"Who needs healing the most?"

"Everyone needs healers at times."

"What happens if you need a healer? Or your father? How many healers are there in the palace?"

"Oh . . . the poorer people don't have that many healers, and the Hall is closer to them?" Lerial pauses. "Then why didn't you tell me that then?"

"I did. You said that there had to be another reason."

Lerial doesn't remember that, but he can sense that there is no evasion in his aunt's reply. "Then there must have been."

"There is. There are several. Would you care to think what they might be?"

Lerial thinks and finally says, "Because putting it there shows that Father cares about the people. It's more visible there."

"Good."

"Why couldn't you tell me that?"

"You weren't able to consider the political reasons then. What else?"

Lerial shrugs. "I can't think of another reason. Not right now."

"Who are the healers . . . most of them, anyway?"

"Daughters . . . women of the Magi'i . . . most of them, anyway."

"Where do they live?"

"Father and Mother . . . and you . . . located the Hall there so that they'd all have to leave where they lived to go to the Hall?"

"Actually, it was your grandmother who made that point. She made it rather strongly. She said that the elthage and the altage classes of Cyador had become too separate from the people they ruled. She also made the point that the poorer folk wouldn't travel to a healing hall in the middle of dwellings of those better off, and that defeated half the reason for even having a Hall of Healing in Cigoerne."

Lerial could see that. What he couldn't see was his grandmother thinking that way.

"She was very proud, Lerial, but she was anything but stupid or unobservant, something that your grandsire never understood. Had he listened to her, we all might still be in Cyad, enjoying the pleasures of the City of Light."

"You've never said anything like that before."

"I have. Just not to you. I told Lephi the same thing when he was your age. He insisted that I was mistaken. Assuming I'm still around when Amaira is old enough to understand, I'll tell her, and Ryalah, in turn. Why am I the one? Usually, some things are better left unsaid by parents, and it might be better if someone else told Amaira . . . perhaps . . . well . . . we'll see when the time comes."

Lerial can see that . . . mostly. Sometimes, more than sometimes, he does listen to his parents, even when he doesn't agree. After several moments, he asks, "Will Amaira and Ryalah be healers?"

"They have the order-talent, but healing takes more than talent, just as it takes more than the ability to recognize, summon, and direct chaos to be a full magus or even a white wizard."

From what Lerial has gathered, although no one had actually said it in as many words, "white wizard" was the term used by the Magi'i for those chaos wielders who were lesser in ability than a truly accomplished magus, those whose talents tended to be limited to throwing firebolts and other forms of lesser destruction.

The walls around the Hall of Healing are formed of comparatively small sandstone blocks mortared in place and about two yards high. There are two gates, both of iron grillwork, and both open, although they are generally closed every night after dark, when a few Lancers guard them, mainly to keep lawbreakers and other minor miscreants from sneaking in and robbing the ill of what little they have. Emerya and Lerial ride in through the north gate, the one reserved for healers and Magi'i, and Emerya leads the way to the modest stable set against the north wall.

"You can leave your mount for the Lancers to groom," advises Emerya. "They don't have much else to do."

Lerial is glad of that suggestion, especially since he has only groomed his mount a handful of times, under supervision, more to let him know what is required than to make him proficient.

After dismounting, Emerya strides toward the doorway on the north end of the Hall, that entry barely standing out with the smallest of limestone arches set in the plain sandstone wall, marked with frequent, if narrow, windows. Lerial hurries to catch up to her. Once inside, in the main corridor that runs the length of the building, he almost stops in his tracks after two steps. That is how powerfully the sense of chaos strikes him.

Emerya lets the head scarf slip off her hair and away from her face, easing that end of the shimmersilk fabric back over her shoulder as she glances back at him. "Come on. You'll get used to it. You'd better, if you want to ride patrols."

Lerial swallows and follows her along the corridor to the first door, then inside. An older woman in pale green—a healer's aide—glances up from where she sits behind a narrow table desk. "Will you need an aide today, Lady Emerya?"

"My nephew has some healer talent. We'll see how he does." Emerya smiles.

"There are several children in the receiving chamber. One has been there more than a glass," offers the woman.

"We'll start there, then." Emerya takes a basket from a small and doorless cube-shaped cupboard, one of several, set in the wall.

Lerial watches as she extends an order mist over whatever is in the basket, then reaches down and picks up an empty basket, which she hands to Lerial. She slips her arm through the arched high handle of her basket, and nods to him. In turn, he leaves the chamber, but nods at the older woman before he leaves, empty basket in hand.

As they walk down the corridor, Emerya says, "That's Demeyla. She's in charge of the healer aides."

"What do the aides do?"

"What you're going to do. You'll see. The basket is for wastes and soiled dressings. Other than that, I'll tell you as we go along. Each one will be different; so there's no point in my trying to explain before. The receiving chamber is the last door on the west side . . . or the first door the way people needing healing come in."

There are a half score raised pallets spaced along the wall of the narrow receiving chamber, each one set between a pair of windows. From what Lerial can see in a quick glance, all but two are taken, most with a person sitting or lying on a pallet, accompanied by someone else.

Beside the first pallet is a woman, standing over a boy who sits on the pallet, his legs over one side. He looks to be younger than Ryalah. He is barefoot and wears shorts and a ragged shirt. Even from several yards away, Lerial can sense the chaos mist surrounding him.

The woman, a good head shorter than Lerial, smiles tentatively as she sees Emerya—or more likely the healer's green tunic and trousers—but the smile immediately fades as her eyes return to the boy.

The boy's hair is black and raggedly cut. His skin is darker than that of Amaira, but still only a light olive-tan, although it is clear to Lerial that his parents must both be Hamorian.

"Ask her what the problem is . . . in Hamorian," murmurs Emerya.

"What might be the problem?" asks Lerial politely, stopping less than a yard from the pallet and the mother.

"Show him, Therylan," replies the woman in an accented Hamorian he does not recognize, certainly not the way in which people from either Cigoerne or Afrit speak. *Is she from Heldya . . . or Merowey?*

Lerial looks to the boy.

"It hurts here." The boy lifts his tattered shirt to reveal a huge ugly pustule half the size of Lerial's hand on the right side of his abdomen, roughly at waist level. Pus oozes from the center of the circular wound, although it is not properly a wound, Lerial realizes, or not one caused by a weapon.

"That looks like a pincer-bug bite that wasn't tended properly," says Emerya in Cyadoran. "Ask her how it happened."

"Do you know how he came by the injury?"

"I do not know. There was a small sore there the day before yesterday. It was bigger yesterday. Today, it is much worse."

Lerial nods, then looks to Emerya.

"What do you sense?"

"There's orangish-reddish chaos in the center, and a white chaos mist around it, with a faint grayish outside that," Lerial replies in Cyadoran, "and chaos mist all around him."

"The gray is what's left of the body's attempt to fight off the wound chaos," explains Emerya. "He's more ill than he looks."

"Could he . . . ?"

"If we don't do something, yes. First, we need to clean away the pus and clean the skin around the wound. I think part of the bug's pincer is still in the wound. That might be what caused this to be so bad. We'll have to get that out. Put your basket at the upper end of the pallet, away from him. When I tell you, have him lie back on the pallet. Take his hands and hold them, gently but firmly. Tell him there's something in the sore that is causing the hurt." Emerya turns slightly and eases a small folded cloth from the basket, which she has set on the end of the pallet away from the boy. The cloth is one of many stacked at one end, Lerial sees. He also can make out a corked bottle.

Belatedly, he places his basket where Emerya has indicated, then turns back to mother and son. "First, the healer will clean away the pus. Then I will have the boy lie back on the pallet. I will hold his hands while she removes one of the things that is causing the hurt. She will clean away more pus after that." Lerial is guessing slightly, but that seems to be what will have to happen.

The mother nods, if tentatively.

"Lie back, please," Lerial says gently, easing the child back, then pulling the tattered shirt up and away from the wound with one hand before taking the boy's hands in his. He has the feeling that everyone in the receiving room is watching him.

Emerya takes the dry clean cloth and gently begins to wipe away the pus, working from the outside toward the suppurating center. Then she drops the first cloth square in Lerial's basket and uncorks the bottle, pouring the clear liquid on another cloth that she uses to further clean the skin. That cloth also ends up in Lerial's basket. Next she takes out a pair of long-necked cupridium tweezers.

Lerial firmly but gently holds the boy's hands as Emerya gently probes the wound. He can sense that she is using order ability somehow to direct the tweezers or move what she seeks to the tweezers—he is not certain which . . . or whether both, but he can definitely sense the ugly reddish-white of what she removes . . . as well as some orangish-red left in the wound.

The boy does not squirm, and only whimpers once. Lerial is not certain whether that is because he is brave or Emerya gentle, or both.

"Try to ease some order into that wound chaos," Emerya murmurs. "Not too much. Just a drop or so at first."

Lerial manages to concentrate a drop of blackness right on the orangish point . . . and that fades so that only the white wound chaos remains, if with the faintest shade of orange.

"About half that . . . again."

About half is all he can manage, and even so, the sweat is beading on his forehead.

"Good. Straighten up. You don't want to drip sweat on him."

Lerial straightens up. Then he watches as Emerya coaxes more pus from the wound and cleans it again . . . and again, then dresses it with a soft cloth secured at the edges with gum-tape strips.

When Emerya finishes, she speaks to the woman in Hamorian. "He is to be quiet for an eightday. If his skin around the wound gets red or has red streaks bring him here quickly. If it does not, he should be healed by the end of an eightday, but he should be careful not to poke or push where the wound is for much longer."

"Thank you, honored healer. Thank you." The woman bows several times before she picks up her son and carries him out of the receiving room.

Before Emerya can move to the next injured person, Lerial asks in a low voice, "Why did you have me talk to them?"

"Because you speak Hamorian without an accent, and that seems to put people at ease. That's even truer for those who aren't from Cigoerne."

After dealing with the boy, Lerial is glad just to watch and hand things to Emerya as she sets set the broken arm of a girl not much older than Amaira. Her mother insists that the girl had fallen, but once the arm has been splinted and the two have left the receiving chamber, Emerya turns to Lerial and asks in low-voiced Cyadoran, "How do you think she broke that arm?"

From the question alone, Lerial would have known that the mother had lied, but he has also sensed that in the way she had answered. "Someone else broke it."

"Most likely her father. Did you see the bruises on her arms?"

"I didn't see bruises, but there were places of white fuzziness."

"That kind of fuzziness usually means bruises or some sort of injury. Sometimes, though, it just means that a more severe injury is healing. You have to look closely because the presence of free chaos isn't always bad. It may just be fading away, and in healing that's good."

"Make way! Make way . . ."

Emerya and Lerial look up as two men rush in carrying a burly older man with a blood-soaked arm, and blood dripping everywhere.

"Cleaver handle broke . . . cleaver cut through his arm!"

Lerial watches intently as Emerya wraps a large cloth bandage around the man's arm, above the gaping wound, then tightens it with a smooth stick, just enough to stop the gushing of the blood, before cleaning the wound, then stitching it, and then binding it, immediately loosening the tourniquet.

"See what you can sense in the arm below the wound," she murmurs to Lerial.

Lerial's head aches, but he concentrates. "There's order there. There's chaos around the wound."

"If you leave a tourniquet on very long, the arm won't recover."

Lerial can sense what she does not say—that it might not anyway. He has another thought. "You had me put order on the wound chaos. Why couldn't we just . . . well . . . bleed way the chaos?"

"There are two reasons for that. First, it's harder for a healer to do that. Second, you can bleed away the chaos force in the body to the point where order will become too strong . . . and the person will die."

Order . . . too strong?

"Lerial . . . order and chaos in the body have to balance, or at least come close to balancing. Hasn't Saltaryn taught you anything?"

"I . . . I just didn't think of it that way."

"As a healer you always have to keep that in mind."

Although her words are quiet, Lerial feels like wincing, but he just nods.

By midafternoon, after following Emerya through the Hall of Healing as she tends to those whose injuries have left them bedridden Lerial comes to a realization. "It seems to me that a good half of the healing you've done today deals with small wounds or minor injuries. Sometimes, it's things caused by the body itself, like boils."

"You're right. What would have happened to that little boy, though, if we hadn't cleaned and gotten rid of the worst of the wound chaos?"

"It would have gotten worse. He might have died."

"It's better to heal, Lerial, when injuries are small. It takes less effort, and a healer can do more for more people."

"You come here most days. Are there that many . . . ?"

"Many come here from well outside of Cigoerne. The way that little boy spoke, he was originally from the part of Merowey just to the southwest of Cigoerne."

"Why do you heal those not from Cigoerne?"

"They could not have traveled that far. They live near here. But . . . even if they did not, we should let them suffer and perhaps die?"

"No . . . I didn't mean that." *Not exactly.*

"Your father rules a land that is more than ten times the size it was when we came here. Every year another village, sometimes more than one, asks to become part of Cigoerne. We protect them and heal them as we can. That is what a good ruler does. The Dukes of Merowey and Afrit have been forced to recognize your father as ruler."

"But not as their equal."

"Not yet. That *will* come. After all, he is Cyador's heir."

The way Emerya says that contains a certainty that chills Lerial, even as he thinks he should be cheered by it. So he merely nods and follows her to the next ward.

By the fourth glass of the afternoon, when Lerial accompanies Emerya from the Hall, he is exhausted. His boots feel heavy, and his feet ache from being on them all day. Trying the small amount of healing that Emerya has let him do has left him without the ability to focus even the smallest bit of order.

IV

Late on fiveday morning, after his lessons with Saltaryn, Lerial watches two of the Lancers assigned to the palace guard detail sparring in the exercise yard to the west of the palace stables. He can do this without being too obvious by using a small window in the stable. After several moments, he realizes that he can sense the order and chaos flows, if as almost vague misty shapes, that would reveal their bladework in darkness.

Useful at night, but you need to be able to hold your own in full light. Still, he has to admit that he is learning from Emerya, and what he is discovering will be useful somewhere and at some time.

When he leaves the stable a half glass later, he is about to cross the courtyard when a voice calls to him.

"Lord Lerial?"

Lerial turns to see Undercaptain Woelyt walking toward him. "Yes?"

"I happened to see you watching Forran and Ghestyn sparring, and I realized that your brother has not yet returned from his patrol." Woelyt smiles politely.

The undercaptain is close enough that Lerial can sense he has something in mind, and Lerial has few doubts about what it is. He just waits.

"Your father suggested several sparring sessions, and we have only had one this eightday . . ." After a slight pause, the undercaptain goes on. "I doubt that he would be pleased with me if I did not mention the matter."

Lerial understands all too well that Woelyt cares less about sparring than in making certain that Lerial's lack of practice is not blamed on the undercaptain. He can hope that the undercaptain has other duties. "Perhaps now?"

"Now would be excellent, and since the wands are already there . . ." Woelyt smiles.

"Then we should do so." Lerial forces a smile and walks with Woelyt toward that part of the courtyard where he has just observed the Lancer rankers sparring.

As they near the worn green tiles set in the limestone courtyard paving, one of the Lancers appears with a pair of wooden wands. "Sers."

"Thank you, Ceaslyr," says the undercaptain.

Lerial nods politely as he takes one of the wands, then tries to concentrate on Woelyt as the undercaptain takes a position just inside the circle. After a moment, Lerial edges forward, wand in a guard position, not only watching Woelyt, but trying to follow the order patterns as the officer feints a thrust, before coming up with a backcut.

Lerial has sensed the second movement even before Woelyt has begun it, and he manages to beat it aside.

"Good," murmurs the undercaptain.

The single word distracts Lerial so much that he has to jump to the side to avoid Woelyt's wand, and he staggers slightly. *Concentrate!* Lerial pivots slightly, getting his feet slightly farther apart to put himself in a more balanced position.

Even so, Lerial has to back away quickly, circling in order to recover and be able to try to hold his ground.

By the end of a quarter glass, Lerial is sweating heavily, but he realizes that Woelyt has seldom managed to touch him—except with each attack, the undercaptain is getting closer to doing so, not because Lerial cannot sense what the other is about to do, but because his arms and even his legs are getting heavy.

Finally, after another long series of passes and more effort than Lerial would like in sliding and avoiding the officer's attacks, the undercaptain's wand twists Lerial's weapon out of his hand and then hits Lerial's thigh with enough force that the youth staggers back, even though Woelyt turns the wooden wand at the last moment so that the flatted side strikes, rather than the edge.

"You've improved," says the officer, lowering his blade. "I tried to pull that last strike."

"That wasn't your fault," replies Lerial. "I just got too tired to slide or block it."

"You're young and don't have your full strength. You also aren't spending enough time practicing. You need to take a heavy wand and practice every move, time after time, just by yourself, without stopping until your arms and hands cannot hold the wand. Then rest . . . and do it again . . . do that for a glass every day for an eightday or two, and you'll be surprised at the difference it makes."

Lerial hasn't thought about it that way, but that is what Emerya has been having him do, in her own way, in dealing with sensing order and chaos. He takes a deep breath. "Then . . . in a few moments, I suppose I'd better try again . . . if you have the time."

Woelyt smiles warmly. "We can do two more sessions with a break in between before I'll have to leave on my rounds." The officer pauses. "While you're catching your breath, let me show you another way to deflect a blade, one that doesn't leave you so open for a counterthrust."

"That would be good."

"We'll do this slowly. I'll start as if you've knocked my wand up with a low counter coming up. You make a straight thrust at my gut—slowly. This is just to show you how it works . . ."

Woelyt goes through the motions slowly, then goes through them a second, and a third time. After that, he has Lerial try to replicate the move. It takes Lerial almost a score of attempts before Woelyt nods.

"You've got it well enough that, if you practice it some tonight and first thing in the morning, you might be able to work with it in sparring. Now . . . you should be ready for another round."

Lerial forces a smile, trudges to the edge of the circle, and lifts his wand.

When Lerial leaves the Lancer's exercise area, more than a half glass later, he understands three things. First, what Emerya's exercises have given him. Second, that he doesn't have the physical strength and endurance to take advantage of what he has learned, or, rather, not for very long. Third, even if he had more strength, that he doesn't have the technique he needs.

From the Lancers' outer exercise yard, Lerial makes his way into the palace and then to the north courtyard, the most private of the three, and cooler than the south courtyard, especially beside one of the fountains. He sees that his mother is seated at a table near the west fountain, and he eases toward the east one, only to find Amaira and Ryalah seated at a small table there, with several small dolls. One is a Lancer, another a healer, a third a magus, but he cannot make out the others.

"You're all wet," Ryalah declares.

Seated in the chair beside Lerial's sister, Amaira says nothing, but her eyes are fixed on Lerial.

"I am. I was practicing blades with Undercaptain Woelyt. I sweated a lot."

"Is he good?"

"He's better than I am."

"Is he as good as Lephi?"

"He's better, I think."

"Lephi says he'll always be better than you."

Lerial keeps the wince he feels to himself, even though he suspects both girls can sense his discomfort. "Right now, he's bigger and has more experience. It won't always be like that." Lerial feels that, and he *knows* that will be true, even if he cannot explain why to himself, much less anyone else.

"He says you have too much order to be a good Lancer," Ryalah adds.

"You do have order," says Amaira more softly.

"Your mother says I can get much better." Lerial laughs gently. "If your mother says so, I'm not going to argue with her."

Amaira grins and shakes her head.

"Lerial!" calls Xeranya from the other end of the courtyard..

He turns to see her beckoning. "I'll be right there." Then he looks back to the girls, taking in the dolls. "You're fortunate Father isn't around."

Amaira nods solemnly.

Ryalah nods as well. "We only play with them when he's gone."

"That's wise." With a smile, Lerial turns and walks toward the other fountain.

As he nears his mother, he sees her slip a thin volume under a leather folder before she turns and smiles at him. "I didn't see you come in. Viera saw you sparring with the undercaptain. Your father will be so pleased that you've been diligent in that."

Lerial hadn't seen Viera, the oldest and only surviving family retainer who had accompanied his grandmother from the destruction of Cyad to Hamor. "I hope so." *He's more likely to be concerned that I haven't practiced enough or learned enough. He's never satisfied.* Lerial does not dare voice such thoughts. He even worries about thinking them. "What are you reading?" he asks, glancing at the leather folder and what lies under it, because he cannot make out what the volume might be.

"An old book of verse." She slides the leather folder aside to reveal a thin volume whose cover is a shimmering silver, touched with a hint of green. "Your grandmother gave it to me. It will go to your daughter. Your aunt has the other copy. There were only two made. Hers will pass to Amaira. If you do not have daughters, your copy will pass to Ryalah."

"Might I look at it?" Lerial isn't all that interested in verse, but he has never seen that kind of binding, and that suggests the book is clearly old.

"Carefully." Xeranya lifts the small volume and extends it to him. "I wouldn't let your father know you've read it. You know what he thinks about verse and playacting."

Lerial nods. "I won't." He won't not just because his mother has asked, but also because she is absolutely right about the way Kiedron feels about verse.

"It is a part of your heritage, the heritage of Cyador. If you and Lephi do not carry on that heritage, who will?"

Lerial nods, then opens the cover gently, although the volume does not feel old, and turns to the first page, which holds only a title: *Meditations Upon the Land of Light.* The characters are strangely angular and hard to read. He turns the page and reads another set of lines, "*To those of the Towers, to those of the Land, and to those who endured.*" Below them are a name and a title, "*Kiedral Daloren, Vice Marshal, Anglorian Unity.*" Lerial has not read or heard of either Kiedral Daloren, whoever he might have been, or the Anglorian Unity. He has heard of the Towers.

"There really were Towers . . . Mirror Towers?"

"Once . . . yes. Your grandmother told me that Kiedral was the second Emperor of Light."

"Who was the first?"

Xeranya shrugs and offers a wry smile. "I asked. No one knows."

Lerial frowns and turns to the first verse.

For all those who braved dark translation's hell
and fought the Forest bravely if not well,
may these words offer consolation's praise
the remnant of past Anglorian days,
and hopes for Cyad's shining, mirrored ways . . .

He slowly closes the book and looks to his mother. "It doesn't make much sense."

"Poetry usually doesn't make sense to you when you're young. I'm just now beginning to understand some of it. Later . . . you might appreciate it. In a way, I think it's all about the founding of Cyad and Cyador and what the writer felt about starting over in a strange land, so far from the Rational Stars. Your grandmother said it gave her hope. Someday, it might help you."

Hope . . . from old verses?

Xeranya extends her hand, and Lerial returns the volume.

As he walks away to wash up and change to cleaner garb, he can't help but continue to wonder how old verses could help anyone . . . and him, because his mother has not mentioned Lephi, or his daughters, and she never would have omitted his older brother unintentionally.

Never. *Why would she give her copy to your daughter? And not to Lephi's. That doesn't make sense.* It especially doesn't make sense because Lephi is the heir, Cyador's heir, and his parents are both practical. Very practical.

V

On sixday, Lerial's leg is indeed bruised, and a bit stiff, but he makes his way along the palace corridors to meet with Saltaryn, trying not to limp. He practiced with a wand for more than half a glass the night before, if in his chambers—where no one could see—but the extra practice hasn't loosened up his leg, and he certainly doesn't feel any more accomplished with the wand, although he thinks he has the movements right for what Woelyt had showed him.

Lerial reaches the study before the magus does, but chooses not to sit down. Saltaryn will not be late, and Lerial does not want to seat himself, only to stand when the magus arrives. He waits only a few moments before he sees Saltaryn approaching, carrying the leather case, more like an oblong box with strap handles.

Saltaryn studies Lerial as he nears the youth, then purses his lips and frowns. "You're still more black, except where you're bruised on your leg."

"I got the bruises sparring with Undercaptain Woelyt. He was showing me moves I didn't know."

"Are you practicing with order?" Saltaryn sets his case on the table.

"I beg your pardon, ser?" Lerial tries to keep his voice calm. "Practicing with order, ser?"

"Are you trying to gather order or trying to heal people?"

"I went to the Hall of Healing several days ago to see what healers do. That was all."

"If you want to be a magus, you need to learn to control chaos before you work at all with order. I suggest you stay away from the Hall . . . that is, if you want to remain among the Magi'i."

Lerial doubts that, as the son of the Duke of Cigoerne, and the grandson of the last Emperor of Light, he will be denied elthage rights, but . . . he could be declared unfit to be a magus, and that would certainly bring his father's wrath down upon him. "I haven't been to the Hall of Healing except that one time, and I don't plan to go again any time soon."

"Good. Now . . . let us see how you have progressed with the candle exercises." From his case, Saltaryn produces two candles, so stubby that they are barely three digits long, for all that they are set in ornate and polished brass candleholders. He sets them on the side of the table away from Lerial. "Do you see the candles?"

Of course. "Yes."

Saltaryn takes out a thin brass frame, perhaps three hands high, from which hangs a black cloth that extends down far enough that its base droops on the table. "Take a chair and seat yourself against the wall so that you face the candles."

Lerial does so, watching as the magus then places the frame before the candles. The frame is high enough and wide enough that Lerial cannot see the candles.

Saltaryn then does something with his hands. "Where are the candles?"

"Behind the drape."

"Are they?" Saltaryn lifts the drape.

Lerial sees no candles. *Is he using chaos to hide them?* He concentrates, trying to feel for the candles with order.

"You're using an order-probe," observes the magus. "That will tell many Magi'i exactly where you are."

"I was trying to see if you had hidden them behind a chaos screen or something." Lerial refrains from pointing out that many of the stronger Magi'i, those using chaos, often cannot sense order. He understands what Saltaryn means—he cannot trust that other Magi'i will not sense what he does with order . . . at least, from what Emerya has said, not unless he becomes very skilled, and that doesn't appear likely any time soon.

"That comes later." Saltaryn lifts the leather case beside the drape frame. The candleholders with the candles are there, behind where the case had been. He lowers the case. Even without probing, just passively sensing the movements of Saltaryn's hands, Lerial can tell that the magus is moving the candles, but not exactly where, or whether he has moved one or both.

"I want you to tell me where the candles are—without probing."

Lerial knows he could do that if he were closer, but he is sitting almost five yards away, and the candles and their holders are small. Still . . . he concentrates, trying to get a sense. "I think there's only one behind the drape."

"Think?"

"There's one."

"Good. We'll try again."

After several more trials, Saltaryn straightens. "You seem to be able to sense where the candles are without probing. Now . . . I want you to light whatever candles I put behind the drape, using only the smallest possible amount of chaos, just barely enough to catch the wick on fire."

"Yes, ser."

"Why am I asking you to do this with the smallest amount of chaos?"

"To teach me better control of chaos?"

Saltaryn nodded. "There's another reason that goes with it. Can you think of what that might be?"

"So someone will have a harder time sensing what I'm doing?"

"That's a good reason, especially for you, but it's not linked to control."

Lerial frowns. *What does he have in mind?*

Saltaryn smiles. "How did you feel after the lesson where you first had to light a candle?"

"Tired. Very tired."

"That's because you worked hard. Directing and using chaos takes strength . . ." The magus lets his words hang, waiting for Lerial to reply.

"Oh . . . you want me to only use as much chaos as necessary so that I don't get tired and can do more if I have to."

"That's right. Especially if you have to use chaos in battle, you don't want to get any more tired than you have to." Saltaryn moves one candle. "Try to light it that way now."

Lerial tries to focus the smallest bit of chaos on the candle. From across the study, even that takes some effort . . . and nothing happens.

"You'll need a bit more chaos," offers Saltaryn.

Lerial tries again . . . and again.

Finally, after close to a quarter glass of effort, he manages to light a candle.

"Good! Now do it again."

Lerial refrains from groaning or sighing and makes another effort.

Then Saltaryn puts two candles behind the drape, and when Lerial has managed to light those, the magus says, "Light both of them at once, not one at a time."

Finally, Saltaryn says, "Good. You're using just the right amount of chaos. When you practice any magely skill, try to determine how to do what you're doing with the least amount of effort and chaos."

"Yes, ser." Lerial blots his forehead with the back of his forearm. He is sweating once more, but not so profusely as if he had been sparring. He is definitely doing better in handling chaos, but he could not have gathered much more free chaos than what he had used . . . at least, it doesn't feel that way. Yet once he has mastered the knack of determining just how much chaos he needed, at the end, lighting the candles was almost easy. *Is that because you're using the order to control it more effectively?* Emerya had said control of order would help, but that raised another question. Why is Saltaryn so worried about Lerial's use of order, especially if it helps in handling chaos?

"Now we need to move on to history." As he talks, the magus collects the items he has set on the study table and replaces them in the leather case.

Lerial notices that the brass of the holders now appears tarnished, yet the metal had been polished when Saltaryn had taken them from the case. *Did my use of chaos do that? Or was that caused by what I did at first with too much chaos?* He can think of no other reason than chaos being the cause, and, somehow, that bothers him.

"Lerial?"

Lerial stiffens as he realizes he has not heard what Saltaryn asked. "Ser? I'm sorry. I was still thinking about the exercises."

"I asked you whether you had considered what we discussed yesterday, about the dangers of a ruler who is also a strong magus?"

"I did, ser."

"And?"

"The greatest danger is to the ruler himself. He's likely to think he is more powerful than he is."

"Why? If he's a powerful mage and knows his power, why would he think he is more powerful than he knows himself to be?"

"Because most of a ruler's power comes from those who follow him. Just because he's a strong magus doesn't increase the strength of his Lancers . . . or increase the golds in his treasury . . ."

"Don't you think, if his Lancers know he is powerful, that they will be more confident and more effective?"

"That could be . . ." Lerial has his doubts.

More questions follow.

"What did you think about Tafoyan's *Historie of Afrit*?"

"What was the most notable accomplishment of Lorn and why?"

Then, after history, comes Saltaryn's perusal of the essay Lerial has written comparing the trading practices of the factors of Merowey with those of Heldya and of Afrit.

"Your penmanship is adequate, but far from outstanding, and your 'R's are too sloppy." The magus pauses, then asks, "What did you mean by this sentence? 'The traders of Heldya have no idea of fairness'?"

"They'll bargain for the cheapest price they can get, no matter what it costs to grow or make something."

"That's most likely true, but that doesn't mean that they have no idea of fairness, does it?"

"No, ser."

"Then you need to write what you told me, not what you wrote." Saltaryn adds, "If you desire to be accurate. There are times when honesty should be tempered, as you will learn, but when you temper it, always remember what you are doing."

More questions follow, almost line by line.

Finally, after Saltaryn has disposed of the essay, he reaches the part of the lessons that Lerial hates—the mental arithmetic problems that Saltaryn recites.

"If you have a company of ninety-seven men, with ten spare mounts, and each mount requires a minimum of a half-basket of grain a day, how much grain will you need for a nine-day patrol?"

"Four hundred eighty one and a half baskets."

"What about your mount?"

Lerial manages not to sigh. "I'd need another four and a half baskets."

"What about grain for the horses pulling the supply wagon?"

"Eighteen more baskets for two supply wagons. That's . . . five hundred four baskets."

Saltaryn nods. "You look at the payroll ledger for a company of Mirror Lancers, and the weekly payroll shows payment of two hundred twenty silvers? How many Lancers understrength is the company?"

Lerial blinks. *Understrength?* Then he remembers that the payroll has to include the captain, an undercaptain, and a senior squad leader in addition to the rankers. "Seventeen rankers, or seven rankers and no undercaptain." He pauses. "Most likely, seven without an undercaptain."

"Why do you say that?"

"Because my father wouldn't allow a company to patrol seventeen rankers below complement." *Not when we're usually outnumbered anyway, for all the companies stationed on the borders.*

"I'll accept that."

Lerial waits for the next problem, understanding the necessity for being able to handle figures in his head, but not particularly caring for the exercises.

After another half glass of exercises, Saltaryn smiles. "You're showing much more discipline in studying. Your father will be pleased to hear that."

Lerial nods politely, thinking, *Not pleased. That's what he expects.*

When Saltaryn and Lerial leave the study, Lerial wonders if he should seek out Woelyt for another round of sparring.

How will you get better and be able to best Lephi if you don't keep trying? Especially after Woelyt told you that you needed to practice more. He takes a deep slow breath, then walks along the main floor corridor that leads toward the outer courtyard and the Lancers' practice area.

Unsurprisingly, Woelyt is available, as if the undercaptain has expected Lerial to appear, and Lerial suspects that the officer just may have . . . or that

Saltaryn has informed him when Lerial would likely be finished with his lessons.

Although the soreness in his leg turns out not to hamper him as much as he had feared, he still has difficulty in responding to anything new or different that the undercaptain brings to bear. After the second round of sparring, while he is catching his breath and trying to cool down somewhat, he turns to Woelyt and asks, "How long do you think it will take before I can defend against something I've never seen before?"

"When you're first sparring it seems to take forever," replies Woelyt with a smile. "The longer and harder you practice, especially with those who are better than you are, the sooner you'll recognize and be able to defend against moves you haven't seen. It's mostly recognition in time to use defenses you already know."

That doesn't give Lerial much cheer, true as he suspects the officer's words are. Still, he perseveres until Woelyt has to leave on his rounds. Then he trudges back into the palace and makes his way to the north fountain court, which he finds empty. He isn't certain whether he's relieved or unhappy to find no one else there, although he wonders where his mother and sister might be . . . or Amaira, for that matter.

After he feels cool enough that he won't start sweating heavily after he washes up, he heads for the bath chamber. He needs to write another essay for Saltaryn, who was less than pleased with his last effort, and that is likely to take much of what is left of the afternoon.

That night, after dinner, he makes his way to his aunt's chambers.

Emerya does not invite him in, but steps into the corridor. "Amaira's fighting a little flux."

"What about tomorrow?"

She smiles and shakes her head. "For now, Lerial, I think you've learned enough."

"Has Father or Mother—or Saltaryn—said anything? Is that why you don't want to teach me more?"

"Saltaryn has expressed some concerns," Emerya admits. "But I have taught you all you should know about order right now."

"I don't know that much."

"You know enough . . . for now. We'll see how you do with what I've showed you."

Lerial can tell that there will be no changing her mind. After a moment, he ventures, "I understand, I think, but there is one thing . . ."

"Oh?"

"Saltaryn had me practicing lighting candles I couldn't see from a distance . . ."

Emerya raises her eyebrows, so white that they are almost invisible.

"Just across the study. Even that isn't easy. The candleholders were bright and polished when we started, but when we ended, they were tarnished."

"Did Saltaryn handle them?"

"He did, but they were tarnished all over, not just where he touched them."

Emerya nods. "Saltaryn doesn't have the most precise personal control over his use of chaos. The best of the Magi'i handle chaos with order in a way that the chaos stays outside their bodies. They're the ones who live the longest. I've told you about that, remember?"

"But they aren't the strongest."

"They don't *seem* the strongest," replies his aunt. "There's a difference. That's another reason why you need to follow the rules and techniques I've showed you. They're harder, but they'll serve you well."

"I'll never be a healer or an ordermage."

"You can't say that." She pauses. "You can't ever be *known* as a healer or an ordermage, especially not if you end up leading Mirror Lancers."

"Because ordermages and healers aren't supposed to kill people?"

"They're not thought to be capable of it. That's not quite the same thing . . . if you think about it. If I were you, I would think about it . . . a great deal." She stops for a moment, then says, "You could be a healer, Lerial, but that wouldn't be good for you, or for Cigoerne. For now, you've learned all you need to know."

"I'm still having problems with my sparring."

"It's only been an eightday or so. Everything takes time."

"But . . ."

"I need to see to Amaira, Lerial."

"Oh . . . I'm sorry."

"That's all right. Just keep working on what I showed you." She smiles, then slips back into her chambers.

For a long moment, Lerial just stands there. Then, he turns and begins to walk back toward his own quarters, thinking.

. . . You can't ever be known to be a healer or ordermage. . . . not if you end up leading Mirror Lancers . . . His aunt's words keep running through his thoughts.

VI

For the next eightday, Lerial dutifully continues his lessons with Saltaryn, followed by sessions with Undercaptain Woelyt. While he feels he is getting better and is able to avoid the worst strikes and bruises, the undercaptain still disarms him regularly, even though Lerial has taken to practicing even more by himself. He no longer gets that tired holding the wand, but he is all too aware that he does not have the physical strength of the undercaptain, or even of Lephi, who returned from his first patrol late the previous evening.

When Lerial rises on sevenday, he sees no sign of his brother, who does not rise for breakfast and is doubtless sleeping in, although their father has always insisted that sevenday morning is for work and that only on that afternoon and eightday itself are the two excused from duties and lessons. Lerial finds he is annoyed, but not especially surprised, since their father's rules seem to him to be applied less rigidly to Lephi. *That's the way things are, and will always be.*

He eats his breakfast quietly, with Ryalah, Amaira, and Emerya, although his mother arrives as he is finishing, then heads for his lessons with Saltaryn. The magus is less demanding on sevendays, and by late midmorning, Lerial is finished. Lephi is still not up.

So Lerial seeks out Undercaptain Woelyt and spends a good glass accumulating more bruises and, hopefully, getting better in using the sabre.

After cooling down and cleaning up, Lerial returns to his chambers to work on an even longer essay for Magus Saltaryn. Lephi does not come by, and Lerial is not about to go looking for him. Instead, he finishes the essay and practices some with the sabre wand, if not strenuously enough to work up much of a sweat. Finally, it is time to head down to the main courtyard for refreshments before dinner.

He reaches the east door to the courtyard just after Lephi. His older brother's face is lightly tanned, as dark as it will likely ever get, but his short-cut hair is now almost white-blond, and his green eyes appear paler to Lerial. He even looks more confident as he fills a glass with red wine, not watering it, and settles into the chair across the large courtyard table from his mother.

Lerial moves toward the refreshment table where he half fills his glass with light lager, knowing that he can drink two half glasses without comments from his mother or aunt, when drawing a full glass would draw a cold look or a few words.

"Emerya!" calls his mother.

Lerial turns to see his aunt approaching with Amaira and Ryalah. Immediately, he sets down his glass and pours redberry from the crockery pitcher into two small tumblers, which he carries to the table where the girls usually sit.

"Thank you," says Emerya quietly, before turning. "What do you say, girls?"

"Thank you," chorus the two.

"You're welcome." Lerial smiles as he steps back and watches the girls sit down.

Ryalah sets the ubiquitous pegboard on the table, then takes a swallow of redberry, but Amaira takes only a small sip.

Lerial cannot sense any chaos in his cousin, but she is very quiet, even quieter than she had been at breakfast. Rather than say anything, he waits while Emerya takes a goblet and pours a small amount of white—or light amber—wine into it. Then he follows her to the large table and sits to his mother's right, putting as much space between himself and Lephi as possible.

"How is Amaira?" asks Xeranya, looking to Emerya. "She seems better. A bit pale, though."

Both women look at the smaller table where Amaira and Ryalah sip redberry juice from the small tumblers.

"Her fever is gone, and she's eating now. She gets tired by the end of the day." Emerya takes a deep breath. "It's been a long eightday."

Lerial nods. He'd been able to sense that just from his aunt's demeanor over the past days.

"Tell us about your patrol," says Xeranya, looking proudly at her older son.

"It was just a patrol," replies Lephi. "We rode southwest from Cigoerne along the Thylan River road for almost four days. One day we rode through Teilyn, as you requested, ser." Lephi looks at Kiedron, who has entered the courtyard from the west entrance unnoticed and who nods. "We didn't see anyone we shouldn't have, and none of the people along the road had been raided. It wasn't until we got to Barteld that we heard about raiders. The captain said that was a bad sign. Usually they don't come north of Narthyl."

"That's not good," Emerya agrees.

From his studies with Saltaryn and glasses spent memorizing maps, Lerial also understands. One of the reasons his father has been able to claim the territory he has for the duchy of Cigoerne is that, except for the lands near the Swarth River immediately west of Cigoerne and along the smaller Thylan River that flows into the Swarth a kay or so south of the city, most of the land claimed by Kiedron consists of hills covered with sparse grass, with occasional wooded areas. Rather . . . most of it had been grassland, but Lerial's grandmother had insisted on using the mages and the Lancers to build ditches and canals off the Thylan and a few smaller streams. Over just a few years, more people have appeared and begun to farm lands that only needed water, and the use of irrigation for some pasturage has also created some herds used for dairying and cheese-making. The fact that raiders are appearing some sixty kays north of Narthyl, which is the largest town in the south of Cigoerne, is definitely a cause for concern.

"What happened?" asks Lerial.

"I was going to get to that," replies Lephi, "if you'd given me a moment."

"You might let Lephi talk, dear," adds Xeranya mildly.

Lerial nods, seething, and takes a sip of his lager.

Lephi does not immediately speak, clearly letting the silence speak for him.

Lerial takes another sip of his lager, thinking he'll be angel-cursed if he'll utter another word.

At last, Lephi clears his throat and says, "For two days we patrolled the area around Barteld. We saw some tracks, but we never saw the raiders. Then a herder sent word that he'd seen riders heading west . . ."

West? wonders Lerial.

". . . and the captain figured out that they were riding toward a hamlet southwest of Bartheld where there's a little lake, and they've got orchards and sheep there. He had us ride late that evening, and we got there before the raiders did. They didn't show up until the next morning, and we ambushed them. Only a few got away. We only captured a handful, but all but one of them died of their wounds."

That doesn't surprise Lerial. The grassland raiders tended to fight to the death if they are surrounded.

"How big was the band, dear?" Xeranya inquires.

"About a score. There might have been a few more."

"Did you fight any of them?" asks Ryalah loudly from the small table.

"No," admits Lephi. "The captain had me with the reserve squad. We were posted between the raiders and the hamlet, just in case any raiders got by first squad."

"What did the raiders look like?" asks Emerya.

"They wore those loose baggy white tunics and baggy trousers, like all the Meroweyans do."

"Only the raiders in the north of Merowey do that," offers Emerya gently. "That's because the land is so dry there."

Lerial could have said the same, but he is glad that his aunt does.

"Of course," agrees Lephi genially. "That's what I meant."

"Did they look thin or gaunt?" presses Emerya.

Lephi frowns. "I don't know."

"What did the captain say about how they fought?"

Lerial can tell that Emerya is worried, but he doesn't understand why.

"He did say something about it being easier than usual. Why?"

"They're avoiding Narthyl because it has a garrison there. Your company was sent out to patrol an area north and west of Narthyl. That likely means that the grassland nomads are short of food. We didn't have much rain this winter, and the hill grasses here are already browning."

"I'm afraid you're right, Emerya," offers Kiedron as he nears the table. "The southlands are dry, and last fall's harvest in the north of Merowey was scanty. That's what all the traders have been saying as well. The Ministry records show we've been getting more hides as well."

Hides? What do they have to do with it? Lerial wonders, but does not ask, not with Lephi ready to show his superiority.

Kiedron walks to the serving table and pours himself a goblet of the red wine. "It's not much better to the west of here. That's where I've been with Fifth Company. We're even seeing raiders and poachers from Afrit there, and the hill forests are drier than usual." He sits down between his sister and his consort so that he is on Emerya's right.

"Did you come across any raiders from Afrit?" asks Xeranya.

"One of the squads did, but we killed only two. The others fled into the woods. The area was rocky and dangerous, and I didn't want to risk the mounts, not over raiders who were more like poachers."

"They're hungry," observes Emerya.

"Then they should poach in Afrit," retorts Kiedron, "except they know Atroyan—or Rhamuel—will execute their families if they're caught. We can't do that, because we'd have to go into Afrit to do it, and the poachers know that. So they try to steal game, crops, or livestock from Cigoerne. Even if they get caught, their families are safe."

"A cruel choice," says Emerya.

"It's a cruel choice for us as well," points out Kiedron after taking a swallow of wine and setting the goblet on the table. "If we don't kill at least a few of them, even more will come sneaking into Cigoerne and steal from our people. We're not a wealthy land, not yet. Duke Atroyan could spare some wheat-corn or maize flour for his people, but he chooses not to. You know we've sent what we can to Narthyl and some of the hamlets when we could."

Emerya nods slowly, and Lerial gets the impression that she does not fully agree . . . or that there is something left unsaid, if not both. But then, that is often the case.

"Lephi's patrol seemed to go well," suggests Xeranya.

"That's what Captain Jahaal told me at the Lancer headquarters. They did run into some raiders, but not as many as I feared from the earlier reports."

"That may be because many are too weak to cross the hills."

"It's possible, and I'm grateful for that. We don't need hordes of poachers, raiders, and beggars. It will be worse after harvest. The water level in the Thylan is low, and it's continuing to drop. If it gets much lower, we won't be able to use some of the older irrigation ditches unless they're deepened, and some of the growers aren't listening. By the time they do something, it will be too late."

"You can't order them . . . ?" says Xeranya.

"I'd rather not. If I do, then I'll have to punish those who don't. If I punish them enough that they understand, they won't be in any condition to dig ditches . . . or harvest their crops."

"What about having some of the Mirror Lancer trainees, the rankers, that is," suggests Emerya, "work on some of the ditches?"

"Majer Phortyn is already assigning that duty for disciplinary punishment. That will help some, but not enough. He's always believed in punishment tasks, rather than flogging."

"With his background, how could he not?" asks Emerya.

"He's worked hard." Kiedron gives his sister a hard glance.

Lerial wonders what lies behind the look, but says nothing.

"Could some of the Magi'i help, Father?" asks Ryalah, timidly.

Kiedron laughs, heartily. "I would that they could, little one, but using chaos to dig in the earth is tiring, and there are better uses for the Magi'i."

Also, reflects Lerial, earth tends to absorb chaos, so that chaos isn't that helpful in digging through soil. In the moment of silence that follows, he turns to his father. "Why weren't there any Magi'i in the Mirror Lancers . . . or in our Lancers?"

"There were more Magi'i in Cyador. It was a far bigger land, but we still have Mirror Lancers."

"But we don't have firelances or mirror shields."

"They're still Mirror Lancers, and their training and tactics are better than any other troopers in Hamor or Candar . . . or anywhere else," replies Kiedron. "We have over fifteen companies now to protect our people. That's another reason why Cigoerne has grown and prospered."

"And because Grandmother chose where we could settle wisely?"

"That's true, but it doesn't matter how well you choose if you can't hold and defend what you have." Kiedron's voice is jovial, but Lerial can sense, both by the slight edge to his father's words and by the increase in the chaos surrounding him, that Lerial's question has annoyed him.

"Strong Lancers are everything," adds Lephi in a pontificating tone.

Lerial debates contesting that, saying that Lancers cannot defend if they don't have a strong land with crops and herds, and crafters to support them, but he decides against speaking out.

"I understand you've been most diligent in your sparring," Kiedron looks at Lerial and goes on, in an almost patronizing tone. "If you keep working you might even be their commander when Lephi is ruler of Cigoerne."

Lerial keeps a pleasant smile on his face. *I hope that's a long time coming.* "You didn't tell me why there are no healers—"

"Men aren't supposed to be healers, except maybe if they're officers, and they can do a little healing for wounded men. Healers feel too much to be effective fighters . . ." Kiedron shakes his head. "Feeling pain and suffering is necessary to be a good healer, but all that feeling would keep a Lancer from being effective in battle."

From beside her brother, where Kiedron is not looking, Emerya gives Lerial the smallest of headshakes. Lerial represses a smile.

"Besides," adds Lephi, "people think healers aren't strong, and it wouldn't be good for us if the barbarians think our officers are weak."

"There's strength, and there's strength," Emerya says calmly. "It takes a certain kind of strength to face wounds and fluxes and blood all over everything and to do the best you can do . . . and know that it might not be enough. I've seen Lancers able to cut down barbarians with ease pale and almost faint when they see a woman or a child who's been badly hurt and bleeding all over everything."

Surprisingly, at least to Lerial, his mother nods at Emerya's words.

Kiedron almost frowns, Lerial thinks.

Instead, his father declares firmly, "We need both kinds of strength." Then he turns to Xeranya. "What might we be having for dinner?"

Even as he understands that his father has ended any further discussion of healers, Lancers, and strength, Lerial wonders why his father has done so.

VII

Lerial wakes early on eightday, but does not rise immediately. Instead, he lies on top of the covers, trying to cool off, because even before dawn on the third level of the palace the air is so still and hot that it might well be an oven, but the sheet gets damper with each moment, and he sits up. He does not cool down, not when there is no breeze coming through the windows, but at least when he sits up, he gets no hotter and his sweat doesn't soak the sheet.

As he sits there looking toward the window, and the heat-silvered green-blue sky beyond, he cannot help but worry. Since his father had stopped Emerya's comments about healers, Kiedron had not said a single word to Lerial, either in the courtyard or at dinner . . . or after. Lerial cannot remember that ever happening. Ever.

Finally, he stands, then walks slowly to his dressing chamber, where he washes and dresses, wearing the lightest cotton undertunic and tunic that he has. Then he slips from his rooms and makes his way to the back stairs, moving as quietly as he can down to the family breakfast room. He hears nothing, suggesting that no one else is up yet, but when he steps into it, he stops short, for his father is sitting alone at the end of the table.

Kiedron gestures, pointing to the chair beside him.

Lerial swallows, then walks to the chair and seats himself.

"It's time we had a talk, Lerial."

"Yes, ser."

Kiedron turns in his chair to face his son directly. "Your mother and I think that you need to spend some time away from Cigoerne."

"Ser? To Afrit?"

Kiedron shakes his head. "I wouldn't send you that far now. I mean outside the city."

Lerial understands the reasons why his father has never called the lands he holds anything other than Cigoerne, particularly given the uneasy relations between Cigoerne and Afrit, although, properly speaking, only the small city on the Swarth River is Cigoerne. That ambiguity can be confusing at times, but his father has declared that it is something they will have to live with for a time yet.

"You need to see how life is away from here."

Lerial is still thinking about what his father has said—that he wouldn't send Lerial that far *now*. That suggests he might in the future.

"Lerial . . ."

"I'm sorry, ser. I was thinking about what you said." Before his father can say more, he adds, "I've seen much of the duchy, ser."

"There's seeing, and there's understanding. Tomorrow, we'll be riding to Teilyn. You need to experience another side of life. I've made arrangements for you to stay with Majer Altyrn."

"Majer Altyrn? I thought . . ."

"That he was dead? Far from it. He is older than your grandmother would be, but in good health, and he has lands and a nice dwelling, a villa, really. He has no sons, only daughters, and they're between your age and Ryalah's. He's agreed to have you—they call it fostering in Afrit and Heldya—and to teach you more about arms and tactics . . . and about managing lands and other things."

Leaving the Palace . . . and Aunt Emerya?

"But . . ." Lerial bites off what he might have said, instead just asking, "Why?"

Kiedron takes a deep breath, one of the few times Lerial has ever seen him do so, a sign that his father is anything but pleased.

Is that because you question him . . . or because you've really displeased him?

"I'll excuse that question. The fact that you asked it is reason enough, although your question is another indication of why we feel this is necessary. This is not my decision alone. I've talked it over with your mother and even with your aunt. All three of us agree that this will be good for you."

Even Emerya? Lerial can sense the truth of his father's words. The fact that his aunt agrees with his father to send him away feels like a betrayal. *Why would she agree to that? Why?*

"Lerial . . . it is never good to act out of anger. Nor to learn out of anger. What one does and what one learns are colored by anger. You are of the elthage, and you would be Magi'i even if you were not my son. Using chaos with a clear mind is difficult enough. Trying to master even a modest ability with anger and rage will lead to trouble and more trouble . . . and most likely an early death."

But I'm not angry at everyone, just at Lephi . . . and that you don't see how he manipulates everyone . . . just because he's older and handsomer and charming when he wants to be.

"You're angry now. I can see that. Anger isn't good for a magus. It isn't good for a Mirror Lancer, and it's even worse for a man who will give commands or orders to either. Unless you come to understand that, you won't be very good at anything. That's another reason why you need to be away from the palace."

Lerial does not reply.

"Lerial . . . have you nothing to say?"

"No, ser." *Not anything you want to hear.*

"Young man . . . with every moment your actions show why you need to leave. I won't say more, except that I hope you think over why this is so."

"Yes, ser. I promise to think it over." *Except that I've thought it over more than you can imagine, and it still comes out the same way.*

"Good." Kiedron nods toward the sideboard, where melon slices have been set out on a platter, as well as fresh bread, and some cheese. "Get yourself some breakfast. After that, pack up some of your garments. You'll need riding gear, and work clothes and your heavy boots. Two sets of good green tunics and trousers should be more than enough. In addition to learning from Majer Altyrn, you'll be doing the duties a son would be doing. The experience will be good for you."

"Yes, ser." *And you and Lephi will be happy that troublesome Lerial is out of sight and out of mind.* Lerial stands, inclines his head politely, and then makes his way to the sideboard. The melon slices are pomats, juicy but small and not quite bitter, and definitely not his favorites, and the fresh bread is rye, rather than the dark sweet loaves he prefers, but the molasses has to be saved for other uses. That, he knows. There are a few slices of ham, though, and he takes one. He isn't all that hungry anymore.

When he turns back to the table, his father is standing by his chair.

"I have to leave, Lerial. We need to inspect the irrigation works on the West Branch, and that will take all day. I want to get back in time for dinner, though."

"Lephi's going with you?"

"He is. Assuming you learn something in the next year or so, you'll be doing the same when you're his age."

Next year or so? Lerial tries not to swallow. *Exiled for a year because you don't like Lephi's arrogance?*

"Believe me, son. This is for the best."

Best for whom? Lerial manages a nod. "I hope all goes well with the irrigation works."

After his father leaves the breakfast room, Lerial seats himself and looks at his platter. Belatedly, he realizes something else. It wasn't what he'd done the evening before. His father has said he'd talked matters over with his mother, Emerya, and that he'd made arrangements with the majer. All that couldn't have been done since yesterday. Teilyn is a two-day ride.

They've been planning this for days . . . weeks. He looks toward the empty doorway. *Could Lephi have maneuvered it all?* From what Lerial had seen, that wasn't impossible. Far from it.

Finally, he takes one of the melon slices. It tastes bitter, but he doubts that is just the melon.

VIII

Lerial wakes early on oneday and immediately washes and dresses for the ride to Teilyn. Given that the town is at the foot of the Wooded Ridges, more than thirty kays away, he and his father, and their escorts, will be in their saddles a good day and a half. He has already laid out the most comfortable riding clothes he possesses. He eats quickly, alone, and hurries to the stables with the kit bag he has packed. There, he immediately saddles the brown gelding and ties the bag behind his saddle before leading his mount out into the courtyard.

His father is mounted and talking with an undercaptain whom Lerial has not met, and a squad of Lancers is drawn up behind them. Lerial mounts and guides the gelding to within a few yards of the two men and waits. After a time, Kiedron motions for Lerial to join him, and they ride out of the palace grounds behind two Lancers. Behind them are the undercaptain and the rest of the squad. Once outside the walls, the outriders immediately turn south, past the Ministry and across the square to take the southern boulevard that will eventually become the southwest road that leads to Teilyn . . . and not all that much farther, at least according to the maps Lerial has studied.

Since the sun is barely above the horizon and below the roofs of Cigoerne, Lerial cannot see it, except when they ride past the east–west streets that run toward the river. He wants to ask his father what he had been talking over with the undercaptain, who had looked rather concerned, but decides against that. Instead he asks, "Who is the undercaptain? I've only seen him from a distance, and I don't recall meeting him."

"That's Undercaptain Helkhar. Majer Phortyn thinks most highly of him."

"He seems most diligent."

"That he is. He is perhaps overconcerned with our safety."

Lerial immediately understands and keeps his voice low as he asks, "That the Duke of Cigoerne is riding so far with only one squad of Lancers?"

Kiedron nods. "We're well within the duchy, and having a larger escort would only reduce the number of Lancers available to deal with raiders and poachers."

"Are there more because of the poor harvests in Merowey and Afrit?"

"There seem to be more. That *might* be the reason."

From his father's tone, Lerial can tell that Kiedron has said all that he is likely to, and the last thing Lerial wants to do is upset him again. "Thank you, ser."

"You're welcome."

Lerial wonders what else might be happening, especially with Afrit, but he decides against doing so until they have ridden well away from the city. Instead he concentrates on observing the road, since he has only ridden for little more than a glass along it in the past. Perhaps three kays beyond where the city seems to end, if the end of close-set houses and the beginning of small cots on plots of land marks such a point, the road roughly follows the western side of a large stream or very small river, no more than six or seven yards across. If the maps are correct, the river is the Lynaar, and Teilyn sits north and west of where it flows out of the Wooded Ridges.

It is well past midmorning, after two brief stops to water the mounts and take a break, before Lerial asks another question. "Might I ask what I should know about Majer Altyrn besides the fact that he was the officer in charge of the Mirror Lancers who accompanied you and Grandmother, and Aunt Emerya on the *Kerial* from Cyador to Cigoerne?"

"You might. He was the most senior officer in the Mirror Lancers from the time he left Cyador until he took a stipend. Your grandmother insisted I promote him to commander before that happened. I did, but everyone still calls him Majer Altyrn."

"Why?"

"That was his request, because, until recently, we never have had as many Lancers as would have been commanded by more than a majer, not back in Cyador."

"We have more than fifteen companies, you said. That's close to two thousand Lancers, and that doesn't count the trainees or those you could call up."

Kiedron nods. "In Cyador, five companies comprised a battalion, and a battalion was usually commanded by a submajer, but sometimes by an overcaptain. Majers often commanded entire outposts patrolling hundreds of kays, sometimes over a thousand Lancers."

"But wasn't the Emperor Lorn only a majer when he ascended the Malachite Throne?" Lerial knows this to be true, but phrases it as a question.

"That was an unusual time. He was never even the second or third in command of the Mirror Lancers. He was named the heir to the throne by the Emperor Toziel. Toziel had no blood heirs."

"What about Alyiakal?"

"He was captain-commander of the Mirror Lancers and took the throne when the previous Emperor and his entire family perished. That is why Toziel designated Lorn as heir. Cyador must always have an heir."

Cyador must have an heir—not always had to have an heir. That puzzles Lerial, perhaps even more than the fact that Alyiakal has never been well regarded by the Magi'i, although Saltaryn has admitted to him that some histories had suggested Alyiakal could have been a magus, but that his talents lay more on the order side, and for that reason he followed his family tradition as a Mirror Lancer. *Did he have a choice?* Based on what has happened to himself already, Lerial has some doubts. *But Alyiakal surmounted all that and ruled Cyador.*

By a glass past midday, Lerial can see that the Lynaar is markedly narrower, showing a width of five yards, although the stream does look deeper than it was closer to the city. The fields do not stretch as far to the west as they did, and the grasses that are already beginning to brown are shorter than those to the north. Some of the land used for pasture bears the mark of having been overgrazed, as well, and that concerns Lerial, although, again, he does not make that observation to his father.

"Where will we be stopping tonight?" asks Lerial.

"We have another three glasses to go. Are you getting saddle sore?"

"No, ser. I just wondered, because you hadn't said."

"We'll be stopping at Brehaal. There's a Lancer post there. More of a way station for the dispatch riders, but there are bunks enough and officers' quarters and a good spring. The town . . . well, you'll see."

Some three and a half glasses later, Lerial does indeed see.

Brehaal appears to consist of a score of dwellings, few of which he would call houses, and some of which are less than cots, scattered not quite randomly on a low flattened rise to the west of the river road. Several modestly large buildings are dug into the north side of the rise. All the buildings have lanes that join a road leading straight to the river road. Between at least two of the buildings is a smooth expanse of polished stone, and above the stone surface are what appear to be long lines of tables. Beyond the dwellings stretch short, almost scrubby trees, with ditches between them.

Lerial looks at the trees more closely, then realizes that there are two types. As they ride closer, he recognizes one kind, but not the other. Finally, he turns in the saddle. "Ser . . . I can see the apricot trees . . . but I don't recognize the other."

Kiedron's laugh is almost kindly. "You wouldn't. Those are young olive trees. It's likely to be another ten years before those bear sufficient fruit."

"But . . . ?"

"Who would plant trees that take more than twenty years to mature? And why? Your grandmother. Olives are good to eat, and the oil is useful in many ways. It makes a bright lamp flame also."

"Then these are your lands?"

Kiedron nods. "Someone has to plant for the future, and not just the present. You and Lephi and your children will benefit."

As his father talks, Lerial realizes the tables set on the stone pavement must be drying tables for the apricots. "Is this where the apricots you sell to the Heldyan traders come from?"

"From here and from some lands near Narthyl." Kiedron gestures ahead. "There's the Lancer post."

Past the dwellings and well past the fruit barns, on the south end of the rise at the right side of the road and facing the stream, is the outpost. Barely visible above a wall—likely mud brick covered with a white clay plaster—is a long structure with a single set of gates. The walls around the building and its courtyard look to be less than fifty yards on a side.

Lerial understands, now, what his father had meant when he'd said little about the town of Brehaal. That fills him with foreboding, since Teilyn is another half day's ride and even farther from Cigoerne.

Teilyn

IX

Well before noon on twoday, Lerial's legs and buttocks ache, even though they did not leave Brehaal until well after seventh glass, and his back twinges now and then, but he isn't about to say anything. More time passes before he can make out the line of hills ahead that must be the Wooded Ridges. Directly before him, on his right, are fields with rows of some sort of green plants that are no more than waist-high. Cots are scattered here and there.

The column slows as they approach a narrow stone bridge, waiting for a horse-drawn cart to cross. When Lerial rides onto the short bridge, he looks down to see that it crosses an empty irrigation channel, although the mud at the bottom is still damp. He glances to his left, where a heavy wooden water-gate, set in crude mortar and stone and similar to many they have passed on their journey, blocks the flow from the Lynaar. The channel continues for only fifty yards to the west, where it splits at a diversion gate that, in one position, sends the water to the northwest and in the other to the southwest, both heading toward orchards. Between the two orchards, which look to contain apricot trees, is another, one of olive trees, but no ditch leads to the olive orchard.

"There's no water going to the olives," he observes.

"They get enough from seepage," replies Kiedron. "The trees won't grow that fast, nor yield nearly so much when they mature, but there's only so much water. For any lands away from the Swarth, water is a problem. You'll learn more about that, I'm sure, from Majer Altyrn. Listen to him, because it's something you'll need to know."

Know about water? Still, Lerial doesn't question his father, because Kiedron, for all that he has upset Lerial, has never knowingly lied to him. That, Lerial could have sensed.

Barely visible beyond the fields ahead is Teilyn, which appears to have close to a hundred houses or other structures. To the west are more fields, and beyond them, sparse grasslands.

Lerial stifles a yawn. He'd not slept well the night before, even though he'd had a small sleeping chamber to himself—a chamber barely big enough for the narrow pallet bunk and a stool, with pegs on the wall. After seeing that his father and Undercaptain Helkhar occupied similar spaces and that the

Lancers slept in crowded bunk rooms, he'd felt comparatively fortunate . . . and the pallet hadn't been that hard. He just hadn't slept well.

"How are you doing?" asks Kiedron.

"A little stiff, but fine."

"Good. You'll get over that."

"Where is the majer's . . . villa?" Lerial has to think for a moment about what his father had called the majer's dwelling.

"It's on the lower slopes south of town, not far beyond most of the other houses, a bit more than a kay out."

"Will you stay with the majer or start back . . . or are you riding somewhere else?" asks Lerial.

"There's an actual Lancer outpost, a real one, at Teilyn," replies Kiedron. "It's also south of town, about halfway to Majer Altyrn's place. It's the base for the regular patrols along the foot of the Wooded Ridges. The officers' quarters there are adequate, and I wouldn't want to impose on the majer's hospitality."

Lerial is surprised at the concern in his father's voice, especially since he's seldom heard it, especially about people outside the family. "Will you ride any patrols?"

"Not unless the post captain reports something strange. I need to get back to Cigoerne before the Heldyans get more restless."

"Are they going to be a problem?"

"They're always a problem," replies Kiedron dryly. "That's why Duke Atroyan's father let us purchase the lands around Cigoerne. This year might be worse."

"I hope not, ser."

"When others depend on you, Lerial, you can't rely on hope. Not if you want to carry on the heritage of Cyador."

Lerial nods, wondering why so often his father's words seemed designed to keep him from talking. Instead, he concentrates on the buildings as they ride into Teilyn.

The houses in Teilyn are largely constructed of brick, some of mud brick covered with a white coating that, in many cases, bears a pinkish tan tint, and some fewer and larger ones of fired brick of a rusty color. None of them are more than a story high, and all appear to have tile roofs. Lerial keeps looking at the dwellings and then to the Wooded Ridges, then back to the dwellings. Finally, he asks, "Why are the houses all of brick?"

"With all those trees so close?" Kiedron laughs softly. "For several reasons. First, the ground up on the ridges is rough and the undergrowth is thick and often thorny. It's hard to get logs down. Second, the trees are a mix of all sorts, but most of the wood is soft. Third, brick houses are cooler in the summer and warmer in the winter. Fourth, the clay here is very good and easy to get to."

There is a modest square located to the west of the road, which has become the main street, if the only paved street in the town, unlike all the streets in Cigoerne, and on its edge are a small inn, a chandlery, and several small shops. Farther south of the square, Lerial sees a blacksmith shop. In far less than half a glass, they are riding away from Teilyn through more fields, orchards, and scattered cots, but the road has begun to rise, so gradually that Lerial does not even realize it, until he glances back north.

Ahead are the walls of the outpost, and it is at least twice the size of the way station post at Brehaal. Even from a hundred yards away, the gate guards are obvious, although the heavy wooden gates are open and swung back. There is also a single narrow lookout tower rising another two yards above the middle of the north wall. Lerial smiles when he sees the awning above the lookout. *But it makes sense, especially in summer.*

As they ride closer to the outpost, he sees that, farther south, between the trees on the tall hills that comprise the Wooded Ridges, at irregular intervals, jagged spurs of red rocks jut up. Around the base of the rocky spurs the vegetation appears sparse, but elsewhere the mixed forest appears thick and almost impenetrable.

Once they have ridden past the outpost, Kiedron points south and west of the road. "There's the majer's villa."

Lerial can only see a low structure barely rising above the orchards north of it, but before long, the outriders turn their mounts through a pair of yellow brick posts and onto the packed clay lane, smoother than the slightly rutted main road. The lane runs some three hundred yards to the villa, a two-story squarish structure perhaps forty yards on a side situated on the slightest of rises facing the river. On each side of the lane is a meadow of sorts, with grass perhaps calf-high, as if it had been grazed, but not recently.

When they are within a hundred yards of the villa, Lerial can see that there is no portico, only a brick-paved square some fifty yards on a side before the east entry, while the lane splits, one branch leading to the square and the other angling to the northwest and the outbuildings. Unlike the majority of houses in Teilyn, the majer's villa is built of the yellow-tinged rusty fired brick, as are the outbuildings. All have roofs of the same reddish yellow tile as the buildings in Teilyn.

A slender man with iron-gray hair stands waiting in the afternoon shade just in front of the entry door.

"Ride forward with me," orders Kiedron quietly.

Lerial does, and the two rein up some four yards short of the man, who wears a plain white tunic, if in the style of the Mirror Lancers, and matching trousers. His black boots are shined, and he smiles at Kiedron.

"Welcome, Lord Kiedron. I see you got here without any problems."

"Thank you. We did indeed. I must say that you're looking well, Majer."

"Working hard will do that." The majer looks from Kiedron to his son. "Welcome to Kinaar, Lord Lerial."

"Lerial . . . please, ser."

Altyrn smiles. "So be it. Welcome, Lerial. I daresay you will find life here very different from that Cigoerne. In some ways, at least. I will walk around to the stables with you." He looks to Kiedron. "You will stay for dinner?"

"Dinner, I won't refuse, but I need to meet with Captain Graessyr before that."

"In two glasses, then?"

"I'll be here." Kiedron looks to Lerial. "I'll leave you in Majer Altyrn's most capable hands and will see you at dinner."

"Yes, ser."

"Good." Kiedron smiles, then inclines his head, and turns his mount back toward the waiting squad.

Lerial watches his father until he and the squad are well on the way back to the river road, then turns to the majer, who has not said a word. "I'm sorry, ser."

Altyrn smiles, an expression that is both enigmatic and sad, all at once, before saying, "I understand." He points toward the lane leading around the north end of the villa. "This way." Then he walks beside the gelding as Lerial eases him forward. "The first building on the right is the quarters for the unattached men who work here. The second is the stable. The third is the barn, and the fourth holds quarters for the unattached women. There's a line of cots on the south side for the couples and families who work here. The other buildings to the west are the livestock sheds."

Lerial does his best to try to recall exactly what the majer has said, then asks, "What sort of livestock? Father didn't tell me much."

"He always has been closemouthed. That's a good trait for a ruler, not quite so good for a parent, I've discovered."

Lerial glances at the walls of the villa, noting that while there are numerous first-level windows, they are all narrow and tall—too narrow for anyone to squeeze through. "He gives short answers to questions, too."

The majer nods. "That's a habit hard to break."

The area between the outbuildings on the north side of the villa and the villa itself is also brick paved, and there is a simple fountain midway between the villa and the stable, where water flows from a spout into a circular basin. Lerial assumes that there must be some piping somewhere that drains the excess so that the fountain does not flood the paved area that strikes him almost as a courtyard without walls.

Lerial dismounts outside the stable, then leads the gelding inside, following the majer, who steps through the wide stable door and points.

"The third stall on the right is yours. You have to groom your mount . . . you do know how to do that, don't you?"

"Yes, ser. Father insisted on that." *If not that often.* Lerial pauses, surprised that the stable has a brick-paved floor. The only other stable he has seen with such a floor is the one serving the palace, not that he has been in more than a handful of stables. "I only have a travel brush."

"There are brushes in the tack room. You're also responsible for feeding your mount and cleaning the stall every day. I'd suggest first thing in the morning and late in the afternoon or early evening, but that's up to you. The soiled straw and offage go into the old cart on the side of the stable. The shovel, the pitchfork, and an old broom are on the peg racks over there. Put them back clean whenever you aren't using them."

"Yes, ser." Lerial hasn't had to clean a stall, but he has watched the palace stable boys do just that.

"The feed barrels are in the storeroom beside the tack room, but you'll have to carry water from the outside fountain. When you finish unsaddling and dealing with your mount, we'll get your kit to your room, and then I'll show you around."

Somehow Lerial finds that the whole process of unsaddling the gelding, racking the saddle and blanket, and grooming the gelding takes longer than he recalls. He does remember to check the gelding's hooves, but he sees no stones or cracks, and the shoes look sound. He makes his way to the fountain through the late-afternoon heat that feels hotter than it probably is because there is no breeze at all. He half fills the bucket from the stall, then frowns and pours a little out. The gelding will be thirsty, but he is not that hot, because the pace from Brehaal had been deliberate. Still . . .

He carries the water bucket back to the stable and watches as the gelding drinks. Then he finds a grain barrel and half fills the feed bucket in the stall. By then, his undertunic is soaked, and sweat pours off his forehead

Finally, he closes the wooden stall half door, lifts his kit bag, and walks from the stable toward the courtyard fountain, where the majer has appeared, as if he had known when Lerial would finish.

"Maeroja and the girls will likely be in the courtyard, enjoying the cool." Altyrn looks at Lerial. "You could use that as well."

"It's hotter here than in Cigoerne, and there's no breeze today."

"There usually is, but it's been drier and calmer this summer. We've had to use more water from the Lynaar. That was one reason why I wanted these lands, and your grandmother and father were kind enough to grant them."

"I don't see any ditches . . ."

"I put them underground, and they leave the river farther uphill. That way there's pressure for the fountains and the water's cleaner."

Lerial hadn't thought about either, but he nods.

The north entry to the villa is just a simple recessed arch with a single ironbound door, but as Altryn opens it Lerial can see that the wood is thick, and the back is also ironbound with a double set of brackets for bars. Once they are inside, the majer immediately closes the door.

"We leave the shutters closed and don't dally with the doors until it's late in the evening and it's cooler outside."

While Lerial would not have called the wide corridor especially cold, the air is definitely cooler inside the villa.

"Most of the dayrooms are down on the ground level—the library, the winter dining room, my study, Maeroja's study. There are root cellars and storage areas below. The kitchen is on the west end . . ."

Lerial listens.

The corridor is not that long, no more than ten yards before they walk through an open door and into a center square courtyard. A roof that extends some four yards from the villa runs all the way around the courtyard, creating a covered terrace that surrounds the center fountain, which contains four sprays, each one situated so that it geysers into the air opposite the middle of each wall. A walk runs from each spray to the terrace, and between the four walks are four small gardens. The one that is to Lerial's immediate right, as he follows Altyrn to the left, appears to contain miniature fruit trees.

"Maeroja is quite the gardener . . . and quite the grower. I just listen to her."

Lerial is certain that is something his father would never have said. "How did you meet her?"

"Did you mean to ask if she happens to be local?" Altyrn's voice is dry.

Lerial is so taken aback that he blurts out, "I never even thought of that."

Abruptly, Altyrn laughs. "Good for you." Then he glances toward the woman and the three girls who stand waiting for them just around the corner of the courtyard. He shakes his head. "The girls actually put on dresses. I haven't seen them that fancied up in eightdays."

Since Lerial's sister and cousin are younger, and since his mother and aunt are healers, he can't recall, offhand, seeing many dresses around the palace in Cigoerne.

The majer stops short of his family. "Lerial, might I present my wife, Maeroja, and my daughters, Rojana, Tyrna, and Aylana?"

Lerial sets down his kit and inclines his head. "I'm honored to meet all of you, and I do appreciate your kindness in allowing me to be here." Even though he suspects that the majer may not have had that much choice, his father would not have imposed if the majer had not been at least somewhat willing.

"We're the ones who are honored," replies Maeroja.

As Lerial looks at Maeroja, she seems to be only a few years older than he is, but he has to doubt that, since the tallest girl is less than half a head shorter than he is, suggesting she is close to his age. Maeroja is also, he realizes, rather striking, with jet-black hair, a slightly tanned skin, and penetrating blue eyes. Her smile is warm, but . . . unsettling, almost ironic, he thinks. He almost stammers, but manages to respond. "Not . . . from what I see. I'm the one most honored."

Altyrn smiles, then says to his wife, "Lord Kiedron will be returning for dinner in little more than a glass."

"We will be ready." Maeroja turns her eyes on Lerial. "I thought the girls could show you to your chamber, and you might wish to wash up before rejoining us for something cool to drink before dinner."

"I would appreciate that very much."

"Rojana . . . if you would show Lerial?"

The tallest girl, who has her mother's complexion and hair, but her father's gray eyes, smiles. "Lord Lerial . . ."

"Lerial . . . please. I'm just a younger son."

"This way . . ." Rojana turns and walks south to the corridor in the middle of the east side of the villa, then steps inside.

Lerial can see that the corridor continues to the main entrance and a circular entry hall, although the light is dim, yet Rojana does not continue toward the hall, but heads up the narrow steps, open on one side except for a railing. Lerial picks up his bag and follows her. The two other girls trail him.

At the top of the steps Rojana pauses, then walks back toward the courtyard along a hallway directly above the one below. "Everyone's chambers overlook the courtyard. The upper balcony goes all the way around it." She turns right at the balcony and follows it around until she stops at a door just past midway along the north side of the villa's upper level.

"This is your chamber. It has a small washroom through the door. There are two buckets to bring up water. You can get cool water from either the outside fountain or the spout beside the fountains in the courtyard. Later we can show you the upper cistern that holds warmer water. It's on the roof balcony. We did fill the tub and buckets for you this time. There is a drain for the waste water."

"Where does it go?"

"The pipes take it to the ditch that serves the front meadow."

Since Rojana does not open the door, Lerial depresses the door handle and pushes the door open. He steps inside, and she follows. Her sisters do not. The chamber is long, some seven yards, he judges, but only four wide. There are three long and narrow windows set in the north wall, about twice as wide as those on the lower level, and one on each side of the door from the balcony. The furnishings are simple and sparse—a single bed, a doorless armoire, a dresser with three drawers, a flat-topped storage chest at the foot of the bed, a narrow bedside table, and a writing table-desk and a chair. There is one wall lamp suspended from a brass arm and a lamp on the table-desk.

"This is very nice," he says, nodding to Rojana. "Thank you."

"There's also a set of work trousers and a work shirt in the armoire. Papa said he hopes they're close enough to fit you, but he didn't want you spoiling riding clothes working with him."

Lerial manages to stifle a rueful smile. The majer has used his daughter to deliver a tactful announcement of what awaits him. "That is thoughtful. I didn't bring anything like that."

"Mother thought you wouldn't." That comes from the youngest girl, who stands in the doorway, a serious expression on her face.

"Your mother was right," replies Lerial.

Rojana eases back to the door. "Is there anything else you need?"

"I wouldn't think so, but I'll let you know if there is."

After the three leave, Lerial closes the door, then carries his kit bag to the chest, where he places it and opens it. First, he unpacks and places his garments in either the armoire or the dresser, setting aside a clean set for dinner. Then he disrobes, washes and shaves, although that takes little time, given that his beard is still fine and uneven. Before dressing in his own garments, he does try on the work clothes. They fit, although they are a shade large.

Less than half a glass later, dressed in clean clothes, he leaves his chambers and retraces his steps back down to the courtyard.

As he nears the majer and his family, gathered around a large circular table under the terrace roof, Lerial can't help but overhear a few words between the girls.

". . . said he wouldn't take long . . ."

". . . because you like him . . ."

"Ssshh!"

Lerial keeps a straight face as he stops short of the table. "Thank you. The quarters are lovely." "Lovely" isn't really the right word, but "more than ample" sounds condescending, and "adequate" would be arrogant. "Perfect" would be an obvious exaggeration.

"We hope so," replies Maeroja. "Your rooms are the same as those of Rojana, and all the chambers are similar."

"I do appreciate them." He turns to the majer. "And the work clothes."

"Good. Working here can be a dirty business." Altyrn gestures to the chair to his left, with an empty mug before it. "You can sit down."

"Would you like lager, ale, or redberry?" asks Maeroja, gesturing to the three large pitchers in the center of the wooden table.

"Lager, please."

"That's the pitcher with the gold stripe."

From that, Lerial understands that he is to pour his own . . . and he does so.

"How was the ride?" asks Altyrn.

"Long. I'm not used to that much time in the saddle. But it was interesting. I've never been this far south."

"It's different, and it's not . . . just like most places."

"Dear . . . don't be quite so obscure," suggests Maeroja with a gentle laugh.

"By that," adds Altyrn, "I meant that people don't change much in what they feel, but how they express it may be very different. That's one way of looking at it."

At that moment, a young man in a tan shirt and shorts emerges from the corridor leading from the main entry door. "Ser . . . Lord Kiedron is approaching."

"Thank you, Rhewen." The majer stands and looks at Maeroja and Lerial. "I'll greet him myself."

Since no one else moves as Altyrn leaves, Lerial remains with Maeroja and the girls, although he feels awkward doing so . . . but the majer's words had been a command of sorts.

"He does have a way of making his wishes known without stating them," Maeroja says to Lerial, her tone matter-of-fact.

"I'm gaining that impression, Lady."

While the majer's wife does not flush, Lerial can tell that his salutation has embarrassed her, but what else could he call her. Not to address her would be presumptuous, if not rude.

"If you must address me," she says with a slight twist to her lips, " 'Maeroja' might be better."

"I did not wish to presume," he replies gently.

"That would not be presumptuous." She smiles softly. "I do appreciate the honor, undeserved as it is."

After those words, Lerial is the one trying not to blush.

"How old are you?" asks the youngest girl.

"Almost sixteen," he answers, adding, "Aylana," as he finally recalls her name.

"You don't look that old. You're thin, too."

"That's likely one reason why I'm here. My father wants me to learn things from your father."

"You'll learn," says Rojana. "Father will see to that."

Both her sisters nod.

"Enough, girls." But there is a trace of an amusement behind Maeroja's words.

Lerial takes a careful swallow of the lager, darker than he would prefer, and, after swallowing it, he finds it is likely also stronger and a shade more bitter. Still . . . he would prefer lager to ale . . . and definitely to redberry. "Do you brew your own lager and ale?"

"We do, but only enough for Kinaar. The barley takes too much space for us to grow more."

Lerial is pondering that, given that there seems to be plenty of land, when Altyrn and his father step out onto the terrace. As Kiedron approaches the terrace table, Maeroja rises, and so do Lerial and the three girls.

"It's an honor and a pleasure to see you again, Lord Kiedron," Maeroja offers.

"It's my pleasure as well. It's not often I can dine with just a family, other than my own."

Lerial can sense the truth of his father's words, and he cannot help but wonder how much he does not know about what has occurred involving the majer and his wife . . . and his father.

"It's still our pleasure," adds Altyrn. "You have had a long day. Perhaps we should adjourn to the dinner table?"

"That might be for the best. I will need to leave quite early tomorrow."

The dining chamber is off the terrace, but has three sets of wide sliding doors that are open so that the chamber shares the cool of the courtyard. On colder evenings, Lerial imagines that they are closed. Altyrn seats Kiedron at the head of the table, with Maeroja to his left, then takes the place to the Duke's right. Lerial is seated beside Maeroja, with Rojana beside her father, and the middle daughter, Tyrna, to Lerial's right, and Aylana beside Rojana.

Once everyone is seated and a serving maid fills each goblet, Altyrn raises his. "To the Duke, Lord Kiedron, without whom Cigoerne would not be."

"I'll only drink to that, if I can reply that I wouldn't be here without you," answers Kiedron, lifting his own goblet.

Altyrn does not offer a demurral, Lerial notes, but adds, "To what has come to pass." He glances across at his wife, who smiles.

Once more Lerial feels that there is much passing by him, but he drinks with the others, and after a moment lifts his goblet of lager. "Might I offer thanks to Majer Altyrn and his lady for their kindness in taking me in to teach me what I must learn?"

"You may indeed," says Kiedron, his words warm.

After that toast, Maeroja says, "The dinner tonight is simple, but one you have always enjoyed."

"It wouldn't be the roasted fowl and mushrooms, with glazed lace potatoes, would it?"

Both Altyrn and Maeroja laugh, if softly.

As the server dishes out the main course to Kiedron—Lerial notes that there is no appetizer or salad—the Duke looks to Rojana. "You've grown quite a lot since I was last here, and you take after your mother, not that you wouldn't look good taking after your father . . . but I do think that gray hair looks better on him."

The girls all smile.

He's never joked that way at table in Cigoerne.

"I would guess that Lerial takes more after your sister, with the red hair," observes Maeroja.

"He does, in that and other ways. That's one of the reasons I thought some time with you might do him good."

"How is she?" asks Altyrn.

"She's well, and I don't know what the healers in Cigoerne would do without her . . ."

For a time, the conversation remains firmly away from personal observations, if ranging from the weather to timbering, the possibility of Meroweyan raiders, and the ambitions of the Duke of Heldya.

Then Kiedron asks, "How is the kiln working these days?"

"There are some who want bricks every year. We fire it up when times are slower in the fields."

"What about our venture?"

What venture? Lerial is not about to ask, but he listens intently.

"We sold some ten stones worth last year. Half of that went to pay off the ironmages who made the threading machine and . . . well, and the interest, because we had to borrow from the moneylenders in Swartheld to pay the ironmages, but it can handle ten times that much, and it will be years before we can produce that much. We also needed more kettles."

"You're getting . . . what?"

Altyrn glances to Maeroja.

She nods.

"A hundred a stone."

A hundred what a stone? Lerial wonders. *Coppers, silvers, golds?* It must be coppers or silvers. What could possibly cost a hundred golds for a stone's worth? A half-yearling lamb cost between five coppers and a silver, and a yearling colt between three and five golds. For a hundred golds, his father could almost supply an entire squad of Lancers with mounts and gear . . . well . . . not completely, but close.

"You're going to expand?" asks Kiedron.

"We're working on it. We'll need more trees."

Kiedron nods, but does not ask more, and the conversation reverts to more on the weather and the likelihood of famine in parts of Heldya and Merowey.

Dessert consists of a fried molasses sweetcake, followed by tiny glasses of a sweet white wine. Lerial has to admit that the wine, as dessert, isn't bad.

Before long he is walking with the majer and his father out to the front entrance of the villa, where two Lancers wait for the Duke.

At the entry, Kiedron turns to his son. "I expect you to obey the majer and learn from the experience, Lerial."

"Yes, ser."

"Good." Kiedron nods, then adds quietly, "Just be careful." Then he turns abruptly, walks toward his horse, and mounts. In moments, he and the Lancers are largely lost in the dimness of late evening.

Just be careful. The concern in those words confuses Lerial, because he's seldom heard that from his father. He stands there, watching, until he can make out no sign of the riders. Then he turns.

Altyrn has waited. "He does care, you know? He just feels he can't show it."

Then why has he brought me here?

"You'll understand in time," adds the majer, almost as if Lerial has spoken. "You probably need a good night's sleep. Morning comes early. I'd suggest wearing the work clothes and your worst boots."

"Yes, ser."

Altyrn closes and bars the main entry door, and the two walk back toward the courtyard terrace.

X

On threeday morning, before sunrise when the sky is as much gray as greenish-blue, there is a rap on his door.

"Time to get up," calls a girl's voice.

Lerial struggles out of sleep, then sits up . . . and finds that every muscle is his body feels stiff and sore. In the dimness, he struggles into the work clothes and boots, washes his face, and finally makes his way downstairs. He is the last one to the breakfast room . . . where the girls are already eating. All three are dressed in faded brown trousers and long-sleeved shirts.

"A little stiff from all that riding?" asks Altyrn.

"A bit more than a little, ser," replies Lerial.

"Nothing like a good breakfast and some exercise to take care of that," says Maeroja. She gestures toward the empty chair at the table. "Are you better with a shovel or a hoe?"

How is he supposed to answer that? He's never used either. After a moment, he replies, "I suspect I'm equally bad with either."

"You've trained with wands," says Altyrn. "You'll be better with a shovel. You and I and Rojana will be working with the crew extending the ditches for the meadow we'll be switching to growing more mulberries."

Mulberries? Lerial has heard of mulberries, but never tasted one. "How do they taste?" He slides into the chair beside Rojana.

All the girls smile.

Lerial has the feeling that mulberries are not something that people eat, but, if that's so, why is Altyrn going to grow more of them?

"They're not bad in a pie, especially if you thicken the filling and add raisins," replies Maeroja. "Do you remember shimmercloth?"

"Grandmother had a scarf and a blouse of it."

"It's highly prized, but no one in Hamor knows how it was created. We do . . . or rather my husband does, and it's taken years to build up enough silk moths, but we can't raise any more without more fresh leaves to feed the larvae."

"You're growing shimmercloth?"

Altyrn shook his head. "It's not quite the same, but the threads and fabric are much the same. The silk moths are different here, and it took years to get white mulberry seeds from Candar."

Lerial cannot say that he understands, but he decides against revealing more ignorance immediately. Instead, he looks at the platter and bowl before him. The bowl contains a grayish porridge of sorts that looks to have raisins mixed into it. On the platter is a piece of browned egg toast, with a slice of hard yellow cheese on the side and a strip of fried meat that might be ham. In his mug is some sort of liquid.

"There's raisin-berry syrup in the pitcher," Aylana advises him. "It's good on the egg toast. Don't hog it."

Lerial can't help but smile slightly at the words of the youngest girl, reminding him slightly of his own sister. "Thank you. I won't."

Since everyone else has already started to eat, Lerial does not hesitate . . . or not much. The porridge is better than it looks, and the combination of egg toast and syrup actually tastes good. The cheese is far stronger than he imagined cheese could be, and he has no idea what the meat might be, except that it is strong . . . and it's not mutton, beef, or ham. He decides not to ask. The greenish liquid in his mug turns out to be a type of greenberry juice he's never tasted, almost too tart for his taste at first, but it does go with the breakfast in a way he cannot explain.

When he finishes his last bite of the porridge, Maeroja hands him a small jar. "Put some on your face and neck, evenly and all over. Otherwise your skin will burn and blister. Especially yours."

Lerial takes the jar.

After returning to his chamber and slathering his face and neck, Lerial makes his way down to the main level, where Rojana and Altyrn wait for him. He and Rojana walk side by side behind Altyrn, out through the center courtyard and then through the corridor on the west side of the villa out across the paved area toward the outbuildings.

Rojana, who carries an oddly shaped piece of wood, points to the brick shedlike building ahead that appears to have a white awning suspended above the tile roof. "That's the cocoonery."

"The what?"

"Where the silkworm eggs hatch. It can't be too hot or too cool. That's why they hatch and are fed during the spring and the early summer. Even with the awning it gets too hot after that. Then the cocoons have to be boiled . . ."

"But who does all this?"

"Tyrna and Aylana are good at teasing out the silk strands, and Father pays some of the local girls to help. We'll have to get more when we build another cocoonery."

"That sounds like a lot of work."

"Shimmercloth is worth twice its weight in gold. That's what Father says."

Lerial swallows, as all the pieces come together and he realizes what the venture his father had mentioned the night before had been . . . and that Kiedron had been talking about a hundred golds for a stone's worth of shimmercloth. *No wonder no one in Cigoerne wears anything made of it.* "I haven't seen any here . . ."

"We need the golds more than the cloth."

So does my father. The realization strikes Lerial almost like a blow as he realizes that, except for the two shimmercloth items belonging to his grandmother, he has never seen any around the Palace.

The majer stops outside a small building that Lerial hasn't even seen initially. "Wait here."

Lerial waits, but only for a few moments before the majer reemerges with two spades. He hands the one with the longer shaft to Lerial, the shorter to Rojana, then gestures to the southwest. "You and Rojana are to dig a section of ditch, just past the stone marker at the corner of the pasture. Where you start is marked out with yarn, and there's another strand that marks the line you take. She has the gauge for how deep and wide the ditch is to be. I'll be working with the men lining the ditches with clay."

Dirt isn't dirt? He waits to ask until he and Rojana are well away from the majer. "What's special about the clay? I mean, different from the dirt?"

"Clay is what you make bricks of. You can line ditches and ponds with it so that water doesn't seep out. The dirt here has too much sand in it, and lots of water would seep away if we didn't use clay."

"Digging isn't something I think of women doing," Lerial says as they near the stone marker.

"Why not?"

"I . . . I just don't think of it that way."

"You don't think women have to work?"

"It's not that. My aunt and my mother work. They're both healers, and they go to the healers' hall every day. My aunt works hard at it. Sometimes . . . sometimes . . ."

"Sometimes what?"

"I don't know that most people could do what she does. She has to help broken arms and legs heal, and sometimes she has to watch people die."

"Is that what she says?"

"No. I've seen it happen."

"You were in the healers' hall?"

"Just a few times." Lerial doesn't want to admit he'd only been once.

"Can you heal?"

"My father says I should be able to once I learn how to handle a sabre better."

"That's stupid. Learn how to kill better so that you can heal."

"It's not that. I'm of the Magi'i, and my tutor says I have to learn how to handle chaos first before I work with order."

"He's stupid, too." Rojana actually snorts.

"There's the yarn marker." Lerial points, not wanting to admit he has always had doubts about Saltaryn.

When they get closer, he wonders why the beginning marker was needed, since the section of ditch already dug ends abruptly right there. A single dirty white strand runs straight west, although Lerial can only see it for perhaps twenty yards before it is lost in the sparse green and brown grass.

"You dig out the grass," says Rojana. "I'll shape the sides and bottoms behind you."

"I can do that." Lerial lifts the spade and attacks the grass.

By midmorning, he is no longer stiff, but his arms both burn and ache. To cut through the grass roots at times requires him to put his boots on the edge of the iron spade, and the balls of his feet are beginning to ache as well.

He stops for a moment and asks. "What do you graze on the front pastures?"

"Goats."

"I didn't see any."

"You can't let them graze too long. They'll rip up the grass roots. Father doesn't like goats."

"Why goats and not sheep?"

"The sheep don't do well here." Rojana lifts another spadeful of earth out of the bottom of the ditch lays it on the ground, then takes the wooden gauge and places it in the ditch. Her lips tighten as she sets aside the gauge and lifts the spade again, shaving a digit's worth of earth from the bottom of the ditch. "You need to keep digging. I've almost caught up with you."

Lerial looks back across the field to where Altyrn is working with two men and an older woman. One man shovels clay from a handcart into the unfinished ditch while another uses a long-handled tamper with a flat bottom to tamp it into place. Altyrn measures and adjusts the depth with a small sharp spade. The woman sprinkles a dark liquid over the tamped clay and smooths the surface.

"How far do we have to dig?" Lerial asks tiredly.

"To the end of the yarn. It's just even with the stone field marker."

He glances toward the stone marker a good fifty yards away. "We might finish by midday. Then what?"

"We start on the next ditch from the east end."

"How many ditches do we have to dig?"

"As many as it takes." Rojana lifts another spadeful of dirt. "Six, Father said."

Lerial looks around the field and calculates. What he and Rojana have done is perhaps a sixth of one ditch. Three days for two ditches . . . *Twelve days of digging ditches?* While Lephi is learning more about sabres and riding patrols?

His eyes burn for a moment.

Then he attacks the dirt and grass once more.

XI

On fourday morning, Lerial is even sorer than he had been on threeday, and his hands are red and almost raw in places. His face feels warm, but it is not red, and he applies the ointment Maeroja had supplied to him. When he reaches the breakfast room, he sees that the majer's consort is seated, as are the girls, but the majer is not there.

"He'll be here in a few moments," says Maeroja. "He had to give some instructions to the field crew." Before Lerial can seat himself at the breakfast table, she says, "Let me see your hands."

Lerial shows her the backs of his hands, even as he realizes that there is the faintest hint of something different in her voice, almost an accent, a way of speaking that he has not heard or, if he has, does not recall.

"The palms, please." There is a certain knowing irony in her voice.

He turns his hands over.

"You won't be able to use them for days if you don't do something about them." Maeroja looks to Tyrna. "Go get the ointment."

The middle daughter slips from her chair and scuttles out through the door to the kitchen.

"You'll also need some gloves for a time, until your hands toughen. I'll put on the anointment after you eat. Its smell isn't perfume, but it does work."

"Thank you." Lerial slides into his chair and looks at his empty platter, then realizes that everyone's is empty. Although his mug does contain the green juice, he decides not to drink because it's clear that no one else has. Just as he is wondering how long they will wait for the majer, Altyrn steps into the breakfast room and seats himself. Tyrna is right behind her father, a jar in her hand, which she delivers to her mother before reseating herself.

"Did everyone sleep well last night?"

The girls nod. Maeroja smiles. Lerial nods belatedly. He had slept well, but that was because he'd been so exhausted that the early evening warmth in his room hadn't kept him from falling asleep—a warmth that might well have in Cigoerne.

"Lerial's going to need gloves today," Maeroja says, her voice matter-of-fact, "and anointment."

"I'll get him gloves after breakfast."

Once Altyrn lifts his mug, a server quickly dishes out breakfast, and the girls begin to eat. So does Lerial.

"What was the trouble?" Maeroja asks.

"Naaryt is worried about the axle on the cart. I told him to only use half loads of clay. I'd like to get the ditching done before we get any rain. That way the clay can set. What about the cocoonery?"

"Another few days before the worms start hatching. I've made arrangements with Zierna if we need more leaves. I'd rather not use the red mulberry leaves, but we can always do what we did last year."

"I'd feed the worms on the southeast section with the leaves from the reds. There's something about that part of the tables that the worms don't do as well there."

"The heat . . . even using an awning in front of the wall, it's hotter there."

Altyrn nods. "It's always something." He continues eating, methodically alternating bites of egg toast and porridge.

As soon as Lerial finishes eating, Maeroja says, "Let's get that anointment on your hands."

Whatever the substance is that she works into the skin of palms and fingers, it smells faintly of something unpleasantly wild as well as something similar to pine, if more acrid.

"Now," she says as she finishes, "don't touch anything for a bit." She smiles at Rojana. "You open the doors until you get to the field today."

"Yes, Mother." Rojana grins.

Lerial can't help blushing slightly, and he hopes no one notices.

Before long, Lerial and Rojana follow Altyrn out of the villa.

There, the majer stops abruptly. "Just wait here. I need to get those gloves for you, Lerial." He hurries back inside the villa.

"Father won't be long," says Rojana. "He never is. Mother says that he's always been in a hurry."

As the two of them stand by the west entrance to the villa, two older women walk by some five yards away, talking to each other. One glances in

Lerial's direction, if briefly. They are conversing in Hamorian, and Lerial strains to catch what they are saying.

"... a cousin or nephew of the majer from Cigoerne ..."

"... trouble with his family, most likely ..."

"... he worked hard yesterday ..."

"... see how he does today ... and tomorrow ..."

Although Lerial strains to hear more, the two women continue walking across the courtyard and toward the cocoonery, their words becoming indistinct and unintelligible.

Rojana looks at Lerial curiously. "You speak Hamorian?"

"Of course. Why?"

"I wouldn't have thought ..."

"My grandmother insisted. Both my brother and I do."

"Does Father know?"

"I thought ..." Lerial shakes his head. "I don't know. I never mentioned it. I thought most ... younger people whose parents came from Cyador had their children speak both tongues."

Rojana shook her head. "Father says many of the Lancer families won't teach their children Hamorian."

"He would know." Lerial frowns. "I can't say that I think that's a good idea."

"Not speaking Hamorian is a terrible idea."

Lerial refrains from grinning at her quiet vehemence.

At that moment, the majer steps out of the west door to the villa and walks toward the two.

"I think this pair will fit." Altyrn extends two gloves of heavy leather, with patches of a darker leather at the base of the palms. "You can get them as dirty as you need to, but don't get them wet. Wet gloves are hard on hands."

"Yes, ser." Lerial eases on one glove, then the other. They're slightly large, but not noticeably so. "Thank you."

"There's one other thing, Father." Rojana looks at Lerial.

"Ser ... I don't know if my father mentioned it ... but I do speak Hamorian."

"He did not," replies Altyrn in heavily accented Hamorian. "How well do you speak it?"

"I'm told that I speak it like any other young Hamorian, ser," Lerial answers in Hamorian, "but I couldn't say if that's true or not."

Rojana grins.

Altyrn shakes his head. "It's true enough, wouldn't you say, Rojana?"

"It's more than true. He has the northern accent, though."

"You were taught by someone from Swartheld?"

"Yes, ser." *Several people, but all from the north of Afrit.*

"Obviously arranged by your grandmother, as you said. She had reasons for everything, and seldom were they wrong. Now . . . let's get your spades from the equipment shed. Just do as well as you two did yesterday, and we'll make good progress."

"Yes, ser."

Once Altyrn has handed them the spades and the wooden gauge that Rojana takes, the two walk toward the field with the uncompleted ditching.

When they reach where they halted digging the afternoon before, Lerial grins and asks, "You want me to do all the heavy digging again?"

"Unless you want us to take longer to finish," rejoins Rojana sweetly.

Lerial sighs, loudly and for effect.

"You don't do that well."

"Sighing, you mean?"

"What else would I mean?"

He shakes his head and starts to dig through a clump of tough and wiry grass.

Almost half a glass passes before Rojana pauses and asks, "Was your grandmother as fearsome as they say?"

"I never thought so. She was determined, and what she said was usually what happened." *At least until a few days before she died.* "How did your parents meet?"

"I don't know," Rojana confesses. "I've asked Mother, but she just said that it was something that was meant to happen."

"But she's not from around Cigoerne or from around here. She doesn't look like anyone I've ever seen." Lerial realizes that what he's said isn't coming out the way he intended. "I mean . . . she's beautiful . . ." *That's not any better.* He flushes. "Nothing I'm saying is coming out right. But do you . . . ?"

"I understand. She is pretty. I'm glad I look more like her. She comes from Heldya, but that's all I know."

"You don't know your grandparents, then?"

Rojana shook her head, then lifted another spadeful of dirt from the bottom of the trench. "Father's parents had already died when he came to

Hamor, and neither of them talk about Mother's. What about you? Besides your grandfather who was Emperor?"

"I told you about my grandmother. My mother's parents died after they came to Cigoerne. That was the year when so many died of the flux."

"Your mother's a healer. Why couldn't she do something?"

"She had the flux herself, and she was with child. My aunt was in Narthyl, tending to all the Lancers that had been wounded in the first big attack by the Heldyans." After a moment, Lerial added, "There aren't that many healers, just like there aren't that many Magi'i who are strong mages . . . or white wizards."

"Can you throw chaos, the way they say the white wizards can?"

Lerial shakes his head, then considers. "I can light a candle or a lamp with chaos. I've never tried more. My tutor said I shouldn't try without a magus nearby."

"Could you be a healer?"

"Men aren't healers."

"That's not what I asked."

Could you be . . . "My aunt said I might . . . well . . . she didn't actually say that, but she showed me some of the things that healers can do."

"Why couldn't you heal your hands, then?"

"Can you lift your boots when you're standing and your feet are in them? Healing's sort of the same thing. A healer uses her own strength to use order against the chaos that grows in wounds or in the body when it has a flux. Using your own strength to try to heal your own injuries would weaken you in other places in your body." *Or something like that.* Lerial *thought* he'd remembered what Emerya had told him.

"Oh . . . that makes sense." After a moment, Rojana adds, "There aren't any real healers here in Teilyn."

"There aren't?" That surprises Lerial, but as he thinks it over, he realizes it shouldn't. There are only a handful of good healers in the city of Cigoerne, and it's far bigger than Teilyn.

"The Magi'i don't like to live away from Cigoerne. That's what Father says."

". . . and most healers are from the Magi'i," concludes Lerial. "That doesn't mean that there can't be healers and Magi'i born from parents who aren't Magi'i. Alyiakal's father was a Mirror Lancer."

"Who's Alyiakal?"

"He was one of the great Emperors of Cyador. Some of the great healers didn't even have altage parents. That's what my aunt says."

"I'll bet they all consorted Mirror Lancers or men who were Magi'i."

"Why do you say that?"

"Because it's true."

"How do you know that?"

"How do you know it's not?"

Lerial starts to retort, then stops. After several moments, he finally says, "You're right. I don't know that it's not true."

Rojana grins.

"We'd better get back to digging." Lerial shifts his grip on the shovel.

Shortly after midday, Altyrn calls them to a meal under one of the olive trees in an adjoining orchard, if bread and cheese washed down with juice for Rojana and lager for Lerial count as a meal. The three sit in the shade as they finish their fare.

"You two have been working hard," says the majer.

"It's the only way we'll get done, ser," replies Lerial.

"That's true . . . but it's dangerous to look at things that way. People who just want to get done with whatever they're doing often don't do a good job. You two are working hard and well. That's good."

"Thank you, ser." Lerial is embarrassed to say that, but not to acknowledge the compliment would be discourteous.

"Why is digging an irrigation ditch well a good thing?" This time, Altyrn looks to his daughter.

"Doing anything well is better than doing it badly."

Altyrn laughs. "Those are my words coming back to me. Why is doing something well worth it, even if the work is unrecognized or if time will undo it?"

Rojana glances at Lerial, but does not speak.

"Lerial?" prods the majer.

"I think that it's important. I don't have the words to explain it."

"You might try."

"Ser . . . I . . ." Lerial shrugs helplessly.

"You need to think about it. I'll give you a hint. What remains of Cyad, once the mightiest city in the world?"

"Nothing," rejoins Rojana.

"Exactly. Think about it." Altyrn rises. "Time to get back to work."

Throughout the afternoon, at least occasionally, Lerial considers Altyrn's question. If all work, even the greatest works, are doomed to fall and be forgotten, why does it matter for him—or anyone—to do a good job, especially of digging a ditch?

He feels as though the answer to that question should be obvious, and yet, he cannot come up with a response that satisfies him.

XII

For Lerial, fiveday isn't much different from fourday, and neither is sixday, just more digging, followed by more digging. Lerial finds that his hands, with the help of Maeroja's anointment and the heavy gloves, are both recovering and toughening, and his pale skin has actually tanned somewhat, with the help of the ointment. He still has no answer to Altyrn's question, and certainly not one with which he is personally satisfied, but the majer does not ask or even remind him of the question.

Why is doing something well important when in the end nothing is left? Those weren't Altyrn's words, but his question had amounted to the same thing. *But did they?*

Much as Lerial pushes the question away, it keeps coming back into his thoughts, as do other thoughts, such as why the majer even asked the question.

"Have you had to dig this much before?" Lerial finally asks Rojana sometime before midday on sixday, setting down his shovel for a moment.

"No. Father insists that we must know how to do everything on the lands." Her face turns sober. "I told him that I didn't want to work in the cocoonery. It's boring and tedious work, and everyone there . . . they're all women, and all you do is make sure that the worms aren't too cold or too hot and cut leaves and make sure that there are plenty of leaves in close to each one. If any die, you have to make sure they are dead and lift them out and clean up where they were."

"It does sound tedious . . . but so is digging ditches."

Rojana sets a spadeful of dirt from the bottom of the ditch on the edge, lays down her shovel, and uses the wooden template gauge to check the depth and width of the trench. "It's outside, and it doesn't smell as much. I don't mind teasing the silk strands out of the cocoons. That's tedious, but you can see where everything's going."

"You remember your father's question to me? Has he ever asked you questions like that?"

She laughs. "All the time. He's asked questions from the time any of us could talk."

"And?"

She shrugs. "Sometimes I agree with what he wants us to think about. Sometimes I don't. He doesn't seem to care whether I agree. He gets angry if I don't think about why I feel the way I do." She pauses. "Sometimes, I even think he wants me to disagree with what he's hinting."

"What does your mother think about it?"

"She asks questions, too. Not as often. Hers are nastier."

Nastier? Somehow, Lerial doesn't think of Maeroja as nasty.

Rojana looks at Lerial. "She's not nasty. The questions are."

"Such as?"

She shakes her head. "They're about women things . . . I don't want to talk about them. Aren't there men things you don't want to talk about?"

Lerial thinks for a moment, then replies, "There are, but no one's ever asked me questions about them."

"That's because men don't want to think about them."

"And women don't?"

"It's not the same." Rojana picks up her spade.

Lerial takes the hint and resumes digging.

By midafternoon, a silvery haze covers the sky, but there are no clouds, and Lerial observes, after blotting his dripping forehead with the sleeve of his work shirt, "It's not going to cool off much tonight."

"It never does in summer."

"Less than usual tonight. That's because of the silver haze. It keeps the air warmer, and there's never any breeze"

"Why is that so?"

Lerial stops digging for a moment. "I don't know. I asked Saltaryn, but he couldn't tell me."

"Who's Saltaryn?"

"He was the magus who taught me."

"Is he really a magus? One who can throw chaos-fire?"

"I suppose so. Anyone who is a full magus has to be able to do that."

"Do you know that he can?"

"He could form a globe of chaos-fire on his fingertip and make it dance around or fly through the air to light a candle."

"Have you ever tried to throw it?"

"I'm not supposed to," Lerial replies. "I told you that."

"You never answered my question."

"I tried when I was younger. I couldn't. I haven't tried since I learned how to light a candle with chaos."

"Why not?"

"Because Saltaryn said I shouldn't."

"Did he tell you why?"

"Because it would have been dangerous, I suppose."

"But he didn't tell you that, did he?"

"No," Lerial admits.

"So you really don't know if you can throw chaos-fire."

This time, it is Lerial who resumes digging without answering.

Even so, Rojana's question, like her father's, lingers in his thoughts all through the afternoon . . . and through dinner, solid and tasty as the fowl stew is.

So, later that evening, a good glass after dinner, Lerial makes his way outside and across the paved bricks behind the villa until he is behind the stable. Then he stands there, feeling hot and sticky, even though he washed up thoroughly after returning to the villa when he finished digging for the day. Overhead, the sky is darkening into a purple overlaid with the hint of silver.

Finally, he takes a deep breath and concentrates on focusing chaos, visualizing a small ball of chaos-fire at the tip of his outstretched index finger. Then he tries to throw the fireball, both with his arm and his thoughts.

The small fireball dribbles from his hand and plops on the brick paving.

Lerial shudders. Something about the chaos-fire feels . . . ugly . . . almost unclean, and there is almost a smell, like brimstone . . . except he knows that the odor isn't exactly in his nose, but more in his thoughts. *Why would it be that way?*

He sighs. He supposes his effort proves that, if he practices more, he might be able to throw chaos-fire like a white wizard . . . but the thought of doing so troubles him . . . and he has the same feelings he did when he'd seen Lephi tormenting the cat with tiny fireballs. He hasn't forgotten that Lephi was caned because he'd used chaos, not because he'd hurt the poor cat.

He turns and walks slowly back toward the villa, lost in mixed thoughts . . . about what Saltaryn had said about mastering chaos first, about what Emerya had implied about the need to understand the flow of order to be able to master chaos, and about Rojana's question . . . and why she had pressed him. He has almost reached the north entrance to the villa, when a voice brings him up short.

"Lerial . . . you're out here late."

He looks up with a start to see Maeroja standing by the entry. "I've been thinking." That is certainly true.

"Might I ask . . ."

"About order and chaos . . . about a lot of things . . ."

"You're a very serious young man. You remind me of what I think Altyrn might have been years ago, when he was young before I met him. He had to learn to laugh, you know?"

Lerial still cannot imagine the majer laughing—at anything. *How could anyone think that he and I might be alike?*

"He does laugh. He keeps much laughter to himself. You should laugh more, too. Life is too short not to laugh."

As Maeroja talks, Lerial is reminded once more of the hint of an accent he does not recognize . . . but only a hint. "One must have something to laugh about."

"One can laugh about anything . . . if you look at it from the right point of view." She smiles. "I will not keep you." With that, she turns and reenters the villa.

After several moments, Lerial follows, but he does not see Maeroja, although he thinks he hears her steps on the stairs to the upper level.

XIII

An eightday passes in which Lerial digs and digs, not only ditches, but holes for the small mulberry trees that have been rooted from cuttings and then transferred to the holes that he and Rojana dug. Then, over the following eightday, the slope and gradients of the ditches have to be adjusted so that just enough water reaches each tree. Some rooted cuttings do not survive, and that requires transplanting more rooted cuttings. By late summer, an orchard of knee-high mulberry trees stands where there had once been a pasture, and Lerial has calluses on his hands and muscles hardened by the kind of labor he'd never imagined. He has given up thinking about Lephi or why his father had sent him to Kinaar, at least most of the time.

Then, after breakfast on oneday, Altyrn draws him aside.

"Ser?"

"From now on," the majer says, "you'll work as usual in the morning. In the afternoon, we'll start your training. You didn't think that wouldn't come, did you?"

"I wondered, but it didn't seem as though what I thought mattered."

"Self-pity isn't terribly useful, Lerial. Very few people care if other people feel sorry for themselves. Why do you think I've made you work this hard? And Rojana, for that matter?"

"To show me that I'm not that special? And to make me stronger."

"You are different, but not special. You're of the Magi'i. You can't escape what you are, but too many of the Magi'i have no idea what the life of those under them is like. You've had more than half a season of hard work, with more to come. I doubt you'll totally forget it. I hope you won't. It would be a pity to waste it. What you have to learn now will make what you've been through seem pleasant."

Lerial doesn't want to think about that. "Why . . . Rojana?" he cannot help but ask.

"Do you think you're the only one with illusions? Hers are slightly different from yours, but she also needed to understand that you and the Magi'i are only different, not special."

"Will she keep working in the morning as well?"

"She may be doing different tasks at times. That all depends on what is necessary, and what the lands require. Even rulers, if they wish to be successful, must understand what their lands require. This morning, you'll both be helping with the barley harvest."

Helping with the barley harvest doesn't sound that bad to Lerial, and better than digging. "Yes, ser."

Altyrn turns and beckons to Rojana, who walks to join them. "You'll need hay rakes. You two will follow the men with the scythes and rake the cut stalks into neat piles. Try to keep the heads of the grain in each pile in the same place. I'll show you how once we get to the field . . ." Altyrn goes on to explain as he leads Lerial and Rojana across the paved space behind the villa.

Lerial glances to the south, where he can just make out the hillside grapevines—the ones that supply the grapes for the raisins . . . and for some small amount of wine, or so the majer has said.

Altyrn stops at the small equipment building, where he steps inside and then returns with two wooden rakes. He hands one to Rojana and the other to Lerial.

Even the teeth are wood, Lerial notes.

"You'll have to rake firmly, but gently. If you break the teeth, you'll have to spend time in the evening cutting and carving a new rake head." With that, Altyrn turns and continues westward.

The sound that comes from the cocoonery as they pass is like rain, although Lerial cannot imagine rain falling inside that shed, much as he has learned that the sound is that of thousands of silkworms chewing mulberry leaves. "It's hard to believe they're so noisy," he murmurs to Rojana.

"Before long they'll start spinning their cocoons. Then you won't hear anything. It still smells."

Rojana and Lerial follow Altyrn down a narrow lane past the north side of the new mulberry orchard, with mostly brown pasture to the right, before reaching a field of golden tan grain. Three men with scythes have begun to work, their scythes moving in unison as they walk and cut the stalks, leaving the fallen grain, still on its stalks, and stubble only a few digits high.

"If you'll hand me your rake, Lerial . . ."

Lerial does.

"This is what I want from you . . ." Altyrn demonstrates, using a firm but gentle motion to gather the stalks sideways, so that each line of stalks ends up essentially as an unbound bundle. "Aylana, Tyrna, and I will gather these into the cart. Once everything is gathered, we'll take the sheaves to the threshing barn. Lerial, you'll be alternating turning the threshing drum with me and the other men, but we won't be doing that until it's all cut and in the barn. That will take several days."

"How many fields have to be cut and gathered?" asks Lerial.

"Five about this size," replies Altyn.

"That's what it takes just to make the lager?"

"For about twenty-five people for a year, yes, with enough left to sell maybe ten barrels, except we sell it in kegs, not barrels."

Lerial is still thinking about that long after he has begun to rake the stalks of grain into the loose sheaves or bundles. It is harder than Altyrn has made it look, far harder. His only consolation is that Rojana appears to be having the same difficulties.

"It's harder than it looks," he finally says.

"Father has a way of making things look easy. They aren't."

By midday, Lerial has discovered that barley raking is just as hard as digging, if in a different way, and there are muscles in his shoulders that ache. He is more than glad to surrender his rake to one of the women who works on the majer's lands, and is struck by how easy she also makes the rake-gathering look.

He has to hurry to catch up to Rojana and Altyrn.

"You both can have some lager and bread and cheese before you start your afternoon lessons."

They eat at the courtyard table not far from the fountain. Lerial appreciates the coolness brought by the spray, although there is so little breeze that the comparative cool barely reaches where they sit.

As Lerial takes a last swallow of lager, Altyrn clears his throat, then speaks. "Lerial, we'll begin with sparring. I'd like to see what you know . . . and what you don't. After that, we'll see about your other skills with arms. Lessons after that." He looks to his eldest daughter. "Rojana . . . I expect more attention in your history studies. Few women . . ."

"Few women have such opportunities away from Cigoerne. I know, Father."

"You know, you say, daughter, but how can things change if women like you do not know both the good and the evils of the past." Abruptly, Altyrn addresses Lerial. "Why did an Empress never rule Cyador? Cyador, not Cigoerne."

"Ah . . . there were always male heirs."

"There were not. Both Alyiakal and Lorn had no imperial blood. Not that we know, anyway. There may have been others whose blood was not as it was supposed to be. That's not something we'll ever know." Altyrn pauses. "Why were there no Empresses who ruled? Did your magus tutor not address that question?"

"Ah . . . no, ser. Custom?" Lorn ventures.

"Custom, indeed. We have women who are ironmages. Why are none of them called magus? They have the same talents as a magus, and some are more skilled in handling chaos than many men who are Magi'i. Your own grandsire had almost no ability as a magus, yet he was considered of the Magi'i."

"Another custom, ser?"

"Why such a custom?" Altyrn looks back to Rojana. "And why did the Emperor Lephi decree that women who were not ironmages should wear either chains or the wristbands of a healer?"

"He did that?" Lerial blurts out the question unthinkingly.

"He did indeed. Can either of you think why all that might be so?"

"Men didn't want women to have power," declares Rojana. "Is that it?"

"We don't know. We'll never know." Altyrn smiles, an expression ironic, yet warm. "So why are questions like that important . . . if we can't ever know?"

Lerial looks to Rojana. She offers an enigmatic smile, one that instantly recalls to him that her mother has the same expression. The enigmatic similarity so disconcerts him that, for a moment, he forgets the majer's question.

"You have no thoughts on that?" presses Altyrn. "Either of you?"

Lerial wrenches his attention back to the majer and throws out the first thing that comes to mind. "If we don't know, that's because no one thought of asking the question . . . or, if they did, they were too afraid to ask."

Altyrn actually looks stunned, if but for an instant. Then he smiles. "That's an excellent answer! And it's likely true. There are two reasons I can think of why obvious questions like that are never asked. The first is what you said. Can you think of the second?"

Lerial cannot.

Rojana does not speak either.

"The other is because the question does not occur to anyone. Why does the sun rise?"

Lerial blinks. "It always has."

"Why? Will it always do so? People don't ask questions, or stop asking questions, when they feel they can't do anything about something . . . or they don't want to." The majer shakes his head and laughs softly. "You two will have me talking all afternoon. Think about questions, though. And, Lerial, have you an answer as to why we should do tasks well when no one will remember or nothing will remain?"

"No, ser. I've thought about that. I don't have an answer that makes sense."

The majer nods, then turns to Rojana. "Read the next chapter in the history while I'm working with Lerial. I'll have questions for you when I return."

"Yes, Father."

Altyn rises from the table.

Lerial follows, as does Rojana, and as he stands beside her, Lerial realizes that Rojana is taller than she had been when he'd come to Teilyn, only a few digits shorter than he is. *Why didn't you notice that before? Or that she and her mother are tall for women?*

He is still pondering that as he walks beside Altyrn past the main entry corridor and then around the corner to the middle of the south side of the courtyard to the south corridor out to the south entrance. The majer halts beside a narrow door, the last one, which he opens. Beyond the door is a long and narrow chamber, with weapons racked on each side.

An armory. Why on the south side? Because when the villa was built, the dangers came from the south?

Altyrn lifts two full-sized wooden wands from a rack.

Lerial notes smaller wands as well. "You've taught the girls to handle sabres as well, ser?"

"Her mother and I have. They're likely not as accomplished as you are, but they will be in time."

The majer closes the armory door and leads the way out to the paved "courtyard." There he stops and hands one of the wooden wands to Lerial.

Lerial takes it, finding it much heavier than the wands with which he has practiced, and certainly heavier than a standard Lancer sabre. He hefts it, frowning.

"It's heavier than what you'll use. There's a reason for that. More than one, actually." Altyrn smiles. "Take your position."

Lerial does so.

"Now . . . begin an attack."

Lerial moves forward cautiously, then has to dart sideways, barely able to deflect the majer's wand. Yet the majer seems barely to have moved.

Watch his order flows! The words come into his mind from somewhere, words with the feel of his aunt, for all that he knows he is warning himself. He steps back and tries to concentrate on both watching Altyrn and sensing what the flow of order around the majer indicates.

Lerial's next attack is better, but his defense is shaky, and the majer's wand strikes Lerial's calf, hard enough to sting and likely leave a bruise.

"A real blade would have cut through and left you lying on the stones." Altyrn's words are matter-of-fact.

Nodding, Lerial steps back and straightens.

After another series of engagements and disengagements, Lerial begins to sense more clearly what the majer's intents and possible attacks and defenses are . . . but even when he can sense what will happen before it does, he finds himself on the defensive, unable to counter what the majer does.

After almost a glass, Altyrn steps back. "That's enough for today."

Lerial is soaked all the way through, but, despite a glass of sparring under the summer sun, the majer sports but a sheen of perspiration on his face and a few damp patches on his work shirt.

"You need to cool down and wash up. When you've done that, meet me in the courtyard at the table. Just wait if I'm not there. I may need to spend more time with Rojana."

"Yes, ser."

Lerial cannot say that he is displeased, but at the same time, he is angry, angry with himself for not being able to counter or avoid what he knows is coming, angry once more with Lephi and his father for sending him away . . . and angry for reasons he cannot even name.

By the time he has cooled down, washed up, and made his way back to the fountain courtyard, most of his anger has subsided.

Tyrna and Aylana are sitting at a small table near the fountain, in much the same fashion as Amaira and Ryalah did in Cigoerne, although they are engaged in a board game that he does not recognize. Even so, at the sight of the two girls at the table, a wave of loss and sadness sweeps over him, and he turns away, standing there for a time before he feels enough in control to continue toward the fountain.

"What are you playing?" he asks.

"Capture," replies Tyrna.

"She's better." Aylana's words hold an irritated edge.

"You'll get better," says Tyrna encouragingly.

Lerial can sense the honesty and the affection behind those words, and he says to Aylana, "You're very fortunate to have a sister who cares."

"She still wins all the time."

"That will change if you keep working at it." Lerial looks up as, from the corner of his eye, he sees Altyrn enter the courtyard. "It's time for my lessons."

Aylana sighs loudly and says to Tyrna, "I get the first move this time."

Lerial walks toward the larger table, reaching it just before the majer, who gestures for him to sit down. Lerial seats himself as the majer does.

"I know nothing about the elthage skills," Altyrn begins. "I won't even attempt to instruct you in such matters. As your father's son and as the brother of the heir, you will be called upon to lead Lancers. If you fail at that, you will not only suffer and possibly die, but so will others. If you are a good leader, but cannot defend yourself with a blade, others will have to die protecting you. Likewise, if you become a master blade, but cannot lead, you will still die, because there will be no one left to protect you." The majer pauses and looks to Lerial, as if expecting a response.

"You're telling me that I have to be a good leader, a good tactician, and a master blade . . . or I will fail."

"Sooner or later, unless you are extremely fortunate . . . yes. And fortune is a most fickle lady and a worse mistress." Altyrn smiles encouragingly. "You have the makings of a good master blade, if you will apply yourself. You have the ability to anticipate, which many never have, but you have less than no idea how to best counter what you anticipate. That . . . I can teach you, if you are willing to learn."

"I felt that, ser. I could almost see what was coming, but not how to best react."

"You don't have the moves. They have to be so drilled into you that you almost do not have to think. Because you are thinking, you are too slow. If you work, we can remedy that. The same principle applies to tactics. One must recognize what is developing before it occurs . . . and act before your enemy knows that you have recognized what he is doing."

"How am I to do that?"

"First, I will instruct you in the basics, what every ranker must know before he rides on his first patrol. Then we will, at times, ride various places, and I will show you how attacks might develop in various places, in the woods, in undergrowth, in the hills, in the sands . . ."

Lerial listens, almost overwhelmed by just the description of what Altyrn expects.

Abruptly the majer stops. "What you need to learn is much. That is because much is expected of you, and that is because you have great advantages in life. A man who does not know how to appreciate and to use his talents and position to their best will soon waste both. I trust you would prefer not to do that."

"No, ser."

"Let me ask you this. Why does your father have power? Why is he Duke of Cigoerne?"

For a moment, Lerial is at a loss. *Why is he Duke? Because he is.* That is not the answer the majer wants, though, and Lerial struggles to come up with a reason. "Well . . . he has the Mirror Lancers, and they obey him. And he is the son of the Emperor of Cyador."

"Cyador is gone. Little more than toppled stones remains. As for the Lancers, *why* do they obey him? He is only one man, and they are many."

"They respect him."

"Do they? Or do they obey him because he can pay them? Or pay them more than others do? Or do they respect and obey him because the senior majer does? Or their squad leader does? Or is it because obeying him is the only way they can be Lancers, and that is what they wish to be? Or do they obey because they fear if they do not, they will be executed for failure to obey?"

"It could be any of those," admits Lerial. "Or some of them."

"If you are a leader, you need to know which support your leadership. What do all of those questions tell you?"

Lerial does grasp that. "The more reasons a leader is respected and obeyed, the stronger his ability to lead?"

"Good. Then why should you be a master blade, if you can pay for the best Lancers?"

Lerial remembers that answer from his father. "Because you're not asking them to do something you can't do."

The questions go on seemingly endlessly, but it is only half a glass later, when Altyrn says, "That's enough questions. We'll start with what a Lancer squad is, what it does, and how it operates."

Lerial nods and listens.

XIV

For the next two eightdays, as summer turns to harvest, even if the days and nights are no cooler, Lerial continues the same pattern of work in the morning and sparring and arms practice in the afternoon, followed by studies of tactics. On fourday, slightly before midmorning, he is working with Rojana in the small lemon orchard, picking only the lemons that are the right size and shade of yellow. He picks those that can be reached from the ground, and she is the one who climbs the tree.

Lerial hears several yells, and then a harrowing scream.

Before he can say a word, Rojana calls down from the tree, "Something's happened! A little boy was hit by the brick wagon." She scrambles down the tree, then grabs Lerial's arm. "This way!"

Lerial has to run to keep up with her as she races up the lane in the direction of the villa, then crosses the space in front of one of the olive groves and nears the narrow brick-paved road down from the brick kiln.

The teamster is still seated on the wagon seat, holding the two-horse team steady. All the color has drained from his face. Another man and a woman kneel beside the large rear wheel of the wagon, loaded with the same kind of yellow-rust bricks as those used to build the villa and pave the area around it.

A boy stands on the shoulder of the road. He is stone-faced. "I didn't mean to hurt him bad . . ." His words are in Hamorian, and are almost defiant.

"What happened?" demands Rojana as she nears the wagon.

The teamster is the one who answers. "One of the boys pushed the other, and he lost his balance and fell under the wheel. I couldn't stop in time . . ."

Rojana turns and hurries to the rear of the wagon. Lerial follows. They both look down on a boy, slightly younger than the one standing back from the road.

Lerial gapes. Blood still flows from a wound on the inside of the boy's upper arm. The flesh is mangled, but only on the underside, as if the iron tire of the wagon had just clipped his arm. How that could have happened without the boy having his entire arm crushed, Lerial has no idea. Even so, the child could die. The woman is trying to stanch the flow of blood, but her efforts appear ineffectual. The man, possibly the teamster's assistant, just stares.

Rojana grabs Lerial's arm again. "Do something! You must have learned something from your aunt . . ."

Lerial pulls off his shirt, then kneels down as Rojana pulls the woman back. The only thing he can see is that there's too much blood. He quickly wraps the shirt around the boy's arm above the wound, ignoring the moans and cries as he does. The shirt stops some of the blood flow, but not enough.

"Get me a short stick!"

In moments, Rojana hands him one, and he ties a knot above and below the stick, then turns it a turn, then another. A third turn is enough to stop the blood flow.

Now what do you do? He has nothing with which to clean the gaping gash, and he's not certain he would even know how to sew up the wound.

"We need to get him somewhere where we can clean the wound and sew it up. As fast as we can."

"Mother can do that!" says Rojana. "You keep him from bleeding while they carry him to the villa. I'll have Mother meet you in the courtyard by the fountain."

Lerial can do that. He also tries to infuse a little order to the boy's arm as he walks beside the teamster's assistant, guiding them toward the closest door—the one on the west side of the villa.

Maeroja is waiting when the teamster lays the boy on the courtyard table, and Tyrna has a bucket of water and clean cloths.

Lerial keeps the tourniquet only as tight as necessary and tries to stay out of Maeroja's way as she cleans and wound and begins to sew it closed. After several stitches, she looks at Lerial.

"Do you see what I'm doing?"

"Yes, Lady."

She frowns at the term of address, but only says, "I want you to do the next stitch. You'll have to do worse in the field."

Lerial sees that there is no way to decline. He takes the needle.

"Keep it close to the last stitch."

Lerial manages two more stitches before she takes the needle back.

"You have to tie the last stitch, or the wound will open again."

He knows that, but watches closely to see how she does it.

When the boy's arm is stitched up and wrapped, Lerial immediately loosens the tourniquet. There is less order in the lower arm than he would like, and he tries to infuse just a bit more. That effort leaves him light-headed, and he has to put out a hand to the table to steady himself.

"You're white," says Tyrna. "Does seeing blood do that to you? It does to Aylana."

"No," replies Lerial. "It was . . . something else." He stands there and listens as Maeroja speaks to the child's mother in a lilting but fluent Hamorian . . . with an accent he has heard before . . . or not exactly . . . although he cannot recall where he has heard that before. He also realizes that he has never heard Maeroja speak Hamorian before.

". . . you must keep this dressing on for the next two days. Keep it clean. Then come back here on sixday. We will see how it heals." She pauses, then nods toward Lerial. "You are fortunate that . . . Lerial was close. Otherwise, your son might have bled to death."

The woman looks to Lerial . . . and then away, almost as though she does not wish to see him.

Rojana offers Lerial a warm smile, one that leaves him disconcerted.

Why? Why would her smile do that? Is it because he is light-headed?

Once the mother and her son have left, Maeroja looks to Lerial. "You did what the healers do, after I closed the wound, didn't you?"

"I was worried that the tourniquet was on too long. I tried to strengthen the order in his arm below the wound."

"He is fortunate in more ways than one."

"He is," replies Lerial. "If Rojana had not seen what happened and insisted we go see, we might not have gotten there in time."

"She thinks quickly, but so did you." Maeroja smiles. "I think the lemon grove can wait until tomorrow. You two just stay here. I'll have one of the girls bring refreshments. You both could use them. You especially, Lerial."

"I could." Lerial hates to acknowledge weakness, but he is still light-headed and more than relieved to be able to sit down, although he does choose the smaller table.

After Maeroja and Tyrna leave, followed by Aylana, Rojana sits across from Lerial. "You never said you were a healer."

"I'm not. I know a little bit about healing, and I can focus a little order and a little chaos. That doesn't make me a magus or a healer."

"Then you could be a healer, couldn't you?"

"I could probably heal a little. Maybe more." Lerial isn't about to admit that he could be a healer, especially if that means giving up the possibilities of at least leading Mirror Lancers and undertaking the other tasks of a true magus.

"You don't want to be a healer?"

"Some healing skills are helpful for an officer who leads Mirror Lancers, especially after battles."

"There's already too much fighting."

"It's necessary."

"It wouldn't be if people didn't fight."

"What would you do if there weren't any Lancers, and Meroweyan raiders tried to take your sheep and all the crops?"

"We'd have to fight, but they wouldn't have to attack."

"What if they're attacking because they have no food?" countered Lerial.

"It's still not right."

"There are a lot of things that aren't right, but happen. We have to be prepared for them."

"We shouldn't start them."

Lerial thinks about that, then decides not to reply as one of the serving girls appears with a tray. She sets it on the table.

"Thank you," he says, but she does not reply, only inclines her head and backs away.

Lerial wonders what he did to frighten or offend her.

"Saenja almost never speaks."

"Do you know why?" He looks at the tray that holds two mugs, one filled with a greenish juice and the other with dark lager, and a platter with thin slices of what looks to be ham, as well as cheese and a loaf of dark bread. He sets the juice in front of Rojana. "Do you want some bread?"

"You need it more than I do."

Lerial breaks off a chunk of the bread and cuts away a chunk of cheese that he wraps in a slice of the ham. He alternates mouthfuls of the bread and the ham and cheese, interspersed with swallows of the lager. Before too long, the headache he has not even realized he has begins to vanish, along with the light-headedness.

"I thought you'd be full of yourself," Rojana declares. "You're not. Not too much, anyway. That's good."

If that's a compliment, I don't want an insult. "It's hard to be too full of yourself when you have an older brother who can drub you in sparring."

"He won't be able to do that if you do what father says." Rojana sips the juice. "I'll be glad when I can have lager or wine. They taste better."

"I'm sure they do." Lerial looks at the platter. It is empty, but he doesn't recall eating all that, and he is certain that Rojana ate far less than he did.

"You don't like letting people know what you feel, do you?"

"It's dangerous when your father is the Duke."

"That's sad. No one will ever know how good you are."

How do you answer that? "I just try to do the best I can."

"I'm glad."

For a time, neither speaks.

Then Saenja reappears and takes the tray and the mugs. Even before she leaves the courtyard, Altyrn enters from the north corridor and walks toward the two. "Time for studies, Rojana, and, for you, Lerial, sparring."

"Yes, ser."

Both Lerial and Rojana stand immediately. Rojana inclines her head to her father and then offers a long look at Lerial before she leaves, moving in the direction of the study.

A thoughtful expression appears on the majer's face, then vanishes. He gestures toward the south corridor from the courtyard, and he and Lerial walk side by side toward it. "Maeroja said you were very quick-thinking this morning."

"Rojana made certain I was," says Lerial dryly.

"She's like her mother in more than looks. Listening to the right woman can save a man, and listening to the wrong one will like as not destroy him. So will not listening at all, but it takes longer." Altyrn pauses. "Listening to any young woman at your age is dangerous . . . but you'll learn that soon enough, and nothing I say will change that."

A tenth of a glass later, Lerial is wielding off attacks by Altyrn and trying to mount his own. For a time, he feels as though he is barely holding off the older man. Then, Altyrn recovers with his wand too low.

Lerial reacts by beating down Altyrn's wand and thrusting, only to find that the majer has dropped to his knees and come up under Lerial's wand with his own.

"That's another trap. Be wary of any opening when your blade is higher than the other man's."

Lerial wants to shake his head. The more he learns, the more he discovers it can be used against him.

"Don't look so hangdog," says Altyrn dryly. "I have learned a few things over forty years as a Lancer."

Forty years . . . and his face is wrinkled and his hair is gray and thinning, and you still have trouble laying a blade on him. "Yes, ser."

"Just remember . . . the same thing will happen to you. If you learn what I'm trying to teach you, someday you'll be looking at a worried young fellow, wondering if you looked that green." Altyrn raises his wand. "Try again."

Lerial takes a slow deep breath, squares his shoulders, and lifts his wand.

A good glass later, after Altyrn has run Lerial through learning another set of responses to various attacks, and called an end to the sparring for the day, Lerial washes up, changes into dry garments and makes his way down to the study.

"You're getting better," Altyrn announces as Lerial enters, then motions for him to sit down at the round table. "You can't see it yet, but I have to use more and more things you haven't come across to surprise you. That's good."

Lerial hasn't thought of it that way.

"You do need a lot more practice, though. Every move needs to be smoother and without hesitation. In another few eightdays, we'll go over to the post, and I'll have some of the better blades there spar with you."

Another few eightdays? How long are you going to be here?

"There's still so much that you need to learn. I wish that I had some of the books that were lost in Cyad . . ." Altyrn glances in the direction of the courtyard, his expression almost morose. "That's why you have to listen to me, because so much of what we had only remains in memory."

Lerial does not comment, since the majer has said something similar several times over the past season. He also knows what Altyrn has said before, that when those who hold those memories die, even less of the knowledge and lore of Cyador will remain.

The majer straightens. "What sort of a stream path or road is dangerous to follow?"

"If there are trees close to the road, especially if the stream is deep." That much, Lerial knows. "Or if the road is muddy."

"There's another kind of stream road to be wary of, especially in the drylands," adds Altyrn. "Those are the roads in narrow and dry canyons, if you can see a storm in the upstream direction. Drylands don't hold water, and a strong cloudburst can fill a small canyon and drown an entire company."

Lerial frowns.

"Take my word for it. Every few years, it happened in the Grass Hills. It's happened once here, about five years back. The only thing that didn't make it worse was that the patrol was only a single squad. Still . . . losing twenty-one men at once . . ."

A good two glasses later, Lerial retreats to the courtyard with a small volume written in Hamorian—*Necessary Skills of War*—one of the few Hamorian books on tactics worth reading, according to Altyrn.

He has some time before dinner, and the courtyard is quiet. He opens the book and begins to read. . . .

> How battles are waged is of the greatest importance to a land. Their outcome is a matter of life or death, the path to either survival or destruction. For these reasons, one must approach battles and their conduct only after studying all that lies behind and beyond them. . . .

True enough . . . but obvious. Lerial winces and leafs through the book to another section.

> *Victory is the only object of battle. If a victory cannot be obtained expeditiously, weapons are blunted and morale depressed. For there has never been a war that is drawn out from which a land has benefited. Likewise when armsmen attack cities and not warriors, their strength will be exhausted without commensurate reward. . . .*

Lerial has no doubt that reading *Necessary Skills of War* will indeed be a battle. Still, he turns back to the first page and begins again . . . taking a deep breath.

Dinner comes . . . and goes, and there is no mention of the accident with the boy, but Altyrn and Maeroja do talk about the reports of more Meroweyan raiders near Narthyl and even crossing the hills to the northeast of the Clyan River.

As Lerial listens, the question that had come to him that morning resurfaces in his thoughts. Who had spoken like Maeroja? Who?

During the remainder of dinner . . . and afterward, Lerial tries to recall who it might have been. Then . . . as he is about to drift off to sleep, the answer comes—*Kyedra!* The daughter of Duke Atroyan. Yet it wasn't quite the same.

He is still pondering when sleep claims him.

XV

By the middle of harvest, Lerial has worked at some aspect of bringing in every crop on the majer's extensive lands, but under the majer's direct supervision, and seldom with Rojana anymore, although he sees her doing harvest chores as well. As part of his studies, he also has to draw up orders of battle for the company stationed at the Teilyn outpost, as well as organization plans for a company and a battalion, make up equipment lists, and plan logistics for campaigns into Merowey and Heldya . . . and those are just the beginning.

"So far as I know, your father is not planning anything like that," Altyrn tells Lerial, "but he might . . . or your brother might."

Much more likely Lephi, thinks Lerial.

On the fourth threeday of harvest, after breakfast, Altyrn says, "We're going over to the outpost at midmorning. You need to spar with someone besides me. I've already talked to the captain. They aren't riding out this eightday. They didn't have orders yesterday, anyway. Wear your oldest pair of greens and riding boots, not work clothes."

"Yes, ser. What do you want me to do before that?"

"I don't recall that you've written your father since you've been here. This would be a good time. That way, you can have it sent with the next dispatch pouch to Cigoerne."

Lerial would rather dig ditches or be battered in sparring than write a letter to his father, but only says, "I'll do that, ser."

"It doesn't have to be long," replies Altyrn, "but give him an idea of what you've been doing."

"Yes, ser."

Lerial returns to his room, where he looks out the small, high window for a short time, trying to work out what he might say that is true, but that does not reveal his feelings. Finally, he seats himself at the small table-desk and begins.

> Dear Father—
> I should have written sooner, but I have been working hard. I am learning all the aspects of how an estate must work. Commander Altyrn has made certain I know exactly how each task must be done. I have dug ditches and helped build brick walls. I have harvested olives and barley, and seen all the processes by which your venture is conducted. The commander has also instructed me in arms, logistics, and tactics.
>
> His family has been most gracious, and my quarters are more than adequate for all my needs . . .

After that, finding words is more difficult, but Lerial adds another few paragraphs describing the villa and the grounds, mostly in case his father chooses to share the letter with his mother and the rest of the family. When he finishes, he signs and seals it, then dresses in the greens and boots and makes his way down to the inner courtyard.

He has been there only a few moments before the majer appears.

"Since you're ready, we might as well ride out now. Go saddle your horse. I'll be with you in a few moments."

"Yes, ser." Lerial nods, then makes his way from the courtyard, sensing the majer's eyes on him.

After grooming and saddling his mount, Lerial leads the gelding out of the stable into the paved area he still thinks of as the outer courtyard, for all that the only walls are those of the villa and the outbuildings. He has ridden very little since he arrived at Kinaar, and only around the majer's lands. He also realizes the fact that he has not ridden much hasn't bothered him in the slightest.

"Where are you going?"

He turns to see Aylana and Tyrna walking toward the villa from the cocoonery, although it is properly no longer that, since all the worms have spun their cocoons, and now all those involved are extracting the strands from the cocoons and turning them into proper silk thread. "Your father and I are riding over to the Mirror Lancer post in a bit. How is the threading going?"

"It's boring," declares Aylana, offering an exaggerated sigh. "I'd rather gather rotten apricots."

"You'll be gathering overripe olives in a day or two," interjects the majer, who has ridden into the unwalled courtyard from the south. "Those few that there are."

From that, it dawns on Lerial just how long the majer has been working on his lands . . . and that he had to have been doing some of it while he was still heading the Lancers . . . or Maeroja did.

Both girls make faces at their father's words.

Lerial represses a grin, then immediately mounts and rides to join the majer, watching as the two girls hurry into the villa. "They do have opinions."

"They'll have to learn when to express them and when not to," replies Altyrn. "Fairly soon. Almost no men like women who appear strong-willed, but there are some who like honest opinions in private." He turns his mount toward the lane leading to the main road and the Lancer post.

The two are on the road before Altyrn asks, "Did you meet Captain Graessyr? Or Undercaptain Shastan?"

"No, ser. We rode straight to Kinaar."

"They're both altage, through and through, for all that Shastan is the son of a local grower. Graessyr's mother is from altage stock, but don't ask about his father."

"Yes, sir." Lerial understands both what Altyrn means and why Graessyr has been posted in Teilyn.

"They'd take a charge single-handedly to save you or your father. One of your responsibilities will always be to avoid putting officers in such a situation. You need to be able to handle a blade well enough so that it is absolutely clear to your Lancers that you do not need special protection. Do you know why?"

"Because we don't have enough Lancers and any that are protecting me cannot be used to deal with raiders or attackers. That weakens the force." Lerial remembers that from something Lephi had said.

Altyrn nods. "It also gives them confidence to see that you know something about the business of arms." He does not say more, and before long, they are riding up to the open gates of the brick-walled post.

"Good morning, Majer," calls out one of the guards from his shaded post beside the gate.

"Good morning, Seimyrt. Is the captain around?"

"He's in his study . . . or somewhere in headquarters."

"Good. We'll find him."

"Headquarters" turns out to be a small yellow brick structure in the middle of the walls, directly across from the stables before which Altyrn reins up. Lerial ties his mount next to the majer's horse, and the two walk across the brick pavement.

Two rankers nod and murmur "ser," as they cross paths with Lerial and Altyrn.

The majer responds with a nod and a smile.

The interior of the headquarters building is simple. Behind the entry door is a large room, empty except for a table-desk at one end, behind which is seated a squad leader who stands as Altyrn enters. There are two half-open doors in the wall at the end of the room.

"He's in his study, ser."

"Thank you." Altyrn makes a gesture that takes in the space around them. "This is where the officers brief their men. The officers' studies are behind those doors." He strides toward the door on the right, opens it full, and motions for Lerial to step inside, then enters and closes the door.

"Can't stay away from here, can you, Majer?" The black-haired captain stands as he speaks.

"You're not rid of me yet." Altyrn grins, then eases to one side, leaving a clear path to the table-desk. "I don't believe you've met Lord Lerial."

Lerial takes the hint and steps forward. "I'm pleased to meet you, ser."

"And I you." Graessyr smiles pleasantly. "Your father said you would be staying at the majer's. You've been there quite a while."

"I've had much to learn, ser."

"That's why we're here," Altyrn says, moving forward slightly. "As I told you the other day, I think that Lerial needs to spar with someone a bit younger than me . . . someone with more energy."

The captain laughs, a raucous barking sound that lasts but a few moments. Then he shakes his head. "I'll spar with him, but don't give me those words that suggest you're a tired old man. I see how hard you work."

Altyrn cannot hide the faintest hint of a smile. "He does need to spar with someone besides me."

"That's something I can accept. Blunted blades and padding or wands?"

"Let's try blunted blades and padding. He hasn't done that." The majer grins. "Might be because I don't have either." He pauses. "One other thing. Lerial has a letter for his sire. Could you send it with the next dispatch rider?"

"We can do that."

Lerial takes out the sealed missive and hands it to the captain. "Thank you, ser."

"That's not a problem. Might as well get started." Graessyr slips from behind the desk with an easy grace, for all that he is not only broad but more than half a head taller than Lerial, and leads the way from the study, and headquarters, to the armory.

In less than a quarter of a glass, Lerial is wearing what amounts to padded armor, with plates sewn into the padding in strategic places. The padding is thick enough that he is sweating even before he thinks of picking up the blunted blade that Altyrn has set on the wooden bench.

He reaches out and grasps the blade, lifting and turning it. It feels lighter than the wand he has been using in sparring with the majer . . . and yet it doesn't.

"You shouldn't have a problem with that," Altyrn says.

"Is that why . . . ?"

The majer nods. "Let's go."

The captain is waiting outside at the edge of the sparring circle, marked in black bricks and wider than the circles at the Palace, Lerial notes.

"Yes, it is wider," Altyrn says. "That makes it harder."

Everything here in Teilyn is harder. Why should this be any different? Lerial takes a position inside the edge of the circle opposite Graessyr.

"No leg cuts," Altyrn orders. "You make the first attack, Lerial."

Lerial prefers to have others move first so that he can observe and gain an idea of what they have in mind, but then Altyrn knows that. He moves forward, careful to watch the captain with both eyes and order-senses.

Graessyr keeps his blade slightly lower than the majer does, but Lerial suspects that is only because Lerial is shorter, and the difference in height would make it easier for him to attack the majer's legs, even though there will be no leg cuts—not with blades, blunted as they are.

Lerial feints, but the captain only shifts his sabre slightly. Then Lerial begins what he hopes looks like a feint, but is actually an attack.

The captain's blade flicks almost effortlessly to deflect Lerial's thrust, and Lerial has to dance aside and retreat, then finds himself defending against a sabre that seems to come from everywhere for the next moments . . . until he begins to get a sense from the order flows of what the captain's intentions are. Even so, Lerial finds himself on the defensive most of the time, taking hits on the padded armor, and blows he knows have been pulled.

He keeps working, though, and feels that, after a time, he is getting better at defending, and he actually manages a partial strike on the captain before he's forced back into fighting defensively.

"That's enough," Altyrn finally calls out.

Lerial steps back, but keeps his blade up until he is well away from the captain.

"Good!" says Graessyr, lowering his blade. "Stay in the habit of keeping your blade ready until you're sure that you don't need it." He hands his blade to Altyrn. "You can take this. I need to get out of the padding before I boil myself."

Lerial feels the same way, but walks to the bench beside the armory door, where he lays the blade before beginning to struggle out of the damp and heavy padded armor.

"I can see the majer's been working you hard," observes the captain from beside Lerial as he also pulls off his own padding. "You've got the basics down well, and they're smooth, but you have to back off too much when something you don't recognize comes at you . . ."

Lerial listens as Graessyr explains. He tries not to move too much, despite the feeling that his legs could cramp any moment, and the stinging in his eyes from the sweat that still flows down his brow and face. When the captain finishes his comments, Lerial nods and says, "Thank you, ser."

"You're more than welcome." Graessyr smiles at the majer. "Every day this time?"

Every day? Lerial manages not to wince.

"That would be best, I think," says Altyrn.

"Next time, he should have a go with Shastan. He's got some tricks that I don't."

"Good." Altyrn nods and turns to Lerial. "Rack the padding and the blade, and then join me at the stable. We need to get back to Kinaar."

"Yes, ser."

By the time Lerial has racked and put away the padded armor and blunted blade and made his way back to the stable, he has begun to cool down slightly. He also feels bruises in places he has not noticed before, but he mounts easily and rides across the courtyard toward the gates beside the majer.

Altyrn does not comment on the sparring until he and Lerial are mounted and a good hundred yards south of the post gates. Then he turns in the saddle. "When you see something you recognize, your defense and reactions are excellent. When you don't, you're awkward enough that you could get spitted."

Wouldn't anyone? Lerial manages to nod.

"You don't have any instincts with the blade. You've probably got more of the healer blood in you than is good for combat. I thought as much, but that's one reason why I wanted to watch you with someone else. We'll have to do something about that."

"What would that be, ser?"

"You'll have to spar with a lot of different Lancers. The more different men you're against, the more comfortable you'll be with a blade, even if you run up against something you've never seen before."

Lerial has a sinking feeling that he never realized just what it would take to become good enough with a blade in order to be able to hold his own against Lephi . . . or anyone else with skill, for that matter.

"You didn't think it was going to be easy, did you?" asks Altyrn genially. "Why do you think I've worked you so hard in the fields?"

"I did think that, ser. I did." He also realizes that he couldn't have even held a blade against the captain for more than a small fraction of a glass if Altyrn hadn't required him to spar with the heavier wooden wand.

He just wonders what else lies before him and what else will be required of him.

XVI

The next two eightdays are, if anything, harder than those that preceded them, with fieldwork following the morning sparring sessions with Captain Graessyr or Undercaptain Shastan . . . or one or two of the more experienced Mirror Lancer squad leaders. All of them have more energy than Majer Altyrn, but, from what Lerial experiences, none has the technique of the former commander of the Mirror Lancers. Even so, Lerial finds that he still does not respond well to any new move, or at least not as well as the majer would like. Then, after Lerial is truly exhausted, Altyrn requires more study and thought. With most of the crops in, Lerial has doubts whether there is that much heavy fieldwork remaining, but then concludes, morosely, after being required to dredge and clean irrigation ditches, that it is more than likely the majer will always have something else planned . . . something requiring enough brute force that he won't even have the comfort of Rojana's presence, not that he has had that comfort for the better part of a season.

On a mild midmorning on the next to last fiveday of harvest, under overcast skies that promise a cooler day than any recently, Lerial is riding from Kinaar to the Lancer post with Altyrn, wondering with whom he might be paired. He has sparred often with Captain Graessyr and Undercaptain Shastan, both of whom have more energy than Altyrn, but who lack the seemingly effortless polish of Altyrn's technique.

"Once harvest is over, I'll have time to give you some instruction with a lance," Altyrn says conversationally.

For a moment, Lerial isn't certain what to say. "Lances? Do the Lancers use them much anymore?" For all that his father's troopers bear the name of Lancers, Lerial has only seen them with lances on a few ceremonial occasions in Cigoerne. In fact, he cannot remember exactly when the last time might have been.

"There are times when they're most useful," replies the majer.

Lerial nods, although he has his doubts, then asks, "What about firelances? Have you ever used one?"

"Years ago, before the Accursed Forest destroyed Cyador."

"I thought my grandmother brought some with her."

"She did. They lasted about a year after we took over Cigoerne. They served their purpose. The lances we use now are more durable, and they're especially useful against raiders. That's because a Lancer can strike while staying beyond the range of those curved blades they use."

"Aren't the Meroweyans the only ones who have curved blades?"

"Some of the Heldyan raiders from the south have them, too. You'll never carry a lance on a patrol. Officers don't. But you need to know something about them so that you don't give a stupid order."

All too often Altyrn mentions the necessity for Lerial not to give stupid orders, as if he is ever going to give many orders, not if his father and Lephi have much to say about it.

In moments it seems, although it is more like a quarter glass, Lerial is once more donning the padded armor and picking up the blunted blade that has become all too familiar to him over the past eightdays. Although Lerial feels that he equips himself quickly, Undercaptain Shastan is already waiting for him. The officer is taller than Graessyr, not a small man by any stretch, and broader, with big hands and feet. In the past, Lerial has been hard-pressed just to avoid being struck too often.

"Let's see what you can do." Shastan's words carry a note of amusement, as if the sparring is a game whose conclusion is foregone.

Almost foregone, thinks Lerial as he raises the blade and moves into the circle to meet the undercaptain. Shastan's blade flicks out, casually, and Lerial slips the half feint–half attack, moving not to his right, but his left, trying to catch the undercaptain by moving to his strength, rather than away. Shastan moves with Lerial, coming back with a cut that Lerial has to parry backhanded, then scramble to his right.

The undercaptain starts a straight thrust . . . and Lerial dances to the side, but Shastan pivots quickly, with more grace than Lerial would have expected from a man so big, and his blade comes up and strikes Lerial's with so much force that the entire blade shivers in his hand, and he can barely hang on . . . with the result that, although Shastan is open for a moment, by the time Lerial can regain full control of his sabre, that opportunity is gone.

"You needed to slip or slide that," comments the undercaptain, launching another attack. "Trying to block an attack squarely will wear you out even if you succeed."

Lerial tries an attack, and for a moment, Shastan retreats a step, but Lerial finds it hard to follow the order patterns when he is attacking, and he loses his concentration for a moment, then finds himself again on the defensive.

His arm is getting tired when he sees Shastan overreach himself.

Rather than take the obvious opening—too obvious—that the undercaptain has left him, Lerial feints as though he will, then drops not quite into a crouch and comes up under Shastan's blade. Just as he is about to strike the Lancer officer on the thigh, Shastan makes a throwing motion, flinging sand and grit into Lerial's eyes before he can close them. The combination of the burning and the blurring of his vision leaves Lerial largely blinded.

Even so, through the stinging of the sand in his eyes, for a moment, Lerial almost lashes out, but instead, uses his order-preception to sense what his watering eyes cannot show him. As he can see more clearly, he still wants to lash out at the dirty trick. *Never fight in a rage!* The words that Altyrn has pounded into him cool him enough, and he concentrates on following Shastan's movements as much through the order flows as through his still blurry vision. Somehow, he manages to ward off the officer's attacks, both with the moves Altyrn has drilled into him and by circling toward Shastan's left side.

He keeps blinking, and finally his eyes clear, and he starts another attack.

"That's enough!" Altyrn calls out.

Shastan backs away.

After a moment, so does Lerial, but he does not lower the blunted sabre until he is outside the circle. Absently, he sees that Captain Graessyr has joined the majer.

"You held a solid defense even when you could barely see," observes Graessyr. "That's good."

When I couldn't see at all. "I just tried not to make any mistakes or give him an opening."

"Sometimes, that's all you can do," says the captain.

Altyrn nods, then gestures for Lerial to head to the armory.

Lerial nods, blots his forehead with the back of his left hand, and heads for the equipment storage room. Behind him, he catches a few words.

". . . not bad . . ."

". . . not for an officer trainee . . . he has to do better . . ."

". . . young still . . ."

". . . doesn't matter . . . Afritans don't care about age. Raiders don't either."

Lerial frowns at the seriousness in both men's voices, but he continues walking. He has just racked the padded armor and replaced the blunted sabre when Captain Graessyr enters the armory, holding a sealed envelope.

"This arrived for you late last evening." The captain extends the envelope.

Lerial accepts the letter. "Thank you." He will not open it until he is back at Kinaar and alone.

"You're doing well with the sabre," adds Graessyr. "You're holding your own against Shastan, and that's not easy."

Need to do better than hold your own. "I'll be happier when I can hold my own against you and the majer."

"That all depends on you, but you've made a good start."

"Thank you, ser."

Altyrn appears in the doorway. "Next eightday, you'll start exercises in using that sabre from the saddle. That's in addition to sparring."

Exercises? Not sparring?

"Practicing bladework against another while mounted is too dangerous," says the majer, adding after the briefest pause, "Even the Lancers don't do it. It turned out that more of them were hurt in practice than on some patrols where they encountered raiders. The exercises will give you enough training."

"Especially with the majer directing you," adds Graessyr, with a laugh. "We'll see you tomorrow."

"That you will," replies Altyrn as the captain leaves the equipment chamber.

Lerial and Altyrn walk without speaking to the stable.

"Why did he throw that grit at my face?" asks Lerial, once they are in the saddle and well clear of the Mirror Lancer post.

"I told him to," Altyrn says.

"Why?"

"Why do you think?"

Lerial considers, if but for a moment, before replying, "To surprise me . . . to show me what could happen."

"That was part of it. It wasn't the only reason."

"Oh . . . because I don't always react well when I come up against something new?"

"You're getting a lot better at that. I thought you would with more experience."

"I was still angry."

"You will be for a while if you fight much. When men are losing or want a quick victory, they'll try anything. You surprised me, though. You were deliberate, more than I expected."

"I surprised you, ser?"

"You're always well mannered, but beneath it all, you're carrying a lot of anger . . ."

You'd be angry, too, if your parents threw you out and stuck you two days' ride away with almost no interest in what you were doing.

". . . but you held yourself in check." Altyrn smiles. "That's good, because I think anger runs in your family. Your grandfather was always angry. Might have been one of the reasons he brought down Cyador."

He brought down Cyador? "What?"

"That wasn't what he meant. He wanted to rebuild Cyador, but he was impatient. He tried to do too many things at once. He wanted to build fireships. He wanted to push back the Accursed Forest. He wanted to reclaim the lands the barbarians had overrun. That was because the copper mines in the west were mined out, and Cyador needed the copper near Lornth. Everything he tried took longer than he thought it should. That made him angry. Then the wards that held back the Accursed Forest weakened, and more and more Magi'i were sent to contain the Forest. So were too many Lancers, and many died. The Lancers fighting in Lornth were defeated because there were too many barbarians and not enough Lancers. That angered your grandsire more, and he took the white wizards who were holding back the Accursed Forest and sent them to conquer the barbarians. That made the Forest stronger, and the dark angels called on it to help them. They destroyed most of the powerful Magi'i, and then there was no one to hold back the Accursed Forest when the dark angels called upon it to destroy Cyador."

Lerial is silent for a time. He knows that the dark angels and the Accursed Forest called upon the very earth and the seas to bring down Cyad and Cyador, but he has never heard the story told the way the majer tells it.

"Mind you," the majer goes on, "that's not the way you should tell the story, but that's the way it happened. You and your brother need to know what really happened. Trying to do too much too fast is bad enough. Doing too much too fast and doing in anger always leads to trouble. You can't afford that."

What am I supposed to do? Wait until I'm as gray as you are?

When the two rein up outside the stable back at Kinaar, the majer looks to Lerial. "I need to ride out to the woodlot. When I get back, we'll have something to eat, and then we'll ride up to a place on the Wooded Ridges. You need to do some thinking about how trees and hills lie and what to do in various places." Altyrn smiles. "That way you can read your letter, and you won't be thinking about it when you should be looking and listening."

"Ah . . . yes, ser."

The majer is riding off even before Lerial has finished dismounting. Since it will be a while before he rides out again, Lerial leads the gelding to his stall and unsaddles him, giving him a quick brushing. Then he makes his way to the villa and finds a corner well away from the fountains where he breaks the seal and opens the letter. The handwriting is not his father's, but his mother's.

> Dearest Lerial—
> I hope this finds you in health and enjoying life away from Cigoerne. Ryalah and I miss you. So does your aunt Emerya. She asked me to tell you not to forget your lessons, especially when you practice with wands.
>
> There have been more attacks by Heldyan armsmen coming across the Swarth River to the southeast of Narthyl, and your father has been gone from Cigoerne most of the time since you left . . .

Lerial lowers the letter. He has been gone more than two seasons, and his father has been in Narthyl or south of it most of that time? That doesn't sound good.

> . . . has sent word that he and the Mirror Lancers have been able to deal with the armsmen from the east without serious casualties so far. He has ordered Majer Phortyn to raise and begin to train another two companies. Lephi is riding more patrols now. Those are mostly to the west and south of Bartheld . . .

Riding patrols and glorying in it, no doubt. Lerial forces himself to concentrate on the letter.

> . . . Your aunt has been conducting the tests for apprentice healers. She said that you have the talents for that, even if men

> are not usually healers. She also said that those Lancers who serve under you will be fortunate because you will be able to do field healing when the time comes.
>
> With all the hot weather we have had, the olives from our older lands are ripening sooner, and it is likely that the amount of oil pressed will be more than last year, and that is good, because food will be scarce in parts of Cigoerne . . .

Lerial reads the rest of the letter impatiently, but all it contains is news about crops, weather, and the low state of the Swarth River. He frowns as he sees his mother's initial at the bottom of the next to last page. Did she add something else?

The last page is from Ryalah, each word painstakingly written.

> My dear brother—
> I miss you. I wish you were here. Amaira wishes you were here, too. We both think you should come home. Mother says you will. She says it will be a while.
>
> Your sister Ryalah

Lerial can't help but smile at the simple words. He also wonders just how long "a while" might turn out to be.

XVII

Over the next several eightdays, Lerial continues to receive sabre instruction and bruises from both Captain Graessyr and Undercaptain Shastan . . . followed by a glass or more of instruction and exercises in handling a sabre while mounted. The one matter about which he is certain is that he sleeps well, possibly because the nights are cooler, but mainly because he is worn out by dinner.

At perhaps a half glass past midmorning on a cool but sunny fourday, when Lerial and Altyrn ride back to Kinaar from the Lancer post, Altyrn clears his throat, then says, "Tomorrow, we're going to take a short journey west, for several days. You and me, and several Lancer rankers I've persuaded the captain to let accompany us."

"Is something the matter?" asks Lerial.

"No. You need to know more about the Wooded Ridges and terrain than you can learn near Teilyn. I have some maps in the study I want you to learn this afternoon. Memorize as much as you can before dinner."

"No sabre practice on horseback, ser?"

"You've had more than enough to know what to do if you get attacked. Your defense is better than most. It's your attacks that are weak, but you're not likely to be attacking much."

On this trip . . . or any time? Lerial suspects it is the latter, but there is little point in asking, because Altyrn would point out that, either way, it makes little difference, something that Lerial already knows.

Once they are back at the villa, Lerial unsaddles the gelding, grooms him, sees to his water and feed, and then makes his way to his chamber. There he washes up and heads down to the lower level and the majer's study.

Altyrn is seated behind his table-desk, but rises immediately and walks to the circular table. Spread there is a large map. Beside it are several sheets of paper which appear to contain smaller maps. The majer gestures. "These are the best maps we have of the lands to the south and west of Teilyn. Learn everything you can before dinner."

Lerial frowns, thinking about all the details a map can hold.

"When you command Lancers, and it's likely you will at some time, you may not even have maps. If you do, you will have little time to study them, and you won't take them on a patrol or into a skirmish with raiders. They're too valuable to risk losing. At times, the details on them may have been discovered and paid for with blood." After a slight pause, Altyrn adds, "I'll be back in a while."

Lerial seats himself at the table. He begins by looking at each of the maps briefly. The large map is one of all of Cigoerne and only shows Cigoerne and the towns, but not the smaller hamlets. The hills and woods are outlined, but not in any detail. The smaller ones show the streams and hills around various towns, some of which Lerial has never heard. He concentrates on the map that shows the lands around Teilyn, making an effort to mentally picture where each is in relation to Teilyn and the Lynaar River, even if it is little more than a stream. Then he attempts to picture the Wooded Ridges, which have a shape almost like an "L" with the lower shorter part running north–south, beginning less than two kays south of Kinaar, and with the longer leg running west for well over a hundred kays, perhaps as far as two.

Hearing footsteps in the hallway and sensing someone approaching, Lerial looks up, but Rojana enters the study, not Altyrn.

"Oh! I thought Father was here."

Despite the surprise in her voice, Lerial feels she is not all that disconcerted at seeing him rather than her father, but that she was looking for Lerial. "He just left. He didn't say where he was going."

Lerial hears what he thinks are another set of boots, but far lighter. *Aylana?*

He discovers how mistaken he is when Maeroja enters the study. She looks to her daughter. "I wondered where you were."

As the two stand there, just inside the study, Lerial glances from one to the other, realizing that Rojana is slightly taller than her mother.

When did that happen?

He also sees that she is every bit as striking as her mother, perhaps more so because of the gray eyes she has inherited from her father.

"I was heading to the courtyard . . . I heard someone here . . ." Rojana breaks off her words.

"And you wondered if it might be Lerial. It is, and your father has set him a long afternoon of studying. Your interrupting won't help him." Maeroja smiles.

Lerial senses a knowing sadness behind the smile, but he says, "I have all afternoon."

"What my consort has set you to do will likely take longer than you have." Maeroja once more looks to her daughter. "You can tell him whatever you have in mind at dinner." After the slightest pause, she adds softly, "Or afterwards."

"Yes, Mother." Rojana turns to Lerial. "Until dinner." For a moment, she smiles as she adds, "Father will ask you where the steepest hills are."

"And where the soft and swampy ground is likely to be," adds Maeroja as she glances toward the study door.

Rojana follows the unspoken command and leaves the study, followed by her mother, who gently closes the door behind herself.

The steepest hills? How is he supposed to discover that from the maps? Lerial shakes his head, then begins to inspect the smaller maps. After a time, how long he cannot say, he discovers two maps that look to be more crudely drawn that have many thin lines on them, and little else but the names of towns and hamlets. There is something . . .

He looks at another map of the same area, which, although larger, covers a greater area. Finally, he understands, he thinks, all because he knows that there is a bluff overlooking the river north of Cigoerne. The approach from the north is too steep, and that same bluff on one of the roughly drawn maps has many tiny lines so close together that they almost merge. That would suggest that the closer the narrow lines are to each other, the steeper the slope.

He finds himself nodding at the ingenious way the majer has used—for the less finely drawn maps must be his—to indicate hills and valleys . . . except the two maps that show that only cover the area to the south and west of Teilyn. How is he supposed to determine steepness from the other maps?

From where the hamlets are? Where rivers and streams are shown, there the land will be lower, he knows, because water always seeks the lowest level. He does discover that high points in the hills are marked on one map, at least in places, with a circled "X," but only on that one map. Then there is the problem of determining distance between places, because only the large map has a legend explaining how many kays are represented by a digit.

Less than a glass before dinner, Altyrn returns, stepping into the study and closing the door behind him. He carries a long object wrapped in oiled cloth, which he sets on his table-desk before turning to Lerial. "Before I ask you about the maps, what can you tell me about them?"

"Distance is different on each one. Only one indicates the scale, but I estimated on the others. Two of the small maps show the steepness of the land. They look as though you drew them . . ." Lerial goes on to explain what he thinks he has discovered. When he finishes, he just stands beside the table and waits.

An expression that might be puzzlement crosses the majer's face, then vanishes. "You have not studied maps before?"

"No, ser. I've looked at some in the palace library, but no one has taught me anything or explained them. I gained the impression that such studies were beyond my years."

"You've figured out more in an afternoon than some junior officers know after their first tour. Still . . . there are a few things I just might be able to teach you." A wry smile appears on the majer's face. "There is a system for indicating more about those circles that you referred to as the topmost point of a hill or mountain. If the circle is open, there are few trees. If there is an 'X' in the middle, that means the area is both rocky and wooded. If a single line, it is heavily wooded . . . lightly crosshatched areas are swampy . . ."

Even after Altyrn's explanations, Lerial feels satisfied, as much as because the majer also appears pleased with what Lerial has ascertained.

"We should join the others on the terrace," the majer finally says. "Tonight's dinner will be the best either of us is likely to have for several days. You will need to pack your gear tonight, because we'll leave right after sunrise tomorrow. Just one set of spare greens and a riding jacket and gloves. There is one other thing you'll need that you didn't bring."

"Ser?"

Altyrn walks to the desk and unwraps the oiled cloth from what it protects, then extends it to Lerial, who gapes for a moment at the leather sword belt and scabbard, and the sabre within the scabbard.

"This is yours now. You'll need it from now on. You shouldn't ride anywhere without it, and it's probably best you wear it if you're on foot outside of any place you don't know is absolutely safe."

Lerial takes the sword belt. "Thank you . . . I can't tell you . . ."

"You already have." Altyrn smiles. "You can leave it here for now. Just pick it up before you go to bed."

"Yes, ser!" Lerial looks over the leatherwork more closely. While the workmanship is excellent, it is also clear that the belt has been worn. He eases the sabre from the scabbard. His mouth opens. He has never seen a blade such as the one he holds.

"It's good steel covered with order-forged cupridium. It may be the only such blade in the world now. How old it is, I don't know, but I've tested the temper. It's better than anything forged today. The belt and scabbard—and the grip—are much newer. It was in the armory of the Palace of Light. We took every weapon we could to the *Kerial,* and when I found that one . . . I must confess I took it personally. But I feel that it should be restored to your family through you."

Lerial senses the faintest emphasis on the last two words. "I will do my best—"

"I have no doubt of that. Just do it well enough that you can pass it on."

"Yes, ser."

"Now . . . let's have a drink before dinner."

Lerial walks from the study and along the corridor beside Altyrn, pleased, but still puzzled by the gift of the sabre.

As they enter the courtyard, Lerial sees that Maeroja and the girls are already seated at the table where the family sits before dinner, although the table has been moved away from the fountains.

"In another few eightdays, we'll likely be having drinks before dinner in the salon on the cooler evenings," Altyrn muses. "We're enough south of Cigoerne that it gets a bit more chill in autumn and winter." He smiles as he adds, "We need to use the hearths more often."

"They say the Duke of Afrit's palace in Swartheld doesn't even have hearths."

"I wouldn't know. Your father might . . . or your aunt."

Lerial conceals a frown. Has Emerya been a guest in Swartheld? No one has ever mentioned that.

"She was the healer who accompanied the Duke's brother back after he was wounded in the last full-scale border fight years ago."

"I knew she healed him when no one thought he would survive. I didn't know about her going to Swartheld."

"Your father didn't like it, but it was important that Rhamuel survived in health. If he hadn't, peace with Afrit wouldn't have been possible." Altyrn laughs softly and ruefully. "It's always a mixed blessing when the brother of the ruler gets too closely involved in battles. Of course, Rhamuel underestimated just how good the Mirror Lancers were. But after he lost most of his force, he and his senior officers managed to get the point across to his brother that leaving Cigoerne alone was preferable to losing more armsmen, especially when the Heldyans took the opportunity to raid the Afritan towns across the river and north of Luba." The majer smiles at his consort before he seats himself at the table. "Good evening, dear."

"Good evening. I see you're filling Lerial in on the past."

"Some of it, anyway."

Lerial takes a seat beside Maeroja. "I knew about the last battle. I never heard much about what happened afterward." He pours himself a glass of the dark lager and takes a small swallow.

"The usual," replies Altyrn. "No one was happy. The Afritan traders had hoped to take over Cigoerne, and they couldn't. The Heldyans wanted to take over Afritan lands to the east, and the peace allowed Duke Atroyan to send all his forces there, and the Heldyans actually lost lands and towns to Afrit. That made Huisyl—he was Duke of Heldya then—mad at us, and that is why his son still sends armsmen and raiders to plague us."

"You two can talk of all this tomorrow."

Although Maeroja's words are soft, Lerial senses the iron behind them, but manages to conceal his smile of amusement.

"That might be best," acknowledges the majer. "How is the weaving coming?"

"As always . . . slowly, but we will have more shimmersilk this year. The girls made the difference, I think . . ."

Before long, Maeroja rises, as does the majer, and everyone follows them into the dining chamber. Dinner is roast suckling pig, with cheese-lace potatoes, and beans. The conversation stays firmly on what is happening around the estate, the weather, and concerns about water, since there has been little rain over harvest—good for harvesting, but not so good for the next crop year.

In the pleasant gloom following dinner, Lerial and Rojana sit at a small courtyard table well away from the fountains, whose cooling mists are largely unnecessary in early fall.

"You will be leaving before long," she says.

"Have your parents said anything?"

She shakes her head, a gesture he senses through the order flows more than he sees in the dim light. "Father is working you hard. He is trying to teach you everything you can learn as quickly as possible. He would not do that were your time here not drawing to an end."

Lerial can sense that she has not said all that she might. "Time has passed so quickly."

"It has."

The silence draws out between them.

"I will miss you," she says softly.

"I'll miss you," he says, realizing with surprise that he means the words.

"It's better this way."

Lerial realizes what she is really saying . . . and why Altyrn and Maeroja have minimized the time they have spent together. "Better? I wonder. Does anyone know what is better for someone else?"

"Mother says that you are meant for greater deeds than anyone knows."

"She does?" *Great deeds . . . from a second son shuffled off away from Cigoerne?*

"Father says never to doubt what she says will be."

Lerial wants to ask what these "greater deeds" will be, but decides that he does not want to know . . . not enough to ask.

"That is another reason they have kept you occupied every moment . . . and me as well."

"I had thought as much." *If only lately.* But he doesn't have to admit that . . . and his own slowness in seeing it.

"Father would be proud of you."

Would be? "He would be . . . if what?"

Rojana looks flustered for a moment. "He is . . . he won't tell you that. I overheard him saying that you worked far harder than your father did."

"He trained my father?" This is something that Lerial has never heard.

"Oh, yes. He didn't tell you?"

"No. Father just said that your father was the most senior officer in the Mirror Lancers and that he accompanied my grandmother and father and aunt to Hamor on the *Kerial*." Actually, as he speaks, Lerial realizes that the person who told him that had been his grandmother, not his father.

"He started teaching your father arms on the ship. He did tell me that."

"Did he say anything else about that?"

Rojana shakes her head.

"What do you learn in your studies?" Lerial asks, although he already has some idea from what she has said on the occasions they had worked together when he had first come to Kinaar . . . and from what Altyrn has mentioned in passing.

"Mother teaches me accounts and how to keep a proper ledger, and how to estimate costs for the season ahead. Father is teaching me how to use a knife and a blade . . . not the same way you do . . . and I'm learning history and mathematics, and writing and rhetoric . . ."

"Your mother keeps the accounts?"

"Father says she's far better at it than he is."

Lerial can see how that might be.

"I'm trying to learn about the laws of Cyador, too. Father found an old book somewhere. It has all the laws. He says that the time may come when we'll need better laws, and someone needs to know what the old laws said."

That does surprise Lerial.

"Mother says that women need men to make the laws because they won't obey them otherwise, but that women need to persuade men as to what the laws should say."

"Rojana," Maeroja calls gently. "It's time for bed. Lerial and your father have a long day ahead of them tomorrow."

Lerial stands immediately, but Rojana rises more slowly, her eyes fixed on him.

"You will be careful?" she says, her words both a question and a gentle command.

"As much as I can be."

"Good."

The two walk across the courtyard to where Maeroja stands.

Maeroja looks at Rojana. "It's time for bed. I need a moment with Lerial."

Her eyes wide in the dim light, Rojana looks at Lerial. "Good night, Lerial." Her voice is steady, but her eyes glisten.

"Good night, Rojana."

Rojana inclines her head to her mother, then turns and walks toward the villa entrance and the steps beyond to the upper level.

"You understand, I hope," Maeroja says.

"That she's fond of me? Yes."

"It's best that you leave it that way, Lerial."

Why? After a moment, he decides to ask just that. "Why do you put it that way?"

"She's my daughter. You're the Duke's son. You will consort whomever your parents choose . . . or, if matters worsen, whomever you must. Rojana cannot help you. Encouraging her affection will only hurt her."

Lerial nods slowly . . . as he recalls a time when he sat in the palace courtyard with the daughter of the Duke of Afrit. *Was it planned that long ago?*

"You do see."

"I see. I don't have to like it."

"I'm glad you don't . . . and, in time, you will also be glad. In time." After the briefest pause, she adds, "Good night, Lerial," her voice almost an older echo of her daughter's. Then, she too turns.

For a time, Lerial stands alone in the courtyard, before he turns toward the majer's study to reclaim his sabre.

Much later, as he lies in his bed, eyes wide open, wondering what the morrow will bring, Lerial's thoughts drift back to what Rojana had said . . . and what his father had not. Yet, if the majer had trained his father, and his father has sent Lerial to Kinaar, that must mean that his father thinks highly of the majer . . . and that Lerial is worth that training. And the ancient sabre suggests that the majer believes that as well. But why has his father never said anything? Why does it seem as though nothing Lerial has done is enough? And what great deeds could he possibly accomplish? Cigoerne is a small duchy compared to Afrit, and especially to Heldya or Merowey.

For all that he wonders and ponders, Lerial can find no answers before he drifts off to sleep.

XVIII

The sun is barely above the low rolling hills to the east of the Lynaar when Lerial and Altyrn ride down the lane to the main road. Altyrn wears a worn Lancer riding jacket, along with Lancer greens, without insignia, as well as a Lancer cap, also without insignia, although Lerial can see the brighter green of fabric once covered by insignia.

"You haven't said much about where we'll be going and what we'll be doing," offers Lerial once they are headed north toward the Lancer post.

"I haven't. That's true." Altyrn grins, something he doesn't do that often, Lerial has noticed, and even the majer's smiles are often guarded. "First, you need to see more of Cigoerne. You also need to compare what maps show to what you see with your own eyes."

"To be able to see in my mind what a map shows?"

"Partly . . . and partly to see what even the best maps do not show."

"What else?"

"That's enough for now, don't you think?"

What that tells Lerial is that the majer has something else in mind.

When they ride into the fort and rein up perhaps ten yards from the small headquarters building, Lerial immediately sees a group of Lancers ready to mount at the near end of the stables. There are ten rankers—and a junior squad leader.

A junior squad leader . . . and ten rankers? Just to accompany the majer and him? Either the majer is more worried about Lerial's safety than he will admit to Lerial, or he has far more in mind than just a journey to educate Lerial. *If not both.* And Captain Graessyr is not likely to allow eleven Lancers to go off with Lerial and the majer, is he, just for an uneventful ride. But if Lerial is that important . . . why is he being allowed any freedom at all?

Lerial is still trying to decide if he is reading too much into what he sees when Captain Graessyr appears on the steps of the headquarters building and calls out, "If you'd spare me a moment, Majer?"

"Just stay here," Altyrn tells Lerial, before he rides over to where the captain stands on the steps up to the small headquarters building. Graessyr moves closer to the majer and his mount and speaks in a low voice.

Lerial struggles to hear the words, but can only make out a few.

". . . sure this . . . wise?"

". . . necessary . . . more . . . think . . . someone . . . family . . . see . . ."

". . . careful . . ."

Altyrn nods once, then twice, then remains by the steps when Graessyr reenters the building, only to emerge in moments carrying a jacket and a Lancer cap.

"Lerial." Altyrn motions.

Wondering exactly what the two want, Lerial urges the gelding forward and then reins up beside the majer. "Ser?"

"The majer and I have been talking," Graessyr begins. "If you wear a different jacket when you're riding with him and the others, people might take too much of an interest. We'd both feel better if you wore a Lancer riding jacket and cap. No insignia. Just so you don't stand out."

"Yes, ser. I can see that makes sense." Lerial slips off the gray riding jacket and folds it, then turns in the saddle and eases it under the straps holding his kit in place. He takes the Lancer jacket from the captain.

"It should fit."

Lerial dons the jacket, leaving it unfastened, and nods. "It does." He takes the cap, and adjusts it so that, as far as he can tell, it sits on his head in the same way as the Lancers wear theirs. He finds that it is more comfortable than it looks. "It fits, ser."

"Excellent." Graessyr steps back. "A good journey to you all."

For all the heartiness in the officer's voice, Lerial can sense a certain concern. That concern is scarcely allayed when, after the riders have left the post, two rankers ride out and take positions as scouts or outriders a good hundred yards ahead of Lerial and Altyrn.

Lerial debates asking the question that springs to mind for the time it takes to ride some fifty yards, then turns in the saddle and addresses the majer, who rides beside him. "The majer ordered the rankers to accompany us. He's not happy about it. Why did you do it?"

"Of course, he's not happy. You're second in line to be Duke of Cigoerne, and he's in charge of patrolling this part of the duchy. If anything happens to you, he doesn't want to explain how it happened."

"You told him I needed to see more of the duchy, and blackmailed him into supplying half a squad of Lancers."

"I didn't ask for anything," replies Altyrn. "I just told him what I planned to do and why. He insisted."

"How could he not?"

"Exactly. That's the first lesson. Sometimes, it's just better to do something than try to persuade someone. You have to be prepared to carry out your plan without them, however, and it had better be good, or you won't be convincing. At least, not until you're much older and more skilled at misrepresenting the situation."

"We're going to do more than ride around this part of Cigoerne, aren't we?"

"There wouldn't be any point in going to all the trouble of possibly angering your father for just that, would there?"

Lerial sees no point in even contesting that. "So what are we going to do?"

"If I tell you first, then you'll never really understand."

"But you wanted me to study the maps . . ."

"That's different. Some things, like reading or knowing maps or handling a blade or riding, you have to learn the basics first. But there are other things where book learning, or tales from an old Lancer, makes it harder to learn."

"Such as?" asks Lerial.

"If I told you, that would amount to the same thing." Altyrn offers a rueful smile. "Now . . . look at the part of the Wooden Ridges that is closest to the river. Where would be the best place to approach it if you thought there might be archers hidden in the trees?"

Realizing that the majer has said what he is going to say about the purpose of the journey, Lerial turns his attention to the trees, a mixture of pines and broadleaf types. "I'd come in from the north, along that gentle slope that goes south from your southernmost barley fields."

"That's the easiest for riders, and it's open," replies Altyrn. "Don't you think the archers would know that? Wouldn't there be more of them there?"

You should have thought of that. "The horses would have trouble climbing the slope to the east, if they could do it at all."

"Does every attack have to be mounted?"

Lerial pauses for a moment. "On foot, the Lancers could take cover behind the boulders, and they could be within yards of where the trees get thick before they'd be exposed."

"That's true enough, but a bow has a longer range than a blade . . ."

Lerial takes another long look at the Wooded Ridges. Even what might have been a pleasant ride that morning is turning out to be more than he expected.

XIX

Lerial continues to puzzle over what Altyrn has in mind beyond teaching him tactics suited to various kinds of terrain. Less than two glasses after they leave the Lancer post on fiveday, they reach the end of the road—rather the point where it turns into a path impassable to all but the smallest carts—but they continue south for another kay before turning west on a trail that winds up a low and wide valley through a less densely forested section of the Wooded Ridges. They bivouac that night at a crude way station that, according to Altyrn, dates back to the first days of the duchy, and then depart just after sunrise on sixday, following the trail through sparsely wooded low hills to the west and south of the higher wooded ridges.

Sevenday dawns cool with a silver haze across the green-blue sky, and Lerial rides behind Altyrn along a section of the trail that is too narrow for two mounts side by side. Riding in front of Altyrn is Chaarn, the junior squad leader, although he looks to be close to the age of Lerial's father, if not older. One of the rankers is roughly two hundred yards forward of Chaarn, and a second is about a hundred yards ahead.

By standing in his stirrups, Lerial can see that they are riding out of the sparse trees and toward a valley of low rolling rises covered in sparse browned grass that might have once been knee-high. He also sees what might be a thin trail of smoke farther to the west, but, other than that, and the trail that has obviously been used recently, he can discern no sign of anyone living in the valley. But then, he reflects, he has not seen any brooks or streams, and certainly no lakes, since they left the second old way station that morning.

By the time they leave the trees, it is midafternoon, suggesting that the distance was much farther than Lerial realized. He rides up beside Altyrn, but the majer says nothing, and Lerial has nothing to say that would not sound inane. So he studies the valley, or what of it he can see—which holds a few scattered clumps of trees and long browned grass that may stretch for kays westward, just below the Wooded Ridges to the north, or end just beyond the next rolling rise.

"If you're patrolling in areas like this," Altyrn says after a time, "you need to watch for tracks near clumps of bushes like those." He points ahead to a patch of foliage some thirty or forty yards across that might barely reach shoulder height on his mount. "Raiders and even Heldyan armsmen like to hide there and attack from the rear when you've passed. The Merowyans usually don't, but enough do that you need to be careful when you're patrolling anywhere."

"From the rear? Not from the side?"

"Just try to turn your horse quickly when arrows or spears are flying at you and when everyone else is attempting the same thing." Altyrn's voice is dry. "The Meroweyan raiders sometimes have spear-throwers, too. That means they can get off several spears from farther away and with more force."

Spears?

"Once you get away from the Swarth River this far upstream, or away from the port cities on the coast, there's much of Hamor that hasn't changed in hundreds of years," the majer replies to the unasked question.

Lerial nods and asks, "Why is that?"

The majer offers a sweeping gesture. "There are more fertile lands closer to the coast and the river, and here there is little those with golds want. Why else did the Duke let your grandmother purchase the rights to the lands your father could hold?"

That, unfortunately, makes sense to Lerial, far too much sense.

"What the present Duke's father did not understand was that knowledge also has value. He came to understand that late, if at all, and it was a bitter draught for Atroyan to swallow when he became Duke. But his sire needed every gold he could lay his hands on. He was not the wisest of rulers."

The way Altyrn explains reminds Lerial that the Duke had not been that much older than Lerial is now when he became Duke.

Another glass passes, and after Lerial and the others ride over yet another rise, the lead scout halts where the trail intersects a wider path, one that is almost a road heading north into the Wooded Ridges. He points south, and Lerial follows the gesture to see a small herd of goats trotting north toward the scout. Behind the goats are close to forty people, some leading horses. All of them are walking quickly. Some of the smaller children are running.

"They must have sighted raiders." Altyrn urges his mount forward. Lerial and the others follow.

While Lerial reins up behind Altyrn, the other Lancers ride past and then form up in a five-abreast front some fifty yards south of Chaarn, Altyrn, and Lerial.

When the people near, Altyrn rides to them and stops a white-haired man and asks him something.

"There are raiders coming. We must go to the caves," declares the old man. "There are many, but they do not know the forest or the caves as we do."

Lerial can see that he has few teeth.

"How many?" asks the majer.

"Too many." The old man shrugs. "We must go." He hurries off.

Lerial looks south along the trail that is almost a road, making out what he first thinks in a haze beyond a rise several kays to the south, except he understands that what he sees is dust.

"They won't stop at the hamlet," says Altyrn. "What they want are the women and the goats."

"Not any of the grain or crops?" asks Lerial.

"You can't carry much grain on a horse."

"Shouldn't you . . . Majer?" asks Chaarn, not quite looking at Lerial.

"Send out a scout to see how many there are. If there are only a handful or two, we can't leave these people to them."

"Yes, ser." Chaarn nods and rides toward the Lancers.

Altyrn dismounts, then hands his horse's reins to Lerial. "Hold him for now."

"Yes, ser."

Lerial watches as Altyrn unfastens a narrow leather case from behind his saddle, opens it, and takes out an almost circular construction that appears to be made of some sort of polished horn or the like. A second case holds a quiver. He looks at Lerial. "It's a horn bow. Some of the nomads near Atla use them. They're very effective."

"How did you find out about them . . . or get one?"

"Maeroja knew about them. She persuaded a friend to obtain it for me. It took me almost a year to learn how to use it properly."

Altyrn strings the bow, a maneuver that takes both coordination and strength. When he is finished, the almost circular object is a relatively small double-curved bow. Then the majer takes out the quiver and straps it in place on his right side. Lerial wonders about that for a moment, then realizes that the majer will be holding the bow in his left and nocking the arrow and drawing the bow with his right. Finally, the majer slips what looks to be a guard on his thumb. Then he takes the reins from Lerial and remounts.

More than half a glass passes before Chaarn returns and reins up. "There are two groups, ser. Six or seven riders are headed this way. They're moving quickly. The scout says that there may be more, but he's only seen tracks."

"If there's anyone left at the hamlet, there's not much we can do. There might be more coming, but if we stop the first group, that might give the locals a chance to make the woods."

Chaarn looks anything but happy.

"I can pick off some of them before they even get close." Altyrn pauses, then adds, "You know how the captain—or the Duke—would feel if we didn't do something."

"Yes, ser."

Lerial can feel the tension. "If we leave now, everyone will think I ordered it to save myself. I can't let something like that happen. It would reflect badly on my father and Cigoerne." Lerial makes a rueful face. "Especially since I have an older brother."

"He's right, you know, squad leader." Altyrn laughs. "You can't answer that. Don't try. We'll stay behind your men."

The squad leader nods, if reluctantly. "We need to move to the top of that rise." He points to the slight crest in the trail some hundred yards south. "If they see us there, they might decide against pursuing the locals."

"And they might not," replies the majer. "But it's worth a try. Let's go."

Chaarn turns his mount and starts back toward the waiting Lancers.

Lerial rides beside Altyrn as they follow.

"Why do you think the raiders won't turn back?" asks Lerial.

"If the Meroweyans have ridden this far, they're desperate. They're not likely to turn around for ten Lancers. I've seen a score attack an entire company. They all died, of course."

But we're far less than a company. "You think they'll have a score of riders?"

"More or less. That's the size of most raiding parties. I'm hoping that they've split their force." Altyrn pauses, then clears his throat, and looks directly at Lerial. "You're right about your not being able to ride away and leave the local people. That doesn't mean you're going to be in the front when we deal with these raiders. You and I will ride behind the Lancers, and you are to remain behind them. Do you understand?"

"Yes, ser." While Lerial would like to think that he is ready to ride patrols, he knows that it would be foolhardy to think he is as accomplished as the rankers accompanying them.

Once they have reached the top of the rise, the ten Mirror Lancers form a five-man front, two deep, with the middle rider at the point of a wedge. Altyrn reins up several yards back from the middle of the second line of riders.

"You stay here. I'm going forward, but I'll be back."

"Yes, ser." Lerial understands, but still resents what he sees as being overprotected, even as he understands the position in which his presence has placed both the majer and the Lancers. Rather than dwell on that, he stands in the stirrups of the gelding and looks south from the low crest of the trail, which stretches in a straight line south for more than a kay before curving westward around a rise. To the right of the road is an open gully, but one so eroded and shallow that it presents no barrier to a man on horseback. Beyond the gully is a patch of scrub brush and trees, no more than a half kay long and less than that east to west, and behind the miniature woods is a grassy rise, just high enough that Lerial cannot see what lies beyond it, although he could see beyond when he had been farther north on the trail. To the east of the road crest, and especially to the southeast, there is an endless expanse of browning grass.

He concentrates on the raiders. They ride slowly, at a walk, toward the Lancers, almost as if the Lancers do not exist. There are nine raiders mounted on horses that range in color from gray to black, and in coat pattern from solid to dapple. No two mounts are even close to the same in color and coat. Nor does any raider appear to be wearing exactly the same garments as any other. The raiders ride three abreast and are already less than half a kay from the Lancers, and still they do not charge, nor do they raise bows. Although Altyrn has told Lerial that some raiders have spear throwers, Lerial sees no spears.

Abruptly, arrows start to strike near the raiders. Then one mount stumbles as a shaft goes through its neck, and a raider slumps forward in his saddle as an arrow slams through his chest.

A shrieking cry comes from somewhere among the raiders, and the remaining eight riders spur their mounts forward into a headlong charge up the very slight slope toward the Lancers.

More shafts fly toward the raiders, then stop as Altyrn slings the bow over his shoulder and rides back toward Lerial. At the same time, the first line of Lancers charges down the road at the raiders, while the second line turns westward.

Lerial wonders why, but only for a moment, because he sees another group of raiders riding out of the small forest toward them.

"Draw your sabre," Altyrn says as he reins up beside Lerial. "If you need it, it won't do you any good in the scabbard."

Since Lerial has already begun to do so, he merely nods. He should have unsheathed it sooner.

Only when the second group of attackers are less than fifty yards from the remaining Lancers, perhaps even closer, do the Lancers charge, clearly waiting as long as possible to remain closer to Lerial and the majer, but also not wanting to take a charge standing still.

Altyrn swings his mount more to the west, and Lerial does the same.

Then, Lerial sees two riders galloping around the clashing raiders and Lancers, heading directly for the two of them.

"Get moving!" orders Altyrn.

Lerial does not respond immediately, instead studying the raider headed toward him. The angular rider has his blade leveled almost as if it were a spear.

Lerial knows that the motion is the beginning of a feint of some sort, then reacts by jabbing his heels into the gelding's flanks. With the slight jump as the big horse starts to move, the raider's blade wavers just slightly, enough that Lerial can sense and anticipate the move. He starts to strike in a way that would leave him open, then ducks and slides the larger blade, acting as the majer has taught him in coming in lower than the other, and then manages to come up as he passes the raider and slash just the sharpened tip of the sabre across the side of the raider's neck, before turning the gelding right, again as Altyrn has instructed him, so that he always has the other rider in sight.

From the corner of his eye, he can see that whatever the majer has done must have been successful, since there is no one that close to Altyrn.

Lerial can see that the rider who had attacked him is slowing . . . or his mount is. The rider has dropped his sword and is clutching at his neck. Lerial quickly looks around. The Mirror Lancers seem to be scattered around the crest of the road. While he sees several raider mounts, they are riderless, and he sees no raiders nearby, except the one who had attacked him He looks more to the south, still keeping his sabre at the ready, and finally sees two raiders riding southward along the trail, fast enough to raise dust.

"Are you all right?" asks Altyrn, riding up.

"Yes, ser. He didn't touch me." Lerial glances back toward the raider, who looks to be trying to dismount, except that he slides out of his saddle and hits the ground. His horse stops.

"I'll check. You stay behind me."

Lerial rides behind Altyrn, then reins up short of the fallen raider.

The man who lies on the ground is bearded and grizzled, and his frayed and faded brown shirt and patched riding jacket are covered in blood still oozing from the slash across his neck. His mouth opens and the only words that Lerial can hear, in a strangely accented Hamorian are,

". . . by a boy . . ." He tries to get out something else, then shudders and moves no more.

Lerial can sense the linked order and chaos begin to unravel . . . until both dissipate unseen into the autumn air that suddenly feels cooler than it actually is. A cold chill settles over Lerial, as if death itself stood at his shoulder. *Why?*

After a long moment, Lerial says, "He's dead."

"He is." Altyrn looks up as Chaarn rides up.

"They're either dead or gone. Mostly dead."

"What about your men?" asks the majer.

"Hualsh's got a deep slash in the shoulder. He might make it. Sparan took a spear through his ribs."

"Let's see them." Altyrn looks at Lerial.

"I'll see what I can do."

They ride after Chaarn toward a group of Lancers. Most are mounted, in a semicircle, facing south. Three are not, but only one of those is standing.

Even before he dismounts, Lerial can sense that he can do nothing for the man who took the spear through the ribs. The shaft went through at a downward angle, and chaos is everywhere within Sparan. He looks up helplessly. Lerial touches his forehead and lets the smallest amount of order flow. "Just take it easy." He hates saying something like that, but he doesn't want to admit he can do nothing.

Sparan grimaces, clearly trying not to moan, as Lerial turns to the other wounded man, who holds a blood-soaked cloth or folded shirt against his upper chest, almost at the shoulder.

Altyrn looks down from where he remains mounted. He nods at Lerial, as if to tell him to do what he can.

"Does anyone have any ale, lager, brandy?" Lerial asks.

"Will that help with a wound that deep?" asked Chaarn, who has barely reined up beside the majer. "Their blades aren't exactly clean."

"It will help, and I need all the help I can get. What about a needle and thread or something."

"I have that," admits Chaarn. "I'd rather not do a field dressing if anyone else can."

Lerial bends over the wounded Hualsh, easing the cloth away, slightly. While blood is flowing, more than oozing, it isn't spurting. He straightens and takes the canvas pack that Chaarn hands to him. Inside are two needles and strong thread as well as what looks to be cleaned raw cotton.

He uses his order senses to feel out the wound, thinking about what Maeroja had said and shown him about stitching wounds. He just hadn't expected to have to do it so soon.

"Here," says Altyrn, handing a bottle to him. "Brandy."

After cleaning the wound as well as he can, Lerial ends up closing it from both ends, but leaving a small opening in the middle, which he packs with the cotton. He is guessing that is the right thing to do, because he feels that the wound will need to drain. Then he presses more order deep into the slash, trying to turn the wound chaos into a dull pink, rather than an angry whitish-red. He stops as his vision narrows, and sparkling lights flash across his vision.

"I . . . can't do more . . . now." His knees are weak, and he rocks back. He can barely sit up on the matted grass.

"Drink this," says Altyrn, seemingly suddenly standing beside him and offering a bottle.

Lerial drinks the bitter ale, and the narrowness of vision retreats slightly.

"What . . ." Chaarn doesn't finish what he is saying, or maybe Lerial doesn't hear it.

". . . he's part healer. He put order into the wound. With the brandy and order, Hualsh might make it."

Lerial hopes so.

"We were lucky," murmurs Chaarn.

Altyrn nods, then offers a rueful smile. "Not just because . . ." He doesn't finish the sentence, but says, "You've sent a scout?"

"Two, with orders to turn at any sign of raiders."

After a time, and several more swallows of the warm and bitter ale, Lerial gets to his feet. He is still slightly light-headed, but he manages to mount and square himself in the saddle. Although he has his suspicions, he asks, "What do we do now?"

"We'll check the village to make sure that raiders who fled aren't there. If it looks like they've all cleared out, we can head back to Teilyn."

"You don't think they stayed, do you?" asks Lerial.

"I'd be surprised," answers Altyrn, "but I've been surprised before. That's why Chaarn sent scouts."

Lerial doesn't have an answer for that. He also wonders why they have to check the village if the squad leader has sent scouts, but he doesn't ask, not wanting to appear denser than he must already seem.

His light-headedness is almost gone by the time a glass has almost passed, and the flickering flashes in his vision have vanished. By then Sparan has closed his eyes and moans softly between intermittent gasps and gurgles. Hualsh's eyes are closed, but his breathing is more regular, and Lerial can sense that the remaining wound chaos has not increased.

He looks once more at Sparan, knowing that he can do nothing that will change matters. But . . . still . . .

"Don't even think about it," says Altyrn from where he stands a yard or so away from Lerial.

"I feel stronger now."

"Even your aunt couldn't do anything. That spear went through his lungs and gut. You're weaker than you think. You could kill yourself and not save him."

Lerial frowns. "Have you seen that?"

After a moment, Altyrn shakes his head. "I could see how much it took out of you for Hualsh, and he still may not make it."

Lerial glances back at Sparan, whose moans are even softer, then looks up as he sees two Lancers riding up the trail from the south.

Before long the two scouts are reporting to Chaarn and Altyrn.

"Village looks to be empty . . . fresh tracks of three mounts headed southwest."

"Lerial and I will check out the village." Altyrn looks hard at Chaarn. "Then we'll be back. You'll find a place to stay tonight? Somewhere close?"

"That might be best. Hualsh shouldn't be moved much right now. I'll send Naekyr and Alakan with you."

"We'll be very careful, but it's necessary."

Chaarn nods.

Lerial thinks the nod is reluctant.

Once they have started south on the trail behind the two Lancers, he asks, "Why do you need to see the village?"

"We both need to see it, for rather different reasons." Altyrn frowns, then goes on. "It's been years since we've seen a band of raiders that large this far north. I'm getting the feeling that it's drier than we thought in Merowey, and that's going to mean more raiders and trouble. A lot more, and Graessyr won't want to hear that, much as he needs to know."

Lerial does not comment on how the majer has avoided answering his question, knowing the Altyrn will not say what he does not wish to reveal and hoping that those reasons will become clear before they return to Kinaar.

The trail is empty except for the four riders, and Lerial sees no new tracks, except for the pair left by the fleeing raiders, and no dust hanging in the air. Little more than a kay from the site of the skirmish, the trail curves around the end of a low rise, and less than half a kay ahead, Lerial can make out the hamlet. As they ride closer, he sees that the hamlet, if it can even be called that, consists of eight dwellings with sloping sod walls. Only the two largest have chimneys, ugly constructions of rocks held together with sun-hardened clay.

"Did you check the huts?" Altyrn asks the Lancers.

"Yes, ser. No one there. It looks like the raiders—the ones who ran off . . . well, they might have stopped here."

"Any bodies?"

"No, ser."

"Then they didn't kill anyone. Could you tell what they took?"

"No, ser. A couple of the huts are a mess. There's no blood anywhere."

"That's good. The locals got off easily, then."

Easier than the Lancers did, muses Lerial.

Altyrn looks to Lerial. "Ride over to the closest one. Dismount and look inside. But have your sabre out and ready . . . just in case."

"Yes, ser."

When Lerial dismounts, he hands the gelding's reins to the majer and walks slowly to the first hut. The walls are made of chunks of sod, stacked on top of each other. There are only two crude windows, with what looks to be a crude wooden square the size of the window opening beneath each. *Solid wood shutters?* What passes for a door is the same, and there is not even a wooden door frame. A sour and acrid odor assaults Lerial as he nears the door, and he raises the sabre as he takes one step . . . and then another. But he can neither see nor sense anyone beyond the entry, and he steps forward.

The hut seems to consist of two chambers. One contains the hearth, a long table made of saplings fastened together with the top side cut or scraped flat, and four backless benches constructed the same way. The odor is overpowering and gets stronger as he peers into the other chamber, clearly used for sleeping, given the pallets there. Except they are not pallets, but raised earthen beds filled with leaves.

Lerial scans the chamber and makes his way out of the hut, trying not to retch. Once outside, he swallows twice, choking back bile, then says, "There's no one in there."

"Take a quick look inside the next two," Altyrn orders.

"Yes, ser."

Altyrn walks his mount and Lerial's toward the second hut, following the young man, but his bow is once more out, and he surveys the hamlet, his eyes never stopping.

Lerial looks into the next two, quickly, but carefully. Although they have no chimneys, they appear to use a window to vent their hearths. The stench is similar in both to the first.

"Mount up," Altyrn says quietly as Lerial emerges from the first hut.

Lerial is more than glad to do so, and they are well away from the hamlet before he speaks. "How can they live like that?"

"Teilyn was much like that when I was granted my lands," replies Altyrn. "Most of the dwellings were either sod or log-walled. There are a few of the log dwellings still."

"Then . . . you . . . made it what it is."

"Maeroja and I did much. The most important was building the brick kiln and the sawmill . . . and showing people how to use mud brick. With bricks and planks, people could build better houses. We also piped clean water down from the hill spring."

"Piped?"

"We fired the pipes in the kiln. That was hard. We broke a lot. Bricks are much easier, at least once you get the hang of it."

As he looks northward to where a mounted Lancer waits, Lerial wonders just what else Altyrn has done . . . and how much of it his father knows.

XX

Sparan dies just before dawn on eightday morning. The Lancers bury him on the hillside where he fought, but remove his personal articles and place them in the dead Lancer's kit bag, which they tie to his saddle.

When Lerial checks Hualsh, the wounded Lancer appears slightly stronger, or his order flows do, but Lerial worries. From what Lerial can sense, the wound chaos has not increased and might be just a touch less. *But is that what you want to believe? How can you tell?*

"How does he feel?"

Although Altyrn's voice is low, Lerial starts, because he has not heard the majer approach. He turns, and after a moment, he says, "He's stronger than yesterday . . ."

"But you worry."

Lerial nods.

"It would be better for him to stay here for a few days. We don't have that choice."

"Because of me?"

"Partly. It's also because Graessyr and your father need to know how bad things could get. The raiders haven't come this far north and east in years. If they're coming here this soon after harvest, there are likely more of them near Bartheld and Narthyl. The longer before he knows, the more growers will suffer." Altyrn adds, "That's going to make things difficult for your father . . . and for everyone in Cigoerne."

"Because the Heldyans—or the Afritan poachers—will take advantage of it if Father sends more Lancers south?"

Altyrn nods. "It's possible."

"We need more Lancers, then."

"If he raises more than the two companies Majer Phortyn is training now, that will leave fewer men in the fields. That will make planting harder and slower in the spring. It takes seasons to train a Lancer. You knew how to handle a blade and ride, and look how long it's taken you."

"And I'm not even as good as they are," says Lerial.

"No . . . you're better than the newer Lancers. You're just not as good as the experienced squad leaders and officers. You're probably better than the very junior undercaptains, but you should be better than that before you can ride patrols."

Why? Lephi likely isn't that much better. "Because I'm Father's son?"

Altyrn offers a sad smile. "No. Because you're part healer."

Lerial doesn't know quite what to say to that. Saltaryn has said that a youth of Magi'i blood should avoid healing until he mastered chaos. Was what the majer has told Lerial what Saltaryn had really meant?

"A Lancer officer who is part healer cannot afford to think about what he does in battle. He must be so well trained and skilled that his body will instantly do what needs to be done."

"Why is that?"

"Healers are steeped in order. Order opposes death. In battle, you have to seek the death of those you oppose. If you don't, you'll be the one who is most likely to die. You will have to lead men. They will know, before long, if you hesitate to kill when you must."

Lerial understands. He doesn't like it, but he does understand.

"Now . . . we need to pack up and head out."

"Yes, ser."

As he begins packing his kit bag, Lerial can only hope that Hualsh can survive the ride back to Teilyn. His eyes drift toward the hillside . . . and the single grave that holds Sparan . . . and the larger and shallower one that holds the bodies of twelve Meroweyan raiders.

XXI

Just before midday on threeday, Altyrn and Lerial ride up to the villa south of Teilyn under a cloudy sky with a cool wind blowing out of the southwest. Lerial is grateful that Hualsh appears to be healing, or was when they left the Lancers at the post, and that the Lancer's wound chaos is less each day. Even so, Lerial worries. He also worries about the quick conversation that Altyrn had had with Captain Graessyr, mostly because of the looks the captain had given him.

As they near the stables, Lerial finally asks, "Did I do something I should know about?"

Altyrn offers a puzzled frown, then abruptly shakes his head and laughs. "You're asking if I was telling Graessyr that you'd made some sort of mistake? No . . . we weren't talking about that at all. He was impressed with the fact that you'd used your sabre as you were taught and that you helped heal Hualsh."

"Couldn't you have stopped the bleeding and sewed up the wound?" This is something about which Lerial has wondered for most of the journey back to Teilyn.

"I could have. So could Chaarn, but Hualsh had a better chance with you. I saw what you did with that boy who had his arm ripped by the cart wheel. I might stitch a little neater, but there's more to healing than that. You have the touch. For you, it's a curse and a blessing. If I were you, I'd not let anyone outside your family know. Graessyr won't say anything, and I told Hualsh that he shouldn't. He'll keep his mouth shut about that."

Altyrn's last words carry a conviction with which Lerial isn't about to argue, especially when he sees Maeroja and the three girls waiting by the north entrance to the villa, less than forty yards away. Maeroja's eyes are fixed on Altyrn, and Lerial can sense her concern.

Apparently, so can the majer, because he eases his mount toward her. "We're fine, dear one."

"I only counted nine rankers, and one of them was wounded."

Lerial realizes that she must have been watching—or had someone watching—when they rode past the villa to the post. *She had someone watching every day?*

"We ran into a raiding party in the south valley. They won't be doing any more raiding," Altyrn says dryly.

Rojana looks up to Lerial. "There's blood on your sleeve. Were you wounded?"

Lerial has forgotten the blood, most likely from when he sewed up Hualsh's wound. "No . . . that's likely from when I sewed up a wound one of the Lancers got from the raiders."

"Likely?" asks Maeroja. "There were other possibilities?"

"It might have been a raider's blood," he admits. "I did have to use my sabre." It feels strange to admit that the weapon Altyrn has given him is indeed his.

"He used it in self-defense," Altyrn adds. "The raiders attacked us."

"Don't they always?" Maeroja's voice is cool.

Altyrn looks at her, and Lerial feels that he is almost pleading, if silently.

"I'm sorry," she says. "I had so hoped . . ."

"So had I. I had hoped . . . this early in the fall . . ." The majer looks to Lerial. "We need to get the horses unsaddled and groomed, and we both need baths and clean clothes."

"You certainly do." Maeroja's voice is warmer.

As Lerial and Altyrn ride toward the stables, Lerial continues to puzzle over the words the majer and his consort exchanged, as if somehow Altyrn has done something he had promised he would not . . . and was apologizing for having done so. *But what he does every day on the lands takes more effort than the journey did . . . or has he promised not to fight the raiders?*

It takes Lerial longer than the majer to unsaddle and groom his mount, and by the time he has finished, the majer has left the stable. Lerial gathers his gear and lugs it to his chambers, and he is grateful that someone—most likely one of the girls—has carried water up to his bath chamber. When he is finally washed and dressed in clean greens, he makes his way down to the courtyard. He looks around and finds that the only ones in the courtyard beside him are Aylana and Tyrna, and they are gathering up their dolls and placing them in a leather case.

"You took a long time," says Tyrna, almost accusingly.

"I had to groom my horse and see to his water and feed." Lerial pauses. "Were you the ones who carried water to my room?"

"We helped Seltha," announces Aylana.

"We did most of it," adds Tyrna.

"Thank you."

"You're welcome." Tyrna smiles.

"Your mother was most worried when your sister saw the blood on my sleeve," Lerial keeps his voice puzzled.

"Father's not supposed to fight raiders anymore. He promised."

"Tyrna!" interjects Rojana, who is walking from the north door toward the terrace table. "You're not . . ." She shakes her head.

"He's almost family," replies Tyrna. "Father said so."

"So did Mother," adds Aylana.

Rojana offers a rueful smile to Lerial. "I'm sorry. It's just . . ."

"You all worry about your father."

"He's supposed to take care of himself . . . and . . ."

"He didn't have a choice . . . and he agreed to train me, and none of us thought we were going to have to fight raiders when he took me to see places he thought I should see. None of you thought that, either."

"He shouldn't have," says Tyrna.

"Fought raiders," explains Rojana. "Not taken you . . . I mean, he should have taken you, but . . ."

"He didn't expect raiders," Lerial says. "He really didn't. When they showed up, he let the Lancers take the charges. There were two lines of Lancers, and we stayed behind both of them. It was just that there were more raiders, and some of them got around the Lancers."

"He said you killed one of them," says Rojana. "Did you?"

"Yes. He was charging right at me. I wasn't trying to kill him. I was just trying to hit him with my sabre so that he wouldn't kill me."

"You'll have to kill more raiders if you go on patrols," observes Rojana.

"If I go on patrols . . . that's possible."

Rojana is about to say something when Maeroja appears.

"Lerial . . . girls . . . we're having beverages in the salon. It's too chill out here."

Lerial inclines his head. "Thank you. I didn't know."

"That was why I sent Rojana." Maeroja looks at her eldest daughter.

"They were talking about the raiders . . . and Father . . ." Rojana's voice is low.

"I don't imagine that Lerial missed our concerns," replies Maeroja briskly. "He senses more than most."

Lerial has the feeling that Maeroja meant "most men" or "most Magi'i,' although she had not uttered either phrase. "I could see you were worried. I'm sorry about the blood. It was where I didn't see it."

"You worried about the wounded Lancer, didn't you?" asks Maeroja.

Lerial nods.

After the slightest hesitation, Maeroja smiles, then gestures to the girls. "We shouldn't be leaving your father alone in the salon."

Aylana and Tyrna turn and hurry toward the north door. Rojana glances at her mother, then follows her sisters.

Maeroja says, "If you would escort me, Lerial?"

"With pleasure." As he speaks, Lerial wonders what is coming next.

"You are a healer, and yet you will have to lead Lancers and kill men. It will take great strength. At times, if you are too merciful, even more will die."

Great strength? "I must confess that I have been so concerned about the strength required to master the blade that I have not considered that great strength might be required to deal with possible success in using it."

"You say that so well I find it hard to believe that you have not."

"I have worried that I may not be able to meet the expectations of others." That is certainly true. "And . . . Lady . . . I am sorry if my father's requests for my learning have caused you concern and pain. I would not have wished that . . ."

Maeroja's laugh is low and rueful. "It is not your father's request that caused the concerns, but my consort's sense of duty and rightness. It was his feeling that you needed to see what you might otherwise never behold."

"And has it been his idea that I also spar with the Lancers?"

"Yes."

"Then I owe you both . . . deeply."

"If you survive, Lord Lerial, you will more than repay those concerns. What my consort has done beyond what your father requested is in the hope that you will be able to help your father and your brother triumph over what must come."

"Attacks by Afrit?"

"Afrit will be your greatest worry, but not for the reasons you think." Maeroja pauses at the north courtyard entry.

Not for the reasons you think?

"Afrit is not nearly so powerful as Duke Atroyan would have the world believe." She continues into the inside corridor and toward the archway into the winter salon. "Your grandmother understood that. So does your aunt, but I am not so certain that your sire does." She stops in the archway. "Perhaps I should not have voiced my views, but I trust you will keep their source to yourself . . . as few would respect the judgment of a mere woman."

"I respect your judgment . . . and your views."

Her smile is softer. "You did not have to say that. Your words and actions already have. Let us join the others."

Lerial follows her into the salon.

"I have your wine, dear," says Altyrn. He is seated in a leather armchair, while the three girls occupy a leather couch. Pitchers of juice, lager, and wine rest on the sideboard.

While Maeroja takes her place in the smaller chair beside her consort, Lerial walks to the sideboard and pours himself a mug of lager, then takes the straight-backed chair at the end of the couch away from the majer, but facing Altyrn.

"It was quite a journey," Altyrn begins. "It didn't start out eventful at all. We rode to the Lancer post and then back south to the west trail. You girls have even ridden the first part of that . . ." He goes on to describe all that occurred until the part when the Lancers saw the locals fleeing up the road. Then he looks to Lerial. "Since I am suspected of telling matters either more or less dramatically than they may have happened, I'd be obliged if you would tell everyone what occurred after that."

Lerial almost wants to suggest that, in turn, the majer might wish to add to anything he might say, but decides against that, since he might not have seen what the majer did. "The majer suggested that the squad leader immediately see how many raiders there might be. I fear I may be to blame for the fact that we did not depart and leave the poor locals to what might have otherwise happened. It occurred to me that if we followed what some might have called the prudent course, over the years ahead it would be said that the son of Duke Kiedron fled in terror from the first raiders he encountered. I thought this would not be good for Cigoerne or my father . . . or for me, or for men I might have to lead in the future. So when squad leader Chaarn reported to the majer that less than ten raiders approached, I suggested that, if there did not appear to be any more, we should attempt to show force to encourage them to turn away. The nine raiders—I believe there were nine—rode forward at a walk, then burst into a gallop and attacked. The squad leader deployed his men in a five-abreast, two-deep, formation with the majer and me behind them. Just as the nine attacked the Lancers, another group charged over a hill and up through a gully. Half the Lancers turned to engage them, but they were outnumbered and two or three got past them. One of them charged me, and one charged the majer. The other one . . . I think he turned to try and attack the Lancers fighting the first raiders from behind, but I didn't have time to think about that because I had to deal with the man coming at me. I managed to slip his blade and get a cut across his neck with a back cut as he went past." Lerial pauses, then adds, "When I looked around after that, two raiders were galloping off, and the rest were dead . . . or dying." He looks to Maeroja. "So it's my fault that we stayed." He thinks about apologizing, but decides against that, because he knows what he did was right for Cigoerne, even if it was not right for the majer. Instead, he turns his eyes on Altyrn. "I think you saw and could explain more of what happened after that."

After a rueful smile, Altyrn continues. "Two of the Lancers were badly hurt. One was fatally wounded, and Lerial gave him some order comfort before attending to the wound of the second. The first Lancer died that evening. The second looks as though he will survive, but likely would not have without Lerial's skill . . ." Altyrn summarizes the remainder of the journey, ending with, ". . . and you saw us riding up the lane to Kinaar." He smiles and says. "In a bit, I think we'll all be ready to eat."

"You think there will be more raiders?" asks Maeroja, in a tone that is just short of not being a question.

"I fear it is likely, but that is a matter with which the Duke and the Lancers will have to deal," replies Altyrn. "I think my journey with Lerial will be the last to the south valley or anywhere that far for some time. If it is up to me," he adds in a lower voice.

Lerial sees the almost concealed wince on Maeroja's face. *Does he mean that Father might call him back to duty? How could he?*

"You won't take us?" asks Aylana. "That's not fair."

"Dear one . . . I will take you on journeys, perhaps to Cigoerne and other places. We just will not be riding into places where there may be raiders."

"That's fair enough," says Maeroja.

Both Tyrna and Rojana nod.

"Now . . . we should eat." The majer rises from his chair.

Lerial follows the majer and his consort, walking almost beside Rojana. She glances at him for a moment, but says nothing. Lerial isn't certain what the glance might mean and is not about to ask.

After everyone is seated, Altyrn looks to Maeroja.

She nods, then says, "We offer thanks to the powers of order and chaos, and to the Rational Stars for the safe return of those who have traveled . . . and for all those who travel into danger."

"Thanks be to the Rational Stars," murmur the girls . . . and their mother.

Dinner is a fowl casserole with dark bread, the first Lerial has seen at Kinaar, and the girls are each allowed a quarter of a glass of white wine, also another first, clearly a quiet celebration of gratitude.

After he has served Maeroja and himself, the majer looks to his youngest daughter. "Aylana, you've heard what we did. Tell Lerial and me what you have been doing, if you would."

"It's not that exciting."

The majer waits.

"Well . . . we've been learning how to use the threader, and I can even do it . . . if Tyrna helps . . ."

From that point on, the conversation throughout dinner, and the honeycake dessert that follows, remains firmly on what has happened at Kinaar.

When everyone has finished eating, the majer clears his throat. "Girls . . . you may be excused. Your mother and I need a few words with Lerial."

Maeroja also looks at the three girls in turn.

"Yes, Father."

Lerial notes that all three immediately rise, incline their heads, and depart without another word. He does not sense that either the majer or his consort is concealing strong feelings. So he waits for Altyrn to speak.

Finally, the majer speaks. "Your father left the decision to me as to when you were ready to return to Cigoerne. I will be frank with you, Lerial. You have great . . . possibilities, but your strengths can also be weaknesses. It is clear you can use order skills to anticipate what I do with a sabre, what anyone does with a sabre. At the same time, those order skills will make it difficult for you in any prolonged battle."

Lerial almost asks why, before remembering the cold chill that had enveloped him just after the raider died. "Yes, ser. I had a feeling about that."

"You need to keep working on your blade skills, but there is little more that you can learn here, and, after what we encountered in the south valley, I fear you will be needed elsewhere before long."

Lerial has his doubts about that.

"You'll be riding back to Cigoerne with the dispatch rider and some other Lancers early on fiveday."

"With the dispatch about the raiders, ser?"

"No. Captain Graessyr had a rider leaving the post within a glass of the time he found out. That couldn't wait."

Lerial feels stupid for his question. *Of course it couldn't wait. What were you thinking?*

"You will always be welcome here." Altyrn smiles.

"And we would be most disappointed if you are near here and do not stop for at least a brief visit," adds Maeroja.

"The girls have benefited from your being here as well," Altyrn goes on. "All of us will miss you."

"I will miss you," Lerial replies.

After a time, as he walks back toward his chamber, Lerial realizes the words he has thought he spoke in courtesy were in fact all too true. He will actually miss Kinaar . . . and the majer and his consort . . . and the girls, especially Rojana. He also wonders if he will see her that evening.

He does not, and eventually, he drifts into an uneasy sleep.

XXII

Almost the moment Lerial finishes his last sip of the greenish berry juice at breakfast on fourday, Altyrn looks across the table at him. "No work on the lands today. You need to get ready for your journey back to Cigoerne. The regular dispatch riders leave at the hint of first light, and they ride straight through. You'll need everything packed and ready before you turn in this evening."

"That's a long ride for a mount . . ." *And longer than you've ever ridden at one time.*

"They'll have spare mounts at Brehaal. You'll have to lead your gelding for the last half of the ride." The majer rises. "Come with me. There are a few things you'll need."

Lerial wonders what the majer has in mind, but follows him to his study. He watches as Altyrn opens one of the small doors in the tall cabinet against the side wall and extracts something.

Then the majer turns and hands Lerial a pair of grayish green gloves that look never to have been worn. "I noticed you don't have a good pair of riding gloves."

"I couldn't—"

"They're yours. Captain Graessyr also said that you're to keep the riding jacket. It's cut to allow more movement in the saddle than your old jacket. Besides, the old one is too small. You've broadened across the shoulders."

Lerial had wondered about that when they had set out on the ride to the south valley, but that memory had slipped his mind—until now. "You don't think that . . . on the way back to Cigoerne . . . ?"

"I doubt that seriously, but you never know where you'll find raiders, or brigands. Also, no one thinks about things like proper blades, jackets, and gloves until after the need is obvious. Sometimes that's too late. This way you'll have them when you need them. And . . . the sabre does belong in your family." Altyrn pauses. "I wouldn't mention that to anyone, not for some time."

"I won't, ser." *If I did, Lephi would insist that it belonged to him, and Father would likely agree.*

"Good . . . because it's better suited to you than either your father or brother, and a blade and its wielder need to fit each other."

Lerial knows that the majer understands his father's abilities with a blade, but how does he understand Lephi's? *And why does the blade fit you better?*

"Your brother stopped by here on the way to one of his patrols. Your father sent a note asking me to give him some pointers in bladework. I did."

"He didn't mention that." Lerial now recalls Lephi's mention of Teilyn, but he'd never mentioned the majer. *That would be Lephi.*

"I don't imagine that he did. Lephi's more like your father. You take more after your grandmeres on both sides."

"I never knew Grandmere Althya." *Except that she perished in Cyad . . . and no one talks about her.*

"Quite a woman she was, and an outstanding healer, I heard tell. She was a redhead, too. There was a portrait in the Palace of Light . . . looked quite a bit like her. Have no idea who it was, except she had to have been an Empress in the old times."

"The old times? How could you tell?"

"It was hung in a back hall, but the painting was excellent, as was the frame."

"Ser? What should I have asked you that I didn't and that I need to know?"

Altyrn laughs, warmly, then shakes his head. "I didn't expect that, but it's a good sign." He gestures to the circular table. "We might as well sit down."

Lerial seats himself and waits.

Altyrn takes the seat across from Lerial and clears his throat. "You need to think about men more than weapons. Weapons are necessary, but it's always men who use them. You need to understand what your officers and squad leaders think and know. You need to talk to them. Never be familiar, but never condescend to them. Always consider the men you work with and against. In some ways, men who are weak within themselves are the most dangerous, especially if they have taken great pains to conceal their weaknesses. Because they are weak, they tend to be ruthless when it is not necessary. They can seldom be trusted to keep their word, except when it suits them. That is, I believe, and it is only my opinion, because they know they are not trustworthy, and therefore believe no others can be trusted." The majer offers a rueful smile. "The truth is that most men are weak in this way.

The most dangerous are those with power. People say that the most dangerous man is the one with nothing to lose, but they forget that every man has his life to lose, and that is the most precious thing of all to most. Never threaten to kill a man. Decide whether to kill him or not. Then do it. If you threaten and don't kill him, he'll never believe you again, and you'll always have to watch out for him, even if you put him in jail in chains."

Lerial nods slowly. "What do you think of Duke Atroyan?"

"You cannot trust the Duke or any of his family, the Duke least of all."

"Have you met him, ser?"

"I've never met him, but I've watched him when he has met with your father and your grandmere. He is a man who believes almost any man can be bought . . . and that those few who cannot need to be killed quickly and quietly." The majer smiles again. "I'll give you another piece of advice. You likely won't pay it much heed, but I'd be remiss in not offering it to you."

"Ser?"

"A woman's beauty has nothing to do with her character or temperament. Some men claim that you can't trust beautiful women, and you can trust those who aren't. That's sowshit. Some beautiful women are honest and trustworthy. Some are not. The same is true of those who are not beautiful. If you treat any woman badly, matters will get worse for you. An untrustworthy woman will become more so, and a trustworthy woman will likely become less so." Altyrn laughs softly. "By the way, that applies to men as well."

"Will you tell me what you know of Afrit and Swartheld that I'm not likely to know?"

"Swartheld is a port. That means you'll find almost anything there . . ."

Lerial listens for almost a glass before the majer stops.

"I've said more than enough, and more than you'll remember. You need to see about organizing your gear."

"Yes, ser."

Still thinking over his conversation with the majer, and puzzling over the matter of the ancient sabre that is now his, Lerial carries the riding gloves back to the chamber that has been his for more than two seasons. Once he climbs the steps, he sees Seltha and Maeroja coming from his chambers, Seltha carrying a large stack of his uniforms.

"You'll have to pack most of your uniforms late this afternoon or early this evening," Maeroja announces, adding with a smile, "There's no way we're sending you back with any dirty garments except those on your back."

"I didn't wish to cause you any trouble . . ."

"You haven't. It's a good thing it's sunny, if a bit brisk. They all should dry." Maeroja stops, but motions Seltha to continue toward the steps down to the main level. "I couldn't help but notice that you don't carry any . . . personal . . . items."

Lerial offers an amused smile. "I'm sure you noticed that before now."

Her smile is open and warm. "I did. Is that by choice or training?"

"Choice. The personal things that matter are those I remember."

"You're like my consort in that respect. That seems to be a Lancer trait. It's rare in a healer."

"You think I'm really a healer, don't you?"

"You don't have all the training you need, but . . . yes, you're a healer." Her smile turns sad, or more reflective. "People will say that healers can't be Lancers . . . or they can't kill. Or that Lancers can't be healers. That's nonsense. It takes more strength to heal than kill . . . and to see those you've treated die, and then try again. Any fool trained with a sharp blade can slaughter people."

"You know more about healing than you let on."

"I have the skills, but not the touch with order. My sister was a healer."

The way Maeroja mentions her sister suggests that her sister is no longer alive.

"I'm sorry."

"You see? I didn't even have to say that I lost her. You sense more than you think you do. In the life the Rational Stars have chosen for you, you will need to take care not to reveal what you feel . . . especially in Cigoerne or Swartheld . . . or Heldya, should you be sent there."

It is more than clear to Lerial that both the majer and his consort believe he will be sent wherever in Hamor that his father, or his brother, feel will serve their interests . . . and possibly those of Cigoerne . . . and they believe it will be soon.

"Are you from Heldya once upon a time?" Lerial has always wondered, but he realizes this may be his last chance to ask.

"In a way. I was born there. We left long before I was old enough to remember anything. I grew up near Amaershyn."

That makes sense to Lerial, since Amaershyn is the westernmost large town—or small city—in Heldya and some hundred and fifty kays south of Cigoerne. Unfortunately, it is also a Heldyan garrison town, and was the staging point for Heldyan forces when they made attacks on the Duchy of

Cigoerne. *But how did she and Altyrn meet?* Lerial does not recall his father sending Lancers against Amaershyn, and it is unlikely he did so in the time before Lerial was born, but not impossible, even though Amaershyn is a walled city larger than Cigoerne. *But maybe it isn't any longer.* Lerial pushes away those thoughts.

"You need to get on with whatever you need to do, and I have a few things yet to do today." Maeroja smiles, then hurries past Lerial, leaving him standing outside the door to his room, his at least for one more day.

He makes his way inside and begins to organize his things.

That doesn't take long because, with most of his clothes being washed, he has very little left to organize. So before long, he heads back down to the courtyard, which is not quite chill and more than slightly breezy. For a time, he stands, watching the fountains, thinking that Kinaar is indeed much quieter, more peaceful than will be the palace to which he will be returning—until his father sends him off somewhere else.

"Lerial . . . ?'

He has been so lost in his musings he has not even sensed Rojana's approach. He turns.

"You'll be leaving before dawn tomorrow, won't you?"

"That's what your father tells me."

"Please be careful." Rojana's voice is low as she looks into his eyes. "Really careful."

Lerial tries not to frown. Why is Rojana so concerned? Both her parents have made it clear by words, in the case of Maeroja, and deeds, by the majer, that there can be nothing between the two of them . . . and even Rojana has maintained a certain reserve around Lerial.

She hands him a small black silk pouch. "This is for you."

As he takes the pouch, Lerial can feel a heavy oblong shape inside the smoothness of the silk. "You don't have to . . ."

"Gifts aren't gifts if you have to."

He can't help but smile, partly because she is so right, and partly because her voice is so like her mother's.

"It's a lodestone. It will help you. It's something I feel. Tyrna, Aylana, and I wove the pouch."

Lerial knows that lodestones fashioned into needles are used as compasses on ships, but how will a solid block of lodestone help him? Yet . . . he feels there is something Rojana is not telling him. "There's more, isn't there?"

After a moment of surprise, she nods. "One of the old books . . . there's a mention of lodestones and ordering order." She pauses, then says, "I don't know how you could order order . . . but maybe you can."

Lerial smiles. The small pouch and the lodestone certainly can't hurt him . . . and maybe, just maybe, he can figure it out. "Thank you."

Rojana looks intently at him. Her eyes are bright. "Take care. You *must.*" Then she turns and moves away, first walking quickly and then running.

Lerial finds that his own eyes are burning . . . but she has vanished from the courtyard . . . and what could he do, even if he ran after her?

He fingers the silk pouch and the lodestone beneath the silk . . . then turns and heads for the north corridor. Perhaps a long walk will help. *Perhaps . . .*

XXIII

In the dimness well before dawn on fiveday, Lerial begins to dress, thinking over the events since he arrived at Kinaar more than two seasons ago. He also worries about Rojana, who had not appeared at dinner the night before. He does not believe he has led her on, and he has been careful never to suggest that there should be anything between them. Yet he is aware, if only through watching and listening, that hearts do not always listen to words or prohibitions.

He pauses. *Is that the difference?* He shakes his head. He has certainly not listened to prohibitions in other areas, and that is why he was sent to Kinaar. The fact that he has listened to the warnings and words of Maeroja and Altyrn about their daughter suggests that his feelings about her are not that deep in his heart . . . and yet . . . he cares, and does not want her hurt. *Much as you care for Ryalah . . . or Amaira?* With a certain physical attraction added in, he admits to himself.

After pulling on his boots, he stands and walks to the bedside table. From there, he picks up the black silk pouch and fingers the oblong lodestone within through the silk. It is not quite a perfect oblong, but when he studied it the night before, it appeared that it had not been cut or ground, and that it had been formed naturally, however such stones occurred. *By the workings of order and chaos within the earth?* He smiles and slips the pouch into the inside pocket of his Lancer riding jacket, then straps on the sword belt and sabre.

He takes a last look around the chamber, picks up the kit bag, and leaves the room, for possibly the last time in his life.

Altyrn is already in the stable, saddling his mount by the light of a single dim lamp, when Lerial arrives.

"Good morning, ser," Lerial offers.

"It is morning, and they seem to come earlier with each year . . . or maybe the nights are just shorter."

Only a thin glow barely illuminates the eastern horizon when the two lead their horses out of the stable and mount. Lerial glances toward the villa. Just away from the lamp set on a bronze bracket by the north door stand Maeroja and the three girls. All are fully dressed. He guides the gelding toward the four and reins up short of Maeroja.

"I cannot thank you enough." Lerial means every word. "For everything."

"We enjoyed having you here, especially the girls," replies Maeroja. "You are always welcome here."

"Always," adds Rojana.

Lerial senses *something* behind that single word, and he can see that her eyes are bright. They may even be red, but even with the lamplight illuminating her face at an angle, he cannot be certain. "Thank you. And thank you for your gift. It means more than you know." *Even if I cannot accept it in quite the way you meant it. Or the way I think you meant.*

Rojana continues to look at him, and the obvious hurt tears at him.

"Please come back." Aylana's voice is not quite plaintive.

"That's up to the Duke, but I will if I can. I don't think it will be soon, though." Lerial doesn't know what else to say, but manages. "All of you . . . please take care."

"We will," promises Maeroja.

As he and the majer ride down the lane toward the main road, Lerial can sense eyes on his back. At least, that's the way it feels.

He does not speak again until they have nearly reached the road. "I have to thank you again, ser. I don't know that I could have learned so much anywhere else."

"Given who you are," replies Altyrn, "you likely couldn't. That is why your father sent you here."

Lerial still isn't certain he wants to give his father that much credit. "My father . . . or my mother?"

"It was your father's choice. I'd be most surprised if your mother and aunt weren't the ones who suggested it. But . . ." Altyrn pauses for several moments. ". . . even if it happened to be their suggestion, your father had the wisdom to accept it and carry it out. That's one of the most valuable traits a leader can have—to see the wisdom of good suggestions made by others and to accept them and carry them out."

Lerial has to admit that the majer has a point. *A very good one, whether you like it or not.*

"You made quite an impression on the girls," observes Altyrn after several moments of silence, "especially Rojana."

"I'm sorry. I tried not to—"

"You were a perfect gentleman, Lerial, and that just made you that much more attractive to her. I couldn't have asked for a better first infatuation for her."

Lerial isn't so sure that Rojana's feelings are merely infatuation. "I think I hurt her"—*You know you did*—"and I didn't mean to, but I didn't know how not to hurt her in some way or another."

"You were gentle. That's all you can be when something like that happens."

"You're not too upset?" Lerial has to know.

"I'm upset that she's hurting. Any father would be. But that's not your fault. As you said, you didn't lead her on, and you didn't take advantage of her. You might be the one for her, but she's not the one for you. No matter whom you consort, you'll cause her grief and pain. The Stars know I've caused Maeroja more pain than I ever intended."

"I'm sorry about what happened in the south valley—"

Altyrn waves off Lerial's words. "She was worried. Pain is different. In time, you'll understand. I hope you do. Most leaders and rulers do . . . if they're good at leading."

Lerial worries about the majer's words about pain, especially given how much Lerial had ached in the first eightdays at Kinaar. Altyrn is clearly talking about something far greater.

"You don't have to worry about that yet," adds the majer.

"Is there anything else?"

Altyrn laughs. "Be a little late now, wouldn't it?"

"I can try," responds Lerial lightly.

In the dimness, Lerial feels as much as sees the good-natured headshake that is the majer's response.

Just before they reach the post gates, Lerial turns in the saddle. "Ser . . . I want to thank you again."

"You're more than welcome. I hope whatever you've learned will stand you in good stead."

"I'm sure it will, ser."

The half squad of Lancers accompanying the dispatch rider—and Lerial—are mounting up when Lerial and Altyrn ride through the post gates. At the head of the column of riders, two abreast, stands Captain Graessyr, beside another mounted Lancer, an older and slightly grizzled man with the insignia of a squad leader. The squad leader's complexion is even darker than Amaira's, suggesting he comes from a local Hamorian background.

Lerial reins up short of the two, as does Altyrn.

Graessyr looks at Lerial, nods, then turns to the older squad leader. "Lerial . . . this is Squad Leader Eshlyn."

"I'm pleased to meet you, Squad Leader. I appreciate your escorting me back to Cigoerne."

"We appreciate having you ride with us, ser."

Lerial notes the Hamorian accent in the squad leader's words, but just replies, "I hope you don't mind if I learn what I can from you on the way."

Eshlyn grins. "Don't know that it's much, but you're welcome to try."

Lerial couldn't help but grin. He likes the squad leader immediately, more on feeling, but, usually his feelings are correct. *And now you're heading back to where no one thought they were.*

"Don't hesitate to tell him if it's a stupid question, either," says Altyrn cheerfully.

"I won't. You know me, Majer." Eshlyn turns to Lerial. "You ready, ser?"

"I'm ready."

"Let's head out!"

Lerial offers a last smile to Altyrn, then turns the gelding to come alongside the squad leader.

XXIV

Because Lerial does not wish to seem too forward, he is mostly quiet during the first few glasses after leaving Teilyn, asking an occasional question about the area through which they are passing or about riding formations or other Lancer matters.

Perhaps a glass before midday, the squad leader says, his voice even, "Captain Graessyr said you and the majer ran into some raiders."

"We did. I don't think he expected them so soon after harvest."

"One of the men who went with you said you wanted to fight."

Lerial is stunned, but manages to offer a rueful laugh. "Not exactly. I didn't want them to fight, and I wasn't looking to . . . but . . ." He shrugs. "If I said we shouldn't fight, all Hamor would know in eightdays that the Duke's son avoided a fight with a bunch of raiders. That wouldn't be good for my father, and it wouldn't be good for the Lancers."

"Killed one of them, didn't you?"

"Two—maybe three of them—got past the Lancers, and one charged me. I managed to slip his blade and slash his throat. That was all. All the other Lancers took care of the other raiders, except the ones that the majer got with his bow and the one he killed when they charged."

"You healed Hualsh. Said he wouldn't have made it without you. Most healers don't carry sabres."

"I can heal a little," Lerial admits, "but I can also use a sabre."

"That's what Chaarn said. Ser . . . do you mind if I ask whether you plan to ride patrols like your brother does?"

Lerial gets the feeling that Eshlyn's question is anything but casual. "I don't mind. I'd always thought I'd ride patrols. Nothing's changed that. As for riding the way my brother does, I can't answer that because I don't know anything about how he rides a patrol. I still have a lot to learn. That's one reason why I've asked some of the things I have."

Eshlyn nods. "What did you think of the raiders?"

"They must be desperate to ride so far into Cigoerne. The ones we saw, their bodies, anyway, they looked like they hadn't been eating all that well. Are they always like that?"

"Sometimes. More the last few years, it seems."

"You've been in the Lancers for a long time, it seems. What do you think about those raiders being so far north?"

"Not so long. Seven, eight years. Think the same as you, ser. Trouble. Folks who go raiding when the harvest is barely in . . . means they don't have enough food for the winter. Or they've had a flux, and they need women. Or someone's taken over their lands. Any way you look, it's trouble."

"What about the Heldyans?"

Eshlyn snorts. "Raiders with uniforms. The ones across the river, anyway. Duke Khesyn just sends out his troublemakers to keep us busy. Offers a half a gold for every Lancer they kill."

"Half a gold? Why?"

"Must have his reasons. Majer Altyrn said it was to keep Cigoerne from getting too strong."

Why would Khesyn care? Heldya is more than five hundred kays east of Cigoerne and close to eight hundred from Swartheld. "How often do they cross the river?"

"Three, four times a season. Try to watch for small patrols. Easier to kill a Lancer if we're outnumbered." Eshlyn offers a sly smile. "At times, we run a half squad on the river road. When they're looking. Keep a company hidden. Works pretty well if we don't do it much."

"Your idea?"

"No. Majer thought that up. Submajer Jhalet told us to keep doing it. Heldyans still don't get it."

"That's why you don't think the ones across the river are their best armsmen."

Eshlyn nods.

Lerial takes out his water bottle and has a swallow of the lager from Kinaar, then replaces it in its holder.

After several moments, Eshlyn asks, "That's not a new sabre, is it?"

"It's new to me . . . well, in the past season. It came from Cyad, though."

"I thought so. It's cupridium, but it looks heavier, and that's an old, old design."

"The majer had me sparring with heavier blades."

"The captain says you're better with it than most new undercaptains."

"So does the majer. He also said that's not good enough. From just what I saw in the south valley, he's right."

Eshlyn actually laughs, if softly. "I'm not sure anything's good enough for the majer. That's why the Lancers are what they are."

Lerial can definitely see that, and from Eshlyn's questions, Lerial gets a definite feel that, much as he hates to admit it, his father was right to send him to Kinaar, especially since it's clear that Eshlyn, and probably most Lancers, aren't likely to blindly follow him or Lephi, whether or not they're the Duke's sons. "I take it he's the reason why Afrit and Heldya haven't taken over Cigoerne."

"As much as anyone is . . . excepting that Duke Kiedron knew to back the majer all the way."

Lerial can't say much to that . . . and doesn't. Since Eshlyn isn't inclined to say more, another glass goes by without much passing between the two.

Finally, Lerial asks, "How did you come to be a Lancer . . . if I might ask?"

"Simple enough. My da was a goat herder, south of Ensenla, little place called Penecca. Just north of the border between Afrit and Cigoerne. Was then, anyway. Now Penecca's part of Cigoerne. That's another story. I had three older brothers. Herd wasn't big enough all for us. So I was looking. One day a bunch of Afritan armsmen rode through headed south. They took a third of the goats. Butchered some right there, and ate 'em for supper. Took the rest with them. Two eightdays later, they're riding back. A lot less of them. Some were wounded. They took a couple more goats. I snuck up to their camp and listened. Didn't hear that much, except that they'd tried something, and they'd got whipped by some Lancers." Eshlyn grins. "Knew I wanted to be part of anything that'd pay back Duke Atroyan. Walked all the way to Cigoerne. Guards at the gate to the old Lancer post wanted to turn me away. Submajer Jhalet—he was a fresh captain then—he said anyone who walked eighty kays to join the Lancers ought to be given a chance. The majer agreed. Here I am."

"I'm glad you are." Lerial nods. He isn't certain he would have had that determination, not walking eighty kays into an unknown land.

He's worried enough about returning to Cigoerne.

Cigoerne

XXV

A good glass past sunset on fiveday, with barely the faintest trace of twilight left in the western sky, Lerial, Eshlyn, and the half squad of Lancers accompanying them ride into the north courtyard of the palace. Lerial is stiff and sore in a few places, but not nearly so much as he thought he might be.

Undercaptain Woelyt strides forward to meet them. "What detachment is this? No one was expected at the palace this evening."

Eshlyn glances to Lerial, who eases the bay he has ridden for the latter part of the day forward.

"I fear I'm the cause of the unexpected detachment, Undercaptain."

Woelyt looks up quizzically, starts to say something, then stops. After a moment, he goes on. "Lord Lerial . . . there was no word . . ."

"No . . . I imagine there wasn't. When Commander Altyrn felt my training was completed, he sent me back to Cigoerne with the dispatch rider and this escort party." Lerial inclines his head. "Squad Leader Eshlyn was kind enough to take on the duty."

"Ser." Eshlyn nods to the undercaptain. "We were to escort Lord Lerial to the palace and then continue to Lancer headquarters."

"I won't keep you," replies Woelyt. "You're relieved of escort duty. Report to headquarters as ordered."

"Thank you, ser." Eshlyn gestures, and one of the rankers rides forward holding the lead to Lerial's gelding.

Lerial takes the lead. "Thank you." Then he turns back to Eshlyn. "And thank you . . . and your men."

"Our pleasure, ser."

Lerial has the feeling that the squad leader actually means it, especially since he smiles before he orders, "Squad! Turn! Forward!"

Neither Woelyt nor Lerial speaks for a moment

Finally, the undercaptain looks up to the still-mounted Lerial. "I didn't recognize you at first."

"I doubt I'm much taller," Lerial says wryly.

"Some, but you're broader across the shoulders and not so pale. You ride like an officer . . ."

Lerial can sense relief behind Woelyt's words. *Did I ride that badly before?* Somehow . . . he doesn't think that is it.

". . . I'll send a messenger to let your mother know you've returned."

"My father?"

"He's in the north with the Lancers. Near the border. There have been more raids."

"Have many been hurt? Crops or herds lost?"

"A few. Your father had posted more patrols there before the raids began."

Lerial nods, then dismounts and begins to walk both horses toward the stable. "I need to get the horses settled."

"The duty ostler can handle that, ser."

Lerial smiles. "Tonight, anyway." He understands Woelyt's unvoiced hint that his mother would prefer to see him sooner, rather than later.

Even so, after turning the mounts over to the ostler, he does carry his personal gear up to his own dark chamber before heading down the corridor to his parents' rooms. He steps into the sitting room to see his mother and aunt sitting in the armchairs at each end of the settee. A single wall lamp is lit. Stifling a grin, he says, "I'm sorry to be late, but we rode straight through." He makes his way to the settee, prepared for a gentle grilling, and seats himself, sitting forward and adjusting the sabre and scabbard.

"That's a long ride for one day," offers Emerya.

"We headed out well before sunrise. The Lancers had spare mounts. So I have two stabled here. Tomorrow, I'll need to return the bay to Lancer headquarters."

"Majer Altyrn . . . he did not send word to expect you."

Lerial notes the concern in his mother's voice, but before he can say anything, Emerya speaks.

"The majer can't be too displeased. Lerial's wearing a sabre."

"Oh . . . I didn't notice, dear. Was that a gift?"

"It's an old Lancer sabre from many years ago that he had. He thought it suited me, and I think he was right."

"Why was your return so hasty?" presses Xeranya.

So hasty? After two seasons? Lerial pushes those questions away. "The majer took me on a long ride through the southern valley south of the Wooded Ridges. He persuaded Captain Graessyr to provide a half squad of Lancers as an escort." Lerial pauses just slightly before continuing. "We ran into a band of Meroweyan raiders."

"You didn't . . . ," begins Xeranya.

"We didn't have much choice." Lerial is trying to keep his response ambiguous, without explaining why he felt they had no choice. "They attacked us. The Lancers took the brunt of the attack."

"You had to fight—personally—didn't you?" asks Emerya.

Xeranya glances at Emerya, not quite quizzically.

"He's changed. More than meets the eye," replies Emerya, who then turns her gaze on Lerial. "What happened?"

"Some of them got past the Lancers . . ." Lerial goes on to explain all that happened, although he does not actually say that he killed the one raider, and ends up by saying, "We rode back the next day, and the majer sent word to Cigoerne. He arranged for me to leave two days after that . . . well . . . a full day and two nights after we got back."

"He shouldn't have . . . ," begins Xeranya.

"He didn't have any choice. He was using the terrain to teach me tactics. There haven't been raiders that far north in years." Lerial's words are matter-of-fact, not with effort or deceit, but because they're true. "Even the majer's consort was upset and surprised that we encountered raiders."

"I would think so." Xeranya's words are cool, too cool.

For a moment, Lerial doesn't know what to say, but he does want to know more. "Why? Because she's Heldyan?"

"That's true."

"I know," Lerial replies. "She said she was born in Heldya and raised in Amaershyn."

"She's a very lovely person," adds Emerya. "The majer was fortunate to find her."

"She was more fortunate that he did." Xeranya's voice remains cool.

"She's been good for him, and he deserves that after all he's done," replies Emerya.

"I can't deny that," replies Xeranya in a tone that belies her words. "Anyway, we're glad you're back safely."

"Lephi's out on patrol somewhere?"

"He's in Narthyl," affirms Xeranya. "With Overcaptain Carlyt. There were reports of some Heldyan armsmen on the west side of the river."

"Weren't there Meroweyan raiders near Narthyl as well? Earlier?"

"There were," answers Emerya.

So Lephi has an overcaptain to watch out for him. Rather than say that, Lerial merely nods and waits.

"We shouldn't be keeping you up longer," Xeranya says. "We'll see you in the morning."

"What about the girls?"

"They're both fine," replies Emerya.

"Good."

"It is getting late . . . ," offers Xeranya.

Lerial doesn't press or question, but stands.

So does Emerya. "I need to check on Amaira."

"I will see you both at breakfast." Xeranya remains seated.

Once Lerial and Emerya are out in the corridor and well away from his parents' chambers, Lerial looks to his aunt. "She wasn't all that pleased to see me."

"She's worried. Wouldn't you be if one son just came back from a fight that wasn't supposed to have happened, another is riding patrols where there might be Heldyan armsmen, and your consort is fighting raiders and who knows who else in the north?"

Lerial can see that, but still thinks his mother was rather cool. "Why doesn't Mother like Maeroja?"

"She thought Altyrn should have consorted a Cyadoran. There were so few men, except for the Lancers, and most of them were rankers," replies Emerya. "There were only a handful of officers, all junior. As the senior Lancer officer in Cigoerne, the majer should have consorted one of the Magi'i young women. That's what Xeranya felt. She's never forgiven him for that."

"Why?"

"Her sister Zanobya was interested . . ."

"I thought she ran off with a merchanter in Swartheld."

"She did. After Altyrn ignored her advances. She was never happy here. She missed the luxuries of Cyad."

"We have everything . . ."

"Lerial . . . we have *nothing* compared to what we had in Cyad. The palace here is the size of a villa that a small outland merchanter in Cyad might have possessed. The Palace of Light towered into the evening, ablaze with lights. The streets were all paved with white stone, harder than a cupridium blade. The awnings were all green, all the same shade. The piers where ships from across the seas docked were of white stone. Every delicacy appeared at table . . ."

"You've never said . . ."

"None of us ever have. Your grandmere would have torn out our tongues. What's past is past—that was what she always said. She told us that

Cyad had once been a tiny town, and that we had to rebuild just as those from the Rational Stars had to rebuild."

"She said all that?"

"She did. She was right. We can't dream about a past we can never reclaim. The future is all we can change."

Abruptly, Lerial truly understands. His aunt was born in the height of luxury and has lost more than anyone who survived the fall of Cyador. She has no consort and no hope of one. She has no real position in Cigoerne. She has only her healing and her daughter . . . and scandal behind Amaira's birth, and some small security in living in a palace that is nothing compared to where she had been raised.

Emerya says nothing in the dimness of the corridor.

Lerial looks toward the steps some twenty yards ahead, and the palace guard stationed there, and then back to his aunt.

"That's not anywhere close to a standard Lancer blade, you know?" Emerya's voice is matter-of-fact.

"I know. But the majer said it should belong to me."

"So it should. So it should." She offers an enigmatic smile, then says, "You killed the raider who attacked you, didn't you?"

"How did you know?"

"You'll come to recognize that, and other things, if you continue developing your abilities. You've been healing, haven't you?"

"Yes."

"Good." She pauses, then adds, "I'd avoid Saltaryn until your father returns. You might spend time sparring with the more experienced Lancers at headquarters—using blunted blades and armor—and occasionally accompanying me to the healing hall."

Lerial frowns. *Why is she suggesting both, when Saltaryn . . .* "You think I need both skills. Might I ask why?"

"You might. Those who rule and those who advise rulers must always balance contradictions in order to succeed. Usually those conflicting contradictions involve power. Learning more about healing and more about war will begin to teach you balance . . . and that will prove useful."

"You haven't advised either Lephi or Father that way."

"Why do you think that?"

"I don't think you have. You've said they're order-blind." After a long moment, he asks, "What do you expect of me?"

"To be the best person you can, and you can't be that unless you develop all your skills."

Lerial cannot argue with that . . . although he knows his father would oppose what Emerya is proposing . . . if he knew.

"Good night, Lerial."

"Good night." Still thinking about all the undercurrents behind the evening's conversation, and his mother's coolness, he makes his way toward his chamber. At least . . . his chamber for a while.

XXVI

Sixday morning, after breakfast, Lerial rides along the southeast boulevard toward the Lancer compound that holds the headquarters building. He is leading the bay he borrowed to complete the journey from Brehaal the afternoon before, and four Lancer rankers accompany him—the fewest he could persuade Undercaptain Woelyt to provide as an escort . . . and that few only because Lerial is wearing Lancer gear. Since it is almost winter, not that winter is especially cold in the north of Hamor, except for perhaps a few eightdays near the middle of the season, the sun is not all that high in the eastern sky, and Lerial is grateful for the jacket and visor cap.

As he rides, junior squad leader Jhubyl beside him, Lerial studies the houses and shops that flank the boulevard. He cannot help but think about his aunt's words. The largely brick dwellings, with their reddish tile roofs, even those of two stories, look somehow shorter and more squat than he remembers. *But how much of what you see is colored by what Emerya said about Cyad?*

Abruptly, he turns in the saddle. "Jhubyl . . . what other towns have you seen along the river?"

"Ser? On the Swarth? Not all that many. Naemersuh, Penecca, Saarthyn."

Of course he wouldn't have seen that many. Most of the towns in Cigoerne aren't on the Swarth. That was because it had always been too easy for the Heldyans to raid towns on the west bank of the Swarth. So most towns were on the Thylan or the Lynaar, or on smaller streams. The continual Heldyan raids were also another reason why Duke Atroyan's sire had been willing to allow Lerial's grandmere to purchase lands on the west bank.

"What other towns have you been through or posted in?"

"Been in Bartheld, Brehaal, Teilyn . . . lots of hamlets . . . places without names . . ."

"How many have brick houses like the ones in Teilyn or here in Cigo-erne?"

"They all have some . . . excepting maybe Penecca. Not many have lots, though."

"Have you ever seen Amaershyn?"

"Just from across the river. There are some bigger places there. Least-wise, looks that way. Hard to tell with the walls, though."

Lerial thinks about asking what Jhubyl recalls of Cyad, but then realizes that the squad leader likely isn't old enough to recall anything, if he even came from Cyador, and that is unlikely, given his slightly darker complex-ion.

As they ride up to the gates of the Lancer compound, one of the duty guards calls out, "Jhubyl! See you got caught bringing back the mount the Duke's boy borrowed."

Before the squad leader can answer, Lerial replies good-naturedly, "No, he got tasked with escorting the Duke's boy who's bringing back the mount himself."

The duty guard, who looks younger than Lerial himself, gulps visibly and looks to Lerial. "Ah . . . sorry, ser."

"It's a fair question," Lerial adds to the guard as he rides past, "but better asked more privately." He smiles politely.

"Yes, ser."

Once they're well past the young guard, Jhubyl shakes his head and laughs softly. "He'll think twice before wising off on duty again."

"At least, wising off loudly," replies Lerial. "You'll have to lead the way to the stable. I've not been here before."

"You haven't, ser?" Jhubyl is clearly surprised.

"The only Lancer posts I've visited are the ones at Brehaal and Teilyn." Lerial does not point out that he is only barely old enough at sixteen—*much closer to seventeen now*—to be considered for a beginning Lancer ranker. "I'd also like to see Majer Phortyn . . . or whoever's in charge if he's not here. Where would I find him?"

"In the headquarters building. That's the six-sided one in the middle of the courtyard there." Jhubyl points. "Might be better if I went with you. Begging your pardon, ser, but you look much like a green recruit."

"That might be for the best."

Once Lerial has turned the bay over to the duty ostler and made temporary arrangements for his gelding, he and Jhubyl walk across the courtyard from the stable to the headquarters building.

Once inside, Jhubyl steps forward, toward the older ranker who is seated behind a table-desk in the foyer, then halts. "Lord Lerial, here, just got back from Teilyn."

The look of boredom vanishes from the ranker's face.

"If Major Phortyn has a moment," says Lerial politely, "I'd like to talk to him, if he's here, or whoever's in charge, if he's not."

"He's here, ser. If you'll let me see if he has a moment."

"Thank you."

The ranker knocks on the study door, then opens it, and slips inside, returning almost immediately. "Please go in, ser."

"Thank you." Lerial eases past the table-desk and through the open study door, closing it behind him.

Phortyn stands behind a table-desk only slightly larger than that of the ranker's in the receiving area. He is a small and wiry man at least several digits shorter than Lerial, with the weathered face of a fair-skinned man who has seen too much sun in his life. His gray eyes are hard. "Lord Lerial. You wished to see me?"

"I did, ser." Lerial waits.

"You're wearing Lancer gear, I notice."

And not all that favorably. "That is what Majer Altyrn and Captain Graessyr suggested. I'm not wearing insignia, and I know I'm not a Lancer."

"Then why the gear and why are you here, if I might ask?"

Lerial doesn't care for the majer's tone, but he smiles apologetically. "Majer Altyrn felt that my wearing Lancer gear would call less attention to me and create fewer problems for the Lancers who escorted me. I'm here because Captain Graessyr was concerned about the raiders we encountered and felt that there would be more trouble over the winter. When I returned to Cigoerne, I discovered that my father is dealing with raiders in the north, and my brother is riding patrols in the south."

"And might I ask what that has to do with your presence?"

"It's likely that I may be called to do something earlier than my father thought would be necessary. I've spent the last two seasons working with a sabre under Majer Altyrn and Captain Graessyr. They think my technique is sound, but that I need more experience against other experienced Lancers. I'd like to see if that is possible."

Phortyn's expression remains impassive, but Lerial can sense that the majer feels strongly. About what, Lerial cannot tell, and he again waits.

"Why now?"

"So that I can learn enough to be effective on patrols when the time comes and so that those Lancers with whom I may have to ride will be confident in my abilities and will not feel that I am a burden that detracts from their duties."

"You're practical. I can see that. Two seasons with Altyrn?"

"Yes, ser."

A wintry smile crosses Phortyn's lined face. "I suppose we should see. Because you are the Duke's son, I'd like to see what you can do with wooden wands first. I'll match you with Captain Chaen. He's in charge of blade training."

"That's fair," replies Lerial. "You only have my unsupported word." *And I need you to trust my word.*

"Scarcely unsupported, but no man is the best judge of his own abilities."

Lerial does not contest that.

"Well . . . let's find the captain."

Captain Chaen is near the armory. He is also wiry, as many Lancers appear to be, but is a good head taller than Majer Phortyn. A quizzical look crosses his narrow face and vanishes almost immediately as Phortyn and Lerial approach.

"Captain . . . I'd like you to spar with Lord Lerial here. He's requested the opportunity to spar with more experienced Lancers. I'd like your opinion as to whether that would be beneficial for him at present. I thought you might start with wands."

"Yes, ser." Chaen looks Lerial over. "You've had some experience?"

"I've spent the last two seasons training under Majer Altyrn in Teilyn."

Another quizzical look appears and vanishes even more quickly than the first as the captain says, "Let me get a pair of wands." He steps into the armory and returns carrying several wands. "If you'd choose one?"

Lerial immediately decides against the smallest wand, then takes the largest and hefts it, then sets it aside. There is something wrong about its balance. The third wand is acceptable, although lighter than he would ideally prefer. "This one."

Chaen nods slightly and returns the other two wands to the armory, returning with yet another wand similar to the one Lerial has taken, if somewhat more battered. "The nearest exercise circle is over there."

Lerial follows the captain and takes a position on the south edge, but to the west, so that neither he nor the captain would directly face the morning sun.

Chaen advances, and Lerial steps forward, concentrating, then slipping Chaen's opening attack and countering. The captain parries the counter, and Lerial forces Chaen's wand down, but has to retreat and slip Chaen's counterattack—simply because the captain is stronger. Even so, Lerial manages to avoid being struck, although twice he has to move quickly and is almost hit.

After less than a quarter glass, Chaen steps back, then lowers his wand. "You've trained with more than wands, haven't you?"

"Blunted blades and padded armor," Lerial admits.

Chaen turns to the majer. "I'd like to see what he can do with a blade and not a wand."

Phortyn nods, almost grudgingly, Lerial feels, then walks away. Chaen motions for Lerial to enter the armory.

Lerial is glad for the respite as he dons the padded armor and selects a blunted sabre from among those hung on one wall of the armory. Chaen is noticeably stronger than either Graessyr or Majer Altyrn, although Lerial questions whether Chaen's actual technique is as good as the older majer's. Then, strength is a form of technique as well, since a stronger man can wear down one with less strength and stamina, assuming that the technique of the stronger fighter is not significantly worse.

Majer Phortyn is nowhere to be seen when Lerial takes the circle again against the captain. For the first few engagements, Lerial feels hard-pressed, as though he is barely avoiding being struck or being maneuvered into ever more dangerous positions, but he slowly begins to gain an awareness, a sense of knowing, and then, for several moments, perhaps longer, Lerial has the absolute sense of knowing where the captain's blade is going to be . . . and for those moments, he is able to slip, deflect, or parry, and even attack once and score a solid but not overpowering strike on Chaen's breastplate.

The captain dances back. "Would have been better with a side cut there."

Lerial nods. "I can see that, ser, but I didn't know how to get there from the parry."

"Oh . . ." Chaen shakes his head. "For a time there, I forgot you haven't been at this that long. Let me show you how to go from either a block or parry into a side cut that won't expose you."

Lerial concentrates as the captain demonstrates and then walks Lerial through the moves. It takes several times before Lerial feels he knows what to do . . . and he hopes he can remember when the next opportunity arises.

After that, Chaen steps back and walks over to Majer Phortyn, who has reappeared.

"Well?"

"He's better than most juniors. He even pressed me once or twice. He's right, though. He needs more experience against different people. He was a bit awkward with me to begin with, but once he saw what I was doing, he got better quickly."

Phortyn frowns, if momentarily.

"If he can be here early every morning," Chaen goes on, "we can work him in with the officers. It would be good for them as well."

The majer turns to Lerial. "Can you be here at seventh glass every morning? Every morning but eightday mornings?"

"Yes, ser." One way or another, Lerial *will* work that out.

"Then we'll see you at seventh glass tomorrow."

"Yes, ser."

The majer turns and walks several yards away from the sparring circle, beckoning for the captain to join him. Lerial waits, uncertain of what to do, not wanting to turn his back on the officers and knowing he should not interrupt their conversation. He listens, as well as he can, low as their voices are.

". . . could be a problem . . . want to take that on . . ."

". . . wish more of them were like that . . ."

". . . least knows what he has to prove . . . most don't . . ." Phortyn says more before he turns and walks back toward the headquarters building, but Lerial cannot catch the words.

Even so, that grudging and limited approval from the majer is encouraging, in the sense that he is willing to look, if skeptically, at what Lerial can and will do.

Chaen walks back toward Lerial, then halts. "Might I ask why you did this yourself, Lord Lerial?"

"Because I fear that I may be needed sooner than expected, and because my father may not return from the north that soon. If I waited, that time would be lost, and perhaps some of the skills I have learned so far, if they are not reinforced."

Chaen offers a faint smile. "I hope you are wrong. Even if you are, more training and experience cannot hurt."

The two walk back toward the armory, Lerial hoping that he has not stepped too far out of line, but feeling that he is doing what is right . . . and necessary.

XXVII

When he returns to the palace, Lerial simply tells his mother and his aunt, and Undercaptain Woelyt, that he is supposed to continue the training begun by Majer Altyrn by learning more about arms at Lancer headquarters. While Emerya hides a faint smile, she says nothing. His mother merely says, "Doing what your father arranged is for the best."

Undercaptain Woelyt nods approvingly, especially after Lerial tells him that Captain Chaen is in charge of his sparring and training. "Good man. Strong as an ox with a blade. You hold your own against him, and no one will beat you down just on strength."

On sevenday, Lerial spars first against Chaen—with blunted blades and padded armor, and then against Veraan, a young undercaptain, "young" meaning likely only a few years older than Lerial himself. Lerial discovers that what Altyrn and Chaen had earlier observed is indeed true because it is quickly clear that Lerial is far better than the young officer. He also understands Chaen's reasoning about the two pairings. The first is to show the other officers that Lerial is good enough to go against the senior captain, and the second is to show the junior officers that Lerial is already above them . . . and that his working with more experienced officers is not a result of favoritism, but skill.

While he does not spar on eightday, he is at Lancer headquarters before seventh glass on oneday, twoday, threeday, and fourday, and he spends more than a glass in padded armor working against various officers. Then he returns to the palace and studies the handful of tactics books from his father's small study, as well as the maps of the areas around the lands held by his father. He does write as gracious a letter as he can to Majer Altyrn, thanking him for his hospitality and all the instruction provided, and arranges for it to be dispatched.

In his sparring, one thing does not change immediately. For the first few moments, even for a fraction of a glass, of each session with an officer with whom Lerial has not sparred, he feels awkward and has to be especially alert and careful, although by the end of his session on fourday morning, he is beginning to feel as though the awkwardness and uneasiness is not lasting as long as it once did.

Because his presence at Lancer headquarters rests on both his position and a certain sufferance by Majer Phortyn, Lerial makes a continuing effort to be polite and deferential to all the Lancer officers, without being obsequious or fawning. He does make a practice of taking a second set of greens with him to headquarters and washing up in the officers' quarters after his sessions, because he is invariably soaked and smelly when he finishes.

On fourday, this is especially necessary, because he has promised to meet Emerya at the Hall of Healing after he has finished his sessions at Lancer headquarters and to spend the day at the Hall.

He is just finishing donning clean and dry greens when Lauxyn, one of the older undercaptains, appears. He is the only undercaptain, besides Veraan, whom Chaen has allowed to spar with Lerial, perhaps because Lauxyn is clearly more experienced, and most likely a former squad leader recently promoted to undercaptain because of his skills.

"Might I ask why you work so hard, ser?"

Sensing honest curiosity, rather than scheming or some other chaos, Lerial decides to answer, if cautiously. "I don't ever wish to be a burden on any Lancers." He grins ruefully. "At least not any burden that I can possibly avoid. Being as good as I can with a blade and learning as much as I can might just help."

"They say the Duke is good with a blade."

"He is. That's another reason."

Lauxyn nods politely. "How long will you be doing this? Do you know?"

"At least until my father returns from the north. After that, he'll decide. He wanted me to improve my training in his absence." That is somewhere between a guess and a fabrication, but it is certainly not impossible, given his father's expectations.

"You could ride some patrols now."

"I hope I've learned enough for that, but that's for my father and Majer Phortyn to decide."

Lauxyn offers a brief smile. "You should be ready when they decide." He slips away, leaving Lerial alone in the small chamber.

After Lauxyn leaves, Lerial straps on his sabre, then dons his unmarked Lancer visor cap and stuffs his damp training greens into the kit bag, before making his way to the stable and his waiting escort, again headed by Jhubyl, who alternates with Fhanyd, the other junior squad leader in the company assigned to the palace.

In moments, the five riders are outside the headquarters' gates and following the river boulevard north toward the Hall of Healing.

"You're sure you don't mind riding around with me?" asks Lerial.

"No, ser. It beats the duties at the Palace. Besides, that's part of what we're there for. It's more interesting than checking guard posts . . . or making sure the younger rankers aren't messing with the kitchen girls . . . on duty, that is."

As they ride through the River Square—almost due east of the palace—Lerial glances at the river piers . . . and frowns. There is not a single flatboat tied up there. And the only sailing craft are two used by the Lancers on their patrols. He cannot remember a time when he has seen the piers so empty.

Because the harvests were so poor in the south? Or could the Heldyans have blocked the river at Amaershyn? Or just coincidence?

Much as it could be, Lerial has trouble believing it is coincidental. *But it could be.*

North of the River Square are the factorages of the larger merchanters in Cigoerne. Even they look less busy than he recalls. Is it that he remembers just the busier times? He looks toward Jhubyl. "Are things here quieter than usual?"

"It'd be hard to say, ser, but I can't say I've often seen the river piers so empty."

"That's what I thought, but I wondered if it was my imagination."

"Be mine, too, then, ser."

"I know the Heldyans blocked the river at Amaershyn some years back. Do you think they could have tried that again?"

"I wouldn't know, ser. The captain didn't mention anything this morning, and there wasn't any watertalk like that at headquarters."

Still . . . Lerial wonders.

When they reach the Hall and rein up outside the stable, Jhubyl asks, "You're sure you don't want us to stay?"

"Thank you, but I'll ride back with my aunt and her escorts."

"Yes, ser."

Jhubyl and the rankers do wait until Lerial has seen his mount stabled and walks into the Hall of Healing before they turn and ride westward toward the palace.

Lerial makes his way to the first door inside the Hall and enters.

The older woman in pale green, perhaps the same one who had been sitting behind the table-desk the previous time he had been in the Hall, looks up. "Lord Lerial, Lady Emerya requested that you join her in the receiving room."

"Thank you." Lerial smiles and turns, making his way along the long corridor to the south end of the building and the receiving room.

He is about to enter the receiving area when Emerya steps out. "Good. You're here."

"Why did you want me to come today?" asks Lerial.

"I'd appreciate it if you'd come every day after your sessions with the Lancers. We're shorthanded here. We had to send the men who are healers north to help your father's wounded. We'll see what you can do—or help me do—today. If you can do what I think you can, you can treat lesser wounds by yourself before long."

"Father's wounded? And you didn't tell me?"

"He's not wounded. He sent word to your mother yesterday. A large group of raiders attacked Penecca. He and his Lancers drove them out. A company of Afritan armsmen attacked. They claimed that Penecca belonged to Duke Atroyan. Your father and his men killed a great many of them, and the rest fled, but many Lancers were wounded. Your father fears that there will be more Afritan attacks."

"I didn't think men could be healers." Lerial knows that's not strictly so, but he finds he's slightly irritated, especially at not having been told what has happened in the north.

"That's not so, and you know it."

"Why didn't you tell me about Father?"

"Your mother asked me not to last night."

"She didn't say anything this morning." That's not exactly fair, Lerial also knows, because he left before his mother had come down for breakfast. *But someone should have told you.*

"Lerial . . ."

"Someone should have told me."

"You'll have to take that up with your mother." Emerya looks at Lerial. "We need to get to work. Come with me."

Lerial follows her from the receiving room back to the entry room, where Emerya insists Lerial leave his sabre, and then to a room with a woman lying on a pallet. She is young, perhaps not even as old as Lerial, and her bulging abdomen and the pain in her face indicates why she is there. The fact that most poor women give birth at home suggests that she is in some sort of danger . . . or that the unborn child is.

"What can you tell me?" murmurs Emerya.

Lerial does his best to sense the order patterns around the young woman. He swallows.

"That's what I thought. But what do you sense?"

"The child is weak, and there's all sorts of chaos around her stomach . . . her abdomen . . . like she's been beaten . . ."

"She has, but that's just part of the problem. Can you strengthen the order of the child? Just a tiny bit . . . too much could kill her."

"Her?"

"You'll learn to sense the difference. I need to help the mother."

"I can do that."

While Emerya and a midwife help the girl, Lerial stands back slightly and eases tiny flows of order into the child, as directed by Emerya.

More than a glass later, a baby girl rests in the arms of her mother.

Emerya turns to Lerial. "Thank you."

"You could have done what I did."

She shakes her head. "Not at the same time. There was chaos all around the birth canal. I had to keep that from her and from the child."

When they leave that chamber, they find that a woman perhaps ten years younger than Emerya stands out in the corridor. She wears faded brown, and her head scarf is worn and has fallen away from her face and across her shoulders. Her face is damp. With her is a grizzled man.

"You should not be here," Emerya says quietly to the man. "This part of the Hall is for those who need healing."

"How is she?" pleads the woman. "My Irnina?"

"She will be well. She has a daughter."

"A daughter?" growls the man, whose skin is darker than Emerya's and Lerial's, but much lighter than that of most Hamorians. "She should not have . . . she has brought dishonor upon my house!"

"Why?" asks Lerial politely. "Because she bore a child?"

"Because she is not consorted and the child is a girl. Unwanted boys are worth something." He turns away and marches toward the south entrance to the Hall.

"But how is my Irnina?" asks the woman.

"Her body will heal from the beating," replies Emerya. "Her daughter will be healthy."

"Let her stay here, I beg you, Lady Healer."

"She can stay for a few days."

"Thank you . . ."

Lerial eases back while Emerya talks to the girl's mother. His eyes turn to follow the older man, but he has already left the Hall.

For the remainder of the day, Lerial does what his aunt directs. He even cleans a workman's wound and stitches it closed, if under Emerya's close watch, and helps her set a broken arm.

Slightly past fourth glass, Lerial washes up for the fourth or fifth time since he entered the Hall and then reclaims his sabre, and joins his aunt and her Lancer escorts outside the small stable by the north wall. The sky is clear, but a cool wind blows out of the southeast as they mount up and then ride out through the gates toward the Palace. Lerial rides beside Emerya.

"There weren't that many people who needed healing today," he says.

"Some days are like that. Some days the receiving room is filled, and the sick and injured spill out into the Hall and outside the south entry." Emerya pauses, then asks, "What did you think of the father of that woman who had the little girl?"

Lerial can sense that the question is more than casual. "He didn't seem to think women are worth much. Especially girls. A lot of Hamorians don't, it seems . . . at least from what I've heard."

"Did you like Maeroja?"

Lerial frowns. What does Maeroja have to do with Hamorian men valuing women? He guesses. "She left Heldya because she felt unvalued? Is that why she consorted the majer?"

"Not a bad guess," says Emerya dryly. "She's somehow related to the Duke of Heldya, and Maeroja is not her birth name. She's never said what it was, and I'd guess she never will. She was rowing a small boat across the Swarth River, and several flatboats with Heldyan armsmen were chasing her. Majer Altyrn used the firecannon on the *Kerial* to destroy two of the boats. That was the last time the cannon was used. . . ."

There is something more behind those words, but Lerial cannot say what and loses some of what his aunt is saying.

". . . turned part of the river to steam. Altyrn and his Lancers rescued her, and he insisted that she change into a Lancer uniform. Then he used a firelance on her clothes and the boat and had it beached on the west side of the Swarth, farther downstream, later that night."

"Why were they chasing her?"

"One of the Duke's close friends tried to take advantage of her. She gutted him with his own blade and fled. So did her sister. The mob killed her sister . . . after . . . Maeroja hid for days before she found a boat that wasn't closely watched . . . but there was a reward for her return."

"All Hamorians are like that? About women?"

"Most of them. Not all, but most. We didn't wear head scarves in Cyador, you know? Oh . . . Cyad wasn't perfect for women, either. Your grandfather gave in to the demands that women be put in their place. He was the one who insisted on the gilded chains for women who weren't healers."

"He was?" This is something that Lerial has not heard.

"Mother—your grandmere—collected all the chains from every woman on the *Kerial* and had them melted down. The gold helped pay for the lands that are now Cigoerne."

Lerial is more than a little confused—not about women being less valued, or valued little, but as to why Emerya has brought up the matter.

"You're wondering why I'm telling you all this?"

"Yes," he admits.

"Lephi is like your grandfather, and your father. I don't wish to see Amaira or Ryalah, or their daughters or granddaughters, treated the way women were in the last days of Cyad or in the way the Hamorians treat them."

"Or the way that man did."

Emerya nods.

"What do you think I can do?"

"Far more than you think you can right now. I don't expect anything from you now. I just want you to think about it."

"I will," he promises, knowing that he owes her that, and possibly much more.

His aunt does not offer another word on the ride back to the palace.

Once they arrive, Lerial dismounts, then grooms the gelding and sees to his feed and water before leaving the stable. He is headed toward his chambers to wash up before going to the north courtyard for refreshments when Saltaryn steps out of a doorway.

"Lord Lerial."

"Magus Saltaryn."

"I understand you have been back in Cigoerne for almost an eightday, and yet I have not seen you."

"I've been busy with arms training at Lancer headquarters . . . and studying tactics and maps as well."

Saltaryn looks to say something, then shakes his head. "Perhaps that's for the best." He smiles, almost sadly. "Best of fortune, Lord Lerial."

For all of his acquiescence, Saltaryn does not sound exactly pleased, but Lerial merely says, "Thank you. I appreciate that."

Saltaryn steps aside, and Lerial continues to his chambers.

XXVIII

Lerial is about to leave the officers' quarters at Lancer headquarters on sixday, after changing into clean greens, when his fingers touch the silken pouch—and the lodestone—he still carries. Why, he isn't certain, except that Rojana had intimated that it was important. Yet while he can sense the faintest flow of order and chaos around it, it is comparatively faint, and he wonders how that might help with handling order. And where did Rojana find it? He pushes away his thoughts on why she has given it to him and slips the pouch and lodestone into his jacket when he hears voices outside.

He thinks he recognizes Lauxyn as one of the two speakers, but not the other man's voice. He stops and listens, but the voices fade, and he can sense the two men moving away. He eases to the doorway, but sees neither. He feels that they have walked around the corner, and he makes his way to the edge of the building and halts, listening.

". . . don't know what you're talking about."

Those words are Lauxyn's. That, Lerial can tell.

"You and Chaen . . . sucking up to the Duke's son . . ."

Lerial *has* to know who is accusing Lauxyn and the captain. He feels that whoever the other man is, he has to be an undercaptain, from the tone of voice and the words used. It's likely that neither man will be looking down, and that the unknown officer might not see if Lerial peers around the corner well below eye height. So he squats and slowly looks, knowing that a sudden movement is more likely to catch someone's eye.

The second officer is Undercaptain Veraan, and his concentration is on Lauxyn.

Lerial moves back and continues to listen. He wishes he could use order to conceal himself, the way some of the great Magi'i were said to be able to do, so that he could move closer, but he cannot. So he remains behind the corner, catching fragments of what passes between the two undercaptains.

". . . don't think the captain would appreciate your views on that."

"I'll deny it . . . and my family will back me up . . ."

Lerial wonders from what family Veraan comes. Perhaps someone at the Palace will know. He stiffens as he senses the two moving, but they are moving away from him. He waits until they have moved well away from the quarters before he begins to walk toward the stables. He does not look back.

Over the past few days, he has been able to sense a certain sliminess about Veraan and wonders if that happened to be one of the reasons Chaen had chosen the slender blond undercaptain as an example when Lerial had first begun to practice with the headquarters' Lancers.

Again, he rides from Lancer headquarters to the healing hall, where he spends the remainder of the day. Emerya was right. This time, unlike on fourday and fiveday, there are many more people needing healers. He ends up dealing with small injuries that have been neglected and worsened, such as animal bites that have turned bad—but not too bad—and a thorn wound that has filled with pus, and before he realizes it, it is past fourth glass and Emerya is informing him that it is time to leave.

He washes up one last time, then makes his way to the stable, where he mounts the gelding and joins his aunt and her escort for the ride back to the palace. For a time, he rides beside her without speaking, glancing toward the heavy clouds to the south and wondering if they are harbingers of the usual winter rain.

"Your stitches are better," Emerya informs him, "and your use of order is more measured."

"Thank you." He pauses, then asks, "What happened to the young woman . . . you know, the one—"

"Whose father thought his granddaughter was worthless? Her mother and an aunt took her away last night. That's what Elnora told me this morning. They said she would be going to live with relatives. They didn't say where."

"What about the child's father?"

"That may be the problem," replies Emerya. "They wouldn't speak about that."

"You don't think . . . ?"

"In healing, you'll see the best and worst of people, more so than in fighting and battles . . . although your father might disagree with me. But then, there are many things about which we don't agree. How was your morning?"

"I'm getting better with the sabre. It's helpful to spar against different officers. There is one thing, though . . ." Lerial turns in the saddle and looks at his aunt.

"Yes?"

"There's an undercaptain at headquarters that I overheard talking about how important his family is. His name is Veraan. I wasn't about to ask him who his parents are, but I wondered if you might know."

Emerya smiles. "It's good you didn't ask, but I don't know everyone of either elthage or altage background here in Cigoerne, not anymore. Oh . . . I might know the parents, if you knew their name, but their children?" She shakes her head.

"I can ask Woelyt if he knows."

"That might be best . . . if asked casually."

Lerial doesn't bridle at her suggestion, not in the way he would have, he realizes, if either Lephi or his father had uttered the same words.

Once they reach the Palace courtyard, and the stables, Lerial takes care of the gelding first and then sets out to find Undercaptain Woelyt, but he doesn't have to look far, because Woelyt is walking toward the stable.

"Good afternoon, ser."

"Good afternoon, Lerial. How is your sparring coming?"

"Well enough, I think. I learn a little more every day."

"Your father will be pleased with your diligence."

"No. He'll expect that. He'd be displeased if I weren't diligent."

Woelyt laughs, if gently. "I can understand that."

"I've run across several undercaptains you might know. One is Lauxyn. He seems good with a sabre."

"He is. He's like me. We came up through the ranks."

"Then there's a younger undercaptain . . . Versaan . . . Veraan . . . I only sparred with him once."

"Oh . . . Veraan. He's pretty junior."

"He was talking about his family . . ." Lerial lets the words just drift, not quite finishing the sentence.

"He's the type. His father's a magus, Apollyn, I think. Doesn't matter who your father is. If you're not good with a blade, you'll still end up dead." Woelyt tilts his head. "How did you do against him?"

"Captain Chaen said he was overmatched against me."

Woelyt cannot quite hide a satisfied smile. "Then you must be doing well."

"The time with Majer Altyrn helped a lot."

"I'm sure it did. I never got a chance to serve under him." Woelyt shakes his head almost regretfully. "Those that did say that he was a fine officer."

Lerial smiles as he replies, "He still is. He's very practical, and I think he and Captain Graessyr talk often."

"Good for Graessyr. Smart, too." Woelyt smiles. "Maybe we should spar when you have some time."

"We should." With a parting smile, Lerial heads for the Palace proper.

By the time he arranges for his soiled greens to be washed and finally reaches the courtyard, his mother is sitting at one of the tables sipping white wine and talking with Emerya. Ryalah and Amaira are at another table, intent on their pegboard. Lerial pours himself a glass of pale lager, perhaps two-thirds full, and takes a seat at his mother's table, to her left.

"You took a while," observes Emerya.

"I had to . . ." Lerial stops as he sees Ryalah marching toward them, her face intent. "What is it?"

"Amaira said you can't go on patrols. She said you're too little."

"I need more training," replies Lerial. "Father will decide when I'm ready."

"I don't see why Lerial can't go on a patrol with Father. He went on a patrol with the majer." Ryalah looks to her mother.

"That was different," says Lerial. "It wasn't really a patrol."

"You fought raiders," insists Ryalah.

"Lerial could go with the majer because the majer isn't Father," replies Xeranya. "He has to know more to go on real patrols, and he can't go with Father, because he's second in line to the throne . . ."

Lerial is struck by his mother's reference to the throne, especially since there is no throne in the palace and since there's no possibility of his father or Lephi ever returning to Candar to rule a Cyador that no longer is.

". . . and if anything happened to both of them, and that can happen in fights, then only Lephi would be left."

"I suppose that wouldn't be good," offers Ryalah.

"Dukes and their heirs should never be fighting in the same places, and preferably not even at the same times," says Xeranya. "There must always be an heir. Now . . . you and Amaira can play at your table or up in your playroom."

"Yes, Mother."

Lerial can sense that behind Ryalah's acquiescence is a certain anger. As his sister walks back to rejoin her cousin, he looks to his aunt inquiringly.

"She's getting to that age where many things are becoming a question of what she sees as fairness," Emerya says quietly.

"She'll have to learn that life isn't always fair," replies Lerial's mother. "It's something we all learn, sooner or later. It costs more the older you are when you learn."

"It's not fair!" Those words come from Ryalah as she glares across the small table at her cousin.

Emerya and Xeranya exchange glances. Then Emerya smiles ruefully and rises. "I'll be back in a moment."

Rather than follow the argument between the girls, Lerial looks to his mother . . . and sees a white oblong shape on the table. "Is that a letter from Father?"

"It is."

"How is he doing?"

"He's well."

"What does he say about the raiders?"

"There are raiders, but they have run them off."

"And the Afritan armsmen?"

Xeranya hands the missive to Lerial. "You can read it for yourself."

Lerial feels he is supposed to refuse the offer, but he does not. Instead, he accepts the letter and begins to read.

My dear—

It appears we will be patrolling the northern borders for several more eightdays.

The Lancers have done well, but it may be well into winter before I can return.

There have been fewer raiders over the last eightday, but there are Afritan patrols just north of Penecca almost every day. It is as if they will wait until we leave before coming south and destroying the town. This is something we cannot allow, particularly now. So we must stay and wait. There are also some Heldyan armsmen across the river who watch us both. That is another reason why we must remain for now.

I am glad to hear that Lerial is training with the Lancers. That will do him good. It will prepare him better for the time when he must ride patrols, and that time may be sooner than either of us might have wished.

The closing is "All my affection."

Somehow, that is so like his father. Lerial does not shake his head, but returns the letter to his mother. "Thank you."

"You're welcome. You should know."

More is implied in those words, but Lerial does not pursue the implications. He understands all too well why his father and several companies of Lancers must remain in the north, especially given that Penecca is only some fifty kays north of Cigoerne. He is saved from the continuation of an awkward silence by the return of Emerya, who now pours herself a glass of lager and sits down at the table, but not in the space between Xeranya and Lerial.

Emerya takes a last look at the small table and two very quiet girls, then lifts her glass and takes a deep draft. When she finishes, she glances at Xeranya, then Lerial, offering an inquiring look.

Lerial offers a smile and says, "Mother, I ran across the name of a magus today. He's the father of an undercaptain by the name of Veraan. The father's name is Apollyn. I wondered if you knew either."

"I don't know the son, but I'm not surprised he's a Lancer officer. Apollyn always did have an excessively high opinion of himself. He wanted to be the tutor here at the Palace. Does the young man take after his father?"

"I don't know. He does say his family is important. What's Apollyn like?"

"He thinks he is important. He claims that his lineage dates back to a first magus in the time of Lorn. Chaaryn . . . or maybe it was Chyenfel. He barely was accepted as a magus, but he consorted with Myra—she was healer from a merchanter family. Very intelligent and perceptive woman . . . enough that she brought all the jewels she could find on the *Kerial.* She even had a number of fire emeralds."

"Like the one in the ring you got from Grandmere?" Lerial has only seen the ring a few times, but he recalls its brilliance and its unmistakable golden-green glint . . . and the fact that there are so few that even a small one is worth more than a hundred golds, and the one in the ring is anything but small.

"Yes. Your grandmere didn't discover that until later. She used those to set up a merchanting factorage—"

"Myrapol House?" asks Emerya. "Is she the one?"

"She *was* the one," replies Xeranya. "She died of a strange flux several years ago. We couldn't save her. Apollyn had a new consort in less than a season—much younger, and far less perceptive."

Lerial nods. "I'd say that Veraan takes after his father."

"Then avoid him if you can. I always have thought his father was a serpent, for all of his warm voice and superficially charming ways. Perhaps more charming than, say, Polidur or Scarthyn, who are almost as venomous."

While his mother has often hinted at her dislikes . . . and made inferences, Lerial has seldom heard such a quietly scathing judgment of a magus, or anyone, from her. He wonders what else she is not saying. "Is there anything else I should know?"

"I believe that's enough, dear."

As Lerial senses his aunt's suppressed amusement, Xeranya turns to Emerya. "I'm glad I've provided you with some amusement, Emerya."

"You have. It has been a very long day. Lerial was most helpful."

"I'm glad of that. Perhaps we could discuss other matters. Do you think we'll have rain this evening? There are clouds in the south."

Emerya shakes her head. "It doesn't feel like it to me. What do you think?"

"I fear you're right. That will make it easier for Kiedron in dealing with the Afritans, but matters will be worse by spring . . ."

Lerial listens.

XXIX

Another two eightdays pass, and, while there are several more letters to Lerial's mother from his father, there are none to Lerial. There is one from Lephi to Xeranya as well, but all it says is that there are some raiders in the south, but not many, and most flee at the sight of the Lancers. The predictions of his mother and his aunt also prove to be true, for, while the clouds of winter roll across Cigoerne, they do not offer the heavy rains that have characterized the early winter eightdays in past years.

Lerial is not certain exactly when it happens, but by sometime late on the first sixday of winter, he has become fully aware of where his opponent's blade will be—before it's there, and he has finally reached the point where he can actually do something with that knowledge . . . and he has not only the technique, but the strength—except when it comes to brute force against Captain Chaen . . . and then he must find ways to exploit technique. He is still weaker than he would prefer on attacks, but almost never can any of the Lancers with whom he has sparred at headquarters penetrate his defenses, largely because, he suspects, he can discern their attacks almost before they develop.

As Lerial is taking off the padded armor outside the armory, Captain Chaen appears. "You've improved measurably over the last three eightdays, Lord Lerial. I'd say that you could hold your own against most now, certainly on defense . . . although it's better not to be defending."

"Am I good enough that Lancers wouldn't worry about that?"

Chaen smiles. "Any Lancer would worry about you, your brother, or your father, but not because you can't handle a blade."

"I wouldn't be as able to do so without your instruction, ser."

Chaen shakes his head. "Majer Altyrn's instruction. I just provided enough different officers so that you could learn how to handle different approaches."

"You showed me things I didn't know," Lerial points out.

"I'll accept that I helped a little," the captain replies. "You don't really need more work . . ."

"But I need to keep in practice, just like your officers, ser."

"Fair enough." Chaen smiles. "Then I'll see you tomorrow."

"Yes, ser." After the captain leaves, Lerial makes his way to the officers' quarters to wash up and change.

When he is finished, he walks back toward the stable. He has planned to ride, as usual, to the Hall of Healing, but when he nears the stable, he sees that there are five rankers with Squad Leader Fhanyd, rather than four.

"Ser," says Fhanyd deferentially, "Lady Xeranya sent a messenger to inform you that she would appreciate your presence at the Palace."

Has something gone wrong? Father? Lephi? Afritan forces riding toward Cigoerne? Lerial pauses slightly to collect himself, then asks, "Did she say why?"

"No, ser." Fhanyd adds after a moment. "It might have to do with your brother's return."

"Is he all right?"

"He looked to be fine, ser," says one of the rankers, presumably the one who had brought the message.

Lerial mounts, then turns to Fhanyd. "If you would send one of the men to the Hall of Healing to inform the Lady Emerya that I've been summoned to the Palace . . . and that it's unlikely I'll be able to be at the Hall this afternoon?"

"Yes, ser." The squad leader turns in the saddle. "Rykkar, ride to the Hall of Healing and give a message to the Lady Emerya that Lord Lerial has been summoned to the Palace and that it is unlikely he will be able to be at the healing hall this afternoon." Fhanyd turns back to Lerial. "Is there anything else, ser?"

"No, thank you." *Not since I don't really know why I've been summoned.*

On the ride back to the Palace, Lerial says little, composing himself for what he fears will be a quiet ordeal of sorts, since he suspects he is being summoned to a small private welcome home for his brother, given that the Lancer messenger had said Lephi appeared well.

He doubts that Emerya has been summoned, but he could be wrong. *Not that you feel you are.*

He also doesn't like the idea that his father is still fighting Afritans, while Lephi is safe . . . *because if anything happens to Father . . .* There's nothing he can do about that possibility, nothing at all.

When he reaches the palace courtyard, Lerial follows his usual pattern of unsaddling and grooming the gelding before he walks to the Palace . . . and turns over his soiled and damp uniforms to one of the maids. Lephi and his mother can just wait a little longer.

He finds his mother and Lephi seated in her salon, with a fire in the hearth, although the Palace does not seem that chill. Lephi has a crystal goblet half filled with red wine resting on the side table beside him. Lerial also notes that he not only wears the uniform of a Lancer officer, but that it is complete with the insignia of an undercaptain.

Both turn to look at him.

"Welcome home!" Lerial makes sure that his greeting is said warmly. There's no point in angering his mother.

Xeranya looks up from her chair with a worried expression. "I wondered what was keeping you, Lerial. I did think that Emerya could do without you for one afternoon so that you could welcome your brother home from patrol."

"I came directly." Lerial offers a pleasant smile as he turns to his brother, who remains seated. "You're looking well. Doing patrols must suit you."

"You look good as well," returns Lephi. "All that extra training must have some benefits. But I suppose you need that to balance the effects of healing."

"It works out." Lerial turns to the sideboard, hoping for some lager, but there are only pitchers for wine. He doesn't really feel like wine, but knows that he is expected to take either the red or the white. He pours less than half a goblet of the white, as the less objectionable of the two vintages, then seats himself on the settee between the armchairs occupied by his mother and brother. Once seated, he lifts the goblet. "To your safe return."

"Thank you," replies Lephi. "I really wasn't in any danger."

"Any patrol could be dangerous. That's something that Majer Altyrn pointed out."

"He must be very old now," says Lephi, after a sip of his wine.

"One wouldn't know it from all that he does. He still handles a wand well."

"That's not the same as a blade."

Lerial refrains from pointing out that the wands Altyrn used to show him moves were actually heavier than real sabres. "No, they aren't, but they do take effort." He smiles again. "Tell me about your patrols . . . well . . . what you haven't already told Mother."

"I haven't said much. We were waiting for you."

"I appreciate that. I came as soon as I knew." *Even if I didn't gallop back in joy.*

"Well . . . as I was telling Mother, patrols aren't quite like what people imagine. There's lots of riding, and most of the time very little happens." Lephi looks guilelessly at Lerial and then continues. "In time, you'll find that out . . . I mean, whenever you start riding patrols."

"I'm sure I will . . . whenever that is." Lerial takes the smallest sip of the wine, which reminds him of vinegar, and offers an attentive expression.

"Anyway . . . we ended up almost three days ride south of Narthyl . . ."

Lerial continues to smile, knowing he is facing a long afternoon.

XXX

Lerial does not see Lephi on sevenday morning, not that he expects to, as early as he leaves for Lancer headquarters. When he returns from the Hall of Healing that afternoon, after riding through a cold south wind that promises either snow or icy rain, he finds Lephi in the main salon, wearing the dress uniform of a Mirror Lancer and talking with their mother. Lephi does not rise when Lerial enters..

"You're going somewhere?" asks Lerial.

"In a while. There's a reception at the villa of First Magus Tyrsalyn. His daughter is pretty enough, but some of her friends are stunning. You should come," suggests Lephi.

"I wasn't invited."

"Who's going to deny the son of the Duke, even the younger son?"

"Even so . . . I think I'll pass."

"You're worried about being too young?" Lephi shakes his head. "Some of the girls will be younger than you are."

"You could go," says Xeranya in a tone that conveys the opposite of her words.

"He could if he wanted. No one will care if he comes with me," Lephi replies.

Exactly! No one will care, except for the wrong reasons. "I think I'll pass. It's been a long week."

"All that bladework tiring you out, brother?"

"Healing is tiring as well."

"Healing?" Lephi raises his eyebrows.

"Yes, healing," says Emerya firmly.

Lerial has sensed her arrival, but has said nothing.

Even Xeranya nods at Emerya's words.

"I suppose a lot falls on you, being the most accomplished healer," Lephi says graciously, not quite pointedly avoiding acknowledging his mother's nod.

"It often does." Emerya moves to the sideboard and pours herself a glass of lager.

Lerial takes the opportunity to do the same, then seats himself on the settee beside his aunt.

"Lerial . . . you never did say how you were coming along with blades," says Lephi.

"Better," replies Lerial.

"That's good. You needed a lot of improvement." He smiles. "We could spar sometime, and I could show you what I've learned."

"Well . . ." Lerial pauses, then goes on, trying to be noncommittal enough, even slightly reluctant enough, that Lephi will insist because he sees a certain weakness in Lerial, "that might be good. Most days, though . . ."

"You don't spar with the Lancers on eightday. They never do."

"That's true. We could spar tomorrow."

"Excellent! I look forward to it." Lephi sets his glass of wine, still more than half full, on the table beside him, and rises. "I must be going before long." He looks to Lerial. "You're sure you don't want to come?"

"Not this time." Lerial smiles politely, with a touch of warmth. "Perhaps when I'm recognized in my own right, as you are." He can sense that Emerya blocks revealing something, almost as if a black haze surrounds her for a moment.

As soon as Lephi leaves, Xeranya looks to Emerya. "What was it that upset you?"

Emerya smiles and shakes her head. "I almost laughed, and that would have upset Lephi . . . unnecessarily." She looks at Lerial. "Do you really think you'll ever be recognized in your own right?"

Not without accomplishing far more than Lephi has. "You're saying that we're only recognized because of our parentage."

"At present . . . isn't that true?" Emerya responds. "Isn't that always true of the children of those with power until they come close to or exceed the accomplishments of their parents?"

"Sometimes," adds Xeranya quietly, "that's true even when a child accomplishes more than the parent."

Lerial understands what she means all too well. His grandfather, from what he has learned in recent years, apparently took actions that led to the destruction of Cyador while his father has built a duchy from almost nothing.

"What people believe is often not true," Emerya agrees, "and sometimes it is most unfair."

"People believe what they wish to believe." Xeranya's words are cool, almost dismissive, yet Lerial senses a weariness behind them. Then she smiles. "We do have a warm dinner, a very gentle burhka, one that even Kiedron would like."

"Will we have snow, do you think?" asks Lerial.

"What do you think?" counters Emerya.

Lerial frowns. Emerya is asking as if he were a weather magus. "I don't know. I've heard that some ordermages and healers can sense what the weather will be. That's why I asked."

Xeranya shakes her head. "Not me. Sometimes your aunt can."

"How do you do that?"

"If a storm is strong enough or near enough, I can feel the patterns of order and chaos." Emerya shrugs. "It's still a bit of a guess, because I've never been able to figure out all the patterns. I do know that when the conflicts between order and chaos are, I'd guess you'd call it 'level,' and the clouds are flatish . . . we usually get a gentle rain . . . and when there are towering white and black clouds, especially white at the top and dark at the bottom and there's a chaotic swirl that's a dull whitish red, that's often going to be a strong thunderstorm. Now . . . the clouds are too far away."

"There are high gray clouds," ventures Lerial.

"High can also be far away."

That makes sense to Lerial, and he sits back slightly and takes a swallow of the lager he has not even sipped.

Lerial is more than happy to have a quiet dinner with his mother and aunt and the girls . . . and then to read in the salon before a fire . . . because a cold rain has begun to fall, and his own chamber will be chill and damp—fine for sleeping, but not for reading—and he only has a single lamp.

That night, after he closes the book on the history of eastern Candar, with the puzzling entry on Duke Heldry, who supposedly stood and challenged a massive thunderstorm, and was thereafter called "Heldry the Mad," he returns to his chamber and opens the shutters. Standing at the window, he tries to sense the clouds above. They do not feel all that "flat" to him, not in the order-sense, but then, the icy rain seems to come and go in gusts and spurts. After that, he tries to see just how far he can extend his reach in feeling what the order currents above are doing. After less than a fifth of a glass, he is exhausted.

Finally, he closes the shutter and climbs under the blankets he so seldom needs.

On eightday, Lerial rises late, for him, at seventh glass. In time, he makes his way down to the breakfast room, which his mother and Emerya are already leaving. Doubting that Lephi will be up any time soon, he takes his time with the bread, cheeses, and the late melon that have been left for him. After eating, he finds Ryalah and Amaira playing with their dolls next to the low fire in the salon. Emerya is using a lap-desk to write something and looks so intent that Lerial does not interrupt her, but amuses himself by listening to the two girls at their play.

How much time has passed he has no immediate idea when Lephi enters the salon carrying a pair of wands.

"There you are. I thought we were going to spar. That is, if you're up to it. It is a bit chill compared to in here."

Lerial stands and stretches. "I suppose we could do that. The south courtyard or outside by the stable . . . where the Lancers practice?"

"The south courtyard might be better. It's . . . less obvious."

"You're right about that." Lerial does not smile, but follows his older brother from the salon along the main front corridor south to the side hall leading to the courtyard. He thinks he can sense someone behind him, but when he glances back, he can see no one.

The courtyard doesn't feel that cold to Lerial, certainly no colder than does the practice area at Lancer headquarters at seventh glass in the morning.

"Take your pick." Lephi extends both wands.

Lerial hefts one, then the other, just to make sure that neither is terribly out of balance. Neither is, and he takes the one that is slightly heavier, then walks to the circle and waits for Lephi to join him. He doesn't have to worry about the sun because there is still a high overcast.

"You ready?" Lephi steps into the circle and raises his wand.

"When you are."

"Then start."

Lerial feints an attack, but just enough of one to encourage Lephi to try a counter. Lephi does, and Lerial slips it, leaving Lephi slightly out of position. Rather than take that advantage, Lerial circles toward Lephi's uncovered side, forcing his brother to retreat and turn. Then Lerial engages Lephi's wand, sliding it up before dropping and starting an underthrust, but waiting just long enough that Lephi can recover.

Lephi charges forward, almost spinning his wand in a circle, but Lerial has already anticipated the attack and slipped past it, striking Lephi's wand on the back edge and forcing his brother into another quick recovery.

The pattern continues for a good half glass, until Lephi steps back. He is breathing heavily. "It was a long night last night. You should have come.

There were some young ladies there who would have been very pleased to appreciate you."

Stepping back himself, Lerial replies, "There will be other times, I'm sure. It's been a long week for me as well."

Lephi lowers his wand. "You've got a good defense, but you never attack. That's not the way to kill raiders or win battles."

"I'm sure, with more practice, I'll learn better attacks." As he stands there, Lerial realizes something else. He has barely raised a sweat. Part of that may be due to the colder weather . . . but not all of it.

"You don't even have any attacks." Lephi's tone is not quite scornful.

"Then I must have a great deal to learn."

"Yes, you do."

Lerial does not reply for a moment because, again, he has the feeling someone is watching, but he sees no one.

"Here. You can take the wands. I got them out." Lephi extends his wooden wand.

"That's only fair," Lerial agrees.

Abruptly, Lephi turns. "I'll see you later."

As his brother hurries off, Lerial senses that Lephi likely drank more watered lager that morning than he had realized. With a faint smile, he heads for the western door to the south courtyard, since that's the closest one.

He is not totally surprised when Emerya steps out of the gloom of the archway. "You were watching, weren't you?"

"The last part. You've gotten a great deal better . . . and much older."

Lerial suspects he knows what she means, but only says, "I've tried to learn as much as I can from the Lancers."

"You've learned more than that. I wonder how Lephi will react if he ever discovers just how good you've become."

"I've had more time to practice. He's been on patrols."

"He's three years older, and he certainly had the time to practice before he was old enough to go on patrols." Emerya smiles. "But you wanted me to say something like that."

Lerial finds himself flushing. "I suppose I did."

"You're bright enough to know that showing up your older brother is unwise, but still young enough to want praise."

"Doesn't everyone want praise . . . or to be appreciated?"

"We all want it. I don't think it's a desire we ever outgrow . . . but it's dangerous to need praise when you have power, especially if you're a ruler or close to a ruler, because you can be manipulated by those who provide the praise. You can feel that they're the only ones who truly appreciate you. Your father understands that. He doesn't like it, but he understands."

Lerial can see what Emerya is not saying. She is worried that both Lerial and Lephi will always be governed by the need for praise . . . and possibly that Lephi is even more desirous of such praise. *Or is that what you want to believe?*

"By the way, that comment of yours last night was masterful. Unfortunately, Lephi is so preoccupied with himself that he missed it."

"The one about recognition? It was perfectly true." *Except for the last few words.*

"You know that it's possible that Lephi just might think over your sparring and realize that you were playing with him?"

"It's possible," Lerial concedes, "but then he'd have to admit that I'm better. As long as no one else knows it, and I don't say anything . . . One way or another, he probably won't want to spar with me again. Even if he thinks he's better, and he might cling to that feeling, he knows that I've gotten better, and that the next time might turn out worse."

Emerya nods. "You're sounding like Grandmere."

"Is that bad?"

"Not with me."

But it might be with others. "Thank you. I'll keep that in mind."

"Do you want to ride down to the healing hall with me? I just want to make sure there's no one who needs a strong healer."

"I can do that. I'd like to."

"Good." Emerya smiles.

Before that long, they are riding northwest on the boulevard.

After a time, Lerial asks, "How do you do a concealment?"

"Why are you asking me?"

"Because I sensed someone was following and watching me . . . and I didn't see anyone. But you were there all along, weren't you?"

"I might have been." Emerya glances back.

"The Lancers always give us space."

"It's a matter of controlling the flow of order and chaos around you." Her voice is so low that Lerial can barely hear it. "Light is a mixture of order and chaos. If you can keep the light from touching you, then no one can see you. If you don't keep the flows smooth, though, people will know something is wrong because where you stand will look like everything is wavering . . . or worse. I can't tell you how . . . not exactly. I just worked at it until I could. Oh . . . there's one other thing. When you're in a concealment, you can't see. You can only order-sense. If you're not good at it, it's better if you stand in the shadows."

"That's it?"

"Is being good with a sabre just holding a blade and waving it around?"

Lerial laughs, if softly, then says, "Yet another thing for me to work on."

Emerya nods. "That's life. Working on one thing after another."

Lerial senses that there is much left unsaid, but he does not press. Not now. For a moment, he wonders why she has told him so easily. Only for a moment. *Because she knows it will not be long before you will be riding patrols . . . and she thinks you need more skills than you have with the blade.*

That thought chills him . . . more than the icy wind blowing out of the south.

XXXI

Lerial once more rises with the dawn on oneday and rides to the Lancer headquarters, and then after practicing with the officers, to the Hall of Healing. Over the next eightday, he seldom sees Lephi, except every so often at dinner, when the two brothers are polite and cheerful, but not especially close. Lerial continues to try to sense the currents in the air and the sky, but without clouds or storms, it is hard for him to determine what the flows of order and chaos he does sense might mean, although he has the feeling that he can sense flows farther away than he could at first. He also tries to work out how to manipulate the flow of order and chaos around himself . . . but cannot seem to manage it, because when he affects one part of the order or chaos, everything else changes. At times, he wants to yell in frustration, but even that is not possible within the Palace, not without raising more questions he certainly does not wish to answer.

On threeday, Lerial returns from the healing hall to find Lephi in the salon. "How was your day today?"

"He's had quite a bit to do," says Xeranya.

"I've had to make a number of arrangements. I'm heading out again on patrol. Father is dispatching me to Fourth Company. They're posted at Sudstrym."

Fourth Company? Lerial frowns, then nods. "The one that patrols the river opposite Amaershyn? Are the Heldyans gathering forces there . . . or does Father want you to have more experience in watching them?"

Lephi shrugs. "His dispatch didn't mention either. I'd judge he just wants me to have experience in all kinds of patrols."

"He'll need that," says Xeranya, quickly adding, "So will you, Lerial, once your father starts sending you on patrols."

"At least, you won't have to worry about rain," Lerial comments.

"Now you're a weather magus, as well as a healer?" asks Lephi sardonically.

"The skies are clear. It's cold, and there's no wind. You don't have to be a weather magus to see that it's not likely to rain any time soon." Lerial isn't about to admit that he has tried to sense the order flows in the skies above, trying to feel what the weather might be. But then, there have been no storms since he began trying.

"Wait until it rains tomorrow, and I get soaked on the ride to Sudstrym."

"You won't get soaked tomorrow. As you said, I'm no weather magus. So I won't even guess about what will happen on fourday."

Lephi rises from the armchair and picks up his Lancer cap, then nods to Xeranya. "I'll be late tonight, but I'll see you in the morning."

"Take care this evening."

"I will." Lephi turns to Lerial. "I'm going over to Submajer Jhalet's. You're welcome to come."

"I'll pass, thank you," replies Lerial.

"You won't always be able to pass, you know?"

All the more reason to do it now. "I know. But I lack your sociability, and I wouldn't wish it to reflect upon you." Lerial smiles politely.

Lephi shakes his head. "You'll never get consorted to the right kind of girl if you don't practice."

"There are a few other kinds of practice that are more important at the moment . . . as you pointed out the other morning."

"So I did. Those are more important, particularly if you can only handle a few kinds of practicing at a time." Lephi ignores the pointed glance from their mother.

"If I don't see you in the morning"—*And I'll be demon-cursed if I will*—"have a good and safe journey to Sudstrym."

"I'm sure I will, rain or no rain." With a nod to Lerial and a smile for his mother, Lephi leaves the salon.

There is a long moment of silence, during which Lerial walks to the sideboard and pours himself a glass of amber lager, then seats himself in a straight-backed chair, rather than the armchair Lephi had vacated. He takes a swallow of the lager.

"You haven't been very warm toward your brother," says Xeranya. "Especially since he is going back on patrol. He could be hurt, you know?"

"I think Lephi can take care of himself, Mother." *He certainly thinks he can.* "Besides, it's unlikely the Heldyans will send forces across the river when they haven't done that in years."

"They did once. They could again."

"Was Majer Altyrn in charge of the force that caught them?"

"He was. He had to cross the Swarth to do it. He burned part of Amaershyn."

"I didn't know that."

"It was before you were born. He also destroyed several other towns."

"Why did they cross the river?" Lerial has an idea, a vague recollection.

"They were angry that he'd turned the firecannon on their ships. They wanted to teach your father a lesson. He hadn't been Duke long at that time."

"And the majer ended up teaching them a lesson?"

"Duke Khesyn's father didn't want to lose more men attacking Cigoerne at that time. Matters have likely changed."

"Why? Because Khesyn has learned that Father is tied up dealing with Afritan armsmen and raiders in the north?" Lerial looks up as Emerya enters the salon, readjusting her head scarf so that it is merely a scarf and not a head covering.

"That's right," says Lerial's aunt. "Khesyn would be a fool not to have realized that as Cigoerne has gotten stronger, Afrit has continued to decline. If he can destroy us, then there's no bar to his taking over Cigoerne . . . and in a few years, or sooner, he can march north along the river and push back Atroyan's forces until they only hold Swartheld."

"Father must know that."

"He's known it for years. That's why he's kept expanding the Mirror Lancers."

Xeranya shakes her head. "I still worry about his doing it with so many outland rankers."

"They're more loyal than some of those born here in Cigoerne." Emerya pours herself a lager, then moves to the armchair and seats herself. "Being a Lancer is a far better life than they'd have had as a goatherd or a raider. Besides, they tell others, and more people want to be ruled by Kiedron than Atroyan or Duke Casseon of Merowey, not that he really rules the northern part of the lands he claims. He can't even collect tariffs. His tariff-farmers won't enter the woods, and Casseon won't send armsmen to collect them."

"Some of the people to the west are already trading with our factors. But . . ." Xeranya frowns. "I still worry."

"Those elders of the forest towns to the west can see how Khesyn treats those who don't bow to his beck and call. They also see that Kiedron is the only thing that stands between Khesyn and them." Emerya takes another sip of lager. "The southern types . . . they don't understand. They just like to raid, and Casseon has never done anything about it, so long as they raid us or Heldya."

Some of what the two are discussing, Lerial has heard before—many times—but not the business about the hill towns and hamlets. "Then . . . those raiders . . . the ones that attacked the majer and me . . . they had to be from the south and not the west."

"I'm sure they were," replies Emerya. "The forest people are mostly peaceful. The fact that they're starting to trade with us is good."

"Some of the factors are complaining about tariffs, again," ventures Xeranya.

"Kiedron has to pay the Lancers. Even Atroyan recognizes that. It's why he's relatively honest in remitting tariff shares. It's less costly for the merchanters in Swartheld that way. All they care about are golds." Emerya's tone is between sardonic and scornful.

"Does Atroyan recognize that . . . or his brother?"

"Atroyan still listens to Rhamuel. How long that will last . . ." Emerya shrugs.

Lerial cannot help but wonder how Emerya knows that, but before he can ask, his aunt looks at him with an expression that clearly suggests he should not. Much as he would like to know, he decides he will pursue that question in private with her, rather than antagonize her in front of his mother.

"Do you think," Lerial asks, looking to his aunt, "that Duke Khesyn will risk sending whole companies of armsmen across the river?"

"Khesyn is usually shrewd," replies Emerya, "but like all shrewd men, he is also capable of incredibly foolhardy acts. While I would judge he would not, it isn't beyond possibility."

At that, Lerial feels a chill, for while he finds Lephi insufferable at present, he doesn't like the idea of his brother and the Lancers facing Heldyan armsmen, especially given Lephi's unrealistic views of his own abilities. Yet, especially with his mother present, he can't say that, either. So he takes a swallow of his lager and nods, deciding to listen to what his mother and aunt may say before dinner.

He also thinks that he had best find a way to learn to do a concealment . . . and anything else that he can do with order.

XXXII

When Lerial returns from the Hall of Healing late on a cloudy and cool sixday afternoon and is preparing to lead the gelding into the stable, he sees Undercaptain Woelyt standing by the stable door, apparently waiting for him.

Why? Is there some problem with the rankers who've been escorting you? Or have you done something wrong?

He stops. "Good afternoon, Undercaptain. Is there something . . . ?"

"Not exactly, Lord Lerial . . ."

Lerial nods. "But . . . ?"

"I notice that you've not asked me to spar with you for some time," ventures Woelyt.

"I'm sorry. I hadn't meant to offend you, ser," replies Lerial. "I've been working with Captain Chaen at headquarters, and I really didn't wish to impose upon you."

"I can understand that, Lord Lerial, but since your father will likely ask me what I think of your progress . . ."

Lerial immediately understands the position in which his thoughtlessness has placed the undercaptain. "If you are free, Undercaptain, I would be more than happy to spar with you at present . . . as soon as I can stable my mount. I do understand, and I would not wish my thoughtlessness to reflect unfavorably upon you."

"If it would not be an imposition . . ."

"Not at all." And Lerial means that completely. He also realizes that his father, upon his return, will indeed most likely talk to the undercaptain. *Another thing you didn't consider.* "I'll only be a few moments. If you'd see to the wands . . ."

"Yes, ser."

Lerial unsaddles and grooms the gelding quickly, then hurries out of the stable to the courtyard exercise circle where the Lancers practice.

Woelyt is waiting. He extends a wooden wand.

"Thank you." Lerial takes the wand, realizing that it feels much lighter than he recalls. Is that because he is used to a heavier blade? He runs through several moves, then nods as he takes his position.

Woelyt does not bother with a feint, but begins with a direct thrust attack, one that Lerial parries easily, realizing almost immediately that the order flows around the undercaptain reveal his intent even before his wand moves, more so than with most of those against whom Lerial has sparred in recent eightdays. Rather than press, Lerial takes a guard position and waits for the next attack, which comes after a feint toward his shoulder. This time, Lerial slips the attack and comes in low and strikes the undercaptain on the thigh, returning to a guard position almost before Woelyt can react.

"You've gotten faster . . ."

"I've had more practice," replies Lerial.

For almost a half glass, the same pattern repeats itself, but Lerial is not about to call a halt to the sparring, not until Woelyt is satisfied.

Finally the undercaptain steps back. He offers a rueful smile. "You've gotten so much better that it's hard to believe."

Lerial smiles in return. "You've had to do all the duties of a Lancer officer. All I've had to do is concentrate on learning things." *Not all of them having to do with sabres and tactics, but learning all the same.* "And I've had the advantage of working against a lot of different officers."

"It shows." Woelyt inclines his head. "I appreciate the sparring, ser."

"Thank you. I do apologize for not thinking about keeping you apprised of my progress." Lerial grins. "You did suffer through my awkward sessions and gave me a good start, and I do appreciate that."

"Thank you, ser."

By the time Lerial leaves the outer courtyard, the slight sweat he had worked up, given the winter air and the breeze, has vanished. He is already cool by the time he reaches the Palace proper and heads up to his chambers to wash up before meeting with his mother and aunt in his mother's salon. He is still surprised at how much he has progressed with the use of the sabre. While he knew he was better, especially after sparring with Lephi, he had felt that Woelyt was better than his own brother. *And perhaps he is.*

He smiles at the thought.

After washing, as he is walking down the hall toward the staircase to the salon, he hears high voices.

"It's not fair! You always win, except sometimes you let me!"

He recognizes Ryalah's voice immediately.

"I do not," Amaira replies. "I win when you make mistakes. You win when I make mistakes."

"It's still not fair!" Ryalah's voice rises into a shriek.

"Girls!"

Lerial does not recognize the older voice, but assumes it must be that of their nurse.

As he nears the next door, it opens, and Ryalah runs out. Tears are streaming down her face, so much so that she runs right into Lerial—or would have had, except that he reaches down and scoops her up.

"Now . . . now . . . you almost knocked me down."

"Put me down!" Her small fists pound on his shoulders. "Let me go!"

Lerial can sense the fury within her, almost like a grayish chaos. After a moment, while he continues to hold her, he tries to soothe her by creating what feels like mist of order, holding his affection for her, and letting it settle. The fists stop pounding, and heaving sobs follow.

"She . . . makes . . . mad . . . not . . . fair . . . never fair . . ."

He says nothing, knowing that nothing he says will matter at the moment.

The nurse stands in the doorway, looking at him.

Lerial can sense her fear as well. "It's all right. She'll be fine in a bit."

". . . will . . . not!"

"All right," he says reasonably, "you won't be."

"You're making fun of me!"

Lerial says nothing and keeps holding her.

Finally. Ryalah looks at Lerial, their faces almost touching. "Please . . ."

"If you'll be good."

"She isn't fair . . ."

Lerial continues to wait, still holding her.

"I'll be good."

"Good."

"I don't have to like it," Ryalah adds as Lerial sets her on her feet.

"No, you don't," he agrees.

For a moment, a look of puzzlement crosses her face. Then she smiles at him. "You're funny."

"Sometimes. Not very often. It's even harder to be funny than good."

Ryalah turns to the nurse. "I'll be good."

As the little blond heads back into the playroom, the nurse murmurs, "Thank you, ser."

"You're welcome."

Lerial hurries down the steps and finally reaches the salon.

"You returned to the Palace some time ago," observes Xeranya, almost tartly, as he enters.

"I had to spar with Undercaptain Woelyt. He hasn't worked out with me for some time, and Father will wish to hear his judgment on my progress as well as that of Captain Chaen." Lerial does not wish to mention the time he has spent with Ryalah and Amaira. He walks to the sideboard for a lager.

After a moment, Xeranya nods. "Of course. Of course. It's good that you're realizing the impact your actions have on others . . . or should I say the impact the failure of your actions might have on them?"

"We all realize that sooner or later," adds Emerya from the settee. "Later for some of us." A ruefully amused smile flits across her lips and face and vanishes. "How did the sparring go?"

"The undercaptain was pleased with my progress."

"Excellent," says Xeranya. "Your father has been worried about that."

"Some of us take longer . . . or at least it seems that way," replies Lerial.

Emerya, her head turned toward Lerial and facing away from Xeranya, lifts an eyebrow in warning.

"Anything worth doing is worth doing well," Xeranya continues, "and that takes time and effort."

"I've discovered that." Lerial seats himself in the armchair nearer to Emerya, then takes a swallow of his lager. "What might we be having for dinner?"

"A green goat curry, I think. I told the girls to finish up the meat we had."

Lerial thinks about commenting on green goats and decides against it.

"I hope you told them to make it mild," says Emerya.

"I did."

"Thank you," replies Emerya.

Lerial is thankful as well. He takes another small swallow of lager and fixes a pleasant smile upon his face, ready to listen . . . although his mind is on concealments . . . and raiders and patrols.

XXXIII

Eightday morning, Lerial wakes up early, despite a gloom more like that created by a heavy overcast late in the afternoon. Yet when he opens the shutters of his chamber, there is no overcast, but there are low dark clouds moving swiftly to the south, with no sign of rain. The air is cold and gusts around him, although it is not chill enough for snow, or even for sleet or icy rain. As he stands at the open window, he finds that he is both unsettled and irritable, perhaps because, once more, this time on sevenday afternoon, after returning from the Hall of Healing, he had tried in yet another fashion to create a concealment . . . and had only succeeded in exhausting himself.

He shakes his head and turns away from the window, his eyes lighting on the black silk pouch on his table-desk.

Rojana had said an old book claimed that a lodestone could help with ordering order. *What about ordering the flows of order and chaos?*

With a smile, half amused and half rueful, Lerial walks to the table-desk and eases the lodestone from the silk pouch, leaving the pouch on the wooden surface. Holding the lodestone in his left hand, he concentrates on sensing the tiny flows of order and chaos, except that the flows are not either, but a combination of each.

He looks around for something made of iron, then sees his sabre, in his sword belt scabbard and hung on the rack beside his armoire. He moves the lodestone toward the blade, still concentrating on sensing the flow of order-chaos. The flow seems to strengthen as the lodestone nears the blade. Lerial moves it back and senses the lessening of the strength, except that is not quite right. The strength does not so much change as that the pattern shifts.

Surely, you can do the same . . . can't you?

He moves the lodestone nearer and farther from the sabre, watching, sensing, before he tries to add what he feels is a duplication of the pattern, and he feels the lodestone pull more strongly toward the sabre.

So you can make a small lodestone stronger? So what? Except . . . somehow . . . he feels that there must be a connection between the flow of order-chaos from the lodestone and the flow of order and chaos necessary for a concealment. *But what?* The fact that doubling the pattern strengthens the pull of the lodestone?

He tries to manipulate the circular waves around each end of the lodestone, but the waves or patterns immediately reform. After a time, his head throbs slightly, and he lowers the lodestone. Then he notices that it appears brighter outside, and he walks to the window and looks out. The clouds still cover the northern sky, but there is a break to the south, and a shaft of light arrows an angle though that aperture in the clouds.

There is . . . something . . . about that.

Then he smiles. *So obvious that you almost didn't see it.* The light shaft doesn't spread . . . or not that much. That means that the light patterns travel in a straight line. The fact that an image is reflected in a mirror is another indication of that, but Lerial has not connected the two until he saw the shaft of sunlight. The lodestone bends order and chaos into a set of circles . . .

He takes the lodestone once more and tries to duplicate the patterns of order-chaos, but with light as well. For a moment, only a moment, there is a pinpoint of light, at the end of the lodestone—at each end. When he sees that, he is surprised enough that he loses his concentration, and the additional brightness vanishes.

But why brightness? His aunt said that, if he did manage a concealment, he would not be able to see. That had to be because . . . why? He thinks for a time. He knows he cannot see in darkness. No one can. That means light is necessary to see. *Obviously!* But he is missing something. Black cloth, black anything—if it's left in the sun—gets hot. White doesn't get as hot. The sunlight heats things. Does that mean that sunlight, or some of it, is caught by dark objects? That would mean less is caught by light ones.

He continues to ponder. But . . . if his order-chaos pattern around the lodestone keeps light away, and that caused the brightness, why wasn't there brightness when Emerya created a concealment? She had been standing in the shadows, and more light would have made an aura around her, and there hadn't been one.

Lerial rubs his forehead, still trying to puzzle it out.

But your pattern was inside the lodestone pattern . . .

Is that it? The shaft of sunlight went on and on until it hit something and lit it up, like sunlight lights everything. *Unless it doesn't touch it!*

He nods to himself. The trick, or skill, is to figure out how to use order flows to bend light around himself, not to contain it in the way that the lodestone bends its attractive force around its end. Somehow . . . he has the feeling accomplishing that is going to be far harder than figuring out what he has to do.

Still . . . he has a much better idea of what is involved. *And it took you a long time and much effort to become better with a blade.*

He squares his shoulders and takes a position in front of the mirror.

XXXIV

While the skies are overcast or cloudy on most days in Cigoerne as winter proceeds, there is only one other light rain over the next several eightdays besides the one that occurred the night of Lephi's return, but the weather turns markedly colder. Every morning, and every afternoon, Lerial struggles with using order to create a concealment, and slowly begins to be able to hold the patterns for perhaps a tenth part of a glass. At times, however, if he does not concentrate closely, small iron objects fly toward him, or rather toward either the lodestone . . . or his sabre. That worries him, because spears and arrowheads are made of iron, and what good is a concealment if holding one will attract weapons?

He wishes his progress were better, and he has to remind himself that Emerya had told him almost a year before that using order would be far harder than merely mastering the skills of handling a sabre . . . and his struggles with mastering the concealment technique are yet another proof of that.

On fourday of the third eightday of winter, there are so few injuries and illnesses that both Emerya and Lerial leave the Hall of Healing just after midday. As he rides beside his aunt, Lerial can see his breath steaming, and he is very glad for the Lancer riding jacket—and the gloves Altyrn had given him.

Lerial, Emerya, and their Lancer escorts are still a good half kay from the Palace when Emerya straightens in the saddle and says abruptly, "Your father must be back."

Lerial almost asks how she knows, but then sees that the ducal banner flies above the guardhouse by the main gate to the palace grounds. "I hope that means that the fighting around Penecca is over."

"So do I, but it might also mean that both sides remain there, and that your father sees no point in staying, since nothing will change over the winter."

Lerial frowns. He has not thought of that.

"Not all battles are won in great fights. Some are won by not fighting at all," Emerya says.

"How can you win by not fighting?"

"Cigoerne today is more than two-score times as large as the lands your grandmere purchased from Duke Atroyan's father. Not a single field was added by fighting."

"But the Lancers fight all the time. They fight raiders, and Afritan and Heldyan armsmen."

"They fight to protect those who have chosen to be part of Cigoerne. Chosen," Emerya adds firmly.

Lerial considers her words and then replies. "Duke Atroyan and Duke Khesyn can't like that. Why have they let it happen?"

"They thought the lands were not worth fighting over, but when our engineers and Magi'i made them worth more, they wanted them back." She pauses. "You're right, though. I fear those times are over."

As they ride through the Palace gates, Lerial sees only a few signs of his father's return—more Lancers in the outer courtyard, dealing with mounts, carrying gear into the stables and the Lancer barracks, and unloading several wagons.

Because he has made a habit of unsaddling and grooming the gelding, and because he stops to wash up somewhat, he knows he will likely be later than Emerya in arriving in the salon to greet his father, but Lerial sees no point in altering his pattern, since no one seems to care that much about his presence.

When he does reach the salon, his father is seated in one of the armchairs, with his mother at the end of settee closest to him. Emerya sits at the far end of the settee.

"Ah . . . Lerial, you're finally here," says Xeranya. "I would have thought you'd have made a greater effort to greet your father."

"I hurried as I could, ser," Lerial says to his father, "but I did have to see to my mount."

"Do you always unsaddle and groom him?" asks Kiedron politely.

"Yes, ser. Well . . . ever since you sent me to Kinaar."

Kiedron looks to Emerya.

She nods.

"It's a good habit to nurture," remarks Kiedron.

"Lerial has changed many of his habits for the better," says Xeranya.

The way his mother utters her words suggests that there might be times when Lerial should not be a servant to even the best habits, but Lerial says, "I'm glad that you're home and well, ser. Very glad." *For more reasons that you know.*

Lerial catches the briefest sense of surprise and amusement from Emerya, a feeling he also senses that his mother does not catch. *But she's a healer, too, like Emerya.* Except, he realizes, and has to accept, that Emerya is the stronger . . . and more sensitive. *Do they go together?*

"I'm very glad to be here." Kiedron gestures to Lerial. "Go get yourself a lager, or whatever, before I tell you all about what happened . . . and what we face."

Lerial moves to the sideboard and pours a glass not quite three-quarters full, then sits in the vacant armchair facing his father.

"What I did not convey is that the elders of the Afritan town of Ensenla have made overtures to me. They have been less than pleased with Duke Atroyan, particularly in the way in which his officers and armsmen have treated their young men and especially their young women . . ."

Lerial nods, thinking about the two healer trainees who fled to Cigoerne.

". . . this has clearly reached either Arms-Commander Rhamuel or Duke Atroyan, if not both, or so many Afritan armsmen would not have been sent to our northern border from the river westward. It is also possible that the overtures have not been made truly by the elders, but by those close to Duke Atroyan as an attempt to entice me to act to expand the borders of Cigoerne. This is something that we have never done. We have only accepted those towns and lands that honestly wanted our protection. At the moment, I have no way of knowing whether these supposed overtures are a true offer or a ruse that will allow Atroyan to assert to Duke Khesyn and Duke Casseon that Cigoerne is ambitious and dangerous and that the three should unite against us."

"Casseon may talk, but he would have to bring armsmen all the way from Nubyat, or even from Dawhut, and that's hundreds of kays just to our southern border," Emerya points out.

"We cannot afford to have any of them think we are too powerful or aggressive," Kiedron replies. "Atroyan would like nothing better than to have Khesyn attack us in force. I know you believe Rhamuel thinks that is unwise, but Atroyan has ignored his brother's advice before."

"True," admits Emerya. "It did not work out well, but Atroyan does not seem to learn from his mistakes."

"People often think things are different, even when the same problem occurs again," suggests Xeranya.

Kiedron clears this throat. "All this brings me back to you, Lerial."

"Yes, ser?"

"I sent a letter to Majer Phortyn, inquiring about your progress." Kiedron pauses. "He sent back a dispatch."

Lerial waits, wondering how favorable the majer's evaluation might be.

"He admitted that he was surprised by your initial effrontery, but also equally surprised by your level of skill, and especially pleased by your dedication to improving your skills. According to Captain Chaen, while your attacks could use some work, your defenses are excellent." Kiedron actually smiles. "It appears your time with Majer Altyrn was worth it."

"Yes, ser. You were absolutely right to send me there."

"We do occasionally know what might be helpful for our children."

Xeranya nods in agreement.

"Your presence in the south and your clear ability to get along with Majer Altyrn," Kiedron continues, "may prove valuable in ways I had not anticipated."

"Ser?"

"I'm getting there. In addition to the problems with Khesyn and Atroyan, the unsettled state of the lands that border Cigoerne on the south and theoretically belong to Merowey has resulted in far too many raids and raiders over the last ten years. Part of the problem is that Duke Casseon is both arrogant and does not believe as we do."

Lerial offers a quizzical frown.

"Duke Casseon forbids the use of chaos in his domains. He claims it is evil and must never be used."

"But . . . both order and chaos are forces. How they are used determines what they are."

"Not to someone like Casseon, but Casseon isn't the problem. Not directly. His lack of control of the northern part of his lands is. Your experience with the majer is just another example."

Emerya and Xeranya exchange glances, and Lerial senses a certain puzzlement from his mother. He also feels his father is enjoying drawing out what is coming next, as if almost challenging the two to figure out what he is about to reveal.

"To put the matter in simple terms, the elders from the hill towns north and east of Jabuti, believe they are almost a land unto themselves They have sent an actual petition requesting that I consider ruling Verdheln."

"Verdheln?" Xeranya frowns.

"That's what they call it. They're even willing to provide Lancer trainees . . . and an advance on their tariffs, in golds, to show their sincerity. They worry greatly that they will suffer worse than have our towns, not because many of the raiders have decided to attack their towns, but because they fear Casseon will insist they open their lands and allow in all from Merowey. This troubles them. Enough that they would have me rule them."

Lerial almost swallows. If the hill towns are the ones whose locations he has studied on Majer Altyrn's maps, their acceptance of his father's rule will more than double the size of the lands held by Cigoerne. In time, his father might rival Atroyan in holdings. *But not in the number of people or the wealth of those holdings.* And that might be another problem.

"Will you accept?" asks Xeranya warily.

"How can I not? The situation is getting more dangerous every year. . . ."

"We're spread too thin as it is," says Emerya. "Even if you can raise more Lancers from those towns, it will take more golds to pay them and time to train them. Who can you spare, with the Heldyans on the east and Atroyan on the north?"

Kiedron smiles. "I have asked Majer Altyrn to oversee the training of those men, and I can spare two squads to support him, but . . . the elders want a pledge that I will not abandon them."

Lerial has a strong feeling about what is coming next.

Kiedron turns back to Lerial. "You can do two things at once. You can obtain more Lancer training, and you can represent me to the hill peoples. You are younger than I would prefer to be riding patrols, but accompanying Majer Altyrn would not be exactly the same. You have already shown, according to the response I received from the majer, that you can defend yourself in battle. That is important, because fighting when you can die is not the same as sparring, even with blunted blades. Your presence will assure the hill peoples of my faith in them. There are more towns hidden in and around the forests than Casseon realizes, and we will be able to use some of the Lancers we train for them in places other than defending against raiders from the south."

"What about arms?" asks Emerya.

"I have known for years that the time would come when we would need more weapons. Every year we have arranged for more sabres to be forged than we would need. An additional fifteen or twenty blades every season seems like nothing for the smiths of Luba . . . and our own ironmages have also been forging."

"How many more companies can you equip?" demands Emerya.

"Seven, perhaps eight."

"You can't take on Heldya or Afrit with twenty-some companies."

Kiedron shakes his head. "No. And we may have twenty-five companies. But it's enough to keep them from wanting to take us on. We'll just keep building up the Lancers, and Atroyan and his merchants will be happy that we're taking the losses."

"Until when?" Emerya's words are flat.

"Until they leave us alone."

Lerial can sense the evasion behind those words, and he knows that his aunt must be able to do so as well, but Emerya only nods, if slowly.

"When do I leave for Teilyn?"

"It will take several days to complete arrangements for the wagons to take the supplies and weapons you and the majer will need. I hope to have you and the two squads on the way no later than sevenday . . . eightday at the latest. Oh . . . and I've asked Majer Phortyn to tell as few people as possible and only to say that you will be accompanying Majer Altyrn on a mission to train townspeople in the west."

"I've been working with the Lancers every morning."

"You can keep that up for the next day or so. After that, you'll be busy. Oh . . . we'll also need to get you some additional uniform greens and undercaptain's insignia."

"I'll be an undercaptain?"

"Provisionally. Once the majer feels you can handle those duties, he will have the authority to make the rank permanent."

"You need me to have that rank now . . . well before we arrive in the hill and forest towns."

Kiedron nods. "I hope that it is otherwise, but this could be the beginning of even more troubled times." He smiles brightly. "That's enough for now. I want to hear what's been happening here."

Lerial manages a pleasant expression, but the fact that his father has said "enough for now" means there is more, and it may well not be all that pleasant.

XXXV

When Lerial makes his way down to breakfast, early as it is on fiveday, he arrives just behind his father. They are the only ones in the breakfast room besides the serving girl, who immediately leaves.

"Good morning, ser."

"Good morning, Lerial," replies Kiedron as he seats himself. "You're off to practice with the Lancers after breakfast, I presume?"

"Yes, ser." Lerial sits down at the table.

Kiedron nods and pours himself some greenberry juice.

Lerial refrains from wincing. Even the thought of greenberry makes his mouth pucker, although he had managed a green juice at Kinaar, but it had not been so sour-bitter. Instead he fills his mug with lager and takes a swallow. Flat as the warmish lager is, he finds it far better than most juices.

"You know I wrote to Majer Phortyn about your blade training and received his reply. I also talked to Undercaptain Woelyt early this morning. He was less guarded. He said that you'd become his superior with a sabre and that there was no way in which he'd wish to face you in combat." Kiedron pauses, waiting for the serving girl to serve him egg toast and ham strips. He continues to wait until she serves Lerial and then leaves. "He also said something else, with which I was most pleased. He said that you were most courteous and thoughtful."

"The undercaptain was most diligent in assuring I practiced before I went to Kinaar. I wouldn't have been able to take advantage of the majer's training without what I learned here."

"Your aunt says that you've also been helping at the Hall of Healing."

"Yes, ser. What she taught me was what helped save a Lancer when we were attacked in the south valley." Lerial follows his father's example and drizzles berry syrup over the egg toast.

"That's good." Kiedron pauses and frowns. "You may actually have the abilities of a healer, but it would be best if you continued to let the Lancers believe that you've learned only enough to be useful in battlefield healing."

"Yes, ser. I'd thought that already because of what you said earlier."

Kiedron laughs. "I should have sent you to work with the majer sooner."

"Begging your pardon, ser, but I wouldn't have known enough to benefit from it much sooner."

"That's probably true." Kiedron takes another swallow of the greenberry juice. "It's probably best that you keep doing what you've been doing until the end of sevenday. I have asked Emerya to have you help with the worst and most difficult healing that may be required."

"Last moment experience?"

His father nods. "It may be useful. I do not know whether the hill people even have healers, but it is possible you will encounter raiders." Kiedron smiles. "I wouldn't have thought of sending you with the majer, except for his dispatch and Majer Phortyn's views. It's better that you go than Lephi, though."

"Because it won't take him away from patrols?"

"In a way . . . but it's not what you think. Cigoerne is a small land, at least as lands in Hamor go, and everyone knows what I do and decide in days. If I send Lephi to Jabuti, too many will think I'm keeping him from danger. The danger is likely the same in either place, as you have already discovered. But I would have to send him if I did not think you were able to handle the matter."

"But because I am younger, and you have made me an undercaptain earlier than you wished, everyone will say that you are risking your own son for Cigoerne?"

"They will not say that. They likely will not think that. They will think it is a matter of course. But if I sent Lephi . . ."

"They would think your sons received special treatment."

"I see you understand."

Lerial understands. In a way, though, it bothers him.

"It disturbs you," Kiedron continues, clearly reading his son's face. "It should. You should understand, though, that any ruler, especially the Duke of the smallest land in Hamor, does not rule just by force. Nor can I rule Cigoerne by tradition. Nor will Lephi be able to rule by tradition. It takes generations to rule by tradition. Tradition is not sufficient by itself, either." He looks at Lerial. "Then what else allows a Duke to rule?"

Lerial has no idea. "Ser?"

"The people have to believe that you can rule. They do not have to agree with everything I do. They don't even have to like me. They do have to respect me."

"And you will lose respect if you are seen to subject their sons to danger while shielding your own?"

"How would you feel if I sheltered Lephi and sent you to fight the Afritans?"

Lerial doesn't have to answer that question . . . and he knows his father knows that.

"Some rulers do not understand that, Lerial. I would not have you or Lephi fail to know the importance of respect . . . or what undermines that respect."

"That is why you were leading at Penecca."

"I try to lead carefully," Kiedron says dryly. "There's no point in being foolhardy, but, yes, I have to be there."

"Mother worries."

"She always has, but she understands. So does your aunt."

"Understands what?" asks Emerya from the door to the breakfast room.

"The need for a ruler to be respected, especially when his power is not overwhelming." Kiedron's tone is dry and sardonic, yet somehow guarded.

"That's true. Respect is essential for a ruler to be successful over time. It's also true of anyone with power. Your Majer Phortyn is well aware of that."

"Emerya . . . ," begins Kiedron, his tone cool.

"He's well aware," Emerya continues, seating herself and looking at Lerial. "Because he's barely altage, he would not take a consort because the ones he wanted wouldn't have him, and he feels he has had to earn the respect of everyone, especially after the unfortunate incident with Sypcalyn."

"That was years ago," says Xeranya from the breakfast room door. "Just because Sypcalyn was named after a hero in the time of Lorn didn't make him great. Both he and Phortyn haven't been as respectful of the Magi'i heritage as they might have been. So that broken lance didn't make all that much difference."

"We've been over that before," Kiedron says firmly, lifting his mug and taking a swallow of juice, then several mouthfuls of egg toast and ham.

Lerial does the same, although the ham is barely warm, tough, and chewy. He feels that his father has said all is he going to say, at least while Emerya and his mother are at the table.

That proves to be true, since Kiedron finishes eating quickly and leaves. Lerial realizes he may be late and also hurries off to saddle his mount.

Once he leaves the palace, Lerial's day is mostly like every other day, except for a brief period at the Hall of Healing when Emerya insists that he help in setting the broken bones of a mason on whom an entire trestle of bricks had fallen. One arm has broken bones protruding from the flesh.

When they finish and leave the surgery, Emerya looks to Lerial. "Thank you for the extra order. It may not be enough, you know."

"I could sense that."

"You should not attempt that kind of healing on the battlefield unless the battle is over, and there are no other wounded to help."

"Because I could do nothing afterward?"

"Can you even sense order now?"

"Barely."

"Exactly." Emerya nods.

Lerial has to have some bread and rest for more than two-fifths of a glass before he can resume giving even limited assistance to Emerya, but there are no other serious injuries for the remainder of the day.

When he returns to the Palace, there is a tailor waiting outside his chambers, and Lerial invites him in, where the man takes measurements quickly.

"Three regular riding uniforms and one dress uniform," he says when he finishes. "The riding uniforms will be ready by sevenday at noon. The dress uniform will take longer, of course, but your father said you would not be needing that immediately . . ."

"I don't imagine that I will," replies Lerial with a slight laugh.

He sees the tailor out and is about to close the door when he sees Emerya walking toward him. He waits.

"I'd like to talk to you before you go down to the salon for refreshments."

"I can talk now."

"My chambers, if you would."

"Of course." Lerial feels like shrugging as he walks beside Emerya. It doesn't matter whose chambers to him. If Emerya has something to say, it doesn't matter where she wants to say it, although he does wonder what she has in mind . . . and the fact that she doesn't want to say more at the moment, even though there is no one else nearby.

Once they are alone in her sitting room, seated in the two chairs that are neither really armchairs nor plain straight-backed chairs, Emerya looks at Lerial. "There are some things you should consider while you are away from Cigoerne. Why do you think Duke Atroyan hasn't mounted a campaign against Cigoerne?"

"Because we protect part of his borders, and we're not a threat."

"That's true, but it's not the entire truth. We could kill five Afritan armsmen for every Lancer we lost and still be destroyed to the last person. Think about that."

Lerial nods. "But why would they want to lose so many when we are not a threat?"

"Is an infant a threat?"

Lerial understands that. "You mean because we only had a few hundred people when you came here, and now there are thousands?"

"That's part of it. The last count showed that more than forty thousand people live within the boundaries of Cigoerne, and it could be much more. Most came from Afrit, some from Merowey." Abruptly, Emerya says, "You met the Duke's daughter years ago. Did she have any cousins?"

Lerial frowns. *What does that have to do with Afrit not attacking Cigoerne?* "She didn't then," he replies cautiously.

"She doesn't now."

"How do you know that?"

"People do send letters up and down the Swarth River, Lerial. People have always written letters." Emerya offers an enigmatic smile. "Sometimes, they've even written poems."

She stands and walks to her table-desk, where she takes out a thin volume. The binding is not leather, but something that shimmers a silver-green.

Lerial realizes that it must be the other copy of the volume his mother had once shown him.

"This book is older than it looks. It is almost as old as Cyad. I want to read you some lines."

Lerial waits, wondering of what use ancient words might be.

His aunt the healer begins, still standing.

"I have no soul,
but a nibbled kernel . . .
feelings dried and stored
on the shelves of self
in the deep cellar where
provisions must be made.

Provisions must be made.
I made them
gleaning
those wild leftovers of

unharvest days,
hoarding hard-to-come-bys
of cold reason
against colder seasons.

Provisions must be made,
and I have made them."

There is a silence after she finishes, and Lerial wonders what he is supposed to say.

Before he can compose his thoughts, she says, "I don't want you to ask me what the words mean. I don't want you to tell me what you think they mean. I just want you to think about them . . . and keep those thoughts to yourself." She turns the silvery pages once more and reads briefly once more.

"Worlds change, I'm told,
mirror silver to heavy gold,
and the new becomes the old,
with the way the story's told."

"What are you trying to tell me?" Lerial can't help asking that, even though Emerya has said she won't explain.

"I've said all I'll say. If you can't figure it out, I can't help you."

"I think I understand." Before she can reply, he asks, "Why don't you and Mother like Majer Phortyn?"

"I don't trust him. She recalls the time he was overheard saying that too many of the Magi'i were broken-down remnants of a great past." She gestures. "You can go now. I'll be down in a few moments."

Lerial rises. "I will think about the verse."

"Good."

Once Lerial is out in the second level corridor, he thinks about her admonition. *If you can't figure it out, I can't help you.* There are so many meanings behind those words . . . so many . . . And yet, his mother has once told him that she had found meaning in the words as well.

As he walks down the hallway toward the steps, he manages not to shake his head. Somehow the business about letters . . . that had seemed so out of place . . . and the fact that his aunt knows that Kyedra, the Duke's daughter, who must be about the age of Rojana, has no cousins.

Then . . . it strikes him. Amaira! How could she have . . . ?

Lerial has always wondered about who Amaira's father is . . . or was. He has even thought it might have be Rhamuel, the brother of the Duke of Afrit, the one whom Emerya had healed after his failed ambush on Lerial's father, but it has never been something anyone talked about.

But how could it have been anyone else? And how could his father or mother—or his grandmother—even have known until it was too late?

But if Emerya is writing letters to Rhamuel . . . and his father knows . . . as he must . . . ? And what purpose was reading the poetry meant to convey? Except that it was written by the second Emperor of Light?

He smiles wryly. His aunt has asked him to think over the poetry while he is gone . . . and it is clear that there is more behind those words than he understands . . . and that there is a message his aunt does not wish to convey directly. *Or feels that you won't understand or appreciate it if she does?*

XXXVI

The remainder of sixday and sevenday both pass quickly, and almost before Lerial knows it, he is saddling the gelding well before dawn on eightday morning and strapping his kit bag behind the saddle. When he leads the gelding out of the stable, he sees his mother and sister, as well as Emerya and Amaira, standing by the side entrance to the main part of the palace. He mounts and rides over to them, where he reins up.

"Take care," his mother offers.

"I will." *As I can.*

"Good-bye," says Ryalah.

"Good-bye . . . and don't get too mad at Amaira."

Ryalah makes a face back at him, to which Lerial grins.

Amaira looks at him and barely murmurs, "Good-bye."

"Good-bye . . . but don't let Ryalah play too much on the fairness business."

His dark-haired and dark-eyed cousin smiles shyly, and then looks away.

"Trust yourself," are the first words from his aunt, followed by, in a lower voice, "in all things."

"That's harder than it sounds."

She nods and then smiles.

Lerial manages not to swallow as he turns the gelding toward the four rankers who are his escort to Lancer headquarters. The very fact that his mother and aunt are both there to see him off brings home the fact that his training mission with the majer is in fact the same as a patrol. He knows his father has said that . . . but when he had heard those words, they had just been words. *Is that why he isn't here? Because it would emphasize even more that there's danger?*

Lerial decides that is most likely, but he keeps a pleasant expression on his face as he rides up to Jhubyl, the junior squad leader, "I see you drew the early morning duty."

"Figured someone from the Palace Lancers ought to see you off, ser."

"Oh . . . I'll be back. Just not for a while."

Once they are through the gates, Jhubyl says, "I hear you're going out into the hill country."

"In that direction, with Majer Altyrn. He's going to start training some of the hill types to be Lancers."

"That's what the watertalk is. Do you think that's because the Heldyans are up to making more trouble?"

"Since when have either the Afritans or the Heldyans not made trouble?" Lerial counters genially, trying to avoid confirming or denying the rumor.

Jhubyl laughs. "You sound just like Undercaptain Woelyt, ser."

Lerial just hopes that he can handle all aspects of being an undercaptain, especially since all too many eyes will be on how he acts and carries out his duties. *Even if you are being used as a sort of replacement for Lephi.* That doesn't mean he can't do the job better than his older brother could. *Not at all.*

As he rides along the southwest boulevard toward the Lancer headquarters compound, he cannot help but think about how much his life has changed over the past two seasons. *Was it all because he listened to Emerya . . . and that provided the initial spark for change? Or would it have happened anyway?*

He shakes his head. Change would have happened in any case, but without Emerya's help, he wouldn't have been nearly so well prepared . . . and he is anything but certain he is prepared for what will occur in the seasons ahead.

Teilyn and Beyond

XXXVII

Lerial waits until the column—two squads and three wagons—is well out of Cigoerne before considering more than exchanging pleasantries and giving necessary orders to the two squad leaders. It is slightly unnerving to realize that he is officially in command, although Majer Phortyn had drawn him aside before they had departed from headquarters. The majer's comments had been short and politely blunt.

"Lord Lerial . . . or Undercaptain Lerial . . . you're the only officer. That puts you in command. That means the lances stowed in the wagons are your responsibility. No one will make off with those. The paychest is another matter. Don't keep checking it. Just make sure it's never unguarded . . . or that your squad leaders do. They will if you don't get in the way. Relay all orders through your squad leaders. I suggest doing it quietly enough that they can offer advice if you've not thought of anything. Before you order anything else, talk to one of the squad leaders."

"Yes, ser. In short, rely on them to keep me from making a fool out of myself." *And damaging Father's position.*

"Keep that in mind, and you'll do fine."

"Thank you, ser."

Phortyn had actually smiled when he'd stepped back.

Now . . . some three kays south of Cigoerne, Lerial rides beside Juist. The senior of the two squad leaders is blond, and his weathered fair skin bears sun-scars, suggesting a Cyadoran heritage and giving Lerial an opening for finding out more about the squad leader.

"As I'm sure is obvious," Lerial begins, "I'm so new to the Lancers, except for training in Teilyn and headquarters, that I don't know anything about you or your rankers. Have there been other Lancers in your family?"

Juist laughs. "Don't know that there've been other than that, among the men, that is. My da was a Lancer. He always said one of his greats, way back, had served under the great Lorn, and I was named after him. Could be a tale." The squad leader shrugs.

"You expected to be a Lancer from the beginning, then?"

"Couldn't see myself doing much else, ser. Not much for grubbing dirt or hewing timber. Don't have the skill with my hands to be a crafter, and I'm not much for staying in one place."

Lerial is certain Juist has more skills than just with a sabre, but he only says, "What's the most important thing you tell a new man, the thing that every junior officer ought to know, the thing that's so basic that most don't?"

Juist looks startled. Then he laughs again, almost ruefully. "Ser . . ." He shakes his head before smiling. "You really want to know, ser?"

"I suspect you feel I won't like it, but if I don't, I should know."

"I tell them that unless an undercaptain's been a squad leader, he won't know sowshit, and that they need to look to their squad leader."

That scarcely surprises Lerial, and he nods. "About how many undercaptains are like me, that have no real experience?"

"Begging your pardon, ser, but, from what I hear, you didn't piss in your britches when a raider charged you, and you killed the bastard. That's more than half the undercaptains in the Lancers can say."

Lerial isn't surprised at that. With only fifteen companies or so, there are likely only twenty undercaptains, thirty at the outside, and half are doubtless the sons of former officers. Then there is the fact that many patrols don't encounter raiders, especially large numbers of raiders. "That's true, but I didn't have to give orders. All I had to do was defend myself."

"That's good. Be better if all officers went through that before they give orders."

"What else should I know?"

"You're asking me?"

Lerial grins. "You said every ranker should look to his squad leader. The majer told me the same, that I should look to you and Kusyl."

"Majer's got some sense." Juist smiles. "Appears you do, too." He pauses. "Don't know where to start."

"Anywhere you want. We've got two days before we get to Teilyn."

Juist is silent for a time, and Lerial wonders if he has been too direct with the weathered squad leader. Finally, the older man speaks. "Rankers don't have to know what you have in mind. Squad leaders do. They need to know what you want done. Suggest what you think will work. See what they think . . ."

Lerial listens and keeps listening.

Sometime after midday, Lerial switches from riding with Juist to accompanying the other squad leader. In appearance, Kusyl is far different from Juist—black-haired, brown-eyed, with a swarthy complexion and deeply tanned skin. He is also smaller and wiry.

Lerial wonders about his background, but decides not to presume, "Might I ask how you came to be a Lancer?"

Kusyl snorts. "What else would I be, ser? Father was a Lancer . . . excepting he didn't survive the mess the Accursed Forest made. Just lucky to be here. Ma was a nurse for the consort of a magus and got on the *Kerial* 'cause someone thought she was Magi'i, too."

Lerial manages not to wince and wonders what he can ask next, but doesn't have to because Kusyl keeps talking.

". . . used to get mad about that . . . excepting that, as Ma said, we'd been dead if'n she hadn't come. When I got older, I looked at what I could do . . . and when I heard they'd give preference to the sons of Lancers . . . well . . . turned out better for me than my da. Got a consort and two boys . . . good pay . . . and, begging your pardon, ser, your sire's a Stars-better ruler than his sire . . ."

"So I've heard." Lerial makes his comment as wryly dry as he can.

Kusyl chuckles. "Fact that he's sending you off says a lot . . ."

Such as? That Father risks himself and his sons? That's obvious, but there's something else about what Kusyl is saying, but Lerial can't put his finger on it. He tries to keep that in mind as he asks another question. "What do you think most junior officers forget in dealing with squad leaders?" Lerial grins and adds, "Besides the fact that the squad leaders know more than fresh undercaptains?"

Kusyl does laugh, if for a moment, before replying. "Everything takes longer. Everything. The more men you got, the longer it takes . . ."

From that point on, the conversation follows a line similar to the one Lerial has had with Juist. There are exceptions, and one strikes Lerial as something he never would have considered.

"No squad leader wants to worry about an officer who's leading a charge. Same way, no squad leader likes an officer who's so far behind that he's not even there. Doesn't mean there aren't times when you shouldn't lead. Means you shouldn't do it much. Only when there's no other way . . . or when you've lost the squad leader in the fight."

By midafternoon, Lerial just hopes that he can remember a fraction of what he has heard . . . and that he can make sure nothing happens to the paychest. He also knows he needs to keep practicing the concealment . . . with enough concentration that he doesn't inadvertently draw iron toward himself.

XXXVIII

By late on oneday afternoon, Lerial has alternated riding with the two squad leaders over the two days it has taken to get to Teilyn, trying to draw each of them out, both to learn what he can and to learn about each of them. He has largely managed to avoid revealing many details about himself, although he is well aware that in the process of conversing with the two squad leaders he has doubtless revealed more about himself than he realizes.

As they near Teilyn, Lerial studies the town, with its mud-brick houses and tile roofs, their white mud-plastered walls pinker than he recalls. Still . . . the streets are straight and the road, once they enter the town, becomes the brick-paved main street, and the side streets are also straight, if unpaved. Abruptly, it strikes him. *The entire town was built—or rebuilt—under a plan, most likely the majer's.*

How could he not have seen that before?

Because you weren't thinking about it.

Interestingly enough, when they pass through Teilyn and near the Lancer post, Lerial does not notice anything new. But then, he'd been in the post scores of times. The duty gate Lancers barely nod as he and Juist lead the two squads and the wagons through and rein up outside the small headquarters building.

Captain Graessyr stands there, waiting.

"Two squads reporting for duty with Majer Altyrn, ser," Lerial announces.

"Squads accepted for duty, Undercaptain." Then Graessyr smiles. "Didn't think you'd be back here, did you?"

"No. It makes sense, though."

"After you and the squad leaders settle the men, we should talk."

"Yes, ser," replies Lerial.

"Oh . . . and you can use a spare mount to ride over to the majer's villa afterward. He's expecting you for dinner."

"Thank you, ser."

"Be the least we could do."

Lerial turns to Juist. "You have the squad." While the words are a formality, they are also expected, Lerial knows. "And the paychest." Those are not.

"Yes, ser. I have the squad. We'll put the paychest in the strongroom first off."

Lerial nods an acknowledgment.

Once Lerial dismounts, he watches as the chest is carried into headquarters. Only then does he lead the gelding into the stable, where he unsaddles and grooms him before heading to the headquarters building. He leaves his kit with his saddle, uncertain where he will be sleeping.

Graessyr is waiting for him in the captain's study and gestures for Lerial to sit down in the straight-backed chair in front of the narrow table-desk.

"What do you know about the hill towns?" The captain's voice is direct and serious.

"I know what the maps show. The majer had me study them until I could draw them from memory. I know what he told me, and that they're almost independent. Other than that . . ." Lerial shrugs.

"The maps aren't as reliable as they could be. Oh . . . all the larger towns and hamlets are there. We've been sending out scouts for years. What do you know about the people?"

"I don't, ser."

"No one knows that much, but there are two or three things you need to keep in mind. First, make sure you and the Lancers keep your hands off their women. You won't have any problem, but some Lancers might. The forest women are beautiful, but they're all Kaordists, and they don't play around, especially with strangers. They supposedly consort for life, and they have a tendency to slice people in half who don't respect their women. Respect means keeping your hands off. The majer will fill you in on more, but it will take the two of you and the squad leaders to make sure the rankers don't mess with the women. You think the Afritans are touchy about that . . . it's nothing compared to the hill people. That's another reason why their elders are approaching the Duke. His high and mightiness, Duke Casseon, thinks anyone north of Jabuti or Clyanaka is a peasant to be used in whatever way suits him or his men. He's a strict ordist . . ."

Ordist? It took Lerial a moment to place the term—a believer in the supremacy of order over chaos, who forbids the use of chaos.

". . . and the hill people are anything but."

With that statement, his father's plans make much more sense. It's also a possible reason why Duke Atroyan's sire allowed the Magi'i to build Cigoerne.

"Did your father ever say anything about that?"

"He said that Duke Casseon didn't believe as we do and outlawed the use of chaos as evil."

"By anyone except his own mages. That's another problem that the hill people have with him." Graessyr straightens. "That's all I have, and I don't want to keep you from a far better meal than you'd get here."

"It won't be a problem . . . ?"

"No. I do appreciate your asking, but officers can eat where they want when they're off-duty. So can rankers, but they need permission from their squad leaders."

"Ah . . . quarters, ser?"

"There are two small chambers for junior officers. Take your pick . . . if that's your choice."

Lerial has the sense that what Graessyr offers is another test, of sorts. "It would be best if I were here." That is true for a number of reasons, and he also recalls that his father did not sleep at Kinaar.

Graessyr nods. "I can see that."

After he leaves the captain, Lerial returns to the stable and carries his gear to the visiting junior officers' quarters, then returns and saddles the spare mount—a mare. For perhaps the first time ever, he rides alone in making his way from the post to Kinaar.

When he nears the north entrance to the villa, Altyrn steps out to greet him. "Welcome back."

"I didn't expect to be here quite so soon."

"Expectations can be misleading." Altyrn looks up at Lerial. "No one would ever know."

"What? That I'm who I am?"

"Or that you're as young as you are. That's good. You didn't mention your age to any of the Lancers, did you?"

"No." Lerial grins ruefully. "I never thought of it, one way or another."

"I shouldn't be keeping you here. Maeroja will be happy to see you . . . and the girls, of course."

Lerial dismounts and walks the mare across the brick pavement to the stables. While he stalls her, he does not unsaddle her, since he will not be that long.

"You're staying at the post, I see," offers Altyrn as they walk back to the villa.

"It seemed to me that was best . . . for several reasons."

The majer nods. "I can see that."

"I'm sorry . . . I hope my being here isn't what dragged you into training the hill Lancers."

Altyrn laughs, a gentle ironic sound. "I suggested making overtures to them years ago. Obviously, your father never forgot."

"Oh . . . I didn't know."

"There's no reason you would." The majer pauses. "I'd appreciate it if you wouldn't mention it at dinner when the girls are present, though."

"They're still upset about what happened in the south valley?"

"Tyrna and Aylana have trouble with the concept that duty never truly ends."

"And Maeroja and Rojana understand it, but don't like it?" asks Lerial.

"Something like that," replies Altyrn dryly. He leads the way through the north entrance into the courtyard and then around to the salon.

Only Maeroja is there, and she rises from her chair and offers a warm smile. "It's good to see you."

"It's good to be here." *If not under the circumstances.*

"I imagine you're thirsty." Altyrn gestures toward the narrow table against the salon wall.

"I am at that." Lerial realizes that he didn't even stop for a drink at the Lancer post. "Very thirsty."

"Go ahead. I have to finish up going over the girls' lessons, Rojana's especially." With a cheerful smile, Altyrn turns and leaves the salon.

Lerial pours himself a mug full of the dark lager, then takes one of the straight-backed chairs facing Maeroja. After a swallow of the lager, he looks directly at her. "I'm sorry about this."

"Things are as they are," she replies.

"But if my father had not sent me here . . ."

"The hill people would still have petitioned your father. He would have requested the same of my consort . . . and you would likely not be with him." She holds up a hand to forestall any objection Lerial might have. "Your father is sending you because you have done well here. Otherwise he would have sent your brother. You are the better choice. I cannot say that I am happy. I worry that every time he leaves Kinaar he will not return. Yet he has built the Lancers from two companies into a force that sustains a country. I cannot ask him to abandon all that he has built."

The implication is clear enough for Lerial—*just as you cannot ask your father to abandon what he has created.*

After a moment of silence, Maeroja says. "I see you understand. But then, you would likely not be here if you did not."

"How . . . is Rojana?"

"She will recover. All who harbor more than childish desires do."

Lerial nods thoughtfully. He wouldn't have put it that way, but her words make sense.

"Tell me . . . what did you do once you returned to Cigoerne?"

"What the majer taught me how to do . . . keep working to get better . . ." Lerial describes what has happened in the season since he has left Kinaar. He has barely finished when Aylana bursts into the salon.

"You did come back!"

"Just for dinner," Lerial replies.

"You can't stay longer?" asks Tyrna, close behind her younger sister.

"No, he can't," says the majer, who accompanies Rojana into the salon. "We have to leave in the morning. What the Duke has asked of us is very important. It might mean the difference between our keeping Kinaar . . . or losing everything."

"That sounds important," says Aylana solemnly.

Both her sisters look at her.

"It is indeed," says Altyrn cheerfully. "And Lerial and I will tell you all about it when we return."

From that, and Maeroja's slightly forced smile, Lerial understands that the conversation during refreshments and dinner will be light . . . and as cheerful as possible. He can't blame either the majer or Maeroja.

XXXIX

Majer Altyrn arrives at the Teilyn post just before sunrise. He wears the riding uniform of a Lancer majer; that is, the same greens as all the Lancers, but with the collar insignia of a majer. Once he arrives, he gathers Lerial and the two squad leaders.

First, Altyrn looks to Juist and Kusyl. "You know about the squad of replacement Lancers accompanying us as far as Tirminya?"

Both squad leaders nod. Lerial does not, although he found out about the replacements that morning, only because, he suspects, Graessyr did not wish him to be surprised. He also learned that Altyrn had added a number of wooden wands of his own to those in the wagons and borrowed even more from Graessyr's armory. That didn't surprise him, either. What did was that he hadn't even noticed the additional Lancers at the post, and that bothered him. *Another reminder of what you don't know . . . or what you don't know enough about to notice.*

"They'll ride in the middle. You two will alternate van and rearguard."

"Yes, ser."

"What about the wagons, ser?" asks Juist.

"We'll take them as far as we can beyond Tirminya, except for the supply wagon for the post there. If we don't get heavy rains, we might be able to bring them all the way."

"They have roads and wagons there?" asks Kusyl. "The hill people, I mean?"

"They have better roads than in the south valley, and they use carts and small wagons." The majer answers questions for almost a fifth of a glass before he says, "It's time to head out."

From Altyrn's replies and certainty, Lerial gets the strong impression that at least some, if not all, of the majer's knowledge comes from his own observations, the result of many scouting trips beyond the "official" borders of Cigoerne, suggesting yet another reason why Maeroja and their daughters are concerned about him—the fact that he has already faced more than his share of danger. *And why Father picked him . . . again.*

Once the squad leaders leave, the majer turns to Lerial. "We'll be heading back into Teilyn, and then west out of town on the north valley road. It's a half-decent road for close to fifty kays, and not bad for another ninety or so, until we reach Tirminya. After that . . . well, it's like all the other trails."

"Tirminya is a border post, then?"

"Of sorts. The hamlets for another twenty kays or so to the west claim allegiance to your father, and they're so poor that Atroyan doesn't care. He'll care more once he learns that the hill people have agreed to allegiance with your father." He pauses. "Time to mount up."

No sooner are Lerial and Altyrn in their saddles than Graessyr walks out from the headquarters building to Altyrn. He carries a dispatch bag that he hands to the majer. "Give my best to Captain Dechund."

"He'll appreciate the gear as well." Altyrn's tone is dry.

"He should." Graessyr laughs genially. "He's getting it and his replacements two eightdays earlier than he would have."

"Anything in the pouch I should know about?" asks the majer, as he straps the dispatch pouch to his saddle.

"Approval of some promotions from junior squad leader to squad leader, and a warning to be aware of more raiders and poachers . . . and a notice that the paychest in the supply wagon has to last until the second eightday of spring."

"He won't like that."

"No post commander does." Graessyr steps back. "I won't keep you."

Altyrn nods and turns his mount toward the head of the column. Lerial follows, and in less than a tenth of a glass, the column heads out through the gates.

Over the next six days, as they ride along the north valley road, through hamlet after hamlet, the names of which few are familiar to Lerial, and those only as names on a map, roughly two-thirds of the time, at Altyrn's suggestion, Lerial alternates riding with either Juist or Kusyl. The remaining time is spent riding with the majer at the head of the Lancers, if behind the scouts.

At night when it is dark, and when no one is looking, Lerial continues to work to strengthen his ability to hold a concealment. While he feels he is improving, there is no way to tell because any use of it around the Lancers would reveal that ability . . . and the ability of an officer to vanish would not be the best talent to reveal.

Close to midday on eightday, Lerial sees a line of dwellings ahead, in the middle of a patch of taller, if browning grass. To the northwest is an expanse of short brown and dusty grass as far as the eye can see. To the south, no more than three kays away, the ground rises into what must be the northern side of the western end of the Wooded Ridges, and just beyond the line of dwellings, west of a depression marked by a sparse line of trees, possibly a small stream, are the white walls, most likely mud brick, of a Lancer outpost.

"Is that Tirminya?" Lerial asks Juist.

"That's Tirminya. Swore on the Rational Stars I'd never set eyes on the place again."

"Why not?"

"No women, not to speak of, except in the taverns . . . and they're not much to speak of. You're always riding north to deal with poachers or south through the gap to deal with the Meroweyan raiders that sometimes hit the west end of the south valley."

"Did the raiders used to come this far north?"

"That's what all the older squad leaders said," replies Juist.

"But no one wanted to move the post?"

"Move the post south, and you'd have more poachers from Afrit, maybe even come into Tirminya."

But why . . . Lerial swallows and asks, "And there aren't enough Lancers to garrison two posts this far from Cigoerne?"

"Not for as few raiders as there are."

"What about raids from the west?"

"Never happened. Hill folk believe in live and let live. Poachers never came back. Neither did Meroweyan raiders, I heard tell."

Then why do the hill people want to declare allegiance to Cigoerne? The only answer that Lerial can come up with is that Duke Casseon has moved armsmen against the hill people . . . or threatened to do so. *But Merowey is so much bigger than Cigoerne . . . Do they hate Casseon that much?* Otherwise, why on earth would they ask for protection and allegiance from Cigoerne?

After a moment, and upon reflection, Lerial understands. The hill people wouldn't ask for allegiance with Afrit because Atroyan wouldn't extend himself that far, and it's more convenient for him to have the hill people as a buffer between his lands and the lands Casseon actually controls. Khesyn would see no benefit and only losses in doing so. Their only choice to maintain their way of life is to appeal to Cigoerne.

You should have seen that earlier.

At that moment, Altyrn rides forward from the rearguard and motions for Lerial to join him.

Lerial eases the gelding forward. "Ser?"

"You must know that's Tirminya?"

"I thought it was from the Lancer post, but I asked Juist if it happened to be," Lerial confesses.

"We'll likely not get that warm a welcome here. The post has enough bunks, but Captain Dechund won't relish feeding us and providing fodder. The mounts need rest. At least a day, maybe two." Altyrn's tone turns wry as he goes on. "We can't afford to spend the golds your father sent to make the captain's go farther . . . and Dechund will know that. He'll understand, but he won't like it, especially when he finds out who you are."

"Yes, ser." Lerial almost asks why the captain has to know, but realizes not telling the officer in charge of the entire area who he is would indicate a total lack of trust . . . and that is something he—*and Father*—cannot afford.

Their way leads to and through the northern third of Tirminya. The road is even more dusty as they ride through the town, a collection of mostly mud-brick structures, although there are at least two dwellings with log walls. Unlike in the hamlets to the east, and especially those near the Swarth River, most dwellings have split-wood shingle roofs, rather than tile or the thatch that Lerial has heard is used in other parts of Hamor. Only a few inhabitants are in the streets, even though it is midday and moderately warm, especially for midwinter. There is no one on the bridge or the road from it to the post.

The gate guards at the post just watch as the three squads and wagons follow Lerial and the majer inside the tall mud-brick walls, walls covered with a mud plaster and then whitewashed. So white are the walls that Lerial feels that there must be years and years of whitewash covering the plaster. The inner courtyard of the fort is paved in mud brick, a patchwork of old solid bricks, some older cracked bricks, and newer bricks.

Outside the center headquarters building waits a captain. Altyrn rides within a few yards and reins up. Lerial eases the gelding to a halt beside the majer and his mount. Dechund is a stocky man, not quite rotund, with short brown hair that is slicked down below the sides of his visor cap and deep-set eyes the color of which somehow Lerial cannot discern. His brow is lined, and Lerial would guess that he is at least fifteen, if not twenty, years older than Lerial himself. His uniform is immaculate, and his boots are polished to a shine that might well serve as a mirror. The captain looks from Altyrn to Lerial and back to the majer. "You're back in uniform, Majer. Did something happen to Phortyn?"

"No. He's well, or was when Lord Lerial here left headquarters."

"Ser." Dechund's nod to Lerial is slightly more than perfunctory.

"I'm pleased to meet you, ser," replies Lerial.

Before Dechund can say anything more, Altyrn continues, "There may be a dispatch for you about our mission. There may not. Duke Kiedron has dispatched us to train Lancers from among the hill people. They've pledged allegiance to him."

"Getting tired of Casseon, are they?" Dechund looks as if he were about to spit, then swallows.

"Wouldn't you?" replies Altyrn genially. "We'll be here for two days, most likely, before we head out." He extends the dispatch pouch. "This is yours, and the third wagon has your supplies. We also escorted your replacement squad."

"My appreciation. You're welcome to what we have, Majer, Lord Lerial . . . It's not much, but it's yours."

"Undercaptain, please," Lerial says firmly, but quietly.

"As you wish, Undercaptain."

"No . . ." Lerial smiles. "As my father wishes . . . and as I understand, for I know far less than the captains and other senior and experienced Lancer officers."

"Undercaptain Lerial has already proved his ability with a sabre against Meroweyan raiders, limited as his experience is," says Altyrn smoothly.

Dechund nods once more, his smile not quite forced. "Once you've seen to what you must . . . my study is yours and at your convenience."

"Thank you. We will join you shortly." Altyrn offers an easy smile before turning his mount toward the stable built against or into the west wall of the post.

Lerial follows. He says nothing while unsaddling and grooming his mount.

"Leave your gear with your saddle," Altyrn tells Lerial as he finishes. "We should meet with the captain."

"Yes, ser."

Lerial follows the majer across the courtyard, feeling that more than a few eyes are on them, hoping that most rest on the majer. A junior squad leader in the anteroom of headquarters gestures to the open study door. "He's expecting you, sers."

"Thank you."

Dechund's study is like the few studies of Lancer officers that Lerial has already seen, with a narrow table-desk and a wooden armchair behind it, two straight-backed chairs, and a stack of file chests. A single bookcase holds few books, and assorted other items, including an odd-looking small brass lantern and several jars.

Altyrn takes one of the armless chairs, and Lerial the other . . . after waiting for the two senior officers to seat themselves.

"I've read the dispatches, Majer. It appears as though you have been assigned a difficult mission. It's one for which the Tirminya post can offer little support, I fear." Dechund offers an apologetic smile.

"Your standing orders will offer sufficient support," returns Altyrn. "It is more than likely that you will need to be more aware of incursions from the north."

"The north, ser?" Dechund is clearly puzzled.

Lerial can sense that without even trying.

"When Duke Atroyan discovers that the hill people are allying themselves with Duke Kiedron, what will be his likely response?"

"I would think he would attack them, would he not?"

"Is any small or company-sized force, or even two companies or three, likely to be successful in penetrating their forests without substantial casualties?"

Dechund considers the question, then frowns. "Are you suggesting . . . ?"

"I would think it highly likely that raids on small hamlets to the north will commence about the time spring planting begins." Altyrn smiles politely. "I have, of course, informed Captain Graessyr of that likelihood, as well as sent a dispatch to Majer Phortyn alerting him to the likelihood of such possibilities."

The captain nods slowly. "I suppose that is possible."

"I thought you might like my views on the matter. You are closer, these days, to the people and the hamlets here, and you will doubtless take the necessary steps as matters develop."

Lerial keeps a pleasant and interested expression on his face as he listens, even as he sees exactly what the majer has done.

Abruptly, Dechund turns to Lerial. "Undercaptain, might I ask your thoughts on the matter?"

Lerial waits a moment before answering. "I am far less experienced in knowing what raids or attacks may occur, or why, or when. Both you and the majer would know a great deal more than I would. I am under the impression that the majer has over the years undertaken some considerable scouting missions, or has at least commissioned them and studied the observations. I do not know what you have done, and so I cannot speak to that. But any thoughts I have on the matter would be mere opinion without facts, and I don't feel that such opinion should be considered." Lerial then smiles ruefully. "Put more bluntly, I don't know enough to express thoughts on the matter, with the exception that Duke Atroyan is not to be trusted in much of anything."

After a moment, Dechund smiles in return. "I can see why you are accompanying the majer."

Lerial understands the veiled insult, but merely smiles. "I am here because, like any undercaptain, I am following orders and will do my best to carry out my duties and to learn as much as I can that will be useful to the Lancers, and to my father the Duke."

The time the captain nods, then smiles once more. "It is good to have you both here, and we certainly will do our best to support you in what lies ahead." He looks to Altyrn. "You have only to ask, Majer."

"Thank you." Altyrn rises. "We will not keep you longer, but perhaps you will be able to fill us in on recent happenings here at the evening mess."

"I would be more than pleased to do so," replies Dechund, standing as he speaks.

Lerial quickly stands as well, not wanting to do so before the captain, but not wishing to lag, either.

Once Altyrn and Lerial leave the headquarters, the majer says, "You've met the captain. We'll talk later . . . on the way west."

That tells Lerial more than enough.

XL

The dinner served at the officers' mess on eightday evening only has two redeeming features. The burhka is hot enough that any taste is lost in the spices, and there is more than enough for the five officers, Altyrn, Dechund, and the three undercaptains—Whalyn, Seivyr, and Lerial. Both Whalyn and Seivyr are older, clearly officers who have been rankers and then squad leaders before being promoted to undercaptains.

The conversation deals largely with the fact that there have been very few raiders or poachers during harvest or early winter, as is to be expected, but that if raiders or poachers show up over the coming eightdays, it will be a sign of poor harvests and lack of game. Lerial says very little, but asks a question or two to keep the conversation going . . . and to give him a better idea about the officers stationed at Tirminya post.

After breakfast on oneday, largely porridge with dried fruit harder than eightday-old stale biscuits, strips of an unidentified meat dipped in hot spices and fried to a crisp, and fresh warm bread that is largely tasteless, Altyrn sets Lerial to studying the maps and reports about the area that had been collected at the post over the years. From a careful perusal of the maps, Lerial notices that towns, hamlets, he suspects, have been added to the main map over the years. This becomes obvious when he discovers an older map at the bottom that shows very little. Even more interesting is the fact that almost all of the "new" hamlets are to the north of Tirminya, ranging from perhaps ten kays north and across a range of almost eighty kays from east to west. The newest additions, if the brighter ink represents those, are the farthest north. *Is that because the people have become more comfortable with the Lancers . . . or less so with Afrit?*

Somewhere close to midday, if slightly after, Altyrn returns to the study shared by the undercaptains of the post, although Lerial has been the only one there.

"Ser?" Lerial looks up.

Altyrn gestures at the map spread on the circular table before Lerial. "What can you tell me about the maps? What did they tell you? Besides what hamlet and what river or stream is where?"

"Hamlets have been added to the main map almost every year. I don't think they just appeared that year. Is it because the Lancers have been charged with scouting out such hamlets . . . or because the people made them aware?"

"Some of each. Also, the lands to the north of Tirminya have been neglected for years by Atroyan and his sire. There are no good roads leading northeast to Swartheld, and there are plenty of forests and timberlands far closer."

"So the Lancers have begun to protect the people?"

"As they can . . . but it's far more than Atroyan has done."

"He's far richer . . ."

"No . . . his merchanters are far richer. There is a difference. What else did you learn from the maps?"

"No Lancers seem to have gone west . . . or they've not reported anything from the west."

"Duke Casseon has claimed the lands to the west . . . as have all of his predecessors," replies Altyrn mildly.

"So Lancers have been ordered not to go into those lands?"

"There are no maps of those lands in Lancer posts . . . except for the maps Duke Kiedron requested of Duke Casseon in order to know precisely where the borders are."

"Then . . . the official border is . . . what . . . ten kays west of here?"

"Fifteen, I believe. Put the maps away. We're going to take a ride through Tirminya. I've arranged to use mounts from the post."

After he returns the maps to the large flat wooden case, Lerial follows the majer to the stable, where his borrowed mount is a dark chestnut gelding, somewhat smaller than his own horse, but he has no difficulty saddling the chestnut, and before long, he and the majer, and four Lancers from the two squads accompanying them, are riding out through the open gates of the post and eastward toward the brick-and-timber bridge over the stream. While there are a few dwellings west of the stream, those are clearly newer, although Lerial had gained the impression the day before that most of the dwellings were of a more recent vintage, most likely the result of the establishment of the Lancer post.

"Those are new?" asks Lerial, gesturing to the dwellings on his left.

"New in the last five years."

The weather and the sun must be hard on dwellings, Lerial thinks, because the structures look older than five years.

"I've been talking to Undercaptain Seivyr," the majer says. "He's the senior undercaptain here. Good man. Make a good captain already. I knew him when he was a raw recruit from Narthyl. He says that some of the people he's talked to on his patrols have seen Afritan scouts within ten kays of Tirminya. They were wearing Afritan Guard uniforms."

"Isn't the official border about that far north?" asks Lerial warily.

"It is." Altyrn frowns. "But there haven't been any Afritan armsmen sighted there in years, and Graessyr hasn't received any reports about scouts. I told Captain Dechund that Afritan armsmen had set up patrols just north of Penecca in the east. Then I asked him if any of his squads had seen any signs of that here."

And he said there weren't any signs of that. But Lerial only asks, "What did he say?"

"I expect you already know. He said he didn't know of any Afritan armsmen being close."

"*He* didn't know. That's an . . . interesting way of putting it."

"I thought so as well."

Once across the bridge, the majer turns south along what passes for the main street of Tirminya. Lerial immediately picks out a tavern, its windows shuttered, unsurprisingly, since there would be few Lancers free to visit until after their duty day ends, especially since it is not an end-day. Beside the tavern is what might be a boardinghouse, but is most likely a brothel, at least at times.

As he rides, Lerial tries to extend his order senses well away from his mount and to those around them. There are so few people on the street that he can sense, at least generally, something about their feelings . . . and the fact that there are only a few people in the boardinghouse. There is a narrow alley between the purported boardinghouse and a chandlery. An older man and woman stand on the narrow entry porch of the chandlery and look at the Lancers briefly, then turn away. Lerial can feel a sense of resignation coupled with something else. *Perhaps grudging acceptance?* He isn't sure.

Beside the chandlery is a carpentry shop, the kind, Lerial assumes, that in a small town handles everything from cooperage to cabinets and simple furniture. Across from the chandlery is a small café. Whether anyone is inside, Lerial cannot see, but he has the feeling he would rather eat at the officers' mess than there. Next is what passes for a square, although there is no one selling anything except a boy standing beside a cart with a few bushels of potatoes.

They continue through the square and down the main street for almost half a kay.

Then Altyrn says, "We'll ride back up and past the bridge road."

Lerial guides his gelding in a turn and ends up riding on the majer's right as they head back north.

Ahead, Lerial senses . . . something . . . in or near a narrow alleyway just short of the south end of the small square. He can't quite determine who or what is there, but there is a sense of both chaos and purpose. Although he cannot say why, he draws his sabre.

Behind him he hears one of the rankers murmur something, but he concentrates on the alleyway as he rides past, almost even with Altyrn. He can still sense purpose and chaos, but sees no one, even as he feels that there may be a man standing in the narrow shadow next to the building that has no signboard over its doorway.

Then the man moves, and for a moment, Lerial can sense that he is an archer. Almost without thinking, he twists in the saddle and slashes with his sabre. He is astonished to see the two halves of the arrow tumbling in front of him, but not so astonished that he does not try to create a concealment as he wheels the gelding toward the alley. Yet as he rides toward the narrow alley, another shaft whistles toward him and strikes his upraised sabre, and the figure in the shadows turns and runs. That is what Lerial senses. He drops the concealment as he reaches the alley, where he reins up, because the narrow way appears empty, and he cannot sense anyone hiding in the nooks in the buildings on each side.

After a moment, he turns the gelding back toward the street, where the four rankers wait, sabres out. Altyrn stands beside his mount, holding the remnants of the two arrows. As Lerial watches the majer slips the broken arrows into an otherwise empty saddlebag, then remounts.

"Did you see him well enough to describe him?"

"No, ser. He's gone. I couldn't see where."

Altyrn nods. "You scared him off. There's not much else we can do here, and riding into a narrow alley isn't the best idea after someone's already taken a shot at us. We might as well head back to the post."

While Altyrn's voice is calm, Lerial can sense a certain turmoil within the majer, that and a measure of worry and concern. Yet it is clear that the majer has no interest in trying to find an assassin who tried to kill him, and that puzzles Lerial.

Lerial can also sense a certain fear and confusion from the rankers. He is afraid he knows why. *Yet what else could you have done?* He doesn't know, but, as they ride up the main street and then west over the bridge, Lerial keeps trying to sense if there is anything else that presages dangers. He senses absolutely nothing else remotely chaotic or dangerous, only the irritation of an older man leading a mule pulling a cart as they ride past.

Once they return to the post, Altyrn reins up outside the stable, dismounts, and hands the reins of his horse to one of the rankers, saying, "If you'd have someone unsaddle and groom him."

"Yes, ser."

The majer looks to Lerial, who has also dismounted. "Take care of your mount and wait for me. I'm going to tell Dechund what happened. As the post commander here, he needs to know that there are idiots who are careless with bows. There's not much he can do, but he will have to send a report to Graessyr and to Lancer headquarters."

Lerial dutifully unsaddles and grooms the chestnut, then waits just outside the stable door. The winter sunlight feels good, perhaps because he has felt slightly chilled since the unknown archer had shot at the majer. He frowns. *You knew he was targeting the majer. How?* He is still thinking about that when Altyrn returns.

"We need to take a short walk, Lerial," Altyrn says. "To inspect the outer walls."

"Yes, ser." Lerial knows full well the walk will have nothing to do with the walls.

Neither says anything until they have walked back out through the open gates and around along the north wall. The majer gestures toward the wall, then asks, as he drops his hand, "How did you do that? In town."

"Do what, sir?"

"You turned as if you knew that assassin was there. I'd looked at the alley as we neared, and it was empty."

"I have a little talent with order-sensing, ser. I've been practicing, and it's easier when there aren't many people around. I felt danger and drew my sabre and turned. The rest of it? I don't know. When I saw the arrow, I just tried to knock it out of the air, and I rode toward him, but he was faster than I was."

"He likely ducked into one of those buildings, but by the time we could have gotten into them he'd have been gone. There also might have been another man just waiting for that." Altyrn keeps walking, but looks directly at Lerial. "I could have sworn that, for a moment, you weren't even there."

"I was very much there, ser. He shot a second arrow. It almost hit me."

"There is a reason, you know, why I told you to let Lancers do the charging."

"I know, ser, but I had the feeling you were the target."

"That won't help, exactly, if you're the one who gets shot, Lerial."

"Yes, ser." *Either way, you lose if I fail.*

"That said," Altyrn adds with a smile, "I greatly appreciate what you did, and I have absolutely no doubts that Maeroja and my daughters would appreciate it even more, were they to find out. Which they will not until much, much later." He pauses. "Do you understand?"

"Yes, ser."

"There's also the problem that the rankers saw what I did . . . and what I didn't. You had to draw the sabre before he loosed that shaft. You have good reflexes, but they're not that good." The majer looks at Lerial and raises his eyebrows in inquiry.

"I did. I sensed danger, but I worried that I was deceiving myself . . ."

"I can understand that, but . . . officers are supposed to be cautious if they feel something is not right. That caution doesn't help your men if you don't warn them as well."

Lerial can see that. He can also see that he is not used to thinking about the responsibilities even a junior undercaptain has to others.

"Just keep that in mind."

"I will."

"There's one other thing. You wondered why I didn't try to chase the fellow who shot at us. That's a typical ambush trap, the kind the Afritans use. You shoot at someone. If you kill them, you succeed. If you miss, you run like you're fleeing the dark angels and hope that some idiot will follow helter-skelter and get shot by a second group of archers." The majer shrugs. "It could have been either way, and it's hard to tell in a small town like Tirminya. You did the right thing by not chasing down that alley. It's not always possible . . . but think before you pursue."

Lerial can sense that there is more the majer is not revealing. "Is there anything else?"

"Not about that at the moment."

Lerial ponders what Altyrn has said about the archer behaving the way Afritan archers do, but earlier reporting the archer as an idiot with a bow to Dechund.

The majer continues to stroll along the path that parallels the north side of the Lancer post, his eyes apparently on the wall. He says nothing.

After a time, Lerial ventures, "Ser?"

"Yes?"

"Isn't it strange that there are Afritan Guards or scouts out here at the same time that Duke Atroyan has forces stationed just north of Penecca?"

"Why do you think that?"

"Well . . . are the ones here to draw men away from Penecca . . . or is it the other way around? Or could Duke Atroyan be planning an attack on all of Cigoerne?"

"What do you think?"

"I don't think he wants to spend the golds and the armsmen to fight against us. Not from what you've said."

"Then why would he station men on our northern borders? Or appear to be ready to attack?"

Lerial considers, then says, "Perhaps to keep Lancers in the north of Cigoerne so that the ones in the south will be outnumbered by the Heldyans?" He frowns. "But if that is the goal, wouldn't that cause a problem if Duke Khesyn sends more armsmen and we're defeated?"

"It would indeed. Since Duke Atroyan doesn't want that to happen, why might he be doing what he appears to be doing?"

"To weaken both Khesyn and us?"

"That would be my guess. I'd judge it's your father's as well. I wouldn't be surprised if he's moving some of the more experienced companies south and replacing some of the more experienced companies in the north with less experienced ones . . . or perhaps rotating less experienced troopers or squads into the fighting in the south so that they're amid more experienced Lancers."

"To give more rankers experience in fighting trained armsmen, rather than raiders or poachers?"

"I would, and I would think that Majer Phortyn would consider it. That is, if your father has not done so already." Altyrn shrugs. "Right now, I don't know, and I'm in no position to advise."

Let alone command.

The majer points to the walls. "How high are they?"

"Three yards, perhaps three and a cubit."

"Could they withstand a siege?"

"Not for long."

"Then why have such walls?"

"They protect the men from surprise attacks . . . and if anyone did want to attack, they'd have to bring more armsmen and equipment out here. And a whole lot of wagons with supplies. It probably wouldn't be worth it."

"Good. Just remember. Anything that ties up great numbers of an enemy's forces and resources with little expense on your part is valuable."

"But, ser . . . there's a whole company here."

"There is, indeed, but what else does a company in a place like this do besides patrol and train?"

Lerial doesn't understand, and his face must betray his confusion, because Altyrn laughs, not sardonically, but generously. "First, the Lancers reinforce the image of your father's power here. Second, they spend their coppers and silvers here. Would there be taverns and the like here if there were no post? Third, they buy provisions here, and that makes the people more prosperous. When they're more prosperous, some of those golds spent on the Lancers come back to your father in tariffs. Fourth, most posts away from the larger towns pick up recruits because there are usually younger sons who have few prospects."

What the majer says makes sense, and it reinforces some of what Saltaryn had tried to convey to Lerial, but with more real-life examples.

As they walk back toward the main gates of the post, Lerial realizes that the majer has not said a word about Captain Dechund . . . and is not likely to do so—not until they have left Tirminya well behind.

XLI

The remainder of oneday and twoday are far less eventful. Lerial spends more time studying maps. He also watches closely as the post rankers replace an axle on one of the post's supply wagons. By the time he and the majer join the three other officers for dinner on twoday night, Lerial is more than ready to leave Tirminya post, and he can certainly see why Juist was not impressed with the time he had spent there.

When the five gather at the small table, with Altyrn at the head, and Dechund to his right, and Lerial his left, Dechund smiles broadly. "I did break out some of the better lager for dinner tonight. It'll be a while before you see it's like again, I'd wager."

"I won't be taking that wager," returns the majer. "We do appreciate the lager."

The meal is better than that of the previous two nights, if marginally, consisting of tenderized mutton cutlets and sliced boiled potatoes, both smothered in a brown cream sauce, with boiled turnips. There is more than enough, even though Sevier and Whalen take rather substantial helpings.

Lerial even finds the lager not bad at all, although he would not call it good, but, rather, adequate.

"What do you think you'll be able to do with those forest types?" asks Dechund after taking what looks to be the last swallow of lager from his mug.

"Who knows?" replies the majer. "We have orders, and we'll do the best we can. Predicting about what you don't know isn't a good idea for any officer." He looks to Lerial. "For that matter, it's not a good idea for anyone."

"They said the women are beautiful," says the captain. "That could be why the Meroweyans are thinking of moving north. You think that's why you ran into raiders in the south valley? That they're having to move out as more small growers move north?"

"That could be."

"You never said much about what happened with the raiders. I mean with you and the raiders this last time."

Altyrn clears his throat, then looks to Lerial. "There's a dispatch I left on the table-desk in my quarters. I meant to give it to Captain Dechund before dinner. Would you mind? I'd rather not put that off until later. Especially not in the morning. Things get misplaced in dim light when you're setting out."

Lerial can sense that, again, Altyrn is telling the truth, but in a somewhat shaded way, and it puts him in an awkward position. As an undercaptain, he should immediately jump up. As the Duke's son and potential heir . . . Lerial decides he's still an undercaptain and likely will be for some years yet.

"I'd be happy to get that, ser," he says as he rises.

"Thank you. I do appreciate that." Altyrn lowers his voice and murmurs, "And take plenty of time."

Lerial can tell that the majer truly does appreciate his fetching the dispatch, and that not only surprises Lerial, but concerns him as he leaves the small mess room and hurries toward the guest officers' quarters. *Why does he need plenty of time?*

The quarters that the majer has been occupying are not any larger than those in which Lerial has been sleeping, and scarcely any better furnished, save that the table-desk looks newer and the pallet firmer.

The dispatch that lies on the table-desk, weighed down by a small brown leather-bound book, is a single sheet of paper, not folded or sealed. Lerial reads it, since he assumes it is not that confidential. It is addressed to Captain Graessyr.

> *. . . pleased to inform you that we have arrived at Tirminya post without any untoward events, and that we are leaving on threeday morning of the fifth eightday of winter. We have delivered the paychest to post Commander Dechund, and have escorted his replacement Lancers to the post. We have seen no sign of raiders or of Afritan troops thus far.*
>
> *The Mina River is running lower than in the past, and that may be a sign of difficulties in the seasons ahead, unless there is more rain . . .*

When he finishes reading, Lerial lowers the dispatch. It is signed and sealed at the bottom, but not folded and sealed again. He can't help but frown. Exactly why does the majer need such an innocuous dispatch so immediately? Or what does he want to tell Dechund and the two undercaptains without Lerial around?

His eyes go to the small volume, and he wonders what it might be. He does not pick it up, but does look at the front cover and the spine, but there is no title or other indication as to what the volume is. Lerial decides against opening it, but does take some time to survey the small room. There isn't much to observe, except that the chamber is neat, and nothing is out of place, and not a piece of gear or clothing is visible. In fact, the only personal items in plain view are the dispatch and the brown book. All of that suggests that Altyrn had in fact planned to leave the dispatch and then send Lerial to fetch it.

After a time, during which he does nothing but stand and think about why the majer may have done what he did, Lerial takes the dispatch and steps out of the small quarters, gently closing the door and then walking from the quarters across the courtyard back to the mess.

When he nears the half-open door to the mess he slows and listens.

". . . and that's why I sent him off . . . Good lager . . . have to admit . . ."

". . . better lager than you'll get at most messes . . ."

". . . we do appreciate it . . . knows what they drink in the hills?"

Lerial frowns at that statement by Altyrn, since he is more than certain that the majer knows full well what beverages are drunk by the hill people.

". . . but you need more of your own lager. I'll even pour it . . ."

Lerial coughs as he nears the door, then steps inside. "I'm sorry, ser, it took a few moments." He offers an embarrassed smile as he extends the dispatch. "The lager . . ."

"It happens to the best of us." Altyrn takes the dispatch and looks to the captain. "Didn't even put the final seal on it. You can do that and send it, though."

"I'd be happy to," replies Dechund.

"Well . . . be up early tomorrow morning." Altyrn stands abruptly, and his jacket sleeve catches the edge of the lager pitcher, but he grabs the pitcher with his other hand, catching it before it can tumble to the floor. Even so, most of the remaining lager, not that there was apparently much, sloshes out onto the wooden floor. "Sorry about that. There wasn't much left, though, and I did save the pitcher." The majer sets the pitcher on the table. "Our thanks again."

Lerial is impressed at Altyrn's quickness in catching the pitcher, but he can also sense a certain worry from the majer as they leave the mess, but he does not ask or speak, even after they are crossing the courtyard back to the officers' quarters.

When the two are well away from any building, apparently alone, Altyrn says quietly, "I hope you didn't mind, but I wanted to tell the others about what occurred in the south valley, without you present, because, if you were, they'd be skeptical about my version of events."

That statement is clearly true and unshaded. Yet that leaves Lerial even more puzzled about Altyrn's motives and why he needed Lerial out of the mess room, because Altyrn had definitely been concerned about something . . . and Lerial has his doubts about what that might be. All he says in reply is, "I can see that, ser."

"We'll talk more tomorrow."

"Yes, ser." One thing about which Lerial is certain is that the majer neither likes nor trusts Dechund . . . and from what Lerial has seen and sensed, he shares Altyrn's concerns.

Still . . . it is a while before sleep finds him.

XLII

Altyrn and Lerial and their squads and wagons are up even earlier on threeday, preparing to leave well before sunrise.

"What about the lances, Majer?" asks Kusyl. "When should we start riding with them?"

"Not now," replies Altyrn. "If we run across raiders, sabres should be enough. If things change, we can get to them quickly enough."

"There won't be many raiders near the Verd," adds Seivyr, who has appeared from somewhere in the low light. "Came to see you off, Majer."

"That's appreciated, Seivyr." Altyrn pauses, then adds, "You know . . . there have been reports of Afritan armsmen. I wouldn't be surprised if you might not get some sort of night attack. I'm just an old careful majer, but it wouldn't hurt to make sure the gates are closed at night for a while. And that they stay locked."

"I've been thinking that myself."

"You wouldn't want any trouble that way. It's easy to overlook an unbarred gate or one with a slipped bar."

Altyrn looks from Seivyr to Lerial. "You'll ride with Kusyl and his squad."

"Yes, ser."

As the majer has ordered, the squads ride out through the gates before the sun even peeks over the horizon, with Altyrn leading the way beside Juist. The road west from Tirminya looks no different from the road into the border town, just a dirt track running through barely rolling hills and paralleling the north side of the Wooded Ridges. While there are groupings of growers' steads, either around springs or small streams, it appears to Lerial that most of those living at the south end of the grasslands that, according to the maps, stretch close to two hundred kays to the north–northwest are herders of some sort, mostly of sheep, although he does see an occasional herd of cattle, but no goats.

Is the absence of goats because they tend to destroy the grass? Lerial doubts that, suspecting that the reason is merely that either sheep or cattle pay more for the herders.

Once the column is on the road west, and all the Lancers and wagons are in order, Lerial turns in the saddle and says to Kusyl, "I haven't seen that many Lancer posts. Just Lancer headquarters and the posts at Teilyn and Brehaal . . . and now Tirminya. How does Tirminya compare to others?"

"Some are better. Some worse. Both Seivyr and Whalyn are good undercaptains. Seivyr'd make a good post captain. Rankers are mostly solid, even the replacements that rode with us." Kusyl pauses, seeming to gnaw at his upper lip for a moment. "Place like Tirminya is hard on the rankers. Have to watch the men close."

Especially the squad leaders do. Lerial doesn't say that, knowing it wouldn't be right, in some fashion. "Because it's so far from everywhere?"

"Partly. Also because there's no real backup. That's one reason why a post like Tirminya has five squads instead of four, and two undercaptains instead of one."

"Did any of the squad leaders at the post say much about raiders or poachers . . . or Afritan armsmen?"

"They've seen some, mostly to the north, but sometimes to the west. Usually not more than a squad." Kusyl paused. "Come to think of it, Gaehorn said he'd never seen more than a squad at a time."

Lerial asks questions intermittently for almost a glass before Altyrn rides back and orders him, if quietly, to ride forward and take the lead position with Juist and his squad. That alone tells Lerial that the majer doesn't expect trouble any time soon.

Once Lerial has ridden beside Juist for a time, he asks the same sorts of questions of the older squad leader as he had of Kusyl, and then listens. The answers are similar, except in one case.

". . . got the feeling that there haven't been as many poachers and raiders from the north lately," Juist says. "Might be because the Afritans have some patrols going. More than they used to." He looks to Lerial. "You have any thoughts on that, ser?"

"I do know that there have been more Afritan armsmen lately just north of Penecca. They might be trying to weaken us by keeping Lancers from being moved south to deal with the raiders from Heldya. There are more Heldyan forces on the east side of the river recently."

"Friggin' Heldyans . . ." murmurs Juist, almost under his breath. "Begging your pardon, ser."

"I don't think the majer's all that fond of them, either. He hasn't said anything, but I've gotten that impression."

"No one with brains would care for them, not from what I've seen."

"Have you had to fight them?"

"Only once. Saw one of them cut the throat of his own wounded. Man had a broken leg, and his mount was down. Could have lived. Grabbed his wallet, too."

"That sounds like a raider."

"It wasn't. Heldyan squad leader." Juist shakes his head.

After another half glass, Altyrn returns, then motions for Lerial to ride with him, well ahead of the squad. Lerial eases the gelding forward, wondering what the majer has in mind.

"I've not been neglecting you," Altyrn says. "I wanted to learn what Juist and Kusyl saw and learned while we were at Tirminya post. Did you talk to them about that?"

"Yes, ser. I mean, I asked what they thought of the post because I hadn't seen that many . . ." Lerial goes on to relay what he has learned.

When he finishes, the majer nods. "Good. You need to talk to them often, but not just for the sake of talking. Never be familiar, and never condescending."

Lerial does not point out that the majer has said that to him before. Several times, in fact, but that indicates to him how important Altyrn feels that advice is.

"What did you think of Captain Dechund?" Altyrn's voice is pleasant.

Lerial detects no strain or chaos around the majer and decides on an accurate, but cautious reply. "There's something about him that concerns me, but I couldn't say why exactly. Then, it might just be the business about his not knowing about Afritan patrols. Both Kusyl and Juist heard about patrols from the squad leaders at the post."

"You're being cautious."

"Yes, ser. I don't have the experience to take risks about things I don't know enough about. Especially when I don't have to." He manages a rueful grin as he looks at Altyrn.

"You're right. For now. But you won't always be in that position, you know?"

"I know, ser, but I can hope I've learned more by the time I have."

"You just might." Altyrn chuckles. "Now, let me tell you what I know about the land and the people in this part of the north valley . . ."

Lerial listens, but not for long, because in little more than a third of a glass, a scout gallops back along the dirt road from a low rise roughly half a kay ahead. The scout turns his mount to ride alongside the majer. "There's a squad of Afritan armsmen up ahead, ser. Just beyond the rise. They seem to be waiting for us."

"Could there be more concealed somewhere?"

The scout considers, then says, "Be hard to do that. Over the rise there, the land's flat as a table for more than a kay in any direction."

"They haven't used the rise for cover or for position. That suggests they want to talk. Still . . ." Altyrn turns to Juist. "Ready arms."

"Ready! Arms! Pass it back!"

"Do you think they'll attack?" asks Lerial as the scout heads forward to join the other Lancer who waits where the road reaches the top of the rise.

"Anything's possible, but I don't think so. The squad leader is in a difficult position. If he lets us pass without asking what we're doing, he'll be censured or worse. If he attacks, he might be killed, and he'd certainly lose most of his squad, if not all of it. If he threatens, he can't back it up, unless he's been sent out ahead of an entire company. And if that's the case, we'll just politely agree and alter our plans. I don't think that's likely, but we'll have to see. They wouldn't pick an area with no cover unless we've surprised them. That suggests the squad is more for reconnaissance or to show Atroyan's banner."

"Belatedly trying to establish what he believes are his borders?"

"Atroyan's often been belated in his actions . . . and that can be dangerous for everyone."

Once Altyrn and Lerial ride over the top of low ridge, Lerial can see the squad of Afritan armsmen, who wear the dull crimson tunics that Lerial remembers, but not the iron breastplates. The troopers are drawn up some three hundred yards west on flat ground. Lerial is surprised to see that one of the Afritan armsmen does in fact bear a banner, although in the quiet air it droops against the staff, and Lerial cannot make out the design, only that the narrow banner is the crimson of Afrit.

A single armsman rides forward to meet them, reining up some twenty yards from the two scouts, now only a few yards before Altyrn.

"Column. Halt," the majer orders. "The undercaptain and I will meet the Afritan squad leader."

Once the Lancers have halted, Altyrn nods to Lerial, and they move forward. The majer reins up several yards short of the Afritan. "Greetings, Squad Leader."

"Greetings." After a pause, the squad leader says, "Do you plan to cross into Afritan lands?"

"We do not," replies Altyrn. "According to the maps sent to Duke Kiedron by Duke Casseon, the lands to the west and south of Tirminya belong to Duke Casseon. We're on a trade mission to some of the forest towns located within those borders."

The squad leader nods. "Might I inquire as to what towns, ser?"

"Apfhel, and then Verdell. After those, that depends." Altyrn smiles politely. "I am most certain that Duke Atroyan would not wish you to trouble yourself with a mere two squads and an old majer doing his best to do a job that any bright captain could do."

Lerial can easily sense the confidence behind Altyrn's words . . . and the slight emphasis on "two squads."

"We're just patrolling the border, ser. There have been reports of poachers."

"That is true . . . although I believe you have strayed a bit farther south than the accepted borders of Afrit, and that might upset Duke Casseon. I do appreciate your concerns, though. Most poachers have come from the north, and Duke Kiedron will be pleased to learn that Duke Atroyan takes his responsibilities so gravely that you are patrolling so diligently. We, of course, are relieved of the burden of dispatching them." Altyrn smiles once more. "Although my men do appreciate the opportunity to use their weapons, there is little satisfaction in dealing with mere ruffians."

For a moment, the Afritan squad leader frowns. Then he nods. "We wish you a successful mission. We will be on our way."

"We wish you well," replies Altyrn.

Both Lerial and the majer watch as the squad leader rides back to his men, and they turn and hard north along a narrow path that cannot really be termed a road.

"Do you think they'll set up an ambush?" asks Lerial in a low voice.

"No. Half the men in his squad are scarcely older than you are. He just wants to send a dispatch saying that he stopped us and warned us . . . and be able to report what we said we are doing."

"I don't think he expected to come across two squads here."

"No. He didn't. That might affect your father as well."

"You think he might consider attacking Penecca because he thinks there aren't as many Lancers there?"

"That's possible. It's also possible that he might have to consider putting more armsmen here and away from the north border nearer the river. There's also the problem that it will be days, maybe an eightday, before Atroyan finds out. He also can't be certain that we'll be doing what we said we were."

Which we aren't . . . or not exactly. Lerial can see how important it is not only to know what has happened, but to be able to judge what will happen . . . and he wonders if he will ever have that kind of skill in judgment. *Lephi won't. That's for certain.*

Altyrn looks at Lerial. "That's a very serious expression on your face."

"I was just thinking about how my father has to decide what to do when he only knows what happened days before."

"An effective ruler is one who can determine what others will do before they do it."

Lerial considers those words. He can anticipate where an opponent's blade will be before it is there, but is there any way his skills with reading order-chaos flows can help him anticipate what others will do in other areas . . . or over time?

XLIII

For the next two days, while Lerial, Altyrn and the two squads pass through small hamlets, and see isolated steads and occasional flocks of sheep, and in one case, goats, neither Lerial, the majer, nor the scouts see any other signs of armsmen, poachers, or raiders.

There are scattered clouds, but no rain, and that is anything but good, Lerial knows, for the coming crop year, and especially for the herders. He does do his best to study the clouds with his order senses, and try to determine the patterns within each. After a time, he begins to get a feeling of which clouds might produce rain . . . or snow, if the weather continues to chill, since he is now wearing his jacket closed and more than glad for the heavy gray riding gloves that the majer had given him.

As the afternoon draws out on fiveday afternoon, Lerial can see that the low rolling hills behind them are giving way to lower and lower rises until the ground before them is almost flat, although the Wooded Ridges to the south appear to be higher above the plain, and he can see wooded hills in the distance to the west and west–northwest. The grass before them is all tannish brown and no more than calf-high.

Altyrn calls a halt for the evening at an abandoned stead that consists of little more than collapsing sod walls that had once been several barns and a grassed-over hummock that might have been a house. There is a well, however, with a wooden cover, and a recently used firepit, as well as signs that others have used the ruins as a way station, although not within the last few eightdays.

As he is tethering the gelding to a tieline anchored in one of the sod walls, he asks the majer, "If there's a well here, and grass, why was the stead abandoned?"

"It's a shallow well," says Altyrn. "It's likely there's no water in summer and harvest . . . The lands here are dry, and there aren't any streams until we get much closer to Apfhel."

"When will that be?"

"If we don't run into rain or raiders, we should reach the beginning of the forest road late tomorrow morning." Altyrn glances toward the scattered clouds and then toward Lerial.

"They don't feel like rain clouds. If they get lower, there might be a quick shower, but I don't think so."

Lerial looks toward the firepit where two Lancers are struggling with a striker and kindling to start a fire with a few scraps of wood and some brush. "They'll need more wood."

"Juist has already sent men to that grove over there."

Lerial follows the majer's gaze and sees a line of trees, most likely the remnants of a windbreak.

"Most of the wood will be green. It's too bad there aren't any camma trees around."

"Camma trees?" Lerial has never heard of them.

"Cammabark is an excellent firestarter. You have to get it just right, though. Too dry and it explodes. It only grows in certain places. The people of the Verd limit where it can grow, obviously."

Cammabark? Lerial is still pondering over that when he realizes the majer has left to talk to Kusyl.

The evening meal is mainly bread and cheese, with baked roots of some sort that Altyrn has directed several rankers to dig up on one side of where the stead house had stood. The roots are chopped up and added to dried mutton that has been soaked in boiling water and then fried over the cookfire. Lerial eats the roots and mutton, not exactly with enthusiasm, but at least he isn't hungry when he finishes.

Later, after dark, he slips away from the fire and back behind one of the sod walls where he creates a concealment, then eases back toward the gathered Lancers, moving slowly and cautiously, since he cannot see from within the concealment, but only sense the other Lancers through his sensing of the flow of order and chaos around them. He gradually makes his way to where Kusyl and Juist are seated on a low hummock that might have once been a sod wall, then halts and listens.

For a time, the two squad leaders talk about the day's ride, and the weather, and about various individual Lancers. Lerial takes in that information, hoping the more he learns about the men and the way the squad leaders talk and handle them, the better he will be if he has to lead real patrols.

After a moment of silence, Kusyl clears his throat and lowers his voice. "What do you think of the undercaptain?"

"What should I think?" replies Juist, his voice carrying a trace of amusement.

"He's not what I thought he'd be."

"That's bad? He asks good questions, mostly, anyway."

Lerial winces at the "mostly," but continues to listen.

"You heard what happened in Tirminya?"

"The business about him cutting an arrow in half with his sabre?"

"Don't laugh. Two of my boys saw it. He cut one shaft in half and knocked another out of the air. And . . . like for a couple of moments . . . he moved so fast they didn't even see him."

"That's a problem?" asks Juist ironically. "He's spent most of the last year training with a sabre. Two seasons with the majer. That's more blade training than most officers get in ten years."

Lerial can sense that there is something about what Juist is saying. He isn't lying, but . . . there's a mixture of order and chaos around his words. Withholding information perhaps?

"There's more there," says Kusyl flatly.

"He's from the Magi'i. Be surprised if there isn't."

"If he's a magus . . . why is he an undercaptain?"

"Word is," says Juist, "that he's a decent field healer."

"Oh . . . sowshit."

"Hasn't stopped him from slicing a raider's throat from ear to ear."

"Still strange . . ."

"He's the Duke's son. How is he going to learn anything if he doesn't see what we do? Anything happens to the Duke or his older brother, and he's the Duke. Even if it doesn't, he's likely to be leading in the field. Be thankful the Duke has enough sense to send him out before he's in charge of anything."

"That's why . . . the majer?"

"Take you this long to figure that out?"

"Sort of thought so all along."

"If the undercaptain needs to know something, tell him. He's still young enough to listen. Won't always be that way, from what I've seen."

Those words bother Lerial. Is Juist talking about Lephi . . . or his father . . . or just officers in general after they become captains or overcaptains?

"He doesn't say much. Just asks questions."

"How else is he going to learn?"

"Still . . . something about him . . ."

"You don't like it when you can't figure out an officer, do you?" asks Juist.

"Nope. You're no different." Kusyl chuckles.

"Not much. Except there are times you don't need to know and, if you're smart, you don't try to learn."

"Oh?"

"Like the majer. Looks like a white-haired old officer. He's done things I'd never want to do. Why do you think the Duke sent his son to train under him? You notice that the undercaptain always says 'ser.' He's a lord, and he's real polite to the majer. Not just words, either."

"Never thought of it like that."

"Best you do." Another silence falls between the two before Juist says, "What ever happened to that girl you met in Barteld?"

Lerial slips away and makes his way back toward the wall where there are no horses tied before he releases the concealment and heads back toward the fire.

He is a good fifteen yards away when Altyrn appears. "Where have you been?"

"Walking around. Trying to do it as quietly as possible . . . just for practice."

"I see." Altyrn pauses. "I've got fairly good eyes at night. I didn't see you."

Lerial shrugs. "I don't know what to say, ser. I wasn't about to wander off."

There is the slightest pause. Then the majer says, "All the best leaders and rulers have special talents. The very best, though, know when to use them, and when not to."

"I'm learning that, ser, but sometimes you have to practice for a long time before you know enough to understand when to use something and when not to. I can sense where most blades will be just before they get there, but it took more than two seasons of practicing with you and the Lancers at Teilyn post before I had enough skill to use that sense."

"I thought that might be the case. Some healers can sense where people will move before they do."

"I've tried that . . . but I can't do that." *Not yet.*

"You never know what you can do unless you work at it."

Lerial grins. "I didn't say I wasn't working at it, ser." *And a few other order skills.*

"Good." Altyrn clears his throat. "None of that will help much, though, if you don't get enough sleep."

"I was about to turn in."

"Good night, Lerial."

"Good night, ser."

XLIV

Less than two glasses after the Lancers set out on sixday morning, they reach a point where the trail makes a wide turn from its previous heading of west–southwest to a definite southwest direction, straight toward the Wooded Ridges, except that Lerial suspects that they are far west of where the Wooded Ridges end. *How can you tell? The forest on the hills extends for over a hundred kays.*

Another glass passes before Altyrn gestures. "See those posts? That's where the forest road begins."

Lerial looks at the two timber posts close to a half kay ahead, one on each side of the dirt track, and a good kay from the trees that begin halfway up the slope to the low ridge before them. "That's the forest road?"

"That's the end of it. That's where Verdheln begins."

"And what we've ridden across for the last four days belongs to Duke Casseon?"

"Some of the forest people think those lands belong to your father. He certainly has more claim to them than Casseon."

"Because the Lancers occasionally patrol them, and Casseon's men don't?"

"That's the main reason. The other is that Casseon's armsmen would have to cross their lands to reach the north valley."

As Lerial nears the posts, he notes that the road beyond is not all that much to speak of, except it is wide enough for a wagon and a mount abreast, unlike the track that they have followed for the last three days, which barely accommodates two mounts side by side.

Once the column passes the posts, Altyrn calls a halt and summons Kusyl forward so that Lerial, the two squad leaders, and the majer form a loose mounted circle.

"We're now within the borders of the lands claimed by the forest people," Altyrn begins. "As I told you last night, they don't attack without provocation. They have a guardpost at the edge of the forest. Undercaptain Lerial and I will lead the way until they agree to let us enter the forest."

"Ser, begging your pardon . . . ," ventures Juist.

"We'll be quite safe so long as we don't behave discourteously. You'll see."

"Yes, ser."

Lerial can sense that both squad leaders have their doubts.

Altyrn clears his throat, then continues. "Apfhel lies about ten kays ahead. The road follows the top of the ridge line and will turn in a more westerly direction once we're inside the forest. The clearance between the road and the forest is only a matter of a few yards. Kusyl, if you'd convey that to the teamsters."

"Yes, ser."

Once Altyrn and Lerial resume riding up the sloping road toward the woods, Lerial studies what looks to be a largely unbroken stretch of forest, yet there are also thin trails of smoke rising in places, suggesting dwellings with chimneys. The trees at the edge of the forest appear to be relatively evenly spaced, but their trunks are so close together that it would difficult for a man to slip between them and impossible for a horse, especially with the thick bushes that fill the spaces. Extending from the trees is an area of grass still partly green and considerably longer than that on the plains the Lancers have been crossing.

Lerial sees why this is so when he is within a hundred yards of the forest. There is a low stone retaining wall some twenty yards in front of the trees, with the only break in the trees where the road passes through them, and there the retaining wall angles back parallel to the road. The wall is not merely constructed of local stones stacked roughly on top of each other, but of roughly cut chunks fitted carefully together, although the exposed sides of the stones are not rough-dressed, but either smoothed by time and nature or surfaces created when a larger stone was broken or cut. *Why would the grass above the wall be greener . . . ?* Even as he thinks that, he recalls the ditches he and Rojana had dug the previous summer and he turns to the majer.

"Do the forest people line the uphill side of the wall with clay or something?"

For a moment, Altyrn looks taken aback, before he says, "Why do you ask that?"

"The grass above the wall is longer and greener. Water runs downhill, but—"

"They must do something like that. I never considered it."

That statement surprises Lerial, because he can't imagine the majer not considering almost everything, especially since the way Altyrn has phrased his answer suggests that he has seen the wall and the grass before. Still . . . "You've been here before? Or did you know about the posts from scouts or from other roads?"

"All three."

Lerial glances to his right and to his left, but the low wall, showing less than a yard between the lower ground and the grass growing over the upper edge of the top course of stones, extends as far as he can see in either direction. "The forest people must have been working on the walls for a long time." After a moment, he adds, "And there must be more of them than most people think."

Altyrn looks as if he might speak, then closes his mouth and nods.

Lerial can sense the majer's surprise, and that bothers him. Why should the majer be surprised at his observation of the obvious?

"What else can you tell about the forest people from that?" Altyrn asks as they ride toward the road gap in the wall.

"Only that that there are more people in the woods," Lerial confesses. "It just struck me when I saw the wall, I suppose, because of the difference in the grass, and I asked how that could be . . . well . . . and the rest made sense."

"I'd have to admit," Altyrn says slowly, "that I've seen that wall before, and others, and what you said didn't occur to me. I've always felt that there are more towns and people hidden here than either Atroyan or Casseon knows. Then, perhaps Casseon does know."

"And he's indicated that he wants more tariffs from them?"

"I have my doubts that he's collected much in the way of tariffs before now. It may be that he feels cheated and has plans for collecting them. Or the elders here fear that may be the case soon. We'll find out before long."

As they near the road gap in the wall, two men dressed in brown appear from out of the trees. Neither bears arms, but their garb is identical, as if a casual uniform of some type. One is gray-haired, the other much younger, perhaps only a year or two older than Lerial.

Altyrn and Lerial rein up, and the majer raises his hand to signal the same to the Lancers behind them.

"What brings you to Verdheln?" asks the older man in Hamorian with an accent that Lerial has not heard before, one similar to that of Afritan Hamorian, but softer.

"The request of the elders," replies Altyrn. "They sent a petition to Duke Kiedron for him to provide Lancers to train other Lancers chosen by the elders. Would you like to see the petition and a copy of his response?"

"If you have it, ser, that would be helpful."

Altyrn lifts the dispatch pouch, opens it, extracts two documents, and leans forward to extend them to the older man.

The border guard takes them and looks them over, then returns them to the majer.

"You are the majer named in the Duke's missive?"

"I am."

"Who is the other officer with you?"

"I'm Lerial, the younger son of Duke Kiedron. He sent me as a token of his good faith."

"You wear the uniform of a Lancer."

"All sons of the Duke serve as Lancers," replies Lerial. "He would have it no other way." Lerial tries to use a hint of order to emphasize the truth of his words.

The younger man takes a step back and murmurs, "He holds the black, not the white. But . . . it must be."

"I can raise some chaos, if you'd prefer," Lerial says quietly.

"That will not be necessary," replies the older man. "I will be your guide to Verdheln. Wait a moment until I return." He turns and walks back into the gap in the trees through which the road passes.

Several moments pass, and then perhaps a tenth of a glass. Lerial begins to worry, although he senses nothing out of the ordinary. *But then, wouldn't harmful intent be ordinary for those who are evil?* He realizes that he has never considered that possibility, and he looks to the majer.

"They expected us, but they couldn't have known when we'd arrive. He's likely saddling his horse."

"He is indeed, ser," replies the younger guard.

"Is this your normal post?" asks Lerial.

"We all spend time serving, either on the borders or doing other things," replies the young man. "That's before we take up our life-work. For some, working the borders is life-work. Not for most."

"And you?"

"I will be a woodworker."

"You have fine woodwork here, I have seen," adds Altyrn.

The young man does not reply, but steps back as the older man rides forward on a gray gelding.

"I am Yulyn, a wayguide for outlanders and those who need my services." He inclines his head. "We three can ride abreast. I will answer what questions I can." He turns the gray.

Altyrn rides up on Yulyn's left, and, after a moment, Lerial moves up on Altyrn's left. As they ride forward Lerial sees two lines of dressed stone crossing the road, with a deep groove or channel between them. The groove is just back from the thick line of trees, and there are two long structures even with the stone, one on each side of the road.

"Are those where the road gates are stored?" Lerial asks.

"Yes. We seldom need them, but they are there in case of such need," replies Yulyn.

The forest behind the gates remains thick and dense on both sides of the road, a mixture of trees and thornbushes, and, contrary to what Altyrn has said, that forest comes right to the edge of the road. That is, it does for almost a hundred yards, after which there is another set of structures holding road gates. Beyond that are grass and bushes bordering the road's shoulder, cut to roughly knee height . . . or perhaps, thinks Lerial, they were cut shorter and allowed to grow higher. The cut area is only about five yards from the shoulder to the tree line, and the trees are spaced farther apart than Lerial would have guessed from what they have just passed through. It is all too clear that the trees have been grown along the edge of the forest to provide a natural barrier. How many raiders or poachers would want to try to go through a barrier of that length and difficulty?

"Are the trees that thick all the way around the lands of the forest people?" Lerial asks.

"I would not know that, ser. The woods are that thick wherever roads lead into or out of Verdheln."

More likely that they extend only for a few kays . . . except the stone wall had to be more than five kays in each direction.

Lerial does not ask another question, not then, but studies what he sees. Before long they come to narrow fields that are separated from the next set of fields by a section of forest as wide as the trees. Each section is higher than the next, in a series of terraces, and there is a narrow ditch at the base of each terrace. Each terrace slopes just slightly downhill, so slightly that it is barely perceptible.

For the next two glasses, Yulyn leads them along the road, which, although of packed clay, is largely free of ruts and mud. It is also level and cuts through low hills. Lerial wonders at the effort necessary to dig out such places. They pass narrow clearings, some holding fields and others pastures or meadows, and in places they even pass orchards, although with the leaves largely the gray of winter, it is difficult for Lerial to determine some of the trees, although he does see some apricots, but no olive trees. He also sees people everywhere, if only as individuals or in small groups, and few look in their direction for more than a moment or two, perhaps because they see the wayguide, or perhaps because they are confident that raiders or poachers are unlikely to enter Verdheln. Those whom Lerial sees look little different from other Hamorians, although they do appear somewhat better clad than the fieldworkers Lerial has seen in Cigoerne.

"We are nearing Apfhel," Yulyn announces.

Less than a fifth of a glass later, the woods end abruptly—except they don't, Lerial realizes. Rather they are thinned, leaving narrow ways on which stand modest timber dwellings with plank siding and wooden shake roofs. The chimneys are stoutly built of rough-cut stone. While each lane and the houses situated on it are surrounded by trees, there are no trees close to any house, which seems paradoxical to Lerial, after seeing how the trees are everywhere.

"We'll be heading to the council building," says Yulyn.

They continue riding along the road, which has become the main way through Apfhel, and after passing perhaps ten sets of alternating side lanes and trees, they come to a cross street, stone paved, but barely wide enough for two wagons abreast.

"To the right," says the guide.

Lerial and Altyrn turn with Yulyn.

The paved street is lined with single-story shops of various sorts. As they ride past, Lerial sees a shop that resembles a chandlery, set beside another that displays various types of cloth. There is also an inn, with stone walls, and Lerial realizes that all the other shops are of timber—except for the smithy farther along on the right side, which is also of stone, and set apart from the others. Ahead, Lerial can see a stone structure that looks to be octagonal, set in the middle of an octagonal green. The green is raised and bordered by a wall, its top course of stones only about a cubit above the pavement of the street that surrounds it. The hitching rails that flank the beginning of the entry walk are polished wood set in sturdy posts.

Yulyn reins up. "One of the elders will be waiting inside."

Altyrn nods to Lerial and then dismounts and ties his horse to the rail. Lerial follows his example, and the two take the walk to the entry. The door lever is not of metal, but polished wood, and the door opens easily.

A young woman stands from behind a well-crafted table-desk set in the center of a modest anteroom. "You must be the leaders of the Lancers from Cigoerne. The elder is expecting you. He is in there." Her accent is similar to that of the guide, although Lerial doubts either would call their intonation an accent. She points to a door to her left.

"Thank you."

Both the majer and Lerial nod to her. Lerial can sense neither chaos nor danger as he follows, but his hand is still near the hilt of his sabre.

Inside the small chamber are a circular table of polished dark wood and four armless wooden chairs. Standing beside one is a silver-haired man in green, whose long-sleeved tunic is trimmed in brown. "I am Elder Moensyn. Welcome to Apfhel." He looks to the majer. "You are?"

"Majer Altyrn, of the Mirror Lancers. This is Undercaptain Lerial, the younger son of Duke Kiedron."

Moensyn nods, then addresses Lerial. "You are truly just an undercaptain?"

"A very new undercaptain, Elder Moensyn. I have barely finished training." In the larger sense, Lerial believes, that is true.

"Does your older brother command a group of Lancers?"

"No. He has only been riding patrols for a year. He is assigned to a company in the southeast of Cigoerne."

"You have no other siblings?"

"A sister only. She is six . . . seven now." As he corrects himself, he realizes he has missed Ryalah's birthday. He also realizes that Moensyn must be an ordermaster from the flow of darkness around the elder.

Moensyn frowns just slightly. "As the son of the Duke, with his heritage, are you not of the Magi'i?"

"I am. My talents lie more in order, though." Lerial knows he is not telling Moensyn any more than the elder can sense.

"Yet you are effective with a sabre?"

"Enough to defend himself most effectively," interjects Altyrn smoothly.

Lerial can sense a veiled feeling of exasperation on the majer's part.

"You must pardon me, Majer," says the elder, "but it is my task to ascertain you are those you purport to be."

"That may be," replies Lerial, "but as an ordermaster, you should now know that."

Moensyn looks taken aback, if but for a moment, before he replies. "I do. I apologize for any inadvertent offense I may have created."

"What exactly do you expect of us?" asks Altyrn.

"Here in Apfhel, we expect nothing. We will provide lodging and food for the night and morning, and tomorrow Yulyn will guide you on your way to Verdell. The High Council will tell you where you are needed. You will be staying at the travelers' hostel just beyond the western end of town." Moensyn smiles. "The other elders and I would hope that you two would join us at the Copse Inn for dinner. It's the inn you passed on the main street."

"We would be delighted," replied Altyrn. "Once we have seen our men settled."

"Of course. Perhaps in two glasses, or somewhat earlier?"

"Between a glass and a half and two glasses, I would judge," replies the majer. "If there are no difficulties."

"There should be none, but we will wait on you."

"Thank you."

Moensyn inclines his head, and the two Lancers nod in reply, then leave the council building, nodding in turn to the blonde who stands as they pass. Lerial does note that she is extremely attractive . . . as he has been warned.

As they ride toward the west side of Apfhel, Lerial is definitely puzzled. The town is orderly and clearly prosperous, and certainly nothing like anything he had expected. With all the prosperity and with what appear to be solid defenses and border guards, why are the elders requesting aid from his father?

Less than a half kay from where they turned off the paved street and onto the main road west, Lerial sees a small, single-storied stone building that isn't a shop or a dwelling, set, again in an octagonal green. The structure is long and narrow with a tower at one end that holds a pair of spires. Yet the spires are very different. One is shimmering silver, and the other a warm bronze. The silver spire is straight, narrow, and several cubits higher than the bronze spire, which appears as if wide rounded coils had twisted around each other and narrowed as they rose in a most even fashion to a rounded nub at the top, while the tip of the silver spire is almost like a mirror lance. *Or what a mirror lance must have looked like,* muses Lerial, since he has never seen one.

He shifts his weight in the saddle and points, asking Altyrn in a low voice. "What's that?"

"I think it's the local temple of Kaorda—the mighty god and goddess of order and chaos."

"The god and goddess have the same name?"

"No. Kaorda has two attributes," replies the majer. "As I understand it, there is the orderly male side and the chaotic female side. According to the Kaordists, half of Kaorda's face is male, and of unsurpassed and rare beauty and composure. The other half is female, but of a dark beauty that shows chaotic and demented passion."

"Some would say that it is the purity of unchecked passion," interjects Yulyn, looking back at them.

"Are there any statues of the god . . . goddess?" asks Lerial, wondering how such a visage might appear.

"Oh, no," replies the guide. "Trying to create an image of Kaorda would be blasphemy."

"Blasphemy?" Lerial almost laughs, except he can sense just how serious Yulyn is. Making a statue would be . . . blasphemy? Trying to show what their deity is would diminish it? Ironmages and builders in Cyad often made models to see what something looked like or whether it would work. Saltaryn had been quite clear about that. Either a god exists, or he or she doesn't. If a god doesn't exist, what harm could a statue do? And if the god of the Kaordists does exist, how could a graven image diminish what exists? "What would happen if a stonecutter or a wood carver tried to make such a statue?"

"They would not. Not in the lands of the Verd." Yulyn's voice is firm.

Lerial wonders how the Kaordists express their belief, but he can sense that pushing his questions further is unwise. "Thank you for explaining."

"You are welcome."

A tenth of a glass later, Yulyn turns south off the main road and down a smooth packed clay lane that leads into an open space that holds several long timber buildings, all of one story, as well as a stable as long as one of the buildings. The guide reins up at the end of the nearest building, which resembles a barracks of some sort.

"This is the hostel. It is yours for the evening. There are several cooks and provisions, and you can request what can be prepared from those. I will meet you here in the morning, at sunrise."

"Thank you," replies Altyrn.

As the guide turns his mount and then rides back toward the main road past the column of Lancers, Lerial wonders if his questions have upset

Yulyn—although he has discerned none of the usual signs of anger shown by the order and chaos flows around the man. Or is Yulyn always that abrupt? There is also another question.

Lerial turns to Altyrn. "This travelers' hostel is more than large enough for two squads of Lancers. Are there that many who travel here?"

"I would not have thought so," admits Altern, "but the forest people are said to be most practical."

It takes nearly a glass for Altyrn and Lerial to make arrangements with the cooks and to settle the men. The hostel buildings are indeed like barracks, although there are several small individual chambers, and Lerial takes one, and Altyrn another, but the accommodations are far better than any the Lancers have had since leaving Teilyn.

More than a glass and a half later, Altyrn and Lerial, accompanied by four Lancers, ride back into the center of Apfhel and rein up outside the Copse Inn. They leave their mounts with the Lancers and enter the inn.

A slender older woman with silver and blond hair steps forward as Altyrn and Lerial step into the small entry hall. "The elders are in the small dining chamber. If you would follow me?" She pauses. "I noticed you have escorts. We will feed them as well."

"Thank you."

"We thank you for coming."

The majer nods in reply.

Lerial does not frown, but wonders at the concern her words have not expressed.

The woman steps down the wooden-walled hallway, a space neither narrow nor especially wide, to the first door on the right, where she stops and gestures. Lerial follows Altyrn into the chamber where four people are standing there and apparently talking turn. Elder Moensyn is accompanied by three other elders—one man and two women, all standing near the front of the chamber. One of the women is silver haired, while the other man and woman are both younger, perhaps fifteen years older than Lerial at most.

"Welcome. This is Elder Sherita," says Moensyn, nodding first to the silver-haired woman, then to the black-haired man, "and Elder Chevaen, and Elder Dalya." Dalya is the younger strawberry-blond woman. "We should be seated. You have ridden long days, I am certain."

"You might say so," replies Altyrn genially, "but the quarters at the hostel are excellent. I would not have thought so many travelers or traders would come from the north and east."

"Oh . . . they do not. The hostel also houses those who are learning service in the woods many times during the year. We are fortunate that only a few are here at present. That is also why your wayguide has requested you depart early tomorrow. There are no other hostels large enough for your forces between Apfhel and Verdell."

Lerial can sense the truth of that, but from the maps he has studied, Verdheln extends much farther to the south. Why is the major town so far north when Verdheln is a part of Merowey?

The table in the small dining chamber is round. Lerial finds himself seated between Chevaen and Dalya, and across from Altyrn, who is seated between Moensyn and Sherita. *You're between the two younger elders, and Altyrn is between the two older ones.* Lerial doubts that pattern bears any resemblance to coincidence. At each place is a wide platter of golden brown. For a moment, Lerial thinks it might be polished wood, but then sees that it is crockery, or perhaps something between crockery and porcelain. There is also a slender mug of the same substance.

Once everyone is seated, Moensyn clears his throat and speaks again. "We are honored to host Majer Altyrn, the most renowned Lancer of Cigoerne, and Undercaptain Lerial, who is also the son of Duke Kiedron. They have come with their men to assist us with certain concerns of the High Elders."

How does he know Altyrn is the most renowned Lancer? Lerial wonders. *From Altyrn's past visits? Or was there something in the documents Altyrn showed him?*

Moensyn gestures to the pitchers on the table. "We can offer you greenberry juice or melomel. The greenberry pitchers have a green stripe."

"We do not have lager or ale," adds Chevaen, "but the melomel is similar to a slightly sweet golden lager, I am told, although I have not tasted a golden lager, I must admit."

Lerial is not certain he wishes either, but decides on the melomel, as the lesser of evils, and starts to reach for the pitcher, but Dalya is quicker, and fills his mug.

"That's a good choice," she says. "At least for me, it is. The greenberry's too tart." She looks to Chevaen. "Some prefer it that way."

"Just be thankful Moensyn didn't offer leshak," comments Chevaen. *Leshak?*

At his expression, Dalya explains. "Leshak is made from greenberries and white grapes, and you don't want to drink much if you want to be able to do much of anything at all . . . even if it is sweet and doesn't taste that strong. Sweet can be powerful." Her last words were edged, but Lerial does not feel that they are aimed at him.

He takes a sip of the melomel and finds it sweeter than any lager he has tasted, but not overpoweringly so, although he doubts that it has the thirst-quenching ability of a good pale or amber lager. "Are there only four elders in Apfhel, or are you four just those dining with us?"

"There are only four elders in any hamlet or town in Verdheln," declares Chevaen.

"Four seems like a strange number," ventures Lerial.

"It makes perfect sense." Chevaen smiles broadly. "If the council, of elders, that is, cannot decide by three to one, it's not a good idea."

"That still doesn't make it a good idea," adds Dalya quietly. "It just makes it a popular bad idea." She looks directly at Lerial. "Might I ask how long you have been a Lancer?"

He finds her gaze, especially with her gold-green eyes, more than a little disconcerting, but he smiles in return. "Not that long. I trained with arms for almost a year before my father and Majer Phortyn decided I was ready to be an undercaptain." Lerial knows he is stretching the truth in one way and understating it in another, since his studies have been to prepare him as well, and they have gone on for years.

"Have you used your sabre in a real fight?" asks Dalya.

"Unfortunately, yes."

"You're young to have wounded or killed a man." Her words contain sadness.

"It wasn't my choice." *Not if you wanted to live . . . and hold your head high.* Before either can reply to that, he quickly says, "I must confess that I had no idea about how well planned and organized Verdheln seems to be."

"Moderately well planned," replies Chevaen with a slightly twisted smile. "Not nearly so well organized."

"The way the trees form a living barrier near the road, and the raised stone wall that is sealed to keep water in . . . That would seem . . ." Lerial leaves his sentence unfinished.

"Tradition and custom," says Dalya. "Those are custom. We live with and by the trees and in harmony, as we can, with the land."

"You wear blades at your side," Chevaen adds. "Here, weapons are knives and staves."

"And bows for hunting," adds Dalya.

At that moment, two servers appear with platters, which they set in the center part of the table, spaced equally around it.

"The main dish is huuras. That's ghanos marinated in spices, then grilled and served with a mild cream sauce that's seasoned with just a touch of honey-burhka sauce. The tubers are baked and covered with the same sauce, and the bread is a kind of acorn loaf."

For a moment, Lerial struggles to remember what a ghano is, then recalls that it is essentially an overgrown ground squirrel. With that thought, he just hopes the sauces are good.

For a time, as everyone serves themselves, there is little conversation, and Lerial takes small bites of everything. The acorn bread has a taste of bitterness. The ghanos strips, at least presented as they have been, are close enough to fowl that the slightly gamey taste is not off-putting to Lerial. The tubers are bland, but with the sauce make the best part of the meal.

Lerial addresses his next statement to Chevaen. "Verdheln looks like a well-established land, for all your demurral about the lack of organization, so organized that I must wonder what assistance we and the Lancers can provide."

"That is up to the elders of the High Council to say," replies Chevaen, in a tone that is not quite sneering.

Lerial takes several more bites before saying, "We passed a Kaordist temple on the way to the hostel. Perhaps I am mistaken, but I had heard that the people of Verdheln accepted the reality of both order and chaos, while Duke Casseon has forbidden any use of chaos to his people."

Chevaen nods. "That is so."

Dalya looks as though she might say something, pauses, and finally speaks. "We accept the reality of chaos and the fire that it can bring, but fire is deadly to the trees near our dwellings."

Near our dwellings? Lerial frowns, if inadvertently. "Is it not dangerous to trees everywhere?"

From across the table Sherita laughs. "Fire thins the underbrush and keeps the forests healthy. We let the fires burn away from our hamlets and towns, but we prefer not to thin them in the same fashion."

"I have heard it said that Duke Casseon has chaos mages among his armsmen," Lerial says. "Do you know aught of that?" He tries to keep his tone guileless.

"His armsmen have burned hamlets south of the Verd," admits Moensyn from across the table. "I have heard word that suggests the burning was not from torches . . . but that is likely a matter better addressed to the High Council."

Lerial is getting an idea of why they are in Verdheln.

"Perhaps it should be," adds Sherita, in a tone that essentially negates any possibility of further information along those lines.

Lerial has the definite feeling that any more questions along those lines will merely upset the elders, although he is puzzled by one matter, and one which he can bring up, while seeming to agree with Sherita. "I've never heard of councils of elders, but, begging your pardons, and hoping I am not offending, none of you seem that ancient."

Dalya laughs, then turns to Moensyn. "Would you care to explain?"

"The term 'elder' refers to those who are respected and productive members of each community," Moensyn says. "Also, no one can be an elder without having served the community without recompense for at least two years at some time in his or her life."

"How does a community define what is productive or what is service?" asks Altyrn, surprisingly to Lerial.

"Service is what benefits all members of a community, not just a few," replies Moensyn. "Things like building or smoothing the roads, building repairing the forest walls, planting trees where they are needed, digging wells, or maintaining the water or waste channels . . ."

"Most people choose to do service when they are young," adds Chevaen, "and there are other forms of service as well." He offers a sidelong glance at Dalya, who ignores it.

"And productive?" presses Altyrn.

"Productive is anything that adds, overall, to the community," replies Dalya.

"That's . . . rather general," observes Altyrn.

"Life is rather general," returns Sherita dryly.

Lerial can sense that the elders all seem in agreement, despite Chevaen's apparent snide reference aimed at Dalya.

Moensyn gestures. Although Lerial sees no one besides those in the dining chamber, the servers return and remove the dishes before each person, placing in front of each a small plate, in the center of which is something that vaguely resembles a small mounded pastry.

"Honey nut-cakes," explains Sherita in reply to Lerial's quizzical glance.

Although Lerial is definitely fond of honey, he takes a small first bite . . . and is relieved that the confectionery, infused with honey, almost melts in his mouth. While there is a layer of crushed nuts, there is definitely a flour of some sort, but it is unlike any he has tasted, and he wonders if it is a nut flour. *Or what kind of nut flour.*

After all have finished the honey nut-cakes, Moensyn coughs, then says, "We would not keep you . . . knowing you have a long ride ahead of you tomorrow."

Altyrn smiles in return. "That is true. We do appreciate your hospitality and kindness and your telling us more about Verdheln."

"It is the least we could do," replies Sherita. "You needed to know more about the Verd."

There is a definite note of truth in her words that strikes Lerial, almost as if she wished to say more . . . and could or would not.

"We are thankful." Altyrn begins to stand and glances at Lerial.

"We are indeed," adds Lerial as he also rises.

"We wish you well on your journey to Verdyn," replies Moensyn, standing in turn.

"Thank you."

Lerial follows Altyrn through the inn and past the silver and blond woman, who nods politely, and out to the narrow covered front porch. In moments, the Lancers appear, mounted and leading the mounts for Lerial and the majer.

"Were you fed?" Altyrn asks the lead ranker.

"Yes, ser. Best fare we've had since we left Cigoerne."

"Good." Altyrn mounts and waits for Lerial to do the same before he says, "We need to talk once we get back to the quarters."

"Yes, ser."

On the ride back west to the hostel, Lerial does his best to extend his senses, feeling for any sort of danger, but he can sense nothing. Nor is anything amiss when they reach their temporary quarters.

Once Altyrn shuts the door to his small chamber, he turns to Lerial. "What did you think of the elders?"

"They're mostly honest. They know more than they're telling us . . . and they're worried."

"About us?"

"I don't know. I don't think so . . . but I'm not sure."

"They're more than polite," rejoins Altyrn. "It's not just that they have to be, either." He pauses, then adds, "I was doubtful when the one elder said that weapons were staves and knives, and said bows were just for hunting, but I'm beginning to think he was telling the truth."

"You think the forest people have relied on their trees and the distance from the large cities and towns of Afrit and Merowey to defend themselves?"

"That . . . and I'm thinking that all the raiders from the south may not be raiding Cigoerne just because of bad harvests. What if the harvests are so poor that Casseon is taking more to feed the people of the cities?"

"And driving the raiders north? Or do you think he's looking to loot the granaries or the supplies of the Verd?"

"I don't think they have granaries as we know them. Did you see any true flour? But they do have ample food. Does anything else strike you?"

"The roads. They're level, and they cut through hill. They don't seem to have that many people for all that roadwork and stonework."

"They don't. Remember what I told you about cammabark? They drill holes in the ground and then fill them with the dried bark. Then they take a string or a strip of cloth treated with a solution that has some cammabark, and they light it and take cover. The explosion removes rocks and dirt." Altyrn shakes his head. "It's very dangerous, but they're very very careful . . . about that . . . about everything."

While the two talk for another half glass, when Lerial leaves, he feels that they have not uncovered any insights they had not already made by the time they had left the inn.

XLV

Just after sunrise on sevenday the Lancers ride out from the travelers' hostel of Apfhel, on a journey that will last past sunset, according to Yulyn.

As he rides beside the wayguide, Lerial cannot help wonder about the discrepancy between Casseon's prohibition of chaos use among his people but his likely deployment of it against his enemies or those against whom he has a grudge.

All that raises another, and far more personal question. What can he do—if anything—should he encounter a magus or a white wizard using chaos-fire? He understands that some of those in the past of Cyador who were not full Magi'i, like Lorn, have faced chaos-fire and triumphed. Strong ordermasters are supposed to have been able to create order shields against chaos. Lerial is well aware that he is nowhere close to being either a magus or a full ordermage. Yet . . . is there anything he can do? *There must be something.*

Even as he surveys the forest through which they ride, a forest that seems to change little, with its mixture of evergreens and broad-leafed trees, most of whose leaves are winter-grayed, his thoughts keep coming back to the question of what sort of defenses he can develop. After riding a glass and a half, from what he can tell, since it is hard to chart the progress of the sun between the intermittent clouds and the tall trees that leave the road in shadow most of the time, they ride through a hamlet. In the entire ride from Apfhel to the unnamed hamlet, they have passed but a handful of small wagons, two other riders, both in brown, and several young men walking the road, carrying either scythes or mattocks.

Once they enter the hamlet, from what Lerial can tell, there are close to a hundred dwellings, similar, if not nearly identical, to those he has seen in Apfhel. He does not see a Kaordist temple, but perhaps it is farther from the main road than is the one in Apfhel. With the thinning of the trees come rays of sunlight, for which Lerial finds he is grateful, yet before long they are back in the shadows of the main road.

"Are all the roads in Verdheln this shadowed?" he finally asks Yulyn.

"I know of none that are not . . . except where they pass through the great meadows."

"Where are the great meadows?"

"Where they always have been," replies Yulyn with a broad grin. "We will pass through one close to sunset. There are not many in Verdheln, and most are to the west and more to the south."

"You don't clear meadows?"

"If the Verd wants a meadow, there is one. Who are we to change that?"

"But you thin the trees for your towns."

"As little as possible."

"Why is that?"

"Because, where there is forest, there should remain forest."

"Why do you think that is the way it should be?"

"The forest was here before us. It will be here long after we are gone. Who are we to change that?"

Once more, Lerial's questions have brought him to a place where the answers to further questions will reveal nothing new. He leans back in the saddle and glances at Altyrn. The majer looks back with a knowingly amused expression, almost as if he might have once asked similar questions.

Over the course of the day, they pass with a certain regularity through hamlet after hamlet. Not only are the dwellings similar, but the hamlets resemble each other in the way in which the trees are thinned and the distances between houses, as well as the presence of stone-lined waste canals. Although the shapes of the hamlets differ, that is perhaps because of the terrain where each is located.

"We will be entering the great meadow shortly," Yulyn announces late in the afternoon.

Only a fifth of a glass passes before the trees end abruptly, and Lerial rides into an open space, where knee-high grass seems to extend for more than a kay in every direction before him, except for where the road cuts through it. The sun hangs half covered by the trees to the west, and an orange light suffuses the air. In the distance to the southwest, which appears to be the direction in which the great meadow stretches the farthest, Lerial sees a red deer, or what he thinks is a red deer.

Fifty yards or so ahead of Lerial, a coney bounds out of the grass and then disappears into the grass on the east side of the road. Farther to the west, there is a small herd of cattle, less than twenty. Despite the lush grass, not until they are close to the southern edge of the meadow does Lerial see any other animals grazing, and then he nearly misses the flock of sheep almost lost in the grass, their fleeces tinted by the setting sun. Again, there are not that many sheep, not for a flock, perhaps fifty.

The road appears to have cut through the great meadow so that roughly one quarter is to the east of the road, and the remainder to the west and south. By the time they reach the south side, a distance of about two kays, the sun has dropped completely behind the tall trees to the west, and the orange glow is even more pronounced—and the gloom of the road under the towering trees is even deeper.

Lerial is glad that the road is comparatively smooth because it would be hard to see potholes in it, and that becomes more of a concern as the light dims over the next glass that passes before he sees the trees thin once more . . . on the outskirts of Verdell.

"The hostel is on the south side of Verdell, a bit to the west," announces Yulyn, but he does not turn off the main road. Before long, after they have passed more than a score of the lanes between lines of trees, the road turns to the southwest once more. Even in the dusk that is verging on dark, it is clear that Verdell is far larger than Apfhel, possibly even larger than Cigoerne, although that is something Lerial cannot tell for certain.

A slender man with white hair—not silver—stands waiting under a lantern in the entry to the travelers' hostel. "Welcome to Verdell, Majer Altyrn, Undercaptain Lerial." He does not wear brown but a light tan tunic and trousers, although his boots look brown.

"Thank you."

Interestingly enough, the travelers' hostel—or way station—in Verdell is barely big enough to handle the two squads and Lerial and Altyrn without crowding, suggesting to Lerial that the statements of the elders in Apfhel were honest, and that he has indeed read them correctly. That he has troubles him in another way, because it is clear there are more hidden aspects about the people of the Verd than he has realized. He puts those thoughts to the side as he and Altyrn arrange for meals and watch schedules—necessary in case the hostel is not so secure as it appears and also to maintain an orderly and consistent routine.

The late-evening meal, served well after dark, consists of warm nut bread of some sort, bland and not so bitter as the acorn bread of Apfhel, and a meat-and-tuber casserole in a thick sauce that is neither creamy nor cheese but has a slightly nutty flavor, enough that Lerial questions whether everything has nuts in it.

Later that evening, tired as he is, Lerial makes his way to the kitchens, where he finds some embers in one of the large porcelain-fired clay stoves. *Why not iron?* That is another question begging for an answer, but an answer that will have to wait. While he cannot even conceive of how he might create shields, the idea has occurred to him that since order and chaos do flow through and around people—and even objects—perhaps he can find a way to slide chaos bolts away from him so that he does not have to bear the brunt of their power.

He finds a few sticks of dry wood in the bin and feeds them to the coals, watching with both his eyes and his order-senses as the wood catches fire. As more wood bursts into flame, Lerial can sense the interplay of order and chaos, although it is not exactly an interplay, because there is little pattern to the way the forces move around the base of the flame, and the only thing that resembles a pattern is that what seem to be tiny bits of order are carried up the chimney by larger bits of chaos.

Still . . . can he move either the order or the chaos? He has been able to move order, and he can focus chaos to light candles. Here the chaos already exists, and he should be able to move it, shouldn't he?

First, he extends his order-chaos senses and tries to direct the flashes of chaos, but while he can move a few, the others just skitter away. Next, he attempts to gather the chaos flashes into larger flashes. He can do that, but as was the case when he tried to light multiple candles, he can feel the effort and strain of doing so . . . and that approach doesn't seem as though it would be terribly productive. He lets go . . . and a flare of light flashes upward.

Releasing it creates a flare? He's not sure what to make of that.

What would attract chaos? Does order attract it? At that thought, he thinks about the patterns of order around the lodestone, and the fingers of his left hand reach into his inside jacket pocket and touch the silk pouch, feeling the oblong shape there. *Can you copy that pattern . . . or something like it? So that chaos attracts order?*

Lerial frowns. He doesn't want to attract order, just channel it, the way that order circles the end of the lodestone . . . but without coming back and striking it.

He tries replicating the pattern at the end of one of the sticks of wood. There is a circular flare, but it does not last. Next, he tries two lines of the pattern . . . and coils one back into the other. For several moments, there is a matching line of fire, paralleling his tiny lines of order. After a moment, he adds a third line . . . and the circular flame is even stronger. He can even feel the heat radiating.

It works . . . but why?

The problem is that he cannot find and manipulate that much order—more than he can chaos, but still not that much. He tries with four fine lines of order, and the chaos flame is even stronger.

"Cold, are you?" asks Altyrn from the doorway to the kitchen.

"No." Lerial pauses, then decides not to evade the point, at least not by too much. "I'm studying the chaos of fire."

"I thought handling chaos was difficult for you."

"It is. That's why I'm looking at how order and chaos interact in fire."

Altyrn nods, then says. "Just make sure you've banked the embers well when you're finished."

"I will. I won't be that long."

Once the majer has left, Lerial takes a long deep breath.

Should you try five lines?

He does . . . and the heat, for a moment, drives him back, and then it subsides, and only ashes and embers remain in the stove.

Will that work against a chaos bolt? He has no idea, except a feeling that, if he can create that pattern around himself—but far enough away—it *might*.

He knows he has done enough, though, because he feels exhausted. He does remember to finish banking the fire and closes the stove door before he heads for the small chamber where he will sleep.

XLVI

Just before eighth glass on eightday morning, Altyrn and Lerial rein up outside a single-level octagonal building of rough black stone, set in the middle of an octagonal green situated in the center of a paved square. The roof is a low dome of smooth slate, suggesting to Lerial that some form of chaos or order mastery was used to create it. That the elders of Verdheln are meeting with them on the end-day morning also suggests either that they believe the reason for which they have requested the Lancers is pressing . . . or that they do not wish the Lancers to be long in Verdell—if not both.

This time Yulyn dismounts and leads the way into the High Council building.

Once inside, Lerial is surprised, because the front half of the building is simply open, with a raised dais against the wall that divides the building. Two doors at floor level flank the ends of the dais.

Yulyn heads for the door on the right side, then glances back and says, "The small meeting room is here." The wayguide opens the door, then stops and announces, "I have brought the majer and the heir."

"Have them enter."

Of the four elders, two are men, two women. One man is clearly older, with silver and white hair, while the other is a redhead. The older woman has iron-gray hair, and the younger, most likely close to the age of Lerial's mother, is a brunette. Lerial immediately senses that all four elders could be of the Magi'i, were they of Cigoerne, although none of them strike him as exceptionally powerful. Yet . . . there is an almost hidden darkness. The four are seated around a circular table, at which there are two vacant chairs, side by side.

"Please take a seat," suggests the oldest elder.

Lerial lets the majer choose the seat on the left, closest to the young male elder. The elder closest to him is the younger woman. She smiles warmly, if briefly, at Lerial.

When Lerial and Altyrn are seated, the silver-haired elder also smiles, almost apologetically, before speaking. "I am Donnael." He nods to the gray-haired elder. "Ruethana . . . and Klerryt and Essiana." After a moment, he continues, "You have traveled through some of the Verd for the past two days. You have also been here before, some years back, have you not, Majer?"

"I have."

"Do you have questions as to why we have reached out to Duke Kiedron?"

"In a way," replies Altyrn. "I assume you reached out to him because there was no one else to whom you could turn. That raises the question as to why that might be."

"Had we reached out to Duke Khesyn, would he have been receptive?"

"He might have been receptive, but he would not have offered much beyond words, not when Verdheln lies between three other duchies. Duke Atroyan would seem likely to have been more receptive."

"He might well have been. So receptive that everything of value would have been tariffed and all our ways trampled beneath the rush of Afritan traders and armsmen."

"Yet you sought our aid . . ." Altyrn's words are level, neither asking nor concluding.

"We have made clear to Duke Casseon that we wish to retain our own ways, and that we have only requested assistance from Cigoerne in training our own people to defend those ways. We have also made that clear to Duke Atroyan."

The majer lets the silence draw out before he says, "You must realize the risk you take."

"If we do nothing, we lose because Casseon will destroy our ways. If we ask aid of Atroyan we lose as surely as if Casseon's armsmen insist on imposing his ways. What other course would you have us take?"

"You have few choices. How do you know that Duke Kiedron will not require something of you?"

"We do not, but he has not forced great changes upon those in his lands. Nor has he turned women into chattels."

Those words surprise Lerial. While the composition of the councils indicates women have a greater voice in Verdheln than in the rest of Hamor, he had not considered that the people of the Verd would court destruction to avoid letting their women lose their position . . . and that the men would fight what well might be a long and losing battle to retain that custom.

"It is more than a custom," says Ruethana, looking at Lerial after either reading his face or sensing his feelings. "It is what we are. You will also be training archers. Most are women. They are all good with bows. They do not know fighting."

Lerial can sense slight surprise from the majer, but not shock.

"You expect us to turn your people into Lancers in a matter of eight-days?" asks Altyrn.

"In the past," replies Donnael, "Duke Casseon has not brought large forces north before the end of spring planting."

"Then why do you think he will attack this year?"

"Because he will," declares Klerryt.

"We did not worry much when the traders told us of a fort being built in Dhesoryt," adds Ruethana, "until the fort was built. It was finished last summer, and many of the people were driven off their lands and sold at the slave market in Nubyat.

"Now we hear that there are plans for another fort. It will be in Yakaat. There have also been Meroweyan scouts. Some did not return to Dhesoryt, but those that did likely discovered we have built a place to train our Lancers, as you will see. Some may also discover that we have been acquiring horses for them for well over a year."

That suggests they decided to prepare to fight some time ago, reflects Lerial.

"I have no doubt of that," replies Altyrn.

"Where is Dhesoryt?" asks Lerial. "And Yakaat?"

"Yakaat is but thirty kays south of Escadya. Dhesoryt is some fifteen kays southwest of Yakaat."

"Escadya—that's the southernmost large town in Verdheln, isn't it?" asks Altyrn, most likely for Lerial's benefit.

Donnael nods.

"And is that where you want us to begin training your Lancers? The ones you realized you could not train yourself?"

Ruethana frowns. "You assume too much."

"Do I, Elder Ruethana?" asks the majer. "You have no one among your people who knows how to counter the Meroweyans. They are to the south. Where else would we train them? What weapons can you supply?"

"Very few, besides arrows for bows," admits Donnael. "We only have those for which we can trade, and neither the traders of Afrit nor those of Heldya will supply fighting blades. Nor can those of Cigoerne, because your father the Duke"—he looks to Lerial—"purchases any forged or shipped there. What else can we do?"

"You could forge your own," suggests Altyrn.

This time it is Essiana who shakes her head. "We would have to rip open the earth to mine coal or cut great swathes from the Verd to cut trees to make charcoal . . . In doing so, we would destroy all that we hold precious and dear."

"More to the point," adds Ruethana, "we have not the time or the ability to do so."

"Also to the point," adds Donnael, "is that it is to your advantage to help us. If Duke Casseon brings his armsmen and forts close to your borders, you will be pressed on all sides and without any help. Duke Atroyan already regrets the bargain his sire made with Duke Kiedron."

Lerial does not correct the elder, although it was his grandmere the Empress who made the bargain.

"You do have a point," says Altyrn mildly, "but that is why we are here, and why we did indeed bring blades. We will need supplies to reach Escadya . . . and your petition mentioned some shared tariffs to be sent to Duke Kiedron."

"The golds will be dispatched tomorrow. We would request four of your Lancers to accompany our couriers."

"We can do that . . ."

From there the discussion continues into the particulars of logistics and travel to Escadya, and Altyrn's polite but rather direct cautions about the immediate effectiveness of training.

"I think you will find that those we have selected for you to train have great ability," counters Klerryt. "They also know that failure will destroy the Verd."

"That can only help," admits Altyrn.

Lerial can sense that the majer has other concerns, which he is not about to voice, and that the elders know that as well, and will not press him to reveal them. He can also sense the regret and sadness in Essiana, and he wonders, *It is almost that she feels they have already lost.*

A good glass later, Altyrn and Lerial leave the council building, although Donnael draws Altyrn aside for a moment before they depart.

Lerial does not hear what transpires between the two, but the conversation is brief, consisting of only a few short sentences by each man.

Once they're mounted and riding back to the hostel behind Yulyn, Lerial looks to Altyrn. "Might I ask what Elder Donnael wanted to convey?"

"That he was most impressed by the fact that you were here, as only one of two heirs to the Duchy . . . and that we are free to stay another day here." Altyrn clears his throat. "Even though we won't be allowing the men to leave the hostel area, we do need a day of rest for them and the horses." He slows his mount slightly, letting the distance widen between them and the wayguide. "What are your thoughts about what Duke Casseon is doing?"

"Casseon is doing more than merely strengthening his defenses on his northern border," replies Lerial.

"Why? And why now?" asks the majer. "We pose little immediate threat, and the people of the Verd certainly do not. They don't wish to leave the forest. They never have."

Lerial shrugs. He has no idea.

"The only thing I can see is that Casseon wants to take over Verdheln soon, and the only reason he could have for that is that he believes that, between them, Khesyn and Atroyan will either destroy Cigoerne or weaken us so much that Atroyan will be able to take over Verdheln."

"But . . ." Lerial stops.

"But what?"

"If Atroyan wasn't strong enough to take over before now . . ."

"How could he do it now? Especially with the armsmen he's moved near Penecca?" Altyrn offers a sardonic smile. "There's only one way."

If all three of them are acting together. "But if they're acting together . . . ?"

"Why don't they all just attack Cigoerne at once? Because they don't trust each other in the slightest. Our Lancers are strong enough to cripple any one army any of them could mass. What would happen if, say, Khesyn sends a message to your father telling him that Atroyan will attack through Penecca on the first day of spring, then promises to Atroyan to cross the Swarth and attack Cigoerne from the south, while not doing so and sending golds to your father as proof of his goodwill in promising not to attack Cigoerne?"

Lerial understands immediately. "Each of them fears that the other will do something like that . . . but if they adopt a strategy of nibbling at our borders on all sides, no one of them is greatly exposed."

"If any one of them is fortunate . . . and exposes a weakness first, then that Duke reaps great rewards."

"Cigoerne is not that wealthy," protests Lerial.

"Not in golds, but the lands and the crops they produce are, and any of them would like to have them. Also, Cigoerne would offer either Casseon or Khesyn a strong point in dealing with Afrit, and it would strengthen Atroyan greatly if he comes to possess it."

"And the only thing we can do is hold them off?"

"Hold them off and become stronger. If we can help the Verdyn repulse Casseon, then the golds of the forest people and the Lancers that they can provide will make us almost as strong as Afrit. It may be that Khesyn has seen that and suggested to Duke Casseon that his only chance to keep Cigoerne from becoming stronger is to conquer the Verd before Verdheln allies itself with Cigoerne."

Lerial shakes his head. "But the threat of such an attack is what prompted the elders to contact Father."

"I doubt that Khesyn thinks Casseon will be successful, but if the attacks weaken us . . ."

That, Lerial also understands—and the fact that, small as all the attacks and raids are, his father is fighting for Cigoerne's survival. Again.

XLVII

Lerial wakes early on fiveday morning. He washes and dresses quickly, then hurries to meet with Altyrn. He still cannot believe what he and Altyrn have found on the southwest side of Escadya—eight new barracks buildings and two long stables, all well built, if recently, each barracks designed for one company of Lancers. Some of the surrounding woods have also been cleared, enough for mounted maneuvers on a company level, if barely. There are six hundred Lancer recruits waiting to be trained. The downside is that two hundred are women. Another two hundred recruits are expected in another four eightdays.

Altyrn is already in the study reserved for him when Lerial appears at the half-open door. He waves Lerial in. "Close the door."

Lerial steps into the study and shuts the door, then takes the straight-backed chair across from the narrow table on which Altryn has several sets of papers spread out. "Have you decided on which way to organize them?"

"Each company will have to have mixed squads, with three squads of men, armed as Lancers, but with bows as backup. Twenty men to a squad, plus a squad leader, and one squad of archers with thirty women to that squad. That only leaves one smaller squad of archers, and they can be deployed as necessary independently of the other six companies." Altyrn smiles. "The archers might make all the difference."

"Why? Because they can already shoot? Do we know that?"

"Both the men and women can shoot. All the young people here can . . . and most of the older ones. On an open field, archers can wreak havoc on unarmored or lightly armored Lancers, but if armed riders get in close, they can scatter the archers and cut them down unless they flee or withdraw to terrain unfavorable to horsemen."

"So why don't we have archers?"

"Your father has two companies that can be used as either foot or mounted archers. They can be very useful. The problem is that bow-making is time-consuming and takes great skill, and it takes years for an archer to be really good. That doesn't matter as much if you have a mass of archers, and they're shooting into a mass of riders—but all good commanders know that, and they don't order mass charges against archers." Altyrn smiles. "I don't think that the Meroweyans know how good the archers of the Verd are." His smile vanishes. "They'll learn . . . and they have some chaos mages. They can destroy shafts in flight and loft firebolts into archers. It becomes a matter of tactics . . . and strategy. We'll have to think this out—while we're training the men with blades and lances. The other problem is that we don't have enough shafts for fighting a large force."

Lerial frowns.

"They use their bows to hunt. Many of the arrows are used for small game or birds. Most people only have ten shafts suitable for large game—or fighting. Many likely have less than that. We'll see if the people of the Verd can make more quickly, but it takes time, especially the arrowheads for war arrows. I've already sent word that we'll need more wooden wands. I've had to let local woodworkers have several of those we brought to use as templates." Altyrn shakes his head. "I didn't plan on training hundreds of Lancers all at once. I knew we'd be short of wands, even with all that I could beg from Graessyr." He shakes his head. "Six hundred trainees at once."

Lerial almost asks where they all came from, except that he knows. The "recruits" are being told that their years of service will be as a Lancer. He doubts that many will complain, because, if they cannot hold back the advance of Merowey, everything they hold dear will vanish. *Much of that will anyway,* Lerial suspects.

"All that leaves us with a bigger problem."

A bigger problem than training six hundred men and women?

"Leadership. They don't have anyone who's had any experience. That means most of our rankers will have to act as squad leaders, and some as senior squad leaders or acting undercaptains in charge of companies, and you're a provisional acting captain—only here in Verdheln."

Lerial nods. *That makes sense.* So does the majer's unease with having to set matters up that way. "What about pay for the recruits?"

"They get paid what they would for service to the council."

"Do you think Majer Phortyn understands some of the . . . implications?"

"He understands that, no matter how things turn out, it's going to be a mess. Why do you think he and your father asked me?"

"Because no one else could do it," replies Lerial instantly.

"More likely that no one else would do it, not in the way it has to be done." After the briefest pause, Altyrn goes on. "What about you?"

"Where can I be the most useful and effective?"

"Where would you think you would be?" Altyrn smiles.

"The only areas where I really know anything are bladework and healing. The healing isn't going to do much to train them to kill."

"That combination will be more useful than you think. I suspect—I don't know, but I suspect that many of the recruits have order abilities. They're more likely to believe they can do what you tell them because you're close to an ordermage."

"I'm not anywhere near that . . ." Lerial pauses, then asks, "Where did you get that idea?"

"Donnael. He is an ordermaster, I think."

"He is," confirms Lerial, "but why on earth would he say that I am?"

"It might be because he thinks you are."

"I can't do any of the things ordermasters are supposed to do."

"Not an ordermaster—an ordermage. You can heal. You know where a blade will be before it's there. I suspect that when you don't wish to be seen, no one can see you. You have some ability to sense what the weather will be."

"I'll admit I have some talent, ser, but not as much as any true ordermaster."

"Keep working at it," says Altyrn dryly. "Before all this is over, you'll need every skill you can muster."

"Things look that bad?"

"Worse, probably." Altyrn straightens in the chair. "We need to talk about how you're going to train these poor recruits in bladework."

"Ser . . . wouldn't one of the squad leaders be able to do this?"

"Yes, but you're as good as they are with a blade, if not better, and better than any of the rankers who will be acting squad leaders. Also, you don't know anything about how to train a mounted squad to maneuver. They do. I'll help you train some of the squads for now, for the first eightday or so, but I'll also be working with the archers. Now . . . you'll have to begin with group exercises . . ."

As Altyrn explains, Lerial listens closely.

". . . and just remember that you can't teach them everything all at once. Repetition is what teaches physical discipline. It gets tiring on the recruits, and even more tiring for the teacher, but you have to keep that in mind. Now . . . we need to get something to eat." Altyrn stands.

The two walk outside from the small study at the north end of the west barracks and south to the mess hall. There is nothing like an officers' mess, but there are two separate tables, one for the Lancer squad leaders and officers, and one for the Lancer rankers from Cigoerne. As the two officers enter the mess hall and walk toward their table, they pass the ranker recruits lined up to be served. Lerial extends his order-senses as much as he can, trying to catch anything that might be said, but most of the recruits are quiet, at least as he and Altyrn walk past them. There are some comments after they pass, in very low voices.

". . . Lancer officers . . . why . . . ?"

". . . the iron majer . . . the one that forged Cigoerne . . ."

". . . said he's fried men like they were ghanos . . ."

". . . the other one?"

". . . one of the Duke's sons . . ."

". . . young . . . but something about him . . ." That was a female voice.

"He's male . . ."

Lerial doesn't hear the rejoinder, and he's not sure he wants to.

Because they do have the privilege of being served, rather than standing in line, Lerial and Altyrn are barely seated when a mess server arrives with two platters and then quickly returns with two mugs.

"Thank you."

Lerial's words are mirrored by Altyrn's.

Lerial looks at the platter, containing what he would call an egg and ghano hash, with a slice of warm acorn-tuber bread. The only beverage offered is a variation on greenberry. Lerial does not sigh, but he is going to miss lager or anything else he would consider a decent drink. As for the food . . .

"Don't look so enthusiastic," remarks Altyrn.

"No wonder everyone here is so fit looking."

"You'll be glad they are when you have to lead them against Casseon's armsmen."

Lead them? They aren't even trained yet . . . and you're not ready to lead anyone. Altyrn clearly reads Lerial's expression. "You're going to have to lead some of them . . . and you'd better keep thinking about tactics and how to do that with whatever you have . . . and that will mean learning exactly what they can do, among other things."

The "among other things" worries Lerial as much as the idea of leading. He's already experienced some of the majer's other things.

After a moment, Lerial takes a bite of his breakfast . . . and then another bite. His sips of the greenberry are small.

All too soon he is standing beside a handcart stacked with forty-one wooden wands, roughly two-thirds of all those that they have, looking at the forty young men, the first two squads of something like eighteen with whom he will have to work. *And you're the best one to do this?* No . . . Altyrn is, but the majer can't do everything, and the squad leaders can do what Lerial can't. Even some of the rankers can do things Lerial can't.

"You're here to learn the basics of how to handle a sabre. You'll begin with exercises using a wooden wand. That's because we'd like to have you survive training without the wounds you'd end up giving yourself or others if you began with real blades. It will also keep you from damaging the sabres before you know the basics of handling them. It takes time to forge a sabre, and we're likely to be short of blades anyway without losing more when we don't have to . . ."

After Lerial he finishes, he looks around the group and almost asks if there are any questions, but decides against that. Questions can come later.

"Each of you, take a wooden wand and form up in a straight line. Hold it in the hand that is most comfortable . . ." Lerial wasn't about to try to deal with trying to have every Lancer using a blade right-handed, not when it was likely most would end up, after an initial attack, fighting one-on-one, and when few recruits were left-handed. Besides, those few could always be placed at the left end or side of the force—and that would provide additional protection . . . and not run the slightly higher risk of injuring the adjoining Lancer.

He watches as the recruits—mostly young men, but not always—file forward to take a wand from those stacked in the small handcart.

He just hopes he can teach them enough, soon enough.

XLVIII

Each day seems like the one before, and almost two eightdays later, roughly at midmorning, Lerial finds himself instructing one of his "problem" sets of squads. Everything seems to take the two squads now before him twice as long to learn, and they seem to forget twice as quickly. The chill air and brisk winter wind doesn't help either, although it isn't as cold as the gray skies would indicate, but day after day of winter gray wears on Lerial.

He returns full concentration to instructing the group on various ways to slip or parry a blade, when one of the taller recruits asks, "Ser . . . why don't we work more on blocks. They're easier, and there's so much to learn."

Lerial swears that he has explained that at least five times before, but he takes a slow deep breath and smiles pleasantly. "I could say that you need to learn slipping and parrying because it's better technique. Or I could say that you need to learn it because I said so, but the real reason is simple. If you make a practice of just holding up your blade in a block, your arms will get tired quickly . . . and if someone strikes it while they're moving faster or if they're stronger, they'll throw you back or they can shiver the iron of your blade so much that you'll lose control. Also, if you fight the same person for long, they'll see that's what you're doing and come up under your blade with a gut thrust. All of those are good ways to get killed."

"I don't understand, ser." A puzzled expression appears on the pleasant-enough face of the big blond youth—except that he's likely older than Lerial.

"Hold your wand in a block," Lerial orders, as he backs away. "Just hold it there."

The puzzled expression intensifies, but the ranker trainee follows Lerial's instructions.

What Lerial is about to do won't work in a real fight, he knows, but he hopes it will get his point across. *One of them, anyway.* He stops five yards back. "Ready?"

"Yes, ser."

Lerial sprints forward, then, whips the wand into a half-down and half-sideways arc so that both his momentum and the force of his strike land on the wand of the trainee. At that last moment, he also adds a touch of order to the point of contact of his wand, because he can't afford to have it shatter, and it should add more force to his blade.

The effect isn't quite what Lerial hoped, because the rather sturdy and stout trainee rocks back on his feet rather than loses his balance, but Lerial finishes with a back cut that rips the wand out of the other's hands.

Lerial's own hands are tingling, but the trainee is standing open-mouthed.

As Lerial steps back and lowers his wand, he hears a murmur.

". . . giving away a stone, and Storen's a logger . . ."

"That's a crude example of what can happen with a stationary block when you're mounted," Lerial says into the silence. "Technique with strength usually beats greater strength with poorer technique—unless you're lucky. It's not a good idea to trust your life to luck. Pick up your wand." He waits until the former logger picks up the wand before he says. "Turn to your partner. On my signal, those on the left, aim a thrust for the chest. Those on the right, slip the attacking wand, or parry it. Ready! Now!"

For the remainder of his session with those two squads, no one raises any more questions, stupid or otherwise, and Lerial thanks the Rational Stars that his impromptu demonstration worked, because he can see, in hindsight, that it could have gone terribly wrong.

After a third session, Lerial is walking toward the small building that holds Altyrn's study when Kusyl rides by and reins up. "Ser . . . ?"

"Yes, Kusyl?"

"I was riding by a glass or so ago, and I saw you . . . well, it was a strange move . . ."

Lerial frowns. "Oh . . . when I was trying to show what could happen if all they did was block a cut or slash."

"How did you think of that, ser?" asks Kusyl.

"I was just trying to get across what would happen if they're just sticking a blade up in a block. I remembered how much it hurt when I tried that." Lerial smiles wryly. "It would have been easier if I hadn't picked one of the biggest trainees."

Kusyl grins. "Might be, ser, but they'll remember it. Never show anything against the smallest man in the squad. Everyone will think it's because you're bigger. 'Course, I never had to worry about that." The squad leader, who is acting as an undercaptain and training the squads in company-sized maneuvers, grins.

Lerial laughs softly. "Do you have any other suggestions?"

"It helps if you can use a blade with either hand."

"That's a good idea." *If you can find time to practice with your other hand.* "Anything else?"

"Keep it simple. Most of them will forget half what you teach them in their first skirmish, and some poor squad leader will have to beat it back into them again."

"Repeat and repeat," Lerial says dryly, knowing that he is merely uttering what Altyrn has already emphasized.

"And do it again." Kusyl pauses. "I'd still like to know how you did that."

"Luck. I don't think I'll try it again. It was one of those ideas that seemed good at the time, and I was lucky it worked. The problem is, I realized, that an officer—or a squad leader—who's instructing can't afford to make obvious mistakes or look bad . . . and that could easily have gone wrong." *And almost did.*

"That's true, ser."

"How are your squads doing in riding as a group?"

"They all stay together, and they've finally managed not to hit each other with their weapons. In another eightday, I might be able to get them to use real sabres without worrying. That is, if the Meroweyans don't attack first. Have you heard anything, ser?"

"Not so far." What Lerial doesn't say, but Kusyl knows, is that it's a good eightday for a dispatch rider from Cigoerne, and it's still winter. "Have your scouts reported anything happening around Yakaat?"

"They've seen some wagon teams and armsmen accompanying them, but there's only a squad of armsmen staying in the town."

"That sounds like they're sending tools and equipment there."

"Be my thought. Probably send armsmen and engineers right after spring planting . . . maybe before, if the weather holds, and there's no rain."

"If there's rain . . ." Lerial shakes his head.

"Be a bitch either way, ser."

Lerial nods. Even he understands that. Enough rain to slow the Merow-eyans will also slow training the recruits.

"Begging your pardon, ser, but I've got another company coming up for maneuvers."

"Don't let me keep you." Lerial needs to hurry himself, if he is to get back to the drill field in time for his next two squads.

XLIX

At roughly a third of past eighth glass on oneday night, Lerial lowers his ancient but still shining sabre after spending a half glass practicing moves using the blade left-handed. After several days, even the simplest moves still feel unwieldy, but not so awkward as when he began. After sheathing the sabre, he raises a concealment and eases open the door to his small sleeping chamber at the north end of the barracks that does not yet hold Lancer recruits. He tries to move as quietly as possible because he doesn't want to disturb Altyrn, who has just returned to the adjoining quarters. While the majer would not see him, he might see a door opening and closing. While Altyrn already suspects that Lerial can do concealments, Lerial does not wish to reveal any more of his slowly emerging talents than he has to . . . especially since he is still working on developing and strengthening them.

That is why he is headed for the mess hall kitchen, for he needs to use one of the ovens. The kitchen is not deserted until after eighth glass, and the cooks and their helpers arrive well before fourth glass in the morning. The kitchen itself is not locked, although the storerooms holding provisions are, and Lerial has to wait in the shadows while one of the Lancer trainees patrolling the grounds passes by and out of sight.

Once inside, with the door closed behind him, he drops the concealment and makes his way to the bank of ovens. He chooses the center oven, selects several chunks of wood, opens the door, and feeds them to the embers, waiting until they catch fire. Then he sets to work.

He begins by forming order into a fine four-line pattern, similar to that created by the lodestone, then doubles that, and uses it to form a line of flame straight up the middle of the chimney. So far, he feels no strain, and that pleases him. That exercise has burned most of the two chunks of wood, and he goes to the wood bin, where he gets two more billets, and returns to the oven and adds them to the fire. Once they are burning, he concentrates once more, this time trying to focus on creating a twelve-line pattern—four lines of three, because multiples of three seem stronger, although he has no idea why.

He can feel heat from everywhere as he struggles to line up the arcs around the inside of the oven and direct the "order channel" upward through the chimney. Abruptly, a massive wave of . . . something . . . builds inside the oven, and Lerial struggles with order barriers to contain it . . . somehow . . . as chaos shoots up the chimney . . .

. . . and darkness slams into him, along with pain so intense that his entire body vibrates like a lute string plucked beyond its limits . . . that breaks . . .

Somewhere, later, he hears voices.

Where are you?

Even that thought sends a flash of pain through his eyes and skull, but he remembers that he had been trying a twelve-line pattern of order when he'd felt incredible pain . . . and nothing. He can feel cold stone against his cheek.

You're still in the kitchen? What time is it?

He struggles into a sitting position despite the increased pounding in his skull.

". . . warm in here . . . lot warmer than it should be . . ."

". . . Gormish didn't bank the oven properly . . . again . . ."

". . . swears he did . . ."

"Likely story . . ."

Because the speakers are on the other side of the long table, and carry a small single lantern, they have not yet seen Lerial. *So far.*

Lerial raises a concealment, despite the pain so intense that it leaves him almost dizzy, and struggles to his feet, trying to move around the table toward the rear door, away from the two cooks, likely bakers, who have entered the kitchen.

"Someone left the oven door open . . . idiots! Embers burned down to nothing."

"Even Gormish wouldn't do that."

"Make sure they all understand. Can't have this . . ."

The two are so engaged that Lerial manages to get through the door and ease it shut behind himself without them noticing. As soon as he can get more than a few steps away from the mess hall, he drops the concealment. The dizziness subsides; the pain does not.

His head is aching, and he can barely see as he walks through the darkness toward the north end of the barracks. He even has to concentrate on the effort to walk . . . all because he tried a pattern too far beyond his strength? *You should have known . . . idiot . . .*

"Ser?"

"Yes?" Lerial struggles to make out the figure of the trainee watchstander, a figure he has neither seen nor sensed.

"Sorry, ser . . . I didn't know . . ."

Lerial forces a smile. "I was walking, thinking things over. I should have let you know, but my mind was elsewhere."

"Yes, ser."

"Carry on." Lerial smiles once more and resumes his progress back to his quarters such as they are. He hopes the little sleep he will get will suffice to allay the worst of the headache and the pain in his eyes.

He does manage to slip into his quarters and collapse on his bunk without waking Altyrn . . . or at least the majer does not come and inquire.

L

By sixday, almost three eightdays since he began arms instruction with the Verdyn recruits, Lerial is still wondering whether he can teach the would-be Lancers enough to survive, and more than to survive, to prevail against the Meroweyan armsmen. He is tired, exhausted, in fact, by the end of each day, as well as hoarse. Yet he cannot complain about the recruits. They are polite. They do everything he asks . . . and, then, by the next session, it is almost as if they have forgotten half of what they had learned before. *At least, it's two steps forward, and only one back.* And both squad leaders and Altyrn had emphasized that repetition is the way to learning skills.

Unfortunately, that is also true of Lerial himself. That is why, tired as he is, especially after another short session practicing left-handed, he makes his way through the darkness toward the building that holds the mess hall and the adjoining kitchen. Given the incident with the recruit watch patrol on the previous oneday, he has decided that he does not need a concealment, except when he nears the mess hall. He can sense two of the recruits standing outside the nearest barracks, in the darkness a good fifteen yards away. How far he can sense people has also increased with practice. Almost absently, he uses his order-sense to try to hear what they might be saying of interest, if anything.

". . . who's that?"

". . . undercaptain . . . walks like he knows where everything is . . . doesn't have to see it . . ."

Lerial nods. He can definitely sense people and their words from farther away, but it has taken continual effort and practice.

". . . same way with wands, blades, too, I suppose . . ."

". . . and he's the younger heir? . . . really scary . . ."

Lerial frowns. While his ability with a sabre is better than that of many, there are others with better technique, except perhaps on defense, but that is not his technique but his order-sensing skill. Admittedly, his order-senses have improved enough that he no longer needs a lantern or a candle, even in pitch darkness, but he wouldn't have thought of that as scary. *Except that you've grown up among the Magi'i.*

He keeps walking toward the mess hall, but stops in the deeper shadows by the end of the barracks nearest the kitchen, where he raises a concealment. Then he crosses to the rear kitchen door, which he opens when he is certain no one is near or watching. After entering, he closes it and makes his way to the ovens, banked, but still hot. He chooses the center oven, selects several chunks of wood, opens the door, and feeds them to the coals, waiting until the wood catches fire. Then he sets to work.

He begins by forming order into a fine five-line pattern, similar to that created by the lodestone, then doubles that, and uses it to form a line of flame straight up the middle of the chimney. Although he still has difficulty in controlling chaos, except that it is not so much difficulty as that the handling of much chaos becomes extremely painful, especially in his eyes and head, he can do so, but he has discovered that using order to channel chaos is pain-free and comparatively easy when he is dealing with smaller amounts of chaos.

While his ability to gather free order has increased greatly, doing too much is still painful, as his experience on oneday had proven. Yet by twoday evening, the pain had vanished, and by threeday, he had been able to create a ten-line pattern, without pain or strain. It is clear that the more he stretches his abilities, the more he can do the next time—provided he doesn't do too much, as oneday's effort had demonstrated all too obviously.

After warming up with the five- and ten-line patterns, he tries, if carefully, a fifteen-line pattern. He can only hold that for a moment, and he is quick to release it, before he loses control and gets hit with the backlash. Even so, he has proved, if only to himself, that he can increase his ability to channel chaos—at least, fire-chaos. Whether he can use that ability against mage-thrown chaos is another question. Yet he has seen and felt enough varieties of chaos to know that what he is doing should work. *If you can work out the differences.*

After another brief creation of a fifteen-line pattern, he steps back and takes a deep breath. He can tell he has done enough for the night. *Just like bladework . . . practice and more practice . . .* And just like bladework, he is sore when he finishes, except the soreness is a pounding headache and a slight sense of dizziness, but not the intense dizziness that had struck him on oneday.

This time, as he has been after his near-disaster, he is careful to bank the coals and close the oven door. He also raises a concealment before he leaves the mess hall kitchen, one that he does not release until he is in deep shadows of the nearby barracks and he can sense no one nearby. Then he slowly walks back to the north end of the barracks that holds his quarters and Altyrn's.

The majer steps out of his quarters, as if he had been listening for Lerial. "Working late, again?"

"As if you don't," replies Lerial with a smile that he has to make an effort to present. "You're planning for the future. I'm trying to catch up in learning what I need to know to be an effective undercaptain."

"A bit more than that, I think."

"Some, but there's still so much to learn."

"The sabre instruction has been good for you."

"Most of it is just basics."

"That's true, but you're more comfortable with a wand or a blade. I've watched. So have Juist and Kusyl. None of us would want to face you now. You're also more confident in dealing with rankers."

"Those are just part of what an undercaptain does."

"You're right. That's why I want you to work with Juist on maneuvers in the afternoon, starting on oneday." Altyrn holds up his hand. "I know they've only had an eightday using actual sabres in their exercises, and they're not sparring with them, but they need the maneuvers more now. We'll have to rework the training schedule on eightday, but some of the rankers who are good with a blade can take over in running the recruits through drills. I've picked out three who will do it well enough."

"Yes, ser."

"I'm glad to see you're getting more sleep. You looked like sowshit on twoday, and not much better on threeday."

"There's just a lot to do," Lerial temporizes.

"There is, but you'll do it badly if you're exhausted. That can get you—and your men—killed if you make a practice of it."

"I'm learning that, ser."

"I think you are." Altyrn smiles. "Good night."

Lerial returns the smile. "Good night." Then he enters his own quarters. He is so tired that he has no doubts he will sleep. Well, he hopes.

LI

For the first few days he is working with Juist, Lerial remains in the background, listening and observing, even though he will never carry a lance, unlike the officers of the Cyadoran Mirror Lancers.

But those were true firelances, not just well-wrought spear-lances. He pushes away that thought and concentrates on Juist—and his commands—as the recruit squad charges forward toward a line of figures woven out of vines and branches and arranged as an opposing squad might be.

Lerial watches and listens as Juist talks with Dueven, the Lancer ranker acting as squad leader.

"They have to hold the line and keep an even interval. Your second rank is sagging in the middle. After a hundred yards, you'll have a hole there. The moment they lag, you'll have to order them to dress it up. They have to hold line and interval until it's habit they don't even have to think about. You should remember that."

"Yes, ser." Dueven, likely only five years older than Lerial, nods.

"You're getting experience, Dueven. Be grateful. Do it again."

Lerial can sense the exasperation behind Juist's voice, and he almost smiles, not out of malice, but because the squad leader's emotions mirror so much what he has been feeling in conducting blade training.

Once the practice charge through the vine figures is complete, Lerial comments, "They looked better this time."

"They're better," Juist admits. "They're actually holding the lances right, leaning forward, and using their stirrups." He shakes his head. "Never thought I'd see a vine dummy unhorse someone."

Lerial knows better than to ask whether that happened. He's already seen two recruits knock themselves out with their own wands.

Three glasses later, when Lerial nears the stable on his return from maneuvers training, he reins up well short of the open door as a Verdyn Lancer recruit in his undress brown uniform hurries toward him.

"Ser! The majer would like to see you at your earliest convenience."

Lerial can barely resist smiling at the use of "at your earliest convenience," a phrase that he suspects dates from the oldest military organizations, even though he had never heard it until he started training with the Mirror Lancers. "Thank you. Carry on."

He dismounts and turns the gelding over to one of the ostlers for unsaddling and grooming, rather than doing it himself, because, if Altyrn wants to speak with him that quickly, it's likely to be important. He walks briskly through the chill air, across the central open space to the south end of the eastern barracks. He stops before the half-open door to Altyrn's study, a square room with a table-desk and chairs and little else. He raps on the door frame.

Altyrn motions him to enter.

Lerial does, closing the door and taking the chair across from the desk. He sees the majer's bow in the corner, unstrung, but not cased, as if he had just returned from working with the archers.

"We've finally gotten a dispatch from Majer Phortyn." Altyrn's voice is level. "It came back with the Mirror Lancers and the Verdyn who conveyed the golds to Cigoerne."

"Ser?"

"Nothing much in Cigoerne has changed, and that's not good. The

Afritan armsmen are still patrolling the border just north of Penecca in force. Phortyn reports that they have at least three companies there at all times, sometimes five. There are more raids along the northern border farther to the west, and there are more Heldyan raiders crossing the Swarth and attacking the smaller hamlets to the south and east of Narthyl. I doubt they're raiders, or even marauders, but Duke Khesyn would claim that they are . . . and that he is doing his best to control them."

"He'd also suggest that any ruler who cannot control his own lands . . ." Lerial doesn't finish the sentence.

"Of course, but only in the most veiled manner. I'd never be able to write something that indirect."

Lerial knows full well Altyrn could; he just wouldn't like doing it. He also wonders how Lephi is doing with the Lancers who must deal with those raids.

"He also reports that he's had to promote Undercaptain Seivyr to captain," Altyrn goes on quietly.

" 'Had to'? That's an odd way of putting it."

"He informed me that Captain Dechund came down with a nasty flux of some sort. He went out of his mind and wandered away from the post in the middle of the night. They found his body the next day."

"That can happen. If we'd been there, maybe . . ."

"You can't be everywhere. No one can. Seivyr will do better than Dechund, anyway."

Lerial can detect no real sadness on the majer's part. But then, Lerial hadn't been at all impressed with Dechund, for all his perfect uniform and polished boots, and he suspected that the majer has been even less so. "Majer Phortyn doesn't like Seivyr?"

Altyrn offers a sardonic smile. "Not since Seivyr was overheard saying that he needed to promote officers on their ability and not on the cleanliness of their uniforms."

Lerial winces.

"It wasn't an accident that Seivyr was posted to Tirminya . . . or that others with less ability or experience were promoted to captain."

The majer is delivering more than one message with those words, Lerial realizes, but he only nods and says, "I think I understand."

"Good." Altyrn smiles warmly and hands an envelope to Lerial. "There is one other thing. This came for you."

Lerial takes the missive and studies the handwritten address—"Lerial,

Undercaptain, Lancer Detachment, Verdheln." He does not recognize the handwriting. Although it looks feminine, it is not his mother's, and it is too well formed to be Ryalah's. Rather than guess, he will open it, alone. He nods to the majer. "Thank you, ser. Is there anything else?"

"Not until after you read the letter. You'll be wondering who wrote it and why, rather than concentrating. Go read it and then come back."

"Yes, ser."

Lerial makes his way from the majer's study to his own, a space even smaller than that of Altyrn's, with only enough space for a table-desk and a chair, and perhaps one file chest, if Lerial even had one. The sole window fills almost all of the outside wall space. He doesn't bother to sit, but leans against the desk, opens the letter with his belt knife, laying it on the desk, and looks to the signature—that of Emerya. He frowns. Why is she writing him? He begins to read.

> *Dear Lerial—*
> *I trust this letter finds you well and hard at work. That is most likely because of your commander. I am writing because your mother requested it. Ryalah has suffered a terrible flux, but she is on the way to health, thanks be to the Rational Stars.*
>
> *You may have heard that we are beset with annoyances on almost every border, but so far all has gone as well as might be expected. Your father continues to prevail in the north, and the raids in the southeast have not amounted to all that much to date. I did think you might be interested to know about one of the more unusual discoveries. It was made by a squad from Third Company. They were patrolling south of the border more than twenty kays west of Penecca because there had been raiders attacking and pillaging the hamlets. The squad surprised the raiders and killed a number. A few escaped. None were captured. Most of those killed were stripped of their weapons by their comrades, but one dead raider was not. The interesting thing was that his blade was the same kind of cavalry weapon used by Afritan armsmen . . .*

Lerial lowers the letter and frowns. *Weapons stripped . . . an Afritan sabre.* While his aunt has given an explanation as to why she is writing him, he is still concerned. Surely, his mother must have had a few moments . . . or did Ryalah nearly die? Or was it that Emerya wanted to make sure word got to him—and the majer—as soon as possible? It's also clear that his father is all too busy dealing with the Afritan problems . . . or Heldya . . . if not both.

> *. . . Amaira misses you and hopes you are eating well. The weather here has been chill and very dry. It is the driest winter I can recall, and the traders from the south are saying the same thing. From what we hear, that is true in Afrit as well . . .*

In short, there will be more raids and trouble.

> *. . . I want to assure you that Ryalah is well on the way to full health, but it was a near thing, and it is another reason why I am writing, rather than your mother . . .*

Another reason? That's the only one she gives . . . Lerial shakes his head. The other reasons lie in what else she has written.

> *. . . Undercaptain Woelyt also asked me to send his regards. He and his company are being posted to Narthyl in early summer. The Palace guard will be a new company composed of some recruits and some more experienced Lancers. That way they can train those who are not on guard duty . . .*

More companies being formed? Lerial worries about what he is reading.

> *One last caution from an overprotective aunt. When you are called on to do battlefield healing, you must be cold and ruthless. Do not waste order and strength on those who will die no matter what you do. And if you can save three men with lesser wounds, those that would turn to corruption and kill, or one man with a greater injury . . . you must choose the three. You are not only blessed with healing talent, but cursed with being a possible heir of Cyador. That, you must also remember.*

The closing is "With Affection and Concern."

When Lerial finishes reading, he walks the few steps back to Altyrn's study. As close as it is to the evening meal, he knows the majer will not have left yet. Altyrn uses every moment. Lerial tries, but suspects he is not nearly so effective as is the majer.

Altyrn doesn't even look surprised at Lerial's swift return.

"Ser . . . I think you should read this. It's from my aunt, but she usually knows more than she says." Lerial extends the missive.

"I'm well aware of that," Altyrn says wryly as he takes the letter and begins to read. He says nothing until he finishes and hands the letter back. "There's a lot there."

"There's more there than she actually says."

"That's what I meant." He looks at Lerial. "What do you make of it?"

"Duke Khesyn is doing as little as possible, but enough to keep all the Lancers in Cigoerne occupied. Somehow Majer Phortyn is creating more companies, one more at least."

"And?" Altyrn raises his iron-gray eyebrows.

"Casseon is likely to move against Verdheln strongly but cautiously. He has probably sent enough scouts to discover that this post exists."

"He has sent a few, remember? None recently, according to the woodguards. Some might have sneaked past, but that won't change matters any."

"Do you think he knows we're here?"

"To those like Casseon, it doesn't matter. Two squads, an heir barely a man, if he even knows about you, and an ancient white-haired majer?"

"But our Lancers have proven better than theirs," Lerial points out.

"Casseon would say that the people of the Verd are not fighters from the heritage of Cyador. I hope that is what he and his commanders believe. And he will lose men if it will gain him Verdheln and a better position from which to attack Atroyan, should the opportunity arise in the future."

"You're saying that Cigoerne has effectively saved Afrit from conquest. So why is Atroyan attacking us now?"

Altyrn laughs softly. "Who would come to Afrit's aid if your father—or in years to come, your brother—decided to turn on Afrit? If Atroyan defeats your father, now, and is merciful, and he would be a fool not to be, and he's not that much of a fool, who else could the people of Cigoerne support?"

"So that's why Khesyn doesn't want to commit many men to attacking us . . . so that if there's a real war between Afrit and Cigoerne, at the end he can sweep down on Swartheld and take it?"

"Were I in his boots, that's the way I'd plan it." Altyrn stands. "We can't do anything about any of that at the moment, and I'm hungry. I imagine you are, too."

Lerial tucks the letter inside his riding jacket and follows the majer.

LII

Over the next several days, something nags at Lerial, but not until twoday, as he has finished his sabre instruction with the Verdyn recruits, who, he has to admit, are actually able to practice moves with real sabres, although they still spar with wands, does he finally realize what has been bothering him. He almost stops in midstride as he walks toward the stable as it hits him.

Altyrn's near matter-of-fact attitude toward the death of Captain Dechund.

The majer hadn't liked or respected Dechund, but the total indifference—or was it the underlying lack of surprise in Altyrn's feelings?—that was what has nagged at Lerial, without his even realizing it. *But you didn't like Dechund, either, and he was keeping information from Lancer headquarters.* That was clear enough, although Altyrn has avoided talking about it, despite saying that they would later. But "later" had never come . . . and the majer isn't one to forget anything.

"You're looking serious. Very serious," offers Altyrn, standing beside his mount. "What are you pondering?"

Lerial halts, caught off-guard. *What can you say . . . that makes sense without being obvious? Or too obvious?* "Captain Dechund's death. It seems so . . . odd. Maybe 'ironic' is a better word. You can ride out against raiders or armsmen, and nothing happens, and then, something stupid, like a flux, hits you, and it does what armsmen couldn't."

"Life is like that." Altyrn laughs, a sound as much sardonic as humorous. "So is death." He pauses. "I'm sure you've noticed that I didn't exactly express sorrow at his death. I don't know why he wasn't reporting the Afritan patrols, or why he was ignoring the raids close to the border, but those aren't the acts of a good or loyal officer. And to have a situation where an Afritan archer took a shot at two officers in a Cigoernean town next to his post . . . that's not an indication of an effective post commander."

"An Afritan archer?"

"I kept the shafts. Those shafts are only used by Afritan armsmen. The arrowheads were those used on Afritan war arrows." Altyrn shook his head. "Given all that, I trust you can see why I was actually relieved that he died.

I'd cautioned Majer Phortyn, but . . ." The majer shrugs. "I could have sent him the arrows, but they just would have disappeared."

The revelation about the arrows stuns Lerial. The majer is implying that Dechund was worse than incompetent . . . and that Phortyn isn't much better.

"There's nothing more to be said," Altyrn goes on, almost genially. "Seivyr will make a good post commander, and most people will forget or feel sorry for Dechund. In a way, he was fortunate, I suppose, because if we brought the arrows to your father with all the Lancers who saw it happen . . . well, we still behead traitors, but that would have just created bad feelings among the Magi'i toward the Lancers, and that's not something the Duke needs."

Another thought strikes Lerial, one at which he has the feeling of both laughing and being totally appalled. "Majer Phortyn *assigned* Seivyr to Tirminya under Dechund? After his comment about uniforms?"

"He did indeed. That's his prerogative as Lancer Commander. You should know that, but I wouldn't mention it to anyone. Not for a while."

"Yes, ser." Lerial desperately wants to ask why he shouldn't, but decides that he needs to think that over before asking the question. So far, the majer has been right in everything about which he has advised Lerial. *But this?*

An ostler walks Lerial's gelding from the stable. "Seeing as you've been occupied, ser . . ."

"Thank you." Lerial takes the reins and then mounts, his thoughts scattered and less than organized.

Altyrn rides beside Lerial toward the cleared area where the recruit squads—and now companies—practice maneuvers. After several moments, he asks, "What do you think of the Verdyn Lancers, such as they are?"

"They can charge and do basic movements." Lerial pauses. "But, with those brown uniforms, the Meroweyans will know they aren't Mirror Lancers."

"That's likely, but Casseon's men will be surprised to find six companies of any sort of Lancers."

"What about the other two hundred recruits?"

"They're supposed to arrive on fiveday."

"I can't imagine they're all that happy about it all. They work with a will, but there's a . . . something . . ." Lerial shakes his head.

"Fatalism, perhaps? It doesn't matter," replies the majer. "They'd have to fight Casseon anyway, or have most of their young people in slavery or servitude. He's the sort that wants everyone to believe in the same things as he does, and in the same way." Altyrn pauses. "I hope you don't mind my saying this, but that was one of your grandsire's worst faults."

"I couldn't say, ser. I understand he was far from perfect."

The majer nods. "Do you know what one of your father's greatest strengths is? As a ruler, that is?"

"I wouldn't want to guess, ser."

"He doesn't believe that people should all think or believe in the same way, just so long as they follow the laws of the land. None of the other Dukes think that way, and it's one of the reasons why Cigoerne has grown. It's why the elders of Verdheln came to him, and it's also why the other rulers are trying to unite against him."

"Won't that help over the long run?"

"Who can tell? When people are different, and there's no danger, they argue. Sometimes, even when there is danger, they argue more. It's always about whose ways are right. That's one of the clarifying things about a battle . . . or a war. No matter what the mages and philosophers say, whoever wins is right. That's because dead men can't argue, and most historians belong to the winner."

As the winter has waned, and spring is approaching—as is the likely attack of Casseon's armsmen—Lerial can see the growing cynicism of the majer . . . and that too troubles him.

As they rein up on the north side of the maneuver field, Lerial turns to Altyrn. "Do the Meroweyan armsmen wear breastplates the way the Afritans do?"

"Only the heavy cavalry of the Afritans wear armor, and that includes greaves and helmets. The Afritan ceremonial guards wear breastplates. I have no idea why. Casseon might have heavies, but I've not heard of any. Khesyn has at least three heavy cavalry companies."

"Will our archers be able to slow or stop any, if Casseon brings them?"

"That's the idea. Not that all ideas work out."

Lerial decides to stop asking questions for the moment. It's clear that Altyrn's thoughts are elsewhere.

LIII

The first eightday of spring arrives, along with more cold winds . . . and no rain . . . and it passes, and Lerial keeps working on blade skills with new Lancers in the morning. In dealing with some of the less-skilled Lancer recruits, he has begun to instruct them using his wand left-handed, and no one has remarked upon it. But then, transferring a skill from one hand to another seems easier, far easier, at least to Lerial, than learning it completely anew. In the afternoon, he works with and continues to learn about mounted maneuvers and tactics with Juist, and more and more often, with Altyrn. In the evening, he strengthens his abilities to deal with chaos, chaos-fire, hoping that what he is doing will work with mage-created chaos.

Chaos is chaos, he tells himself, even as he wonders whether that is indeed true, much as Saltaryn had once told him that.

Most times, the majer is more than approachable . . . and yet, in some ways, Lerial feels that he does not know Altyrn at all. But then, he has felt the same way about his own father, especially when he had seen him laughing and joking with Altyrn's daughters. *Could he do that just because they were daughters . . . or because they aren't his own children?* He also recalls the great respect that Rojana and her sisters have for their father. *Or is it that there is always a certain distance between strong parents and their children?*

All those thoughts remind him of Ryalah, and the guilty pleasure she and Amaira take in playing with their dolls when Kiedron is not around—and Ryala's almost secretive smile. Lerial can only hope that she is indeed as well as Emerya had written.

More and more, he has come to meet with Altyrn at the end of the training workday, just before dinner, and this fourday is no exception.

"We have a new report from the scouts," declares the majer even before Lerial finishes closing the study door. "The Meroweyans are assembling in Yakaat. They're also readying their forces for what looks like an advance on Verdheln."

"Without building the fort?"

"They've put the people to work on the fort. The armsmen are gathering supplies."

"Raiding the local people?" Lerial does not disguise the contempt he feels.

"Lerial . . ." Altyrn's voice is low, almost tired, but there is iron in that single name.

"Yes, ser?"

"There is great danger in feeling superior to one's enemy. That is especially true of moral superiority. Being a better person—or a better land—by itself does not make one more likely to prevail in battle . . . or in the events that follow a battle. The one who prevails is the one who destroys the enemy's ability to fight. One can win a battle by every measure . . . and lose. But . . . almost never can one lose a battle . . . and still win. There are two ways to lose, and only one to win. All too often it may be the land that we would deem more worthy that loses, because moral worth in itself does not win battles. What wins battles and wars is the ability to prevail and the willingness to do whatever is necessary, however distasteful that may be. There are no moral victories in defeat; there are only ashes and suffering."

Lerial is so taken aback by the iron in the majer's voice that he does not speak as Altyrn continues.

"There are also ashes and suffering in victory, but with victory comes the opportunity to rebuild. Most times." After the slightest pause, Altyrn continues. "If a land is willing and able to raise and train armsmen or Lancers without equal, to forge and sharpen weapons to supply them, and to appoint leaders who are able, perceptive, and determined, that land will prevail . . . even if it engenders suffering, all manner of evils, and the enslavement of much of its people."

"You make it sound as though power obtained through evil will always prevail," Lerial replies slowly.

"It often does." Altyrn offers a bitter smile. "Until that evil makes it impossible for there to be wise and able leaders, and those who have been enslaved revolt or are so beaten down that they can no longer work effectively. History seems to show that power alternates between those who are worthy and neglect their strengths and those who are less wise, often evil, and preoccupied with gaining power at all costs." He pauses. "The people of the Verd are wise in the ways of governing themselves, but they have been too trusting of those around them for too long, and one way or another, what they have been will be destroyed."

"Even if we beat back the armsmen of Merowey?"

"Matters will be better for them if we do, but what was here before will never be again." A sad smile follows. "Now . . . we need to go over what we can do. Once we know for certain that they are on the march, we need to take the road south and take a position outside the Verd."

"Outside?" Lerial cannot help but feel that it is less than wise to abandon the protection of those thick and twisted massive trees that stretch a hundred yards deep around the Verd.

"It is better to choose where to fight than to allow one's enemy to make that choice," Altyrn says dryly. "We may indeed use the trees as a fortress, but if Casseon brings a number of white wizards, any of our forces within those trees could be turned to ashes."

"Old trees don't burn that easily," ventures Lerial, then stops for a moment. "He might actually send white wizards? The Afritans and the Heldyans almost never send them against the Mirror Lancers, do they?"

"Not since the early days," replies Altyrn. "Remember, Casseon like as not doesn't even know we're here. If he does send white wizards, he'll be sending them to subdue a rebellion of his own people . . . and to make it easier by burning into the Verd."

"He'd do that?"

Any ruler is likely to do what he feels necessary. As for burning trees . . . any tree will burn if enough chaos is used, as you should know, and the thornbushes among them will burn hot, especially before their leaves turn from gray to green. The other problem is that those same trees that might offer protection will not allow us to deploy our forces quickly. Remember how narrow the forest road entry to Apfhel is?"

"Couldn't we create another entry point?"

"I already have inquired of the elders as to whether other hidden entrances exist, ones that we could use for attacks, if it appears possible . . . or for a withdrawal, if matters develop otherwise." The majer stands and spreads a map on the narrow table-desk. "This shows the approach road from Yakaat. You can see the hills here . . . and here. We may be able to conceal archers in the trees here, and have them attack the Meroweyan column if it holds to the road. The scouts report that Casseon may be dispatching as many as twenty companies."

"And we have six, and two barely into training," says Lerial, hoping to get a reaction from the majer.

"We also have a stronger defensive position—unless the Duke sends a number of white wizards. I can't believe he won't send some, because it will be far easier for them to burn their way into the Verd than to fight their way in. By the way, that's another reason for assembling outside the Verd. If we don't, they won't even need wizards to start fires everywhere. You're going to have to command a company and one with an assignment of moving to deal with outlying forces. Since you can sense weather, you can sense general forces from a distance, can't you?"

"I don't know how far, ser." *That's because you've never tried.*

"Then you'd better find out in the next few days."

"Yes, ser."

"Another thing. Some of the members of various councils *might* be joining us. They have some order or chaos talents. That could make matters . . . interesting, but we'll need every talent they can bring . . ."

Lerial continues to listen, wondering how he has ended up where he's likely to be in the middle of a war, while his brother just rides patrols and deals with raiders.

LIV

In the dim light before actual sunrise, Lerial glances forward at the scouts, and then back at the Second Verdheln Lancers—second company, "his" company—three squads half-trained in sabres, and a squad of women as mounted archers, although all the men carry bows as well. At least he has four Mirror Lancers as squad leaders, although all are really just rankers acting in that capacity. And while undercaptains do lead companies, Lerial doubts there have been few, if any, as young or inexperienced as he is.

For that reason, Lerial suspects, Altyrn had been quite adamant. "You are *not* to engage any enemy armsmen personally. You are to inflict casualties and withdraw. Do so quickly, and do not linger in any attempt to kill or wound just one more Meroweyan."

Lerial understands that all too well. He also understands the value of his taking a company against Casseon's forces from the beginning . . . and that Altyrn understands that as well, and likes it not at all.

The two scouts ride a good third of a kay ahead of Lerial, riding beside

Korlyn, the first squad leader, a cheerful and round-faced former ranker perhaps seven to eight years older than Lerial. They have not taken the road, for obvious reasons, and are already a good kay south and west of where the long dirt road from Yakaat enters the Verd. Lerial wants to be in position, within a glass of full sunrise, behind the hills he and Altyrn have picked for his attack on the vanguard of the advancing Meroweyan forces. Lerial can only hope that the reports he has from the scouts are accurate enough for what he and the majer have planned. There are alternatives, of course, but they are not likely to be as successful.

There are no clouds overhead, and the wind is out of the south, slightly warmer than it has been over the past few eightdays, but scarcely springlike. The ground is dry, and that is another reason for proceeding at a fast walk. A faster pace would not only tire the horses unnecessarily, but would likely raise enough dust to be seen from a distance, even before sunrise.

Another two kays ahead, the hills are higher on the east side of the road, and there is a slight dry wash between the road and the hills. Lerial's mission is to place the company on the back side of the hill, just close enough so that when they move forward to the crest, they will have a good shot at the Meroweyan column—*if* they can hold that position without being seen by any Meroweyan scouts . . . one way or another.

As they ride southwest through the winter-browned grass and the scattered bushes still showing only their winter-grayed first-year leaves, Lerial keeps glancing to the outriders serving as scouts, but the two offer no signals indicating any sign of the Meroweyan forces. When second company reaches the back side of the hills from which it will attack, the sun has not risen, but Lerial knows that will happen in less than a third of a glass.

Before deciding on exactly where to position the company he waits for the scouts to return and report, which they do in less than a tenth of a glass.

"The Meroweyan outriders are less than two kays away, ser," reports Gherst. "They have road scouts less than a kay from us."

"What about scouts away from the road?" asks Lerial.

"We haven't seen any, but there's more brush on the east side of the hills south of here, and the wash is deeper."

Lerial nods. "Take a position south and east of here, but stay under cover. Don't report to me unless you see a body of armsmen moving against us from any position away from the road. We'll deal with scouts, but I don't want to be hit with a surprise attack."

"Yes, ser."

As Gherst and Vominem ride off, Lerial decides against moving the company too high on the eastern side of the hill, not until the Meroweyan force is closer, although he cannot say why he feels that is a good idea, only that it feels right. He also worries that the sun will be too high by the time the enemy reaches the section of the road beneath the hill, since the plan had been for the Meroweyans to be looking into a low morning sun at the time of the attack.

Still . . . given the height of the hill . . . the sun might still be in their eyes.

Before long, he can sense the Meroweyan vanguard, almost a kay away, but not the end of the column, suggesting that the force extends more than two kays. *Definitely more than two thousand armsmen.* Possibly twice that. He reminds himself that his task is merely to reduce those numbers without unduly risking his company.

Then . . . he also senses a scout, not on the road, but one riding along the backside of the low hills to the east of the road, most likely set out to warn the Meroweyans of any attack like the one Lerial is supposed to carry out. He cannot see the rider, but the scout is definitely moving northward. *If you can't see him, he most likely can't see you.* Lerial turns to Korlyn. "Tell the rankers they'll be in total darkness. I want total silence. Not a word. Not a whisper. Pass it on."

"Yes, ser," acknowledges the squad leader.

Lerial uses his senses to locate more closely the scout's probable path. From what he can tell, the man will pass a good hundred yards above them on the gradual slope, but he will have to see. He waits until the word has reached all squads, then raises a concealment over the company.

Despite his command, there are more than a few whispers and murmurs, and several short commands of "Silence!"

Lerial is impressed, but thankful. *Maybe they've seen more magecraft than you know.*

Slowly, oh so slowly, or so it seems, the scout rides through the matted tan and brown grass northward, if higher on the slope, toward the hillside where second company waits. The swish and crackle of grass is but a faint murmur, and grows, seemingly so loud that the scout sounds as if he is riding right in front of Lerial, even though he can sense that the man is some seventy yards away.

By the time the scout is far enough north of the company that Lerial drops the concealment, hoping that the Meroweyan is out of sight, Lerial himself is shaking in the saddle, feeling wrung out. *Because you've never held that large a concealment for that long?*

He can still see the scout, but the rider does not look back, at least not until he is out of sight. Lerial manages a drink of watered greenberry, wincing as he swallows, but the liquid seems to help, and he extends his order-senses west and south. The Meroweyan force is less than half a kay away from the section of road over the crest of the hill from second company.

"Forward, at a walk," Lerial orders.

He halts the company far enough below the crest that he cannot see over, then turns to Korlyn. "All squads to attack formation."

"To attack formation. Ready bows!"

All four squads shift into a ten-ranker front . . . and wait.

Lerial concentrates on the oncoming vanguard and the companies immediately behind. He cannot sense any other forces flanking those on the road. He continues to focus on the first ranks of the vanguard until they are almost even with second company—again by design, so that if the Meroweyans decide to charge second company once they catch sight of the Lancers, they will have to turn their mounts. "Forward. Fast walk." Lerial and Altyrn have discussed the approach and decided that a quick walk into possible sight of the Meroweyans is better than a faster entry because it will be slower to be noticed and will also allow greater precision for the barely trained rankers.

Lerial leads the way, giving another order. "At my signal. Three volleys! Three! At my signal! Then we withdraw." *Quickly.*

Once they reach the top of the hill, Lerial glances back. From what he can tell, anyone on the road is still looking directly into the sun, because the shadow of the hill stops just short of the road itself.

"Company! Halt."

If the hill had cast no shadow at all, Lerial would have moved the company farther downhill to avoid being silhouetted against the sky. The road is less than two hundred yards away, possibly closer to a hundred and fifty yards, but there is a dry streambed, as the scouts have reported, between the western base of the hill and the road. Perhaps half the vanguard is already past them.

"Nock shafts." Even as Lerial gives the command, he can see gestures from below indicating that they have been sighted.

"First volley!

"Second volley!

"Third volley!"

Lerial is surprised to see armsmen below going down . . . and more than a few, as many as a third of those in the first company, if not more. Still . . . others are turning their mounts toward the hillside.

With a quick shake of his head, he snaps, "To the rear, quick-time! Ride!"

This time the Verdheln Lancers and their mounts move quickly.

"Lancers! Left turn! Left turn!"

From what Lerial can see, only two riders try to turn the wrong direction. But, on the other side of the hill, he can sense chaos building. *A firebolt?*

As the chaos-fire screams down toward the archers, Lerial forces himself to concentrate, as he creates a fifteen-line pattern to angle the chaos to the south. The pattern seems to vanish, but the firebolt angles well to the south, a good fifty yards from the nearest Lancer. As it strikes the ground, a wave of fire washes outward a good five yards in every direction. In instants, there is nothing within that circle except fine drifting ash and blackened earth.

If that hit trees . . . Altyrn's concerns about using the trees as a first line of defense suddenly become much more real. So do his concerns about the Meroweyans as he senses at least one company charging up the hill.

"Company! Quick-time! Forward!

"Quick-time! Forward!" echo the squad leaders.

Lerial, now at the rear of the company, senses yet another chaos-bolt arching down toward second squad and immediately creates a diversion pattern.

The chaos-fire seems to skid above second squad, close enough that Lerial can feel the heat, before almost bouncing farther to the east and landing amid a cluster of bushes. Flame flares skyward.

Lerial is ready to order a full gallop, but he senses that the Meroweyan armsmen have slowed as they near the top of the hill. Nonetheless, he keeps glancing back as the fourth squad leader, Moraris, now at the front of the two-file column, keeps the company moving quickly northward and away from the ambush site.

From the east, Gherst and Vominem come racing forward to join up with Lerial, although they do not reach him until he has traveled almost half a kay.

"They've slowed, ser," reports Gherst, "but they're still following."

Lerial finds himself shivering and shuddering as he tries to reach out to the west to determine the progress of the main Meroweyan force. He takes a deep breath.

"Are you all right, ser?" asks Korlyn.

"A . . . little . . . tired . . ."

Even without trying, Lerial can sense the squad leader's concern. "I'll be fine . . . in a bit."

A flash of dizziness washes over Lerial, and he has to concentrate so much to remain in the saddle that he only catches fragments of the words exchanged by Gherst and Korlyn..

". . . wrong with the captain?"

". . . has to be using order . . . knows where they were . . ."

". . . maybe . . . something . . . see how the firebolts swerved . . ."

Almost a quarter of a glass passes before Lerial can really do much but stay in the saddle. Finally, he is able to ride forward to the front of first squad. "Sorry . . . Korlyn. Are they still following us?"

"Doesn't look like it. Did you keep those fireballs from hitting us, ser?"

"Yes. It took more strength than I thought . . . appreciate it if you'd keep what it did to me between us . . ."

"I can do that, ser."

Gherst and Vominem also strongly suspect that, but, for the moment, Lerial would prefer that the remaining rankers not know just how close many of them came to being obliterated.

Slowly, he works out the bottle containing the greenberry juice and begins to drink, carefully, hoping that it will help with the remaining dizziness. After several swallows, he glances back, but can see no sign of the Meroweyans.

"Begging your pardon, ser . . . but you've not given an order as to where we're headed, except for away from the Meroweyans."

"Back to the marshaling point, and you're right. I'll ride forward and have Moraris pass the order back." Lerial offers a ragged grin. "I appreciate the reminder."

Korlyn nods in return, and Lerial urges the gelding forward.

Lerial's dizziness has almost subsided completely when second company reaches Altyrn's main force, marshaled less than five hundred yards south of where the road reaches the woods. After seeing that his company is fed, and their mounts watered and also given some fodder, Lerial seeks out Altyrn, who is seated behind a small table under a small awning just forward of the low stone wall that contains the green fronting the seemingly endless line of ancient and massive trees that protect Verdheln. The majer looks up from his camp table and the map spread on it, but waits for Lerial to speak.

"We attacked and hit them with three volleys. The Verdyn archers are good. I'd guess that the shafts struck a third to a half of the vanguard. They reacted quickly, the way you said they would. Some of them were starting up the slope when we withdrew. I followed your advice, ser. We didn't stay for a fourth volley."

Altyrn nods. "Did you suffer any casualties?"

"No, ser."

"How close were you?"

"About a hundred and fifty yards."

"You should have hit many from that range. How did you get that close? Didn't they have scouts out to the side?"

"They did . . ." Lerial goes on to explain.

The majer frowns. "I'm surprised some of the rankers didn't give you away."

"I told them they'd be in darkness. They kept quiet."

"What about chaos-fire?"

"They do have at least one white wizard. He threw two firebolts at us—that I saw, anyway. We were already moving, and they missed. One came pretty close. I could feel the heat. I'd guess that by the time the magus or white wizard could throw another we were too far away."

"You don't think he was just tired?"

"Both of them were strong. It seemed that way to me. Each one burned everything to the bare earth across a circle more than five yards across."

"That's only moderately strong. How far were you from the wizard?"

"I don't know. We were more than four hundred yards from the nearest part of the main force. Where the wizard was I couldn't say."

"Most likely not near the front." Altyrn smiles faintly. "Let's say you turned fifty armsmen into casualties. We'll only need forty-nine more attacks like that."

"You're saying we won't get near that many."

"Kusyl's out there with fourth company. He has a different ambush strategy. Let's see how he does. If we're fortunate, between the two of you we might have removed the equivalent of a single company."

"What about Juist?"

"He'll be trying something else . . . later . . . if we get the chance."

"Do you think they'll attack today?"

"Knowing what I know, if I were the Meroweyan commander, I certainly would. Knowing something about them, I'd be very surprised if they attack even tomorrow. While I hope I'm right, we need to be prepared for whatever they might do." He pauses and looks hard at Lerial. "You need something to eat and drink. Do that before you do anything else. That's an order. After that, check your men and mounts again—you were getting them fed, I saw—and come back here."

"Yes, ser."

The majer looks down at the map—an effective dismissal—and Lerial steps back, then turns and heads for the cookfires. His stomach is growling, and his head still aches.

LV

Over the course of the late morning and early afternoon, Lerial tries to rest, and does manage to eat, although he's anything but fond of acorn bread, but the cheese, which has a sort of blue mold through it, makes the bread palatable. Since Altyrn does not summon him, slightly after the third glass of the afternoon, he makes his way back to the awning. The majer is not there. Lerial wonders where he might be, but since he cannot see him, he walks back to rejoin his company.

"Have you heard anything, ser?" asks Bhurl, the second squad leader, a square-faced and stolid former ranker.

"Nothing new. Have you?"

"Word is that fourth company came back in. They lost near-on half a squad to those fireballs. Good thing we left when we did."

Lerial smiles. "We made a tactical withdrawal, and you're right. It was a good thing we did."

"Ah . . . yes, ser."

Lerial can see that Bhurl is having trouble concealing a grin.

Lerial talks in turn to Fhentaar, the Lancer ranker who is third squad leader, and is about to make his way to fourth squad when he sees Altyrn striding toward him. He turns and meets the majer. "I heard that fourth company returned, ser."

"They did. Kusyl was a bit more adventurous than I would have preferred. They took out almost an entire company. It cost them almost a full squad, half dead, and the other half burned or wounded. The archers didn't take any casualties."

Although the majer's tone is level, Lerial gets the impression that Altyrn is relieved that the archer squad has suffered no casualties . . . and he doesn't think that it's because the archer rankers are women. "You have more plans for the archers?"

"Outnumbered six to one, shouldn't we?" The majer's words are sardonically biting.

Lerial feels stupid for asking the question, rhetorical as it was. "I should have asked what they are, ser. It's obvious we need to reduce their numbers while risking our own forces as little as possible."

Altyrn actually grins. "I knew what you meant. Neither your father nor Majer Phortyn would have stopped to think about what you meant, rather than what you said. Most senior officers don't want to guess at meanings in battle. Some can't."

Six to one? That was more than twice what Lerial had estimated. "I couldn't count them this morning, but there had to be more than twenty-five hundred."

"It's difficult to tell anywhere close to exact numbers," Altyrn goes on, "but they've got close to eight battalions. That's if the reports from the scouts are accurate."

Battalions? Lerial has to think for a moment. "Do they have four or five companies to a battalion?"

"Five, usually. That's what I'm basing the number of battalions on. They're settling in for a methodical assault on the Verd. We have to keep them off-balance."

"Using the archers as much as you can from where they can't easily retaliate?"

"That's the idea. They also know that's what we'll have to do. That's why they've set up camp on hilltops surrounded by relatively open ground. Can you conceal a squad for half a glass?"

Lerial considers. "Most likely." Then he adds, "except I can't conceal any dust raised and left behind if they're riding."

This time, Altyrn frowns. After a moment, he says, "You're good in the dark. Are you good enough to locate wagons from a distance?"

"From a kay away, maybe farther."

"That should do. Come and see me in a glass, but have your fourth squad prepare for an evolution after full dark tonight."

"Yes, ser."

With that, the majer turns and heads in the direction of the small awning.

Lerial looks to the south. The Meroweyans are completing positions some two kays to the southwest, opposite the Verdyn position along a ridge that is more like a long hill. Although the largely flat crest of the ridge is a good twenty to thirty yards lower than where Altyrn's forces are marshaled, between the two forces is a shallow valley more than a kay wide. For either force to attack the other directly will require an uphill advance.

Somehow, Lerial doesn't see that happening, not immediately.

But the way they outnumber us . . . At the same time, after the majer's explanations of how the larger three duchies distrust each other, Lerial can see why Casseon would prefer to lose as few armsmen as possible. *That means outflanking us until we're forced to retreat behind the trees. Then they'll burn their way through in so many places that we'll be spread too thin to stop them . . . unless the majer has a better plan.*

Lerial then continues toward fourth squad, slowing as he sees Moraris talking with another Mirror Lancer that Lerial only recognizes by sight and not by name. He stops and slips behind a cart, extending his order sense and trying to hear what the two are saying and what may be passing between the two.

". . . any spare shafts?"

". . . if I did, Moraris, wouldn't be trading 'em to you, not after—"

"I made it up to you, didn't I?"

"Not until . . . you know . . . What about the undercaptain? Green as he looks?"

"Green? Some ways. Stiff . . . like all young officers . . . scary, too. Part ordermage, and he'd take you and me apart with a blade."

". . . until he's against someone out to kill him . . ."

The stocky Moraris shakes his head. "Talked to Juist. Undercaptain's already killed a raider who charged him, even before he was a Lancer. This morning . . . fireballs falling all around us . . . kept his head, got us out . . ."

"An undercaptain you like . . . that's something . . ."

"Don't know about like . . . know it's not good to cross him . . . not because of his da, either . . ."

". . . keep that in mind . . ."

"About those shafts . . ."

"Not on your life or mine . . ." The other Lancer turns away.

Lerial waits a moment, then slips from behind the cart and continues toward the acting squad leader.

Moraris turns and starts, as if he hadn't expected Lerial. "Ser?"

"I saw you talking to . . . ?"

"Saetaln . . . he's got second squad under Shaskyn, I mean, acting undercaptain Shaskyn."

Although Lerial doesn't recall anything about Saetaln, Shaskyn is a senior ranker who had been a squad leader, but demoted a season back for questioning a captain's order. When Lerial had asked why Altyrn had selected him as an acting undercaptain of fifth company, the majer had just said that the offended captain was Akyael, an officer Lerial has never heard of, and said that Shaskyn was good in a fight, and that, one way or another, it wouldn't matter.

Lerial nods and says, "Undercaptain Shaskyn is supposed to be good in a fight."

"Angel-flamed good, ser." Moraris starts to go on, but abruptly closes his mouth. "The past won't matter if we all do well here," Lerial replies. "I wanted to let you know that the majer has something special planned for you, me, and fourth squad after dark this evening. I don't know the details yet, but I wanted you to know."

"We don't have that many shafts left, ser . . . six for each archer."

"I'll let him know that when I meet with him." *If we have to we can take shafts from the first three squads.* "How are things going otherwise?"

"They rode well this morning. Good shots, too. Head archer is really good." Moraris's smile is a little too warm.

Lerial decides he will have to watch that and says, "The majer wants hands off any Verdyn women, archers or not."

"Yes, ser. They are good archers."

"Far better than I'd be with a bow." Lerial smiles pleasantly. "I'll let you know as soon as I can."

"Yes, ser."

Lerial can sense Moraris's eyes on his back as he turns. He still wonders what the squad leader was going to trade to get extra shafts for his squad. He can't fault Moraris's interest in keeping his squad fully armed, but . . .

At fourth glass Lerial makes his way to the awning. The majer is not there. So Lerial waits, glancing around, especially toward the southwest. A few moments later, Altyrn rides up, accompanied by one of the Verdyn rankers, dismounts, and hands the reins to the ranker, who rides away, leading the majer's mount.

"I've been checking the Meroweyan positions and how they line up against us and against the woods." Altyrn walks over under the awning, but does not sit down behind the table.

"What I need for you and your archers to do is to create a number of fires amid their supply wagons. Those wagons are still mostly on the west end of the ridge. That's because it's close to the road. They're worried about rain . . . as if it's going to rain any time soon. It's not looking to be cloudy tonight, and that will make it easier for them to see you. But if we wait until it's dark and cloudy, we'll still be waiting when Casseon's men charge over us. That's why I asked about concealing one squad." The majer pauses. "You can't throw firebolts, can you?"

"No, ser."

"I didn't think so, but it never hurts to ask." He looks at Lerial. "Do you know why?"

"Because sometimes you think something is so, based on what you believe, but it's not, and you won't find out if you don't ask."

"Exactly. Now . . . since you can't throw firebolts, your archers will. You'll need to get close enough to put fire arrows into the wagons and everything around them."

"Ser . . . we're already short on arrows—"

The majer holds up his hand. "You don't need to waste good war arrows. Send some rankers to the third supply wagon. We've got fire arrows there. They're easier and faster to make because we don't need barbed iron heads. We've also got some oil bottles. The archers will have to share, and your squad leader will need to make sure they're distributed so that every archer can get to one quickly . . ." Altyrn continues with his instructions, but when he finishes he asks, "Any questions?"

"How much do you want me to risk the archers?"

"As little as possible, but we need to have enough fire arrows hitting things to get them to burn. The faster they can release shafts the less likely any mages can stop you. I also don't want to explain to your father how you ignored caution and became a dead hero." Altyrn offers a grim smile. "Remember, one of the ways to be successful in war is to make your enemies make all the gallant but useless sacrifices . . ."

Gallant but useless sacrifices . . . Lerial wants to keep that in mind.

". . . should be as dark as it's going to get by eighth glass . . ."

In the middle of the majer's explanation, Lerial realizes something he should have picked up earlier. "Ser . . . ?"

"Yes?" Altyrn's voice carries mild exasperation.

"To get close enough, I think we'll need to move under concealment. I can sense where I am, but no one else can. I need two long, long lengths of rope or really strong cord. That way—"

"I understand. How long? You think twenty yards?"

"At least twenty. Twenty-five might be better."

"I'll have it at the supply wagon later. Now . . ."

Once the majer has finished explaining, Lerial heads back to find Moraris.

The squad leader has an apprehensive expression as Lerial joins him. "Ser?"

"We're going to make a night attack on the wagons marshaled near the west end of the Meroweyan position. With fire arrows. We won't need any more war arrows. You're to take the archers to the third supply wagon and draw special arrows and oil. Let me know if they don't have enough iron and flints." Lerial takes a deep breath. "They're going to have to trust me again, because they won't be able to see for a good part of the approach if I conceal us from their sentries and scouts. If I don't, we won't be able to get close enough to do what we need to do . . . not without taking a lot of casualties . . ."

"Ser . . . best we talk with the head archer. She'll have to instruct the others."

Of course. Once more, Lerial feels stupid, and even stupider for not recalling the name of the head archer—which he ought to know.

"Begging your pardon, ser, but I told Alaynara to stand by. Figured we might need her thoughts."

"We do." Lerial decides to say as little as possible.

The squad leader motions, and a short and squarish woman walks away from the women of fourth squad. She has broad shoulders, reddish brown hair cut squarely a digit or so above the back of her uniform tunic, a lightly freckled face, and a nose slightly too small. Lerial suspects she is among the older rankers, possibly older even than Korlyn, but not as old as Bhurl.

"Ser?" Her voice is neither high nor low.

"We need to talk over the approach to the Meroweyan camp," Lerial says. "I'd thought that you could loft arrows—they'll be fire arrows—up the slope and down onto their supply wagons. You'll have to be mounted. How close do we need to get?"

"Uphill . . . not that much of a slope . . ." Alaynara tilts her head slightly.

"We could do two hundred, but closer is better. First volley will be a guess. Fire arrows, though, they'll let us see the range better than war arrows . . ."

As she talks, Lerial mentally revises some of what he has planned. When she finishes, he says. "The other thing is that to get close enough, we're going to have to ride under a concealment . . . the blackness I used at the ambush this morning."

"How will we know where to go?"

"I'd thought to use cord from rider to rider. I can tell where to go, but I can't be calling out directions."

The head archer nods. "Ought to work. Can't be that much worse than night riding in the deep Verd."

When he finishes with Moraris and Alaynara, Lerial walks to the west end of the Lancer positions and begins to study the Meroweyan positions. He especially notes where there are large clumps of bushes, few as those are. After a time, he returns to second company, checking the tie-line near the woods where the mounts are tethered. That arrangement and the fact that the supply wagons have not been unloaded suggests to Lerial that Altyrn thinks that they may have to withdraw on very short notice. It's not a comforting observation.

Lerial forces himself to eat when dinner is ready—ghano hash between dry acorn bread slices, washed down with either water or greenberry . . . or the combination of the two that Lerial can get down. After obtaining lengths of cordage from the supply wagon, and turning them over to Moraris, he forces himself to take his time getting ready, and he offers last-moment orders to Moraris about a third before eighth glass.

"We'll ride west as a two-abreast column, and then, just before we're opposite the target we'll stop and pay out the cord so that each file can keep position. We'll head south, still east of the road. I'm going to take us beside several areas that have clumps of bushes until we're at a point where I'll raise a concealment. Once we get in range, I'll drop the concealment. When the archers can see the stars, I'll give the command to dip the arrows and then strike their flints and light them. Then they keep dipping and firing them until they're out of fire arrows . . . or if there's a charge headed our way. That's when we turn and leave as fast as we can."

"No concealment on the way back, ser?" asks Moraris.

"There's no reason for that. If they have white wizards, they'll sense where we are from the concealment . . . once they know we're there. And the fire arrows will give away our initial position anyway. They likely won't be looking with chaos senses all the time before we get there. That's too tiring." *That's what your experience says. What if theirs is different?* "If they sense us earlier, we'll just have to break off the attack."

Finally . . . fourth squad sets out westward, parallel to both lines, with Lerial at the head of one file, and Moraris at the head of the other.

When they're opposite their target, Lerial turns the squad and starts south before calling a halt and giving the order, "Pay out the cord to each file."

While he waits for the guiding cord to reach the last ranker in each file, Lerial again tries to sense, without reaching out, whether the Meroweyan white wizards are showing any sign of having discovered them. So far, they are not moving, nor are they doing anything different. *Then, too, they could be watching to see if you get closer, or waiting until you do.*

Lerial is finding that he doesn't like to try to guess what his enemies are doing, even as he knows he must . . . and that he must get better at it . . . so that he is not guessing, but anticipating. *Like with the sabre.*

"Guide cords in place, ser," Moraris says quietly.

"Squad. Forward."

After they have ridden downhill and south, then across part of the small valley, but before they reach the middle, Lerial can sense the supply wagons. Without probing, recalling his lessons with Saltaryn, he tries just to gain an impression of where there might be ordermages or white wizards. There are two, possibly three, white wizards in the middle of the Meroweyan positions, and several farther to the south, although he cannot locate the wizards to the south, most likely because they are beyond his ability to discern clearly. Fourth squad continues at a measured pace, first, because it is quieter, and also safer in the darkness, and second, because slower movements are not as likely to be noticed at a distance by sentries.

Lerial also directs the squad from clump to clump of bushes, in ways that do not markedly extend the distance they must cover, in order to convey the impression that the riders are a scouting party . . . if they are noticed. But with about half a kay remaining to the area from which he wants the archers to loft the fire arrows he says, "Concealment coming. Pass it back. Quietly."

After several moments, he raises the concealment, then makes another effort to try to determine whether the chaos mages might have detected anything. He can sense no changes. He almost feels like holding his breath in the darkness that is far darker than a starry night as he leads the column across the remainder of the flat area and then starts up the gradual slope toward their target.

When they near the area he and Altyrn had picked out, Lerial realizes that they cannot go exactly where he had hoped. Because, even his senses are telling him that the ground ahead is far too uneven to ride across. Yet . . . they are possibly thirty, perhaps even fifty, yards short of where he would like to be, a good hundred and fifty yards from the supply wagons. He lifts the concealment.

"We're fifty yards farther out. Pass it back."

Lerial waits for Moraris to report.

"Fourth squad, ready, ser."

"Strike and light," Lerial orders, hoping that is an accurate order. He has no idea what the proper order might be, but his words seem to have the desired effect because small balls of light appear along the line of archers.

"First volley!" he finally orders, then watches as the arrows arch up and over the crest, trying to follow them with his senses. While a few strike the wagons, most fall slightly short. "Head archer! Most are about ten yards short."

"Ten yards more. Ready for volley."

"Second volley!"

Most of the arrows are in the right range, but many still miss the wagons. One wagon seems to be catching fire, from what Lerial can sense. "That's a good range. Stand by for third volley."

"Ready for volley."

"Third volley!"

This time a few more shafts stick.

"Stand by for fourth volley."

"Ready."

"Fourth volley!"

Lerial can sense the chaos building—somewhere to the south and east of him—but there is nothing he can do but wait . . . and hope he has the ability to divert whatever chaos force is aimed at fourth squad. While the arrows are having an effect, they really need at least one more volley.

The fifth volley goes, and Lerial is about to order the sixth, knowing there are only enough arrows for seven full volleys, when a firebolt flares directly toward him.

Even though he is as ready as he can be, it takes a huge effort to drop the chaos-fire short of fourth squad, more so than angling it away, but he hopes the flare of power will momentarily keep the white wizard from seeing or determining whether his effort was successful.

"Sixth volley!"

As soon as the fire arrows are away, he orders, "Turn and withdraw! On the double!" He turns the gelding, noticing that some of the archers are glancing toward the hilltop. "Withdraw! Now!"

"Forward to the rear!" orders Moraris, urging his mount forward toward the end of the column that has become the van.

The squad starts downhill, but Lerial remains at the back. He tries a quick sensing of the wagons and gets the impression that as many as six may be in flames. Men are scurrying and pulling other wagons away. At least, that is the impression he gets—along with that feeling of building chaos.

The next firebolt is bigger than the previous one, but it arches down toward Lerial, almost as if the wizard intends to drop it right on him.

Lerial concentrates—this time with a terribly fine-lined twenty-strand order loop—and the firebolt strikes the hillside less than thirty yards behind the gelding. Heat hotter than an oven washes over Lerial, then dissipates.

"Captain?" comes a call from Moraris.

"I'm fine. Keep riding! There might be more fireballs."

No sooner are the words out of Lerial's mouth than he can sense more chaos building somewhere behind him, and he wonders if he can divert the next chaos-blast . . . and still function.

The third bolt is more whitish red, somehow *nastier* feeling.

Lerial doubts that he can survive another twenty-line diversion pattern, and he tries two linked ten-line patterns. His mouth opens as the firebolt just disintegrates in midair with streamers of reddish-white flames almost dribbling from the star-sprinkled night sky.

Over the next three or four hundred yards, he can sense no more chaos-fire concentration, but, once more, Lerial's head aches, and tiny flashes of light erratically distort his vision. He keeps looking back, but there are no more firebolts, and once they are close to a kay away from the Meroweyan lines, he begins to breathe more easily. As fourth squad begins riding up the slope on the north side of the valley, back to the Lancer camp, Lerial realizes that, despite the evening chill, he is sweating and soaked, and his entire body is shaking. *Just from diverting three firebolts? Three?*

But then, he'd only managed two the last time.

He takes another look back across the valley. The flames have died down, but there are still some reddish-orange points of light and an overall fire glow. He almost smiles, until he thinks about how many white wizards the Meroweyans have . . . and the fact that at least one of them had known exactly where he had been.

He just wishes he could figure out a way to divert all that power in the chaos-bolts back to the wizards who are throwing it—or at least back at the Meroweyan camp. *You'll have to think about that.* Except . . . to do that, he needs to work with wizard chaos, and that tends to be difficult when, if he fails, he's likely to be incinerated on the spot.

Lerial is so exhausted by the time that he and fourth squad return that he really doesn't want to do anything but collapse into sleep, but he needs to report to Altyrn. After unsaddling and grooming the gelding, quickly and not well, he makes his way to find the majer.

Altyrn is standing beside the awning tent, talking to Juist and Kusyl. Rather than interrupt, Lerial waits until they leave to step forward. "Ser?"

"I could see the fire from here. Did you take any casualties?"

"No, ser."

"Good. Were there any problems or anything I should know immediately?"

"No problems, but they do have at least four white wizards, chaos mages."

"I saw the firebolts. How far do you think the farthest one went?"

"A kay at most."

Altyrn nods and then looks closely at Lerial in the dim light. "Get some sleep. You can tell me the rest in the morning. Early."

"Yes, ser. Is there a problem?"

"Not unless you have one. I need to work out some things with fifth and sixth company."

"No problems, ser." Lerial nods and departs, wondering if and how he has disappointed the majer. He stifles a yawn.

He can worry about that in the morning . . . and he knows he will.

LVI

The next morning Lerial wakes up early, stiff from a night on a bedroll—especially in his shoulders and neck—and very worried. Although it is before sunrise, the gray has faded, and the sky is largely clear, but he can see a few scattered clouds on the horizon to the south, although it will be later in the day before those clouds get near enough for Lerial to determine whether they might bring rain. After readying himself for the day and then checking with his squad leaders, he hurries to find Altyrn.

The majer is at the table under the awning, looking at the maps and talking to Juist. He beckons for Lerial to join them, but continues to talk to the acting undercaptain. ". . . can take the trail on the back side of the wash a kay west of the old quarry there . . . bring you within striking distance . . . bluff there . . . have the first three squads use their bows to target the rankers, and the archers put fire arrows into the supply wagons . . . no casualties . . . if possible . . ."

"That's going to make them mad," observes Juist.

"It probably will. Since they intend to kill us all anyway, what difference does it make?"

At the ironic tone in the majer's voice, Juist shakes his head and chuckles.

Lerial can sense that there is far more behind the majer's comment, but not what.

"Do you want us to do anything on the way back?" asks Juist.

"Get close enough to the Meroweyan lines here that they can see you returning, but not close enough for them to be able to send out a force able to reach you before you rejoin us."

Lerial can see the point of that.

"That's all," concludes Altyrn. "Set out as soon as you can."

"Yes, ser." Juist nods to the majer and turns, smiling wryly at Lerial as he departs.

Lerial steps closer and waits for the majer to speak.

"Give me a brief summary of your mission last night."

"Yes, ser. We headed west in front of our lines until we were close to opposite the objective. Then we headed south, silent riding, and moving from various clumps of bushes at a deliberate pace . . ." Lerial goes on to give a brief description of what happened, but without mentioning his diversions of the firebolts, and only saying that the second one came so close that he felt as though his back had been in an oven.

"So . . . you accomplished your objective last night. No more and no less."

"Yes, ser. We did so without casualties."

"That's always good." Altyrn pauses. "You do realize that they have more than three thousand armsmen. The scouts have reported another five to ten companies on the road from Yakaat. Presumably they are headed here. They'll arrive late this evening, or tomorrow. You heard the strategy I gave Juist for dealing with them."

"It's a variation on what we did last night," offers Lerial

"That's right. Last night, you provided a solid diversion. Very nicely done. It was just the thing to keep them from considering an immediate attack."

A diversion?

"The fact that their firebolts aren't doing the damage they should may be worth more than the casualties they've suffered." Altyrn offers a wry smile. "I'm hoping it also suggests that they wait for reinforcements. Of course, there is the danger that there might be another white wizard with the reinforcements." He looks directly at Lerial. "So far, all we've done is annoy them. We've removed perhaps a company and the supplies for two or three, maybe even five companies. That's only until they get replacements."

"Might I ask, ser, how we can stop so many of them?"

"By killing or wounding most of them. That's the only way I know." After a moment, the majer adds, "I'm working on that. But we need them to feel that, once they have all their armsmen, we'll just whittle away their forces if they wait. They can't live off the land, not unless they get into the Verd, and if they take a measured and slow approach, that will cost hundreds if not thousands of golds for supplies, not to mention the armsmen that Casseon will lose."

"What if they advance with everything that they have once the additional armsmen arrive?"

"We withdraw into the Verd and force them to fight their way in. That will wear out their wizards and their armsmen. We can talk about that later. I want you and second company to make an attack before dawn tomorrow, while it is still dark, most likely on the companies on the eastern end of the Meroweyan lines. This will be an attack designed to see if they will attempt to attack you. So you will need to think about how to provoke them to ride after you and then ambush them when they do."

"What if they don't?"

"Then keep attacking them until you can do no more without incurring significant casualties. Study the lay of the land, and the position of their companies. Think about it, and then come to me this afternoon with your plan."

"Yes, ser."

After he leaves, Lerial reflects not only on what he has been asked to do, but on what the majer has said . . . and what he has not.

What are you missing?

Lerial does not know. All he knows at present is that he is indeed missing something and that every time he attempts to ask questions, the majer avoids answering them. Even if he were the heir—like Lephi—and insisted on answers, Lerial doubts that he would get any more information than he already has.

What can he do? For now, the only thing to do is to study the terrain and the enemy . . . and ask his squad leaders to do the same thing . . . and then see what they have seen before completing his own plan of attack.

All that will go for nothing if the Merowyans attack. But they won't, Lerial suspects, because in everything, so far, the majer has been right. *Is that just experience . . . or does he know something others don't?*

After gathering his squad leaders and asking them to watch the Meroweyans, as they can, over the next few glasses, Lerial decides on riding east to observe what he cannot from camp, and asks Fhentaar to detail four rankers from third squad to accompany him.

"You don't want the whole squad, ser? How about ten men?"

"Four will be fine. I'm not going that close to their lines. I don't want to tire any more horses than necessary in case the Meroweyans change their minds and decide to attack today."

"Yes, ser." The squad leader's voice verges on doubtful.

"The majer says they won't, and I'm not about to question him on that."

In less than half a glass, Lerial leads the four rankers away from camp, riding eastward, staying close to the low stone wall that appears to border the forest, but they have only ridden a few hundred yards when he realizes again and belatedly, that he is not headed due east, but more east–southeast . . .

and that a kay or so farther east, the forest gradually extends, if at a gentle angle more to the south. As he rides slowly through the knee-high grass, green at its base and partway up each stalk, but winter-or-drought-browned at the ends, he keeps a close eye on the enemy lines and reaches out with his order-senses for anyone—especially a mage or wizard—who might be approaching.

All he senses are riders within a few hundred yards of the Meroweyan position. Once they are well east of the end of the last Meroweyan armsmen, he eases the gelding more to the south and downslope so that he can look at the approaches open to second company. One of the first things he notices has nothing to do with the Meroweyans, but with the Verdyn rankers accompanying him. There is not even a hint of a murmur between any of them, unlike any Mirror Lancer squad with which he has ridden.

Lerial does not wish to get too close to his target, nor to stop and study any one point for long, fearing that such might well alert a sharp Meroweyan to a specific point to defend. For that reason, he continues to ride to the southeast, trying to give the impression of surveying the entire east end of the Meroweyan position. For the most part, the slope up to the ends of the ridge shows the same mix of grass and bushes as on the northern side of the ridge, but what Lerial has not realized is that the eastern end extends far more to the south than does the western end, so that the ridge top is roughly triangular.

Would an attack from farther south be more successful? Lerial decides he will have to think about that, since there is also a gully of sorts that runs down from the top of the ridge roughly a half kay south of the front of the Meroweyan position. Attacking from north of the gully could result in being trapped if the Meroweyans sweep downhill and eastward quickly enough. And to attack from south of the gully would require riding up onto the ridge. *But you'd be behind them . . .*

The other thing he notices is that there are tents set up at the rear of the Meroweyan position. Tents may be flammable, and so might their contents—another possibility to consider.

More than a glass later, Lerial and the rankers ride back past the outriders serving as sentries and into what he suspects will be a very temporary camp. Once he has dismounted and unsaddled the gelding, he walks back toward the woods, thinking. The majer wants him to set up an attack, followed by an ambush, but for any attack and ambush to be successful, second company will need more arrows. Fire arrows will suffice for the initial attack, the one to rouse the Meroweyans to come after second company, but to kill or wound armsmen will take more than that.

What about chaos-firebolts?

The only thing Lerial can think about is spreading the archers who will loose the fire arrows far enough apart that it will take a separate fireball for each, with himself amid them, close enough to divert any that might strike an archer—with the rest of the company far enough away that the chaos mages would have difficulty throwing firebolts that far. He considers the terrain once more, then returns to second company to talk to the squad leaders one by one.

Since Fhentaar appears to be the closest, Lerial seeks him out first. "What have you noticed about the Meroweyans?"

"Ser . . . I can't claim to have seen much. Does seem to me that they don't want to fight much unless they got wizards nearby. We attacked the other day. Armsmen didn't move until fireballs were flying . . ."

The big squad leader doesn't have much to add to that, and Lerial moves on to talk to Moraris, whom Lerial cannot help but think of as a would-be trader, and who confirms that opinion to some degree when he says, "They get more upset when they lose goods. Maybe their armsmen know it. Could be they're not too anxious to stick their necks out."

"Why do you think that?" Lerial asks in return.

"They threw fireballs last night, but none of their armsmen came very close. They just did enough so that they could claim they did something."

Lerial finds that interesting and, also, the fact that he caught Alaynara watching the two of them, and that she did not look away when he glanced at her. *Almost as if she were studying you.*

Next, he seeks out Bhurl, who leads second squad, and asks for his observations.

"I can't say that I've seen enough, ser, to say much. They got us outnumbered, and they just sit there. I don't mind that, because every day they wait I can spend working with the squad."

"Just keep doing it," replies Lerial with a smile when he leaves.

Korlyn is waiting for Lerial. "I didn't see anyone shadowing or trailing you this morning."

"I'm sure more than a few were watching. What do you think of the Meroweyans?"

"The southerners don't seem to move all that fast. They don't like tall grass, either."

"When did you notice that?"

"Yesterday. When they charged after us up that hill they all avoided the taller grass."

"Do you think somewhere there are raiders who conceal traps in the tall grass? I can't see why they'd avoid it otherwise. It's not all that high."

"Couldn't say, ser."

"How well do they ride?"

"A little better than our rankers. Not much. They don't ride as well as Mirror Lancers. They're not even close. They're more like mounted foot armsmen. That's the ones we saw anyway."

"How is your training going?"

"They're a little better with the sabres every day. I can't teach them about bows. They know more than I do."

"More than I do also," replies Lerial with a light laugh. "I'll let you know what the majer has in mind for us after I meet with him."

"Yes, ser."

After a time thinking over what he has learned from the squad leaders, Lerial sets out to find Altyrn, although that is scarcely difficult, since he is looking over his maps under the awning. The corners of the maps are weighted down with large stones to keep the brisk cold breeze from carrying them away.

"What sort of plan have you worked out?" asks Altyrn pleasantly.

"That depends on whether we can get more arrows."

"We can spare a hundred more war arrows for you."

"What about fire arrows?"

"How many do you want?

"Two hundred and more oil."

"There should be that many left. How are you going to use them?"

"I think it will take a great number of fire arrows to get the Meroweyans to leave their camp. They're relying on the chaos wizards . . ." Lerial goes on to explain.

When he finishes, Altyrn frowns. "I have some doubts, but the fact that it is not just your opinion, but that of rankers with some experience might lend some credence to that idea. I'd place your other three squads farther downhill . . ."

Lerial listens carefully.

LVII

Even in the starlight well before dawn, Lerial can see his breath as he readies the gelding for the attack, even if it is supposed to be spring. He is glad that he briefed the squad leaders around one of the cookfires the night before. The sky is clear and dark, and the stars offer little light. The company is forming up at the east end of the camp as Lerial rides to the head of the column and reins up.

"First squad ready, ser," announces Korlyn.

In turn, the other three squad leaders report their readiness.

"Company! Forward!"

Lerial has positioned Gherst and Vominem as outriders only about ten yards ahead. There is little point to putting them much farther out, not in the darkness, and not when he is likely to be able to sense any body of riders or armsmen.

Lerial leads second company well to the east before heading south, making a wide circle so that they can come up behind the Meroweyan position from the southeast, but on the south side of the gully running down from the ridge. Should they be detected, there is more than enough open ground to the east and the south, but the gully will protect them from being attacked from the north. He has also decided against using a concealment, trusting to the darkness to provide a certain cover. Besides, he isn't so sure that his use of a concealment might not have alerted the Meroweyan wizards.

By the end of another half glass, second company is moving slowly up the gradual slope on the southeast corner of the triangular ridge. Lerial can sense sentries ahead, but they are only set out a hundred yards or so from the rear of the Meroweyan encampment.

Because wizards are watching? Or for some other reason?

When he judges that second company is somewhat less than a half kay from the sentries, he orders a halt, then gives another order. "Squad one, squad two, and squad three. Take your positions."

Although there is some murmuring and shuffling, and whuffing of mounts, Lerial doubts the sounds have carried upslope to the sentries, but he watches and listens, and gathers in his senses about the sentries, who walk slowly back and forth. There is no change in their behavior.

Korlyn rides up and says quietly, "Squad one in position, ser."

"Good. Stand by."

Shortly, Bhurl reports, followed by Fhentaar.

Then Lerial turns to Moraris. "Squad four. Forward."

"Squad. Forward. Silent riding."

As he rides, Lerial tilts his head, but can sense no clouds near, and there is so little wind in the stillness well before dawn that the archers should not have too much trouble lofting the fire arrows over the sentries.

A third of a glass later, Lerial halts fourth squad, then orders, as quietly as he can, "Fourth squad to positions. Loose shafts when you see the first fire arrow fly." While he remains mounted beside Alaynara to give the head archer the command to begin the fire attack on the east end of the camp, he forces himself to wait as he senses the twenty-nine other archers ride out and take positions in an approximate square, each archer a good five yards from any other ranker. So far, the sentries in the darkness before them have not moved or raised an alarm. *Are they even awake . . . or is it some sort of trap?*

Still . . . he can sense no armsmen near, except for the sentries, and no chaos wizards.

"They're in position," he finally says to Alaynara. "Strike and light."

"Striking and lighting, ser."

After a few moments, the first fire arrow arches into the darkness of the sky and then drops toward the Meroweyan camp. Within a few moments, flaming arrows are raining down upon the eastern end of the camp.

"Enemy archers!" shouts one of the sentries, but he does not advance.

"Fire arrows! Scores of them!" yells a second.

Lerial hears voices, and several loud voices giving orders, but he is too far away to make out what all those orders might be. What he does sense is that, so far, no one is moving toward the archers. Before that long, more than a hundred fire arrows have left the archers' bows, and more than a handful of tents or wagons have begun to burn. Lerial can hear more shouts and orders, and, in the scattered light cast by the fires, see and sense men running, some beating out flames with blankets, but he does not feel the building chaos he had experienced during the last attack.

Why not? Because the archers are spread out . . . and the fire arrows aren't doing that much damage to the armsmen?

Abruptly, a larger tent bursts into a ball of flame.

Within moments, Lerial can sense men running toward the horses on tie-lines, some two hundred yards to the northwest of the westernmost of the fourth squad archers, as well as another group of armsmen on foot beginning to form up. He can also sense chaos probes sweeping the area, followed by a concentration of chaos near the burning tent. Then a wagon goes up in flames, as if it had contained oil.

"Archers! Withdraw! On the double!" While Lerial has not sensed that the Meroweyan riders have finished forming up, they are moving quickly, more quickly than he has expected.

"Archers! Withdraw!" echoes Moraris.

"Keep your intervals!" Lerial turns the gelding and urges him forward, feeling that if the archers group together that could result in a fireball being lofted at them, especially as the chaos near the burning section of the Meroweyan camp continues to build.

For the first fifty yards, Lerial is almost comfortable—until he realizes that there is one company riding directly toward him and fourth squad—a company that is far closer than he had thought. *Were they under a concealment from order-sensing?* That is certainly possible, although that isn't a skill he has even considered, let alone tried to perfect. "Double time! Otherwise they'll catch us before we clear the other squads."

"Double time!" echoes Moraris.

Several moments later, Lerial can sense a mount going down—one of the archers out to his right, but there is little he can do, not with speed of the pursuit. Then two of the pursuing riders somehow get tangled and go down, and Lerial can sense that slows the company riding directly after them. But there are two more companies, and one behind their direct pursuers, and one riding due east, as if to try to cut fourth squad off.

Lerial can only hope that company will turn south before the gully shallows out beyond the base of the ridge. Being chased by two companies is bad enough.

After covering another two hundred yards or so, Lerial can sense that their pursuers have only closed the gap slightly, if at all, and are not pressing so much. Just as he wonders about that, he can feel a ball of chaos-fire heading in his direction. *Can you divert it back into the Meroweyans?*

Even as he thinks that, he summons up a double-pattern of ten fine order-lines, trying to angle them so that they will accomplish his objective.

Whhssst!

The modest fireball slams into the grass-covered ground well behind fourth squad, but well before the pursuing armsmen. Lerial realizes that trying to ride, to use his senses to know where he is going, and trying to redirect chaos-fire, all at the same time, isn't the easiest combination of tasks in the world. Then, too, he can sense that they are nearing the remaining three squads of second company.

"Fourth squad! Close up! On the squad leader!"

"Close on me!" orders Moraris.

As the squad leader draws closer, Lerial calls out. "They're yours now. Set up below."

"Yes, ser."

Lerial slows the gelding and turns more to the east, where he will be on the northwest flank of first squad. In moments, he reins up beside Korlyn.

"Ser?"

"It's me. Ready bows!"

"Ready bows! Pass it on!"

Lerial can feel as much as hear, the pounding of hoofs as the Meroweyans approach. He scans the darkness, sensing, rather than seeing the position of the first three squads, each with a staggered ten-man front, angled so that each ranker can loose arrows straight forward into the pursuers, approximating a partial cross fire. *If the Meroweyans follow fourth squad.*

The first Meroweyan company slows as it nears second company, almost as if the captain knows he is nearing Verdyn forces, but the Meroweyans do continue forward.

At that point, another firebolt arcs toward second squad.

Lerial attempts to divert it, but instead, the fireball explodes above the open ground between the Meroweyan attackers and second company—and knives of pain flash through Lerial's skull, so much so that he can just barely see the oncoming Meroweyans. In the fading glow from the fireball, he orders, "Shafts at will! Loose now!"

"Loose now!" echo the squad leaders.

At that moment, rather than turning or retreating, the Meroweyans spur their mounts forward, directly toward second squad. Lerial belatedly realizes that the southern commander has seen second squad and assumed that second company is massed there.

"Second squad! Bows away! Second squad! Sabres out! Charge!"

As Bhurl repeats the command, Lerial draws his own sabre. Given the relative positions of the squad and the charging Meroweyans, he can only hope that maneuver will give the rankers the best chance.

The first ranks of the attackers charge past first squad, less than ten yards away, as if they have not even seen Lerial and the Lancers . . . and in the darkness, they may not have. But Lerial cannot leave second squad to face a company, or what looks like one.

"First squad on me!" Lerial rides directly into the side and rear of the Meroweyan company. Neither of the first two rankers he cuts down even see him, and the third barely has a chance to react.

Other sabres clash . . . and then, for whatever reason, the attack from two sides in the dark causes enough consternation that, abruptly, the Meroweyan company turns, and riders scramble to head away from the mass confusion, mainly heading due west and uphill.

Lerial waits a moment, then orders, "Second company! Withdraw now!"

"First squad! Here!" shouts Korlyn.

"Third squad . . ."

Lerial turns to the southwest, heading downhill, only to sense a chaos-bolt sizzling toward his regrouping forces. Despite the throbbing in his head, he throws up a diversion pattern.

The firebolt explodes short of second company. Exactly where, Lerial cannot say because the pain is so intense that his entire body feels as though a thousand knives have sliced into him, all at once, and he reels in the saddle. He keeps riding, hoping that the squad leaders can re-form their squads.

"First squad, ser," announces Korlyn.

"Any casualties?"

"All present. Two wounded."

Lerial's eyes continue to burn, but he waits . . . and waits . . . for Bhurl to report. Finally, he hears, "Second squad, two missing, one dead, three wounded."

It could have been much worse. "Thank you."

Fhentaar reports three men wounded, none seriously.

"Fourth company, ser, rejoining," announces Moraris.

"Casualties?"

"One, ser."

"Was that the archer who went down in the withdrawal from the ridge?"

"Yes, ser."

"Thank you. Have fourth squad fall in at the rear. Detail someone to watch for approaching riders."

"Yes, ser."

Lerial can barely stay in the saddle as he leads second company east and well away from the Meroweyan lines and the gully just to the north. He can only hope that they do not run into the third Meroweyan company . . . but given his splitting headache, he cannot sense more than a few yards away.

What a mess . . . That thought is an understatement. He could tell who had been where, but he doubted that anyone else could, and trying to convey orders in that confusion . . . He starts to involuntarily shake his head, but the lance of white-hot pain through his neck and eyes freeze him in the saddle for an instant.

He keeps looking to the west as the sky begins to lighten, but he sees no riders or armsmen anywhere near second company. There are riders and armsmen all over the east end of the ridge, but none appear to be in formation or moving north.

The sky is a medium gray as second company rides the last half kay toward camp. The worse of the pain racking Lerial's body has lifted, leaving him with aches, soreness in places, and a throbbing headache. At that point, Lerial recalls that he has never even questioned the squad leaders on possible enemy casualties. So he rides back along the column and asks each squad leader. In the end, when he returns to the head of the column, the best estimate he has is somewhere over twenty Meroweyan casualties, perhaps twenty-five. Nothing has gone quite the way he'd planned . . . and the plan had been his, even if the majer had approved it.

Three missing, likely killed, one dead, and five wounded. Nine casualties. And Lerial doesn't even want to think about facing the majer.

When second company reins up, Lerial rides to each wounded ranker, checking each, hoping desperately that none need urgent healing. Three appear to have broken arms, without compound fractures, and Lerial has their squad leaders direct them to the two healers provided by the elders. The fourth ranker, from second squad has only made it back with the help of his squad mates, and Lerial accompanies him and the last wounded man to the healers' tent. The fifth wounded ranker has taken a thrust straight into the gut, and he is beyond writhing in pain. Lerial doubts he will last the glass . . . and, again, there is nothing he can do.

So he turns to the other ranker lying on an adjoining pallet, who has a deep slash and gash across and into his thigh. Lerial can sense more than mere wound chaos. He tries to remember the man's name. "Haermish . . . was this a sabre wound?"

"It was more like an axe, ser . . . short axe."

Battle-axes? Lerial has never heard of them being used in Hamor . . . or even in Candar.

"He couldn't have hit you directly . . ."

"No . . . ser . . ."

Lerial immediately infuses a little order into the wound and tries to strengthen the area around the blood vessels.

He straightens, the tent spins around him, and darkness crashes down on him.

He wakes lying on a pallet in the corner of the tent.

No sooner do his eyes open than an older man in deep brown—one of the healers, Lerial can tell from the well of dark order around him—appears. He smiles almost sadly at Lerial.

"What is it?" Lerial's voice comes out as a croak.

"You cannot do that often, Captain."

"What?"

"Kill and heal."

"How is he? The one with the gash? Haermish."

"You did enough, Captain. He will live. He won't likely walk that well."

"How did . . . you know?"

"There was no one else who could have . . . and order flows around you and through you, even now, weak as you are." He extends a mug. "Drink this."

Whatever it is, Lerial realizes as he sits up slowly and takes the earthenware mug, it smells absolutely terrible. "What is it?"

"What we drink when we try to heal too much."

Lerial begins to drink, trying to ignore the taste and smell. When he finishes, he sees that the healer has left and is splinting the arm of one of the second company rankers. Rather than move or say anything, he remains sitting on the pallet for a time until the residual dizziness subsides. Then he stands, slowly and carefully. The older healer nods to Lerial as he leaves, but does not speak.

Once outside the tent, Lerial makes his way to see the majer.

Altyrn is once more under the awning, studying maps and making notes on a separate paper. He looks up. "You took your time."

"I made sure the wounded got to the healers' tent."

"That's not your job. That's what squad leaders are for."

"I had to heal a serious wound. You told me never to do that in the field while in command." That is not precisely what Altyrn had said, but it is close enough. Surprisingly to Lerial, the majer nods. "Fair enough. Tell me what happened."

Lerial does. He is so tired that he doesn't bother to skirt around diverting the firebolts, and the majer doesn't remark on that, confirming Lerial's impression that Altyrn had already deduced his ability in that area.

"What sort of casualties did you inflict?"

"It was hard to tell . . . ," Lerial begins.

Altyrn cuts him off. "You have no idea how many casualties you inflicted?"

"Not really, ser. I saw two Meroweyans killed and another two wounded. I could see two others go down when their mounts hit holes in the ground or something. My squad leaders report that they saw or their men saw another twenty casualties. We know that they lost men to war arrows, but not too many."

"And the scouts reported that they sent out burial details at first light," added Altyrn. "I'd judge from all reports that you might have gotten as many as thirty in the skirmish, and possibly more from the fires in the camp. Say, fifty at the outside, and you lost nine rankers. Even taking out five of theirs for every one of ours . . . we lose."

Well aware of this, Lerial merely nods.

"On the other hand, five to one isn't bad for a young very junior undercaptain in your boots. You don't have the experience . . . and experience is paid for by making mistakes. Usually undercaptains have experienced squad leaders and senior officers. Our only experienced squad leaders are acting undercaptains, and I can't be everywhere. Some of the rankers acting as squad leaders don't have as much experience in fighting as you do. In the end, though, all of those difficulties don't count. You . . . and I . . . we have to find ways to do better."

"Yes, ser."

"Get some food and rest." The majer offers a smile, fleeting as it is. "I'll need you later."

LVIII

For the remainder of threeday, Lerial rests, eats what he can, watches the Meroweyans, sees to the details of notifying the family of Arsenor, the Lancer who had died of his gut would, checks on the other wounded from second company, all of whom appear likely to recover . . . if not for a time. He rests some, when he can. He also wonders if Lephi has had any experiences like his own. *How would you find out? He likely doesn't even know you've left Cigoerne.*

Fourday is not much different, except that no companies attempt attacks on the Meroweyans, who, from what Lerial can see and the scouts report, are occupied in readying for some action.

When Lerial asks Altyrn what he thinks, the majer smiles grimly. "They'll attack tomorrow morning, but not before seventh glass or more likely eighth. We'll arrange all the rankers on foot with bows ready. We'll loose every shaft we can into the attackers, and then withdraw. The councils sent a wagonload of war arrows, thank the Rational Stars. The Meroweyans will have to hack or burn their way into the Verd. That will keep the entry points narrow and enable us to attack them in positions where they can't overwhelm us with sheer numbers. At least for a while."

"How will you know where they'll attack?"

"You and the few Verdyn ordermages will tell me. So will the scouts posted in the barrier trees."

"You never did plan to stand up to a massed attack, did you?"

The majer shakes his head. "I'm sure the Meroweyans know that as well, but if we hadn't mustered out here, they could have begun attacking the Verd with no casualties at all . . . and at their leisure. Now they know that we can continue to bleed and harass them as long as they do not attack, and they know that they would lose many more armsmen that way. I wouldn't be surprised if the commanding officer has doubts about the whole idea of attacking Verdheln. That doubt will cost. If he doesn't have doubts, then they'll lose even more armsmen."

Lerial has to think that over before he nods.

"As for you, get some rest, and make sure your company does as well. I'll send for you if I need anything." With that, Altyrn returns to his papers and maps.

Lerial follows the majer's instructions—or orders, and by seventh glass on fiveday morning second company is lined up on foot with bows in hand and quivers full of arrows a good two hundred yards forward of the tree line, almost exactly where the ground slopes away into the low valley that separates the two forces. All the tents have been struck, and all the wagons have departed into the Verd. So have all but a handful of mounts, including the gelding Lerial rides, and two squads from Altyrn's own first company, although an older ranker acting as a company squad leader is actually giving the commands. First company is posted so that the road from Yakaat to the Verd lies at the point where the rankers of first and second companies adjoin each other. Lerial's second company is to the east of first company, Juist's third company to the west of first company, while Kusyl's fourth company flanks second company on the east. Sixth company is the farthest east and fifth the farthest west.

After surveying the Meroweyan forces, now forming up, Lerial glances back at his own rankers—spread in a staggered double file facing south and waiting, if in somewhat relaxed positions, since Lerial knows it will likely be a glass, if not longer, before the attackers advance to the point where the archers can target them.

At around eighth glass, a series of horn calls echo across the low valley in the cool spring air, and Lerial can immediately see that the dark mass of Meroweyan forces begins to move, although there are gaps between companies. As he watches from the east end of second company, he can see that, at the center of the Meroweyan advance, is a line of shieldmen. Immediately behind them are pikemen, whose weapons extend beyond the shields, a distance even greater than the length of a Mirror Lance. Behind the pikemen, a good five yards back, are armsmen on foot, with small circular shields on one arm and, presumably, a blade in the other, at least when they plan to engage the Verdyn force. On each flank of the foot armsmen are mounted companies.

Lerial calculates that there are roughly two thousand armsmen on foot, in two formations, one group of roughly ten companies, followed by a second. All in all, the Meroweyan force attacking stretches a third of a kay from side to side, more than twice the width and ten times or more the depth of the thin line formed by the six Verdyn companies.

There is certain majesty, Lerial has to admit, to the ponderous and even advance of the Meroweyans down the far slope and across the flat bottom of the valley.

Even when the Meroweyans have almost reached the point where the ground rises toward the edge of the Verd, Lerial can sense no chaos wizards and no chaos. *Have they shielded themselves . . . or are they saving their powers for later?* He shrugs fatalistically. There is no way of telling, and he has no experience in a pitched battle upon which he might draw for even an educated guess.

He hears hooves and glances to the west, where he sees a ranker wearing the green and white sash of a messenger riding toward him. He waits, and the Lancer reins up beside him.

"The majer has orders, ser. Have your rankers ignore the front line and target the foot armsmen or the mounted riders behind them. Then withdraw when ordered, but not before the company to the east of you."

"Inform the majer that second company understands and will obey."

"Yes, ser." The ranker nods, then urges his mount eastward toward fourth company.

Lerial turns to Korlyn. "You heard that. Have all rankers target the armsmen or cavalry behind the shields and pikes. Pass it on. Send a messenger to the other squad leaders."

"Yes, ser."

Another quarter glass passes before the Meroweyans near the thin line of defenders. Then a high shrill and shuddering pipe sound blares out—Altyrn's command to fire at will.

"Fire at will!" Lerial orders, adding "Take your time!" Even though he has briefed the squad leaders on the battle plan, which requires first and second company to loose arrows for longer, which is why his men and women have more shafts than do those in fifth and sixth company, he still wants to reinforce that order.

All the rankers loose the first volley, and hundreds of arrows arc down toward the mass of attackers behind the shield line.

Lerial looks at the advancing Meroweyan line, still moving steadily upslope, but just over two hundred yards away. He can see armsmen begin to drop as the Verdyn shafts sheet down into the central mass of attackers. Still, the shieldmen and the pikemen plod uphill, and the number of armsmen who stagger or fall seems small indeed compared to the total Merowyan host. Lerial looks to the east, seeing that the rankers of Denieryn's sixth company are loosing their shafts as fast as they can—as ordered.

In what feels like a matter of moments, although it is doubtless longer than that, Lerial thinks, a double blare of the battle pipes sounds. He glances eastward. The rankers of sixth company are moving quickly, not quite running, but moving at a trot behind fourth company and toward second company and the road into the Verd. Fifth company should be doing the same, but even mounted, Lerial cannot see if they are.

A series of horn commands comes from the rear of the Merowyan force, and the shieldmen and pikemen pick up their pace, but Lerial can see that they are not moving that much faster, but then they are going uphill while carrying heavy shields and pikes. Still the arrows fall into the armsmen, and he can actually see some few gaps in places.

A triple blare of the battle pipes shrills across the Verdyn lines, and Lerial hears Kusyl's voice from the east.

"Fourth company! Withdraw! Deliberate speed!"

Lerial glances down and along the line of his rankers. Most still have perhaps five or six shafts in their quivers. Those won't last long enough. "Slow your fire!"

"Slow your fire! Pass it on!" repeats Korlyn.

Lerial keeps watching, measuring the advance of the Meroweyans against the withdrawal of third and fourth companies, but as soon as Kusyl rides behind the westernmost ranker of second company, and turns up the road into the Verd, Lerial knows that it will not be long before second company will have to withdraw.

"Fire at will! Rapid release!"

Korlyn repeats the order, and the arrows from second company fly faster. By now, the Meroweyans are only a hundred yards away.

Obviously, Altyrn has been watching as well because, as the last available arrows fly, the battle pipes sound.

"Second company! Withdraw! Deliberate speed!"

In moments, first squad has begun to move up the road, paired with first company's fourth squad. Lerial rides forward, just slightly, ready for any chaos-fire that might be thrown at the retreating rankers, but there are no firebolts, and he cannot sense any white wizards nearby.

By the time the pikes are close to fifty yards away, Lerial and Altyrn's senior squad leader are alone on the road where the Verdyn battle line, such as it had been, and Lerial turns the gelding toward the narrow opening remaining in the road gate, a solid and massive structure almost three yards high, urging the gelding forward, if glancing over his shoulder every few yards of the hundred or so he has to cross before passing through the road gate. The acting first company undercaptain is right behind him. Once through the gate, he looks back, absently wondering how the road guards can even move the gate, even along the narrow and deep polished stone grooves that had been covered with fitted wooden covers. Lerial can only get a glimpse of the Meroweyans before the gate closes behind the other officer and additional barriers are moved into place.

For a moment. Lerial wonders why the attackers have not tried to rush the gate before it closed, but then realizes that after the attacks by the various companies, the Meroweyans expect more arrows if they advance closer.

A series of horn calls rise from beyond the Verd. Lerial can sense that the attackers have halted . . . and that the armsmen and the mounted riders are re-forming or dressing their lines. Then he rides back and rejoins second company, mustered a good hundred yards north of the second road gate. Immediately to the east, under the tall trees, are the company mounts, saddled and ready for use.

When Lerial reins up, Korlyn looks at him. "Ser . . . how many do you think we took down?"

As Korlyn speaks, Lerial order-senses that a smaller group of Meroweyans is nearing the main body of the attackers . . . and among the newcomers are several white wizards.

"Ser?"

"I'm sorry, Korlyn. How many? There were gaps in their ranks, but there were enough that I couldn't count. *But second company alone must have loosed close to a thousand shafts . If one in ten hit someone . . .* "We might have wounded a company's worth." *Leaving us with few if any war arrows . . . and not much chance of getting more soon.*

"If the other companies did as well, ser . . ."

"They couldn't, except for first company. We had more arrows. If we're fortunate, we might have wounded three companies worth." *And that leaves something more than thirty-five companies.* He smiles sardonically. "We only have to keep doing that day after day."

"Yes, ser."

It is almost a shock to Lerial when he realizes that Korlyn believes that is possible . . . but the last thing he wants to do is dash the young squad leader's beliefs. What will surely come will do that all too soon. Lerial surveys the area. Because second company was one of the last to leave, Lerial and his squads are already where Altyrn has positioned them for the attack that will come, sooner or later.

Almost a glass later, Lerial and the others are still waiting. While he has dismounted, he has tied the gelding to the nearest tree. He can sense that the Meroweyans have divided their forces into three bodies. One body remains straddling the road into the Verd. The second is a good kay to the west, and the third a kay to the east. That makes all too much sense to Lerial. They will attack simultaneously at all three points. He can sense two white wizards behind the shield and pike line facing the road gate. There are also white wizards with each of the other two Meroweyan formations, but Lerial has the sense that they are not so strong as the strongest one closest to him.

He needs to do something, but what?

Could you divert one of those firebolts back to the wizard who is throwing it? He had attempted that on the last attack, but all he had succeeded in doing was dropping the chaos into the ground short of his own rankers. *But you were much farther away from the wizard.*

What if you formed a larger pattern, one that attracted the chaos-bolt back toward the wizard who created it? Creating a larger pattern will be difficult enough, but he has no idea how to create flows that will do that. He takes out the silk pouch that holds the lodestone and studies it closely with his order-chaos senses. While there is a pattern at both ends, there is something . . . He concentrates . . . finally sensing that, between the ends of the lodestone, there are flows of order and chaos—or something like order and chaos—and each is like a coil. Can he create a coil like that running from the mage to the chaos-bolt?

Lerial has no idea. Nor does he know if his idea will work, since he does know that he cannot create that large a coil of chaos, even if the pattern lines are extraordinarily fine. *But don't order and chaos have to balance somehow? They must . . . because, if they didn't, wouldn't they destroy each other?* Again . . . he has no idea, but both Emerya and Saltaryn have made the point that the best of the Magi'i always use order to handle chaos. *But you're not the best of mages . . . if you're one at all.* Still . . .

Abruptly, he looks at the first squad leader, some ten yards to the east of him. "Korlyn . . . you're in command for the moment. I'll be back as soon as possible. I need to talk to the majer."

With that Lerial unties the gelding and mounts, setting out to find Altyrn, not that he has to ride far, because he finds the majer standing beside the second road gate, the one some hundred yards behind the outer gate. The gate is not quite closed, with an opening about a yard and a half wide.

Altyrn looks up at Lerial, but does not speak.

"I don't *know* if I can do anything about the wizards, but if I can I need to be close to them." Lerial gestures southward toward the outer road gate. "Close to that."

"Well then," replies Altyrn, "go see what you can do . . . for a while. But don't get yourself incinerated in the process. Oh . . . and don't ride on the road itself, whatever you do. Take two rankers in case you get too involved in ordermagery. Who's in command in your absence?"

"Korlyn, the first squad leader. Traps in the road?"

Altyrn nods. "We don't intend to make it easy for them."

Puzzling over Altyrn's comparatively easy acquiescence, Lerial rides back to Korlyn and reins up. "I'll need two rankers to accompany me, and you're in command until I return." *Or until the majer appoints someone else.* Lerial doesn't voice that thought.

The puzzled expression on the squad leader's face is but momentary as he turns and calls out, "Linstaar, Muaran, you're detailed to the captain. Mount up."

In little more than moments, the two rankers are following Lerial, who turns back and says, "We're not to ride on the road itself once we go through the inner road gate." Both men nod knowingly, almost as if trapping the entry roads is a usual practice.

It probably is. Lerial doubts that such a practice will account for more than a few men and mounts. *But then, if we account for a few men and mounts time after time, it might add up.* That, at least seems to be the hope of the elders and the majer.

Lerial is conscious of Altyrn's eyes on his back as he leads the two rankers through the gate and then continues southward through the calf-high grass toward the outer road gate, behind which wait a half score of men in brown. He brings the gelding to a halt some ten yards short of the gate guards and surveys the gate. From what he recalls when he passed earlier, it is a good half yard thick, if not more. He cannot determine of what the gate is constructed although the back side consists of thick timbers over thick planks. The east end of the gate fits tightly into stone groves in the massive pillar, and from each end of the gate extend stone walls as far as he can see, not that he can make out much beyond ten yards, so entwined are the walls with the trunks of the massive trees on both sides.

Unless the Meroweyans have brought siege engines, and Lerial has seen no sign of such, they are unlikely to breach the road gate. Even with chaos-fire, it is likely to take a number of firebolts. Yet . . . what can Altyrn do?

A wry smile crosses Lerial's face as he realizes that well might be the reason why the majer has allowed him to see what he can do.

He waits almost a quarter glass before he senses the line of shieldmen moving forward, then stopping a good fifty yards back from the road gate. He can also sense a chaos wizard behind the shield wall, flanked by armsmen and then by horsemen.

Chaos builds.

Lerial tries to create the circular spiral pattern he has visualized, but before he can complete it, a firebolt arches from behind the shield wall and slams into the road gate. The gate does not even shiver, although flames flash skyward, followed by puffs of gray-black smoke.

An involuntary "Oh!" escapes from one of the rankers behind Lerial.

You've got to be quicker. Lerial begins creating the pattern the moment he senses that chaos is building around the second white wizard.

The second firebolt arches not toward the road gate, but toward the thick woods to the west of the gate, and Lerial barely manages to throw his pattern into the path of the chaos-fire.

An unseen whip of order and chaos rocks him in the saddle, and a thin line of chaos-fire forms an arch between a point just short of the woods and another point short of the shield wall, where the chaos flares against an unseen barrier.

Shields! Lerial is well aware that some Magi'i have shields, but the appearance of shields among the Meroweyan white wizards startles him, so much so that he is slow to react to the next firebolt, partly because of the throbbing headache the backlash, if that is what it was, that struck him has created.

Belatedly, he realizes that the third firebolt is aimed directly at him, as if the white wizards know he is there. *But why shouldn't they? You know they're there.*

Frantically, Lerial throws together another order coil, stronger, he hopes, and more accurate because he doesn't have to gauge or measure the incoming firebolt—it's headed toward him.

Lerial snaps the order-coil pattern into place just as he feels the faintest heat from the approaching firebolt—and order and chaos flare in a searing pattern!

Lerial almost smiles as he can sense the chaos flashing back toward the white wizard, except blackness smashes him down before his lips can even curl.

He wakes with a start, and the blackness hammers him again, so much that his vision narrows to a point of grayness. He closes his eyes. He is lying on a blanket, but the blanket is clearly on the ground, because he can feel every lump and stick digging into his back.

"Don't try to move, Captain." The voice is a woman's, and he doesn't recognize her, but the accent suggests she is Verdyn. "You're still very weak. You will recover quickly, though." There is a slight laugh.

"It's funny that I'm lying here unable to move?"

"No . . . but the reason is."

Lerial opens his eyes slowly. The woman kneeling beside him on the blanket is silver haired. She is not old, but neither is she young.

"What might that be?" he asks cautiously. He can smell the acrid odor of burning wood and vegetation, but he can see no fire, nor any smoke.

"You almost died from having too much order in your body. It tends to make everything stop."

Too much order? "How . . . did that happen?"

She shakes her head. "I've never seen that before. Your men rushed you here. You weren't breathing, and if it hadn't been for the order you would have died immediately. You would have if we hadn't bled off some of the order and gotten you breathing. Your chest and back may be a little sore." At his puzzled look, she adds, "That's not from what caused you to stop breathing. It's from what we had to do to get you breathing again. Don't move your head, but wiggle your fingers."

Lerial does so.

"Good. Do they hurt?"

"No."

"Lift your arms and put them across your chest . . ." After a tenth of a glass of gentle exercises, the healer has him sit up . . . slowly. After watching him for a time, she nods. "You'll be fine. Just don't do what you did again." She straightens, then turns and walks away.

Lerial glances around. While he had thought it might be twilight, that was because he had been lying in the deep shade and gloom of a space under giant trees of some sort, and it is clear it is still afternoon. Almost absently, he recalls what Emerya had said something like a year earlier, about the body needing to balance order and chaos.

"Ser?" Linstaar hurries toward Lerial.

Behind him, Muaran remains with the three mounts

"Are you all right?" asks Linstaar.

Lerial realizes his chest is sore, not much, but noticeably. "I'm sore. The healer says I'll be fine. What happened? What did you see?"

"Ah . . . ser . . ."

"Did you see anything? Tell me, even if you think it was strange or that you might not have really seen it."

"Ah . . . well, ser . . . There was a firebolt. It was headed right toward us. Then everything got bright, and it sort of split and part of it struck back toward the Meroweyans. That part was sort of golden red and brilliant white. The other part . . . well it was hazy and silver gray . . . maybe silver black. It hit you, ser. You were like a statue. Muaran said we had to get you to the healer, and we did. She did something, and some of the fuzzy blackness . . . well, it sort of flowed off you. Then she made us lift your arms while she pressed on your chest to get you breathing again."

Lerial nods. "Thank you." He decides to stand and does so slowly.

Linstaar recovers the blanket, shakes it out, and rolls it up.

"Is that your blanket?"

"Yes, ser."

"Thank you. Where are we? Or, rather, where is second company?"

"The company's maybe two hundred yards that way, ser, along that path."

"What about the Meroweyans? What are they doing?"

"The ones outside on the road? The guards said that they moved back. The others I don't know."

Lerial is still trying to gather himself together when Altyrn appears.

"They said you were wounded." The majer surveys Lerial.

"In a way." Lerial doesn't know what else to say. "Did it help?"

"You've gained us some time."

"What happened?" Lerial's voice is rough.

"You didn't see?"

"The backlash was . . . rather quick."

"The healer said you got covered in pure order. How did you do that?"

"I was trying to send the chaos-bolt back at him."

"You did that all right. There's a wide blackened space where those two white wizards used to be. All the Meroweyan forces have backed off. They're likely rethinking their tactics." Altyrn studies Lerial. "You don't look that bad for nearly dying. Only like eightday-old sowshit." He shakes his head. "Don't do that again. I don't want to explain that I let you try to kill yourself twice . . . and that you were successful the second time. You're worth far more than one frigging white wizard. Or even two."

"I won't try that again." *Something else perhaps, but with greater care.*

"Good. Go get something to eat and then lie down and get some sleep."

"Now?"

"Now. They don't look like they'll attack soon, and you need the rest."

Lerial decides against arguing.

LIX

When Lerial wakes early the next morning, his eyes are irritated and itching and the smell of smoke is everywhere. He cannot believe how long he has slept. Then, again, the way he had felt when he fell asleep . . . maybe he can. Even so, the first coherent thoughts he has are about what had happened the day before and how he might somehow change the pattern he constructed so that the order doesn't flood back to him. *But how will you know if it will work?*

He doesn't have an answer to that question, and he has scarcely pulled himself together and has just finished eating barely warm ghano-egg hash of some sort, washed down with extra-tart greenberry juice, when Altyrn arrives by the cookfire in the middle of the small clearing.

"You're looking better this morning. Are you?"

"Yes." Considering how he'd felt the evening before, being able to stand and eat without feeling like a stiff breeze would push him over meant he was feeling much better.

"Good. I've got another mission for second company. Second company, not Captain Lerial."

"Yes, ser."

"Late last night, Casseon's forces sent out mages in the darkness to burn gaps in the forest protections—"

"Why didn't you wake me?"

"So you could go out there in the darkness and try to kill yourself again?" asks Altyrn.

"Why didn't the forest just keep burning?" asks Lerial, not really wanting to answer the majer's question.

"It burned enough. The elders have ways of slowing it. Before long, once the embers and coals cool, the Meroweyans will try to move through those openings. At the same time, the forces near here look to be forming into a large body. They'll likely be the ones to attack through the burned out area—"

"Where we were?"

The majer shakes his head and opens a map, handing it to Lerial. "Hold this. They gave up on that and moved half a kay east. The other two groups have split, a larger one farther to the west and the smallest one to the east. For the moment we'll have to do what we can, and leave the rest to what the Verdyn can do without us. Casseon can't have that many mages, and he has two less now. A wayguide will take you and second company to one of the hidden paths in and out of the Verd near the smaller force to the east." Altyrn points to the map. "Here is where you'll be. Here is where the companies you're going to attack are. Once you get the signal that the mage has left to burn another entrance to the Verd, you'll leave the woods and get as close to the companies escorting him as you can. The companies escorting him. Not him. Send one squad to ride through the lines and then race through the lower ground here. If you set your archers here, they should be able to cut down a fair number of them before withdrawing. Then keep riding east until you reach somewhere here. There should be a wayguide there to see you in through another narrow passage. Keep the map. You'll need it."

"You're doing this sort of thing with the other companies?"

"Just third."

"Where will we get more arrows?"

"There are some carts on the way. Once the Meroweyans moved away from the battle sites, the elders sent out youths to gather any that they could find, whether whole or broken. The Meroweyans weren't that interested in picking them up."

"What did that cost them? The youths?" asks Lerial.

"So far, nothing."

"Don't they have archers?"

"Casseon probably does. He likely didn't send many north. Massed archers aren't that useful in wooded lands, except at close range and from behind trees, and the Meroweyans don't like to fight that way. They're also wary of ambushes. So they're leaving the youths alone. For now, anyway. That will change."

Lerial wonders what the majer knows that he can make such a statement so confidently . . . and sadly.

After Altyrn leaves, Lerial slips the map inside his jacket and passes the word to the squad leaders, then goes over the majer's plan with them, deciding that second squad will make either an attack or a feint to draw the Meroweyans, whichever looks to be effective without excessive casualties, depending on what Lerial sees once they encounter the Meroweyans. *The point is to kill them, not to get our Lancers killed.*

After that, while he and second company wait for the carts with the arrows, Lerial studies the map that Altyrn has given him. At the same time, in the back of his mind, the same thoughts with which he had awakened keep coming back. *How can you change the patterns so that the order doesn't come back to you personally?*

Abruptly, he realizes a simple fact—he'd never really directed the coil away from himself. He'd been so focused on capturing the chaos-bolt with the coil that he'd never considered what might happen. He shudders. *It could have been so much worse.*

Then he takes a deep breath and eases out the silk pouch that holds the lodestone, concentrating on it, and trying to see if he can not only replicate that coil pattern, on the smallest scale, but also find a way to split the order on the return. Except . . . *Why split it? You never been able to raise enough order to do things like shields. Why can't you divert it into a shield of some sort, so that when the next firebolt comes . . .*

For the next half glass or so, until Lerial hears the creaking of carts approaching, he is very busy trying out various tiny order patterns with the lodestone. He *thinks* he might have something . . . but that will have to wait while he makes sure that all his rankers are as armed as they can be.

Right after all the arrows are distributed and Lerial gets the reports from his squad leaders, Altyrn rides up, accompanied by a white-haired older man in the near-uniform brown garb that most men of the Verd seem to wear.

He always seems to know just when to be where. "Second company stands ready, ser." *Second company may be ready, but its captain isn't. Not yet.*

"Excellent. This is Wayguide Smathyl. Smathyl, this is Captain Lerial."

"Pleased to meet you, ser." The older man inclines his head politely.

"And I, you."

"Smathyl will be guiding second company to a point where you can leave the Verd some distance east of the main body of the eastern Meroweyan force that appears to be readying itself for an attack through the burned area about half a kay east of here. I'll leave you in his hands, Captain."

"Yes, ser."

"You and your men can ride double file for now, but when we get to the hidden way, there will only be space for one horse at a time."

"Whatever is necessary, Wayguide."

"If you'd follow me, then."

"By squad! Double file!" Lerial orders. "Forward!"

After less than two hundred yards following the main road north, the wayguide turns onto a path barely wide enough for two mounts abreast. From the dust raised on the path, Lerial suspects that other companies have ridden the same way earlier. That thought is confirmed when after almost half a kay, they pass an opening to a small clearing. There, Lerial sees several companies standing down and waiting. He thinks he sees Kusyl, but he is not certain. After that, there is little dust raised by second company on the path, although they only ride another three hundred yards or so, where the wayguide reins up and dismounts beside a thornbush thicket.

"If you would hold the reins, Captain."

Lerial leans forward and takes the reins, then watches as the guide walks to one side. He cannot see exactly what the guide does, but part of the bush rolls aside, revealing a narrow path.

Then Smathyl walks back to Lerial. "Ride and lead my mount until you hear that everyone is on the way. Then stop and wait for me."

Lerial looks at the narrow path and then at the wayguide.

"It's wide enough for a mount and a man, but not two mounts."

Lerial laughs softly. "I'll take your word for it."

It is almost a quarter glass later when Smathyl rejoins Lerial, somehow eases his mount past Lerial, then remounts. Second company begins to follow him along the narrow path that twists and turns through the thickest woods, or so it seems to Lerial. After some time, he finally makes that observation to Smathyl, riding ahead of him.

"That it does, ser, and for a reason. Should anyone find the path, they would be hard-pressed to find their way any place with any speed." The wayguide turns in the saddle and grins. "Not that it's difficult to make such a path. All one has to do is follow ground at the same level through the woods."

At the same level . . . There is something to those words, something that almost but not quite reminds Lerial of . . . But he cannot grasp that elusive thought, and he goes back to practicing creating coil patterns.

Almost a glass later, Smathyl reins up in a small clearing where the path appears to end, with only enough space for a mount and rider to turn. Lerial immediately extends his senses and realizes that open ground lies beyond the clearing, perhaps less than ten yards away, yet he can see no sign of what he senses.

The wayguide whistles an odd tune, and two men in brown appear as if from nowhere to stand in front of the thick thornbush. Smathyl rides forward, and the three converse. Lerial can only make out phrases, even using his order sensing.

". . . almost a kay . . ."

". . . make sure . . . move quick . . ."

". . . little ones . . ."

After a few more moments, Smathyl rides back to Lerial. "It's clear to the south, but the evil ones have split. The larger body is a kay or so to the west. They won't be able to see you because the trees extend farther south just west of here. We'd appreciate it if you'd turn all your riders west quickly so that it looks like you've been shadowing the tree line. The smaller group is almost two kays east, and they've got a wizard who's throwing firebolts at the trees. Not big ones, but making a mess. So far he hasn't started any fires."

"Thank you. We'll be as quick as we can. How steep is the stone wall beyond the grass?"

"Little more than half a cubit. You'll have to walk your mounts down over that." Smathyl pauses, then says, "You're one of the hidden black ones, aren't you, ser? Not that it'd be any of my business . . ."

"I can do a few things . . . some healing, and I can sense the clouds and the weather a little." Lerial smiles wryly. "Just enough to get myself in trouble."

"Anyone who tries to do what's right usually does. That's why so few of power remain good."

Lerial is still thinking about that when the "thornbush" rolls aside and a section of the massive trunk of the tree beyond it swings back, revealing a space just big enough and tall enough for one Lancer to ride through, if by ducking his head.

"Go ahead, Captain." Smathyl gestures.

Lerial cannot sense anyone out on the open grassland, nor can he see anyone through that opening. So he urges the gelding forward and lowers his head. As he rides through, he sees that there are two smaller trees, if substantial in themselves, around which a false trunk has been constructed, so that they appear to be two forks out of the base trunk.

The stone wall is more like a cubit high, and Lerial guides the gelding over it slowly, then calls back. "Watch the drop at the end of the green grass! Pass it back!"

Before long, second company is formed back into squads with a four-file formation riding westward but keeping close to the trees, with a single scout some fifty yards ahead. Lerial keeps checking the map against what he sees and what he order-senses. The breeze out of the north is warmer than it has been, but it is spring, Lerial reminds himself, and there could be a shift and another cold south wind at any time.

Half a glass later, close to midday, the ranker scout rides around a large bulge in the forest, then halts, signals, and heads back toward second company . . . in a great hurry at a canter, if not a gallop.

Lerial frowns. He has not sensed anyone, except a mist like chaos. *A mist like chaos? A chaos concealment!* He bites back what he almost exclaims.

The scout reins up. "They're coming this way, ser, two companies, maybe three, and it's like they knew we were coming."

"How far?"

"Two hundred yards, ser! Maybe less."

Withdraw . . . or fight? If second company immediately flees . . . that suggests that the company is alone . . . and invites further pursuit. "All squads!" orders Lerial. "Line out on first squad! Five front! Ready bows!"

The other three squads have barely formed a line when the Meroweyan riders emerge from around the trees to the west. There are a good three companies, and the lead squads carry spears, not quite so long as the mirror lances that Lerial's company does not have, but long enough.

Lerial waits . . . watching as the Meroweyan horse thunders toward his single company, waiting, judging. At just over a hundred yards, he commands, "Fire at will!"

With the shorter distance, the archers and Lancers only lift their shafts slightly, so that any that might pass between the oncoming riders can possibly hit riders behind. All the shafts are concentrated on the leading squads, and at first, only a mount or two goes down. Then one rider swerves, and two others collide with him . . . and more shafts fly.

Lerial is about to order an instant withdrawal when he senses the concealment mist vanish. Almost simultaneously, a modest chaos-bolt arches over the oncoming riders, now less than fifty yards from Lerial, directly toward first squad.

Lerial immediately tries the best order pattern he has, hoping that this time, the order returning will go where he wants it—and well away from him. As he clamps the order-pattern around the chaos-bolt, a feeling of ugliness, almost like filth or sowshit, grasps him.

WHUMPPPHYT! The chaos-bolt explodes—or starts to—midway between the two forces—and then a brilliant line of golden red sears back behind the attackers. Chaos-fire flares in their rear, far more than the chaos-bolt could have contained. But, with the explosion and the dissolution of the order pattern, the ugliness is gone.

Then . . . a barrier of hazy silver black, like a low wall no more than two yards high, appears just in front of the first line of Meroweyan spearmen. The entire first line hits the barrier and piles up for a moment . . . before the hazy silver black vanishes, as if it had never been, leaving a tangle of men and mounts, and then a huge gust of hot air smashes into first squad, and most probably, the rest of second company.

Lerial is almost torn from his saddle, but manages to keep his seat. He glances around, seeing that two or three rankers are barely hanging on to their mounts.

"Second company! Withdraw! To the rear! Now!" Lerial can sense that, while the attack has been blunted, the armsmen in the Meroweyan rear, at last on both flanks, can easily swing around the mess his very temporary shields have created, and they far outnumber his company, not to mention that they are better armed for riding down his semitrained rankers, already likely short on arrows.

As second company reverses direction and Lerial urges the gelding back toward the rear of first squad, now the front, he keeps pressing his order-senses. What he notices immediately is that there is no sense of chaos amid the Meroweyan force. Either he has disabled or killed the white wizard . . . or he has shielded himself, and there is no way to tell. After several moments more, it is also clear to Lerial that the confusion created by Lerial and second company is apparently enough to stop any immediate pursuit.

Even so, Lerial does not slow the company to a slow walk until they have put a good kay between themselves and the Meroweyans. Unfortunately, after riding another half kay, Lerial can sense yet another difficulty. Not that far ahead—perhaps a kay and a half—is the other Meroweyan group that Smathyl has mentioned . . . and the last thing Lerial wants to do is get trapped between both forces—especially since the force they are approaching has a strong white wizard and since Lerial still feels somewhat shaky after his last encounter with a wizard.

He turns to Korlyn. "We're going to have to head farther southeast. There's another large Meroweyan force ahead." He pauses. "How many shafts do most of the men have? Get me a rough count, if you would . . . and from the other squad leaders."

"Yes, ser."

Lerial keeps surveying the shaded spots under the trees at the edge of the Verd as well as the open grasslands with their scattered clumps of bushes, but he can sense only the two groups of Meroweyans and some scouts for both.

Before long Korlyn returns. "No more than four shafts each, ser. Some only have three."

"Then we're going to have to take a longer ride than we planned."

"Yes, ser."

"On me!" Lerial commands as he turns the gelding more to the southeast.

Once they are farther away from the Verd and the effect of the tall trees, Lerial feels that the wind has also begun to pick up. When he looks more intently to the northwest, he can see dark clouds, and the clouds appear to be moving swiftly across the far reaches of the woods toward them, with the haze beneath suggesting rain. While the rain, if it continues, will hamper the wizard in his efforts to burn through the tree-walls of the Verd, Lerial really doesn't want to be caught in the open in the middle of a rainstorm . . . not that he will have much choice, it appears, given the need to avoid the Meroweyans.

The Meroweyans also apparently see the oncoming rain, and while it is possible that the white wizard may sense second company, the three companies or so of horsemen ride more quickly back westward. Even so, by the time Lerial and his company circle around the Meroweyans and finally locate the wayguides and the second narrow entrance to the Verd, the rain has been falling steadily for almost a glass, and Lerial and all the rankers are soaked through and through.

By then, the rain has also penetrated the forest canopy and falls from the leaves on all the riders as they make their slow way along yet another narrow, turning, twisting, and seemingly endless passage through the Verd, back toward their encampment.

It is well after sunset, or would have been, had the clouds not covered any trace of sun, by the time Lerial settles second company—and after discovering that one of the rankers in first company had broken his arm when the backlash gust of wind had unhorsed him. Lerial has finished a cold and oily meal whose contents he could not have described and is standing just inside a damp tent he understands he will be sharing with Altyrn, although he has not yet seen the majer.

Is there any way you could retain or manipulate that order split from a chaos-bolt? The problem is that it all comes at once, and he has no experience in dealing with that much order or chaos. He is still pondering over that when Altyrn walks stolidly through the rain and into the tent, where he gently brushes the water off the oiled leather jacket he wears.

"What happened?"

"We were attacked even before we could even attempt a fixed ambush . . ." Lerial goes on to relate the details, finishing up with, ". . . and then we rode back along a very wet and narrow passage through the Verd, getting even more soaked before we got here."

"You managed to inflict some casualties. Do you have any idea how many?"

"Maybe two squads worth, between the injuries at that temporary order barrier and the ones brought down by arrows." Lerial shrugs. "We didn't stay to find out."

"You're likely hurting them more with what you're doing to their mages," muses Altyrn. "They burned two more gaps in the trunk wall before the elders could get the rain to strengthen."

"They're weather-mages? Why do they need us—"

Altyrn sighs. Loudly. "Didn't you hear me? They're not that strong, or not that strong without risking their lives. They can make it rain harder . . . or less . . . but they can't create the storms."

That makes sense, unfortunately.

"The damage the Merowyan wizards did was enough. They have three gaps big enough to put a company at a time through." The majer turns and looks out into the dimness beyond the tent. "The rain will help for a few days after it lets up, but then they'll burn another one or two. After that, there won't be any way to keep them out."

"How did Juist do?" asks Lerial, not only wanting to know, but also to change the subject.

"About the same as second company. Kusyl didn't even get close. They were waiting for fourth company as well. He lost eight men. Between the three of you, we cost them another company today."

Lerial understands all too well what the majer isn't saying—that they still face overwhelming odds.

LX

The rain keeps falling sixday evening. It is still coming down on sevenday morning, and from what Lerial can sense in the clouds and in the flow of order and chaos, it will continue for at least several glasses, because he can find no change in the clouds to the northwest, which is from where the light winds are blowing. He still wonders just how the elders had managed to increase the rain.

After dealing with muster and making sure his men are as dry as possible, and having to admit to Alaynara that he does not know whether more arrows will be forthcoming or when, Lerial spends the morning experimenting with various order-patterns, using the lodestone at times, and not at others. He is discovering that, for whatever reason, most likely practice, he is more able to summon free order . . . but he has difficulty in doing much with it. To him, order is more like a flow of liquid, like water, except, unlike water, he has no container with which to hold it, so that he can direct it to some extent, but unless he concentrates—hard—on containing it, it flows from his patterns like water running through his fingers, or oozing from cupped hands.

The other matter that concerns him is the feeling of ugliness or uncleanness that he felt when he had redirected the chaos-bolt. He has always been slightly uncomfortable with chaos, a feeling he had almost not recognized, but the ugliness . . . even sitting on his blanket in the tent, he shivers slightly to think about it. *Was that because you were dealing with more chaos . . . or more closely?* That brings to mind his aunt's caution about always making sure order lies between him and any use of chaos. *But you were using order and not trying to influence the chaos directly.*

Still . . . he has only been using one coil of order, unlike the earlier patterns where he has employed several lines of order. *What if you use just two thinner order lines in the coil shape?*

He sets to work trying to duplicate that. After a half glass he is sweating slightly, despite the slight chill, but he has finally managed to create the small pattern the way he wants it.

He nods happily. Then another thought crosses his mind. *What would happen if you wrapped that order pattern around the lodestone?*

Lerial smiles as he does so—but his mouth drops open as the lodestone, pouch and all, rips itself from his hands and slams into the scabbard of his sabre, lying on the blanket beside him. The lodestone holds to the iron of the blade even through the hardened leather, and it takes a great effort by Lerial to pry it loose. Holding the lodestone tightly and well away from the sheathed sabre, he studies the dark oblong with his order-senses. Somehow, the pattern he has created has become part of the lodestone itself, amplifying the natural order-lines of the stone.

If you did that to any piece of iron . . . would it do that? Lerial shakes his head. To make iron act like a lodestone . . . at the moment, he can think of no reason to do so, but he will keep that in mind.

"If I might ask, Lerial . . . what are you doing?" Altyrn stands just inside the tent, shaking rain from his oilskin jacket.

"Working on trying to get better control of firebolts. Why?"

"Because you were surrounded by something like a silver-black haze." The majer smiles almost slyly. "I recall something you said about not being an ordermage . . ."

"I'm not. I've had a little instruction, and can do some healing. Other than that, I've figured out a few things, but I can't predict the weather, or change it. I can't erect shields against either order or chaos; I can only sometimes shift where chaos goes . . . and that's dangerous. You've seen that."

"I have." Altyrn nods. "I've also seen you destroy two chaos wizards, and you can conceal your entire company from sight."

"Only for a short time."

"Many would consider all of those enough to name you an ordermage, Lerial. Your rankers already do."

Lerial winces. "I'm not that good."

"You may not yet be what you would consider a good ordermage, but you are an ordermage of sorts, and it's foolish on your part to deny it. Denying what you are only weakens you . . . just as exaggerating what you are does. Strength lies in knowing who and what you are—your capabilities and your weaknesses."

Lerial cannot dispute that, and he nods.

After a silence that seems long to Lerial, but probably lasts but a few moments, Altyrn says, "The rain is a mixed blessing. Their chaos mages can't do that much, and that will allow the crafters here to make more arrows."

"That would be good. My head archer was asking about that."

"I will let you know as soon as I do."

"Yes, ser." Lerial pauses, then goes on. "I know that the rain will keep the fires from spreading, but you said they can't do much."

"It's been forgotten, I think, but handling chaos in the rain can be very painful for those who do. At least, that was something I was told a long ways from here when I was a very junior officer."

Lerial frowns for a moment. That's something he has not heard. "Is there anything else that makes it hard for them?"

Altyrn laughs softly but harshly. "An even stronger ordermage. Or having to use chaos in the middle of the ocean or a large lake." After another pause, he says, "I came to see if you had any sense of how long this rain will last."

Lerial is about to protest, then reluctantly smiles. "Wait a moment . . . if you would." He concentrates once more, letting his senses probe the clouds. As before, he can sense no immediate change . . . yet . . . the order flows seem slightly lighter and not quite so strong. He looks at the majer. "The rain *might* start to weaken in a few glasses, but I can't tell if it will strengthen after that . . . or get stronger again."

"I'll see you in a few glasses then . . ." Altyrn gives Lerial a surprisingly boyish grin, "Captain and ordermage." With that he turns and leaves the tent, walking through the rain toward the tent that holds Donnael, who has remained with the six companies for the last three days.

Lerial looks down at the lodestone he is still holding. *What else can you try?*

LXI

By eightday morning the rain has stopped. Only a thin haze remains, a combination of fog and mist that hovers in the forest canopy and higher. The wind has shifted to the southwest and turned cooler, but the Meroweyan forces do not look to move or break camp. Shortly after midafternoon, Altyrn sends out sixth company under Denieryn through the main southern road gate—still unbreached—to see what reaction that provokes. Three companies immediately charge, and fireballs fly. Sixth company loses almost a full squad to firebolts and two stragglers who are cut down by hard-riding Meroweyan horsemen, although archers stationed by the road gate bring down close to another squad of Meroweyan riders who pursue too closely.

"They were ready," says Lerial after hearing from the majer what happened.

"They knew you weren't there," observes Altyrn.

"Do you want second company to try next?"

"You can't do everything," the majer replies.

That's not exactly an answer. While that is Lerial's first thought, he realizes that what the majer means is that if second company is the only one moving against the Meroweyans, sooner or later, the attackers will find a way to trap and outnumber second company . . . particularly since Lerial has no way to shield his position from the Meroweyan mages or wizards, given that, just as he can sense concentrations of chaos, they seem able to know where he is through the concentration of order he has, small as it is.

"Do you think they'll attack this evening?" asks Lerial.

"I'd be surprised. They lost some of those riders because the ground was soft. Every glass the wind holds it dries out the ground and trees more. Tonight . . . well . . . it's going to be a long night," says Altyrn.

By eighth glass in the evening, the first firebolt strikes the edge of the already burned area east of the road-gate, and Lerial goes to find Altyrn.

"I can try to stop them," he says.

"Which ones? How will you keep up? The chaos-fire you saw to the east isn't the only place they'll fire. They've already moved on. Their mages rode up behind a company, threw some fire and withdrew."

Lerial understands all too well, especially after riding on the tortuous paths of the Verd. If second company leaves the Verd, Lerial will likely be immediately outnumbered and forced to withdraw. "So what do we do?"

"Wait. The Verd is still damp, and the elders can minimize the spread. If Casseon's men do attack in the darkness, they'll risk taking huge losses among the trees. They'll likely attack in force tomorrow." Altyrn snorts. "If they attack tonight, I'll have you awakened, never fear. For now, try to get some rest. You'll have plenty to do tomorrow."

Even before Lerial returns to the tent, he can smell the acrid odor of burning wood and vegetation, but he can see no fire, not even a dull red glow.

As he stands there, a short and broad-shouldered figure approaches. "Ser?"

He recognizes her. "Yes, Head Archer?"

"Do you know where we will be riding tomorrow?" Alaynara's voice is low for a woman, but pleasant.

"Wherever the majer sends us. That will depend on where the Merow-eyans are and what they're doing."

"You know you're not what anyone thought?"

What anyone thought? "You mean by 'anyone' the people of the Verd? Or the Verdyn Lancers?"

"Both. It's not as though the Lancers and the people are different." Her smile is somehow sad, Lerial thinks.

"Sometimes, those who are younger don't see things the same as those who are older."

"Especially when the younger ones are fighting and dying. Is that what you mean?"

"I have thought that. What did you mean by my being different? That I'm fighting instead of merely being here and conferring with the elders?"

"Mostly. But you also saved Haermish when it might have killed you."

Her words embarrass Lerial, and he quickly replies, "I did what I could . . . and it was after we got back."

"You like to think of yourself as practical, don't you?"

"I try." He almost laughs, thinking how that description would have amused his father.

"Practicality has to include who we are."

"That's why you're fighting," he points out.

"I thought you would understand. The majer does. I hope your father does also. Good night, ser." With a polite nod, Alaynara slips away into the darkness.

For a time, Lerial stands there. *Did she seek you out just to make that point? Why? You're not even the heir.*

In a way, Alaynara reminds him of Emerya, the same sort of combination of caring and practicality . . . and that reminds him of Amaira . . . and Ryalah, and he wonders how they are both doing . . . and that makes him wonder if Alaynara will end up like Emerya. He is still pondering what Alaynara had wanted when he stretches out on his blanket.

That acrid odor is stronger when he wakes as the sky is beginning to lighten the next morning. He glances at Altyrn's bedroll, which is already rolled up and wonders if the majer ever sleeps. When he looks outside, he can see that the cooler wind has brought scattered clouds, not thin ones, but the puffy kind that may well turn into thunderstorms by afternoon.

After checking with the second company duty ranker, he is relieved to know that there have been no more attacks during the night, not after ninth glass, anyway, and that the fires caused by the white wizards have largely died out. *Because of the efforts of the elders?*

Lerial eats quickly and goes to find Altyrn, whom he finds standing in the narrow opening of the outer road gate. The lines of smoke from cookfires and the fact that there are no forces obviously mustering suggest that they do not plan on an early attack.

The majer turns to Lerial. "Close to midday. They've widened the gap east of here. I could be wrong, but I think they'll attack there in force without their wizards."

"Ser?"

"They have to know that you can't or won't throw chaos. But you can throw it back at them. They don't need chaos to prevail. In fact, it could hurt them. So they'll send the wizards elsewhere to burn other entries and let most of their armsmen push their way into the Verd."

"Shouldn't second company go where they are?"

"We don't know—yet—where that might be. If the Meroweyans attack where it's most likely, fifth and sixth company will be in the trees on both sides of the burned-out area, and they'll be on foot with blades and bows. Third and fourth company will be behind them, but angling in, with half the squads on foot, and half mounted. Their battle line will be the unburned brush and trees. First and second companies will be the farthest back, and mounted, but in the middle of the assault. If we get word as to where the white wizards are, I'll pull second company to ride to where the wizards are. Juist and Kusyl can pull back and in and to cover first company on both sides."

"When do you want us in position?"

"Unless I order otherwise, start moving into place in a glass."

"Yes, ser."

Slightly more than a glass later, Lerial stands at the edge of the burned-out section of the Verd, looking out across a charred and ash-covered waste where only the blackened trunks and lower limbs of the most massive trees remain, jutting into a sky half-filled with white and gray clouds. The burned area is close to four hundred yards wide at the former edge, where even the stoutest trunks have been blasted away by chaos-fire, those ancient and massive trunks that Lerial had once believed could withstand almost anything—anything but fire. The fire-cleared area stretches back a good three hundred yards, but narrows to slightly more than two hundred yards wide where Lerial stands, beside a tree whose lower leaves are gone, but not those in the canopy. Lerial can see the purpose behind the Meroweyan chaos-attack, because the trees are much farther apart farther inside the Verd, separated by as much as five to eight yards behind Lerial. In other areas, he knows, the trees and underbrush are almost impassible, suggesting that the Meroweyans either have had spies posing as traders and scouting the Verd for a time or the white wizards are very accurate in sensing the areas with fewer trees.

Lerial glances southward, but does not see any Meroweyan forces. The wind is gusting at times, and each gusts shifts fine ash. Even with the wind, the sun is much stronger, early in spring as it is, and Lerial wears his jacket unfastened as he stands beside the gelding, wondering if the wayguides or the elders or the scouts will be able to locate the remaining white wizards. *How many did they bring?* He's fairly certain that he has killed two, possibly three. Are there that many strong white wizards in Merowey? Or does Duke Casseon prefer to keep the stronger ones busy and at a distance? *Or both?* The latter possibility is definitely disturbing, but there's little he can do about that now . . . or possibly ever.

Out of the corner of his eye he sees movement, and he reaches out with his order senses, recognizing Altyrn and another rider. He turns and sees that with the majer is an older man in brown, most likely a wayguide—and that suggests that second company is needed elsewhere. Rather than guess, he just waits as Altyrn reins up and merely says, "Yes, ser?"

"You can guess, I'm certain, Captain. This time they've moved some three kays east. That's where they threw firebolts earlier, but not enough to totally break through. Reksyl, here, will guide you as close as he can. If it's a feint, I'd appreciate your returning as soon as possible. But you know that," says Altyrn. "If there is a chaos wizard there, anything you can do would be appreciated, especially to the armsmen with him."

"I understand, ser." *In short, use the chaos, if you can, to reduce the number of Meroweyans we have to fight.*

"I'm sure you do." Altyrn nods brusquely, then says to the wayguide. "Thank you." He turns his mount.

Lerial calls out, "Second company! Mount up! Back to the road. First squad to the east. Double file!" Then he mounts and nods to the wayguide. "If you would, Reksyl."

"This way, ser."

Lerial keeps glancing back, but the squads are following, and behind them, he can see first company shifting position. In less than a fifth of a glass second company is riding eastward at a fast walk. The "road" is more like a path wide enough for two mounts abreast, and the grass at each side extends only a cubit or so out from the packed earth before giving way to underbrush and trees. Lerial feels as though he is riding through a gray-green tunnel, mostly gray, because only the green tips of the new leaves have begun to show and there are not that many evergreens in the Verd. Even the birds are hushed, as if they sense a storm of some sort, even though the rankers are largely quiet.

Lerial begins to sense the chaos to the southeast after they have ridden some two kays. While he is not totally certain, it feels a good kay away, perhaps slightly farther. He turns his head toward Reksyl. "How much farther?"

"A bit more than a kay, ser."

Lerial nods.

"You can sense them." Reksyl's words are more statement than question.

"Somewhat . . . ," he admits.

"You are the . . . youngest officer, are you not?"

"Yes."

"It is a sad time when the youngest son of a ruler must ride into battle with so many men's lives behind him."

"It is a sad time, when any ruler's son must lead men into battle," Lerial replies quietly.

"That is true," replies Reksyl. "That is not what I meant. It is not it at all. You are young to have killed so many."

Have you killed that many? How does he know?

"I am not a powerful ordermage, as are you, but the white touch of death leaves a faint silver mist around those mages who have brought forth death."

"I've never seen that," says Lerial.

"None sees his own mist, and few ordermages are strong enough to bring death and still hold order with power."

Strong enough . . . or desperate enough? questions Lerial silently.

As they ride closer to the burned-out area, Lerial uses his order-senses to discover the formation of the Meroweyan forces. From what he can tell, there are four companies, and one is moving forward, toward the small burned-out part of the Verd edge. The front line, no more than a twenty-man front, consists of men with overlarge shields. Behind them are riders, and the riders also bear the same kind of overlarge shields. Perhaps five yards separates the foot and mounted shield line from a company of horse troopers, and behind the horse troopers are several mounted figures, one of whom is surrounded by chaos—the chaos wizard who will doubtless begin the process of burning a wider gap in the tree trunks that have protected the Verd for so long.

The other three companies are spaced equally far apart, roughly twenty yards of open grassland between each formation, and consist of four squads with two squads in front and two behind, each squad showing a five-man front. To Lerial's senses, all three companies are "misted" in chaos, as if each protects a wizard who has created a chaos blur.

But then, one wizard could have cast that mist, and how can you tell where he is? Or if he is anywhere close to any of the companies?

Ahead, the wide path ends in a narrow clearing, no more than twelve yards deep and perhaps forty long, barely large enough to fit second company.

"The grasslands lie a little more than a hundred yards to the southeast," says the wayguide. "The trees are closer here than elsewhere, but there is enough space for a rider to pass until you reach the thornbushes. They do not begin until you are within fifty yards of the trunk-wall."

Lerial nods, considering. Then turns in the saddle to Korlyn. "I'm going to take second squad with me, closer to the Meroweyans. You're in charge of the rest of the company. Keep them ready to charge—or withdraw immediately." What Lerial doesn't mention is arrows. Only the archers of fourth squad have any shafts left, and those amount to but two or three for each archer. He is holding fourth squad in reserve, to fire several quick volleys to slow a Meroweyn charge, if necessary and practical. He hopes it is not necessary.

"Form up by squads. Five-man front! First squad on me!" Lerial rides to the west end of the clearing, making it easier for the company to re-form from the two-file column. While the squads are moving into position, he uses his order senses to check the Meroweyan advance. By now the shielded line of the Meroweyans is perhaps a hundred yards from the edge of the Verd.

Lerial immediately rides over to Bhurl, the second squad leader. "Have second squad accompany me—now—through the trees to the edge of the burned space. Or as far as we can go," he adds quickly, thinking about the thornbushes.

"Yes, ser." Bhurl turns. "You two! Flank the captain. Second squad! Forward!"

Lerial waits only a few moments for the two rankers to join him before urging the gelding through the trees on the south side of the clearing. While there are small bushes amid the massive trunks, and occasionally smaller and lower trees, covering the first fifty cubits or so is not all that hard . . . not until he reaches the massive and tangled thornbushes that are almost as high as the gelding's ears. He reins up a few yards short of the thorny mass.

At least, the Meroweyans aren't coming through here without clearing the way. Except he knows all too well that they will be clearing the way—unless he can stop them—with chaos-fire.

"Form a line abreast, two deep, as best you can," he orders.

While the Verdyn Lancers are moving into position, Lerial again checks the position of the lead Meroweyan force, but, as he does, he senses the lightest of . . . something . . . tinged with chaos.

Is that what a chaos-sensing probe feels like? That is his guess, but it is only a guess.

The center company of Meroweyans halts roughly fifty yards from the edge of the Verd, or where that edge had been before being turned to ash and charcoaled tree trunks. The two trailing companies halt farther back, perhaps a hundred yards.

"The closest Meroweyans are about a hundred yards away," Lerial tells Bhurl.

"You've got better eyes than me, ser," replies the squad leader.

A modest fireball arcs from the lead force toward the back of the burned-out area, or the thornbushes and trees at the beginning of the unburned woods.

Lerial counters with a small pattern to redirect the firebolt back at the chaos wizard, but he can sense something, shields or the like, and the chaos-fire sprays away from the wizard. Lerial winces inside as he feels the silver-white blackness that Reksyl has said shows death. Although he cannot tell how many armsmen near the wizard have perished, he feels it is more than a single man, but not a large group.

Two far larger firebolts arch north, not toward the edge of the Verd, but toward Lerial and second squad. Given the shields shown by the first mage, Lerial creates two patterns, but both are angle-linked to redirect the chaos back toward the westernmost wizard, the one Lerial feels, although he cannot say why, is the weakest of the three he faces.

The wizard's shields hold, but chaos flashes away from them, and a wave of silvered black-gray death flows from the Meroweyan company.

Even before that chaos subsides completely, three firebolts—one from each Meroweyan wizard—sear toward Lerial.

Lerial has to struggle to complete three coil patterns, and the fireballs fuse—sending flame into the trees and thornbushes less than thirty yards from him—before flaring back toward the westernmost wizard. The wizard's shields tremble, then fragment, and chaos fire splashes out across the entire Meroweyan company.

". . . flaming sowshit . . ." murmurs one of the rankers slightly behind but flanking him.

Sweat runs down Lerial's face, and his eyes sting from the small amount that flows into his eyes. He finds he is breathing hard . . . and that two more firebolts are headed toward him.

It's more than clear that he's in a trap. *But how . . .* He doesn't have time for such thoughts as he wrestles another pair of patterns into place.

The two firebolts fuse, even closer to second squad, and more trees and thornbushes go up in near-instant flame, while heat washes over Lerial and the squad. But the patterns hold, and the redirected chaos-bolt flies toward the chaos wizard shielded by the easternmost company, the stops short of him and sheets in all directions. Another wave of gray-silvered whiteness rolls back toward Lerial, a wave unseen and unfelt by any in the Verdyn force, Lerial suspects, except himself and likely the wayguide, who waits at the back of the clearing.

Another chaos-bolt flies toward Lerial, this one from the easternmost company, but only one. Again, he creates the diversion pattern, but almost as he finishes it, another comes from the closest chaos mage, the one Lerial feels is the strongest.

Lerial can barely manage another diversion pattern, and the wizard's shields shunt the redirected chaos back into the edges of the burned-out area, the corrosive fire disintegrating more of the massive trunk wall that had guarded the Verd for so many centuries. He can feel the trees and the thornbushes in front of him beginning to spin, and knows he cannot divert another chaos-bolt, even a few yards away.

"Second squad!" he manages somehow. "Withdraw now!"

He has to hang on to the gelding's mane, just concentrating on staying in the saddle, as he turns his mount and urges him back through the trees as quickly as he can. He yells out, "Second company! Withdraw now! Now!"

"Ser! Are you all right?" demands Korlyn.

"Withdraw, frig it! We can't do any more here."

"We haven't taken any—"

"That's because none of the firebolts have hit us yet. They will if we stay here. I can't—"

At that moment, another firebolt arches over the trees, right toward Lerial and Korlyn and the center of second company.

Frigging sowshit! Lerial throws up another diversion pattern, a weak one, but all he can manage.

Then heat and hot blackness crush him down.

LXII

You may be the son of a Duke, Captain, but you won't be for long if you keep this up." The gentle words are the first sounds Lerial recognizes as he swims out of a haze of fireballs and darkness, of burning trees and acrid smoke. Except . . . there are no trees, and he is lying on his back in a tent in darkness, and the Verdyn healer is blotting his forehead with a cool cloth. She lifts the cloth.

"What glass . . . what day . . . where . . . ?"

"It's eighth glass in the evening on oneday, and you're lying in a tent on the green in the hamlet of Suaddern." The healer straightens.

Suaddern? Lerial doesn't recognize the name. "The Meroweyans . . . ?"

"They burned their way into the Verd along the south road. They stopped attacking when it got dark and they started losing men in the trees. That's what one of the wounded said."

Lerial cannot help but wonder. "My company?"

"They got back fine . . . mostly."

"We might have lost a few to firebolts."

"Hasn't every company?" Her voice is matter-of-fact. "This time you almost didn't have enough order in your body." She puts a surprisingly strong arm behind his shoulders and helps him into a semisitting position, then puts a mug to his lips. "Drink."

Lerial does. Whatever it is makes tart greenberry juice seem sweet, but even after the first swallow, he can feel some of the pounding in his head begin to ease, if only slightly.

"Drink it all. Keep sitting up, but don't try to stand yet." With that final command, the healer stands. "You cannot do anything with order or chaos for the next day, preferably two. If you do, it will likely kill you. I'll be back later." She leaves the tent, disappearing into the dark.

Lerial forces himself to keep drinking until the mug is empty and he can set it aside.

"Ser?"

Lerial turns, and he sees a figure peering in the tent, but he cannot order-sense who it is close as the man might be. "Yes?"

"Korlyn, ser. You all right, ser?"

"The healer seems to think I will be."

"I'm sorry, ser." The way Korlyn is standing, he doesn't seem to want to look directly at Lerial, but then the words tumble out. "I didn't know, I mean, not really, that you were the one keeping that wizard fire from us . . ."

"What happened after that last fireball . . . the last one I saw anyway?"

"The wizard didn't send any more, not that I saw. We got clear pretty quick. First squad . . . well . . . we lost two rankers, and two others got bad burns."

"What about the other squads?"

"No casualties there, ser. Not from the Meroweyans. One of Moraris's archers ripped up her arm on a tree . . . chief archer said she was careless. Wouldn't want to cross her . . ."

Why didn't the wizard throw any more firebolts? Because he thought you were dead? Could it be that when he'd been unconscious the wizards couldn't sense him? Was that why there were more wizards remaining than he'd thought? Because he'd only knocked one of them out? "Did they keep throwing the chaos at the trees?"

"For a time, sir. Maybe, two or three more. We didn't stay to see. Not when you couldn't . . . do what you were doing."

"You did what you were supposed to do. I'd already ordered the withdrawal." *And if I hadn't had to explain . . . but shouldn't you, as captain, have made that clear earlier?*

Korlyn has barely left the tent when another figure appears. While Lerial cannot sense who it is, the man's stance tells him that it must be Altyrn.

"I see that you almost managed to get yourself killed again." Although the majer's voice is dry, Lerial can hear concern behind the dryness.

"I already was trying to withdraw second company before the last firebolt almost hit us. I misjudged a little." Before Altyrn can say anything about that, Lerial quickly adds, "This is new to me, ser, and I'm still learning. I worry that if I don't do as much as I can . . ."

"If you try to do more than you can, then you won't be around for the next attack, and your men will suffer even more. I took the liberty of talking to the squad leaders and pointing out that you were risking your own life trying to protect them from the firebolts. I think you can be a bit more judiciously cautious from now on."

"Yes, ser."

"Your squad leaders didn't seem to know all that happened. They said that all they saw was firebolts beyond the trees."

"That was because we couldn't get through the thornbushes. The white wizards probably burned through them after second company withdrew."

"That's what the Verd wardens reported. The Meroweyans are waiting for the fires to subside. They'll likely attack there tomorrow. Their force may need some reinforcements. The wardens say that the firebolts you turned back incinerated two companies, maybe more. They couldn't tell about the wizards."

"There were three. There are two now." Sparks flash across Lerial's vision, and an unseen hammer pounds his skull. He can tell he is getting tired. *Tired? Just sitting up?*

"The healer says it will be days before you can handle order or chaos again. Why didn't you withdraw earlier?"

Altyrn's repetition of the question tells Lerial that the majer is concerned . . . and that he is very serious about Lerial not overextending himself.

"I misjudged how long it would take, and there was another firebolt that would have hit us. I think that was the Merowyan strategy. To wear me out and then throw several firebolts at once." Lerial isn't about to explain again that he'd already ordered second squad to withdraw.

Altyrn nods slowly. "I'm holding second company out of the fighting tomorrow—unless it's absolutely necessary. If I have to use your rankers, you won't be commanding them."

"Ser?"

"You're just the type who will try to protect them if it's possible. I can't afford that kind of sacrifice. Neither can your rankers. Nor can the Verdyn. Besides, the healer says you'll be too weak."

"She's probably right," Lerial admits. His head is beginning to spin once more.

The healer reappears, holding a large jug. "You need to drink more and then rest." She bends and picks up the empty mug, refills it, and hands it to Lerial. "Drink."

Lerial's hands are shaking, but he manages several swallows of the tart and exceedingly bitter greenberry potion, then holds the mug in both hands, hoping the dizziness and shaking will subside. After several moments, he feels that they have receded slightly, and he takes another swallow. As he lowers the mug, he realizes that the majer has left.

"When you finish drinking that, you need to lie down and sleep." The healer's voice is pleasant enough, but Lerial can hear the tone of command.

"Yes, healer."

"Elizean will do, Captain. Keep drinking."

Lerial finishes the potion and hands her the mug. She does not need to tell him to lie down.

LXIII

The air is still, heavy, and acrid, with the smell of ashes and smoke everywhere, when Lerial struggles awake sometime after dawn but before sunrise on twoday morning to the sound of barked commands, wagons, and horses. He pulls on his boots and as much as staggers to his feet as stands. He is not dizzy, but he does feel unsteady as he dons his visor cap and straightens his riding jacket, then steps out of the tent, aware that his eyes are watering slightly from the acrid smoke.

He glances around, seeing rankers seemingly hurrying everywhere.

"Strike that tent! Now! Majer says we have to be out of here in less than a glass."

"That long? Burned out the woods on both sides of the road gates . . ."

"Takes longer when you got that many troopers . . ."

As Lerial hears those words, two other rankers hurry up, the second leading his gelding, already saddled. The first hands him a water bottle and a small pouch. "These are from the healer, ser."

"Here's your mount, ser. Majer requests you join him." The second ranker points. "He's by the road over there."

"Thank you." Lerial eases the pouch into his jacket and slips the water bottle into the saddle holder. Then, he gathers himself together and climbs into the saddle, the difficulty he has underscoring just how weak he is. He guides the gelding in the direction of the majer, discovering as he nears Altyrn, mounted beside another rider, that he has regained some ability to order-sense, if but to a distance of perhaps ten yards. The lack of range in order-sensing and the weakness in his legs prompt him to lift the water bottle and take a long swallow of the tart and bitter greenberry liquid.

He replaces the water bottle and then takes out the pouch, which, he discovers, contains several hard biscuits. He puts one in his mouth, gingerly, and discovers that, while neither bitter nor tart, it has little taste at all. He eats the first biscuit in moments and then the next, replacing the pouch in his jacket as he reins up beside Altyrn, who is talking to Juist.

". . . those road traps and makeshift caltrops ready to put in place, ser, once we engage them . . ."

"Then take up that position and look like you're going to hold it, but if they start to throw fireballs, fall back immediately behind the log barricade. Have your archers loft shafts into their rear. That's where the white wizards are. Ease back as quickly as you can."

"Yes, ser."

"Go!"

Lerial has only the vaguest idea of what Altyrn has just ordered, except that it sounds like a ploy of some sort. "You're trying to lure them into something?"

"That comes later. I'm hoping that they'll drop fireballs into some bitumen and oil that will surround a mass of their armsmen on three sides."

"If they don't?"

"Then Juist will likely lose the rankers who will have to use torches." Altyrn's voice is steady, as if he were discussing the worms that made shimmercloth fibers. He turns his mount. "Just stay with me and watch. Don't ask any questions until I tell you that you can."

"Yes, ser." The only wagon that Lerial can see around the area where second company had been posted creaks by him, leaving the area with little but flattened grass where tents had been and almost empty of Lancers—except for third company, forming up across the road. To the south, in the direction of the apparently still-intact but useless road gates, Lerial can hear horn signals, but he can sense nothing more than a few yards away.

"We need to move back. This way," commands the majer, turning his horse.

Lerial follows Altyrn along the shoulder of the road, through and past another wider clearing, beyond which the trees are spaced more widely. Some hundred yards later, the majer reins up behind a pair of trees with wide trunks that almost touch. He positions himself so that he can look through the gap at the road that leads to where the roadgates are . . . not that they have done much more than delay the Meroweyans. "Stay behind me."

Third company rides past, and the area where the Verdyn forces had been for the past eightday or so appears empty. For a good quarter glass, nothing seems to move, not even the air, and there are no clouds in the sky that is slowly turning from gray to green-blue as the sun begins to rise, not that Lerial can see it yet, not from within the confines of the Verd forest.

He shifts his weight in the saddle and takes several more swallows of the greenberry liquid, admitting wordlessly that he does feel better, and slightly stronger, as a result of drinking it and eating the biscuits. He shifts in the saddle again.

"Watch," orders Altyrn quietly. "Say nothing."

From the south come sounds, a muted series of vibrations. Lerial stands in his stirrups, so that he can look over Altyrn's head and through the opening between the two tree trunks. He can make out what at first looks to be a huge brownish worm with spikes jutting out and walking sideways on many legs, but then realizes it is a Meroweyan shieldwall some fifty yards wide, centered on the road and moving toward the majer and him. Behind the shieldmen are pikemen, their pikes leveled to discourage a mounted attack. Behind the pikes and shields are footmen, although Lerial can only see their heads, while behind each end of the formation are mounted troopers.

When the shieldmen are about a hundred yards from the majer and Lerial, a wall of flame races from somewhere well to the sides of the road and under the boots of the shieldmen. Several yell, and one man staggers out of formation, his uniform in flames . . . and then another . . . and another. As the shieldmen run forward to keep from getting burned, the pikemen are left at least partly exposed to the arrows that come from all sides. Then two squads of Verdyn Lancers—one from the east, and one from the west—charge the pikemen.

The mounted troopers behind the ends of the line of pikemen move forward, but by the time they get around the chaos of wounded pikemen and disorganized shieldmen, both squads have turned and vanished back into the trees.

"Time to withdraw!" snaps Altyrn, turning his mount and urging it into a canter along the shoulder of the road.

Lerial follows, wondering where or when Juist's men will do what he had heard the majer discussing, because what he has just seen does not match what he had heard between the two.

Altyrn does not slow his mount until they have covered almost a kay and entered a larger clearing. Closer to the north side is a log barricade almost eighty yards long and somewhat more than two yards high that straddles the road. The two sides are slightly angled so that the middle is perhaps ten yards forward of the ends. Lerial can see the tips of spears and caps and the like behind the barrier, and slightly less than two squads of riders in formation at each end. Altyrn keeps riding, circling around the east end of the log barricade and into the trees on the northeast end of the clearing.

Once there, he turns his mount so that he can see the clearing, but so that he is largely shielded by the trunk of the tree. Lerial follows his example and reins up the gelding beside a nearby tree. Looking back, he can see that most of the figures behind the log barricade are crudely formed of vines and branches or other material with caps or scarves or the like on the "head," and that the spears and weapons are merely crude poles with carved points. Still, from a distance, they looked real enough. What is real, however, is the small catapult behind the mock force. Three youths, even younger than Lerial or any of the rankers, wait by the catapult. Behind the catapult are two rows of women archers, presumably from third company.

Almost a glass passes before the shieldwall of the Meroweyans enters the south side of the clearing and moves roughly twenty yards into the clearing before a horn sounds, and the shieldwall comes to a halt, while the pikemen ground their pikes, as if expecting an attack.

Lerial cannot see exactly what is happening, and his order senses have not recovered enough for him to determine anything at that distance, either, but he can see movement.

Then, at some signal he does not catch, a flaming ball of fire arches from the catapult behind the log barrier toward the shieldwall, landing on the ground and spraying feeble shards of burning matter. There is no reaction from the Meroweyan forces. Several moments later, another flaming ball arches over the log barricade, and this flaming ball catches the top of one of the outsized shields, and burning goo splashes on the shield-bearer, who drops his shield and rolls in the grass trying to smother the flames burning his sleeves and chest.

Then a third ball of flame hits another shield-bearer.

The Meroweyan horn sounds, and the pikes level. The shieldwall marches forward, solid step by solid step. Another flaming ball arches into the Meroweyan force, this time into the armed footmen behind the shields.

At that, a chaos-bolt arcs from the rear of the Meroweyan formation toward the catapult, but misses to one side, incinerating three stick dummies. Another chaos-bolt follows. The fireballs are smaller than the ones Lerial has diverted, and he wonders if that is because the white wizards are tired as well . . . or because they have been ordered to husband their chaos strength. The youths sprint away. Two escape. The third, trailing by a yard or so, is enveloped in flame.

With that, the archers loft shafts toward the rear of the Meroweyan troopers.

In response, the mounted armsmen race from each end of the Meroweyan formation toward the small squads of Verdyn Lancers flanking the ends of the log barricade. The Lancers wheel and gallop behind the barricade and then onto the road. As they pass, the archers also turn and run.

Seeing the fleeing Verdyn forces, the Meroweyan riders urge their mounts onward also around the ends of the log barricade. Lerial sees a ranker with a torch running forward, but the Meroweyans don't seem to see him—or are more interested in running down the women archers.

Lerial wonders if something has gone wrong, despite Altyrn's plans . . . and why the archers don't sprint for the trees. Then he sees the Lancers slow and turn.

At that moment, fire erupts, seemingly from the ground, creating a semicircle with each end touching the log barricade, enclosing almost two companies of riders. In addition, after a few moments, the log barricade also begins to burn. Startled by the sudden flame and heat, more than a few of the Meroweyan mounts either rear or balk, but perhaps a squad of riders either crosses the line of flame before it is at full strength or bursts through it anyway, only to find that the archers have turned and begin to loose shafts at those riders. The three remaining squads from third company charge back at the surviving Meroweyan riders. In a matter of moments, none of the less than a score of the attacking riders who escaped the flames remain alive or unwounded. The archers, still carrying their bows, sprint toward the edge of the woods, where, Lerial sees, their mounts are tethered.

"Third company! Withdraw now!" shouts Juist.

"That means us," says Altyrn.

Now? Then Lerial sees that the flames are dying away, even those on the log barricade, and realizes that before long there will be no flame left and no barrier to the companies of armed riders on the other side of those dying flames . . . or the even more riders and footmen on the south side of the barrier. He also sees that two of the third company mounts are riderless and one archer lies motionless on the road, her neck at an odd angle.

Lerial has to jolt himself into motion to turn the gelding and follow Altyrn. They ride for almost a kay before he and the majer reach a wide place in the road where third company has reformed, with Juist positioned at its head.

"Ser!" announces Juist. "Third company stands ready."

"Casualties?" asks Altyrn.

"Two dead, and the one boy who manned the catapult. Two wounded, neither seriously."

Altyrn nods. "Well executed, Undercaptain. Very well executed."

Lerial has to agree, wondering if he will ever be able to do that well, or do that well without using order-chaos skills.

"We'll put back to . . . Nevnarnia and hold there," the majer adds.

Lerial can sense that the majer has to struggle to remember the name of the hamlet that lies to the north of them on the road into Vernheln . . . and eventually to Verdell.

Altyrn gestures to Lerial, then turns his mount, as does Lerial. They ride northward along the road for a time before the majer speaks. "They'll make a good five kays today. With what we've already done and the various traps the locals are setting, we'll cost them another company, or two, with luck."

"Will they keep burning the Verd, do you think?" asks Lerial.

"Not now. There's no point in it. They've breached the barriers, and a runaway fire could turn on them. Once they realize they've lost . . . that's the time for worry."

Once they realize they've lost . . . ? Lerial almost shakes his head. While the majer's hastily trained Lancers and archers might have removed five or six companies—*and maybe three white wizards, just possibly four*—there are still something like thirty or thirty-five companies riding into Vernheln.

LXIV

Lerial did not even recall Nevnarnia from the time when he and Altyrn and the two Mirror Lancers squads had ridden through it on their way from Escadya, and his first glimpse of it at around midday, coming from the south, tells him why.

"The main road doesn't even pass through the hamlet," he observes to Altyrn as they turn up a side road, certainly almost as wide as the route they have been following.

"Don't you imagine there is a reason for that?"

"What? That they aren't a trading town, or interested in that?"

"That would be my guess."

"You don't think the Meroweyans will just march by, then?" Lerial tries to inject a bit of levity into his voice.

"Ignore the first hamlet or town inside the Verd after losing hundreds of men?"

Lerial frowns, realizing that might well be what his father might do . . . but not if all the inhabitants had fought against him. *But then, he wouldn't have invaded if all the people were opposed to his being their ruler.*

"You don't think so?" asks Altyrn.

"No. I agree. I was just thinking that it seems a bad idea to invade another land if it hasn't attacked you and the people don't want you."

"It usually is," replies the majer. "But Casseon thinks the Verd is his land, and the people don't. Most rulers don't take to that. Would you?"

"I suppose not . . . but I think I'd try not to get into that position."

"What if a people believed in everything you hate, that they all wanted to kill every black ordermage who was anything more than a healer on sight, that they put anyone who didn't pay the slightest debt in chains for life and made them work in quarries or on building roads for the rest of their life, and that they used chaos-fire to destroy anyone who might be a magus if he didn't serve the ruler with absolute loyalty?"

"I don't think there could be a land like that, could there?"

"You never know," replies Altyrn dryly. "In your father's position, what would you do?"

"Avoid dealing with that land. I can't see any good coming of fighting it—unless they attacked first."

"And if they did?"

Lerial sighs. "I suppose I'd have to be ruthless to protect my own people."

"And how would that make you different from the ruler of that land?"

Lerial doesn't want to answer that question. Instead, he glances skyward, into a sky that has become almost completely cloudless, with a light and warm breeze coming out of the north.

Altyrn laughs. "Be careful of simple answers, Lerial. Nothing . . . nothing for a ruler or those who serve him is simple."

At that point, Lerial sees ahead, on both sides of the road, where the Verdyn Lancers are setting up another camp.

"We're taking a position on the south side of the town," Altyrn says. "That way, we can take the lanes north and use a back road to return to the main road, if necessary. Along the main roads are where we have to fight. They intend to follow this main road all the way to Verdell."

"You know that?"

"If you don't take the main city of a land, you haven't won. Would anyone think that they had conquered your father's lands without taking Cigoerne proper?"

"But . . ." Lerial pauses and then goes on, "just because someone takes the capital city or palace doesn't mean they've been successful. Not if that's all they hold."

"You're right about that." Altyrn smiles. "I need to think more about tomorrow. If you'll pledge not to use order-skills in fighting, I'll return you to command. Can you do that?"

Lerial has to think about that. *Not to use . . .* But Altyrn has so few experienced officers, and it's incredible that Lerial has more experience than most. Finally, he nods. "Yes, ser."

"I'm glad you actually took a moment or two to think about it," say Altyrn dryly. "Once you've seen to your company, take a little time and ride through Nevnarnia. It always helps to know where you may be fighting. Look for places and positions that will give you an advantage. We may not get that chance, but it's better to be overprepared than not prepared because you didn't think you'd have that opportunity." Altyrn grins. "Besides, it's good practice, and you need as much of that as you can get."

Lerial cannot dispute the majer's words, and it only takes Lerial a little while, less than a tenth of a glass, to find second company, possibly because his men are setting up close to the east side of the road that leads to Nevnarnia. He reins up short of Korlyn.

"You back, ser?" asks the first squad leader.

"I'm back," confirms Lerial. "But I won't be able to protect anyone from firebolts for a while. We'll have to avoid them by not being where they hit."

"Yes, ser." Korlyn's smile still seems to reflect relief, as if he definitely prefers Lerial to be in command.

After speaking with Korlyn, Lerial also meets with each squad leader. He cannot help but notice that Alaynara watches him and Moraris closely.

When he has finished with the squad leaders, he rides north to inspect and study the hamlet. The first dwellings in the Nevnarnia proper are less than four hundred yards from the Lancer encampment, and as Lerial rides closer he finds that the road splits into three forks. He takes the westernmost one that curves into a lane parallel to two others. He can see that hamlet is certainly modest, with perhaps fifty to sixty dwellings spaced carefully along the three narrow lanes. Lines of tall trees run between the houses set back to back on the lanes. As in the other towns he has observed, all the dwellings have plank siding and wooden shake roofs, with sturdy stone chimneys. Most of the dwellings are shuttered. That scarcely surprises Lerial. Outside of the dwellings themselves, he sees no places that would shelter or offer any real cover to mounted Lancers—except in the woods to the west of the hamlet. Nor does he discover any ditches or depressions that would hamper a mounted charge or a foot advance.

As Lerial nears the far end of the lane, or rather, the point where it curves eastward, he sees another small Kaordist temple. He reins up and studies the twin-spired structure with the one spire curved and rounded and somehow off-center and the other spire clean and straight.

Can one really call chaos feminine and order male? From what Lerial has seen of life, little as it may be compared to someone like the majer, men are the ones who are more chaotic. *But then, in most places, men make the rules, and it's hard to argue with that.* Just like it's hard to argue with his father, the majer . . . or even Lephi.

He continues onward, making his way down the middle lane, in the center of which are some shops and a small building that looks as though it is similar to a chandlery. There are a few people on the lanes, less than a handful.

Near the northern end of the last lane on the east, or rather where it joins the curved extensions of the other lanes, and the combined road curves due east, most likely heading back to the main road to Escadya and, beyond there, to Verdell, just short of the last dwelling on the east side of the lane, he sees a man with a ladder. The man sets the ladder down and turns away from Lerial to talk to the woman who is following him. Neither is looking in Lerial's direction.

Lerial definitely wants to know what they're talking about, especially since the few others he has seen have hurried on without looking at him..

Can you raise a very small concealment? He decides to try, perhaps almost a blurring rather than a full concealment. He does not feel light-headed or dizzy and lets the gelding carry him slowly toward the couple, easing to a stop when he can hear their voices.

"If you're staying to fight the Meroweyans, so am I," declares the muscular, graying woman.

"You don't know one end of a sword from the other," declares the stout and half-bald older man in brown.

"Neither do you. Besides, you don't have a sword."

"I've got my bow and a score of good shafts."

"I have mine, and just as many shafts. And I'm a better archer. You know that in your heart, Kaleb."

"You're a stubborn woman, Yasnela."

"Wasn't that what led you to consort me? Least, that's what you always said." The woman puts her hand on her consort's arm. "Together, we've got twice as many arrows."

"Still say you're a stubborn woman."

"We're going to lose everything, no matter what. You know that. We don't do what we can, each of us, everyone's going to lose everything. No sense in asking why it falls to us. It does, and that's that. Now . . . we'll go back to the house and plan this out sensible like."

Lerial does not move as the two turn and walk toward the small brick dwelling, the last one on the lane, away from him. He drops the concealment and smiles because he only feels slightly tired . . . and that might just be because he has had a long day. *At least, that's what you hope.*

He turns the gelding and starts his return south, riding back toward what is likely to be a very temporary camp, his smile vanishing as he thinks over the words of the couple, years older than even his own parents. He smiles wryly as he thinks that, in a way, in their own way, his parents are doing the same thing as the older couple he has overheard.

LXV

Later on twoday, the Lancers from second company join all the other Lancers and archers in creating a set of defenses for Nevnarnia, using shovels and mattocks from two carts that Lerial had not noticed earlier, and he wonders if they had come while he was inspecting the hamlet. Lerial glances into the skies to the south, where trails of smoke still wind into the skies, wondering why the Meroweyans don't press, and watching as the scouts ride up and report to Altyrn, then ride back out.

After a time, well after the fourth glass of the afternoon, he makes his way to where Altyrn has set up his table under the trees to the east side of the road.

"Ser?"

"Yes, Lerial?"

"Why aren't they pushing forward?"

"Because they can't." The majer smiles at Lerial's puzzled expression, then goes on. "The larger a force is, the more difficult it is for it to move swiftly. The roads here in the Verd are narrow, at least for thousands of riders and armsmen on foot. If they try to move quickly, they'll have to form a narrow column, most likely more than two kays long. That would allow us to attack anywhere, and they would lose the advantage of having a much larger force. They're proceeding deliberately, clearing a wider area on each side of the main road. They're using their wizards to do that, and that slows them more, because they don't want them worn out."

Lerial can see that, but that raises another question. "So why are we—"

"Building a barrier instead of attacking them from the woods? That's because they're still too close to the edge of the Verd."

Abruptly . . . Lerial understands. "This is only to give them the impression that we will stand and fight."

"Not exactly. This is likely to be one of the last times we can inflict large numbers of casualties at one time . . . and we need to do it in a way that will anger their commanders to the point that they will vow to destroy us to the last Lancer and officer."

That takes Lerial aback.

"We can't afford to fight Merowey more than once in a generation." Altyrn's smile is both sad and weary. "That's also why you are not—under any circumstances—to attempt to use order until the healer says you can. We will need that skill far more in the eightdays to come than we will now. Your task as captain is to inflict what casualties you can while losing as few rankers as possible. If you and the others can do that, in the end we will win. Now . . . here's what you'll be doing tomorrow . . ." The majer goes on to explain. When he is finished, he says, "I'll give you your final orders tomorrow morning, once we know more about what the Meroweyans plan."

"Yes, ser."

"Eat what you can, and get some sleep. See that your rankers do, too."

By the time the sun has set and darkness has crept across Nevnarnia, the defenses that Altyrn has designed are in place . . . and all the Lancers are tired, but not tired enough that all the companies except second and fifth company mount up and depart, leaving Lerial and Shaskyn and their companies to hold the road and bar the Meroweyans from the hamlet.

A barricade two yards high and woven out of branches and greenish thorns, as well as anchored to sturdy posts at regular intervals, runs across the road and into the trees, extending a good fifty yards beyond the road on each side until it is lost in the thick underbrush, much of it gray-leafed and thinner than would have been the case later in the year. The branches and thorns are of the greenest vegetation available so that the chaos-fire will not spread easily or quickly.

Behind the barricade is an open ditch some three yards wide running from the trees on the east to those on the west. It is only a yard deep, but is filled with sharpened stakes protruding a third of a yard from the base of the trench. Little more than a yard behind the first trench is a second, and deeper trench, also staked, but covered with branches and leaves and then with road clay where the road would have been and grass from the shoulders to the trees. The earth dug from the trenches is piled and packed behind the barricade, more than a yard high. South of the barricade, exactly one hundred yards out, the upper limbs have been stripped from the road side of two tall trees, one east of the road, and one west.

Even though the evening meal is more cold ghano-acorn hash, Lerial is glad for it. He also has no trouble falling asleep.

He is more than surprised not to be awakened early on threeday, although he does wake before sunrise. He washes up from a bucket of water . . . and wishes he could shave. He and second company eat quickly and are making ready when Altyrn strolls from somewhere.

"There's not that much hurry. They're still a kay and a half away, and they're still breaking camp. They've sent scouts this way, and that's suggesting that they'll march on Nevnarnia. If they do, you're to follow the battle plan we went over last night. Second and fifth company will form up about fifty yards back of the barricade. Once the Meroweyans are in range, you're to start shooting the fire arrows into them . . ."

Lerial understands the reason for fire arrows. They don't require the iron heads of war arrows, but the flame can cause damage and often can spook mounts.

". . . there's still always the possibility that the Meroweyans will decide not to attack, but continue on the main road, looking for a back lane to take you from the rear. If that happens, I'll send a messenger with a wayguide who will show you the other lane that will allow you to rejoin the other companies. There will be more than enough time if they try that. We have a few more surprises if they head that way. We'll have other surprises if they don't." With that, Altyrn turns and heads in the direction of fifth company.

Lerial can't help but wonder if his father knows that the majer would be forced to fight a war in the Verd . . . or if he even thought it would come to an all-out fight. Was that why he picked the majer? But then, if he'd known or suspected that training Verdyn Lancers would cause a fight, why would he have said what he did to Lerial, and Lerial had known his father had not been either lying or withholding information. Besides, Casseon had to have made plans before Lerial's father had even decided to send Altyrn and the two squads of Mirror Lancers. Or was the majer supposed to have withdrawn once he knew the Meroweyans were sending so large a force?

The more Lerial experiences in dealing with the majer and the Meroweyans, the more questions he has. He has only pondered matters for a few moments before Altyrn returns.

"Any last questions?"

"No, ser." Lerial thinks he probably should, but he can't think of any.

"You know where to meet us?"

Lerial nods. "Five kays farther northeast on the main road, just past the bridge over the deep creek."

"Good. Do what you can, but save yourself and your rankers."

Lerial watches for a moment as Altyrn rides north and into the hamlet on his way back to the main road by the less direct route. Once the majer is out of sight, Lerial crosses the road to the area where fifth company has loosely formed up. Shaskyn steps forward to meet Lerial. "How do you want to handle this, ser?"

"Follow the majer's orders. Wait until they get well within range, maybe with the lead elements as close as a hundred or a hundred and fifty yards, and then let loose with the fire arrows." Lerial pauses, then adds, "It might be best if one company loosed the first volley, and then the other, and not too quickly, so that they feel like they're under a constant attack."

"Some archers ought to aim toward the rear, too," suggests Shaskyn. "Might stir 'em up."

Lerial nods. "Detail maybe five archers to do that."

The two spend another tenth of a glass working out their plans for the attack . . . and the withdrawal. When Lerial crosses the road to the side held by second company, he finds his four squad leaders waiting, all clearly interested in what the majer had imparted and what Lerial and Shaskyn had decided.

"The simple order from the majer is to inflict as many casualties on the Meroweyans as possible while trying to avoid taking any casualties ourselves. They're a good kay away and taking their time . . ." Lerial goes on to explain.

As he and second company wait for the Meroweyans to approach, Lerial tries order-sensing, and finds that he can now sense people and objects with some clarity for up to a hundred yards or so, a great improvement over what he could do a day earlier, but far from his abilities prior to his being stunned. He also studies the sky, although there is little enough to see, given that there are no clouds and there is only a slight warmish breeze out of the north.

A glass passes . . . and then another half glass . . . before one of the rankers posted in a tall tree calls out, "Riders coming!" A moment later, he adds, "Shieldmen behind them!"

Lerial walks to the gelding and mounts, not because he believes that battle is imminent, but because from horseback he can see over the road barriers. He rides into the middle of the road, where he is joined by Shaskyn. At first, all Lerial can make out are the outriders and scouts, but before long he can see the shields of the front line of the main body, filling the road and the shoulder almost from the trees on one side to those on the other.

"Second company! Form up!"

"Fifth company! Form up!"

All the archers and Lancers are in formation and mounted in a matter of moments. While that reduces the range of the archers, and the speed with which they can strike flame to the fire arrows, Lerial wants to be able to withdraw nearly instantly.

By now, the shieldmen are less than four hundred yards away, Lerial estimates, and the Meroweyan column continues northward at a measured pace.

When the leading shieldmen near a point that Lerial knows is two hundred yards from the barricade, at least two companies of foot armsmen fan out from the rear of the Meroweyan formation and trot into the woods on both sides of the road, obviously determined to make their way around the barricade in order to make flank attacks from both sides. That will likely be more difficult than they anticipate, Lerial hopes, since the armsmen struggling through the underbrush will find thousands of sharpened sticks here and there, barely protruding from the ground and concealed by leaves or hidden in shallow depressions, and often smeared with offal or anything else that might cause a wound to fester.

You'll still have to watch your flanks closely. Some will get around if the attack slows.

"Second company! Bows ready!"

"Bows ready!" echo the squad leaders.

There is something about the vibrations in the air and ground . . . and Lerial realizes that all the Meroweyan foot are marching in time.

Just before the shieldwall reaches the point between the two marked trees, Lerial orders, "Second company! Strike and light!" He waits until he is certain that all the fire arrows are ready, then orders, "First volley! Fire! Strike and light!"

More than four score flaming shafts arch over the barricade and drop down behind the shield wall into the massed foot. Lerial can see no change. The Meroweyans keep marching.

"Second volley! Fire!"

Now it is fifth company's turn, and Lerial watches as Shaskyn's rankers release their two volleys. He can also see Meroweyan armsmen trying to beat out flames here and there, but the foot are so close together that it would be difficult for an individual to break and flee.

"Second company! Strike and light!" Lerial waits only until most arrows are lit before ordering, "Third volley! Fire! Strike and light!"

Even before the fire arrows from that volley are sheeting down into the Meroweyan forces, a chaos-bolt arches from farther back in the attacking force and flares into the middle of the barricade, where vines, sticks, and even a post go up in flames . . . but the hole is little more than two yards wide.

"Fourth volley! Fire! Strike and light!" Lerial can see that the fire arrows are beginning to disrupt and slow the attackers on foot, and there is jostling and even some gaps in the formation.

Two more firebolts sail over the front ranks of the attackers, now little more than fifty yards from the barricade, and burn another set of openings in the barricade, but three gaps in over a hundred yards are not nearly enough to allow the Meroweyan advance to continue, not at more than a crawl.

The next set of fire-arrow volleys from fifth company sheet into the massed armsmen, and a horn signal sounds. The advance halts.

Two more firebolts flare into the barricade, and then another two, and then two more . . . and another two. The last pair are decidedly weaker, but most of the barricade that had barred the road itself has vanished.

Another horn signal sounds, and the shieldmen surge forward, pushing through the ashen remains of the barricade and past the few remaining untouched sections, and Lerial sees that they all wear uniforms of a dull golden brown. Almost in a detached fashion, he also realizes that until that moment, he has never actually seen any of the Meroweyans that close, not in daylight and close enough to see the color of their uniforms.

Some of the shieldmen try to use their shields and belt knives to make their way through the places not burned away, but quickly give up and move toward the openings blasted by the firebolts, and all of them slow, some stumbling, when they come up against the packed earth behind it. Many lose their footing in trying to climb over, not seeing the staked ditch immediately beyond the earth, and plunge into the ditch.

A horn call follows, and the advance stops.

Someone issues a command and the shieldmen begin to use their shields to flatten the ditch stakes in the middle of the road.

"Second company! Strike and light!" Lerial orders. "Direct fire at the shieldmen!"

The hardened wood-tipped arrows and their flaming heads will not do nearly so much damage as war arrows, but they will wound and disable some.

Lerial nods as he sees that Shaskyn has ordered the same, then orders, "Strike and light! Fire at will!"

More flaming arrows fly toward the struggling shieldmen, but Lerial can see that they will soon have a pathway of dirt and shields over the first ditch. He also sees the massed foot clearing the remnants of the barricade, and several shieldmen are breaking down the low earthen wall behind where the others are building up a way across the two-yard-wide staked ditch.

That means horsemen!

Lerial looks across to Shaskyn. "Fifth company! Withdraw! Now!" Then he watches as Shaskyn's squads cease shooting and begin to withdraw.

"Second company! Strike and light! Last volley! Fire!" Lerial checks to make sure that all the fifth company squads are clear and headed north before he orders, "Second company! Stow bows! Turn and withdraw! Turn and withdraw! Deliberate speed!"

Even as he issues the command, he can see horsemen in brown uniforms surging up the road.

"Withdraw now!"

Second company needs no further urging, but Lerial hangs back to make certain all his rankers are accounted for. He takes a quick look south, but it is hard to tell what the toll may have been on the lead elements of the

Meroweyan force. Finally, as fourth squad canters past him to the north, Lerial swings in behind them, but he keeps looking back over his shoulder, watching as the Meroweyan horsemen ride down the middle of the road, then narrow to single file through the barricade and over the open ditch—only to have the first two plunge into the second covered ditch.

If only we had more war arrows. But they don't. *We don't have enough of anything.*

Lerial keeps checking over his shoulder, but the Meroweyan advance has slowed, not quite come to a halt—and even if it had, it would have been a very temporary one, Lerial knows.

By the time he reaches the turn to the eastern lane, he sees uniformed riders moving forward once more, and several carry burning torches.

Should you have stayed and tried to remove more of them?

Much as he knows what will happen to Nevnarnia, once the Meroweyans have gotten through the barrier and over the ditches with any force, second company would have still had to withdraw—*retreat*—or take terrible casualties in blade-to-blade fighting. *And it wouldn't have done anything to stop them.*

As he rides up the eastern lane to the north and east road back to the main road, Lerial looks at all the dwellings—all shuttered and empty. At least, he hopes they are empty. Then he rides forward to the front of second company. He cannot help but wonder what will happen to the older couple whose argument he had overheard the day before. Will they perish as well in the flames that will sweep through Nevnarnia? Or die shooting arrows at overwhelming Meroweyan forces? Or will they escape into the woods, pursued by flames or angry Meroweyans?

LXVI

Lerial keeps a close watch on the main road behind second company as they ride northeast toward the meeting point described by Altyrn, especially since he does not recall the creek or the bridge mentioned by the majer. *Shouldn't you?* His first thought is that there is no reason he should, since it had been almost a season ago and since, until today, he has only ridden this section of road that one time. Yet he suspects that Altyrn remembers all aspects of a road after riding it just once. Does his father? Or Lephi? About their recollections, Lerial has his doubts.

All he can do now is try to keep track of the distance they cover, but in the end it does not matter—*this time*—because once they pass over a bridge after what he thinks have been five kays, he sees that fifth company has already reined up several hundred yards past the bridge, and that Shaskyn is talking to a squad leader. He halts second company and rides forward to join the other two.

"Captain," offers the squad leader, "Majer Altyrn sent me to lead the way to Ironwood." The young Verdyn Lancer grins. "It's not hard to find. Three more kays on the right side of the road."

"Do you know what happened with the majer's company this morning?"

"No, ser. Not really."

That doesn't sound all that promising to Lerial. "And the majer?"

"He's in Ironwood, ser, with first and fourth company. We got there around midday."

"How is Undercaptain Kusyl?"

"He's there with the majer, ser."

Since Lerial can see that the ranker doesn't want to say more, he nods and says, "Lead on. We'll follow behind fifth company."

Lerial cannot help but worry about what may have happened to the two companies that Altyrn used for his attack on the Meroweyans. *But if Altyrn and Kusyl are in Ironwood . . .* All he can do is wait.

The road is completely empty except for the Lancers, although Lerial can see cart and wagon ruts, and signs of heavy traffic—something he has not seen on the roads of the Verd before. There is also a continuing acridity in the air, although Lerial has no idea whether that is a remnant of earlier burning caused by the Meroweyan wizards, the result of more recent wizard-caused fires, or both.

Slightly more than a glass later, the column turns onto a side road. Ahead about two hundred yards are a set of stone posts, one on each shoulder. Lerial has barely passed the stone posts flanking the road, on one of which is chiseled the word "Ironwood," when a ranker rides up.

"Captain, ser, the majer sent me to show you your company's quarters."

Quarters? Since when do we get quarters? "Lead the way."

"Yes, ser."

The road continues through the woods for another four hundred yards or so before the trees thin, and a score of yards past that point it splits into four lanes. The ranker takes the westernmost lane. Lerial can see that Ironwood is laid out in similar fashion to Nevnarnia, except that the dwellings and structures are located along four lanes, rather than three, and the plank siding of all of the buildings has been stained with a gray oil. As in Nevnarnia, the few dwellings Lerial can glimpse on the more easterly lanes are shuttered. When they turn onto the western lane proper, the buildings are unshuttered, and he sees mounts on tie-lines. The dwellings appear to be occupied, or are being prepared to be occupied, by the Verdyn Lancers.

Halfway down the lane, fifth company moves off to the side, and the ranker rides back to Lerial. "The majer says that your company is assigned the next four dwellings—the ones starting after the covered ditch. The fifth one is for him and you and the other officers."

Once the ranker leaves, Lerial assigns the squads to their respective dwellings and stresses that they are to treat them with care—the Meroweyans might burn them, but his rankers aren't going to damage them. Only after he is satisfied does he lead his gelding to the dwelling serving as the officers' quarters. After unsaddling and grooming the gelding, and tying him securely to a brass ring on a stone post, with enough rope to let him graze on what grass there is, Lerial carries his gear into the dwelling. He finds Altyrn there in the main chamber with his maps. He glances around, noting that there are no small items in the chamber, and no furnishings that he would call fine . . . or costly.

"Good afternoon, Majer."

"Good afternoon, Lerial. What do you have to report?"

"We followed your orders. We used almost all the fire arrows, and between us and the barricade and the ditches, they might have lost half a company, possibly more. They reacted better than I thought. The white wizards burned gaps in the barricade and after they lost half a score of shieldmen, someone ordered the others to use their shields to flatten the stakes and then scoop the earth with shields and pile the shields and dirt up to allow the horsemen through. The second ditch took down five or so, maybe more. They sent two companies through the woods, but I couldn't tell what happened there . . ." When Lerial finishes, he immediately asks, "Might I ask what happened with your attack?"

"We had similar results," Altyrn says, his eyes straying to the map on the small table behind which he is seated. "We took casualties, though. How is your ability to handle order?"

"It's returning, but I can only sense things for a hundred yards or so."

"Let's hope you improve more in the next day or so."

"What happened here, ser? What about the people?"

"Everyone's left," says Altyrn. "By the order of the High Council."

"Left? The Meroweyans are a day away."

"The people know what will happen. Word has spread faster than the fire."

"They hadn't even gotten around to burning Nevnarnia when we left," replies Lerial.

"We're fighting in more than one place. I had to send Juist and Denieryn farther west. The part of the Meroweyan force that split off there has already burned two hamlets, and they're advancing on Truyver. It's good-sized town as Verdheln towns go. The people there will fight. Not well, most likely, but well enough, with Juist to guide them, to whittle away a few more companies."

"What about us? What do you have planned for tomorrow?"

"If the Meroweyans stay in Nevnarnia for a day or two, we'll wait and prepare for their attack here. The local people will harass them from the woods. If they move out tomorrow, then we'll withdraw."

"Because we're short on war arrows, fire arrows, and oil?"

"Short?" Altyrn snorts. "First and fourth company don't have any of those, not to speak of. I've got some who have experience as fletchers working on something that might pass for fire arrows. Local youths are bringing in spent arrows and arrowheads. The elders have promised more oil by late tomorrow . . ."

Lerial also understands what Altyrn is not saying—that hand-to-hand fighting with sabres is unwise against an enemy that outnumbers them seven to one . . . although it might only be close to five to one by now.

"They've also promised more shovels and mattocks." Altyrn looks down at his maps.

"If you need anything from me, ser, just let me know."

"I will."

Lerial finds a bedroom and leaves the bed for the majer, while creating a makeshift bed for himself against one wall. Then he goes back to second company and takes inventory of all the weapons, discovering that his archers have only one or two war arrows each, and only a handful of fire arrows, and no oil. The three Lancer squads have less than a score of shafts among them. Unlike Altyrn's company, none of Lerial's rankers have any real experience in crafting shafts or fletching them.

There is a hot meal, of sorts, that night, something with the consistency of stew and the various items sliced as if they had been meant for a casserole, but what they might have been, other than some sort of meat, cheese, and root vegetables, Lerial cannot tell. It doesn't matter. He eats it all.

After he finishes, he makes his way back to the dwelling serving as officers' quarters, where he finds Altyrn in the main room. The leather map case is folded closed, and there is a small fire in the blackened hearth.

"Did you eat, ser?"

"I did."

Lerial can sense the truth of that and says, "Good. If you don't mind my saying it, I do worry about you."

"I appreciate that."

Lerial eases himself into a rickety straight-backed chair and waits.

After a time, Altyrn does speak. "In one of the old books—I wish so many had not been lost in the fall of Cyad . . . One of the greatest privileges of being the head of the Palace Guard was the ability to borrow books from the Malachite Library. I learned so much there." Altyrn shakes his head. "What was I saying? Oh . . . about Lorn and Alyiakal. One book said that even when Lorn was old and looked feeble that his technique with either blade or order and chaos was so superb that no one dared stand against him. He was so able that he could use the strength of his opponents against them. There were similar words about Alyiakal. So many, especially the young, believe strength and power are everything. Some strength and power are necessary for success, but technique makes the difference. Technique is not just important. In the end, it is what decides what will be." A wry smile crosses his face, and he adds, "If you have the weapons and the men." He pauses briefly. "I'm going to take a walk. I'll be back later." With that, Altyrn rises and leaves.

Lerial sits for a time, thinking, but the majer's words continue to ring in his ears. If Altyrn is right, then Lerial should be able to improve his technique with order so that he can handle much stronger chaos mages. *Should? Not if you don't work on it.* He looks into the fire burning in the hearth. *How fine a line of order can you formulate?* He pauses, recalling that he had experienced one other problem. *And how fast can you do it well?*

After several moments, with a sigh, he stands and goes outside to the woodpile, where he looks for the greenest wood. He finally selects three modest lengths that look and feel less seasoned, both to his eyes and order-senses, and carries them back into the dwelling, where he eases them onto the hot coals, then steps back. He hopes what he has planned will work.

After several moments there is a spark, but Lerial cannot even see it, much less sense it.

He concentrates more intently, and by the time several more sparks have popped, he is able to find them quickly, but it takes almost a third of a glass before he is able to find each instantly.

Next comes making a pattern quickly to trap them.

More than a glass later, Lerial feels exhausted, but he is finally managing to catch each spark—a tiny bit of flame and chaos—within a tiny "cage" of order.

The door opens, and Lerial turns to see Shaskyn and Kusyl enter.

"What are you doing?" asks Kusyl.

"Practicing technique," replies Lerial blandly. "What have you been doing?"

"Scrounging through the dwellings, trying to find weapons."

Lerial should have thought of that, he realizes. "Did you?"

"Not a one," admits Shaskyn.

With that admission, Lerial feels somewhat less guilty. Somewhat.

"Technique?" presses Kusyl.

"For trying to divert those chaos-bolts. Fire is sort of like chaos . . . and it's less dangerous to try new things with fire."

"I can see that. I think." Kusyl nods. "I wish you well. I'm turning in."

"Me, too," adds Shaskyn.

Once they have left the main room, Lerial goes out to the woodpile, where he gathers more green wood, then returns to the fire and adds another two lengths of what he has brought in. For all of his resolve, after but a few more attempts, his eyes are blurring, and he knows he can do no more. He just watches the fire until it burns down more and he can safely bank it.

Then he heads for his bed, such as it is, and discovers that Altyrn is already asleep. *You never even heard him come back in.*

Before long, he, too, is asleep.

LXVII

Lerial wakes early on fourday with his eyes burning and their corners filled with sleep encrustations. The still air in the bedroom holds the acridity of wood smoke. Because Altryn is still asleep, snoring lightly, Lerial eases out of the small bedroom, carrying his boots and personal gear, and into the main chamber of the dwelling, where he finishes dressing as quietly as possible. Then he makes his way outside. The entire sky is hazy and reddish to the east, where the sun lurks below the horizon. To the west, the smoky haze is far thicker, and Lerial wonders just how much of the Verd has burned . . . or is still in flames.

He sees smoke coming from the chimney of the dwelling being used as the kitchen for second and fifth companies, and he catches a whiff of something being baked or cooked, but that odor is largely overwhelmed by that of wood smoke.

"Good morning, ser."

Lerial turns to see Alaynara, the head archer of fourth squad, standing at the corner of the dwelling. "Good morning. How are your archers?"

"They're fine. We don't have any shafts. Not many, anyway." She tosses her head slightly, not enough to move her short reddish brown hair.

Lerial answers the unspoken question. "We're supposed to get more this afternoon. It's not likely we'll fight today." He pauses, then says lightly, "I'm not promising."

Alaynara's distant expression softens. "You weren't allowed to be a child long, were you, ser?"

The question takes Lerial so aback that he does not answer for a moment. "I suppose not. What matters now . . ." He struggles for a moment. "What matters now is that others will have a chance to be children when they should be."

Abruptly, Alaynara looks away. "I'm sorry, ser. I didn't mean . . ."

"No offense was meant, and I didn't take any." He manages a smile. "If you and your archers can find any more arrows or anything else that will stop Meroweyans, I'd be obliged if you'd let me know."

"We've been looking. We've found a few shafts that might do in a pinch."

"Good."

"Thank you, ser." She takes a step back, then turns.

Lerial watches as she walks north, most likely toward the dwelling that holds the archers, wondering what prompted her question. *That you look so young for what you're doing?* He isn't about to ask. That might invite a familiarity he cannot afford.

For some reason, her question raises an entire series of questions—those he has not thought about for a time. What is Lephi doing? Is he riding routine patrols or are the Mirror Lancers in the southeast of the duchy fighting pitched battles with the Heldyans? Or do the feint-and-pursue skirmishes continue? Is his father still spending most of his time in the north, keeping the Afritans from sacking Penecca? Have the Afritan forces backed off? Or have they begun full-scale attacks? And how are Emerya, Amaira, and Ryalah faring?

This far from Cigoerne, how will you ever know?

He takes a deep breath, knowing he will get no answers, not soon, and perhaps not for seasons, if it is that long before he can return to Cigoerne.

After mentally going over what he should do, Lerial checks with his squad leaders, eats quickly, and then walks along the lane, testing his order-senses. He is relieved to discover that he can discern objects and individuals almost a kay away. *You might have most of your skill back by tomorrow.* Except he'd been able to sense more than three kays before being felled. *Or in a few days . . . maybe.* He also knows that the Meroweyans aren't likely to stop attacking while he recovers.

He tries to think about weapons . . . and ponders whether they might try making spears or javelins. There is certainly enough wood around. Finally, he returns to Altyrn who is back at his table in the dwelling.

"Ser, I've been thinking . . . What about spears or javelins?"

Altyrn looks up from the square of paper on which he has been sketching a map or battle plan of some sort. "That's a good idea. I've had some of the men working on that . . . and on some old-style spear-throwers. I thought about lead spear points, but the Verdyn don't use lead. They say it's a poison. So we'll have to do with sharpened tips." The majer grins. "Don't look so discouraged. I do have a little experience. In fact, I should have thought of throwing spears earlier, but we've been so used to lances it didn't occur to me. We also weren't expecting an army of four thousand men."

Lerial is glad that the majer used the word "we," but he still feels stupid. What else should he have thought of . . . and hasn't?

"If you or your squad leaders or rankers have any other ideas, please let me know." Altyrn shakes his head. "I'm about out of ideas."

"Yes, ser." Lerial understands what Altyrn hasn't said—that any "new" weapons need to be the kind that they can use from a distance because they don't have rankers to spare. He leaves the majer to his battle plan, if that is what it is.

Lerial meets once more with all his squad leaders and asks for their thoughts on weapons or traps that they can make easily that won't take excessive effort and will be effective.

"Slings, maybe, ser," suggests Bhurl, but before Lerial can reply, the squad leader shakes his head. "They're effective, but it takes time to learn how to do it . . . and you need the right kind of stones, too."

Fhentaar and Korlyn each mention javelins, and Moraris just shakes his head, and says, "The farther a weapon reaches, the more time it takes to make it."

"And usually the more iron," replies Lerial.

Less than a half glass later, just before eighth glass, he is still thinking the matter over when he notices that the majer, accompanied by a squad from first company, rides out. *Scouting for another battle site?*

Over the course of the late morning and midday, the smoke and acrid odor from the west abate somewhat, but the sky remains hazy in all directions, most likely because the air barely moves, with only an occasional light breeze from the north that quickly dies away.

Lerial goes back to the fire in the dwelling, practicing variations in catching and diverting chaos-fire, and trying to do so according to the precepts of his aunt Emerya. He has to admit that he feels less tired working that way, but it takes more concentration, especially at first. After more than a glass, he leaves the fire and walks outside. He is still standing there when Altyrn rides back up and dismounts.

"Where are we fighting next, ser?" ventures Lerial.

"If we get the choice . . . if we do, there's a bridge over a fairly deep stream some three kays east of here. If we remove the bridge we could make it hard for them to cross."

"If we get more arrows."

"There are two wagons on their way. We passed them coming back."

"Do you know how many arrows?"

"Enough for ten to fifteen shafts for each ranker. Just for the companies here. That's a rough estimate. Some of the heads are a bit battered, and they might not fly true, but . . . there are a lot of Meroweyans."

After a time, Lerial leaves Altyrn and walks south along the lane, thinking . . . and trying to sense both the order and chaos around him. When he finally turns back, it is likely close to fourth glass, and he believes his order-chaos discernment is sharper. As he nears the dwelling serving as officers' quarters he sees that Altyrn is sitting on the narrow front porch, talking to Kusyl.

The majer gestures for Lerial to join them. "I hoped you'd be back before long. Practicing again?"

Lerial nods.

"You were earlier, too. I could tell. That main room is like an oven." Altyrn smiles. "That's why we're out here."

"Ser . . . ," ventures Kusyl. "There's a ranker. He's got a messenger sash."

Lerial turns and watches as the rider slows and asks something of a group of rankers sitting in the shade. One of the rankers points southward toward the three officers on the porch.

The messenger urges his mount forward. When he reaches the dwelling, he rides right up to the porch and dismounts, hurrying to Altyrn. His brown uniform is dusty, his eyes reddish and twitching, and his voice hoarse as he says, "Dispatch from Undercaptain Juist, ser. He said it was urgent."

"Thank you. When did you leave him . . . and where?"

"The east side of Truyver, ser. Eighth glass last night. I took two mounts. Had to come the long way."

"If you'd stand by."

"Yes, ser."

Altyrn reads the short dispatch quickly. "Juist and Denieryn have pulled back. Juist reports that they each lost close to a squad. The locals did everything they could. Some flung crocks of burning oil, and they put pit traps everywhere. Juist thinks they wounded or killed more than three companies of Meroweyans. The Meroweyans killed scores of men, women, and even some youths. They bombarded Truyver with firebolts. The entire town and much of the surrounding forest are in flames." He hands the sheet to Lerial. "Read it. Did I miss anything?"

Lerial scans the short sentences, then starts to hand the dispatch to Kusyl. The former squad leader shakes his head, and Lerial realizes that one of the reasons that the man was likely never promoted to undercaptain was that he cannot read or write—or not well. Lerial hands the paper back to the majer. "You said everything that he wrote."

The majer turns to the messenger. "Tell me what you saw, if you would."

"Ser . . . ?"

"What you saw. The undercaptain only wrote what happened. We need to hear what you saw and went through."

"Ser . . . we had trenches . . . good trenches . . . the Meroweyans threw firebolts . . . but the fire didn't touch us. Our archers, they shot over the heads of the shields . . . into the men on foot. We ran out of shafts, and the shields came for us, and some of them got caught in the staked ditch. Their own wizards . . . they dropped fireballs into the ditch . . . killed some of their own to burn away the stakes . . . and then they charged. We pulled back and mounted . . . and the people they threw oil down on the attackers . . . that's when they got to the center of town . . . the undercaptains had us charge one flank . . . They weren't expecting it . . . we killed some . . . then there was fire everywhere. That's what I saw . . . and there was this boy . . . and he was running, and he was all fire . . . and there were others . . . my mate, Fheric, there was a firebolt overhead, and it exploded and part of it went through his chest . . ."

Lerial swallows quietly and listens until the messenger finishes.

"Thank you," Altyrn says quietly. "Just take care of your mount. Then go lie down in the main room. There's water inside. We'll wake you when it's time for mess."

"Thank you, ser. You sure, ser?"

"I'm very sure. You did well to get this here. There's nothing else you need to do for now . . . except to get some rest."

"Yes, ser. Thank you, ser."

Once the messenger makes his way into the dwelling, Altyrn takes the dispatch, folds it, and slips it into the leather map folder, then looks to Kusyl. "Get Shaskyn. We need to go over the plan for tomorrow. Whenever they come, we're likely to face firebolts first, rather than later."

Will you be able to handle them? Any of them? Lerial doesn't know. He can only hope.

LXVIII

Fiveday morning finds Lerial and second company packing up once more and readying for another ride, another tactical withdrawal, in the majer's words. When Lerial is certain his squads are ready, he rides over to join the other company commanders, just in time to hear Shaskyn speak.

"We're . . . just leaving, ser?" asks the fifth company acting undercaptain. "Now, ser, when . . . ?"

"There's nothing we can do here," replies Altyrn. "There are no defensible positions, and we're outnumbered. It's better to spend the time to prepare our next line of defense."

"Seems a shame," murmurs Shaskyn.

Kusyl nods, but adds, "We didn't start this."

"Starting a war is always a bad idea," replies Altyrn, "assuming you can ever figure out who really did."

Puzzled expressions cross the faces of both Kusyl and Shaskyn, and for a moment, Lerial doesn't understand. Then he does, and he nods.

In less than a third of a glass, second company is moving out, if slowly, because Altyrn has assigned Lerial as rearguard. The road, as before, is empty except for Altyrn's forces, but there are enough fresh ruts and tracks to indicate that quite a few of the local people have fled, although Lerial suspects there may be many who live deeper in the woods and who are gambling that the Meroweyans will stay fairly close to the main road to Verdell. Lerial doesn't doubt that, but he does think it will only be a matter of time before the fires set by the invaders will get out of control—if they haven't already in the west where Juist and Denieryn are fighting. When that happens the fire will do to those who are in its path what the Meroweyans haven't.

Lerial also briefly ponders why the Meroweyans have not set more fires after razing Nevnarnia and Truyver. He shakes his head when he realizes that those advancing toward Verdell don't want to end up being trapped by any fire they set, and that they would have to answer to Duke Casseon if they fired every hamlet and town because that would destroy much of the reason for even occupying the Verd. In addition, it is clear that the Meroweyans have waited to march on Ironwood until the fires set at Nevnarnia have died away . . . or been damped down by the elders.

Once everyone is on the main road, the ride from Ironwood to the creek takes little more than a glass.

The bridge is constructed of heavy timbers that join two mortar and stone bases set into the bank on each side. It is wide enough only for a single large wagon, or two horses abreast, but does have sturdy timber posts and railings on each side. The stream is modest, no more than six or seven yards across the water itself, and as Lerial rides across he looks down. The water is clear enough, but he can only see little more than a yard down, suggesting it is deep enough that crossing would be harder than it first appears. He also notices that there are no trees near either bank, although there are more than a few stumps, and all of the stumps are small.

They cut back the trees often, every year possibly. Why? Lerial cannot conceive of what benefit that might convey, but he is certain that there must be one, because it is clear that the people of the Verd do nothing on whim or without a purpose that has been well considered.

Once all the companies are on the east side of the stream, Altyrn immediately sets fifth company to removing the bridge timbers. At Shaskyn's look of questioning, he laughs softly and says, "You're wondering about what will happen if the Meroweyans don't come this way? Then they'll have to go through the woods, and they'll suffer losses there from the Verdyn . . . and they'll still have to face us, but they'll have fewer armsmen. If they don't come at all, then they will have left to return to Yakaat or wherever, or they will find they have to before long. But they're too stubborn and too convinced that they will triumph. They'll be here, possibly tomorrow, probably by sevenday, and certainly by eightday."

"Yes, ser." Shaskyn moves off.

Altyrn turns to Lerial. "You and your company . . . I need you to dig trenches and revetments at the top of the bank. Make the trenches about a yard and a third deep and wide enough for two rankers to pass each other easily. That should give archers enough space. Pile the spoil into a revetment on the stream side of the trench. There should be enough shovels and mattocks in the second wagon."

"How far do you want the trenches to go?"

"Start in the middle of the road and dig out. The farther the better."

As Lerial turns to set his rankers to work, he cannot help but hear what the majer says to Kusyl.

"Once we have enough timbers from the bridge you use some of your men and mounts to drag them south one by one . . . so we'll have a ford there . . . and a surprise . . ."

Lerial wonders what sort of surprise Altyrn has in mind, but smiles wryly, knowing that, whatever it is, it will not be pleasant for the Meroweyans. In the meantime, second company has to dig trenches and build up revetments, both to steepen the bank to make climbing it harder for any possible attackers and to provide greater protection against firebolts.

LXIX

The Meroweyans do not attack on sixday, but smoke rising in lines just to the southwest by late afternoon shows that they have occupied Ironwood. When the lines of smoke are still rising at eighth glass on sevenday, Lerial knows that the earliest an attack will come is on eightday, and that is fine with him, given that his order-sensing is finally at least as strong as it had been before his last encounter with the chaos mages.

He puts some of the Lancers to work extending and strengthening the ends of the trenches, and he watches for a time as Altyrn works with a handful of Lancers, showing them how to use the few spear-throwers that first company has made. *You wouldn't know where to start in making one of those.* After a moment, his next thought is *But you can divert some chaos-bolts, and that's even more important.* But is it? What Altyrn has done improves the strength of at least an entire squad.

Later that morning, Altyrn inspects the trenches and revetments. When he is finished, he turns to Lerial. "They've done a very good job here."

"Thank you, ser. I just applied what someone taught me about trenches." Lerial grins.

The majer grins back. "I told you no knowledge was ever useless."

"Yes, ser. Still, ser . . . when they see all these revetments, won't they just march upstream or downstream to find an easier place to cross?"

"I'm most certain that they will, and there's a place a kay south that looks perfect."

"That's where you had the timbers dragged," Lerial recalls.

"Exactly. The stream widens and is only a little more than a yard and a half deep, if almost ten yards wide. That part is almost fifty yards long, and the banks are less steep there." Altyrn pauses. "There's also an underground spring or stream that enters there, and the muddy and sandy bottom . . . well, the locals call it the bottomless sink. Scores once died there . . . or so the locals claim. At the very least, it ought to leave a lot of Meroweyans stuck or struggling there like grounded geese. I've had fifth company make tracks to and from the water on both sides as if that's where we've been crossing since removing the bridge. We've also piled up the bridge timbers on the east side to form a revetment to block the only place where the stream bank is low." The majer shrugs. "If they're smart, they'll just have their mages topple three or four tall trees here, and then swing them over the stream and send a slew of armsmen across. That would do the job . . . but it would likely cost them another company, maybe more. They'll attack both places . . . and maybe try to cross farther north, even if the forest is thicker there. I've had some of fourth company staking the stream bank to the north . . . just within a yard or two of the water, and there are some locals with bows up there."

"You're giving ground and making them pay for it with troopers . . . until they have no more left."

"That's the idea. Whether it will work . . ." Altyrn shakes his head. "Second company is closer to full strength than any other company, and you're down to four score or a little less, including you and the squad leaders. In rough terms, we've lost somewhere between a company and a half and two companies. They've lost more than ten. That leaves around thirty, twenty-five at the least. We're still outnumbered five to one."

"As opposed to seven to one when they arrived," Lerial points out. "But we have to do better."

Altyrn nods. "They'll have scouts near here within a glass, if they haven't staked us out already."

For all that the majer has said, Lerial cannot sense or see any bodies of men on the west side of the stream whose name he does not know. Nor does he sense more than one or two over the course of sevenday, but those two are mounted, and likely scouts, although they never approach to closer than a hundred yards. They are good enough that even when Lerial looks right where his order-senses tell him they are, he still cannot see them. That worries him . . . a great deal. In time, one of the scouts moves south, and the other north . . . and another appears, if somewhat farther south and just out of sight . . . or where he would be out of sight if Lerial could even see him.

The scout moving north concerns Lerial, although fifth company flanks second, but that thought brings to mind his worries about his own fourth squad. He doesn't feel solid about putting the archers either directly opposite the road or at the northernmost company position in the trenches, which is where they are at the moment. So he walks along behind the trenches until he finds Moraris.

"Ser?"

"We need to talk to the head archer." Lerial would prefer to talk just with Alaynara, but that would be going around the squad leader, and could lead to problems he'd just as soon avoid.

"Ser?" questions the squad leader, again.

Lerial understands that, too, but he just smiles. "I want to hear what each of you has to say about where fourth squad should be positioned. She doesn't have your experience, and you've not dealt with archers very long." Lerial pauses just slightly. "If you'd have someone summon her . . ."

Moraris turns slightly. "Haelcyna . . . I need the head archer. Pass the word."

"Yes, squad leader."

Lerial looks at Moraris, thinking once more how the Lancer looks more like a trader, and asks, "Where do you think fourth squad would be most effective?"

"On the flank. Archers aren't trained or armed to repulse a frontal attack."

"That's true." Lerial nods.

Alaynara hurries toward the two, then stops and inclines her head. "Ser, Squad Leader?" Her voice is low and pleasantly polite.

"We'd like your advice," Lerial admits. "If the Meroweyans attack from the road . . . if they do . . . where would be the best place for your archers?"

"Against a shieldwall front? What do you want us to do? For how long?"

Lerial almost blurts out, "Kill as many as possible, of course," but realizes just before he does what she means.

"They'll likely continue with the shieldwall," he begins, although that is merely a calculated guess on his part. "They'll try to shield those who will make the first attempts to cross the stream . . . try to get them as close as possible to the water before exposing them."

Alaynara nods thoughtfully. "We ought to be to the side some, not so much that we can't shoot down the road if necessary, but we'll have a better chance if we have an angle on the column."

"How do you . . . ?" Lerial shakes his head.

"In some ways, it's like hunting. It's hard to hit a red deer head-on. If you do, there's a better chance of bringing him down with a single shaft, but a greater chance of missing if he moves suddenly. In fighting, it's obvious that you want every shaft to count in some way. If you wound more, rather than just kill a few, the fewer that are left to fight."

Lerial can sense grudging agreement from Moraris. "You two have the same general views. The squad leader doesn't think your archers would be used to their best advantage in a head-on confrontation, and you think a slight angle will allow you to cover both the road and the attack. Good. We'll leave first and second squads where they are, but I'll have you and third squad switch positions." He smiles. "Thank you both."

When Lerial turns and leaves to inform Fhentaar of the change, he can sense a certain veiled amusement from Alaynara. Moraris does not seem upset, even possibly relieved that Lerial has not placed fourth squad closer to the bridge abutments.

Lerial continues toward the bridge, or where it had been, wondering when the Meroweyans will attack . . . and how.

LXX

Slightly before seventh glass on eightday morning, Lerial hears regular thudding sounds, but cannot see anything. He even checks the white and gray puffy clouds for lightning and thunder. While there are certainly flows of order that will likely bring rain and lightning later in the day, he senses nothing within the clouds immediately overhead. Scanning the road and the woods with his order-senses, he finally locates three men some hundred yards west of the stream and on the south side of the road. At first, for just a moment, he thinks that they are swinging at a midsized tree with blades, but almost immediately realizes that they are using axes to cut down the tree, which slowly topples. The axemen move to another tree. Lerial studies the area some more and finds that a squad of armsmen is drawn up near the loggers.

With that information, Lerial hurries along the ground behind the trenches, glancing to the east as he hears a mount whinny. He can sense but not see where the Lancer mounts are tied, in the trees adjoining the road, but a good fifty yards from the back of the trenches. He sees Altyrn in the shade just south of the road and behind the earthworks. Lerial also notices Donnael and Ruethana of the elders walking away from the majer.

Lerial glances up at the clouds once more, wondering if Ruethana is a weather mage as well as Donnael . . . and what they may be able to do, if anything, when the Meroweyans attack. A few yards away from Altyrn, he stops and says, "They're chopping down trees, and they have at least an armed squad protecting them. They're staying off the road and out of sight."

"That makes sense. How long before they have enough trees to create a bridge, do you think?"

"They're working fast, but they'll have to trim the trunks as well. At least a glass."

"More like two."

"We could slow them down with arrows," suggests Lerial.

"How many shafts would it take? Could they even get through the brush and trees? If you were successful, how many arrows would it cost us? And to what result?"

Lerial understands. "Yes, ser."

"Let me know what else you find."

"Yes, ser."

Lerial returns to second company and keeps watching. Before long, the three loggers have felled two more trees of the same size. Other men have joined the first three, but the new arrivals work at cutting away limbs and branches, while the three initial loggers move on to another pair of trees.

Somewhere farther to the southwest, Lerial can vaguely sense both riders and a faint chaos mist, a good indication that the Meroweyans have left Ironwood and are approaching on the main road. There is no smoke rising from the woods, suggesting that the attackers have not put the hamlet to the torch. *But then, no one opposed them there.* So far, they have only fired the hamlets and towns where they were opposed. Lerial shakes his head. The Meroweyan force more to the west fired two hamlets. Then he reconsiders. *You don't know if the people there opposed or attacked them.*

He takes a slow deep breath. There is so much he does not know, and he wonders if war is always like this . . . never knowing everything, and sometimes almost nothing about the enemy, and trying to outthink and anticipate what one's enemy might do.

A glass later, the loggers have stopped felling trees. As well as he can determine from order-sensing, they have cut about ten trees, none of them particularly large, but all moderately tall and straight, and all of those around the trees are trimming them. In time, the men begin to move the tree trunks, all cut to the same length, until they are within a few yards of the grass and low brush flanking the road. By now, Lerial can sense the main body far more clearly, although they are still indistinct to his eyes, over a kay to the west on the road. The shadows come and go as the clouds pass over, seemingly closer together and larger as the morning draws on.

There are few woodland sounds, except for the traitor birds, several of whom apparently are taking delight in flying around the loggers in the woods, alighting on branches and offering their irritatingly cheerful and loud chirps. Only one of the traitor birds come near enough to Lerial so that he can see its yellow-banded black wings, but the calls that sound like *twirrpp* are identification enough.

Lerial senses someone approaching from behind, and he turns to see Altyrn walking toward him.

"Two glasses," says Lerial. "You were right. The shieldmen are half a kay down the road, and they've got ten small to moderate tree trunks cut and ready to go."

Altyrn nods. "They'll bring up the shieldmen to give cover to the men who will carry the trunks toward the stream. Your Lancers and archers are not to fire at them. First company will. Unless something changes, you're to target the main body, but not until they attack and I give you the order."

"Yes, ser."

Once the majer leaves, Lerial turns and tells Korlyn, "I need to talk to the head archer. I'll be back in a few moments." Keeping his head low, Lerial hurries northward along the trench until he reaches fourth squad, about thirty yards north of where the bridge had been.

"Squad Leader! Head Archer!" Lerial waits for Moraris and Alaynara to join him, then relays the majer's instructions.

"The main body is out of range," Moraris points out.

"That's right," says Lerial. "If all of second company looses shafts at a handful of men, what will we have left when two thousand of them storm down the road? The Lancers can use their blades on the handful that might get across the stream now."

"Oh . . . yes, sir."

Alaynara nods. "We'll wait for your order to shoot."

Lerial then hurries to Fhentaar, and then back to Bhurl and Korlyn to relay the majer's orders.

Almost another half glass passes before a horn sounds and the shieldmen start forward, advancing until they reach a position just east of where the shaped trunks lie. They halt and raise their shields. Lerial can sense other armsmen coming forward and picking up the first two trunks, more than a half score to each. Even with that many men, the trees have to be pines of some sort. Oak or lorken would be far too heavy.

Once the two teams are in position behind the shieldmen, the shieldwall begins to advance toward the stream, steadily and stolidly. The main Meroweyan force has now moved up, but has halted on the road behind the point where the tree trunks lie, clearly waiting to see if the shieldwall and the armsmen lugging the trunks can create their own bridge.

Before long, the shieldwall closes on the western bank of the stream, less than fifty yards from the bridge abutment, when it edges toward the upstream side of the bridge foundations, and more toward second company, apparently trying to position the armsmen with the trunks so that the logs will be anchored not only into the earth of the stream banks but rest against the foundation on one side.

First company's archers do not even begin to release shafts until the first shieldmen are no more than a score of yards from the bridge abutments—except Lerial suddenly realizes that the shafts are not arrows but javelins hurled from spear-throwers with surprising force, enough in one case for the javelin to go through the upper part of a shield and into the chest of the shieldman. More than a few shieldmen go down, and the shieldwall slows almost to a halt before others step forward, and even more slowly, the shields advance, then stop a good five yards back from the abutments. Those shieldmen in the center swing out, opening the way for those carrying the tree trunk.

The armsmen carrying the first trunk charge full speed toward the stream, but a hail of mixed javelins and arrows takes down enough of them that they lose control of the log and it slips away and skids partway down the bank before burying itself in the softer earth just above the water. Lerial can see that the end of the tree trunk has been hewn into a rough point, and that means that the rankers intend to drive each of the trunks into the eastern riverbank, but he cannot see at first how they had planned to get it over the water—until he realizes that the armsmen at the front were trying to plant the point while those behind, with the help of the ropes tied to the far end would heave it upright and then let it fall forward onto the eastern stream bank. The simplicity of it strikes Lerial, but he also realizes that simplicity rests on the ability to lose armsmen in the process.

Then a second group of armsmen charge forward with their trunk. Although several fall to javelins and arrows, with great effort the end of the log goes up and slowly reaches a point straight up, and then drops, almost not moving, before speeding up enough that the end that had been at the rear comes down with a thump on the eastern bank, perhaps half a yard above the water and a yard and a half back from the edge of the stream proper. The trunk is angled slightly, but not much.

In the meantime, the shieldwall closes behind the Meroweyan armsmen who have carried the logs and survived, but does not withdraw. Behind it, Lerial can see and sense two more groups of armsmen coming forward. He looks at the single long trunk spanning the stream and wonders why Altyrn has not sent anyone to dislodge it, before realizing that if it took more than ten men to carry and raise the trunk, the majer isn't about to risk the number of rankers it would take to move the trunk—if it even could be moved, buried as it is the soft earth of the riverbank.

Although another shieldman falls to a javelin, and two Meroweyan armsmen go down, the third group of armsmen manages to raise the end of the third tree trunk into the air, but it tilts and comes down—hard—on the bridge abutment in front of the trenches of first company, bounces, the end splintering somewhat before it half rolls, half slides, off the abutment and into the stream, where it lies wedged at an angle between the western bank and the stone abutment, where the splintered end is several handspans underwater.

"Captain!" comes a call.

Lerial turns. Altyrn is practically beside him in the trench.

"Pull out second company. Mount up and head north along the east bank. There are at least five companies coming from the north. They must have crossed more than five kays upstream."

That means he had scouts out that far. "You want second company to move north and stop them?"

"You most likely can't stop them. Do your best to slow them and make them take casualties. The elders are here. They may be able to help with the storm."

Help with the storm? Lerial nods, recalling the rains that had slowed the efforts of the Meroweyan wizards in burning through the edge of the Verd.

"Try not to lose to lose too many rankers. Oh . . . and stay a good two yard from the water."

"Yes, ser."

Altyrn gives a brisk nod and heads up the trench in the direction of fifth company. Lerial turns to Korlyn. "You heard the majer. Pull your squad back to the horses and mount up. Send a ranker to pass the order to the other three squads."

"Yes, ser."

As Korlyn turns to pass the orders, Lerial looks back to the stream and is dismayed to see that the Meroweyans have managed to position another trunk across the river, but, thankfully, it is a good yard away from the first one. *Still . . . if they keep doing it, they'll eventually have a bridge of sorts.* He looks up to see that in the narrow clear space directly above him and the river, the clouds have thickened so that he can see almost no patches of clear green blue. Yet he has no sense of additional order or chaos moving in the clouds, only that the patterns of order and chaos that are always within rainstorms are, somehow, more deliberate. *Trying to figure that out or learn how they do that will have to wait.*

Once he is sure that all his squads are complying with the orders and some of fifth company is moving down into the trench area held by second company, Lerial hurries back to where the gelding is tied and mounts up. Then he leads the company through the woods to the north, not coming out onto the clearer area just above the bank until they are a third of a kay north of fifth company. There is no sense in letting the Meroweyans know that the defenses have been weakened. This way, they may just believe that Altyrn has shifted his troopers. Although Lerial can sense the main body of the attackers is still facing Altyrn, that body definitely feels smaller to Lerial's senses, considerably smaller, than it did days earlier, suggesting that the Meroweyans are not only attacking from the north, but also from the south. Lerial just hopes that a great number of those in the south are having difficulty with the ford trap set by Altyrn.

At the rumble of thunder, Lerial glances up, then tries to sense what may be different about the clouds, but can only feel what he might call smoothness in places. *Technique—technique so good that it goes almost unnoticed.*

While he can sense the Meroweyans ahead, he does not call a halt for another half glass, until the attackers are less than a kay ahead. "Second company! Halt!"

"Squad, halt!"

"Squad leaders! Forward!"

Once the four are gathered around him on their mounts, he explains, "Our orders are to slow the Meroweyans. They'll be here shortly. Here's what we'll do. First squad will be forward, on foot with bows. The formation will be two lines, staggered, so that each ranker will have a view of the enemy. Behind them will be second squad. Fourth squad will be third, and third squad last. All squads will be on foot when they're in the front rank. To begin with, first squad and second squad will be on foot." Lerial has learned that being on foot allows greater range and accuracy for an archer, and he wants the greatest accuracy possible. "Fourth squad will hold first squad's mounts, and third squad will hold second squad's mounts." Lerial again looks to Korlyn. "When I give the order, you're to shoot for the men behind the leading armsmen. Shoot deliberately, but quickly. Korlyn, let me know when your men are down to one shaft. Have them each save one shaft. Is that clear?"

"Yes, ser."

"Then you'll withdraw to the rear and mount up, and then each man will take one or two, as necessary, of fourth squad's mounts and take a position behind third squad. Second squad will shoot down to one arrow per man, and then withdraw and hold third squad's mounts. . . ." When Lerial finishes, he asks. "Are there any questions?"

"Ser . . . ah . . . what do we do after third squad withdraws?"

"We withdraw back downstream and take up a position on the flank of fifth company. That's unless the majer has other orders for us by then. Any other questions?"

"No, ser."

"Then go form up."

Lerial watches as they do, hoping this plan will work better than the last one he designed by himself. Then he rides up and stations himself just at the edge of the trees, even with the front line of first squad.

After a short time, Korlyn calls out to Lerial, "Ser . . . the ground's too soft on the lower slope closer."

"What about a five-man front near the top of the bank?"

"I'd say that would be better, ser."

"Go to a five-man front . . . and pass it back to second squad."

"Yes, ser!"

It seems like more than a glass has passed before the Meroweyans come into view, but it is likely only about a third of a glass. While the sky continues to darken, there is no sign of rain. Lerial estimates that there are probably five companies in all, as Altyrn has said, and they extend back close to a hundred yards. Once again, they advance with foot-bearing shields, but these armsmen carry smaller round shields on their left arms and blades that look somewhat longer than sabres.

Shields and blades make sense with the softer and uneven ground. It also may be that they only have so many troopers with heavy shields. In addition, he can sense the faint chaos mist.

Lerial continues to watch as the Meroweyan foot move forward at a measured pace. He is trying to judge at what distance he should have first squad open fire and wonders when the white wizard will loose a fireball. From what he can tell, there is likely only one with the approaching force, but he has been wrong before in judging what he has faced.

At a hundred and fifty yards, Lerial orders, "First squad! Ready bows! Stand by to fire."

"First squad, standing by," replies Korlyn.

With just under a hundred yards between the forces, the Meroweyans break into a trot or lope toward the outnumbered first squad.

"First squad! Fire! Fire at will!"

In moments, several of the attackers are staggering or down under the continuing assault of war arrows. At least one has tripped on a sawed-off stump or the like, and the attack is slowing, if only slightly.

"First squad, ready to withdraw."

Meaning that they're out of shafts. "First squad, withdraw! On the double!"

Lerial turns the gelding and rides back toward second squad. "Second squad! Fire at will!" He reins up, looking beyond the first lines to the rear of the oncoming force. He can sense the chaos mist, but there is still no sign of a firebolt.

The Meroweyans keep coming, and the gap between the forces is more like sixty yards, although Lerial can see and sense that the war arrows, fired at such comparatively close range are taking a toll, despite the attackers' shields, which are deflecting many of the Verdyn shafts.

All too soon, Lerial orders, "Second squad! Withdraw! Double time!"

He barely waits until the last second squad ranker has slipped past the fourth squad archers before ordering, "Fourth squad! Fire at will!"

The greater number of archers in fourth squad, and the speed with which they release their shafts, slows the Meroweyans, but the attackers are far too close, and Lerial wishes he had ordered first squad to begin shooting far earlier.

Again, he wonders why the Meroweyan wizard has not thrown a single firebolt. *Because he's been told to let the troopers do what they can? Because they've lost too many wizards?* Still, he's definitely glad that he hasn't had to deflect any firebolts.

Overhead, thunder rumbles through the dark clouds, but there is not a hint of rain.

Lerial glances from the Meroweyan foot troopers, still advancing, if more slowly, now only forty yards away and holding their shields in a fashion to guard their chest and guts, and then back to fourth squad, where Alaynara stands in middle of the front rank of the archers, releasing shaft after shaft.

At that moment, he senses a strong buildup of chaos, just before a firebolt arches toward fourth squad from behind the still-advancing Meroweyan shields and foot.

Lerial concentrates, coldly, accurately, and like a crossbow quarrel, the firebolt sears straight back to the chaos wizard who created it—except that the wizard does something, and the firebolt, brighter than ever, and far stronger, slows, then reverses its course, arching higher and angling straight toward Lerial.

Lerial smiles grimly and sets out three fine-linked ten-line patterns, then clamps them around the firebolt. *There! See how you like this!*

WHHHUMPHT!!

Lerial gapes, openmouthed, as the firebolt splits into three unequal lines of flame—the largest one slamming back at the Meroweyan wizard, one fanning down on the lead ranks of the Meroweyan foot, and one narrower beam slashing into the middle of the fourth squad—where Alaynara and three other archers had stood loosing shafts a moment before.

Unseen silver-gray mists, but mists that Lerial can sense all too well, fill the entire area from the front of fourth squad to the rear of the Meroweyan force.

For several moments, Lerial sits frozen in the saddle. *How did that happen?*

With all that chaos in one firebolt . . . why hadn't he considered where some of it might go when it could not return to him and some was blocked by the Meroweyan wizard's shields? Why hadn't he . . . ?

Anticipation! Why didn't you anticipate something like that?

His eyes keep looking for Alaynara and the other two archers.

"Ser!" calls Moraris. "Fourth squad is ready to withdraw!"

Lerial brings himself up short. "Fourth squad! Withdraw! Withdraw!

Withdraw and mount!" He looks to the Meroweyan front, but the shielded foot have halted. *For the moment.*

He tries to see if he can tell anything about the casualties that he and second company have inflicted, but amid the lingering smoke and a misty haze rising from the damp ground that had once held at least a score of Meroweyan foot, he cannot tell.

"Third squad, withdraw now! Third squad! Withdraw now!" While Lerial would like to have Fhentaar's squad use their shafts, the Meroweyans are beginning to regroup, and they are far, far too close.

"Third squad, withdrawing!"

Lerial keeps looking from his rankers to the Meroweyans and back again.

His eyes go back to second company. The archers have reached their horses and mounted, and third squad is beginning to mount. But the Meroweyans, at least some of them, are beginning to run toward second company. Realizing, almost belatedly, that he is the closest one to the attackers, he turns his mount and urges the gelding forward.

By the time he reaches third squad, at the rear of second company, all the Lancers are mounted, and he orders, "Second company! Withdraw! Withdraw on the double!"

Lerial remains near the rear of the company, glancing back and using his order-senses, but before long, the running Meroweyans slow . . . and then stop, and second company is widening the gap between forces on its way south . . . and Lerial cannot help but worry about how Altyrn's remaining three companies are faring against thousands of attackers.

Another roll of thunder echoes across the sky, and he glances up. There is no lightning he can see, and no rain falls.

Once he is certain that the Meroweyans are not pursuing, or not with any speed, and that second company will not be attacked from the rear so long as they keep moving, Lerial eases the gelding forward to the front of the company and slows the pace to a fast walk. Then, he begins to use his order-senses to try to determine what lies ahead of them, except he has more and more trouble discerning anything to the south, other than the fact that there appear to be a chaos wizard and far more men than could be possible for just the three companies that had held the eastern bank of the stream.

"We're going to have to work our way through the trees to join up with the others," Lerial tells Korlyn. "The Meroweyans have crossed the stream and hold the eastern side." *From what little you can tell . . . and if you can find*

Altyrn. As he speaks, droplets begin to fall, and before they have ridden another hundred yards, the rain is coming down steadily, and the drops are cold enough to give Lerial a chill feeling when they hit the back of his neck.

Lerial has a thought and tries to order sense to the north, finding that his ability to find the Meroweyans is far better there. *So the rain affects you as well. Are you using chaos as well as order, then?* He doesn't know, not for certain, and now is not the time to be trying to find out. Instead he attempts to locate the Verdyn Lancers.

After riding another hundred yards, he *thinks* he has located them, if more than two kays away and almost due east of where he is. Next, he tries to find a way through both the trees and rain.

"Second company! On me!"

As Lerial struggles to lead the company through rain and trees, and around occasional large patches of thornbushes, his thoughts keep returning to the short battle on the banks of the stream—if indeed it even qualified as a skirmish, let alone a battle.

It was not quite a rout, but his withdrawal has been hasty indeed. *Still . . . is it a rout when they lost scores, and a white wizard, and you only lost three?* He shakes his head, knowing he could have accounted for more Meroweyans, had he judged the pace of their attack better. *And perhaps Alaynara and those other two archers wouldn't have died.*

LXXI

Some three glasses later, well after fifth glass, Lerial and second company struggle into Bherkhan, the small hamlet where Altyrn has billeted the other three companies. Just off the main road to Escadya and, eventually, to Verdell, Bherkhan lies some eight kays east of the site of the stream battle. Everyone in second company is drenched through, and Lerial is shivering by the time he finally stands in front of a fire in the small dwelling serving as officers' quarters.

"You took a while getting here," observes Altyrn.

"It took a glass or so to get into position and then they slowed down . . . and then they attacked in a hurry, and we did what we could and barely managed to withdraw before we were overrun. They did have five companies, as you informed me."

"The elders sensed a large chaos blast," says Altyrn. "The rain began to fall so soon afterwards that they couldn't tell any more." He pauses. "We were worried."

"You were right to be worried." Lerial can't help but glance around, although he knows that neither Shaskyn nor Kusyl are in the dwelling, most likely dispatched so that they will not overhear what Lerial has to report.

"You didn't look to have lost many, if any." Altyrn's voice is cautious.

"Three. All archers, including the head archer. That's a loss."

Altyrn winces, almost in spite of himself, then says, "She is . . . was . . . Elder Klerryt's daughter. How did that happen? He'll want to know."

The elder's daughter? For a moment, Lerial is silent. "That firebolt . . . the one the elders felt. I managed to stop it, but . . . it exploded above the Meroweyans. I managed to channel most of it back at the white wizard, and some of it at the front companies of the Meroweyans, but one small bit flared back and hit the middle of the front line of fourth squad."

"Frig . . . ," murmurs the majer.

Lerial knows exactly what he is thinking. *With only three casualties, why did one have to be Alaynara?* That might be because he had the same thought, almost continuously, for most of the ride back to Bherkhan . . . and he hadn't even known that Alaynara was Klerryt's daughter. He'd only known that she was intelligent and perceptive—especially perceptive.

"How did you set up your company?" Altyrn finally asks when Lerial does not volunteer more.

Lerial informs him and waits for the majer's reply.

"For that position, that's not a bad plan. How did you do as far as reducing the number of Meroweyans facing us?"

"We couldn't stay to see. I miscalculated a little," Lerial admits. "I waited too long to have first squad open fire, and we had to withdraw before third squad could loose their shafts. Still, the diverted chaos did take out the white wizard and most of a company. The arrows wounded or killed at least another squad, maybe two . . . but that's a guess."

Altyrn nods slowly. "There's always the problem of timing. It's something you'll learn with experience."

"What happened at the stream?"

"We had to withdraw when we ran out of javelins and arrows, but we didn't face any chaos-fire."

"The rain?" asks Lerial.

The majer nods, then goes on. "Without the support of the chaos-fire, they lost almost two companies. That was between what we could do at the bridge and what Kusyl's fourth squad did to the companies trying to cross to the south."

"That's not bad," says Lerial.

"Not bad, but not exactly all that good, either. Our three companies at the stream still lost more than a squad, mostly wounded, but most of the wounded won't fight again this season . . . or this year. We're whittling them down, but they're also taking a toll on us."

"It comes down to who can whittle better, then," says Lerial tiredly.

"Or whether one side or the other can come up with a way to decimate the other without suffering equal casualties." Altyrn looks at Lerial.

"I haven't figured out how to do that, ser." *Not yet, anyway.*

"One thing you should figure out," replies Altyrn dryly, "is that you need to strip off that soaking uniform and wrap yourself in a warm blanket. Let the fire dry the uniform and your boots. There are some things we still need to go over, but they can wait until you do that."

Lerial nods, then sits on an old straight-backed chair to pull off his boots. Even that minor chore leaves him feeling tired, but in a few moments he is indeed wrapped in a threadbare but warm and dry blanket that Altyrn has had waiting.

He cannot help but think about Alaynara . . . and about Altyrn's indirect suggestion that somehow he needs to find a way to make more of a difference. He knows the majer is right, because the events of the past eightdays have made it more than clear that, when he cannot use order, he is anything but successful as a company commander.

But if there aren't any white wizards around to provide chaos . . . what can you do?

He has to find a way . . . not only to save the people of the Verd . . . but to survive.

LXXII

When Lerial wakes on a cloudy oneday with the rain still falling, if in more of a continual drizzle than a downpour, he is slightly stiff and sore, but otherwise he feels well enough physically, but he could have done without the nightmares about seeing second company being overrun because he hadn't anticipated what the Meroweyans did in time to save his rankers and squad leaders. The fact that, in the dream, he had struggled unsuccessfully to use order didn't help his state of mind. The dry uniform was welcome, but, as he dressed, he kept thinking about how poorly he had judged the speed of the Meroweyan advance—and that his order skills are almost useless in battle unless a chaos wizard attacks his company.

You have to do something about that. You have to.

"That's a serious face you've got on, ser," says Kusyl, moving from the back room to stand in front of the low fire.

"Yesterday was serious," replies Lerial dryly.

"That was yesterday. Can't do anything to change what happened." Kusyl shrugs. "A man'll go out of his mind thinking about what he might have done . . . should've done . . . could've done . . ."

That's easy enough for you to say.

Kusyl turns to Lerial. "Might not be my place to say . . . but you got handed a sowshit stew, ser. Couldn't be a duke's son anywhere in Hamor, except here, standing there a few yards from men and wizards that'd love to kill you. Not you as an heir, just love to kill a Cigoernean officer. Thing is . . . you do what officers're supposed to do. You're going to frig it up at times. Everyone does. Doesn't matter. Matters what you do tomorrow." The undercaptain grins. "You think too much about yesterday, you won't be ready for tomorrow."

"He's right about that, you know," adds Altyrn, who shakes the rain from his oiled waterproof, standing just inside the door.

Lerial knows they're both correct, but he has trouble not dwelling on the past. *You always have, whether it was your father or Lephi.* He doesn't know from where that thought came, but it feels true, and he can't help but express a slight sardonic smile. "I think you two have made your point." He manages a grin.

"Good," replies Altyrn. "There's a fairly hot breakfast in the house next door. You might get over there before Shaskyn eats everything."

"That's a good idea," says Lerial. The growling in his guts agrees with Altyrn's suggestion. "I'm on my way." He knows part of his hasty departure is because he is indeed hungry, but part is because he doesn't want to talk about why he should put yesterday behind him, much as he knows he must.

Breakfast is indeed warm, and welcome, especially if he doesn't deal with the thought of chopped ghano, mixed with acorn bread and some sort of eggs, all held together with the bluish cheese. After he eats, he checks with his squad leaders, goes over what arrows and weapons are left, and then reports to Altyrn.

The majer accepts his report and asks, "What are you going to do now? You can't keep checking on your rankers every glass."

"Try to figure out some things . . . and see if I can do them well enough to practice them."

Altyrn nods. "I'll let you know if anything changes. I doubt the Merow-eyans are going to want to ride and march through this." He gestures toward the window. "They might surprise us, but the scouts will let us know." He pauses. "Do you need the fire?"

"Not now, ser. I might not at all."

"Good. No offense, but you've turned some chambers into ovens."

Lerial just nods and sits on the only chair in the main room except for the one Altyrn has pulled up behind his narrow table. He needs to think.

It's not as though ordermages *can't* manage chaos, reflects Lerial. It's that it unsettles them or . . . He isn't sure exactly what, but healers deal with chaos, if in a different way, all the time. So it is the way of handling it. He can direct chaos through his patterns. He's proved that. But to handle it without just redirecting chaos drawn and concentrated by a white wizard . . . that's another thing. He doesn't even like the idea. But . . . he's already had to do things he doesn't like in the slightest, such as killing people and ordering rankers into places where some will be—and have been—killed.

For a time, he goes over what might be possible, but, in the end, much as he worries about it, he needs to look into the clouds. He stands and makes his way to the front door. There is a slight overhang that mostly shelters a narrow area just outside. Lerial slips outside, closing the door behind himself. He does notice, in the gloomy light of a drizzly morning, that the plank siding of all the dwellings in Bherkhan, those that he can see, has an oil finish, but the finish is almost a tan color. *Does every hamlet pick a different shade of oil?* It does appear that way.

Lerial pushes away the thoughts of oil and directs his senses to the clouds above. There is a flow of order and chaos, a pattern, or rather two patterns, because there is one set of flows inside the cloud . . . and a different flow outside, and yet the two interact. There is also more order in the cloud than in the air around it, and Lerial thinks it should be the other way around . . . except . . . a cloud is a structure, while the air is more like chaos. He uses his order-senses to follow the patterns of a section of the clouds just to the east, because he can see them, at least he can see them as well as he can see anything, while staying under the overhang of the roof and not twisting his neck.

The two patterns . . . they're almost like the order line coil creates a related chaos coil . . . of sorts. Except that the comparison isn't quite right, and Lerial cannot think of a way to make it so. *But what would happen if you nudged the flow inside, because that's more like order?*

Lerial does so, and the chaos outside the center of the cloud strengthens, as if more is flowing to join that already there. He keeps watching. Is the patch of sky to the east darkening? It certainly looks that way.

Then, there is a small flash of . . . something, as if chaos had flowed one way, and order rebounded along the same path . . . or maybe it had been the other way. Lerial cannot tell because it has happened so fast, but the thunder that follows suggests that whatever he did triggered a small bolt of lightning.

The rain to the east intensifies, for perhaps a tenth of a glass before stopping. The clouds there, or now more to the south, because they are slowly moving southward, begin to thin, so much so that, for perhaps a tenth of a glass, hazy sunlight filters through that thin film, but before long the order-chaos patterns in the clouds reassert themselves, and a more uniform drizzle dribbles down on Bherkhan once more, except, Lerial notices, the drizzle is finer and lighter than before.

Of course! You changed the patterns, and the clouds rained harder, and that left less water in them . . . Lerial nods, even as he finds himself grinning. *And you did something that created lightning, if only in the air.*

He takes a deep breath, knowing he has a great deal of effort . . . and work ahead of him . . . if he can even make what he has in mind work, but if he doesn't . . .

He doesn't even want to consider those possibilities. Instead, he sends forth his order-senses once more.

LXXIII

Twoday dawns bright and clear—and by midmorning the air is too warm to be merely springlike, as Lerial recognizes as he stands in the sunlight outside the officers' temporary quarters, trying to use his abilities to separate order from chaos in clear air, a task he is finding difficult, but not impossible, as a small cloud begins to form in the air several hundred yards above him. Interestingly enough, the more he makes the separation, the easier it becomes.

He looks up to see Altyrn riding toward him, followed by Juist. From the majer's bearing, and the hint of chaos swirling around him, Lerial can sense that the majer is worried, if not upset, and he releases his hold on the small cloud above him, looking at it for several moment as it drifts southward in the light and warm breeze, still holding its shape. Even though it contains comparatively little moisture, if slightly more than the air around it, while he knows it will dissipate, the process is going to take longer than he has thought it would.

He walks swiftly toward Altyrn.

Even before he has completed dismounting, the majer addresses Lerial. "Muster your company and be formed up in half a glass. The scouts have reported that the Meroweyans are less than five kays away. They're not moving that swiftly, but they're headed here."

"We're withdrawing, ser? Where?"

"All the way to Escadya."

"That's almost fifteen kays, isn't it?"

"We need the distance and the time. We're going to have to let the people do what they can. We still don't have any war arrows to speak of and only a few handfuls of spears that the rankers have made in the last day. There's been no word from Juist or Denieryn. Facing well over a thousand armed Meroweyans with four Verdyn companies that contain only three companies' worth of rankers and no weapons except sabres and a few lances that are useless in this kind of fighting is something I'd rather not do." Altyrn's voice is edgy, something Lerial has not heard before.

"I wasn't questioning, ser. What else can we do that makes sense right now?"

"I know you weren't." Altyrn's brief smile vanishes. "I had to tell Elder Klerryt about his daughter."

"He's here?"

"He and the other elders are already on their way to Escadya." Altyrn pauses, then adds, "What made it worse for him was that she didn't have to serve. She was older and had already done her service as a woodland warden. She was the one who insisted. She told her father that if some offspring of the elders didn't serve, how could they insist that so many other young people should." Altyrn offers a sardonically wry smile. "I thought you might understand that."

Belatedly, Lerial understands some of what Alaynara had meant by saying that practicality included who people were. *She thought you knew . . . and you had no idea.* "Her experience was why she was so good an archer, I imagine."

"Did you talk to her much?" asks the majer.

"Some. About the same as the squad leaders."

"It might help if you wrote a letter to the elder. Not the specifics of what happened. I told him those."

"Just about how good an archer, how good a leader she was?"

Altyrn nods as he ties his mount to the short hitching rail. "Not immediately, but when you have time."

Once the majer walks toward the door, Lerial strides toward the small dwellings holding second company, marveling about the fact that, with roughly eighty rankers left out of slightly over a hundred, it is the closest to full strength of all of Altyrn's companies.

Almost exactly a half glass after Altyrn has informed Lerial of the Meroweyan advance, all four companies are on their way. The main road is damp, but not all that muddy, as they leave Bherkhan, but by the time they have ridden two kays, the packed clay is almost dry.

Since Lerial has not had a chance to write the letter to Klerryt, as he rides beside Korlyn, he thinks about Alaynara . . . and what he could say about her. *All the things you would like to say—that she was kind and perceptive, or that she understood more than she expressed—all those things would likely convey the wrong meaning to her father. And all the other things that you could say—that she was capable, intelligent, decisive, and a good leader and archer—convey so little of what she was.* Lerial also knows that what he had seen in Alaynara might not even be understood by her father. *Some parents understand . . . and some do not.* That is something he knows all too well.

In the end, he knows he will write about those things that express the obvious, then, later, if he meets Klerryt, he will feel his way and perhaps say more . . . or nothing beyond what he will write.

"Ser?" Korlyn finally ventures after Lerial has said nothing for almost a glass. "How many companies do the Meroweyans have left? Has the majer said?"

The squad leader's normally cheerful round face reflects concern, the first time Lerial has seen that. *Or is it the first time you've taken the time to notice?* "He's only said that they have over a thousand men in the force moving toward Escadya. I don't know how many are in the other force, the one to the west. We haven't heard anything from Juist or Denieryn."

"That's not good, is it, ser?"

"It's neither good nor bad."

"But . . . ?"

"If it were truly bad, I think the elders would know and would have told the majer. What it likely means is that Juist and Denieryn have withdrawn, just as we are, and that they haven't fought another battle or skirmish." *That's what you hope, anyway.*

"Like to think that, ser."

Lerial laughs softly. "So would we all."

"You think they've got more of those wizards?"

"I'd be surprised if they don't. They have less than when they started, and maybe we can see if they'll have even fewer."

"That'd be good."

Lerial just nods to that, and Korlyn refrains from pressing.

By the fourth glass of that afternoon, Lerial and second company are riding back into the very area in Escadya where he had spent eightdays training Lancers in blade skills and trying to learn what he could about commanding a company. He glances at the sky once more, but it is clear. *Of course. Once you've finally figured out how you might handle clouds . . . there aren't any.* But that also reminds him of how dangerous putting off doing things can be, no matter how pressed he feels.

Once the troopers are settled back in the barracks they left eightdays before, Altyrn summons Lerial and the other two company officers to meet in a corner of the mess hall.

When Lerial enters and looks around, he can see—and sense—that it is totally empty, except for the four of them . . . and likely has been for some time. As he seats himself across the table from the majer, to the left of Shaskyn and then Kusyl, he says, "Everyone is moving out of Escadya as well?"

"Not everyone," replies Altyrn. "Several hundred people will likely stay and try to hamper the Meroweyans in some way, and some are working on fashioning more spears. There are two wagons full of war arrows, and a cart with spears that just arrived. When we finish here, you need to have your companies re-arm. If the Meroweyans proceed as they have, we will have tomorrow to prepare our defenses for their attack. The people here have been working to create more pit traps in the woods flanking where we will make a stand. We will use the same sort of defenses as at the stream, except they will be on the low ridge just west of Escadya itself, the one that crosses the small meadow that the road runs through . . ."

Lerial listens intently as Altyrn outlines what he has planned.

LXXIV

When he rises on threeday morning, Lerial immediately checks the sky, but sees only high hazy clouds, although, with the tall trees surrounding the Lancer training grounds, he cannot see any that might be near the horizon in any direction. *You're just going to have to practice with the air as it is, clouds or no clouds.*

By seventh glass, second company is at the low ridge—really a gentle rise that is no more than two or three yards above the flat meadow to its southwest, so low that the main road just goes right over it, although time and the passage of people, wagons, and horses have worn down a short stretch near the top of the rise. Lerial has to question how four undersized companies are going to defend a rise that extends close to half a kay.

"You have a doubtful look," Altyrn observes, as he and Lerial wait for Kusyl and Shaskyn to ride up and join them.

"I have several questions," Lerial admits. "How can we possibly defend this? And why won't they just find a way around us?"

"The answer to the first question is simple," replies Altyrn blandly. "We can't. We're only going to use the position to inflict as many casualties as possible before we withdraw."

"They must know that by now."

"They may."

"Then why won't they just avoid us?"

"For two reasons," replies Altyrn. "First, it's not a good idea to put yourself where you might be surrounded, and the Meroweyans can't be certain that we might not have more forces around Verdell. Second, every military leader knows that until you defeat and destroy the forces that oppose you, you can't control or govern a land. Some can't even when they do destroy all organized armed forces that have opposed them, but that's another question. Ask me about that some other time."

Lerial takes that as a veiled suggestion not to take any more of the majer's time, at least at the moment.

"Here come Kusyl and Shaskyn. We need to set the boundaries and the angle of the trenches and defenses."

By midday, second company has completed digging out its share of trenches and is beginning to place the branch and stick figures created in response to Altyrn's request days earlier—to give an impression of a greater force than actually exists.

In between supervising and walking the trenches, Lerial creates order pattern after order pattern, some of which are complete failures, but discovering in the process several with possibilities, including some with interlinked order "coils." Although he has said nothing, he knows that some of his Lancers have cast glances at him and at the occasional small clouds that have formed overhead . . . and then dissipated.

"Ser!"

Lerial turns to see a ranker hurrying toward him.

"Ser . . . the majer requests you join him immediately."

Lerial glances around, but does not see Altyrn. "Where is he?"

"Oh . . . he's over there by the trees." The ranker points to the northwest.

"I'll be right there." Since Bhurl is the closest squad leader, Lerial walks to him and says, "I'll be with the majer over there."

"Yes, ser."

The spot the ranker has pointed out is over two hundred yards away, but since the mounts are on tie-lines almost as far away, Lerial walks the distance. As he nears, he sees that with the majer are two of the high elders of Vernheln—Donnael and Ruethana.

"Captain Lerial, I thought you should hear what Elder Donnael has to report."

"Yes, ser." Lerial moves beside Altyrn and looks at the two elders.

The senior elder's face is drawn and has deep lines Lerial does not recall. His eyes are bloodshot and sunken, and his once silver hair is a yellowed white.

"The small Meroweyan army to the west is no more," announces Donnael.

How did they do that? Lerial wonders.

"You might explain how you managed that," suggests Altyrn.

"The Meroweyans were following the west road to Verdell. The next large town after Truyver is Faerwest . . . or was. They were angry after what your men and our people did at Truyver. When they were thrown back from the stone and earth walls that blocked the entry to the town, they went around the walls. The Lancers withdrew into the town, and the wizards began to bombard Faerwest with firebolts." Donnael's mouth offers a twisted smile. "They did not realize that it is on higher ground and that the stream to the east is deeper than it looks. We started fires behind them . . . and placed a fair amount of cammabark in the right positions . . . we had to strip most of the camma trees there and made certain that the wind was from the west . . . and brought down the only bridge before them, just after the Lancers withdrew across it . . ."

Made certain . . . Lerial can sense that those words are deliberate, and he wonders which of the elders is a weather mage . . . or something like it.

". . . the Lancers were able to kill those few who made it across the river. Some of them perished as well, but the rest should be able to make their way to rejoin you later tomorrow . . . by fiveday at the latest."

After the Meroweyans attack here. But at least, they will reinforce the thinned companies holding the south road toward Verdell, reflects Lerial. "What about their wizards? If I might ask?"

"The greatest of chaos masters would have trouble with the chaos of an entire forest burning. They were not that great. We think there were two. They perished with the armsmen."

"The people?" inquires Altyrn gently.

"I told you about Essiana. Besides her, we lost hundreds . . . but they lost close to two thousand. We will recover what weapons we can when the ashes are cool."

Essiana, one of the elders? She died? She had been the most empathetic, so far as Lerial is concerned, and he is about to ask about her when Ruethana speaks.

"We would have liked to have spared their horses. That was not possible."

Something about those two statements so close together chills Lerial, especially after hearing the almost casual fashion in which Donnael has almost dismissed Essiana's death, and Ruethana has ignored it. *And they don't seem to have the slightest regret over all the deaths.* Given the coldness the two have shown, Lerial can't help but wonder how much Klerryt might really feel about his daughter's death. *That's not fair. You really don't know.*

"The weapons will be useful, if they can be recovered," replies Altyrn.

Lerial has the feeling, although he could not say why, that behind the evenly spoken words, the majer may be at least somewhat disconcerted as well.

"We have people placing traps in the areas you requested." Donnael frowns. "You said that you wanted a number of them to be obvious."

Altyrn nods. "That way they will be more cautious. It also might keep them from spreading their forces too much or putting too many men into the wood. Arrows do more damage among armsmen closer together."

Ruethana smiles coldly. "I can see that."

"We will do what we can," says Donnael. "We cannot call any more storms, not by tomorrow."

Lerial suspects he knows why, but given their attitude toward the death of Essiana and the total lack of regret about killing thousands and losing hundreds of their own people, he decides to press them. "Why might that be?"

"If you do not know, Lord Lerial—" begins Ruethana.

"We can only manipulate the forces that are, not create them," says Donnael, overriding the other elder. "And there are fewer of us now."

"That is too bad," Lerial says, trying to sound regretful. "The storms over the stream battle were most helpful."

"We do what we can, as do you," replies Donnael. "We should depart to allow you to continue with your preparations."

"Matters are well in hand," replies Altyrn with a pleasant smile that Lerial knows is false, or forced. "We will be grateful for anything you can do."

"As we are for what you have already done . . . and what you will do." Donnael's smile is also pleasant, yet distant.

Once the two elders have left, Lerial looks to Altyrn. "They didn't seem all that upset that one of their own was killed."

"She was the one who controlled the fires. Doing that was what killed her."

"She was an ordermage. How . . ." Lerial breaks off his words as he thinks about his own experiences, then says, "I think I see what might have happened."

"What might that have been?"

"You have to keep great amounts of order and chaos either balanced or separated. If you fail with either separation or balance . . . I don't know, but I think . . . I think there was just too much chaos created by the fires."

"Something like that happened to you when you stopped breathing?"

"I *think* so . . . except there was too much order. There had to be too much chaos with that much fire."

"What happened in the west of the Verd won't help us tomorrow," Altyrn says. "According to the scouts, they still have fifteen companies. In actual numbers, we have less than four, perhaps even less than three if we don't count the riding wounded."

"That's why all the stick figures?"

"They've helped before. At the very least, they should slow the Meroweyan advance, until someone gets close enough to see that's what they are. That should give us enough time to bring down more of their armsmen before we have to withdraw." Altyrn pauses. "Is there any possibility that you . . ."

"If their white wizards throw chaos at us, I can often—not always"—*That's not something you ever want to promise as certain*—"divert some of it back onto their forces."

"If you can, that would be helpful."

"I'll do what I can."

"That's all I can ask."

"I'd better get back to my company and make sure the stick figures look as real as possible." *And keep working on some other way to use your abilities against the Meroweyans.*

"Go." The single word is delivered lightly, with a humorous smile, if one that vanishes even before Lerial turns.

The rest of threeday is long, but by the time the sun drops behind the trees at the west end of the meadow, the modest earthworks do indeed look like they shelter more than twice as many Lancers as will be actually holding the defenses.

Lerial is tired, not from what he has to do as company commander, but from what he has been attempting to discover. For all the ways he has tried to use order, by the time he stretches out in the tent he shares with Altyrn, he still cannot find a way to draw enough chaos from the area around him to create more than a tiny fireball. *Chaos wizards can do it. So can great ordermages.* He looks through the darkness at the fabric overhead. *But you're not a great ordermage, and you must be doing something wrong.* Not necessarily wrong, he decides. It's just that he doesn't know how to do it right. Before his eyes close, he just hopes that he can find a way . . . before it's too late.

LXXV

When Lerial wakes on fourday, he has no new ideas.

Perhaps you'll get one. Right now? Not likely. He snorts softly as he pulls on his boots and looks out at the sky that is still gray—but very clear. *And perhaps thunderclouds will appear from nowhere.*

Early as it is, Altyrn is already awake and gone, doubtless looking over the meadow and checking the reports from the scouts and dispatching more scouts. Lerial shakes out his blanket, rolls it up and slips it into the loops on the side of his kit bag, then puts on his visor cap and goes to look for the majer. He finds Altyrn at the edge of the trees on the north side of the meadow, looking southward at the trenches. In the low light before dawn, the stick figures, even from behind, look convincing.

"They don't look bad, ser . . . the stick figures, I mean."

"If they just keep the Meroweyans together for a time, that will be helpful."

"They'll help," Lerial affirms.

"For long enough? We'll see."

"What have the scouts reported?"

"The Meroweyans are forming up in a very small hamlet. They're about two kays south. Might be a little less."

Lerial extends his order-senses. While he can sense a mass of men in and around some dwellings on a lane some two kays south, there are so many Meroweyans in such a small areas that he cannot make out details. "Have you heard any more about Juist and Denieryn?"

"No. We won't hear anything until after whatever happens here today. That's if the Meroweyans even decide to attack."

"You think they won't?"

"You never know until it happens. I just hope they haven't heard too much about what happened at Faerwest. That might decide them against attacking."

Lerial understands that Altyrn definitely wants the Meroweyans to attack, outnumbered as the majer's forces are.

"So that, even if they decide to withdraw, they lose more armsmen?"

"The more they lose here, the less likely Casseon is to consider attacking again . . . or opposing your father. It would be best if we could defeat them decisively, but that's unlikely. If we can hold together for a few more battles, and they keep taking the kind of casualties they have been, they might get to the point where their commander will realize that there's little difference, so far as he's concerned, between a victory and a defeat. That's when things could get very deadly."

"Because he'll be facing one disaster if he continues and another disaster if he has to return to Nubyat?"

Altyrn nods, still looking at the defense emplacements largely garrisoned by stick figures at the moment. When he does not speak for a time, Lerial slips away to seek out his squad leaders and go over the plans for the day. They are simple enough, not that executing them will be anywhere close to that simple. *Or that things will work out even close to what the majer has planned.*

In order to dissuade the Meroweyans from immediately using their horse to sweep over the ends of the ridge beyond the trench, Altyrn has assigned two mounted squads from first company at the east end, and two from fifth company at the west end. The remainder of first company is to hold the center of the trench, with second company on the east and fourth on the west of center. All the mounts for the Lancers and archers in the trenches are on tie-lines on the back side of the rise, close enough for the Lancers to reach them in moments, long moments perhaps, when the time comes for the withdrawal. *The inevitable withdrawal,* thinks Lerial.

Once he reviews the postings with the four squad leaders, he dismisses them to have them position their rankers. Then he grooms the gelding and leads him out to the tie-line below the ridge. From what he can order-sense, the Meroweyans have left their encampment—or most have, since a small group, perhaps a squad's worth of cooks or others, remains—and are proceeding along the main road toward the meadow and the Verdyn emplacements.

He studies the sky once more, but there are no signs of clouds, and the wind is warm and out of the north. He tests the order and chaos in the air by creating the smallest of clouds by separating the order and chaos, then shakes his head, knowing that he is missing something, but is unable to determine what he is overlooking. *Or what you do not know.*

"How long before they get here, ser?" That is the first question Korlyn asks after reporting that first squad is in position and standing ready.

"A glass or so."

"You said fifteen companies?"

Lerial notes the uneasiness in the squad leader's tone and replies, "We don't have to hold the trench to the last ranker. Our job is to inflict as many casualties as possible and then withdraw." *And keep doing it, retreating from place to place, until we destroy them, or they us, or they decide it isn't worth it and go away.*

Korlyn looks pointedly to the east, then asks earnestly, his open round face expressing worry. "How long do you think it will be before they try to circle around the ridge?"

"As soon as they think they can. Our job is to send arrows and spears into their main body so that they don't have time to think about what else they might do."

"What if they don't attack?"

"Most likely they'll get hungry and they'll have to start raiding the local people, and the people will hide everything. Then the Meroweyans will start losing men one by one, and they'll try to take another town. We'll be waiting, and they'll be attacking with fewer men."

"They'll start killing people in the forest steads and smaller hamlets. It'll be hard on them."

"That's possible," Lerial admits.

"What does Duke Casseon really get from all this, ser?"

"He wants to stop the people of Verdheln from becoming part of Cigoerne, because that will strengthen Cigoerne. He thinks that will also protect Duke Atroyan, and he and Duke Khesyn want to eventually take over both Cigoerne and Afrit." Lerial pauses. "That's the way I see it."

"Two dukes who have everything they could want aren't satisfied and want more, and lots of armsmen and innocent people are dying because of it?"

"That's a fair way of putting it. But there's nothing new about that."

"Doesn't make it right, does it, ser?"

"No . . . but right has to be supported by strength. You've seen that, I'm sure."

Korlyn shakes his head and looks as though he is about to say more when Bhurl approaches and announces, "Second squad in position and ready, ser."

"Good. Have the men stand easy."

"Yes, ser."

Korlyn and Bhurl return to their squads, and almost immediately Fhentaar and Moraris report, and then return to their squads. Lerial uses his order senses to check the Meroweyan progress. The lead armsmen are less than a kay from the south side of the meadow, and the green-blue sky remains bright and clear.

A half glass later the first of the Meroweyan forces arrive, a company of mounted armsmen who take a position a hundred yards into the meadow, while behind them the first of the Meroweyan foot form up into a shieldwall that moves forward almost to the mounted troopers, who then ride eastward to a point opposite the end of the Verdyn trench. To counter that, or to give the appearance of it, the two squads of Verdyn Lancers, from first company, ride up to the east end of the trench. Then another company of Meroweyan horse enters the grassy expanse and rides to a point opposite the west end of the Verdyn emplacement. They are countered by Shaskyn's two squads.

More Meroweyan foot form up behind the shieldwall, almost as wide as the trench that holds the Verdyn forces. Behind the shields, armsmen form more closely than Lerial has seen before, and more seem to fill the space until the Meroweyans are more than ten deep.

Farther back, surrounded by another two companies of cavalry, are two chaos wizards, but Lerial can sense no buildup of chaos, only the chaos mist—slightly different for each of the two—that indicates that both have raised a concealment of sorts, and likely some form of shields as well.

A horn signal sounds, and the shieldwall begins to advance, but the mounted companies remain where they have drawn up, some hundred yards out from the trees on the south side of the meadow, on the flanks of the shieldwall. While the riders carry spears shorter than lances and look ready, they have not moved. As the shield wall approaches the bottom of the rise, the foot behind the large front shields lift smaller shields almost overhead but angled to minimize the impact of the Verdyn arrows. The mounted body behind the massed foot moves forward as well, but there is a gap of at least twenty yards behind the rear of the foot and the first riders.

Lerial waits for the order from the majer for the Lancers and archers to begin to fire at the advancing Meroweyans, but even when they are little more than a hundred yards from the earthen walls that shelter the Verdyn trenches, that order does not come.

Then, just after that, the pipes shrill.

"Second company! Fire at will!" Lerial orders.

Arrows pour down at the Meroweyans, and Lerial can see that many glance off the shields of the still-advancing attackers, although the speed of the advance is slowing slightly as the Mereweyans start up the slope, and as some of the shieldmen fall.

At that moment, Lerial realizes that the Meroweyans have not thrown a single firebolt. *Not one.* Someone has realized that he can only respond—not that they know who he is, only that whoever can use order is limited to responding—and they are going to storm the defenses on foot, then have the mounted troopers sweep around the ends of the trenches.

But are you limited to responding . . . or only limited to using chaos through order? He knows the answer, but what other chaos is there to use?

The chaos concealment screen! Can he draw on it . . . and perhaps create a miniature thunderstorm over the chaos wizards? There likely isn't too much water in the air, but . . . *You have to do something.*

He is still trying to think what he can do when the shieldwall halts, partway up the slope, less than fifty yards from the earth ramparts before the trenches. Then, seemingly from nowhere, comes a hail of javelins, javelins with dull metallic points.

"Javelins! Company down!" Lerial drops to his knees just as the javelins arc down and pass through where he might have been standing, or at least close enough that there was a chance he might have been hit.

He hears someone yell, but he cannot see who it might be or where . . . and there are other shouts and yells, but what they signify, it is impossible to tell. Before another set of javelins comes toward them, Lerial lifts his head, then sees one in the grass behind the trenches. He grabs it. Immediately, he can see that the tip is bent slightly, and the weapon feels heavier than it should. *Lead! The points are cast from lead.* That gives the javelin more weight . . . and if the head pierces a man and deforms . . .

He wonders if he can fling it back. *What if you use order to smooth its path, the way you were smoothing the air?* He might as well try. He hurls it as his father once taught him to throw a spear, then reaches out with order to smooth its path.

His mouth drops open as he senses the javelin rip through a shield and into the shieldman. Even though he knows that a few more wounded Meroweyans won't make that much difference, he glances around until he sees the butt end of one in front of him, as if it had stuck in the front side of the packed earth rampart that shields—mostly—the trench in which he stands, his head slightly down. He grabs the javelin and drops back behind the earthen barrier.

Another pipe signal blares, the one that signals the spear-throwers that Altyrn has posted to begin releasing their weapons. Lerial takes the second javelin and hurls it, this time using order not only to smooth and propel it, but to guide it toward the shieldman on the edge of a gap.

The javelin hits with enough force to slam through the shield and throw the man bearing it back into the two foot armsmen behind him. Lerial looks around frantically, finally taking three quick steps to grab another javelin and hurl it back toward the other side of the gap in the shieldwall.

"Fourth squad! Arrows into the gap!" Moraris's voice is shrill, but loud.

Lerial can sense the further slowing of the advancing attackers as shafts pour into the bodies of the armsmen who had held shields high.

The hail of javelins slows, almost halting, perhaps in response to the Verdyn spears, but Lerial knows that respite will be slight.

And still the chaos wizards have not thrown a single firebolt!

What if . . . what if you act as if their shields and concealment screens are like the inside of a thundercloud . . . and just place what order you can above and around it?

Knowing he only has moments to do something before the Verdyn forces must either fight hand-to-hand or beat an immediate and speedy retreat, he extends his order senses and begins to create order lines as parallel as he can make them to the dancing chaos behind the concealment and possible shields of the chaos wizards. A small dark thundercloud appears over the mounted formation within which are the chaos wizards . . . but nothing else occurs.

Lerial feels that he can almost—but not quite—create the force he is seeking.

How can you get more order? Is there order within things . . . not just around them? As there must be within a lodestone?

He fumbles—or he feels like he is fumbling—trying to ease apart order and chaos in both the air above the concealment screen and in the ground below. Someone in the Meroweyan force must anticipate something, because the horn sounds, and the two mounted companies close on the other two surrounding the Meroweyan chaos wizards.

Abruptly, Lerial can sense, almost with brilliant light, the interplay between another level of order and chaos, an interplay *within* all things, from the air he breathes to the ground on which he stands. With that understanding, he begins to separate order and chaos in the ground under the mounted Meroweyan formation.

He has barely begun—or so he thinks—when he senses something—immense power—and he frantically drops trying more order-chaos separation and flings up a triple ten-line order coil with the power going anywhere but along the Verdyn trenches.

HSSSST!!!!

Lightning flares from ground and sky, crisscrossing and searing men, grass, shields, and mounts. Thunder with the force of mighty winds slams into everything, and Lerial can sense armsmen before the earthworks being flattened—just before he is flung against the back of the trench with enough force that for several moments, he cannot move or breathe. Then he struggles up and looks over the embankment as a wave of the unseen silver-gray flows over him. His head feels as though it is being pounded with a wooden mallet, and his eyes burn, leaving his vision blurry. He squints. That sharpens his sight enough that he can make out what lies below the low rise.

Half, if not more, of the Meroweyan foot force is strewn across the grass, much of which retains its tan-tipped green, if with an irregular crosshatched pattern of black lightning burns.

"Fifth company! Charge!"

From the west, Shaskyn's two squads race toward the disorganized remnants of the cavalry around the chaos wizards and, most likely, the force commander . . . if they have even survived. Shaskyn leads that charge, a sabre in each hand, guiding his mount with his legs and knees. Then a squad of first company's Lancers charges on foot from the trenches toward the Meroweyan armsmen remaining in front of the trenches, with fourth company's Lancers following.

Lerial thinks about having second company follow that example, but his eyes go to the mounted riders still swirling around the rear—and Shaskyn's outnumbered squads. "Second company! Lancers! Mount up!" Then he hurries around one of the stick figures, and is about to leap out of the trench, only to hear someone moaning.

That someone is Korlyn, half sitting, half propped against the back of the trench between two stick figures—with a javelin through his lower chest just below his breastbone.

"Ser . . ."

Lerial glances from Korlyn back across the embankment to the south, where he sees the scattered remnants of the mounted troopers starting to regroup, and regrouping around a chaos concealment screen. *Frig!* He glances at Korlyn, seeing the pleading look. He can sense that in all likelihood, nothing he can do will save Korlyn. *In all likelihood . . .*

"Ser . . ."

Nothing he can likely do will save Korlyn from that kind of wound. Yet . . . he might . . .

He wants to shake his head, because the last thing he wants is the Meroweyans to reform and rally to destroy the Verdyn Lancers. If that should occur . . . he doesn't have time to think about that. He has to act. While second company may be tired, the mounts aren't. He looks to Korlyn. "I'll be back," he says, knowing that he will not see the squad leader alive again. "Second company! Mount up! Now!"

"Ser?" calls Bhurl.

"We have to stop them from re-forming . . ." Lerial doesn't need to explain. "Mount up! Now! On me!" He is already trotting back to where the mounts are. "Moraris! Mount the archers and hold them here!"

"Mount up!" echoes Fhentaar.

"Squad one! Mount up! On me!" Lerial yells again.

Lerial chafes at the time it takes before the first three squads are moving around the end of the trenches with three squads abreast in a five-man front. Before them lies a confusion of fallen men, patches of burning grass, and swirls of gray and black smoke. Although he has not heard any commands, the two squads from first company have already joined the fray around where the Meroweyan wizards were, and where, from the diminished chaos shield he senses, one still is. While fifth company is attacking from the west and first from the east, even with blurred vision Lerial can see that the Meroweyans are beginning to re-form in the middle . . . and that is where he leads second company.

"Sabres ready!" Lerial orders, belatedly, hoping that the Lancers have anticipated him and, with a quick glance around and behind him, seeing that some have not and are struggling to draw weapons. With that observation, a single thought crosses his mind. *Is this really a good idea?* Bad idea or not, he and second company are committed, and he scans the still somewhat disorganized Meroweyan horse troopers less than fifty yards away.

The very emergence of another company from the swirling smoke prompts some of the Meroweyans to turn their horses and attempt to flee, but most spur their mounts toward second company, if in a ragged and very uneven line, with gaps here and there. Before Lerial almost knows it, a tall Meroweyan rider waving a very long blade, or so it seems to Lerial, is bearing down on him.

Lerial flattens himself under the wild cut, then uses a thrusting slash, guided more by order-sense than vision, into the brown-uniformed horse trooper's shoulder, half yanking, half slipping his sabre away from the wounded man and using it almost as a short lance against the next trooper—who does not even see it coming. After that, he barely manages to block a side cut from another Meroweyan, and has to lean to one side in the saddle, almost unbalancing himself before managing to regain balance and initiative.

While he is alternately attacking and defending himself, he can sense that the chaos shield is moving away—toward the south, back toward Merowey, and there is nothing he can do about it. *Not yet.* All he can do is cut, thrust, parry, duck, twist . . . whatever it takes to avoid getting hit, reacting to what his order-senses tell him is likely coming.

Then . . . suddenly, it seems, there is no one left to fight, and second company is near the trees on the south side of the meadow, not all that far from the road that leads south back to empty or destroyed hamlets . . . and to Merowey.

Much as Lerial has tried to cut through the disorganized Meroweyan forces quickly, the small band of Meroweyans that surround the chaos wizard are close to a kay south of the meadow.

"Second company! Re-form! On me! Second squad forward." Lerial has to repeat the command several times. Although it seems as though it takes glasses before the company is in a column heading south, with Bhurl riding beside him, second squad behind, followed by first squad, and then third squad, he doubts that it has taken more than a fifth of a glass.

He sets the pace at a walk, a good walk, but running the horses won't help. The Meroweyans have run theirs, and they are already slowing. But he cannot allow the Meroweyans to escape, even if his head continues to throb and his vision to blur.

That he knows, even if he could not explain why that is so.

In less than a fraction of a glass after Lerial begins the pursuit of the remaining Meroweyan forces, he realizes that no one, especially Altyrn, will know what he is doing. He should have thought of that, but it is hard to think of everything. *Especially when your head feels like it's splitting.* For a moment, he looks to find Korlyn, then realizes, with a sinking feeling, that he will not see that round cheerful face again.

He looks to the second squad leader, who has been riding silently beside him. "Bhurl? Is there anyone with us who is only slightly wounded? Someone who could carry a message back to Majer Altyrn?"

"Yes, ser. Jharem could. Slash on his arm. Insisted he could still fight."

"Have him come forward."

In a few moments, a fresh-faced Lancer with his left sleeve cut away and a dressing bound around his arm eases his mount up beside Lerial. Lerial cannot help but think how young he looks . . . and almost smiles when he thinks that Jharem is still probably older than he is.

"Ser? I can still ride."

"I know. That's what I need you to do. Majer Altyrn doesn't know where second company is. He needs to know that. You're to ride back and find him. Avoid any Meroweyans. The message is more important. Tell the majer that second company is pursuing the last company of Meroweyans. Also tell him that there is one chaos wizard with them."

"That's all, ser?"

"That's all. That's what he needs to know."

"Yes, ser."

Lerial watches for a moment, as well as he can, as the young Lancer turns his mount and rides back along the shoulder of the forest road.

"He's a good Lancer, ser," Bhurl remarks. "He'll do fine." After a moment, he says, "Ser . . . how long . . . ?"

"Until we catch them. That's why we're not straining the mounts. They're only about a kay ahead of us."

"You know that, ser?"

Lerial nods, his eyes taking in the hoofprints on the road . . . and a wad of bloody cloth on the shoulder. He looks for other signs that might indicate the state of those they pursue, but there are only the tracks on the road, the occasional burned-out isolated stead dwelling . . . and the continuing quiet in the surrounding woods, as if the smoke and violence had silenced the birds—even the usually raucous traitor birds—and even the insects.

As Lerial rides, trying to ignore the air of unreality created by the alternation of seemingly untouched woods with burned-out hamlets or those clearly damaged just out of vengeance or spite, his thoughts go back to the wounded Korlyn, and the plea in the young man's eyes. *Maybe . . . just maybe . . .*

He shakes his head. *You can't second-guess everything . . . and there will be a greater cost if you don't stop that wizard from returning to Nubyat.* Still . . . he has the feeling that he will always recall the expression on Korlyn's face.

Lerial takes a deep breath . . . only to find himself thinking about all that has happened . . . and Alaynara, who had understood him, almost just by looking at him. *What can you say to her father that's not trite and meaningless . . . or incredibly presumptuous?*

Inadvertently, he finds himself shaking his head once more.

"Ser?" asks Bhurl, riding beside him.

"Just . . . just the . . . the waste of it all," he finally says, unwilling to say exactly what troubles him.

"Yes, ser. Seems like Duke Casseon'd been better not to force himself on people minding their own business."

"You could say that about more than Duke Casseon, but it doesn't seem that some rulers think about that."

"Your father . . . I mean Duke Kiedron . . . he seems to."

"He can't afford to waste Lancers or golds in trying to force people to do what they don't want to do."

"Be good if more rulers felt that way."

"It would." *But it's not going to happen.* Lerial even has his doubts about whether Lephi would be able to refrain from imposing his will by force. *Except Father and Lephi will never have that kind of force. So it won't come to that.*

Lerial retreats into himself, and Bhurl does not press. The two continue to lead the pursuit of the Meroweyans without speaking.

Third glass comes . . . and goes, and still second company is a little less than a kay behind the Meroweyans, who now travel with several wagons, most likely supply wagons joining them from the last Meroweyan encampment, although Lerial had not noticed through his order-senses exactly when that had occurred. The wagons have slowed the retreating Meroweyan horse, but only slightly, and Lerial doesn't want to push his men or mounts. Even at a fast traveling pace, it will be at least another two days before they reach the edge of the Verd.

LXXVI

After another day and a half of pursuing the Meroweyans, Lerial's headache has faded, and the blurred vision has finally vanished. What has not changed is that the Meroweyans remain ahead of them. He is convinced that—just as he can sense the chaos wizard—the chaos wizard can also sense him, because any time that he picks up the pace to try to close the distance between the two groups, within a short time, the Meroweyans also pick up their pace. Even so, by noon on sixday, second company is less than a kay behind the main body of the Meroweyans, possibly even only a bit more than half a kay behind the rearguard. Lerial is beginning to tire of the terrier-and-rat game, and although he would like to think that second company is the terrier, he wonders at times. He is also now easily recognizing the area though which they are passing, especially once they have ridden past the stone posts of Ironwood and are nearing Nevnarnia—or its charred ruins. Close as second company is, they are not close enough . . . yet. Deciding that a sustained pursuit of any sort will turn into a race, he needs to try something different, because, with his forces still outnumbered, he doesn't want to confront the Meroweyans when his men and especially mounts are more tired than theirs are. Since there is often a time gap between when he picks up the pace for second company and when the Meroweyans respond, he has an idea.

He turns slightly in the saddle and looks to the second squad leader. "Bhurl . . . on my command, we'll canter for just a hundred yards or so, and when I give the second order, we'll go back to a walk. We'll be doing this on and off for a time. Pass it to the other squads."

The squad leader's puzzled expression is but momentary. "Yes, ser."

Once the order has been passed, Lerial calls out, "Company! Forward!"

Just on his feelings, although he senses nothing, after only about a hundred and fifty yards, Lerial calls out, "Company! Walk!"

Second company walks for another third of a kay before Lerial repeats the cantering maneuver, this time for a little over two hundred yards before slowing.

"The other wizard can sense where we are, just like you can?" asks Bhurl once the company is at a walk again.

"That's true, but the other wizard doesn't seem to be watching all the time, and I'm trying to use that so that we can get closer without tiring the horses too much."

Bhurl nods. "We might be able to do that."

After perhaps another glass, just after second company has ridden past the turnout on the north side of the main road that leads to what remains of Nevnarnia, has closed the gap to well under half a kay, and been walking at a comfortable pace for the last quarter glass, Lerial senses that the Meroweyans have moved to a fast walk. He smiles. "Second company! Fast walk."

Shortly, Lerial can sense the Meroweyans slowing as they enter an open space, and for a moment he is puzzled. Then he senses something else near the north side of the clearing, a barricade of some sort—*The log barricade and fire pits where the first fights inside the Verd took place.*

The Meroweyans come to a stop, and Lerial wonders why, until he feels that one of the wagons has tilted. After perhaps as little as a tenth of a glass, during which time second company reduces the gap between the two forces to perhaps five hundred yards, although Lerial cannot yet see the rearguard of the retreating force, the withdrawal continues.

When second company enters the clearing with the log barricade, directly ahead is a wagon, still tilted, with its right front wheel caught and the axle bearing at an angle to the axletree. Obviously, the Meroweyans had quickly unhitched the draft horses and unloaded what they could from the disabled wagon and then hurried on.

Lerial looks to Bhurl once more. "Have the company follow me. We'll need to skirt the firepits, or we'll likely lose some mounts the way they did that wagon."

Just beyond the wagon is the back side of the log barricade, and outside of spots where the wood has charred, it appears fairly solid. There are still some stick figures on poles that appear almost untouched.

Lerial can see the rearguard of the Meroweyans ahead. *Should you charge them?* That doesn't seem right, not after all his men have been through, and they cannot reduce the number of Meroweyans from a distance because they have no arrows left, not to speak of.

You'll have to use order and lightnings . . . But that is something he doesn't want to do along the narrow road in the forest, not with the risk of setting yet another fire, and with no elders and no clouds in sight for rain that might damp it. He'd hoped to catch them in one of the clearings or meadows. Now . . .

"Ser?" asks Bhurl.

"We follow until they're out of the Verd."

"Begging your pardon, ser, but . . ."

"I didn't say we'd do nothing. We just can't do it here."

"Yes, ser."

Lerial can tell the squad leader isn't totally happy, but he doesn't want to explain, especially if what he has in mind doesn't work. *It should. You've done it once.* At the same time, Bhurl should know why. After several moments, he adds, "If we attack now, they'll use chaos, and we'll be caught in the middle of a fire, and they might escape . . . or both."

"Hadn't thought of that, ser. Makes sense."

It does, even if it's only a partial truth. He still worries as he finishes guiding the company around the depressions that had been firepits and back onto the road. When they reach the more southern area where the very first skirmish in the Verd had taken place, and where the companies had bivouacked awaiting the Meroweyan assault on the Verd itself, he again guides his men around the low pits that he can sense and back onto the road.

Ahead of them, the Meroweyans are riding through the road gates that they must have opened once they had poured through the gaps they had burned in the tree-wall of the Verd. The riders move in measured steps. Lerial lets them, although he increases the pace slightly, not wanting the Meroweyans to be too far away when second company leaves the Verd.

Once all of second company clears the road gates, Lerial orders the squads to form up on the still-matted grass late in the afternoon on a warm spring day. The Meroweyans have also formed up, but make no move to attack. The Meroweyan force is composed of riders bearing different arms, some with spears, others with small bucklers and long blades, and still others with light armor and curved sabrelike blades, clearly a mixed group of survivors, but a group that numbers more than two companies, while what remains of second company, without fourth squad and with all the casualties suffered since the first attacks, is little more than half a company.

For all the differential in force size, Lerial doubts that the Meroweyans will attack, but he waits to see what they will do.

The two forces face each other, one in dull golden brown and one in forest brown. After some time, perhaps as long as a tenth of a glass, a horn sounds. The first two ranks of the Meroweyans hold fast, but all the other riders begin to turn their mounts.

Are you just going to let them go? For a moment, Lerial is tempted, until he recalls all the burned hamlets, the thousands who are dead and the thousands more homeless . . . and the thought of letting the Meroweyan survivors ride away, as if they had done nothing wrong, is not something he can accept. Nor will it send the right message to Casseon.

He order-reaches out to the ground beneath the middle of the Meroweyan force, seeking a piece of something, something small from which he can more easily separate order and chaos. Almost, immediately separated flows of silvered black and golden red shoot skyward, unseen except by Lerial, followed by brilliant pinpoints of light that all cannot fail to see.

A chaos shield flares in the middle of the Meroweyan force.

In less than a moment, lightning flashes everywhere, crisscrossing and turning Meroweyan riders and their mounts into pillars of flame and then instant columns of ash—except for the small area protected by the wizard's shields.

Lerial creates more order-chaos separation, focusing it on the wizard's shields and simultaneously creating stronger protective order coils before second company.

Lightning rages against the chaos shield, focused chaos against disordered but latticelike chaos . . . and Lerial can feel a tension, as if every hair on his head and body is standing erect, while everything and everyone around him is fixed in place, unable to move.

Then . . . then, a brilliant flash of light sears across Lerial's eyes, momentarily blinding him, as the chaos shield disintegrates, revealing to his senses, but for a moment, a woman in brilliant white, with red hair that is the essence of fire.

The brilliance vanishes. Everything is cloaked in a darkness so profound that Lerial can see nothing, nothing at all. The blackness fades slowly into dark gray, and progressively lighter gray until Lerial is looking southward over what once had been a sweep of tall grass, taking in the yards and yards of smoldering grass, the charred remains of what had been men and mounts . . . and a circle of fine gray ash, and nothing else, that had held a chaos wizard, one lone woman.

How could you have known? Yet he understands that, woman or not, in the end, he could do no different. For all that, he feels like he should somehow mourn, not even knowing what he might be mourning.

Amid that devastation he can make out the three Meroweyan wagons, of which little remains but the iron wheel rims, the iron axle bearing rings, other iron parts he cannot identify with charred wooden remnants that might have been anything. He can feel, through his recurrent pounding headache, that Bhurl and Fhentaar have reined up several yards away, but not approached nearer, whether out of deference or fear, he cannot tell.

"Angel-flamed . . . never see anything like that . . ."

"Might give Duke Casseon something to think about . . ."

"Might. Too bad Moraris couldn't see this," Fhentaar continues in a low voice to Bhurl.

"He'd have asked the captain to spare the wagons so he could trade them," returns the other squad leader.

Moraris would have said something about capturing them, that they would have been worth something . . . After that vagrant thought, Lerial just sits in the saddle and looks across the charred ground. His eyes burn, and his head still throbs.

He feels tired . . . and like sowshit.

What else could you do? You could have lost half the company if you'd charged them with sabres. And yet . . . to strike them down with lightning . . . *But they used chaos-fire against both the Verdyn Lancers and the Verd itself.*

None of that makes him feel any better.

LXXVII

On sixday evening, second company stays in some of the houses in Ironwood that have not yet been reoccupied. Lerial does not bother with detailing Lancers to bury the remnants of the Meroweyans. There are likely no remnants to speak of, and after all his men have done, that is something that the locals can do—or not—as they wish. He sleeps, if not well, with troubling dreams that he cannot recall once he is fully awake. While the throbbing in his head has eased, it has not eased that much, but at least his eyesight is not blurred.

After eating a mixture whose ingredients he does not wish to know for what passes as breakfast, Lerial meets with the squad leaders, and then effectively acting as squad leader for first squad, with those rankers. Then he begins to groom the gelding, under skies that are largely clear, except to the southwest. He also notices a faint acrid smoky odor, the same one that, he realizes, he has smelled ever since he loosed the lightning the afternoon before. Yet the air is clear, without a sign of haze or smoke. Immediately after he grooms and then saddles his mount, a thin man in a faded brown shirt and worn brown trousers approaches . . . just before Lerial is about to order the company to mount up and begin the return to Escadya.

"You're the captain here?"

"I am," replies Lerial warily, trying to be pleasant despite the headache that remains far from entirely fading.

"Mite bit young for that, aren't you?" The man shakes his head. "What happened to those cess-swilling Meroweyans? They be back any time soon?"

"Almost all of them are dead. Those that aren't are wounded or captives in Escadya." Lerial pauses, then adds, "There might be a few wandering around here and there, but they'd likely be near Escadya . . . maybe Faerwest."

"You'd not be stuffing my ears now, would you?"

"No. Most of them are dead." Lerial's voice comes out flat.

"How'd that happen, if you don't mind my asking?"

Lerial does, especially with the annoying, almost whining, tone of the man's speech that seems to worsen the pounding inside his skull, but he manages a smile. "The Meroweyans lost almost ten companies in the skirmishes with the Verdyn Lancers on their march toward Verdell. Some of the Lancers lured one army into a trap at Faerwest, and the elders burned them up in a huge fire. I understand the fire also destroyed the town. The other army, the one that came through here, attacked the Lancers just south of Escadya. More than half the invaders were killed by lightning. The others were killed, wounded, or captured by the Lancers. We destroyed the last two companies just outside the road gates south of Nevnarnia yesterday afternoon."

" 'Destroyed.' Big word for a young fellow like you."

Lerial smiles faintly. "Go and see."

Abruptly, the man edges back, then nods his head. "Be thanking you." With that, he turns and walks quickly away.

Lerial watches him for several moments, then mounts. Second company needs to get back to Escadya.

A glass later, as second company is riding northwest on the main road, empty except for them, he is still pondering why the man, clearly a resident of Ironwood, had so suddenly decided to cut his inquisition of Lerial short. Had it been the certainty in Lerial's voice? Or something else?

He glances up as the light seems to fade, realizing that a cloud must have crossed the sun. *Now there are clouds.* His smile is wry. The smile fades as he realizes he still smells the bitter acridity of smoke, if faintly.

Riding beside Lerial, Bhurl clears his throat. "Been thinking, ser. Might there be many chaos wizards in the Heldyan forces?"

In the Heldyan forces? "I wouldn't know. Before we came to Verdheln, I knew that Duke Casseon had some wizards, but no one seemed to know how many. I've not heard anything about mages or wizards in either Afrit or Heldya. I'm sure there must be some. Why?"

"Couldn't say, ser. Except it seems like . . . well . . . trouble just doesn't visit alone, if you know what I mean. The Afritans are stirring things up. Same for the Heldyans . . . and here comes Duke Casseon."

"They say troubles come triple," replies Lerial with a smile. "It could be that the Duke and the Mirror Lancers have taken care of the others as well."

"Be good if they have." Bhurl nods, then frowns. "You know those wizards . . . they're sneakylike. Can't even see if they're with armsmen. Can make a man a mite skittish thinking about it."

"We managed."

"Yes, ser, we did. Mostly you, ser."

"It wouldn't have been possible without all the Mirror Lancers who came, or the majer, or the elders of the Verd. It took all of us."

"Yes, ser." Bhurl offers a smile.

For the next kay or so, the squad leader's words prey on Lerial, and he can't help thinking, *What happens if you don't see or sense a chaos wizard? What can you do about that? Can you make an order diversion pattern that is part of the flow of order and chaos around you all the time?*

Lerial has the definite feeling that is something he needs to work on . . . and soon, or as soon as his head stops pounding. He also has the feeling that there are other things he needs to do . . . if he could just think of them.

LXXVIII

It is well past seventh glass, twilight is deepening into night when second company rides into the training compound on the south end of Escadya and reins up before the stables. It is more than a glass later before Lerial finishes settling the company and making sure that they have had the first real meal in three days. He acts as squad leader for Korlyn, as he has been doing, although that isn't the best idea, but he has no real idea which of the Verdyn Lancers might be best for the position, and there certainly aren't any spare Mirror Lancers to take the squad. He can still recall, all too vividly, the look on Korlyn's face, when he had left to chase down the Meroweyans.

Only after all that does he seek out Altyrn, who has not intruded.

The majer is waiting, standing outside the study he has used for eightdays, with the door slightly ajar. "Welcome back. I presume you had some success?"

How do you answer that? "I did what I set out to do."

"Come in and tell me about it." Altyrn steps to the side and opens the door, gesturing for Lerial to enter.

Lerial does so and then seats himself on the single straight-backed chair in front of the narrow desk. Absently, he massages his forehead with his right hand for a moment. "Before we start, what about Juist and Denieryn and their companies?"

"Juist is fine. Denieryn . . ." Altyrn shakes his head, then closes the door, and sits down behind the desk. "He lost almost two squads to firebolts, and he was one of the first hit. I've transferred the survivors from sixth company to third to bring it up to full strength. We'll move trainees into the other four companies." Altyrn looks directly at Lerial, then smiles. "You know, when you headed out after the Meroweyans, that's the first time you've taken the initiative to do something well beyond your orders."

"I could see it was necessary."

"It might have been, but you have yet to tell me what it was that you did."

Lerial can see that Altyrn likely has already guessed, but it is good manners, and safer, to describe exactly what happened, not necessarily detail by detail. "We followed them all the way to the road gates south of Nevnarnia and out onto the grasslands. They formed up. They had about two companies worth of mounted armsmen, but all kinds, as if there were a few from one kind of company and a few from others. There was one white wizard. We faced each other, and then they started to turn and leave." Lerial pauses. "I used order and lightning to slaughter them to the last person. She was the white wizard."

Altyrn nods.

"We spent the night in Ironwood and rode back. Here we are."

"Why do you think it was necessary to slaughter them all?" Altyrn's voice is calm and level.

"I don't want to have to fight them again, and the Verdyn shouldn't have to, either."

"That leaves the question of prisoners. There are more than a hundred. Most are wounded. What would you suggest?"

"Make all of them help clean up the mess they made. Then send them back to Casseon . . . unless they want to stay, if the elders will have them, or you think any would make decent Mirror Lancers."

"Some might. We'll have to see." Altyrn clears his throat. "What you did to Casseon's armsmen and wizards was drastic, even for war. Don't you think that your acts will just enrage Casseon and prompt him to send an even larger force?"

"It might. But it might not if he received a dispatch from the Duke of Cigoerne pointing out that two squads of Mirror Lancers and six companies of Verdyn Lancers destroyed over forty companies and at least six white wizards . . . and that Cigoerne has no designs on any other part of Merowey, but does respect the right of the people of the Verd to choose who will rule them, particularly since the Duchy of Merowey has provided neither assistance nor leadership to Verdheln."

"That last part might be a bit strong."

"You're right."

"We don't have to worry about that part of it." Altyrn smiles again. "Your father does. He will worry, but likely not too much. He sent us to keep Casseon from taking over the Verd. We did. Or rather, you did much of that."

"I think there should be very little said about what I did."

"That is your choice. That might be the wisest course, but you will have to see what your father says."

And how it affects Lephi. That could be another problem, one that Lerial has not considered.

"You'll have some time to think about that on your return to Cigoerne. You'll be leaving on twoday."

"I will?" Lerial has not even thought about what he would do, or be required to do, after dealing with the Meroweyans.

"There's nothing else you can do here now. You've certainly demonstrated your father's and your commitment to Verdheln. Your father needs to hear what happened, especially from you. I'll send a sealed and written report with you. Two copies. One for your father, and one to Majer Phortyn. I trust you also won't mind carrying a letter to Maeroja . . . and the girls, of course."

"Not at all." Lerial understands that, especially since he will get to see Ryalah and Amaira, while Altyrn is still mired in Verdheln. Absently, he also wonders how Rojana is doing. Without the lodestone she had given him . . . He returns his attention to Altyrn.

"You'll lead half a squad of mostly Verdyn Lancers. You'll need some Mirror Lancers as well. We'll go over who they should be tomorrow."

"What about you?"

"I'm not done. We need to train more Verdyn Lancers, and give the ones who've survived more training. What do you think about Bhurl as acting undercaptain for second company?"

"He'd do better than Moraris or Fhentaar. You might think about putting Moraris in charge of procurement or supplies. I think he's a born trader."

"That might not be a bad idea . . . if he even wants to stay."

"How long do you intend . . . ?"

"Another season should see them well enough established that they can provide companies to help Cigoerne . . . if necessary. What's important is that they have a core of Lancers who've been through skirmishes and battles."

Lerial stifles a yawn. He *is* tired.

"You need some sleep, I can see. There's one other thing."

"Ser?"

"Did you ever think that, if something happened to me, you would be in command of the Verdyn Lancers?"

"No. Actually, I didn't." That is certainly true enough.

"I'm not chastising you. What you did was the right thing to do. I would be happier if you had made that decision after considering all the factors. Those are things you will need to weigh in the future."

That, Lerial also understands.

"Go get some sleep."

Lerial doesn't protest. He just stands. "Good night, ser."

After he leaves Altyrn's study, thinking about returning to Cigoerne and carrying a report from Altyrn to Majer Phortyn, a thought strikes him. Outside of the letter from Emerya and the one dispatch from Phortyn to Altyrn, they have received nothing from Cigoerne. *Because no one wants to spare men as couriers . . . or because Phortyn doesn't consider Altyrn's task a true Mirror Lancer mission and only sent the one dispatch because it cost him little to do so?*

Another yawn comes over him. He is tired.

LXXIX

A good night's sleep and some solid, if not particularly appetizing ghano-acorn hash for breakfast has Lerial feeling far better on oneday morning when he goes to meet with Altyrn to discuss who might be best to accompany Lerial on his return journey to Cigoerne.

When Lerial enters the small study, Altyrn seems preoccupied for a moment, then says, "I think we'd better go over my report."

"I trust that you didn't identify the ordermage who created those ground lightnings," Lerial says evenly.

"I thought you might say that."

"You hoped I would." Lerial offers a lopsided smile as he sits down in front of the desk.

"That, too, but I've noticed that you don't want much credit."

"I like praise as much as anyone, but I like not being a target even more."

Altyrn extends a sheaf of papers. "Then read."

"You must have been writing all night."

The majer shakes his head. "I've written each section as it happened. You forget less that way. You also have less temptation to revise occurrences in your favor."

Lerial can see both points. He eases the report before him and begins to read. When he finishes, he says, "The only thing I'd suggest is to add something about the loss of not only Essiana, but also a chief archer who was the daughter of an elder on the High Council. And something about the number of hamlets burned and Verdyn killed."

"I'd thought about the hamlets. Why do you want to mention Klerryt's daughter?"

"It's a way of pointing out that the Verdyn are similar."

Altyrn nods. "You're right. That will strengthen your father's resolve to keep supporting them."

Lerial hands the report back.

"For your return party, I'd thought to ask for four Mirror Lancer volunteers, well . . . three now, and six Verdyn Lancer volunteers."

"Three now?"

"Bhurl has requested permission to return with you."

"How does he know I'm going?"

The majer grins. "He doesn't. He requested that he be allowed to return to Cigoerne whenever it was possible and in the interests of the Mirror Lancers. He has a family in Cigoerne, his consort and three children. Most of the other Mirror Lancers do not—or if they do . . ." Altyrn shrugs.

They're in no hurry to return to that family . . . for one reason or another. "Will there be trouble getting volunteers?" Lerial is thinking that some of the rankers may prefer to remain as squad leaders in Verdheln, even if they are not being paid as such.

"We can order some of the Mirror Lancers to go, if necessary, but I doubt it will be. Out of six companies . . . five now, I'm certain we can get six Verdyn volunteers to escort the Duke's son and to have a chance to see Cigoerne." Altyrn's lips quirk into a smile.

"When you put it that way . . ." Lerial shakes his head.

"You'll need to get used to things like that."

Lerial supposes he will, but has another thought. "Fhentaar could handle second company . . . with guidance."

"We'll see. I'll also be sending a request for weapons to train and outfit more companies of Lancers. The elders have agreed that more are necessary."

"There were quite a few weapons recovered from the Meroweyans." Lerial's statement is bland.

"There were. Once we have them all gathered up, we'll send some of those, the ones that aren't suitable for Lancers. Your father or Majer Phortyn can arrange for their sale or their reforging into sabres or lances." A faint smile crosses Altyrn's lips. "There is one other matter. Klerryt and I will be riding with you to Verdell. The full Council of Elders wants to meet with both of us to go over an agreement they wish you to present to your father."

"What sort of agreement?"

"Something to bind him and his heirs to allowing the people of the Verd to retain their own customs in return for their allegiance and tariffs."

There is something about that idea that bothers Lerial. He has no problem with the Verdyn wanting to retain their customs, yet . . .

"You have a problem with that?" asks Altyrn pleasantly.

"I have no problem at all with them retaining their own customs."

"Then why are you looking so concerned?"

"There's just something . . ." Lerial knows there is, but it is a matter of feeling, or more of the fact that what is wrong is so obvious, and yet he cannot put his finger—or his thoughts—on what that is.

"There is indeed. It's only symbolic," Altyrn says. "At one time, Casseon's predecessors promised the same thing. It's very hard for a ruler to bind his successors to a promise, even one in writing, made by a man long dead."

Lerial feels stupid for not seeing the obvious, but he's not about to admit that, except to himself. "They hope that if I agree . . ." He shakes his head. "Lephi's the heir, not me, and I can only try to persuade him."

"They know that, but if you and your father agree, it will be harder for him to ignore the promise, and it may not even come to that."

Lerial can see the elders' point. "That raises another question. I assume I should report to Majer Phortyn immediately upon my arrival in Cigoerne."

"If you still consider yourself a Mirror Lancer."

"Why shouldn't I? I'm not the heir. As an undercaptain, I should report to the majer." *Even if I won't be telling him everything.*

"As an undercaptain . . . that's true." Altyrn's voice is level.

"I'm certain that the majer would prefer that I report initially through the chain of command," adds Lerial. "He doesn't have to know I carry a personal communication from the High Council."

"He could command you to reveal it to him and to remain at headquarters while he reports to your father."

Is he that great an idiot? "Then I would just have to tell him that my orders from his superior—that's my father—were that I should report to the majer first, but that I should then report to the Palace. I would prefer not to have to say that."

"You likely won't have to, but it's best to decide how you would deal with such a situation."

Another not-so-veiled suggestion to anticipate and prepare for all possibilities.

For another half glass, Altyrn goes over the details of Lerial's return to Cigoerne and what he should expect, including what to say to the post commander when he reaches Tirminya. To Lerial, the fact that Altyrn does not refer to Dechund by name suggests just how little the majer thinks of the captain.

When Altyrn finishes, he adds, "By the way, you won't have to write Elder Klerryt."

"Oh?" Lerial is immediately on guard.

"He came to Escadya yesterday to represent the council. Donnael has been ill and has returned to Verdell to recover."

"I should talk to him, then."

"You should. He'll be here by eighth glass."

"That won't be long. I might as well go out and wait for him." *While you think about what you should say about Alaynara.*

"He would appreciate that courtesy."

"By your leave, ser?"

"Of course. I also appreciate the courtesy."

Lerial stands and then makes his way to the hitching rail outside the barracks building that holds the officers' quarters and their studies. There are no riders coming down the lane from the main road, and he turns his thoughts to Alaynara. He is still thinking about what he should say when he sees two riders on the lane. The elder rides in accompanied by a wayguide who looks familiar, but it takes Lerial a moment to recognize and recall Yulyn, who had guided them from the northeast side of the Verd to Apfhel and then to Verdell and Escadya.

"Greetings, Elder, Wayguide," offers Lerial.

"The same to you," returns Klerryt as he dismounts.

From what Lerial recalls, there is far more white in the elder's red hair than there was a season ago, not to mention the dark circles under his eyes. "I thought we might talk for a bit . . . if you have some time."

"I always have time to talk to Duke Kiedron's son."

Lerial stiffens inside at the formality of Klerryt's words and tries to offer his reply in a gentle tone. "I would hope you would also have time to talk to Undercaptain Lerial, ser."

"I would and do." After a slight hesitation, Klerryt adds, "I'd prefer to walk while we talk."

"We can do that." Lerial gestures toward the green in the center of the rows of barracks buildings, then steps up beside the elder, who is just a digit or so taller than Lerial is.

"What did you have in mind?"

"I wanted to talk about Alaynara."

"To offer some trite comments or explanations?" Klerryt's words are softly tart.

"No. To tell you what I learned about her and exactly what happened . . . without justifications or elaborate explanations or rationalizations."

"I'm listening."

"She was very professional. She was the best archer I've ever seen, and she could estimate a distance and put an arrow down almost on a point on the darkest night. That is no surprise to you, I'm certain."

"I can't say it is."

"She was also very perceptive. She once suggested, very tactfully, except it was really a rhetorical question, when no one else was around, that I'd hadn't been allowed to be a child long."

"I don't imagine you were. What did you tell her?"

"That it didn't matter now . . . that what mattered was that other children would have that chance. Somehow . . . that surprised her. At least, I think it did."

"It may well have. Why did you think so?"

"Her voice softened, and she said she was sorry."

Klerryt shakes his head, but there is a wry smile on his face as he looks at Lerial. "That would have been Alaynara. Is there anything else?"

"She was excellent at knowing where the archers should be, and in letting me know in a way that was firm without being challenging." He pauses. "I didn't talk to her that much, but . . ." He shakes his head. "She had picked the position for the archers in the battle at the stream, but we didn't have the chance to see how effective they would be. We were ordered to pull out and move north along the east side of the stream to delay some Meroweyan companies so that Donnael and Ruethana—I think—could call a storm to block the chaos wizards . . ." Lerial goes on to explain how he had positioned the squads. ". . . I misjudged the speed of the Meroweyan advance, but Alaynara had fourth squad cutting down a great number of the leading ranks. There had not been any chaos-bolts thrown. I was prepared for that, and when one came, I redirected it back at their wizard. He did something I hadn't seen before, and it came back at us twice as strong. I must have done something wrong, because when I sent it back, just a tiny blast of chaos flared back—right in the middle of fourth squad. It only hit three archers. The middle one was Alaynara." Lerial swallows slightly, then says. "I had the company withdraw immediately, or they would have overrun us."

Klerryt does not speak for a long moment. "You surprise me."

Lerial waits, unsure of what the elder will say, worried that Klerryt will offer some withering remark, and knowing he has every right to do so.

"You have not offered a single word to mitigate or justify what happened."

"How could I, ser? It was a small miscalculation on my part. That is true, but some under my command died because of that mistake."

"How many others died?"

"None, ser. Not there."

"Were you attracted to my daughter?"

Lerial blinks. *What?* For a moment, he can say nothing. Finally, he says, "I admired her. I didn't think of her in any other way."

"A fair and honest answer. You've worried about her death and talking to me . . . have you not?"

"Yes, ser." *Many times.*

"So here we are. An older man and a younger man. You have risked your life to save our people, and you made a small error of judgment that required your taking an action that led to my daughter's death, but preserved the lives of almost a hundred other young people."

"Then," Lerial is forced to add.

"Then," agrees Klerryt. After another painfully long silence, he continues. "You have not resorted to excuses. You understand more fully than most far older than you would your responsibility. I can mourn the circumstances. I can and do grieve for my daughter. I cannot fault you, especially given the burdens you bear. No leader, no ruler, no officer can protect all of those in his charge from all eventualities. All we can ask is that they have the greatest skill possible and carry out their duties to the best of their abilities. You are what, perhaps eighteen?"

"I'll be seventeen on threeday after the turn of summer, ser."

Klerryt almost stops in his tracks, then shakes his head slowly. "Alaynara was indeed right." His smile is close to bitter. "And so were we."

"You? The elders?"

Klerryt nods. "Your father leads the Mirror Lancers on many occasions, does he not?"

"He does."

"Your brother serves as a Mirror Lancer officer, does he not?"

"He's an undercaptain, too." *Or he was.*

"What of your mother . . . the women of your family?"

"They're healers." Lerial thinks he understands what Klerryt needs to know. "My mother and my aunt serve as healers in Cigoerne. My aunt is the head healer at the Hall of Healing."

Klerryt nods brusquely. "Then you understand why we were right."

"I think I understand that you believe you made the best choice of those available."

"You don't think so?"

Lerial allows himself a wry smile. "I think so, but to say that you made the best choice would sound more self-serving than I'd care to be."

Klerryt laughs softly. "It is indeed a pity . . ." Then he breaks off his words and shakes his head. "We need say no more about what happened . . . at the stream."

Lerial nods, relieved, but still concerned and wondering what may come next, because Klerryt begins to resume his former pace.

"I saw the battlefield . . . you were most fortunate."

"We were. They could easily have overrun us."

"That is true." Klerryt smiles sadly. "But that is not what I meant."

Lerial nods for the elder to continue.

"Pardon me, Lord Lerial, if I sound as though I were a tutor lecturing a pupil, but I know no other way to convey what I must say. It is most important that you understand what you did and what you can do . . . and what could happen if you do not understand."

Lerial does indeed think that Klerryt sounds more like Saltaryn than Saltaryn himself, but the almost gentle way in which the elder speaks suggests that Lerial should indeed listen carefully. *You don't have to agree, but after what you did to his daughter, even unintentionally, you need to listen to him . . . for the rest of your life, if necessary.* "Please go on."

"Order and chaos exist on two levels, if you will. One level is the one on which most of us who have some ability in manipulating order and chaos operate. Most order and chaos manipulation uses, for lack of a better way of saying it, 'free' order or chaos. These are bits or concentrations of order or chaos that are comparatively—comparatively, only comparatively, mind you—easy to bend to one's ability and will. A fire creates a certain amount of free chaos. So does killing someone or something, or destroying something. A well-built structure tends to attract free order. People can attract either. You, by the way, do not. Most great chaos wizards or ordermasters don't." The elder offers another almost sad smile before continuing. "The world and all beyond it are composed of entwined order and chaos, but on a tinier level. What you did was to break apart a few of the most minute pieces of the world to release a great amount of order and chaos. Had you continued for even a few instants more, all that would have remained of you—and all the Lancers and all the Meroweyans—would have been a charred bowl in the ground that might have someday filled with water and have been known as one of the cursed lakes."

Lerial nods slowly, then says, "I could feel an upwelling of immense power, and I stopped and shunted as much as I could away from us."

"You did well at that, for which all of us, save Duke Casseon's men, are most grateful. I can only beg of you to be most careful if and when you attempt that kind of order-chaos manipulation, although"—Klerryt smiles more cheerfully—"I think you have already found that you may not need such drastic measures that often in the future." The smile vanishes. "You had best hope you do not. For most of great power, the more that power is used, the greater the impact on the user, until, at some time, it is used once too often, and it recoils on the user. When that happens . . ."

Lerial can sense that Klerryt believes what he says. "You're saying that I must measure what I do . . . that . . ." He frowns. "How can that be?"

"Why do you think Essiana died?" asks the elder. "She asked too much of herself and her power. That is how most great ordermages die. That is also why the great ones who survive tend to learn more subtle uses of order."

"I admit that I have not attempted much since the last battle," Lerial says cautiously.

"I would suggest that you proceed cautiously, especially at first. I would also suggest you develop some sort of defense . . . shields or something that will protect you at all times. Not all order or chaos attacks with noisy and powerful firebolts."

"You've sensed much of what I've felt, haven't you?"

"Some. Not all. You hold enough order that it is . . . tiring . . . to try to sense everything."

Left unsaid, Lerial realizes, is the fact that, without shields—or something—he likely seems like a blazing fire on a dark night to other order-mages—or Magi'i—or, especially—white wizards and chaos mages.

"I do need to speak to Majer Altyrn, since you will likely not be remaining in Verdheln long."

"Then we should walk back."

Klerryt nods.

Once Lerial has escorted the elder back to Altyrn and slipped back to the small study that is his, for the next day, anyway, Lerial thinks about Klerryt's last words. *What happens if you don't see or sense a chaos wizard? What can you do about that? Can you make an order diversion pattern that is part of the flow of order and chaos around you all the time?* After a moment, he has an additional thought. *If you want to survive, how can you not?*

Although Lerial feels tired as oneday wears on, he cannot ignore the advice and the warning that Klerryt has delivered. Nor can he ignore what he feels—that somehow he must learn greater control over his abilities so that nothing like what happened to Alaynara will happen to anyone else as a result of his lack of understanding or control.

Isn't that presumptuous of you—at your age? But the answer to that question is obvious enough. Whether he likes it or not, he has a certain power. Failure to gain greater control and understanding of that power could easily kill him . . . as he has come close to seeing . . . and that failure has already killed others.

After begging—requesting, really—some acorn bread and the smelly blue cheese from the cooks, Lerial leaves the mess hall with it and walks slowly down to the open area where he and second company had practiced maneuvers so often—maneuvers that they had so seldom used. *Is that always the way of it, that you don't use what you know and you're always confronted with what you don't?* He smiles ironically. *That's because those who oppose you will attack where you're weakest . . . at least the best of them will, and you can't count on often encountering the worst.*

All that is fine, but how is he going to create shields or defenses of some sort, that is, the kinds that work all the time?

He begins by creating a simple coil pattern. That is easy enough. The next step is to link it to the flow of order around himself . . . and that is where he runs into trouble.

No matter what he tries, the moment he stops thinking about the pattern, it dissolves back into free order. What he does discover, though, is that there is a great deal more free order around than he recalls. Except that Klerryt had said—and he doesn't think the elder was deceiving him—that he doesn't attract free order . . . or chaos. So why . . . ?

Because you now sense "deeper" levels of free order?

That makes sense, but whether it's correct is another matter.

By late afternoon, Lerial is no further than he was when he began, not in terms of being able to create shields or defenses that will remain in place when he is not thinking about them . . . although he has developed defense patterns that provide—he thinks—a stronger defense with less effort on his part. He can definitely gather and concentrate more order, and with it, more chaos, but even small concentrations of chaos make him feel very uneasy, even when that chaos is surrounded and shielded from him by order.

In the end, he goes to bed early—worried and tired—on oneday night.

He wakes up more rested, but no less worried, or at least concerned, about his inability to figure out a defense that he doesn't have to maintain actively.

Then again, you didn't have any defenses a season ago. While true, that thought doesn't console him terribly, although it remains in the back of his mind as he is packing his gear and grooming the gelding to be ready to leave the training compound with Altyrn by seventh glass. The early morning sky is hazy, not that the haze will make much difference for the ride, since most of the way is shaded by the tall trees of the Verd.

He does not bother to mount the gelding, but walks him to the north end of the stables where Bhurl, selected by Altyrn as the acting squad leader because he is the most senior, is forming up the Lancers who will accompany Lerial all the way to Cigoerne, as well as those who will ride to Verdell with the majer and then escort him back to Escadya. One of the other three Mirror Lancers is Moraris. That doesn't surprise Lerial at all, because Moraris has always struck him as the kind of man who is more comfortable where there are more people and more opportunities to trade things to an advantage. The other two Mirror Lancers are Taendalk and Khillen, men Lerial scarcely knows except by name. Except for Vominem, he knows none of the Verdyn Lancers by name, although most of their faces are vaguely familiar.

"Morning, ser," Bhurl calls out cheerfully.

"Good morning," Lerial replies with a smile, then mounts the gelding quickly as he sees Altyrn and Klerryt both riding toward the formation.

As the column moves from the training compound, Lerial is riding at the head of the column beside Bhurl, with Vominem a good hundred yards before them as scout, and Klerryt and Altyrn behind Lerial and Bhurl.

"You glad to be headed back?" Lerial asks the squad leader.

"Relieved. Glad to be riding back in one piece. Always the chance that it can happen to you the way it did to Ferragn and Alaarn."

"I was a little surprised to see Moraris . . ." Lerial is not at all surprised, but wants to hear what Bhurl will say.

"He's close to the end of his term. Wants to try his hand as a trader. That's what he says."

"I did overhear him trying to trade for more arrows for his archers."

"Leastwise . . ." Bhurl breaks off with a laugh. "He did a good job with the archers. Had some help from the chief archer. Shame about that."

"A great loss." *In so many ways.* Lerial lets the silence draw out before he asks, "What can you tell me about Taendalk and Khillen?"

"Good men. Taendalk's almost as senior as me . . ."

Lerial listens, trying not to think too much about Alaynara . . . or his own failure to create defenses.

LXXX

The column turns up the paved street in Verdell on fourday afternoon just before third glass, heading toward the octagonal green that holds the black stone building, also octagonal in shape, where Lerial and Altyrn will once again meet with the High Council of Verdheln. This time Bhurl and Klerryt ride at the head of the Lancers, followed by Altyrn and Lerial. After they rein up outside the single-level octagonal building with its low, domed slate roof, Lerial, Altyrn, and Klerryt dismount, and the elder leads the way into the building, through the open area, and then into the council chamber where three others are waiting, rising from their places around the circular table.

Lerial recognizes Ruethana and Donnael, but not the other woman, who, while certainly not young, is strikingly exotic, with an almost silver-white skin, and short hair that is a shade Lerial could only have described as silver blond. Her eyes are black, and chaos radiates from her.

As Lerial and Altyrn move to the far side of the table Klerryt stops beside Donnael, who offers a few words that Lerial cannot make out. Klerryt shakes his head and replies, also in a low tone, then asks something.

Donnael frowns quizzically and murmurs, "Are you certain?"

At least, that is what Lerial thinks he asks.

At Klerryt's reply, Donnael hands the younger elder something wrapped in a brown cloth. Klerryt nods, and moves to stand behind his seat.

"Welcome to Verdell," says Ruethana, in a voice that is but a shade warmer than perfunctory.

"Welcome, indeed," adds Donnael in a far warmer tone, although his voice is raspy and Lerial can see that his one hand, gesturing for them to take the vacant seats at the table, is shaking slightly, while the other hand, on the back of the chair, steadies him. After a pause, the senior elder inclines his head to the silver-blond woman. "This is Khalya, the newest elder."

Khalya inclines her head.

Klerryt takes his seat, and so does Altyrn. Again, Lerial finds himself between the majer and the youngest elder, in this case, Khalya.

As he settles into his seat, Lerial gathers in what his order-senses tell him about the elder who has succeeded Essiana. While she radiates chaos, there is no free chaos actually within her, nor any free order, either. It is almost as though she attracts chaos and then repels it, but that it never becomes a part of her. That may be so, but he cannot determine how she does that, or why there is no more order around her than the usual amount in a living person. Certainly, he has never seen or sensed anything like her. He tries not to look too obviously in her direction and waits for what the elders may say.

"Lord Lerial, Majer Altyrn," begins Ruethana, "you and your Mirror Lancers have accomplished something we doubted was possible. Your efforts have also left the High Council with certain concerns. It is clear that Duke Kiedron prefers a Verd that is part of Cigoerne. It is clear as well that both of you do. Duke Casseon had the same preference, but he did not wish us to continue in our way of life. The concern we have is whether, in the future, Cigoerne will continue to allow us our ways . . . or whether, in time, some future Duke will decide to force the issue the way Duke Casseon did."

Lerial is tempted to suggest that what Ruethana has said is not even a question, but instead he looks to Altyrn.

The majer nods politely back at Lerial.

"Elders," begins Lerial, cautiously, "no one can foresee the acts of future generations. I can only say that my father the Duke has let those people who have asked to be governed by him continue in their old ways, if with several exceptions. He has insisted that girl children be treated as equals with boys"—*At least until they're grown*—"and that the punishments for violation of the laws be the same throughout Cigoerne . . . or no harsher than those levied in Cigoerne. I do not foresee that he will change his views in those regards. Nor would I, were I in a position to do so." But trying to speak for Lephi is something Lerial isn't about to do, nor will he even bring up the matter of his brother being the primary heir.

"We understand that," says Donnael smoothly, although his voice remains hoarse. "We would like you to take a proposed agreement between the High Council of Verdheln and your sire, as Duke of Cigoerne, which, with his signature beside ours, would affirm his agreement with those principles."

"I can certainly convey that agreement."

"Perhaps you should read it," says Ruethana dryly.

"We would be happy to do so," replies Lerial.

Ruethana hands a large envelope to Klerryt, who passes it to the majer.

Altyrn slides the single sheet from the envelope, reads it, and then passes it to Lerial with a pleasant smile.

Lerial begins to read, almost skimming over the prefatory politeness and formality of the greeting to his father, referred to as "Duke of Cigoerne, heir of the Rational Stars," before concentrating on the text that comprises the key section of the agreement. To his surprise, the agreement is almost as direct as Ruethana's words. The last paragraph lauds Kiedron under the notation that the signatories for the High Council freely acknowledge the Duke's aid and assistance without which there could have been no agreement.

After rereading the agreement to make certain that he has not missed anything, Lerial slips the agreement back into the envelope, then says, "I see no problems with conveying this to Cigoerne for my father's consideration."

"Then that is settled," says Ruethana, nodding to Donnael.

"Lord Lerial," offers Donnael, "I will be frank. We appreciated the gesture of your sire in sending his youngest son. We thought that his dispatching you was merely a commitment to good faith. We did not anticipate that you would actually command a company in battle. Nor did we think that the Duke would have sent someone so young . . ."

Barely more than a boy, is what Donnael means, Lerial suspects.

". . . who turned out to be so powerful." Donnael coughs several times, then wheezes.

Lerial cannot help but sense the faint red of sickness chaos in Donnael's chest, but manages a polite smile, rather than the concerned frown that is more like what he feels.

". . . we would like to convey our appreciation, both personally and as representatives of the High Council, for your efforts, one of which brought you as close to death as is possible without dying . . ."

Even with the chaos radiating from Khalya, Lerial can sense some disruption of the flow. *Surprise? Consternation? Anger?* He cannot tell, only that something affected her.

". . . likewise, Majer Altyrn, without your expertise, experience, and capabilities in training and employing the Verdyn Lancers, all would have been lost from the beginning. For those reasons, we would like to present you each with a small token of appreciation." Donnael nods to Klerryt.

Klerryt swallows before he speaks. "The past few eightdays have been difficult . . . for me. You all know why. I asked to go to Escadya. It was not only to relieve Donnael. It was to find an answer. I did not find the answer I sought, but another. That is why I have asked Donnael to allow me to present these to you." Klerryt leans forward and hands Altyrn two objects wrapped in soft brown cloth. "The top one is yours, Majer."

Altyrn takes the top bundle and hands the other to Lerial.

Lerial discovers that the soft cloth is a winter scarf, but it is wrapped around something else—a belt knife in a tooled leather scabbard. The tooling on the front of the scabbard displays an ornate "L" flanked on each side by a cloud, with three stars in an arc above the "L." The hilt is of black lorken, textured with a diamond pattern. He eases the knife from the scabbard, and he can feel the order within the iron. The blade is simple, with a full lower cutting edge, and a double-edged point. The knife itself is older than the scabbard, but certainly not ancient. He looks up. "Thank you. It's beautiful and most effective, I suspect. I hope I will do justice to it and to whoever last carried it."

Klerryt nods. "You already have."

There is little Lerial can say to that except nod.

"We will not keep you," Ruethana says, not quite curtly. "We know Lord Lerial has to prepare for a long ride back to Cigoerne." She rises, as do the other elders, although Donnael is slightly slower.

"Thank you," offers Altyrn as he stands.

After rising, Lerial walks over to Donnael, where he sets the envelope holding the agreement on the table, along with the scarf and knife, then takes Donnael's hand with his own, placing his other hand on the older man's forearm and letting a flow of order go from him to Donnael, directing some of it into the other's chest and lungs. "I do appreciate your understanding, Elder Donnael. I will take the agreement you are requesting and present it to my father with my support for what it contains."

Donnael looks surprised, and murmurs, "You do not have to do that."

Lerial knows he is not referring to the agreement on the table. "I do, as my father's son, for good and trustworthy allies are not often found." He releases the elder's hand and arm, then retrieves the knife, scarf, and envelope, steps back and smiles.

Klerryt escorts the two out of the council building, then stops at the bottom of the low black stone steps and turns to Lerial. "You healed him, didn't you?"

"I hope so. I tried."

The elder smiles. "You did enough that he will recover."

This time. "Thank you for presenting the knife to me. I appreciate that . . . after . . ."

"She would have wanted me to."

Lerial nods. He understands that, recalling again what Alaynara had said to him. He reaches out and grasps Klerryt's hand for a moment. "Take care."

"You as well, Lord Lerial."

"As I can." Lerial offers a last smile, then turns and walks to where one of the Lancers holds the gelding's reins. Before mounting he slips the knife, scarf, and agreement into the top of his saddlebags.

They have ridden for several hundred yards before Altyrn speaks. "You know, don't you, that you're committed to support them?"

"By accepting the knife and scarf?" Lerial shakes his head. "I was committed before that."

"After the stream battle?"

Lerial nods.

"Loyalties outside family are dangerous," Altyrn says quietly.

"Having none is even more dangerous, I think."

Abruptly, the majer laughs. "Let's get back to the hostel and make certain everything's ready for you to leave in the morning."

To
Cigoerne

LXXXI

Six days later, Lerial glances up at the sky and then back at the two packhorses and the last of the Verdyn Lancers in his comparatively small party—just nine Lancers, Bhurl, and himself—the smallest group of Lancers he has led in more than a season. There are no clouds, but a faint haze imparts a silvery sheen to the green-blue sky, and the air is warm for a spring day. But then, Lerial realizes, while he has been thinking of the season as spring, two days earlier, spring had given way to summer.

Now, kays east of the Verd, he cannot help but keep going over the thoughts that circle in his mind. *What did all of this accomplish? Casseon never really held the Verd, and he still doesn't. He lost more than four thousand men and something like six white wizards trying to get something he never really held. The people of the Verd lost thousands, young and old alike, and one of their most talented elders, and it will be years before Verdheln recovers . . . and it's likely never to be the way it was.*

How did it all come about? We were supposed to train Lancers. Lerial shakes his head. Somehow, after training the Verdyn Lancers, he and Altyrn and the squad leaders and rankers ended up leading them. *It seemed so logical.*

His fingers drop to the hilt of the knife from the elders, and, again, he can feel that there is something slightly different about the order contained in the blade and tang, although he cannot explain what that might be, but it is somehow almost reassuring, like the lodestone from Rojana that has provided him with so much understanding and inspiration.

In time, he thinks about Alaynara . . . and then Essiana, not that he knew the elder at all, except through one brief meeting, and about her successor . . . and the fact that, for all that Khalya radiates chaos, that chaos is not a part of her, and yet he could detect no pattern, no mechanism that attracted or diverted chaos . . . as if that ability were indeed a part of her.

His mouth opens, and he shakes his head.

"Ser?" asks Bhurl.

"Nothing. I just realized something." *That is why you can't create defenses that are always there. They're not a part of you . . . and they have to be.*

He is still thinking about that when Bhurl gestures and says, "Believe that's Tirminya over that rise ahead."

Lerial knows they have made better time on the return, largely because they have not had to worry about wagons, just the supplies on the two packhorses, but he still wonders if they are really that close to the post, although they have passed groupings of growers' steads over the past day, and he does not recall that many steads that close together, except near Tirminya.

He extends his order-senses . . . and discovers that Bhurl is indeed right. The post lies less than two kays ahead over the low rise ahead and to the south of the dirt road that they have followed for days, seeing only occasional herds of sheep and one small herd of cattle. "You're right. There's no one on the road over the crest, either."

"You could worry a man, ser, seeing where eyes aren't."

Lerial grins. "As I recall, that came in useful more than once."

"Still worrisome." But Bhurl grins in return.

What's worrisome to Lerial is that, for all his quiet attempts over the journey, he is not that much closer to having figured out how to create continuous shields, or what he thinks of as permanent defenses. He has been able to create what amounts to a continuing "chaos-diversion" shield, in a way, by linking the pattern to his sabre or his belt knife, but if he doesn't renew the pattern every few glasses, and sometimes more often, it slowly disintegrates. On the one hand, he worries that he is overlooking something simple that he should know . . . and on the other he wonders if making such shields a part of himself are just beyond his abilities.

The post gate guards scarcely blink when Lerial, Bhurl, and the assorted Lancers ride up to and through the gates. Lerial has barely reined up outside the stables when Seivyr, wearing captain's insignia on his collars, hurries up.

"Welcome back, ser."

"Thank you. It's been a long ride. I see you're a captain," observes Lerial before dismounting. He really wants to stretch his legs.

"Better late than never." Seivyr's smile vanishes. "Before I forget, I wanted to tell the majer that I did appreciate the caution about the post gates. You'll let him know, won't you, if you see him before I do?"

Lerial nods. "Of course."

"He was right about that for sure. After I took over as acting post commander, I watched especially close. Sure enough, one night, I found a ranker slipping the bar. We tied him up and waited. A squad of Afritan armsmen was sneaking around, and they tried the gates. We killed about half of them. The others got away. I gave the men some of their arrows as souvenirs." Seivyr looks blandly at Lerial, almost as if he knows something. "They weren't even broken."

At that moment, Lerial recalls that Altyrn had never mentioned the assassin who had tried to kill the majer the first time they had passed through Tirminya, except as an idiot with a bow. That is, he'd never mentioned it to Dechund, but Seivyr's words suggest that the majer had told the then undercaptain. "Do Afritan arrows have something that identifies them?" Lerial asks guilelessly. "As Afritan, I mean?"

"There's a mark on the arrowhead," replies Seivyr, "and a red band painted around the shaft above the fletching."

"I wonder if Captain Dechund knew that," muses Lerial.

Seivyr shakes his head. "He never mentioned anything about it." After a slight hesitation, he adds, "Whalyn didn't know, either, not until after the raid."

There is something . . . but Lerial needs to think about it, especially before saying anything, and he asks, "Is Whalyn the only undercaptain here now?"

"He'll be going soon as we get two fresh undercaptains. Be a captain before the turn of harvest, I'd wager. Stands a bit higher in Majer Phortyn's eyes than some."

"That can happen."

"We can talk about it over supper. Whalyn and his two squads won't be back till late. You and the majer ever get into it with the Meroweyans?"

"That will take dinner and more to tell," replies Lerial with a laugh.

"Then I won't keep you." With a smile, Seivyr turns and leaves Lerial and Bhurl to deal with the Lancers and the packhorses.

A good glass later, Lerial and Seivyr are seated in the post's small officers' mess.

"I'm afraid that supper is plain mutton," says Seivyr apologetically.

Lerial looks at the platter before him—just cheesed and sliced potatoes and mutton with gravy, with pickled beets—and he smiles broadly. "After ghano-acorn hash and a few other Verdyn staples, this looks wonderful." He stabs a slice of the mutton and cuts it. "You just don't know . . ."

"The way you're eating, I don't know as I'd want to," returns the captain.

Even the lager, which Lerial once would have called bitter, but passable, tastes so much better than the watered greenberry with which Lerial has had to content himself for so many days. Finally, after enjoying the plain food, he looks up, almost embarrassed. "I'm sorry. I should tell you about Verdheln."

"It's clear that the fare wasn't to remember." Seivyr laughs. "The majer said something about that once. How is he?"

"He's well. He's training more companies of Verdyn Lancers. We had six companies partly trained when the Meroweyans attacked. The majer taught us to use their skills with bows to whittle away their numbers. We lost every skirmish and every battle until the last two, and when it was all over, there were only a hundred or so of their wounded left."

"Begging your pardon, ser, but I think you left a bit of that tale on the table."

"I suppose I did." Lerial takes another swallow of the lager, then clears his throat. "Well . . . first he sent out Juist and his company to shoot arrows into their column, the one riding toward Verdheln, from the west. Then he sent me and second company to attack from the east. When they finally got to the ridge just south of the Verd they set up a long line. We did several night attacks with fire arrows and whittled away some more of their forces. Then they moved up and started attacking the Verd with their chaos wizards. We'd slip out from other places and attack companies on the fringe. That went on for an eightday or so before they burned through the tree-wall and started marching up the main road toward Verdell . . ." Lerial continues in a similar vein for a time. ". . . and then the elders set a fire that trapped the western army between a river and the fire, and that burned up the town, the Meroweyans, and the chaos wizards with them. That left the bigger army, except it wasn't so big by then—"

"You never did say how many men Casseon sent."

"The majer thought it was eight battalions, around forty companies."

"And he managed to defeat them with six green companies?"

"That was with the help of the Verdyn elders, the people, and the order-mages that were in the Verd. One of the elders—the one who called the fire at Faerwest—was killed by bringing up that much chaos."

"What about the bigger army?"

"We met them just south of Escadya. We had trenches across the open meadow. We'd cut down a few of them and put a gap in their shieldwall, but they were about to overrun us when the ordermage with us called on some lightnings, and that killed a bunch of them and disorganized the rest of them, and we were able to take most of them. One company or so fled, and I had to take second company and follow them. We caught them on the grass-lands outside the Verd."

"What happened?"

"None of them survived to make it back to Nubyat." Lerial shrugs. "That was about it."

"You make it sound easy. It wasn't, not knowing the numbers and the majer."

"No," says Lerial quietly. "It wasn't easy. Not at all. You'd know that."

"What did it cost?"

"More than two companies worth of Lancers, several thousand Verdyn killed—maybe a lot more, but who will ever know?—three towns and maybe a dozen hamlets burned or destroyed, one of the senior elders killed . . . who knows how much of the Verd burned."

"And Verdyn is now part of Cigoerne, and likely to stay so." Seivyr nods. "Sounds like the majer. When he sets out to do something, it gets done."

Lerial stiffens for a moment. *But did he set out to do that?* He manages to swallow as he realizes that, in fact, Altyrn has schemed and strategized to turn what might have been an armed annexation by Casseon into an all-out war . . . sacrificing the people of the Verd, or some of them, in order to so weaken and destroy a significant portion of Casseon's armsmen that it essentially removed Merowey as an immediate threat to Cigoerne. By attacking the Meroweyans before they reached the Verd, he had ensured that they would attack in force . . . and everything else followed.

What if the Meroweyans had won? Some of the same things would still have happened, except they would have taken longer. Even had the Meroweyans defeated the Lancers, they would have taken significant losses, and because of the size of the Verd, they would have been tied up for years in trying to hold and rule it, keeping them from threatening Cigoerne.

"He does have that ability," Lerial finally says.

"Dechund didn't understand that. Majer would do just about anything to preserve Cigoerne. But Dechund didn't serve directly under the majer." Seivyr takes a small swallow of lager. "How long will you be here?"

"I'd thought a day to rest the horses." Lerial grins. "And maybe stock up on some decent travel food."

"You think it's decent, and you're welcome to it." Seivyr laughs.

"What can you tell me about Majer Phortyn?"

Seivyr raises his eyebrows.

"Besides the fact that he likes officers with clean uniforms and well-polished boots, and that he's skeptical that Duke's sons can handle a blade or perform in battle?"

The captain shakes his head good-naturedly. "You know that, and that's what you've got."

Lerial doesn't press, and the two talk about Tirminya and the post, and the sightings of Afritan patrols for almost a glass before they leave for their respective quarters.

Lerial is sitting on the edge of the narrow bunk, pulling off his boots, when all the pieces fall into place, triggered by what Seivyr had said earlier about the Afritan arrows. *By the Rational Stars! Dechund didn't die of a flux . . .* Lerial tries to recollect what exactly had happened in the mess the night before they had left Tirminya. *There was more than one reason why he wanted you out of the mess! And spilling that carafe when you came back was no accident.*

But that meant Altyrn had suspected Dechund might be a traitor from before leaving Teilyn. Otherwise . . .

Lerial shivers.

Seivyr had said that the majer would do anything to preserve Cigoerne.

LXXXII

By second glass on oneday, after six long days after leaving Tirminya, even with quick glances at intervals at the jagged spurs of red rocks jutting along the Wooded Ridges to the south of the road, Lerial can easily recognize the landmarks and the most impenetrable-looking sections of the forest, although, after seeing the thornbushes of the Verd, the Wooded Ridges look far more open than he had once thought, and more familiar. *They should, after all the time that the majer had you learning the terrain.*

He still hasn't figured out a way to create lasting order-defenses, although he's gotten quite proficient at creating a variety of defenses in instants, some of which he can also instantly link to his belt knife or sabre. *Which is fine for when you know that you're being attacked, or going to be . . . but that won't always be the case.*

He smiles wryly. As in everything, it seems, being able to anticipate is vital.

Under the late afternoon sun of early summer, the mud-brick houses of Teilyn appear a faint orangish-pink as he and Bhurl ride through the town toward the Mirror Lancer post to the south. At the gate, the guards look from Lerial to Bhurl and then to the brown-clad Verdyn Lancers behind the other three Mirror Lancers in green.

"Verdyn Lancers detailed to escort duty," Lerial explains. "That leaves more Mirror Lancers to assist with training in Verdheln."

"Yes, ser," replies the gate guard, his tone suggesting he's not quite convinced.

Word must travel quickly, or the lookout has already reported, because Captain Graessyr stands waiting by the time Lerial rides to the stables and reins up. Behind him looms Undercaptain Shastan, as massive as ever, also looking concerned.

"Returning from Verdell with dispatches and Verdyn Lancers as additional company," Lerial announces.

"Not that we're not glad to see you, Lord Lerial," declares the captain, "but I was hoping that we'd also be seeing the majer."

"He's fine, but he says he needs another season training the Verdyn Lancers. We took some heavy losses in defeating the Meroweyans."

Graessyr frowns. "I thought you were just training them."

"The Meroweyans didn't wait until we'd finished training the Verdyn Lancers. The majer took command. We fought. We won. It was a mess, and it was costly. I'll be happy to fill in the details after we settle the men. I also need to carry a letter from the majer to his family."

Graessyr smiles, if slightly sardonically. "Spoken like a Lancer. I'll be in my study."

Settling the Lancers doesn't take all that long, and since the duty ostler volunteers to groom and feed the gelding, in little more than a half glass, Lerial is sitting in front of Captain Graessyr's desk, explaining what had happened in Verdheln, in much the same way as he had to Seivyr in Tirminya. When he finishes, he waits for any questions Graessyr may have.

"You took a single company after the fleeing Meroweyans . . . and didn't leave any survivors."

"That was partly because things got out of control with their last chaos wizard," Lerial replies, "but I didn't want there to be any effective fighting forces returning to Nubyat."

Graessyr nods slowly. "Most would say that was carrying matters to excess."

"They might. But with so few trained Lancers remaining and even fewer ordermages, it seemed prudent to do everything possible to reduce the possibility of another attempt to take the Verd any time soon."

"There's one other thing I don't understand," says the captain, smiling as he adds, "or maybe more. If the Verdyn had all those ordermages, why did they need the majer and you to train Lancers?"

"They didn't have that many, and they lost at least one that I know of, and I'm not certain how long the senior elder, who is also an ordermage of some kind, will live after the strain the war put on him. What made the difference was the way the majer deployed the Lancers we had. Even before the Meroweyans managed to burn through the tree-walls to get into the Verd, we'd killed or wounded almost five companies worth of their armsmen . . . well . . . maybe four. Every skirmish or battle, they lost at least five or six times what we did. And the people, they killed or wounded quite a few with their traps and their hunting arrows. But none of it would have worked without the majer holding it all together."

"And you just led a company? That's all?"

Lerial pauses for just an instant, then says, "I'm just a young undercaptain, acting as a captain. That's the way it's reported, and the way it should be."

After a moment, Graessyr nods. "I hadn't thought of it that way. You're right, though. Might I ask . . ."

"I requested that it be that way. The majer had drafted the report along those lines before I read it."

"Is there anything else you would care to tell me?"

Lerial thinks. "I don't know if you heard, but Captain Dechund suffered some sort of flux and wandered off in a brain fever and died. Majer Phortyn promoted Seivyr to post captain."

"Dechund . . . oh . . . he was the one with the clean uniforms and bright boots. Sorry to hear it. Seivyr'll do well, though."

Graessyr's matter-of-fact comments confirm that he has the same opinion as Altyrn does, and that tends to reinforce some of Lerial's skepticism about Majer Phortyn.

"Now, ser, I have a question. What can you tell me about raids by the Heldyans, especially along the river?"

Graessyr snorts. "Not much has changed since you and the majer left. We hear that they kept testing the patrols, but they withdraw if we show any force. I haven't heard anything about your brother. Were there anything wrong, I'm certain we'd know."

"Thank you. Now . . . if I might borrow a mount?"

"I told the ostler to have one ready for you. I'd thought to have four men as an escort . . ."

Lerial wants to deny the escort, but then thinks about Graessyr's position in dealing with the son of the Duke. "I think two would be more than adequate."

Graessyr starts to say something, then shakes his head. "You're sounding like your sire."

Before long, Lerial and two Mirror Lancers are leaving the post and heading south toward Kinaar. He is glad that the majer's villa is close. Less than a fifth of a glass later, he turns the borrowed mount onto the packed clay lane leading off the main road. The lane is just as smooth as he recalls as it passes through the yellow brick posts toward the villa. They have barely covered half the three hundred yards from the posts to the villa when Lerial sees several figures hurry out of the villa and wait by the north entrance. *How long has she had someone posted and watching?*

As he rides nearer, he sees, standing with Maeroja, Rojana, Tyrna, and Aylana. Even before he reins up, Lerial can see the worried expression on Maeroja's face, and he quickly says, "He's fine. The fighting is over, and the Meroweyan force was destroyed. He said he had to stay another season to complete the training necessary so he wouldn't have to go back." Altyrn had never actually said the last words, but Lerial feels that is what he meant. "I have a letter for you. He asked me to deliver it personally." Lerial keeps his eyes on Maeroja, although he can feel Rojana looking at him.

Rojana murmurs something to her mother, and Maeroja smiles. "Can you stay for dinner? I would have asked anyway, but I was prompted."

"I'd hoped that would be possible. I'd very much appreciate that." Lerial turns in the saddle. "You can return to the post."

"Ser . . . ?" ventures one of the Mirror Lancers.

"Give him a good two glasses," says Maeroja.

Lerial laughs. "You can see I'm in good hands. Two glasses, it is."

"Thank you, ser."

As the two Lancers leave, Lerial says, "Can I just stable the mare in an empty stall?"

"We could summon the ostler . . ."

"I can do it, and it's likely to be faster." Lerial rides to the stables, where he dismounts, stalls his horse, then walks back to the north entry, where Tyrna and Aylana are waiting.

"Mother took Rojana with her," announces Aylana.

"They're getting refreshments," adds her older sister. "We're to take you to the salon."

"It's still cold in the courtyard," declares the youngest daughter.

"Have you started this year's worms?" asks Lerial.

"Not yet. Mother says they'll be late." Tyrna turns.

Before she can open the outer door, Lerial steps forward and opens it. "After you, ladies."

"We're not ladies yet, mother says," declares Aylana.

"Rojana almost is," adds Tyrna.

Lerial keeps his smile to himself, thinking of Ryalah and Amaira as he follows them all the way to the salon. Maeroja and Rojana rise as the two younger sisters and Lerial enter the chamber. For a long moment, Rojana looks at Lerial, then drops her eyes.

"Before I forget . . ." Lerial steps forward and withdraws the sealed envelope from his Lancer jacket, extending it to Maeroja. "I might take a walk in the courtyard while you read it."

Maeroja cannot conceal a frown.

"There shouldn't be anything disturbing in it," Lerial says quickly. "I just thought you'd appreciate it without . . ."

"If you wouldn't mind . . ."

"I wouldn't have suggested it." Lerial looks down to Aylana. "Would you care to come with me?"

Aylana looks to her mother.

"I'll read it all to you later."

"We'll all walk in the courtyard," announces Rojana, with a firmness that sounds much like her mother.

Once the four have left the salon, Rojana glances to Lerial. "Thank you. She's been so worried." She pauses. "Father is all right, isn't he?"

"He was fine when I left. He wasn't wounded or injured at all. He was brilliant in the way he defended the Verd—and Cigoerne."

"Cigoerne?" asks Tyrna. "I thought you were in Verdheln. That's what Mother said."

"We were. But we were fighting to keep the Meroweyans from threatening Cigoerne."

"Oh."

Lerial walks toward the nearest fountain, realizing, suddenly, that he had not seen a single fountain anywhere in Verdheln. *Is that because they have plenty of water?* "I like your fountains." He glances back to see that Aylana has stamped her foot and is glaring at Tyrna.

Rojana glances back at her sisters, shaking her head and smiling, then says, "The arrangement was Mother's idea. You won't tell her I said that, will you?"

"No. Not if you don't want me to." *Why would she say that?* "Is that because . . . she missed having fountains?" Lerial barely manages to keep from having said something about Maeroja missing things from home, remembering what Emerya has said about her.

"Father never said. Neither has Mother. I thought you might know."

"He said that it took some effort and special pipes for them." That is certainly true enough.

"You won't say, will you?"

"It's not my place to say."

"You've changed."

Lerial can hear a trace of sadness in her voice as he looks into her gray eyes and says softly, "War, for the first time, must change everyone, don't you think?" He pauses. "I never truly thanked you for the lodestone. What I've learned from it saved my life . . . more than once."

"I'm glad . . . I thought it might help."

"It did. More than you know."

"I wanted . . ."

"I know."

Neither speaks for a moment. Then Rojana looks away.

"Do you think she's through reading now?" asks Tyrna, hurrying toward them.

"We should walk around the fountains once," suggests Rojana.

"I don't want to. I'm cold," declares Aylana as she joins the others.

"You'll feel warmer if you keep moving," says Lerial, reaching out and taking Aylana's hand. "We'll go this way."

Lerial and Rojana manage to coax the other two into two tours of the courtyard before returning to the salon.

Maeroja looks to Lerial and Rojana and mouths, "Thank you." Then she says, "Your father assures us that he is healthy and well. I'll let you all read it later. He also wrote that things would have gone badly without Lerial. He says we mustn't ask Lerial about it. That's because he will insist that your father and the elders and everyone else did it. That's not true, but it has to remain our secret." Maeroja pauses. "We should have refreshments. Lerial has waited long enough."

"Can I have lager?" presses Tyrna.

Maeroja shakes her head. "Not yet. You and Aylana can have a little watered wine, if you like. Rojana, only half a beaker of lager."

"When can I have lager—" begins Aylana.

"When you're the age Rojana is now," says Maeroja firmly.

Aylana's pout is only momentary, perhaps because of the stern look bestowed on her by her mother.

Lerial moves to the refreshment table, then nods to Maeroja. "Wine or lager?"

"Lager, please."

Lerial fills one beaker—that is, two-thirds full—and another one-third full, handing the second to Rojana and the full one to her mother, before returning to the table and serving himself. Then he takes the armchair to Maeroja's left, the one not usually occupied by the majer. After a slow sip from the beaker, he smiles. "This is the best lager I've had, ever, and it's made better by the fact that they don't brew anything like it in Verdheln."

"I'm glad you like the lager," says Maeroja. "Dinner will be simple. We didn't know we'd have company."

"Whatever it is will be far better than anything I've eaten in over a season."

"Could you tell us something about the Verd?"

"Trees and more trees," he begins, "and where the trees end they have grown special trees with such trunks that they form a tree-wall around the forests that comprise the Verd . . ." From there Lerial does most of the talking for a good half glass . . . until he sees a serving girl standing in the entrance to the salon.

"It is time for dinner." Maeroja rises.

Lerial does as well.

"You didn't finish," declares Aylana.

"I'll finish at dinner," Lerial promises.

The main dish—in fact really the only dish—except for fresh-baked bread and pickled carrots, not his favorite, but acceptable—is a large platter of lamb biastras, seasoned with far less chili than at the Palace, with a brown sauce that has a slight fruity taste, rather than the white cream sauce that Lerial associates with biastras. The sweet peppers are an orange brown also. He has four of the tubular biastras, and could have eaten more, except he feels that would be excessive . . . and he has promised to finish telling about Verdheln. He cannot, or should not, talk while eating. So he contents himself with sips of the excellent lager and describes everything he can remember.

"I hope you don't mind," says Maeroja, "but we hadn't planned sweets . . ."

"Stars, no! The biastras and the lager are treat enough." Lerial means every word. Simple as the meal may have been, he has not had anything that good since leaving Kinaar the last time.

Maeroja glances to Rojana. "If you would help your sisters ready themselves for bed . . ."

Lerial can tell that is the last thing Rojana wants to do, but she nods politely and ushers the other two from the table.

"And make sure you wash your hands and faces," adds their mother as the three leave.

"I've truly enjoyed being here, and the biastras and bread were delicious." Lerial knows he needs to be leaving soon.

"Thank you. It was our pleasure, and we cannot thank you enough for the news and for the letter."

"That was my pleasure," Lerial insists.

After a moment of silence, Maeroja fixes her eyes on Lerial. "How much danger does he face in Verdheln? Truly?"

"Very little, if any . . . now."

"You are being truthful, I trust."

"Very truthful. There are only a few handfuls of Meroweyans in Verdheln, mostly wounded and all held captive . . . and no mages or wizards—not Meroweyan ones. There are at present no other Meroweyan armsmen near the Verd, and I doubt that there will be for some time to come."

"What you say suggests that he was in great danger earlier."

"He was in danger. He was most careful. He sent others on the most dangerous missions. He led no charges, but we were greatly outnumbered. He planned thoroughly and well. What he did was brilliant."

"But you went on missions, didn't you? Why?"

"I'm a junior undercaptain, and he's the majer in command. Also, he is more valuable to Cigoerne than I am."

"He would not say that." She purses her lips.

Lerial smiles pleasantly and waits.

"He *knows* how things should be," she finally says. "He claims he doesn't see what will be . . . but he has . . . a certainty."

"He had that about you, didn't he?"

For one of the very few times he has seen, there is a momentary expression of surprise and consternation on Maeroja's face. Then she laughs softly. "I should have expected that. I imagine you know the answer. He also believes that you are . . . let us say that . . ." She shakes her head. "Let us say nothing."

By saying she would say nothing, she has said what she wished to convey, Lerial knows. Since he senses someone—Rojana—nearing and stopping just short of the open doors to the dining chamber, he decides against pursuing that. He is also amused, since there is no way that Rojana could have completed her task in that short a time, which means that she likely turned the task over to one of the servants in order to hurry back and eavesdrop. "I am just the younger son, doing what I can to support my father."

"Doing it rather well."

"Only because of your consort, and all he has done for me," he replies. "I cannot thank him—or you—enough."

"You have already. You can tell me what you will, but you kept him safe." She holds up a hand. "Please . . . no argument. I can see—it is plain to see, for those who observe with more than eyes—that you are not the youth who left here more than a season ago."

"Rojana said I've changed."

"You will change more. We live in a time of great change." A faint smile crosses Maeroja's lips. "You may come in, Rojana."

"The girls are in their rooms and ready for bed," Rojana announces as she steps through the doors.

Lerial looks to Maeroja. "I should be going. It's a bit past two glasses." He stands.

"We'll walk you out to the outer courtyard." Maeroja rises from the table and nods to her daughter. "We're so glad you could stay for a while."

"So am I. And I'm glad that I could bring you good news."

When they reach the north entrance, Lerial can see that one of the villa stable boys has brought the borrowed mare from the stable and holds her reins. Beside the mount, the two Lancers wait, still mounted.

"I hope you haven't been waiting long," Lerial says. "I didn't mean to keep you."

"No, ser. Less than a tenth of a glass. Young fellow here just brought your mount."

Lerial turns back to Maeroja and Rojana. "Thank you both. I can't tell you how much I appreciated the dinner and the company." *Especially since it will be a long time before I'm back here.*

"It was our pleasure." Maeroja smiles.

Rojana's smile is fainter, as if it is an effort, and Lerial wants to comfort her . . . and knows that would be a mistake, because it would give her the wrong impression. Instead, he returns the smile and then mounts.

He can sense Rojana's eyes on his back as he rides down the lane toward the yellow brick posts and the main road.

LXXXIII

Lerial leaves Teilyn before dawn on twoday so that they can reach Cigoerne in one long day. Even so, the sun has set before they ride into the city proper, and the twilight is lengthening into a deep greenish purple when they reach the gates of Lancer headquarters. Lerial frowns. The main gates are actually closed, although the small personnel gate is ajar.

"Detachment returning from Verdheln," he announces.

The shorter gate guard looks hard at Lerial. "Begging your pardon, ser. There are no detachments in Verdheln."

For an instant, Lerial is disconcerted. "Then Majer Altyrn and two squads of Mirror Lancers will be somewhat concerned to learn that they don't exist. And Duke Kiedron will be most upset to think that he dispatched his son with a detachment that doesn't exist." Even Lerial is surprised at the dry and withering tone with which the words come forth.

"Ser . . ."

Lerial surveys the guard, with his crisp greens and polished sabre and almost comments on that, but instead says mildly. "You can let us enter, and lose a bit of face. Or you can deny us and face the consequences tomorrow." Lerial can't help but think about the number of Verdyn Lancers who died fighting off the Meroweyans, especially compared to the guards standing gate duty in Cigoerne.

The other guard peers at Lerial, then swallows, finally saying in a low voice, "Ruefyl . . . that's Lord Lerial you're denying."

"But . . ." Ruefyl looks totally flustered.

"Yes, I am wearing the uniform of an undercaptain. That is because I am one. So is my older brother, who is riding patrols in the south along the river. You might recall that my father the Duke still commands patrols. Or have you forgotten that as well?"

Lerial realizes that he's already said too much and adds quietly, "Just open the gates. It's been a long ride from Verdell."

"Yes, ser." Ruefyl looks totally dejected as he steps back and signals. "Open the gates. Incoming detachment."

After several moments, the gates swing inward, and the eleven riders and two packhorses move through.

As they ride toward the stables, Lerial turns to Bhurl. "I'll need to talk to the duty officer. We'll need bunks for the Lancers, and food, as well as feed . . ."

"We can take care of the mounts, ser."

"If you would. I'll also need a spare mount and two men as an escort to the Palace. They can stay there tonight. I'll return them and the mount in the morning. Then I'll take my own mount back to the Palace."

"Think I can take care of that, ser."

Once he dismounts outside the stables, Lerial takes Phortyn's copy of Altyrn's report from his saddlebags, then crosses the courtyard to the octagonal building that holds the studies for the senior officers—and the headquarters duty officer. He has taken no more than two steps into the duty chamber when a stocky older undercaptain steps forward, as if he has been waiting.

"Lord Lerial . . . We hadn't expected you."

"We traveled from Teilyn almost as fast as a dispatch rider could have." While the undercaptain looks familiar, Lerial doesn't recognize him. "I'm sorry. Our paths have crossed, but I don't believe we've been introduced . . ."

"Haentur, ser. Lauxyn told me all about you. We all wondered where you'd gone."

"To Verdheln . . . with Majer Altyrn to train Verdyn Lancers. We just returned with four Mirror Lancers and six Verdyn Lancers . . . and two packhorses. That's for the duty book. Oh . . . there's one thing. One of your gate guards, Ruefyl, didn't want to let us in. I was perhaps excessive in chastising him when he told me that there were no Mirror Lancer detachments in Verdheln."

Haentur frowns. "I didn't know that, either."

Phortyn hasn't let many of his officers know? "Majer Phortyn's the one who sent us off."

"The majer's not here at present, ser. He's having dinner with Magus Scarthyn."

"He keeps in contact with a number of the Magi'i, I understand. That's not surprising, I suppose, since some have sons in the Mirror Lancers. Isn't Veraan from a Magi'i family?"

"Yes, ser. Magus Apollyn is his father." Haentur glances toward the area behind Lerial. "Be hard not to know that."

"I suppose the majer dines with him often as well."

"I don't know about often, ser."

That is all the answer Lerial will get . . . and all he needs to know. "Well . . . since the majer isn't here, I'd appreciate it if you would leave word for him that I'll be reporting to him first thing in the morning."

"Yes, ser. I can do that."

"And if I don't see Lauxyn before you do, give him my best."

"It's not likely either of us will see him soon, ser. He's riding patrols in the north. Near Penecca, I hear."

"Have there been more raids there?"

"No more, but no less, either. Afritans just like to make trouble."

"I can understand that. Oh . . . Since I'll be borrowing a mount, and taking two rankers as an escort to the Palace, I'll return all three early tomorrow."

"Yes, ser. I'll note that in the duty book also."

"I appreciate it, Haentur."

When Lerial returns to the stables, Bhurl has two rankers Lerial has never seen before mounted and waiting.

"Hope you don't mind, ser. Khersett and Lavoyt are with the duty company. Khersett's the short nasty one. Lavoyt's taller and nastier. Thought that our men had ridden enough, and I've known these two a while. They've never seen the Lancer quarters at the Palace, either."

"So long as I'm not taking them from other duties . . ."

"Ser . . ." Even in the dim light cast by the lantern outside the stable, Bhurl's wide grin cannot be missed. "Don't know that many duties outweigh accompanying you. One thing to face danger in battle. Can't help that, but last thing we'd want is having one of the heirs needing to dispatch a bravo here in Cigoerne."

Lerial grins in return. "Your point is taken." He turns to the two. "I appreciate your willingness to spell some rather tired Lancers."

"Our pleasure, ser," returns Khersett.

Lerial notes that his gear has been shifted to the black mare. He opens one of the saddlebags and slips Phortyn's copy of Altyrn's report back inside, then mounts.

Once they leave the headquarters compound, Lerial asks, "Have either of you heard about what's happened in the south, with raiders and Heldyan attacks?"

"They keep attacking, but not very often, ser," replies Khersett.

"Most of the raiders aren't raiders," adds Lavoyt. "They fight too well, and they know when to back off."

"So we haven't taken that many casualties?"

"Some, ser," replies Lavoyt. "Mostly green rankers who make mistakes."

"Are meals in the taverns and cafés getting dearer?"

"Ser?"

"Are you paying more for lager or ale?"

"Well . . . ," Khersett draws out the word, "the Blue Beaker added a copper to the price of lager . . . maybe an eightday ago. Fhasyl said that was because brewers' grain was costing more. Still think he didn't need to."

Lerial doesn't learn much more by the time they near the Palace, but he can barely see, and only because of the mirrored lantern below, that his father's banner flies from the main guardhouse by the gate. *So he is here in Cigoerne.*

Unlike at Mirror Lancer headquarters, the guards immediately recognize Lerial. *But then, they're from Woelyt's company . . . or are they?* Hadn't Emerya written something about Woelyt being posted to Narthyl?

Lerial only gathers his gear and leaves the mare to the ostler. There are times when he doesn't feel guilty about others grooming his mount . . . and this is one of those times. He has barely walked away from the stable when he sees and order-senses someone headed toward him. As the other nears, he recognizes Undercaptain Woelyt.

"Good evening, Woelyt."

"I'm glad to see you, ser. I thought I might not before we left."

"Your company is being posted to Narthyl?"

"No, ser. I mean, we were going to Narthyl, but Majer Phortyn decided we were needed more in Tirminya. I'm being promoted to captain, and we're headed out next oneday. The captain there and his entire company are being sent to a new post east of Narthyl, I understand. That's where I think we were going, but the majer wants a company with more field experience there. That's to deal with the Heldyan incursions."

"I just came from there. You're likely to be just as busy in Tirminya as you would have been in Narthyl. The Afritans have at least a company just north of there, and they could be a problem. They also have sent some archer assassins to Tirminya . . . and they tried to bribe rankers to open the gates to raids. You'll have to be vigilant. Certainly, my father and I will be counting on you to make sure nothing like that happens again." Lerial smiles. "I can fill in some of the details later."

"I'd like that, ser."

From what Lerial sees and can sense, Woelyt knows nothing about the intrigue involving the late Captain Dechund—and that may well mean that a ranker or a squad leader in Woelyt's company does . . . or has certain instructions. He also wonders just when Phortyn changed his mind. "We'll do that. It may be a day or so, since I need to report to Majer Phortyn in the morning." Lerial pauses. "Do you know who your replacement here at the Palace is?"

"Undercaptain Veraan, ser. He's been assigned a new company . . . some seasoned squad leaders and a few solid rankers, but mostly recent recruits."

Lerial manages not to stiffen. He nods. "I've met him. Have a pleasant evening, or what's left of it. Oh . . . and congratulations on the coming promotion."

"Yes, ser. Thank you, ser."

"You've earned it, and you certainly will at Tirminya." Lerial offers a smile and starts across the courtyard toward the Palace proper.

Someone must have hurried to inform the Palace staff, because a messenger boy runs up to Lerial as he nears the guards at the west end of the north wing entrance.

"Lord Lerial, ser?"

"Yes?"

"The Duke would like to see you. He is in his main floor study, ser."

"I'll go right there." Lerial hands the kit bag to the messenger, then extracts the dispatches from the saddlebags before handing the saddlebags to the messenger as well. "Please put my gear in my chambers, if you would."

"Yes, ser."

"Thank you."

Lerial nods to the guards and then enters the Palace after the messenger, heading for the study where his father handles duchy affairs.

The guard outside the study raps once and opens the door. "He's expecting you, ser."

"Thank you." Lerial steps into the study, steeped in gloom, except for the two lamps at each side of the desk.

"Lerial!" A broad smile crosses Kiedron's face as he stands and surveys his son. He shakes his head. "Had I seen you leading a company I doubt I would have recognized you. You have grown. Oh, not that way, but in the way you carry yourself. Do sit down? How far did you ride today? How did the training go?"

"We rode all the way from Teilyn today. We left well before dawn. As for the training . . ." Lerial is the one to shake his head. ". . . we just finished fighting a modest war." He looks at the two envelopes, then extends the one for his father. "I think you should read this first, ser. I would have left a copy with Majer Phortyn, but he wasn't at the post. We even had trouble getting in. The guards didn't know there was a Lancer detachment in Verdheln. Neither did the duty officer. He said none of the officers he knew had any idea."

"A good commander tells only what needs to be said, Lerial." Kiedron frowns. "A modest war? Casseon didn't actually attack, did he?"

"He sent eight battalions and six chaos mages or white wizards. It's been a long spring in Verdheln, ser."

"Looking at you . . . I did wonder at the change. You led a company, didn't you?"

"There wasn't much choice, ser."

"I'd better read the report before asking more questions." Belatedly, Kiedron takes the envelope, then seats himself.

"Before you start . . . how is Ryalah? I got a letter from Emerya . . ."

"She's fine. Now. Without Emerya . . . it might not have been so good." Kiedron smiles. "But she's like nothing happened." Kiedron lifts the envelope.

Lerial sits quietly as Kiedron breaks the seal, then extracts the sheets and begins to read. After the first sheet, he is frowning, and the frown is even deeper when he sets down the last one on the wide study desk.

"You were fortunate to survive. Hard as it may be, I would like to request that you not tell your mother any of the details of your . . . campaign. She has consoled herself with the idea that you and Lephi have been engaged in politically necessary but not terribly dangerous duties. She thinks that the Heldyans are even more dangerous than what you have been through." Kiedron looks directly at Lerial.

Lerial can see, for perhaps the first time, the lines in his father's face, and sense a certain tiredness behind the firm words.

"Do I have your word?" presses Kiedron.

"Yes, ser."

"Good. I am proud of you, but we will not talk of it around your mother or your sister."

Lerial understands . . . unfortunately.

"Why would Casseon do that?" asks Kiedron, almost musingly. "One would think that he knew I was sending the majer there."

Maybe he did. Lerial does not voice that thought. "According to the Verdyn elders, he did build a fort closer to Verdheln last year and looked to be building one closer this year, but that might have been cover for the attack on the Verd."

"It likely was. Someone must have told him." Kiedron shakes his head. "As long as there are men who revere golds over honor . . . or power . . . there will be traitors, even among those you most trust. Remember that, Lerial. Never forget it."

"No, ser." *Should I mention Phortyn? No . . . not after his comment about the need to be closemouthed.*

Kiedron laughs. "I imagine you're ready for a good night's sleep."

Lerial withholds a smile. Some things never change. His father will always keep the words to a minimum. "That I am. I'll be up early. Majer Phortyn wasn't at headquarters, and I need to deliver his copy of Majer Altyrn's report to him."

"You didn't leave it?"

"No, ser. Majer Altyrn requested that I deliver it personally."

The Duke nods thoughtfully. "I can see that. If Majer Phortyn questions that, tell him that I also ordered that he receive the majer's report personally."

"Yes, ser."

"Good night."

When Lerial leaves the study, his father is still at the desk, his eyes fixed somewhere well beyond the Palace.

Lerial supposes he should see his mother, but when he makes his way to her chambers, her maid informs him that she has already retired for the night. Lerial is somehow relieved at that, although he knows he will hear about his not waking her, but he doesn't really want to explain anything at the moment—especially given the promise made to his father.

He turns toward his own quarters.

LXXXIV

Lerial wakes at dawn on threeday, largely because his stomach is empty and growling. He does wash thoroughly and shave, then dons a set of clean greens that have not been worn in a season. He is about to leave his chamber, when someone begins to pound on his door.

"Lerial!"

He cannot contain a smile as he recognizes Ryalah's voice. He hurries to the door, unbolts it, and opens it—only to step back several paces as his sister throws her arms and around his waist with such force that retreating is the only way to keep his balance. "You're back! You're back!"

"I'm back." Lerial gently disentangles himself, noticing that Ryalah is barefoot and still in her nightdress.

"No one told me. Except Nurse, and she said I couldn't wake you. So I waited until I heard you."

"The only one awake when I got here last night was Father, and he told me not to wake anyone." That is untrue, but Lerial doesn't want to get into more complicated explanations, including the fact that, if he had awakened Ryalah, it would have been glasses later before she would have gone back to sleep.

"That wasn't fair."

Lerial reaches down and scoops her up, wrapping his arms around her and holding her tightly. "I'm just glad you're well."

"I've been well for eightdays. Aunt Emerya says I'm fine."

"That's so good. I worried about you."

"We all worried about you."

As much as Ryalah squirms in Lerial's arms, he sets her down. "I'm just fine."

"Will you stay here now?"

"For a while." Not all that long, Lerial knows, not so long as he remains an undercaptain in the Lancers . . . and while Afrit and Heldya threaten the Cigoerne's borders.

"That's good," Ryalah declares emphatically.

"You'd better get dressed, now," Lerial says. "You wouldn't want Mother seeing you barefoot and in nightclothes."

"Must I?"

"If you want to have any breakfast."

"All right." There is a hint of a pout as Ryalah turns and heads for her room.

Lerial steps out into the hall and watches. His sister keeps turning her head and looking over her shoulder, but once he is certain she is in her room, he quickly makes his way down to the Palace breakfast room.

He is the first there, and has only had a few mouthfuls of honest egg toast with sweet berry syrup when his mother appears and marches to the other side of the table. She looks at him. "You didn't think that I worried about you? You couldn't even stop for a few moments to let me know you were safe?"

You knew she'd be upset. You knew. "It was late, and you left word you were not to be disturbed—"

"With you off in the west and no word from you in almost a season—"

"There was no way to send word, Mother . . ."

"You're the son of the Duke, and there was no way?"

"We were fighting the Meroweyans . . ."

"The Verdyn were fighting them. That is what your father said."

Lerial holds back a sigh. He understands why his father has not told her everything . . . and why he made Lerial promise not to reveal details. She has always been overprotective—*especially of Lephi*—and can worry herself sick. "We didn't have any men to spare, and they certainly didn't. Most of their archers were even women."

"Women in battle as archers." Xeranya gives the tiniest shake of her head, and not a single strand of blond hair moves. "Barbaric."

"But obviously necessary," adds Emerya from the door to the breakfast room. "Welcome back." Behind her are Ryalah and Amaira.

Ryalah grins at her brother.

"Thank you. I have to eat and leave. I need to make my report to Majer Phortyn."

"Aren't you the fortunate one."

Lerial gulps down three more mouthfuls, some lager, and bolts for the stable.

". . . and now you're leaving . . ."

"He is a Lancer officer who has to report." Emerya's voice is soothing and reasonable in Lerial's ears as he slips from the breakfast room

He hurries through saddling the mare, but it is almost half a glass later before he, Khersett, and Lavoyt are riding along the avenue toward Lancer headquarters. With them are two rankers from Woelyt's second squad to accompany him back from headquarters. As he rides he thinks about Phortyn . . . and what he should do about the majer. *Everything is so suggestive, but there's no real proof.* He considers the points—Phortyn's excessive secrecy about Lerial and Altyrn's mission, the assignment of Dechund to Tirminya and the events that followed, not to mention the punitive transfer of Seivyr to Tirminya in the first place, the recent assignment of Seivyr to Narthyl, the last-moment reassignment of Woelyt's company to the northern border, and Veraan's assignment to the Palace, Phortyn's dinners with influential Magi'i . . . some of whom are less than esteemed for their integrity, not to mention the impressions he has gotten from more than a few people. Lerial doesn't like what he sees, but then there's been a lot he hasn't cared for in the last season or so.

What if . . . ? What if you're right? Then what should you do?

One thing Lerial has learned, just from observing Altyrn, is that "unfortunate" events should appear when no one else is around and without any apparent motive. *Still . . . how . . . especially with order . . .*

Abruptly, he understands what he can do. He creates a pattern, one that he links to the iron beneath the cupridium of his sabre. It takes him several attempts before he can do what he has in mind. He can sense that the pattern, with order on the inside, as in a cloud, will attract chaos. He also knows that, as with all the iron-linked patterns, it will not last more than two glasses, three at the most. He releases the pattern and straightens in the saddle. If he has judged correctly, the next time he uses the pattern it will do what he intends for it to accomplish . . . if he needs it.

Should you do it? That is the question that will be determined . . . shortly or later. The gate guards make no comments as the five ride in. Lerial thanks the two headquarters Mirror Lancers, leaves the mare with the duty ostler, arranges for his gelding to be saddled, and walks quickly to the hexagonal headquarters building.

The squad leader at the desk outside the majer's study looks up. "Ser . . . the majer said you were to go in as soon as you arrived."

"Thank you." Lerial slips the large envelope from his jacket, then walks to the study door, opens it and enters, closing it behind him.

Majer Phortyn looks up from behind the desk. "You're not terribly late this morning, Undercaptain."

Lerial steps forward. "Here is Majer Altyrn's report, ser."

Phortyn nods brusquely, but says nothing as he breaks the seal. His gray eyes are like flint as Lerial takes a seat across the desk from him. Then he lowers the sheaf of papers. "It is customary to send reports through the chain of command."

"That was not possible. Both Majer Altyrn and your superior ordered me to deliver the report personally to both you and the Duke as soon as possible. You were not at headquarters when I arrived last night. I understand you were dining away from headquarters."

"I do have to eat, at least upon occasion."

Lerial can sense that something about his remark has stirred the majer's flow of order and chaos. He represses any expression and says, "I'm certain that you're much in demand, ser, with the position you hold, and that must leave you little time to yourself. But, given the nature of the report, and my orders, I obviously could not leave it."

Lerial concentrates on sensing Phortyn, and there is a definite reaction to Lerial's words, although the majer's tone is level as he says, "I can see that placed you in a difficult position. Still . . ."

Lerial does not reply, only nodding in agreement.

"Do you intend to remain while I read the report?"

"I had thought to, ser. That way, if you wished more information, I might be able to supply it. If you wish me to leave, of course . . ." Lerial starts to rise.

"Never mind. You're here." Phortyn offers a smile. "There's little sense in sending you off and then calling you back."

Although Lerial watches as the majer reads the report, Phortyn's posture and countenance offer little clue to his thoughts. The order-chaos flows around him are a better indication, and their flow becomes more agitated when Phortyn is reading the last page.

Finally, the majer looks up. "Rather remarkable, but then, it does show that Duke Casseon's forces are not what they could be." After a slight pause, he goes on. "You apparently performed credibly. I would have expected no less, given the intensive training provided by Majer Altyrn, but it is good to know that he has not lost his touch in training, both yours and that of the Verdyn. It always was his strongest point."

Phortyn leans back just slightly, and Lerial catches a glint of golden green at his belt, above the scabbard that holds the majer's belt knife. *Golden green . . . in the hilt of a belt knife? A fire emerald . . . from a man who has been a*

Lancer his entire life and had nothing when he joined . . . and has no consort from whom he could have obtained something that valuable?

Lerial manages to nod politely, even as he uses his order-senses to verify that the fire emerald is indeed set in the hilt of a belt knife. "Yes, ser. Everyone, I've observed, has their strengths . . . and everyone their weaknesses."

"The higher one rises," the majer says evenly, "the more people seek out one's weaknesses . . . particularly if they are young and apparently untried."

"I've observed that as well, ser. Do you have any questions about the report?"

"Not at the moment, Undercaptain. I may after I consider the report. How many companies is Majer Altyrn planning to train? Do you know?"

"He had talked about beginning with another six or so to bring the Verdyn Lancers up to a full ten companies."

"Once he has done that, perhaps we should dispatch a senior officer to relieve him and take command. Submajer Jhalet . . . or one of the senior overcaptains."

"The majer thought that was likely. He had mentioned only remaining another season or so."

"Wise man." Phortyn smiles brightly. "I will not keep you. I'm certain your family would like to see more of you before your father and I decide on your next posting."

Phortyn has said enough. Lerial reaches out with his order-senses and creates the pattern he had adapted from those used in creating clouds and lightnings—except this pattern is quite small and links securely to the iron in the major's belt knife, with the fire emerald in its ornate hilt, the only place where a Lancer officer might wear such without much attention . . . unless one has seen a fire emerald and knows its worth.

Lerial stands. "Thank you, ser. I appreciate everything, especially your advice." He nods slightly.

"You're more than welcome." The majer rises, his jacket sliding over the knife hilt.

He frowns, as if to say something, then shakes his head. "Until later."

"Yes, ser." Lerial is careful to close the study door firmly behind himself.

Then he makes his way to the stable where the two rankers are waiting.

"We're headed back to the Palace now."

"Yes, ser."

Lerial mounts quickly and guides the gelding through the courtyard, followed by the rankers. He does not look back as he rides through the gates and turns northwest on the boulevard that leads back to the Palace.

It is a good half glass before noon when Lerial finishes unsaddling and briefly grooming the gelding, then makes his way through the warmest morning he has felt in more than two seasons back to the Palace, looking for his mother. He would prefer Emerya, but he has no doubts that she is at the healing hall.

He finds Xeranya in the salon.

"So you have time for your poor mother now."

Lerial represses a sigh, wondering why she sounds more bitter than he recalls. *Or did you just not see it?* "I had to report to Majer Phortyn. Father insisted that I do so first thing this morning. As soon as I did that, I rode straight back here and came to find you."

Xeranya actually smiles. "I'm sorry. I've just been so worried. I've worried about all of you. I thought you were the safest out there in the west while Lephi was in the south fighting Heldyan invaders." Her words are unsteady, as if she is almost on the brink of tears.

Lerial just looks at his mother, sensing that she truly feels that. He doesn't shake his head. "Like Lephi, I went where Father sent me. I did all that he asked."

"It's all so terrible. I thought . . . once Cigoerne was strong . . . that the fighting would stop. It never does."

"It hasn't, but we've lost very few here in Cigoerne. Thousands of people died in Verdheln under the Meroweyan attacks."

"I can't worry about them. I can only worry about Lephi . . . and you, of course, Lerial."

Lerial has the feeling that her last words are an afterthought, but he nods, then goes on, knowing that his words will have little impact for the moment, but feeling they need to be said.

"All those who died or suffered had dreams, too, and many of them were young men just like Lephi, or me. Too many of them died. Because they fought and died, Casseon will not attempt another attack on Cigoerne. The people of Verdyn are part of Cigoerne, and they will fight to the death against Merowey . . . or anyone else, so long as Father allows them their own way of life. There are likely over a thousand more Lancers in training there now."

"I'm just glad you're safe, and I want to see Lephi safe, too."

"Once Duke Khesyn hears about what happened in Verdheln, we may see fewer attacks from Heldya."

"I would hope so."

Lerial smiles. "It's quite pleasant in the courtyard. We could enjoy the spring air. Would you join me?"

Xeranya smiles in return.

After spending a good glass with his mother, Lerial repairs to his chambers and changes into an old set of greens and, after finding Woelyt, works out in the Lancers' courtyard with some of Woelyt's junior rankers. He can only hope, at best, that his efforts will work, and, at worst, that, whether they do or not, there will be no signs of what he has done. By half past the third glass of the afternoon, Lerial is sweat-soaked and calls an end to the combination of exercise and training.

Once it is clear that Lerial has finished, Woelyt approaches. "You're even better than when you left."

"You might call it practice under pressure." *Although most of the practice was with order-sensing and anticipation.* Lerial blots his forehead.

They both look up as Emerya and a Mirror Lancer officer Lerial does not recognize immediately ride into the courtyard, followed by a full squad of Mirror Lancers. Emerya dismounts hurriedly and gestures for Lerial to join her. As he walks toward her, he recognizes the other officer as Submajer Jhalet, the second-in-command of the Mirror Lancers. He also sees a Lancer behind the submajer carrying a small strongbox, one that is anything but light, it appears.

"What—"

"Just come with us. Is your father in his study?" asks Emerya.

"He was when I came out to spar."

"He likely still is, then. This way, Submajer," Emerya orders, in a fashion that Lerial knows would make any Mirror Lancer obey.

Kiedron is indeed in his study. "What's happened that all of you have descended on me?"

"Majer Phortyn died, ser," announces Jhalet. "He left headquarters for a bite to eat at the mess, and then went to his quarters. He did not return for his afternoon meeting with me. The duty officer and I went to summon him, but he did not answer the bell. We had to break the door. He was in his armchair, as if he just dozed off . . . but he didn't wake up. Sometimes . . . sometimes, people aren't dead when they look like they are. So I summoned the head of healing at the Hall."

"He died in his sleep . . . or his nap. His heart may have been failing. It might be why he felt tired and sat down to rest," Emerya says. "There's no trace of poison or chaos. In fact, there was less sign of chaos in his body than in most cases."

"You're certain?" asks Kiedron.

"Absolutely."

Lerial refrains from nodding, maintaining an interested expression.

"There was one thing, though," adds Jhelat. "That is another reason why I am here."

"Oh?"

Jhalet gestures, and the Mirror Lancer steps forward and gently sets the small but heavy ironbound chest on the desk.

"When I was checking his quarters, just in case matters were not as they seemed," Emerya said, "I could sense some highly ordered iron. There was a strongbox hidden in his armoire. The lock was ordered iron. We brought it here, unopened. We also brought the key pouch we found."

Kiedron frowns.

"If there's something of value there," the dark-haired Jhalet adds, "we didn't think it should be left, although I did post guards." He extends the small leather pouch. "We thought it might be best if you were the one . . ."

Kiedron takes the pouch and extracts a leather spring ring on which are three keys, all similar. The lock opens to the second key.

"Let me, ser," suggests Jhalet. "Just in case." He takes out his belt knife, one with an ornate carved hilt, possibly mother-of-pearl, Lerial notes. Then he uses the tip to lift the lid of the chest, standing as far back as he can.

In the ironbound box are hundreds, if not thousands, of golds.

For several moments, none of the three speaks.

"It must be an inheritance or a gift he kept secret." Kiedron looks to Jhelat. "Wouldn't you agree?"

"Yes, ser. It must be."

Kiedron frowns. "He has no children, does he? I know he never took a consort . . . but . . ."

"None that anyone knows of."

"Then it would be appropriate if the golds were held and a set amount given to the widows of Mirror Lancers killed in service, would it not?" suggests the Duke. "As a tribute to the majer's service?"

"Yes, ser," agrees Jhalet.

Lerial looks at the other keys, wondering what chests they might open and where they are. *Will we ever know?* He has his doubts.

"You will make arrangements for him," says Kiedron to the submajer, "and let us know?"

"Yes, ser. Will you take custody of the chest?"

"I think not. It belongs to the Mirror Lancers. Have the golds counted by you and two other trusted officers and kept in the Lancer strong room with a separate ledger for each disbursement. Say . . . ten golds for an officer's widow, or young children, if his wife is dead, and five for a ranker."

"Yes, ser. Very good, ser."

"That should include Squad Leader Juist, who died in Verdheln," adds Lerial.

Kiedron frowns slightly, then nods.

When Jhalet and the Lancer have left, with the strongbox, Kiedron turns to Emerya.

"What do you really think?"

"There's no doubt. His heart stopped. There are no signs of poison, and the mess said that he only had some bread and cheese. If he'd been poisoned at breakfast, he would have died either much sooner or much later."

"Good." Kiedron shakes his head. "I mean, it's good that it's clear he wasn't poisoned. Will you make certain that the other healers know that as well . . . quietly, of course."

"Of course."

"We'll need a new commander. I'd rather not recall Altyrn." He turns to Lerial. "What do you think?"

"I'd agree. He wouldn't decline the post, but you wouldn't be doing him or his family any favors, and you'd still have to find someone to succeed him before too long."

"Is he ill?"

"No . . . but," Lerial answers in a wry tone, "he might be before long if he had to take command again."

"Then we'll confirm Jhalet as his successor and watch closely." Kiedron turns to Emerya. "Is there anything else?"

"No."

"Then . . ."

Lerial and Emerya exchange glances.

"I'll leave you in comparative peace," says Emerya.

Lerial follows Emerya from the study and down the hallway away from the guard before speaking. "You never trusted him, did you?"

"No. You didn't either, did you?"

Lerial smiles sadly. "No . . . but I never had enough proof to go to Father about it."

"Well . . . the way things turned out, you were right." Emerya offers an enigmatic smile.

"Let's just say that we were fortunate this time."

"We were." Emerya glances toward the courtyard. "I need to get back to the healing hall. There have been far too many injuries today. You need to talk to your father a bit more, I suspect."

"I'm just going to tell him what few things I know that led to my suspicions . . . and why I couldn't bring them to him without more proof."

"He'll appreciate your discretion, I'm certain."

Lerial watches as she strides toward the courtyard, then he walks back into the study, closing the door behind him.

Kiedron stands between the end of the desk and the window, looking out into the courtyard, where Xeranya is sitting in the shade, reading something. The cover is silvered green.

Lerial nods to himself and waits.

Kiedron turns. "You had something else to say?"

"Yes, ser. I've worried about Majer Phortyn for some time. I don't think I told you, but only a handful of Mirror Lancer officers even knew that Majer Altyrn and I'd gone, and none of them except Captain Graessyr and Undercaptain Shastan at Teilyn post knew that we were going to Verdheln."

Kiedron frowns. "That's true, but what does that have to do . . . ?"

"Then there was the business of the Afritan archer who tried to kill Altyrn in Tirminya." Lerial goes on to explain finishing up with, ". . . and when I got back here to the Palace, I found out that Woelyt had been reassigned to the north and Seivyr to Sudstrym or a new post that is taking the brunt of Heldyan attacks, and no other than Veraan would be taking over the Palace garrison—when Phortyn has been courting Veraan's father Apollyn, and also Scarthyn. By the way, before I forget, I'd suggest that you ask Submajer Jhalet to replace Veraan with a more seasoned undercaptain, someone like Lauxyn or Haentur. Anyway, I left the majer feeling very uneasy, especially when I saw that he was wearing a belt knife with an ornate hilt that held a fire emerald. I kept thinking that you'd said that someone had likely told Casseon about our mission there. Why else would he have sent so many armsmen? Then there is the problem with that chest . . . and the other keys."

"The other keys concern me as well," admits Kiedron, "but there are times to look and not to look. If other chests turn up, well and good. If not . . ." He shakes his head.

Lerial shrugs. "Maybe I should have told you sooner, but . . . I've never run across anything like this . . . and I wanted to sleep on it."

Kiedron nods thoughtfully. "I can see that." He offers a wry smile. "The Rational Stars were looking out for us."

"It's good they were." *And we won't mention that they had a little help. Not ever.*

LXXXV

Two eightdays later, well past fourth glass in the afternoon, Lerial returns from Lancer headquarters, where he has been assisting Captain Chaen in training new Mirror Lancer recruits, to find himself summoned to his father's study. He suspects he knows why, given that the courtyard is filled with both Mirror Lancers and a squad of armsmen in golden brown uniforms

He steps into the study and inclines his head. "Ser, you requested my presence?"

"I did. Duke Casseon sent an envoy. I've just finished meeting with him. I thought you should know." Kiedron picks up several sheets of heavy parchment and extends them to his son. "I'd like you to read his proposed agreement and tell me what you think." A hint of a smile lingers at the corners of his lips.

Lerial begins to read, skimming the honorifics and niceties and concentrating on the significant sections.

> *. . . clear and obvious that the inhabitants of the Verd, the people of the area that calls itself Verdheln, have chosen to be ruled by you . . . have made that choice with life and blood, as well as with order and chaos . . . as Duke of Merowey, I have striven to keep chaos from my people, another reason for my acquiescence in their choice . . . as an honorable ruler of Merowey I will respect that choice . . .*
>
> *In return, I would trust that you, as Duke of Cigoerne, will ensure that the people of the Verd refrain from any raids or warlike acts against the*

peoples south of the Verd . . . that you will also take all steps to keep raiders from Afrit or elsewhere from using or crossing those lands to trouble my people . . . I would also trust that the boundaries between our lands follow those suggested on the attached map, although we should agree that, if it is in our joint interests, small modifications to those boundaries may be possible . . .

There is a great deal more, but those are the parts that are most important.

Lerial looks up and lowers the papers. "It's a great victory. Cigoerne is now almost as large as Afrit."

"Not really. Afrit is a third again our size, with far more people."

"For now," Lerial points out.

"For now," Kiedron agrees. "I shouldn't question this too closely, I suspect, but even after reading the majer's report, I can't see exactly how he managed this."

Lerial smiles politely. "We didn't, not alone. The Verdyn did, with blood and ashes. The last two battles delivered the final message. Duke Casseon sent something like six chaos mages along with forty-five companies . . ." Lerial suspects there may have been more, but he remains uncertain whether, in some cases, his order-controlled and redirected chaos killed or merely stunned a chaos mage. ". . . in the end a few survivors, if that, straggled back to Yakaat. Casseon knows we had only six companies."

Kiedron laughs, but the sound is tinged with rue and puzzlement. He looks to Lerial. "You had more to do with this than you're saying, didn't you? More than I even suspected."

"I was able to redirect some chaos bolts, ser." That is all Lerial wishes to admit.

"Saltaryn has said you had limited abilities to gather order or chaos."

"Apparently, ser, I have fewer difficulties in turning that which others have gathered against them."

"Apparently."

Lerial steps forward and lays the sheets on the desk. "You'll still have to negotiate a few things."

"Of course." Kiedron smiles. "And you can take my place in periodically riding patrols along the Afritan borders."

"I'd be honored, ser."

"No . . . I'm the one to be honored . . . and relieved."

Lerial returns his father's smile.

Everything will continue as it had before Duke Casseon's ill-considered attack on Verdheld, or perhaps with even fewer border skirmishes and raids . . . at least for a while . . . and that is all anyone can expect.

"Let's go tell your mother and aunt. They'll be pleased."

The two walk from the study toward the sun-drenched courtyard.